The

GUARDIAN

BOOK 2

TO RUN WITH THE SWIFT

Other Books by
GERALD N. LUND

The GUARDIAN

BOOK 2

TO RUN WITH THE SWIFT

A NOVEL

GERALD N. LUND

M.
®

**DESERET
BOOK**

SALT LAKE CITY, UTAH

To family—
An eternal journey

To Lynn
whose unwavering commitment to family binds us together

And to our children, who are extending that commitment
into the third and fourth generation

Visit us at DeseretBook.com

Library of Congress Cataloging-in-Publication Data
CIP data on file
ISBN 978-1-60907-796-9

Printed in the United States of America
Edwards Brothers Malloy, Ann Arbor, MI

10   9   8   7   6   5   4   3   2   1

PROLOGUE

Bombed Ruins, Munich, Germany
May 1, 1945, 10:18 p.m.

The little girl leaned down and screamed in her mother's ear. "Mama! Someone's coming."

The child's voice barely penetrated the heavy fog of exhaustion, making the woman feel like she was smothering. She fought with what little willpower she had left to force her eyes open, but they only fluttered for a moment, then closed again.

Let them come. It doesn't matter anymore.

Sobbing, the girl began shaking her violently, crying, wailing, whimpering in fear. She was only four years old, and she was terrified. But it wasn't enough.

It doesn't matter.

Slowly she surrendered. It felt so good to let go. She had fought so hard for so many days. She had huddled in terror for so many interminable nights. It was time to let go.

Her head lolled to one side as she slipped back into unconsciousness.

●

Her next conscious awareness was that of pain behind her eyes. Yet it felt good at the same time. Confused, she cracked one eye open, then hurriedly clamped it shut again as she realized it was a beam of sunlight shining directly in her eyes, warming her face. With a great effort, she turned her head away and opened her eyes. Slowly, perceptions began to register in her brain.

They were still in the bombed-out shell of a two-story building.

There was no roof, and the sky above was a brilliant blue.

She was no longer cold, and that seemed almost unnatural to her. Except that somewhere in the deep recesses of her mind, she remembered that it was spring now.

There was the smell of something delicious in the air. She sniffed a second time. Sauerkraut and frankfurters. It made her almost dizzy with pleasure.

She turned her head to the other side, trying to comprehend where she was. And why. A stab of fear pierced her as she saw a dark figure kneeling in the rubble a short distance away. His back was to her, and she saw that he was bent over a small, portable burner, like the ones soldiers used in the field. And he was wearing a uniform.

And then she focused on the other, smaller figure to his side. It was her Liesel. She came up on her elbow with a lurch as hope shot through her. *"Schatzi?"* It was the German term of endearment used by spouses for each other.

The man whirled around to face her, and that brought his face fully into the light. One hand came up and swept off his hat. The disappointment stabbed so sharply that she gasped with pain. It was not her *Schatzi*. This man was a complete stranger to her. She saw that he was not in uniform at all. The hat and jacket he wore were those of a farmer. His trousers were plain and worn. His closely cropped blond hair did remind her of a soldier, but he didn't have a soldier's bearing. Light blue eyes smiled out from beneath thick brows. The face was long and narrow, but kindly. He was smiling at her, and she saw that his teeth were somewhat crooked.

"Schatzi? Is that you?" She pulled herself into a sitting position, still hoping.

He got up and came toward her. "I'm sorry, *Frau* Decker, but I am not your husband."

She shrank back. "I . . . my name is not Decker. It is—"

"It is Decker now," he cut in quickly. "You cannot ever use your real name again. Do you understand me? That is very important. Starting right now, you are *Frau* Elizabette Decker.*"

It was as if he were speaking a foreign language. Her mind refused to process the words.

"Where is my husband?"

"In a prisoner-of-war camp. I do not know where."

"Is he dead?" It had been more than three months now since she had been told that he was missing in action and it was assumed he had been captured by the British or American forces.

"No. That has been confirmed. But from this point on, until you are reunited with him, *Frau* Decker, you must tell people that he is dead."

He turned his head as the little girl leaped to her feet and ran to her mother. She dropped to her knees in front of the woman and threw her arms around her. "Oh, Mama. I thought you were dead too." She began to cry with deep, shuddering sobs.

The mother held her close, rocking back and forth, touching her hair and murmuring soothing words of comfort. "No, Liesel. I'm not dead. I feel . . . better now."

The man turned back to her. "*Frau* Decker. Your daughter has a new name too. It is Gisela Decker." He pronounced it slowly—GEES-ah-lah—to be sure she got it.

She barely heard because something else had flashed into her consciousness. She looked around the shattered room. "What do you mean 'dead too'? Where's Willi, Liesel?"

Fresh tears burst out. "Willi's sleeping, Mama. I'm sorry. I'm sorry. I couldn't wake him."

Taking her daughter in her arms, trying to stop the trembling in her body, the mother looked up at the stranger, her eyes imploring.

He nodded. "He passed away just before morning. He is at peace now."

She went numb. Her firstborn gone? Not yet six years old and dead already? Tears trickled down her cheeks as she tried to blot out the pain. She had known her son was close to death. Since they had been evicted from their home, Willi had become the little man of the family. It had been too much for him. She remembered that she had seen it in his eyes last night before she had fallen into her own exhausted sleep.

The man leaned in, eyes soft with compassion, but nevertheless all business. "We must hurry, *Frau* Decker. There is no time to waste. We must go quickly. I have left a note on your son's body so he will receive a Christian burial. But we must go. The Americans are already in the city." He leaned down and gently took her by the arm. "Come. Eat a little breakfast."

As mother and daughter ate their meager meal, the man talked quietly. "My name is Manfred Hoffman," he began. "I am a captain in the army, though I am out of uniform at the moment. I knew your husband well."

"Hoffman?" It was a name she vaguely recognized.

"Yes. After completing my basic training, I was given lieutenant's bars and assigned to your husband's unit in Poland. That was back in 1942. We were together for over a year." His eyes filled with shame. "I was young and impetuous, ready to spit into the face of the world. But fortunately, your husband took a liking to me and took me under his wing."

"I remember now," she said. "It was while he was stationed in Krakow. He wrote of you."

"Yes, in Krakow." He took a quick breath. "After I had been with him for several months, several of us were given weekend passes. We went into the heart of the city. We got very drunk, and . . ." He looked down, not able to meet her gaze. "I did something very terrible, very foolish. And . . . and I was caught doing it. At the very least, it should have cost me my commission. Under these wartime conditions, it could even have gotten me shot."

She was shocked by his words. He seemed so pleasant and so kind.

"Your husband intervened in my behalf. He made it right, using his own funds. No charges were ever filed, and it was never entered into my record." He sighed. "A month later I was sent to the Russian front, and he was eventually transferred to France. I never saw him again."

"That would be my *Schatzi*," she murmured.

She could tell that he was glad to have it said and to be done with it. "I knew that he was from Munich and had family here. He spoke of you and the children all the time. So when I was transferred here two months ago, I tried to find you. I wanted you to know what your husband did for me. I want to help your family in some small way to repay the debt that I owe to him."

He was staring at her, pain darkening his eyes. "I had no idea you were so young. Colonel Kessler never said."

Her head tipped back proudly. "It was an arranged marriage. I was but seventeen. He was thirteen years my senior. But it quickly became a marriage of love. He knew the war was coming and wanted to have children immediately. My Willi and my Liesel were born just fourteen months apart."

Her head dropped and she began to sob. And now, at twenty-four, she was in all but fact a widow. Her firstborn was dead. She and Liesel were on the run, homeless, penniless, without hope.

He went on gently. "But when I arrived here in Munich, things were already terrible. When I went to your villa, I was shocked to find another family living there. They told me that you had sold it to them and gone to Berlin."

"Sold it?" she cried bitterly. "The local *Gauleiter*, an evil little man, used his influence in the Nazi party to have us evicted. When I went to the bank to draw out money to fight them, there was no money there. He produced documents saying that my husband had sold our estate to him. But I knew otherwise. My *Schatzi* would never have sold our beautiful home, even when conditions grew worse."

Captain Hoffman reached out and briefly touched her shoulder. "This is one of the reasons you must leave. They know that as long as you are alive, what they did can be undone." He looked away. "They are determined that you shall not survive the war. They are looking for you now."

"No, I cannot leave. I must get it all back, before my *Schatzi* returns."

"It pains me deeply to say this, but there is another reason you must disappear for now."

"Another reason?"

He nodded grimly. "Your husband was not only a high-ranking German officer, he was also an important figure in the Nazi party here in Munich."

Her face softened momentarily. "He was very important. We were invited to all the parties. It was such a thrill." She leaned in, as if to share a secret. "It was here in Munich that the National Socialist Party had its first beginnings, you know. We even sat at the *Fuehrer*'s table on several occasions and—"

"The *Fuehrer* is dead," he cut in bluntly. "He and his mistress, Eva Braun, committed suicide the day before yesterday in their Berlin bunker. Berlin is surrounded by the Russians and will almost certainly fall today or tomorrow." His eyes held her as if in a tight grip. "You have to leave Munich, *Frau* Decker. The world has much anger toward Germany right now. There is already talk about forming tribunals to prosecute war criminals."

"But my husband has done nothing wrong. He was a loyal and faithful officer and—"

"He was a Nazi," he said bluntly. "And as his wife, you might be under suspicion as well. This is the other reason why you must go."

"I . . . I don't understand. Munich is our home."

"Munich has fallen. The first American troops entered the city two days ago. They hardly had to fire a shot. The city is almost completely deserted. Most of the people have fled to the country. And we must join them. Quickly. Before there is no more escape. Please, *Frau* Decker. I am here to help you. But we cannot delay. We must go."

Almost senseless with grief, but filled with gratitude at the kindness of this gentle man, she looked up, brushing at her eyes with the backs of her hands. "But where shall we go?"

"The first thing is to get you out of the city. Then we shall make you disappear." What he hadn't told her was that *Gauleiter* Werner had already snuggled up to the Americans and was promising to help identify Nazi criminals and other undesirables. This was in exchange for certain considerations, including keeping his estate. It wasn't too much of a leap to realize that *Frau* Decker would be one of those he identified as a problem.

"So is the war over, then?" the new *Frau* Decker asked.

"Not officially yet, but all German forces in Italy surrendered yesterday. And that fat old strutting fool, Mussolini, was caught trying to flee the country and was executed."

Her face was white, her pupils wide with shock. "So the Third Reich is no more?"

He laughed bitterly. "I fear that it fell a little short of the thousand years we were promised."

The trip to the city's western outskirts was one prolonged nightmare, but Captain Hoffman stayed with them all the way. There were many detours. Several of the streets, even the widest boulevards, were choked with rubble. Twice they saw columns of American soldiers coming into the city and ducked into side alleys or blown-out buildings. Perhaps Munich had been mostly emptied, but there were still thousands fleeing the city. A few pulled their things in children's wagons or pushed them in wheelbarrows, but mostly, they had bundles over their shoulders. Some had nothing at all. No one looked at them, and they looked at no one. Everyone averted their eyes as they hurried on, moving west. They were just one more family with gaunt faces, desperate expressions, and vacant, haunted eyes.

By nightfall they were out of the city. Now their protector increased the pace. Little Liesel—now Gisela—began to whimper. Hoffman picked her up, put her on his shoulders, and carried her for what seemed like miles, singing children's songs to her. Finally, he turned off into a narrow country lane. "We are almost there, *Frau* Decker," he said gently.

"Where? Where are we?"

"At the house of a trusted friend. It is a small farm. He will give you food and shelter."

"But . . ." She felt the dismay rising quickly. "But what shall we do?"

"You will rest. I will return as quickly as possible, but it may take a day or two. I must create documents for you and your daughter."

"Documents? But we already have documents."

"No, not anymore. We need identity papers under your new name. Passports. Travel documents." There was a long sigh. "I wish I could stay here with you, but I must return. If I am found out of uniform, I will be shot. And I must see to my own family as well."

"But where are we going?"

"I have a sister who lives in Zurich. She knows of our family's debt to your husband, and she will take you in. As you know, Switzerland is a neutral country, and you will be safe there while other arrangements are made."

She peered up into his face. "When shall we be able to return to our home?"

He looked away. How much should he say? How much did she have a right to know? When he turned back, his expression was very grave. "I cannot say much, *Frau* Decker, because what I know comes from classified documents that I am not at liberty to discuss. But—" He took a quick breath. "But it may be that you may never return to Munich."

Another quick breath, and he averted his eyes. "You may never be able to return to Germany."

Frau Elizabette Decker looked at the haughty woman who stood before her. "A scullery maid?" She was deeply shocked.

Katarina Hoffman Schreiber's eyes narrowed dangerously. "Beneath your station, is it?"

Gisela tugged on her mother's skirt. "What's a skully maid, Mama?"

Her mother barely heard her. Her chest was rising and falling as her breath came in short, angry bursts. Finally, her head came up, and the tired eyes flashed fire. "I come from a house where we had more household servants than your husband employs in his petty little manufacturing shop. And you would make me a scullery maid?"

"And where is your great house now?" Katarina shot back. "And your servants? Tell me, *Frau* Decker. Where are they now?"

"Mama," Gisela cried in alarm, "what is a skully maid?"

Lips pressed into a tight line, Katarina looked down at the little girl. "The scullery is a small room behind the kitchen in large manor homes or villas. It is the room used for washing dishes, scrubbing pots and pans, laundering the servants' uniforms"— she shot a look at the child's mother—"and other of the most menial duties."

Elizabette looked down at her daughter. "A scullery maid is the lowest of all the household servants. And her salary is a pittance." She turned back to face their hostess. "It is an insult, that's what it is. I am the wife of a very important man who—"

Katarina sneered in disgust. "You are the wife of a high-ranking Nazi official who is likely to be charged with war crimes. You are on the run so that you will not be arrested and made to pay for what the Nazis have done to our country. So don't you stick your nose in the air and sniff at me like I am some piece of scum beneath your feet. My husband already thinks I am a fool for helping you."

She started to turn away, then whirled back. She took two steps to the writing desk to her left and picked up a thick manila envelope. Thrusting it at Elizabette, she leaned in close, jaw clenched and eyes cold with fury. "This arrived this morning from my brother. It is all there—train tickets to Marseille, passage for two on a tramp steamer that will work its way eventually to Liverpool."

She looked away. "He has done all this at terrible risk to himself and the rest of our family. You have your travel documents, passports, everything you need. And he left me sufficient money to see you to England. Do you know how tempting it is to throw you and your haughty pride out on the streets and keep the money for my own family? But I will not. We may not be one of the 'noble families of Germany'"— the last was spoken with open sarcasm and contempt—"but in our family we believe in honor and integrity. So you will have your new life. You will go where no one will know who you are or what your husband has done."

"My husband has served the Third Reich faithfully. He will be vindicated."

"No," Katarina yelled, "he will be hanged." And then the tears came. "As will my brother."

That finally punched through Elizabette's outrage and anger. "Your brother? Do you mean Captain Hoffman? But—"

Cheeks stained with tears, Katarina's head dropped. "He was arrested yesterday. Someone saw him out of uniform when he went to help you. They reported him, and an investigation began. When they learned that he had forged documents and purchased train and steamer tickets, they assumed it was for him. He has been charged with desertion."

Elizabette Decker fell back a step, one hand flying up to her mouth. "No."

"Yes," she hissed. "And now you stand here quivering in anger because of your offended pride? Demanding some kind of privileged position? Get out of my sight. If I had not given my word to Manfred, I would send you back to Munich and let you find out for yourself that there are much worse things than being a scullery maid."

—

Summa cum laude: A title given only to those who achieve perfect grades in all classes. In Latin meaning, "with highest praise."

She looked at the diploma, running her fingers lightly across the lettering, smelling the richness of the leather cover.

University of Manchester

Has conferred upon

Gisela Elizabette Decker

Who having demonstrated ability by original research
In the Field of Economics
the degree of

Doctor of Philosophy (Ph.D.) in Economics

with all the rights and privileges thereto pertaining
Issued by the Board of Regents upon recommendation of the faculty
June 16, 1967.

It was signed by the Provost and President and had the university's seal affixed to the bottom. "Not bad for the daughter of a scullery maid," she murmured bitterly. Then, lifting the skirts of her graduation robes, she started for the door. As she walked through the crowds, she had never felt more alone. They were gathered in clusters—graduates and their families, graduates and their friends, graduates and other graduates. *Clusters* was not a word that described her now, nor had it ever been. She had done this on her own, with only her mother to encourage her.

But didn't that define her life? Their lives? From the time they had fled Germany? She shook it off angrily. She had a doctorate in economics. She had earned it through the sheer strength of her own will. Who cared about being a cluster? She was proud that she stood alone. Proud of what she had accomplished. And let the rest of the world rot in hell if that was how they were.

Just as she was about to leave the hall, someone called her name. She turned to see an older man, nearly bald but with a white, neatly trimmed beard. He was waving to her and making his way through the crowd toward her.

She waved and stepped back, pasting on the bright smile again. He joined her, extending his hand. "Hello, Gisela."

"Dr. Williamson, hello."

"Congratulations! Well done."

"Thank you. You are responsible for much of it." And she meant it. Here was an exception. A friend. A mentor. A man instrumental in helping her achieve this day.

"I think not. I was just the midwife. You are, without question, the finest student it has ever been my privilege to mentor. It was a joy."

"And for me. You were much more than a midwife. You do great honor to the title of teacher and educator." She really meant it. Of all her professors, Dr. Williamson was the one she admired the most because he had had the greatest impact upon her. She had chosen him as the chairman of her doctoral committee, and he had championed her throughout her studies.

"Kind of you to say it. Thank you." He hesitated a moment, then, "Are you off so quickly? Not going to join us for some bubbly out in the commons?"

She looked away. "No. I have to . . . I . . . I can't."

"Ah," he said, his face falling, "I heard about your mother. How is she?"

"Still in hospital. Not well. Not well at all. And very disappointed that the doctors would not approve her coming to graduation today." It was a lie, but she had told it enough times that it came easily to her lips.

"Well, tell her for me that she has every right to be proud of her daughter." He glanced down at the diploma. "At least she will have that to look at."

"Yes. She made me promise to come there straightaway."

"Well, tell her what I said."

"I shall."

He turned and started away, then spun back around. "Which reminds me. I just heard a rumor about you." He reached down and took her left hand, lifting it up to show the diamond ring on the third finger. "Well, well. So that dashing young man that I've seen walking you around campus finally came to his senses?"

She blushed slightly as she smiled. "Yes, with a little persuasion. We are to be married next spring."

"Then double congratulations. I hear he is from a prominent banking family in Switzerland."

"Yes. His name is Bernhardt von Dietz, from Bern."

"From Von Dietz Global Financial Enterprises?" He was clearly impressed.

"Yes. He is a great-grandson of the founder."

"Very good, my dear." There was a soft chuckle. "How wise of them to bring an economist of your stature into the business."

She laughed. "That's what I keep telling them."

———

Gisela sat across from her mother in the tiny sitting room of the cottage. Her mother had her diploma on her lap, reading every word again. She looked up, and Gisela was not surprised to see tears streaking her cheeks. "I'm so proud of you, Gisela," she whispered.

"I know, Mama. But your name should be there with mine."

"So you forgive me for all those nights I made you study instead of going out to play?"

"I do now," she laughed. "I didn't then."

"I am so proud of you," she whispered. "So proud."

"I know, Mama." She stood. "Would you like some more tea? Another crumpet?"

"Yes, please."

Moving to the table, Gisela refilled both of their cups from the flowered teapot that had been Gisela's present to her mother on her forty-sixth birthday earlier in the year. It had meant skipping lunch for two weeks, but now it was her mother's most prized possession. She picked up another crumpet—a round, spongy griddle cake smeared with butter—and served her. "Mama, won't you please come with me to Switzerland? Just for a few days."

Panic instantly darkened her mother's eyes. "No, but thank you for asking, my dear."

No surprise there. The surprise would have been if she had said yes. She rarely left the village, let alone the country.

Several years ago, when Gisela was doing her master's degree, she had sought out one of the professors at the University of Manchester Medical School. He was in the department of psychiatric medicine. Telling him only that it was a woman she knew, she described her mother's fear of leaving the village, her reluctance to attend social functions, how her life was limited to the tiny circle of her cottage in the village and the manor house in which she now served as housekeeper.

Yet in Hawkings House, the great manor house whose occupants owned the village as part of their thousands of acres of holdings, she was a woman of confidence, assertiveness, and action. In the English system of household servants, the housekeeper was in charge of all female servants. Along with the butler, she ran the entire household, seeing to it that the family's needs were met with impeccable exactness. Gisela had watched her bark orders at the female staff like a drill sergeant. But when she returned to her little cottage, she underwent a complete change.

The professor had been so fascinated with Gisela's account that he spent over an hour with her, probing for more details, especially about this woman's earlier life. Gisela told him that she was the only child of an upper-middle-class family who took great pride in the fact that they descended from German nobility. At seventeen, she had entered into an arranged marriage with the oldest son of a wealthy and prominent family in Munich thirteen years her senior. It had been a good marriage. He loved her and doted on her. She adored him—even worshiped him. At eighteen, just before Hitler invaded Poland, she gave birth to a son. Just over a year later, she had a little girl. Gisela, of course, gave no hint that she was that little girl. Careful not to share details that might reveal something, Gisela told him the rest of the story.

When Gisela had finished her narrative, the psychiatrist had his diagnosis, using the technical terms for her mother's condition. She was paranoid. She was obsessive-compulsive. She had agoraphobia—a panic disorder stemming from the feeling that one cannot escape from one's current situation. This was often triggered by being around or among groups of strangers. It was a wonder she functioned at all, the psychiatrist concluded. Gisela had lowered her head, fighting back tears. "She is the most remarkable woman I have ever known."

Now, as she set the tea in front of her mother, she bent down and kissed her on the top of her head. Her hair was nearly white now, even though she was not yet fifty. The story of her life was written deeply into her face. "I love you, Mum," she whispered.

Her mother looked up and smiled. "I know."

As they sat together, quietly sipping their tea, Gisela Decker let her mind go back to that first day they had arrived at the great Hawkings House estate. She had been dazed by what lay before them. It was a vast estate of thousands of acres with a nearby village totally owned by the Bremley family. Only years later did Gisela learn that the Bremleys were also an aristocratic family from southern Germany.

In the early 1930s, as the Nazis came to power, Lord Bremley (changed from Bremmer) had seen where Adolf Hitler's meteoric rise was taking Germany. The family emigrated, changed their names, hired tutors to help them erase their German accent, and pledged their complete loyalty to England and the United Kingdom. By the time war broke out eight or nine years later, the people round about their great country estate no longer considered them as German and accepted them fully. They were good landlords to their tenants and treated their household servants firmly but fairly. They also insisted that the children of the servants attend school in the village at no charge to their parents.

Within a year, Gisela was fluent in English, speaking it with a perfect Lancashire drawl. She learned to emulate every little mannerism of her friends until she was far more British than German. And she excelled in school. Oh yes, how she excelled in school.

Somewhere during that time, they learned that her father, still held in a POW camp in West Germany, had been charged with war crimes. Eventually he was convicted and hanged. On that day, her mother changed in terrible ways. From that day on, Elizabette never again spoke of returning to Germany. She never even spoke of her life there. It was as if someone had taken those years from her memory.

—◆—

"Liesel?"

Gisela came awake with a start. She half sat up in her bed, momentarily confused. This was not her flat in Manchester. A soft knock sounded again. "Liesel, it's time to get up. Your flight leaves in a few hours."

"Yes, Mama," she called, shaking her head to sweep out the cobwebs. "I'm coming."

When she came into the kitchen, her mother was peeling her a boiled egg. Her toast was on the plate, the orange marmalade placed just above it. Just as it was every time Gisela returned home. Across from her, her mother's egg was already shelled and waiting. Bernhardt kidded Gisela about not knowing how to crack and peel an egg because her mother always did it for her. It was an exaggeration, but not without some truth.

"Good morning, Mama."

"Good morning, Liesel!"

Gisela sat down, reaching across the small table to hold her mother's hand for a moment. She smiled at this woman whom she loved so much. "Do you know how long it has been since you called me Liesel? Why now?"

Elizabette's eyes finally focused. "I never liked the name *Gisela*," she said. "I wish our Captain Hoffman had asked me what name I wanted for you instead of choosing one himself."

"Mama, I have not been Liesel for a very long time." Actually, hearing herself called Liesel left her feeling uneasy.

Her mother leaned in closer, and, to Gisela's surprise, she looked a little impish. That was something she didn't see very often. "I don't like it because it reminds me of geese. *Gisela. Geese.* I don't like it one bit."

The woman who had just received a doctorate in economics *summa cum laude* laughed aloud. "You never told me that before."

There was a tiny smile around the corners of her mother's mouth. "I didn't want to hurt your feelings." Then she was instantly sad. "That is the one thing I truly regret."

"What?"

"That we abandoned our family name. As if we were ashamed of it."

"But, Mama, we had no choice. It was the only way—"

"I know, I know, Gisela." Then her mouth set. "But at least we did not totally turn our back on our heritage. I don't think I could bear it if we had English first names, too."

"Like Mary Alice. Or Mary Amelia. Or Mary Charlotte. Why is it that every girl in England is named Mary?"

That actually won her a smile. "Or Lady Mary Kathleen Bremley."

Gisela took a bite of toast and washed it down with coffee. "But England has been good to us, eh, Mama?"

She nodded, but her eyes were somewhere else. She did that more and more now—just kind of retreated into herself and pushed the world aside. But then she shook it off. "And why did your Bernie man not attend your graduation? Now that you've proven that you're smarter than he is, he's not going to dump you, is he?"

Gisela hooted. "'Dump' me? I think, dear Mama, that you have been watching too many American soap operas on the telly. But, no, he did not dump me. Bernhardt is in New York. The bank is making a major acquisition. He offered to postpone the meeting so he could be here yesterday, but I wouldn't hear of it. It's just a ceremony, Mama. He'll be back in Bern day after tomorrow. And then we'll both come and see you."

Elizabette's eyes probed her daughter's. "Do you love him, Liesel?"

That took her aback. "Of course I do, Mama. Why would you ask that?"

"He's not particularly handsome, you know. His ears are too big. And he laughs like a donkey. Are you sure you're not just after his money?"

"Mama!" Gisela could scarcely believe that her mother was actually teasing her. "I find him very handsome, and it pains me to hear you say otherwise."

"So you *are* after his money. Good for you." Then she smiled to let her know she was teasing her. "He is a good boy, Gisela. And that is enough. You have chosen well."

Gisela shook her head. Bernhardt was thirty-two, six years older than she was, but he was still a boy to her mother. "I know, Mama. I will be happy with him. He makes me laugh."

"Not many can do that anymore. Marry him quickly."

"Won't you please reconsider, Mama? How can I have a wedding without my mother being there? I'll come and get you, and we'll fly back together and . . ." It was no use. She could already see the fear rising up behind her mother's eyes. "Never mind. Bernhardt insists that on our way to our honeymoon in Thailand we shall come here first and tell you all about it."

Elizabette's eyes were instantly glistening. "No wonder you love him, Gisela."

"I do, Mama. I'm very happy." Then she laughed. "But the money is nice, too. You'll never have to work again. We're going to buy you a new house and—"

And just that quickly, Elizabette retreated into her shell again. Gisela took one last bite of egg, wiped her mouth with her serviette, and stood up. "It's all right, Mama. I know you love your little house. And Lady Bremley would have my head if I took you away from them."

"Yes," her mother said after a moment. "She depends on me. They all do."

"I know they do." Gisela bent down and kissed her cheek. "I've got to pack. Thanks for breakfast."

Schloss von Dietz, Bern, Switzerland
Thursday, November 13, 2008

Gisela Elizabette Decker von Dietz watched her mother as she carefully unpacked her single suitcase and began putting things in the closet or in the chest of drawers. And she marveled. Eighty-seven years of life, and everything the woman owned could still be carried in one suitcase.

But Gisela refused to be sad. After all the years and all the invitations and all the pleading, and after she had given up hope that her mother would ever leave England, it happened. Two weeks before, Elizabette had called and asked if there would be a place for her if she came to Switzerland.

Gisela had been so totally taken aback that for a moment she hadn't known what to say. Then she had blurted out, "Oh yes, Mama. For how long?"

What followed utterly astonished her. After a long silence, Elizabette said, "If it would be all right, perhaps I might come to *stay* with you."

Gisela had groped for a chair, suddenly blinded by tears. "Do you mean it?"

"As long as you can stand me." Then her mother made Gisela laugh right out loud. "With Bernhardt gone now, I thought you might need some company."

That was her mother. Bernhardt had died just over two years ago, but *now* Gisela needed company. More amusing, this was not about *her* needs, of course. It wasn't about *her* being eighty-seven and growing increasingly frail. It wasn't *she* who needed company. She was coming to help her little Gisela, the grieving widow. But that was all right. If that was what it took for her to leave the tiny circle of life that had defined her for more than sixty years now, Gisela would not question it in any way. It was, when she thought about it, absolutely stunning. And with it came great joy.

She stood and went over to help her. "Anina is driving in from Zurich tomorrow and should be here in time for lunch. She's taking the children out of school. They are so excited to see you again, and to know that they will now get to see you more often."

"And Niklas?"

"Niklas is in Paris at the moment. He's leading a team from the bank working on a major acquisition. But he'll be here tomorrow in time for dinner."

"Leading the team? At his age?"

Gisela laughed. Her Niklas had turned thirty-five this year. "He *is* one of the senior vice presidents now, Mama. Bernhardt saw to that. He had Niklas sweeping out branch banks before he was ten. By the time he was fifteen, he was an assistant clerk. He also took a degree from Harvard in economics, and a—"

"Like his mother," Elizabette broke in, pulling a face. "It's sufficient to give one a sour stomach. Two economists in the same family."

"And he got an MBA from Harvard in international banking. So he didn't just skate into his present position."

Her mother's face softened. "Ah, Gisela. He is so like you. So bright. So quick to learn. I'm very proud of him. And Anina too, of course," she added as an afterthought. "She is a sweetheart."

"Now, Mama," Gisela chided. "It is true that Anina was content to marry at eighteen and never set foot on a college campus. But don't sell her short. She had the very good sense to marry one of the Richter boys from Zurich. The *banking* Richters of Zurich. Now the two families—and the two banks—are joined, and we have become Switzerland's third largest bank. And seventh largest in Western Europe. So be kind."

"I wasn't being unkind," Elizabette said tartly. "I am delighted that at least one of the family has something besides Euros and dollars running through her veins. And also, she does produce the most beautiful great-grandchildren in all of Switzerland."

"She does indeed. And all three of them will be with her tomorrow."

"Speaking of which, is your Niklas ever going to get married?"

"Oh," she teased, "so it's *my* Niklas now, is it? And this from the woman who has turned down three proposals of marriage and has been a widow now for more than sixty years."

Just that quickly, there were tears in her mother's eyes, and Gisela instantly regretted mentioning her father. That was really something, when you thought about it. After more than six decades, her mother still wept for the man she had lost. Gisela went to her and took her in her arms, and together they stood there, just holding each other and remembering.

———

They had dinner together in the villa overlooking the Thunersee (or Lake Thun) and the spectacular Swiss Alps in the distance. They spoke quietly of earlier times and of the hardships and sacrifices they had experienced. But as they finished their dessert and the servants began clearing away the dishes, Gisela learned the real reason why her mother had finally agreed to come and live with her.

To her surprise, her mother turned to the butler, who was standing back, making sure that all was being done in order. "Gerhardt?"

Interesting that she had remembered the name of the butler after being introduced to more than a dozen servants earlier.

"Yes, Madame?"

"Would you be so kind as to have someone fetch me the small brief-case from my room, please? It's in the armoire."

"But of course," Gerhardt replied, flicking a finger at one of the maids.

As the girl left the room, her mother further surprised Gisela by standing up. "Would you mind if we retired to the sitting room? I have something I would like to show you."

———

What she showed her stunned Gisela. No, more than stunned. It absolutely astonished her. When she finally looked up, her mother was beaming triumphantly. "Where did you get all this, Mama?"

Elizabette was instantly indignant. "That money you send me every month. You said it was mine to spend as I wished. What of it?"

"I don't understand. You bought these somewhere?"

"No, you silly girl. I hired a top-notch security firm in London to do the research for me."

That was even more shocking. Gisela had been sending her mother a thousand Euros a month for over ten years now, but she had never spent any of it as far as Gisela could tell. So she had roughly a hundred and twenty thousand Euros? That was a lot of money.

Her mother picked up the three manila folders she had earlier extracted from her briefcase and waved them in Gisela's face. "I needed information. My time is running out. And after asking you for the last ten years to help me and getting no response, I decided that if I am to get any peace before I die, I will have to get it done myself. The *Gauleiter* was not the only one who needed attention."

Gisela's face flushed. "I know, but when Bernhardt learned about that, he went into orbit."

Elizabette slammed the folders back down on the table between them. "Well, Bernhardt isn't here any longer. So you'll have to come up with a new excuse. You promised me that you would never forget, just as I can never forget. We have lived with the shame and the dishonor and the humiliation for all these years. Isn't that long enough? Isn't it time we finally did something so that when I meet my *Schatzi* I will not have to hang my head in shame?"

Gisela's head lowered. "Yes, Mama."

"Has all of this"—she looked around at the luxurious room—"made you soft? I understood while Bernhardt was alive. Well, Bernhardt is gone now. And still you sit and do—"

"I get it, Mama," Gisela said sharply. "You don't know what's in my heart, so don't lecture me like I was nine again." Then, to deflect her mother from saying anything more, she picked up one of the folders and opened it. The top sheaf of papers had a black-and-white photo of a handsome man in the uniform of a German army officer clipped to the front page. She stared for a moment, not comprehending. Then it hit her. She knew this man. "Is that Captain Hoffman?"

"Yes, our deliverer. He is gone now, but this has all the information the security company has been able to find on his family."

"Including that cold witch of a sister of his?" Gisela said, bitter with the memory of Katarina Schreiber, who had thrown the title of scullery maid in her mother's face.

"Yes," her mother responded with surprising gentleness, "including his sister." She took the papers, removed the paper clip, and showed Gisela a color photo of a tall, stately woman standing beside a somewhat portly man. They had four children with them—a boy and three girls. The Swiss Alps were in the background.

"You have to remember, Gisela, her brother had just been thrown into prison because of what he did for us. Can you blame her for being angry?"

"Yes." But Gisela didn't really mean it. She knew full well that the woman could have refused to help them and left them to make their own way to England. But she had seen it through for her brother's sake. "And so now, you're going to punish her?"

Elizabette was dumbfounded. "Punish her? I have sent her fifty thousand Euros as a small token of our thanks. Anonymously, of course. And I hope to send her more."

"You *what?*"

"Oh," her mother snapped back, "don't act so shocked. You said it was my money to do with as I chose."

Reeling, dazed, Gisela picked up another folder, the thickest of the three. On the tab were two German words: *Gerechtigkeit endlich. Justice at last.* "And what do you plan to do with these?"

Her mother reached out, quick as the strike of a cat's paw, and grabbed the folder from her. "Never you mind. Since you no longer have the heart for this, I shall take it up with your son."

———◆———

Niklas von Dietz was a man of the world in about every possible way that phrase could be interpreted. He knew people often said that of him—occasionally in his presence—and he never corrected them, because it was true.

As the only son and primary heir of Bernhardt von Dietz and Gisela Decker von Dietz, he had been lavished with attention and pampered with luxury from the day he was born. He did not consciously consider himself superior to others; his exalted status was so deeply ingrained in his nature that he took it for granted, just as he took breathing for granted. *Prodigy. Gifted. A financial genius. Mature beyond his years.* These were all words and phrases people used to describe Niklas, and he took them as his just due.

He was strikingly handsome. Six foot three inches tall. Long, wavy, light brown hair brushed straight back without a part in it. Broad shoulders and flat stomach. Wide-set blue eyes, high cheekbones, and firm jawline. In manner, he was deceptively pleasant, with a smile that could charm a stone gargoyle into life. But underneath, there was this powerful energy emanating from him. Some even called it ruthlessness. Even men much senior to him acknowledged his natural leadership ability and tolerated his meteoric rise through the banking house of Von Dietz Global Financial Enterprises.

Since English was the language of world commerce and business, Gisela and her husband had spoken English in the home as well as German. With perfect ease, Niklas could switch between English with a distinctly Lancashire accent, English with a Boston Yankee accent, and absolutely impeccable German. And since Switzerland had three official languages and required all students to study at least two of them, he was also fluent in French and Italian and could converse to some degree in Spanish and Dutch.

Many a mother and grandmother in Europe's most prominent families were scheming tirelessly to find ways to bring their daughters to his attention. He was surrounded by some of Europe's most beautiful women, and he enjoyed their company, but he never got close enough to have even once been engaged. Much to the disappointment of his mother. She was sixty-eight now and wanted more grandchildren. Anina and her husband had made it clear that three was enough for them.

All of this was playing in Gisela's mind as she watched her son going through the stack of papers and photos one by one. When he finished, he straightened them into a neat pile, then put them back into the folder and stacked it on top of the others. He looked up. "This is amazing. I can't believe how much information she's gathered."

"And that's all you have to say?"

He shrugged. "What do you want me to say? I've already told Granny that she needs much more than this if she hopes to accomplish her purpose."

"Such as?"

"Well, for example, this doesn't have current addresses for everyone. You should also know what their financial circumstances are. How many family members are there? How close are the family ties? Where does the family live? What do they do for recreation and entertainment? Do they have little secrets we can use to our advantage? Do they—"

"I get it, Niklas."

He tapped the folders on the desk. "But I don't think we need to spend a lot of money just to humor her."

"To humor her?" The tartness in her voice brought his head up. "Is that what you think I'm doing?"

"I . . . well, you surely can't be serious about her plans."

"Why can't I? Maybe it's time."

He was genuinely alarmed. "Mama, stop it. This is craziness. Granny is an eighty-seven-year-old woman who is obsessed with the past. Don't encourage her in this. You can see how frail she is." He glanced over at the grandfather clock, which showed nearly ten o'clock. "I mean, look at the time, and she's gone to bed already. She used to outlast all of us."

"All the more reason to delay no further."

He jumped up and began pacing. "Would you put the assets and the reputation of Von Dietz Global Financial Enterprises at risk? Ruin everything your husband and his father and three generations before him created?"

When she said nothing, he threw up his hands. "Think of Anina. Think of your grandchildren, Mama. Would you risk bringing shame on them? On us all?"

"Now you're being ridiculous, Niklas. You know I would never do that."

"Then—"

"But I'm with Granny in this all the way, Son. You need to understand that. She's right. This wrong has gone unanswered long enough. There has to be restitution. It has to be made right to maintain our family's honor. But Von Dietz Financial is part of our family heritage too. So I give you my word that I will never jeopardize that in any way, not legally, not financially. There will not be one Euro taken from the corporation's books. Nor will it involve Anina and the children in any way, shape, or form. They will remain totally innocent of this."

"Well, thank whatever gods there may be that there is some tiny semblance of sanity left in this family."

"Don't get cheeky with me, Niklas. You forget yourself."

He backed off immediately, but he was still agitated. "I can't believe I'm hearing this," he muttered. "From Granny, yes. But not from you." Then suddenly he was up again, too worked up to remain seated. "Why now, Mama? Why after all these years? Why this sudden urgency?"

"You know the answer to that. First and foremost, your father wouldn't hear of it while he was alive. Not any part of it. You saw his reaction when I took action against the *Gauleiter*. After that flaming battle between us, I promised him I would do nothing more. Not while he was alive."

She got up and went to him, taking both of his hands and turning him to face her. "Now, it's Mama I am dealing with. I made promises to her, too. Years ago. And she's come here to hold me to them, Niklas. Why do you think she finally left England? That is an enormous sacrifice for her, as you know. Do I just ignore all that?"

"She's eighty-seven. She's not got that much longer. Just stall her."

Jerking her hands away, Gisela glared up at him. "While she was still in her teens she moved into a house like this. She knew nothing but wealth and comfort and luxury. Like you, Niklas. And then it was all ripped away from her. You think about that. You have never known poverty. You have never known hunger. You have never slept between anything but silk sheets. Everything you have, everywhere you go, anything you do, you are swathed in luxury and privilege. Only the finest for our Niklas. Well, try to imagine having all of that ripped away from you and spending the rest of your life scrubbing floors as a kitchen maid."

He started to turn away, but her hand shot out and gripped him by the chin. "Don't you ignore me. Think about it! Your whole life turned upside down. Not because of mistakes you made, but because evil men wanted what you have. What would you do?"

He pulled free and backed away. "All right, I get it. I'm sorry. But, Mama, you're asking too much. I will not be part of something that risks everything our family has accomplished."

She sat back down and motioned toward his chair. "Sit down,

Niklas. I want to ask you a question. And you have to be absolutely honest with me."

He forced a smile. "Are you setting a trap for me?"

She chuckled. "I surely hope so."

"Go ahead."

"Are your concerns only financial, only about the bank and our other companies? Or do you find what I am suggesting morally distasteful as well?"

"I . . ."

"Come on. You and I both know that your father and his father—and probably several generations of von Dietzes beyond that—didn't mind bending the law occasionally if they could make a profit. And you personally have been part of acquisitions and mergers that have left hundreds, even thousands, of people in financial ruin. I also know that you personally have used considerable sums of von Dietz capital to influence the outcome of deals, or as downright bribes—all off the books, of course. So get off your moral high horse and answer my question."

He glowered at her for a time, but finally he shook his head. "I knew it was a trap."

"And you're caught. Admit it."

"All right. So the moral implications of what you're talking about are not my first concern."

She hooted softly. "More like, 'not *any* concern.' But go on."

"You asked me to picture what it would mean if I were torn from my present life. Well, I'm asking you the same thing. Because if something goes wrong here, we're talking about you spending the rest of your life in a prison cell. And Granny too, for that matter."

"You think I've not considered that? But it's not going to happen."

"Oh, really? Guarantee me that, and you can count me in."

"It's simple. What was your father's favorite saying? You know, the one you heard about fifteen or twenty times a day?"

He hesitated, then smiled. "Plan impeccably. Strike boldly. Exit swiftly. And leave nothing to chance. *Nothing.*"

"Yes. Well, that's your answer." She decided it was time to go in for the kill. "So what if I told you we can do all that Mother wants done, keep ourselves totally safe while doing it, *and* make a ton of profit at the same time?"

"I would say that you were getting senile in your old age."

Her brows lowered. "I'll let that pass, boy, but watch your mouth. I'm not too old to have you stripped of your vice president's position."

That clearly knocked him back. He laughed nervously. "I do believe you could, Mama."

"Not only could, but would. Not for saying you want no part of this. That is your choice. But you start forgetting your place in this family and start thinking you're something really special, and I will feel it is my duty to teach you some humility. Got it?"

"Yes, Mama."

"Good. Here is what I propose. If you are in, I want you to start immediately on a plan for making this work. That would include setting up bank accounts, creating whatever organizational structure you feel is required, recruiting the kinds of people we need, and so on—and all of this totally off the grid. You're the one with the Harvard MBA, so just do it. I know this will take time, especially since we want it seamless and flawless. That will be hard on Granny, but if she knows we're really committed to this, then she'll be all right."

"And where does the funding for all this come from? I'm guessing we're going to need a million Euros just to get under way. And if you agree that we can't take it out of Von Dietz, then—"

"I will fund the initial one million out of my own personal funds. After that, you generate your own income."

"And how do I do that?"

Her look instantly made him color. "Never mind. But here's the deal, Niklas. Everything you make from there on, minus expenses, is yours to keep."

She was pleased to see the greed that filled his eyes almost immediately. "Everything?"

"Yes. So are you in or out?"

Taking a deep breath, he nodded. "I'm in."

Her face was like flint now. "And what is our guiding philosophy?"

"Plan impeccably. Strike boldly. Exit swiftly. And leave nothing to chance. *Nothing.*"

"Good boy. We'll tell Granny in the morning. She was sure you would see it our way."

Schloss von Dietz, Bern, Switzerland
December 24, 2009

One year and just over a month later, on Christmas Eve 2009, Elizabette Decker passed away peacefully at 11:29 a.m. She was eighty-eight years old.

Her family were all there at her bedside. As were the household servants, at Elizabette's request. She thanked them for their kindness to her. She next bid farewell to her granddaughter, Anina, Anina's husband, and their three children. All were crying, but Anina was so distraught she could barely stand. When finished, Elizabette then requested some time alone with her daughter and her grandson.

As the door closed and the two of them moved up to the bed, she reached out and took the hands of Niklas and Gisela. And these were her last words to them.

"Swear to me that my death will not end this. Swear it to me now. Swear it on my grave. Swear it!"

"I so swear," Gisela said in a choked voice.

"It is under way," Niklas said, eyes glistening.

"*Swear it!*" she shouted hoarsely.

"I swear it, Granny. You have our word."

PART ONE

Return

CHAPTER 1

Lakeview Motel, Page, Arizona
June 21, 2011, 11:33 p.m.

Hi! My name is Carruthers Monique McAllister, AKA Danni McAllister to everyone other than my mom.

If you are wondering how and why anyone living in the 21st century could have a name like Carruthers, please see "My Personal Journal: Volume 1, p. 2." The details of how I got my nickname and why my mother steadfastly refuses to call me by it are all found there. It's pretty boring stuff, so I won't repeat it here.

I am currently sitting on the toilet—and FYI, the lid is down, thank you very much!!!—in the bathroom of a motel in Page, Arizona. Mom and my little brother, Cody, are asleep in our room, and this is the only place where I can have the light on without waking them up. We're here because my best bud, Rick Ramirez, is in a clinic a block or two from here with a gunshot wound in his leg. And no, I'm not going to explain that further. See Vol. 1 where all is revealed.

I am 16 years and 9 days old. I will be a junior at Wayne County High School this fall. I am five feet five inches tall, have green eyes and a ton of Irish freckles. I weigh about . . . ha! Had you going there, didn't I? ☺

I have dark, straight hair—like my mom's—which I haven't cut since I was twelve. It is nearly down to the middle of my back now. Usually I wear it in a ponytail, or Mom puts it in a long French braid. It takes a lot of work to take care of it, and so I've been thinking about cutting it off before school starts. But when I told Rick that last night, he told me not to be stupid. He loved it the way it was, especially when it's braided. That's Rick. As usual, I wasn't sure if it was a compliment or a put-down. But, FYI, I won't be cutting my hair anytime this year.

Okay, enough with the introduction stuff. I see that it's close to midnight and I am getting very tired. As is my bottom. So just a quick word about today. Me and Mom and Cody are the only ones still here in Page with Rick. Grandpère had to go to SL to be with Dad, and Charlie Ramirez (Rick's dad) and Rick's sisters had to go back to Hanksville, so they all left yesterday.

The doctors say that Rick can go home today. So Clay—that's Clay Zabriskie, AIC (Special Agent in Charge) of the SLC Regional FBI office—is coming down in a chopper to take us all home. Which is way cool! I'm going to see if the pilot will do a fly-over of Hanksville so we can wave to everybody from the air. Wake them up a little.

It's going to be good to get Rick out of here. The nurses here—especially the single, younger ones—have spoiled him shame-lessly. Another day or two of this and his ego will be bigger than a football stadium. I've told him that several times just to keep him humble.

Seriously, all kidding aside, every day I thank Heavenly Father that Rick is okay. If he had died, I—nope! Not going there. Not now. Not ever. I can't even think about that.

So, before I start bawling my eyes out, let me explain about this Volume 1, Volume 2 thing. On my thirteenth birthday, my grandfather, who lives with us and whom we call Grandpère, gave me my first journal. He encouraged me to keep a record of sig-nificant things in my life. I have been doing that now for three years.

But about a week ago, my family had a terrible experience. A gang of professional thieves tried to kidnap us and hold us for ransom. It was a horrible few days, but we were very blessed, and with the help of God, along with a friend by the name of Le Gardien (French for The Guardian), we managed to escape and stop them. That was how Rick got shot.

As you might guess, during that week I didn't do a lot of writing in my journal. But now, with Rick in the hospital, I decided this was a good time to catch up on everything that had happened. I wrote quite a bit on Monday when Rick was still sleeping a lot because of his pain meds. Then this morning, I left Mom and Cody sleeping in the motel and came down early. Rick was awake and we had a good talk, but he crashed again after breakfast, so while Cody and Mom went back to the motel to watch a movie, I finished the rest of my account.

I was glad I did. A little before noon, Grandpère called from Salt Lake City. (He and my father are up there closing on the sale of the Danny Boy Mine.) After asking how Rick was doing, he asked me if I had my journal with me. When I said yes, he said that it was very important that I write up a full account of all that happened while it was still fresh in my mind. He seemed very pleased when I told him that I already had done so.

What he said next really kinda knocked me off my saddle. He said that he was sending me a new journal. When I told him that I had only used about two-thirds of the first one, and that I didn't need a new one yet, here's kinda how the conversation went from there:

Grandpère: Did you write about the part Le Gardien played in all that happened?

Me: Of course.

GP: In full detail? Even the little things?

Me: Yes, everything. Did you not want me to?

GP: No, I'm glad you did. We need a record made. But Danni, promise me that you'll keep the journal with you every moment until we can put it in the safety deposit box in the bank.

Me—in mild shock: Are you kidding? My journal in a bank vault. What? Do you think someone's going to offer us a movie contract or something? (Ha Ha)

GP—not a hint of a smile in his voice: I'm sending you a new journal via overnight mail. Finish the record up to the sinking of the boat and the arrests. That should be your last entry. Thereafter, write in the new journal.

About then, I didn't know what to say. For some reason I had little chills dancing up and down my back.

GP: You've watched your Dad use dynamite enough that you know what it can do, right?

Me: Yes.

GP: Good. Think of your journal as if it were a dozen sticks of dynamite, okay?

Then he suddenly said he had to go and hung up on me.

Sure enough, my new journal was delivered to the clinic just before lunch. That is what I am writing in now, sitting on the toilet in our bathroom while Mom and Cody sleep. And BTW, the old journal is locked in the motel safe, along with the duplicate pouch. Oh, yeah. That's another story, but not for tonight. It's past midnight. My handwriting looks like a lizard just ran across the page, so good night, one and all. This ol' girl is headed for bed.

The intermittent buzzing, though very far off, was an unwelcome intrusion. I was lost and didn't want to be interrupted. This was bliss that you never wanted to end. And then it started again.

"Carruthers! Wake up."

I cracked one eye open with a tremendous effort. To my surprise, Mom was standing in a doorway, one towel clutched around her, another towel rubbing at her hair. For a moment, I had no idea where I was. "Mom?" I managed to mumble.

Buzz. Buzz.

"Carruthers!" Much sharper now. "Answer the phone."

With a groan I rolled onto my side and started groping for my phone. I recognized the sound now. I had put my phone on vibrate last night so as not to wake up Mom and Cody.

"Not your phone. My phone. There on the dresser. Hurry!"

"Where's Cody?" I said, pulling myself up to a sitting position.

"At the swimming pool. Hurry, Carruthers. I can't get it. I'm dripping wet."

I got out of bed and retrieved her phone, swiped my thumb across the "slide to unlock" button, and put it up to my face. "Hullo?"

"Angelique?"

"No, sorry. This is Danni. I'm her daughter."

"Hi, Danni. This is Clay. Is your mom there?"

"Oh, hi, Clay. Yeah, but she's just getting out of the tub. Can she call you back? Or can I give her a message?"

"Sure. You ready?"

"Uh . . ." I looked around for a paper and pencil.

"It's not that long, Danni," he chuckled. "You don't need to write it down." He paused. "You all right? You sound like you've got a hangover."

"Thanks. What time is it, anyway?" I turned to see sunlight behind the drapes.

"Almost nine. Sorry to wake you up."

"Who said I was awake? What's the message?"

"I talked to the clinic administrator a couple of minutes ago. The doctors have confirmed that Rick will be released today, but they want him to take it easy for at least another week."

"Good luck with that," I said. "He's already saying he won't need the crutches."

"That's a good sign, but the doctors will set him straight on that." He paused for a moment. "Danni, tell your mom that we'll be to the clinic about ten. We'll be coming by car because—"

"Car? I thought you said you were bringing down a chopper."

"We are, but we're going to set her down a little ways out of town. This one has FBI markings on it, and we want to avoid attracting a lot of attention. We'll have a car waiting for us. There are some things I need to share with you guys before we take off. So we'll have a little meeting there at the clinic before we leave."

With that, I was finally fully awake. "Is something wrong, Clay?"

"No, no. Just some logistical things that we need to talk through. No big deal."

I stifled a huge yawn. "All right. I'll tell her."

"Great. See you in about an hour."

⬥

Clay stuck his head into the medical center's conference room at 10:07. He was not in a suit and tie but in jeans, sports shirt, and hiking boots. He looked like one of the locals. He went straight to Rick and shook his hand. "How's the leg coming along?"

"A little slower than my other one at the moment," he said.

Clay's face softened. "As you may remember, I once took a bullet in my right leg, so you have my full sympathy."

He moved down the table, briefly greeting Mom, me, and Cody. Then, taking a seat at the end of the table, he plunged right in. "Okay. We don't want to spend a lot of time here, but there have been some new developments, so we need to make a couple of changes in our plans."

"What developments?" Mom asked.

"First, some good news. Danni's guess that your kidnappers might be Europeans was a good one. We contacted Interpol and—" He glanced at Cody. "Do you know what Interpol is?"

That irked Cody. "Yes. It's like the FBI, only it's in Europe."

"Actually, they have offices in about a hundred and ninety countries, but yeah, that's pretty much it. Anyway, we sent them what little information your family was able to provide, along with a few fingerprints we were able to pull off the houseboat and the vehicles."

"And?" I asked eagerly.

"More than I expected, to be honest. It turns out that they have been tracking a highly sophisticated, very professional group that has been operating in Europe for the last several years. They believe this group is responsible for at least half a dozen kidnappings and extortion schemes.

Mom broke in. "You mean like some kind of political extremist group?"

"No. Their motivation seems to be strictly financial. So far they have raked in about nine million dollars. So you can guess how frustrated they must be with losing your twenty million. But they have no known political or religious affiliation, so far as Interpol can determine."

Mom was not liking this one bit. "So how did they pick a family in Hanksville, Utah?"

"That's what Interpol would like to know. They're sending over a couple of their people to interrogate our prisoners. Not that I have a lot of hope for that. So far the prisoners have refused to say a single word to us. They even refused to talk to their court-appointed attorney."

I raised my hand, but Clay didn't see it. He was extracting a piece of paper from his shirt pocket. "Danni, you and Rick said you overheard some of them calling each other by their first names. Do you remember what they were?"

Rick answered immediately. "The two who chased us into Leprechaun Canyon, the ones Danni called Doc and Gordo, called each other Raul and Lew."

"Yeah," I came in. "Lew was the short, fat one. Raul the tall, ugly, mean one. And El Cobra called his wife Eileen, and she called him Armando."

"Good, that's what I remembered. Interpol thinks the leader of the group is named Armando Mendosa. He is not from Latin America, as you supposed, but from Malaga, Spain."

"Is Eileen Irish?" I asked. "She had a strong accent."

"She is. She's originally from Dublin but now holds Spanish citizenship, probably because of her marriage to Mendosa."

Rick was following this closely. "And Doc and Gordo?"

Clay looked at his list. "Raul is probably Raul Jose Carrero Muñoz. He was born in Colombia, but his family immigrated to Spain when he was a boy. He and Armando evidently were close friends in high school." He smiled at me. "And he is known to have a liking for Doc Martens shoes. Lew is almost certainly Lewis Fortier. He was born in England but lived with his French father in the Basque region on the border of France and Spain for most of his life.

"They're still working on some of the other names, but they think they have identified one from France, two Brits, and one Belgian. Very international."

"So, the three who escaped are probably the two Brits and the one from Belgium," I guessed.

Mom's head swung around. "Escaped? Who escaped?"

Clay was startled, then instantly apologetic. "Sorry, I gave Mack and Jean-Henri that information yesterday. I forgot I hadn't shared that with you yet. But yes, that is correct. As Danni knows, when the gang took off from the houseboat, three boats headed upstream for Bullfrog Marina, but one went downstream with three men in it. We had teams waiting at all the marinas and picked up all of them except the three who went south. They never showed up."

"So they slipped past your agents?" Rick asked.

"Actually, no. Late that afternoon, we got a call from a park ranger. He found an abandoned boat at a place called Crosby Canyon. You familiar with where that is?"

All of us looked at each other, then shook our heads.

"It's a small cove at the north end of Warm Creek Bay. That's the next bay up from Wahweap. There's a back country road that comes right down to the lake at that point. It's the only place on Lake Powell that you can get lake access by vehicle other than the main highways."

"So they had someone waiting for them there?" Mom asked.

Again he shook his head. "We don't think so. Our team did some exploring up the road for a ways. They found a place on a little two-track side road where someone had parked a truck in the underbrush of a dry wash. There were three sets of boot prints around where the truck had been parked, and fresh tire marks leading away from the site. We're pretty sure they initially came in that way, then left their truck there so they could go out that way. Which is actually pretty clever when you think about it. Don't send everyone out by the same route. And it worked."

"Where does that road go?" Cody asked.

Clay's sigh was one of frustration and weariness. "Unfortunately, it splits a few miles above the lake. If you turn west, you come out on US 89 at Big Water, which is just above the Arizona line. If you go east, eventually the road goes all the way north to Escalante. So, several options."

Mom said, "So they got away?"

He shrugged. "Probably. We've put out an APB—an all points bulletin—to every police and sheriff's department in Southern Utah and Northern Arizona. If they did go out through Big Water and cross into Arizona, they probably headed for Mexico. By now they could even be back in Europe."

"Which means they are no longer a threat to us?" Mom said.

"Until we find them, we always consider them a credible threat. But we think it is a very low possibility. The plan seems to have been to have the whole gang scatter to the wind, get out of the U.S. as quickly as possible."

I had another thought. "What about the two locals who came in the pickup to help Gordo?"

"Ah, yes. Thanks to your description of the truck, we picked them up in Salt Lake City. They were a couple of lowlifes, muscle that El Cobra hired out of Salt Lake and brought in just to back up his team. They are cooperating, but they know practically nothing."

Cody abruptly stood up. "So can we go home now?"

Clay pulled a face. "Um . . . yes, but . . . I've got one more thing first."

It was obvious that Clay was uncomfortable. He kept glancing over at me, then away. "Okay, here's the deal. I've been on the phone with Joel Jamison, who is the Deputy Director of the FBI in Washington. He is my direct-line supervisor. We are concerned that if this whole story gets out, we're going to have a media blitz that could greatly hamper our investigation."

"You mean about us?" I asked, somewhat knocked back by that.

He waved his hands in the air, like he was putting up a banner. "Young Teen Thwarts Vicious Gang of Professional Criminals. Boyfriend Shot."

"He's not my boyfriend," I broke in. "We're just best friends."

"That's right," Rick said, blushing a little.

Clay laughed shortly. "Try selling that to the media." He turned back to Mom. "Think about it. Home break-in, family held at gunpoint, twenty-million-dollar ransom, a rhodium mine in the mountains. Come on. If this gets out, there will be a media feeding frenzy."

Mom still looked confused. "Are you suggesting we keep it all a secret?"

"No, that's not possible. When we made the arrests at Bullfrog Marina, there were people around who saw us do that. And then, of course, there's the boatload of people who came over to help Armando and Eileen and who were shot at. They immediately called that in to park headquarters. So far, the press hasn't got ahold of that yet, but rest assured, they will soon enough. Not only will publicity severely hamper our investigation, but it could put you at risk."

Mom's head came up slowly. "What do you mean?"

He shrugged. "Your family are key witnesses in this case. Any convictions will depend heavily on your testimony."

We all looked at each other. This was not good.

He went on quickly. "So, here's what we recommend. There will come a time when we will release the full story, of course, but for now we've put out a brief press release. It states that over the weekend, the FBI and the Utah Highway Patrol cooperated in making a major drug bust of one of the Mexican cartels transporting drugs here at Lake Powell. Your names have not been mentioned, nor will they be for now.

We're saying that this is an ongoing investigation and no further info will be available at this time."

"Um . . ." I raised my hand. "Aren't you forgetting about Rick here? The staff here at the clinic all know that he was shot."

"Yeah," Rick said. "I was thinking about what I might tell people when I show up in Hanksville hobbling around on crutches."

Mom laughed. "You'll be like a field of flowers to a hive of bees, especially with the girls."

To my surprise, Clay was looking at me now. "I was just getting to that." He turned to Rick. "Even while you were on your way here, I talked to the clinic administrator and told him that the gunshot wound was an accident, and that until the investigation into the incident is completed, the person responsible will not be identified." There was a momentary flash of panic on Clay's face. "You didn't tell anyone what really happened, did you?"

"No. Like I said, no one asked me about it."

I smirked at him. "And believe me, Clay, Rick never volunteers any information unless you pry it out of him."

Clay ignored that, and so did Rick. Clay was looking at me again, and, to my further surprise, he looked very apologetic. "But since Rick *is* being released today, we're going to have to release the name of the person who shot him."

"Who?" Rick, Cody, and I all blurted it out together.

He cleared his throat. "Well, um . . . when you think about it . . . uh . . . the angle of the wound is such that it clearly was not self-inflicted. So we can't blame Rick. And . . . uh . . . since we can't say anything about El Cobra's team being on the houseboat with you, I . . . I think we'll have to say that it was a family member."

The silence in the room was total for about two seconds. Then I shot to my feet. "You're telling everyone it was me? But you—"

He held up his hand, cutting me off. "Think about it. Your dad often carries a pistol, but he has a reputation for being very, very careful with his weapons."

Mom saw it now too. "And everyone knows that I don't like guns, even though I know how to use them."

"No!"

"And it's a bit of a stretch that Cody would be handling a weapon on a houseboat."

I turned to Rick, and he had this stupid grin on his face, like he was two years old. I dropped my head in my hands and groaned. "No, no, no."

"Come on, Danni," Clay said softly. "This has to be believable. And eventually the truth will come out. Then you'll be the big hero."

I didn't look up. "Okay. I get it. Danni loves guns. Danni's a ditz. Danni's the perfect fall guy. Or fall girl." I was picturing how this was going to go down in Hanksville. Lisa. Angie. Megan. Rick's friends. All doubled over with laughter. The lunch crowd at Blondie's. The guys at the service station. The clerks at the store.

I moaned inwardly. *Hanksville was only the beginning!* Even though the towns in Wayne County were miles apart, I knew without the slightest doubt that the word would spread to every person within a hundred miles, faster than you could spit at a jackrabbit.

"I'm sorry, Danni," Clay started, "but—"

Waving him off, I glared at Rick, who quickly wiped the grin off his face and was trying to look sufficiently stricken. "One crack out of you, buddy," I hissed, "and I'll shoot you in the other leg. Maybe in both arms, too."

"One more thing," Clay said. "Flying you guys into Hanksville in an FBI chopper is no longer an option."

"Why don't we walk back?" I suggested sarcastically. "Or swim. It might take a little longer, but hey, who cares?"

He laughed. "Thanks, Danni. Thanks for seeing what has to be done." He turned to Rick. "We took that Silverado pickup back to the rental company. Your 4Runner is in the parking lot at Bullfrog Marina where you met El Cobra and Eileen. It has all your stuff in it. So, here's the plan. Even landing at Bullfrog has too high a visibility, so we'll drop you off on the other side of the lake, near Hall's Crossing. Once the chopper's gone, then you can take the ferry across to Bullfrog and pick up your car." He reached in his back pocket, took out his wallet, and extracted two hundred-dollar bills. He handed them to Mom. "Here's enough to pay for your ferry tickets and to grab a bite of lunch before you head back."

She nodded as she took the two bills. "What about our Suburban? They brought me and Cody here in that, and I assume it's still at Bullfrog too."

"Not anymore. Your father took it Salt Lake to join up with Mack. So you and Cody will go back with Rick and Danni. Okay?"

She nodded, visibly relaxing. And I had to admit, it was good to know that Clay had thought of everything and was not taking any chances.

"Mack and Jean-Henri are at my office in Salt Lake right now, giving their statements. They should be back home in Hanksville by late this afternoon or this evening. Then we're hoping things can start getting back to normal for the McAllisters and the Ramirezes."

He stood up. "We have new satellite-capable smart phones in the chopper for you. One for your dad, too, Rick. They have your names on them. They are bug free and encrypted so they are completely secure. Mack already has his. Jean-Henri didn't want one. I had the staff put my number and all of your numbers on each of the favorites list, along with all your personal data—contacts, calendar stuff, and so on. These are your personal phones now, even though they have satellite capability. Any questions?"

No one spoke.

"Then let's go." He stood up and led us out.

As we reached the chopper, the rotor began to spin with a sharp whine even before we were out of the car. One of the waiting agents took Clay aside and conferred quickly with him. He nodded and turned to us.

"Good news," he said. "We received a tip from a service station in Big Water. Last night, three guys in a white Ford pickup truck stopped for gas at the station. An attendant came out to help, but they waved him away." He grinned. "But not before he saw at least one assault rifle in the backseat."

"Our three escapees?" I blurted, delighted with that news.

"We think so. Unfortunately, the guy didn't think to get a license plate number, but he said they did turn south, headed for Arizona, just as we thought."

His fellow agent spoke up. "We're already on it. We've got teams setting up checkpoints along all the major roads as quickly as possible."

"Good. All right, guys. Into the chopper. Rick first."

I was the last to climb in, and Clay gave me a hand up as I did so. "Are you sure you're ready for this?" he shouted as I strapped myself in.

"What?" I shouted back. "Oh, you mean being sacrificed on the altar of shame?"

He laughed. A few moments later, we lifted off and headed east.

CHAPTER 2

By the time Clay dropped us off half a mile above Hall's Crossing and we walked down to the ferry, took it across to Bullfrog Marina, grabbed a bite to eat, and finally approached Hanksville in Rick's 4Runner, it was almost three twenty in the afternoon. Mom was driving. I was in the front seat with her. Cody sat in the back with Rick, giving Rick enough room to stretch out his leg. I could tell by watching his face that it was hurting him, but, of course, he said nothing.

However, when we saw the town in the hazy distance, Rick leaned forward. "Could you get my phone out of the bag, Danni? We should be in coverage by now."

"It's a satellite phone," Cody reminded him. "You have coverage everywhere."

Rick nodded and went on. "Dad's at work, so I told Aunt Shauna that I'd call her and tell her when we were almost home."

"We'll drop you off, Rick," Mom said, "and then we'll get your car back to you tomorrow, or later tonight if you need it."

"No," he said. "Go to your house first. I can drive that far."

I had bent over and was opening the gym bag, but with that I shot him a warning look. He ignored me. But then I think he saw Mom staring him down in the mirror. "Uh . . . or maybe it would be easiest to just have you drop me off."

"That's better," I said. I found his phone. "Want me to dial it for you?"

"Yeah." Another surprise. I did so, listened until it started to ring, then handed it back to him. He took it, wincing as he leaned back again.

I was still watching him when his eyebrows shot up. "Dad?" A moment's pause. "I thought you were working today." He listened again. I could hear the tinny sound of his father's voice through the phone. "Oh. That's good. I'm anxious to see you too. I was going to tell Shauna, but—yeah, I'm fine, Dad. Really." Pause. "Still a little tender, but—"

I shook my head and gave him a pitying look.

"Look, Dad. Mrs. McAllister is going to drop me off. We should be there in about ten minutes, and—"

This time the interruption went on for thirty or forty seconds. Rick's face fell, and his expression turned from surprise to irritation and then finally to dejection. "Okay. Okay. Yeah, I understand." And he hung up.

"What is it?" I asked. I knew him well enough to know that he was not happy.

"We're to stop at the Chevron station. There's a welcoming party waiting for us."

"What?" Mom and I blurted out simultaneously.

"Clay called my dad. That's why he's home early. Clay thinks it's a good idea to get this over with."

"Get what over with?" Cody came in.

Rick pulled a face. "Clay asked Dad to call the mayor and tell him what happened to me. Which he did. You know Mayor Brackston. He's decided he wants to have a 'Let's-Welcome-the-Wounded-Warrior-Back-Home' experience this afternoon. So there's already people gathering at the Chevron station."

"No!" I was genuinely dismayed. "Not today." I wasn't ready for this yet.

"Unfortunately," Rick went on, "Dad agrees. He says the sooner we deal with it, the sooner it will go away. So he's calling the mayor back right now to let them know that we're almost there. Dad will meet us at the station."

"Thanks, Rick," I muttered.

His eyes widened in surprise. "For what?"

"This involves all of us, you know. Not just you."

My mother jerked around so fast, I thought she was going to take my head off. But after a moment, she shook her head and looked away. "I agree with your father, Rick. Let's be done with it and get on with life."

In Hanksville—which had a registered population of 219 in the 2010 census—three is considered a crowd, five, a mob. Mom slowed down as the Chevron station came into sight, and I groaned aloud. There had to be fifty or sixty people milling around, with more coming on the run as we approached.

Someone saw us and started pointing and yelling, waving their arms, jumping up and down. In a moment, the whole crowd was swarming toward us—to the point that Mom had to bring the car to a stop just barely off the highway. As the crowd pushed in, I felt a hand on my shoulder. I turned. Rick managed a tight smile, and I could see the pain in his eyes. "Sorry, Danni."

Talk about feeling awful. *What a self-centered brat you are, Danni McAllister. What makes you think that life is always about you?* I turned all the way around in the seat and reached over and took him by the hand. "No, Rick. I'm the one who's sorry. I . . . ." Suddenly I was fighting this huge lump about halfway down my throat. "There I go again. Queen of Stupid. Miss Insensitive. Danni the Dork."

He smiled. "Are you hoping for a contradiction in there somewhere?"

I swallowed, then swallowed again. "Are you up for this, Rick? How are *you* doing? I mean, really doing? You know that you don't always have to be Mr. Tough Guy."

"Who, me?" But I could see the pain behind the smile, and that his face had a gray pallor to it.

I squeezed his hand gently. "Thank you. Thank you for what you did for me. And I don't just mean taking the bullet. For always being there. For being the kind of friend that others would die for. For always taking my crap and being patient and—" I brushed quickly at my cheeks with the back of one hand.

At that moment, Cody opened the door and started to get out.

"No, Cody!" I barked. "Not yet."

Rick had started to turn too, but he turned back as Cody pulled the door shut again. "It's all right, Danni."

"No, it's not. I want to say something. No, I *need* to say something, and I should have said it before this. Maybe a hundred times so you'd know I really mean it." For a moment, I thought he was going to say something, but he didn't. He just waited.

"Underneath this tough-talking, butt-kicking, Super-Chick front I put on, I'm just really. . . scared. And—"

I had to stop. I was starting to lose it and I couldn't do that. If the floodgates opened, I might not get them shut again. And with all of Hanksville just outside the window, this wasn't a good time for the dam to break. So I took a quick breath and finished. "I need you, Rick. Like Mom says, you're our rock in the river, the stone that deflects the flood, keeps the rest of us from drowning. So—" I sniffed quickly a couple of times. "So, thank you."

For what seemed like a long time, his eyes pulled me into his, expressing so much without him saying a word. Then that slow, cowboy grin stole across his face again. "Does this mean you're sorry that you shot me?" he asked.

I half laughed, half sobbed. "More than you can ever know. More than you can ever know."

About then, we saw Rick's dad and Mayor Brackston pushing their way through the crowd toward us. I nodded at Cody, and he opened the door. The mayor was hollering for everyone to get back. They did so, moving back maybe an inch or two. Beyond the crowd, I caught a glimpse of Officer Shayla Blake leaning against her Utah Highway Patrol cruiser. She saw us and waved before the crowd shut her off from view again. I wondered if that was Clay's doing too. Maybe provide a little crowd control. It surely wasn't normal for her to be hanging loose here in our town.

But then, Cody jumped out, grinning like some clown in the circus. He pushed the door all the way open so those closest to the car could see inside. Rick had started to get up, but fell back a little as a roar went up. People applauded, laughed, yelled, shouted out questions at him, and pushed their way in closer.

He turned and looked at me, almost bewildered. "Would you like me to call out the Royal Guard, your Majesty?" I asked.

That won me a blistering look. I laughed. Maybe this wasn't going to be all bad after all.

"Danni," barked my mom, "don't just sit there. Help Rick out of the car." She was opening her own door even as she spoke.

By the time I got out and pushed people back enough for me to get around the open door, Charlie Ramirez was to us. The mayor was right behind him, looking a little flushed. With good reason. In addition to the temperature approaching a hundred degrees, this was a pretty big day in sleepy little Hanksville. "Get back, people," he shouted, wading into the midst of the crowd. "Give him some air."

Oh, that was rich. As if the crowd were sucking up all the oxygen in Wayne County or something. But it worked. Quieting, the crowd fell back, forming a semicircle around the 4Runner. With more room to maneuver now, I went around to the back of the SUV, opened the rear window, and got the crutches out. By the time I came back, Rick was standing up, leaning heavily on his father's arm, holding his left foot a little above the ground. He took the crutches, slipped them under his arms, wincing noticeably as he did so, then stood alone.

That broke things open again. "You okay, Rick?" "Welcome home, Rick." "Hey, Rick, can we autograph your cast?" At that last one, Rick reached down and touched the leg. The clinic in Page had cut off the left trouser leg of his jeans to make room for his bandage. It was now about the same length as a pair of shorts. This left his bandage clearly visible to all. "It's not a cast, Kenny," he called back. "Just a bandage."

Mary Anne Jessup, who was the same age as me, waved a hand with a pen. "I'll sign it anyway." Everyone laughed, and it did give me some pleasure to see Rick flush a little beneath his tan.

"Sorry, Mary Anne," I called out. "Doctor's orders. No girls over two years old autographing the bandage." The crowd loved that, and applause broke out again.

Mayor Brackston waved his arms. "Okay, folks. Let's get Rick over into the shade. We've got a chair over there for you, Son," he added to Rick. Then back to the crowd, "Rick's agreed to say a few words to you, then his father is going to take him home. Let him get some rest." He flashed a quick grin at me. "And that *is* the doctor's order."

People were already moving before he could finish. No surprise. Anyone with half an eye knew instantly that only about half the crowd was going to fit in the shade of the service station. The rest would be in full sunshine.

I stepped up to Rick. "Here. Let me help you."

He gave me one of his looks. "Okay," he whispered, "but remember, head lower than the king's at all times."

If I hadn't been still pretty choked up from before, I might have brained him at that point. But I also decided that the Royal Subjects might not take too kindly to one of the lowly maids smacking the king on the back of his head with her fist. Without waiting for me, he moved off, carefully keeping his left foot off the ground.

The crowd was mostly quiet as he sat down heavily in the folding chair that had been set there for him. His father took the crutches and stepped back a foot or so. I stayed beside Mom and Cody on the front edge of the crowd. Rick looked around, saw me, then said, "Oh no you don't, Danni." He pointed to a spot beside him. "You're right here."

"Yes, m'lord," I murmured, then moved up beside him.

Mayor Brackston, beaming broadly, looked directly at Rick. "Okay,

Son. All we've heard is that there was an accident on the houseboat. Tell us what happened."

Rick glanced up at me briefly, then turned his attention to the circle of faces. "Well, there's not that much to say. We were on the houseboat, me and the McAllisters. We had been . . . um . . . doing some target shooting on the way down to the lake earlier, and—"

"Come on, Ramirez," someone called from behind us. "Spit it out."

"Uh, yeah," Rick said. "So . . . um . . . anyway, we were . . . uh . . ."

Ezekiel Howell, whom everyone called Zeke, cupped his hands to his mouth. "Whadja do? Shoot yourself in the leg?"

Some laughed, thinking it was only a joke; then they saw Rick's face. I heard another woman gasp. "He shot himself?"

Rick gulped a couple of times, then smiled. "I tried that, but I missed both times. Nearly shot off my toe, though."

More laughter rippled through the group. The audience was getting their money's worth. This was turning out to be entertaining as well as informative. I leaned over and whispered in his ear. "Just say it!"

He ignored me and went on. "So, anyway, we were in the houseboat, just sitting around . . . um . . . and—" From my position standing above him, I could see beads of perspiration forming along the line of his dark hair and around his temples. I decided it was time to end his agony and mine.

I took a step forward, cleared my throat, and jumped in with both feet. "What Rick is trying very hard to say, without actually saying it, is this. I had just finished cleaning my dad's pistol. I reached for my rifle, which I thought I had unloaded when we got back to the boat."

All around me, eyes were growing very large, and the crowd had gone completely still. I rushed on. "My hands were slick with gun oil. When I picked up the rifle, it slipped out of my hands and hit the floor. Hard. It went off. Unfortunately, Rick was directly in the line of fire and took the bullet in his upper left thigh."

The buzz of shock and surprise rolled outward as people gaped at me. Again, individual voices seemed to jump out from the general noise.

"It was Danni?" "Danni shot him?" "Oh, my goodness." That was from Elmira Peterson, who was eighty-something and had never said anything harsher than "Oh, my goodness," in her entire life.

I raised my hands, and gradually the noise died out again. "I am not proud of what happened, and for reasons I think you will understand, I find it very painful to speak of it. So I will not be answering any questions. I have apologized to Rick profusely, and, knowing Rick as most of you do, you will not find it hard to believe that he frankly forgave me."

I turned and gave Rick my sweetest smile. "Of course, once he met a very lovely nurse at the Lake Powell Medical Center, he found that much easier to do."

His face instantly turned beet red. "Not!" he blurted, as the people roared with laughter and clapped their hands. Turning back to the crowd, I raised my hands high over my head, holding them together as if I were handcuffed. "And with that," I cried, "I am surrendering myself to Officer Shayla Blake of the Utah Highway Patrol, who will put me in chains and drag me off to jail, where I will await trial and sentencing and possible execution."

For a moment there was shock, then the laughter broke out again. I smiled. "Seriously, folks. This is Rick's day. Not mine. I'm going to bow out now."

"Poor Danni."

I turned, my stomach dropping like a rock. I knew the voice as soon as it spoke. It was Lisa Cole. Standing with her were three of my other so-called friends—Angie Roberts, Megan Davis, and Brianne Linford. I suppose Lisa's look was meant to be sympathetic, but to me it was this awful, condescending smirk. I pushed past them, pretending I hadn't heard.

"Way to go," Lisa said. Then she put her cupped hand up to her mouth and whispered to the others, but loudly enough for me to hear, "Danni Oakley rides again." The other three burst out laughing.

Danni Oakley? What was that supposed mean? Then it hit me. *Annie* Oakley. Star of the old Buffalo Bill Wild West Show back in the late 1800s. Most famous for being a crack shot with pistol and rifle. I whirled on Lisa. "Cute. I didn't know they had summer kindergarten going right now."

Not waiting to see her reaction, I pushed my way through the crowd, anxious to be out of all this. There were some other smirks and critical expressions, but mostly the faces were sympathetic and understanding. A few reached out and touched me as I passed. There were murmurs of condolences and "It could happen to anyone." Which only made things worse.

———

In a moment I was clear and joined Mom and Cody, who were with Officer Blake now. I was seething underneath, but I kept throwing little smiles at those who were staring at me like I was in a zoo. After a moment, everyone turned their attention back to Rick, who was saying something I couldn't hear.

Mom came over and put an arm around me. "You did well, Carruthers. It can't be easy, trying to make yourself look stupid."

I made a face. "Oh, I don't know. I've had a lot of practice."

Cody grinned and poked me. "You can say that again."

Mom glared at him. "Not funny, Cody. Not now."

But even as I was tempted to hit him with a blistering put-down, those more tender feelings came over me again. I stepped forward and put my arms around him. "I love you, Little Bro. Warts and all." Then, before he could answer, I turned and said, "Hello again, Officer Blake."

"Shayla," she said, coming forward to shake my hand. Then she gestured toward the crowd. "Big day in Hanksville, right?"

Mom laughed. "You'd think so, wouldn't you."

I nodded, only half listening. *Danni Oakley?* There had to be a good answer to that.

Then Shayla was shaking her head. "Oil on your hands? I don't think so. Was it El Cobra who shot him?"

I leaned back against the white cruiser, still smoldering. Lisa and her groupies had pressed in right around Rick now. So Mom answered for me. "Yes. Danni made him so angry, he smacked her across the face. When Rick saw that, he went after him like a heat-seeking missile, and El Cobra shot him."

"I thought so," Shayla said. "Clay told us about his plan to keep the lid on things for a while." To me: "I wondered how you would pull it off." She gave me a warm smile. "You did good, Danni. It was very believable."

"Thanks," I said glumly. Mom moved closer and slipped her arm through mine. As I was about to say something to her, the crunch of tires on gravel sounded behind us. We turned as a large SUV pulled off the highway and came toward us. It skidded to a stop, and instantly the doors popped open and a bunch of kids my age started tumbling out. Two-thirds of them were girls. I took one look and groaned. "No! Tell me this isn't happening."

"Who is it?" Mom asked.

"Kids from high school, from Loa and Bicknell." Those towns were about an hour away. How could they have heard about this so quickly? But I instantly knew the answer. Facebook. Twitter. Cell phones. Texting. This was the day of instant communication, especially among my generation. With my luck, the exploits of Danni Oakley were already beaming out across the ether.

Suzanne Callas was a senior and good friends with Rick. She was driving. As the kids piled out of the car, she saw me and waved. "There's Danni," she called, and they all turned and started toward me.

I raised my hand and pointed. "Rick's over there," I called. "By the building. He's answering questions." Like a flock of birds in midflight, they spun and headed the other way. I looked up at my mother. "Can we just go home now, Mom?"

Her eyes darkened momentarily. "I think we owe Rick more than that, don't you?" Then, more softly, she said as she patted my hand, "I know this is hard, Carruthers, but eventually the truth will all come out."

Maybe so, but "eventually" wasn't much comfort at the moment.

For the next ten minutes, we stood there watching. Gradually, the crowd began to disperse until it was mostly older teens, including the carload from Bicknell. From the occasional glimpse I got of him, I could tell Rick was getting tired, and it surprised me that his father didn't end it. But I thought I understood why. As Clay had suggested, this was pretty sensational stuff for our little community. So the best thing for it was to get it all out now, then let it die away.

Just as that thought came, I heard Suzanne's voice rise above the others. "So, Rick. I hope this doesn't mean you won't be going to the school dances this fall. That would be a real tragedy." General laughter, mostly female.

Then Lisa's mousy whine broke through it. "And I'd suggest you not ask Danni Oakley to any of them. Wouldn't want you getting shot in the other leg."

The others loved that and howled with laughter. What really hurt, though, was that Rick was laughing too. That did it. I started away. "I'm walking home, Mom. See you there."

She grabbed my arm and pulled me to a stop. And she didn't do it gently. "You will not leave, Carruthers. Not until Rick does."

And with that rebuke, the thoughts came flooding in again. *Look at him, Danni. See how tired he looks. The smile is there, but it's strained. Why not worry about his wounded leg instead of your wounded pride. Do something for him. He needs you for once.*

Suddenly this simple but brilliant thought came into my mind. I pulled the cell phone from my pocket and started to call up SIRI. Then I saw Mom and Shayla's looks of surprise. "Excuse me," I said, and walked away a few yards.

Once I was alone, I got the phone up, then held my thumb down on the home button for two or three seconds. In a moment, SIRI's dispassionate voice came on.

SIRI is one of my very favorite features on the iPhone. It is a speech-recognition software application that serves like a "personal assistant." It allows you to tell the phone what you want it to do, and it pretty much does it. Rick had showed me how to use it. He used it so much, I told him once I was getting jealous of SIRI. That made him laugh, and, in response, he pushed the button and brought her up. "SIRI, will you marry me?" he said. "I'm sorry," came the dispassionate response, "but I am not the marrying kind." After that I forgave her.

"What would you like me to do?" SIRI asked.

"Send a text."

Almost instantly her pleasant but dull voice responded, "To whom shall I send it? I need a contact name, phone number, or email address." The microphone again lit up and beeped twice.

"Can you make it come from CNN or Fox News?"

"I'm sorry, I do not know how to do what you ask."

I punched the button again. "Just do it, SIRI," I barked.

There was a long pause, then, "Please give me a moment. I am working on your request."

I felt a hand on my shoulder and turned to see Mom staring at me. "What are you doing?"

I shook her off and quickly walked a little farther away. She didn't follow. A moment later SIRI came back. "I can send a text from the Associated Press. Would that be sufficient, or would you like me to keep trying?"

"Associated Press is perfect!" I nearly shouted it. This just might work.

"Okay," SIRI said, ever the patient one. "To whom would you like this message sent?"

I didn't hesitate an instant. "Lisa Cole."

A moment's pause, then, "What would you like to say to Lisa Cole?"

I put the phone up close to my mouth. This I had already decided. "News Flash, period. Regarding Chris Hemsworth, movie star, period." I hit the microphone to stop the recording. Instantly my words were translated into print, including the correct punctuation. I hit the record button again. "Word just received that Australian-born Hemsworth, star of the much-anticipated 'Avengers,' to be released in May 2012, is vacationing at Lake Powell, in Southern Utah, period."

I stopped and waited for it to show up on screen. I immediately saw I had spoken too quickly and "just received" came out as "justice sees." I highlighted the two words with my finger and typed in the correct spelling. Then I started recording again, turning my back so I didn't have to watch Mom glaring at me. "Hemsworth has announced a press conference to be held at Bullfrog Marina today at—" I glanced at the time at the top of my phone—"At 5:30 p.m. Hemsworth will be signing autographs immediately afterwards." Then I tapped the stop recording icon. A moment later the full text appeared.

SIRI came back in. "Would you like me to send your message now?"

"Yes," I said with delicious satisfaction.

There was a soft chirp, and the message moved up to the "sent" window. Feeling an enormous sense of satisfaction, I walked quickly back to Mom, Shayla, and Cody. From their expressions, it was obvious that I hadn't been as clever as I thought. They had heard it all. Cody held up his hand and gave me a high five. "Wicked!" he said. Mom just shook her head. Shayla was looking at me with both admiration and a touch of awe.

But there was no chance for any more discussion. A short blast of rock music blared. Lisa had her back to us, but I saw her grab her phone and hold it up. I held my breath and crossed my fingers. All we ever heard from Lisa in the last few months was Chris Hemsworth this, and Chris Hemsworth that. He was the most attractive man in the world. He was hot. He was awesome. He was . . . Then words would fail her and she would just shake her head and sigh. She had already made her mother promise to drive her to Salt Lake City for the first night's showing of *Avengers,* even though the movie was still ten months away from being released.

She gave a shrill squeal and started jumping up and down, shouting, "Omigosh! Omigosh! Chris Hemsworth. Omigosh!"

Everyone gathered in around Lisa. Her voice was shrill as she read the message to the others. In less than ten seconds, Rick was totally—I mean like totally—forgotten. He was ancient history. Kids huddled in. Someone asked her to read it again. Then Lisa said, "I'm going. Who's going with me?"

"What about your mother? Don't you have to ask her?" someone asked.

"For Chris Hemsworth? Are you kidding? Who's going with me?"

I couldn't believe it. It was like someone had fed a bunch of squirrels some nuts laced with amphetamines. Kids were yelling and running for their cars. Some were calling their parents on a dead run. A moment later, Suzanne Callas evidently got that permission, because she called out that she was leaving right now and those who wanted to go with her had better get in the car.

As her car took off, quickly followed by another, then another, I felt a pang of guilt. Some of these kids were good friends. Great friends. I had only meant for Lisa to get distracted. But there was nothing to be done about it now. I looked at Mom and hung my head. "I'm sorry, Mom. I didn't mean for that to happen."

She smiled a tiny smile. "Perhaps not. But it worked. Look."

I turned in the direction she was pointing and saw that, with the exception of one or two people slowly walking away, Charlie and Rick Ramirez were alone. Rick's dad was handing him his crutches. I took off at a swift walk and caught them just before they reached their truck.

Rick turned as he saw me coming. He cocked his head slightly. "Did you have anything to do with what just happened?"

"Who, me?" I asked innocently. "Whatever made you think that?"

"Oh, just a BMW convertible with a live license plate and writing on the windshield."

I fought to keep a straight face. "I think any relationship between that and what just happened is purely coincidental."

"Yeah, right," he growled. But then his face softened. "Thanks, Danni. I am very tired. I wasn't sure how to break it off."

I saw Charlie watching us, a funny expression on his face. *Whoops.*

Shouldn't have mentioned the BMW. But I just smiled. "Put him to bed, Mr. Ramirez," I said. "Hog-tie him in if you have to. Okay?"

"You have my word on that," he said.

"'Bye, Rick. Talk to you tomorrow."

He pulled a face. "Even if I'm hog-tied, I can still talk on the phone. How about tonight?"

"Shall I actually call you?" I teased. "Or should I just send you a text?"

———

Because we hadn't been home for over a week, before we left town Mom and Cody ran into the grocery store and bought enough food for dinner and breakfast. I stayed in the car to catch up on my phone messages. I was still checking my Facebook page to see what I had missed when we turned into the lane that led to our house and, a few moments later, into our driveway.

That's when Mom's voice startled me and I looked up. "Oh my word."

I saw nothing unusual and looked at her. "Oh my word what?"

"On the front porch."

We were passing the barn and the equipment shed and approaching the house now, so when I turned my attention to the front of the house, I saw immediately what she was seeing. "Omigosh," I squealed. "What is it?"

She turned and smiled. "I'm not sure, my dear, but I think those are roses."

She opened the garage door but didn't pull in. I was out of the car and trotting for the porch before the engine even died. Cody was right behind me. Pulling up at the bottom step, I stared at the spray of color before me. "Oh! My! Gosh!"

What we were looking at was a clear glass vase, large enough to hold probably two or three gallons of water. It was one of the largest flower vases I had ever seen. And from it, in a spray of brilliant crimson, erupted an armful of roses. I beg your pardon. No one person could have held that many roses in her arms. It would take two people at least to encircle the bouquet.

"Wow!" Cody breathed as he hopped up on the porch and started walking around it.

"Wow, indeed," Mom said, coming up to stand beside me.

"Who's it from?" Cody asked. Then he bent down. "Here's a card." He straightened with a small, brown envelope in his hand. He started to open it. "It says it's for you, Danni."

"Then give the card to Carruthers, Cody. Let her open it."

Still in awe at what stood before us, I managed to open the envelope and remove a card with a floral pattern on the front. I opened it and started reading. "It's from Clay."

"Clay?" Cody said. "Why Clay?"

"Read it out loud, Danni," Mom said. So I did.

Dear Danni,

As promised, here is a small token of our appreciation for an amazing week. I know I promised you several semi-trucks full of flowers, but my wife assures me that this is even better.

Mom's face was wreathed in smiles. "She got that right," she murmured.

The florist told me that red roses signify love, respect, and courage. I cannot think of three better words to represent what you are and what you stand for. Working with you and your family in these difficult circumstances turned out to be one of the most significant experiences of my entire career. I consider it an honor to call you and your family my friends.

Earlier, I mentioned having your family and Rick's family up to our home for supper sometime so you can meet my boss, Joel Jamison, the deputy director from Washington. My wife has a better suggestion. Each year, it is a Zabriskie family tradition to

*gather all of our family for the Fourth of July. We do a parade in
the morning, a picnic supper in the evening, then the big fireworks
show that night. It would be an honor to have your two families
join us. Since the Fourth is on Monday this year, and since we
have to get an early start to get a good spot to watch the parade, we
would reserve rooms for you near our home in Sandy for Sunday
and Monday nights. The deputy director will be here Tuesday by
noon so he can meet you all.*

*Talk to your folks and Rick's. If that agrees with their sched-
ules, let us know.*

With warm affection,
Clay Pigeon

I looked up, finding Mom's face a little blurry all of a sudden.
"What do you think?" I asked.

She laughed. "What do you think I think?" she exclaimed. "Of
course, we'll go."

"Yes!" Cody yelled, punching the air.

Then Mom got this mysterious smile. "Maybe we can talk Dad into
going up early enough on Saturday so you and I could buy us each a
nice dress to wear. You know, something that would look good for a VIP
from Washington."

I saw through her subterfuge immediately and smiled sweetly back
at her. "Wonderful. Maybe you could buy me two or three, just to be
sure we find something we both like."

For a moment, she was startled, then she threw her head back and
laughed. "Oh, Danni, Danni, Danni. Wherever did my little Carruthers
go?"

CHAPTER 3

The house smelled musty to me as we walked in. The last time I had been here was two days after my birthday. Without saying a lot, we went to work cleaning up the worst of the mess. There was broken glass from the picture that still hung crazily on the wall and from the lamp that had been hit by a stray bullet. We couldn't do anything about the bullet holes in the walls. Dad would have to patch them up later.

By unspoken agreement, none of us talked about that night.

The phone rang about an hour later. I was closest to it, so I turned off the vacuum and started toward it. "I'll get it," I called. Mom, who was in the kitchen, came to the door to watch.

"Hello?"

"Hi, Danni boy."

A rush of warmth and longing swept through me. Though we had talked on the phone, I hadn't seen my father since Sunday morning on the houseboat. It was wonderful to hear his voice again. "Hi, Daddy."

"What time did you guys get home?"

"Around five. Where are you? How did the closing at the bank go?"

"We just turned off I-70 onto Highway 24. We'll be there in about an hour. Is Mom there?"

Mom was already at my side. I handed her the phone and went back

64

into the kitchen, wondering if he had deliberately ducked my question about the bank closing.

"Where are they?" Cody asked.

I told him. Then I had another thought. I stuck my head back into the family room. "Mom?"

She looked up.

"Can I talk to Grandpère when you're done?"

Waving a hand to let me know she'd heard, she turned away again. I watched her closely to see if anything seemed to be wrong, but she was clearly just happy to be talking to her husband again.

They talked for only a few more minutes before she called to me. "Carruthers, Grandpère's on."

As we passed each other, Mom called out to Cody, "They'll be here in less than an hour. Let's get some supper started."

I took the phone. "Hello? Grandpère?"

"Hi, Squirt," he said.

I chuckled. He hadn't called me that in a long time. "How are you and Dad? Really?"

"We're fine. Really." I could hear a bit of a teasing note in his voice. "We're both tired and ready to be home, but all is well."

"Good." I hesitated, then plunged. "Grandpère?"

"*Oui?*"

"Where is *Le Gardien*?"

Long pause. "You saw it sink in the lake."

"Yes, I did. But I'm pretty sure I also saw you fish it out again. Do you still have it?"

"No."

"Where is it, then? Please tell me, Grandpère. I'm too exhausted to play games tonight."

"As am I."

"Then just tell me."

"Tell you what?"

"Do you have it with you?" I blurted, feeling my temper rising.

After a very long day that included "Danni Oakley" in it, I wasn't in much of a mood to be teased.

"No, I do not."

My heart sank. "Then where is it?"

"If I don't have it, how can I answer that?"

"You swear you don't have it?"

"I swear."

"On Grandmère's grave?"

"I see," he said, clearly disappointed. "So my word's not good enough."

"I didn't say that."

"Yes, you did." Then his voice softened. "I know today has not been a good day for you. We'll talk more when we get home. But I will say this much. I hereby state clearly and unequivocally that I do not have *Le Gardien*. However, I am confident that one of these days it will turn up. Does that satisfy you?"

It did not. The disappointment was like a knife. "Whatever. Good-bye, Grandpère." I hung up the phone and stood there for a few seconds, suddenly realizing just how utterly tired I was. After briefly indulging myself in a pity party, I raised my head. "Mom?"

"Yes, dear?"

"Do you need help with supper, or can I start bringing our stuff in from Rick's car now?"

"We're okay. Bringing in the stuff would be good."

There wasn't a lot to bring in. It wasn't like we'd packed well before leaving. I took Mom's and Cody's stuff in first, taking it to their rooms. On my way out again, I stopped in front of the roses, now placed on the coffee table in the living room. Here was a bright and beautiful exception to an otherwise bleak and dreary day. I lingered for a moment to enjoy their beauty.

I was feeling a little guilty about my conversation with Grandpère. Regretting my snappishness, I started to send him a text, then changed my mind. Why was I the one feeling guilty? Irritated all over again, I went out to the car. Taking my bag and the duplicate pouch in one hand

and Dad's rifle in the other, I went back into the house. I locked the rifle in the gun closet, then stopped for a moment at the kitchen door. "Do I have time for a bath?" I called.

Mom turned. "I expect Dad and Grandpère in about twenty-five or thirty minutes. How fast can you be?"

"Not that fast. After that tiny bathtub in the motel, I plan to spend at least an hour in there."

"Yeah, me too."

"Okay, I'll wait. Let me take this stuff upstairs, then I'll come down and set the table."

"That would be great."

As I turned and went up the stairs, letting the bag and the pouch almost drag along the carpeting, I realized that my exhaustion wasn't just mental and emotional. I was physically spent, and soaking in a hot bath sounded absolutely divine.

In my bedroom, I tossed the bag on the bed, then bent down and put the duplicate pouch in the bottom drawer of my dresser—the one with the most room. As I straightened again and started toward the door, I stopped dead, my head jerking forward. There, right before my eyes, hanging on its wooden peg alongside the mirror on my dresser, was *Le Gardien.* With a low cry, I sprang to it. I gently took it in my hands, loving the feel of its roughness in my hands. I put it to my nose and was not surprised to smell a faint, moldy scent. At that moment, my phone chimed again. I took it out and looked at the screen. It was from Grandpère. *You still there?*

I called up SIRI again and quickly dictated: *Yes. And looking at* Le Gardien *hanging on the wall. You can be very vexing at times.* "Vexing" was a word Grandpère used on me and Cody all the time when we were doing something he didn't like.

Moi? Long pause, then the phone chimed again. *You up to a random thought???*

From you? You don't do random, remember?

No answer for almost a minute, then came this: *If thou hast run with the footmen, and they have wearied thee, then how canst thou contend with horses?*

I stared at it for several seconds, not comprehending. This time, I typed with my thumbs. *Huh????*

I waited over a minute, but there was no answer. By then, I knew there wouldn't be one.

———◆———

I am one hundred percent better than I was an hour and a half ago. Mom cooked spaghetti and meatballs for supper. We still had a couple of loaves of garlic bread in the freezer, so we had that, too. It tasted like pure heaven. I ate three pieces and Cody ate five. After reminding us that the loaves were actually French bread, Grandpère had three himself. For dessert we had root-beer floats. Yum! After four days of continental breakfasts at the hotel and eating lunch and supper with Rick at the clinic, this was divine.

And finally, I got my bath. Even more sublime than food. Steaming hot water, bubbles thick enough to lay your head on. It was wonderful.

While we were eating, Dad said he needed to talk to all of us after supper, but Mom and I both begged him to let us take our baths before doing so. He reluctantly agreed. I didn't get to soak for a full hour like I planned, but I did wash my hair and put some body lotion on. After being out so much in the sun this last week, my skin was totally dry.

Mom is taking longer than me and isn't out yet. So even though Dad, GP, and Cody are down waiting for us, I'm writing in my journal until Mom comes out.

I won't have time now to tell you all about what happened today when we got back to Hanksville, but I'll write about it to-morrow. Let's just say, it wasn't pretty.

I called Rick about ten minutes ago. He sounded way tired, but, like me, he's glad to be home. He won't say much, but I can tell today has been rough on him. He's still got some pain pills from the doctor, but he stopped taking them yesterday. Said they made him nauseous. I told him I was going to rearrange his facial features if he didn't take some tonight. That sounds kind of rude, but the way I said it, he knew what I was trying to say. To my surprise, he agreed, just like that.

Whoops. Mom's out of the tub. Gotta go.

Mom and I came down the stairs together, arm in arm. The male half of the family were sitting in front of the television, watching a European soccer match. Dad turned it off as soon as we appeared at the bottom of the stairs. "We're in here," he called.

Dad and Cody were on the couch. Dad scooted over so Mom could sit between them. She did, putting one arm around Cody and the other through Dad's arm. I went over and plopped down beside Grandpère on the love seat and cuddled up to him. One part of me was still irked at him for playing with me, but I had *Le Gardien* back, so I pushed it aside. He seemed to feel the same because he put his arm around me and squeezed me tightly.

"Now, this is nice," Dad said. "Back home at last."

"If you don't mind the bullet holes," Mom quipped.

"I'll bet we're the only ones in town to have them," I said. There were a couple of polite smiles, but otherwise the joke fell flat. Come to think of it, it wasn't very funny.

Dad cleared his throat. "Okay, it's time to catch you up on what happened in Salt Lake." Another pause, then a deep sigh. He turned to Mom. "We didn't close the mine sale today, Angelique," he said, his voice low.

Shock registered on her face. "You didn't?"

"We felt like we had to say at least something to the Canadians about what had happened. Clay asked us not to give any details, but we did tell them that something had come up that put the mine at risk. And with that, they backed out."

Me, I was reeling, but what Mom said next was remarkable, considering the implications of what had just been said. She took both of Dad's hands in hers. "Oh, Lucas, I'm so sorry. You worked so hard for this."

I felt ashamed. My first thought had been for the money. I was some-what gratified when Cody burst out, "So no twenty million dollars now?"

"'Fraid not, Son." There was a low, hollow laugh. "You know what they say: Easy come, easy go."

"They were honorable about it," Grandpère said. "They did give us five hundred thousand dollars for those four bags of ore. But we'll have to pay all of our expenses for opening up the shaft and finding the ore. So, we're not broke. It's just that . . ." He shrugged.

I sat back, sick at heart. Twenty million dollars. Gone. I wanted to cry, but when I saw that Dad was watching me closely, I forced myself to smile. "So no car when I turn twenty-six?"

He gave a soft bark of laughter. "Yeah, and there goes my red Ferrari, too."

Mom was staring at him. "What red Ferrari?"

"Just a dream, my dear. Just a dream." Then he grew more serious. "The five hundred thousand is a great blessing. We'll still pay off the mortgage, maybe buy Mom a new dress." He was putting a brave face on it, but I could tell he was pretty devastated.

"And don't forget," Grandpère broke in, "we still have the mine. The twenty million dollars isn't gone; it's just in a little less available form."

Dad half turned so he was facing Mom. "Which reminds me, Hon. Jean-Henri and I need to go up to the mine. We need to seal it up, secure the shaft until we decide what to do with it." He looked at Grandpère. "In fact, maybe we should wait on going up to Green River and get it done."

"Green River?" I said. "What's in Green River?"

"Grandpère wants to take your journal up and put it in a safety deposit box."

"Oh, yeah."

Grandpère spoke up. "I know the mine is urgent, Mack. But so is the journal. We need to get that in a secure place."

"Can't the mine wait a couple of days?" Mom asked. "Can't we have even one day's rest?"

Dad's head swung back and forth slowly. He spoke first to Grandpère.

"I'll lock it in my office safe. If we're going up to the mine, we need to make an early start." Then he turned to Mom. "No, Angelique. We really can't wait on the mine. If word somehow leaks out about the rhodium, we'll have people swarming the place. And right now, they can get in with a crowbar or a pair of bolt cutters."

Mom didn't like it, but she finally nodded her acceptance. "In a way, this is a relief," she said, looking now at me and Cody. "Your father and I have been worried about you kids getting spoiled if we had twenty million dollars lying around the house."

I forced a smile. "It would take a lot more than that to spoil us, right, Code?"

"Heck, yes," he drawled. "Twenty-one million at least."

Dad seemed pleased that we could joke about it. Again he spoke to Mom. "On the way down, Jean-Henri and I talked about what we might do to make it up to you and the kids."

"And?"

"We have a proposal. I'll give you a hint, then you have to guess. What have I been promising to do for you ever since our honeymoon?"

Her eyes grew wide, then her hand shot out and grabbed his arm. "Really?"

"It wouldn't be much of a second honeymoon if we took the kids, but that is a consideration. What do you think?"

"Oh, Lucas. Yes! Yes! Yes!"

"What?" Cody cried.

I felt like my face was going to split in two. I knew exactly what he meant, and this was one seriously wicked piece of news. "Hey, Code," I said, "think about where Mom and Dad went on their first honeymoon."

He looked at me, blank for a moment, then his jaw fell open. He spun back around. "France? We're going to France?"

Dad was all smiles now too. "We're not talking right away. Maybe next spring, when school's out."

Cody started whooping and hollering and doing a little Irish jig in a seated position. I was sorely tempted to join him, but Grandpère reached across and took my hand. He squeezed it softly. "Not just France, Danni. I want to take all of you to Le Petit Château, where I was born. I'd especially like you to see where your great-grandmother Monique LaRoche lived and where I grew up as a boy. Maybe we could even retrace the journey your great-great-great-grandmother, Angelique Chevalier, took when she fled Germany to escape the mob that killed her parents. Would you like that?"

"Are you kidding me? I would die for that."

Mom's eyes were glistening all of a sudden. "Oh, Dad, I would love that too. Very much."

It was amazing how the mood in the room had changed so dramatically. Nowhere was that more evident than in Dad's countenance. He was literally beaming. "Maybe in the next few months we can get a few more bags of ore out of the mine and have the Canadians refine it for us. I was thinking maybe we'll take a month for the trip. So that is going to be expensive."

"Can we go to Italy?" I burst out. "Italy has the best-looking men in the whole world."

Mom laughed at that, but next to me I heard a gruff harrumph. "I beg your pardon, *mademoiselle*. What did you just say?"

Big mistake. I had said that once before, a few years back, and got an instant reaction then too. So I gave him the same answer as before. "I said that, after we get to see all of France, which has the handsomest men in the world, maybe we could go to Italy, even though the men there are ugly and painful to look upon."

"Ah," he said, stroking his goatee in satisfaction, "that's what I thought you said."

—◆—

We talked excitedly for a few more minutes, each of us throwing out things we'd like to do. Finally, Mom stirred. "It has been a very long day. I think it's time we all go to bed."

As she started to get up, Grandpère waved her down again. "Before we do, there's one more thing. I need Danni to go up and get the journal."

"My journal? The old one or the new one?"

"The old one. Since we're not going to Green River tomorrow, Mack, I'd like to lock it in your safe until we can."

Glancing at Mom, I saw she was a little bothered by this, as was I. Seeing that I hadn't moved, Grandpère nudged me a little harder. "Go on."

Shrugging, I left. I ran lightly up the stairs and about thirty seconds later came back down again. I started toward Grandpère, holding the journal out to him, but he motioned toward Dad. Dad took it and went into his office.

When Dad came back, Grandpère stood up. "Okay. Now to bed."

"Wait," I said. "I have a question for you, Grandpère. Why didn't you tell me you put the pouch back in my room?"

"Because you didn't ask me."

"Yes, I did."

"No. You asked me if I had it. And I didn't."

"What did you do? Stop in here on your way to Salt Lake after you left us in Page so you could leave the pouch?"

He shrugged. "I needed some clean clothes, so, yes, I stopped by the house."

"Why didn't you just give me the original pouch before you left the clinic?"

He shrugged. "I was afraid you'd stick it away somewhere and it would go moldy."

I threw up my hands. "But why didn't you just tell me that, Grandpère? I've been really worried about it, and—"

"And where is it now?" Grandpère cut in.

I just stared at him in amazement. He wasn't going to answer me. "It's upstairs hanging on its hook," I said tartly. "Does that meet with your approval?"

"Danni," Dad said sharply. "Watch your tongue. I know you're tired, but you will speak to your grandfather with respect."

"Sorry," I mumbled.

"I love it when you are overcome with such sincerity," Grandpère said dryly. Then he bored in again. "And what about the duplicate pouch? Where is that?"

I sighed. "In the bottom drawer of my chest of drawers. Do you want me to get them, too? Put them in the safe with the journal?"

That seemed to catch him off guard. He considered it a moment before he shook his head. "No. We're going to bed in a few minutes. But otherwise, I would say yes."

Sometimes when Grandpère was chiding me about something I had done wrong, I could tease him out of it. I decided to try that now. "If it will make you feel better," I said with a smile, "I'll sleep with it under my pillow, take it in the bathtub with me. Maybe even sit on it when I'm watching TV. Would that satisfy you?"

Bad choice on my part. "That's my concern about you, Danni," he said. "You seem to think this is all some kind of a joke." He leaned in, his jaw set, eyes pinning me back. "You go off and conveniently forget it. You leave it on the bus or in an unlocked car."

I rocked back, deeply stung. Mom sprang to my defense. "That's not fair, Dad. Danni's been very careful with it lately."

He barely acknowledged her. "I mean it, Danni. This is too important to have you treat it as if it were a pair of your old cowboy boots."

"All right!" I snapped. "I get it, already! Now can I go to bed?"

It shocked me to hear those words come out of my mouth, and to hear the tone of voice I had just used with him. I never spoke to my grandfather like that. My head dropped and I looked away. "I'm sorry, Grandpère," I whispered. "I didn't mean that. You're right. I have been too casual with it. I haven't taken it seriously enough. I'll try to do better. I am trying, Grandpère. I know I'm not perfect, but . . ."

He stood up so he was towering over me. He wasn't angry. But there was this intense sadness in his eyes. "I want you to listen to me very closely, Danni, for what I am about to say comes only after much reflection."

I braced myself.

"What you and Cody and Rick did this last week is nothing short of astonishing. Really quite miraculous. I am very proud of you."

I blinked. That wasn't what I expected. "Thank you."

"There were moments of absolute brilliance." He paused. "But that doesn't excuse the times of folly. Sometimes you acted like you were twenty-something, but sometimes it was like you were ten years old again."

That hit me hard and I rocked back a little. "I—"

He went right on. "I waited until you were thirteen before passing *Le Gardien* on to you. That was three years ago. Don't you think it's time you grew up?"

"Dad," Mom broke in, "aren't you—"

"Danni needs to hear this," he said curtly. Then he turned back to me. "The pouch is not your personal genie. What? You don't like the speed limit, so you rub the pouch and change the signs? You nearly cause a terrible accident because you're irritated by a slow driver? What's next? Ordering up a strawberry shake when you're hungry? Having it take your exams for you?"

I was staring at him. How did he know about the speed limit sign? Or Miss BMW? I went on the offensive quickly before he could start talking about me and the redneck in the big pickup truck. "Who told you that? Rick? Cody?" I shot Cody an icy look, but he was vigorously shaking his head.

"That's not an answer," he fired right back. "That's a dodge. You are the keeper of the pouch, Danni, but that privilege can be lost." He reached down and took my hand, and his voice softened. "We don't choose to be the keeper of *Le Gardien*. It chooses us. And while it is a burden we do not seek, it is, nevertheless, a responsibility we cannot neglect."

Inside me I was teetering between tears and anger. I decided the latter was the best offense. "Maybe it was foolish," I snapped, "but those very incidents later helped me and Rick escape. Where do you think I got the idea to put writing on Officer Blake's rearview mirror? Or to cause the engine of her patrol car to stop working? That came from the pouch too. And besides, I didn't tell *Le Gardien* to do those things. They just happened."

That didn't faze him. "The Guardian carries out the wishes of your heart, Danni. And that is what I am talking about. It's not so much what you *do* that brings its influence, but what you *are*."

That hurt. As much as anything he had ever said to me. I blinked quickly and looked away, fighting desperately not to cry. My chin dropped and I could feel my lower lip start to quiver. "You are right," I whispered. "I was stupid. I did make mistakes. What can I say? I *am* only sixteen years old, in case you've forgotten."

His eyes never wavered from mine. "In France, during the war, we had fourteen- and fifteen-year-old girls in the Resistance. Some of them were caught and tortured by the Gestapo. Please don't use your age as an excuse, Danni. You are better than that."

I dropped my head. "I give up, Grandpère. I'm sorry. I'm sorry I am a disappointment to you."

He leaned forward and took both of my hands. "*You* are not a disappointment, *ma chérie,*" he said with infinite gentleness. "Not in any way. But what you *do* sometimes is. And to let those things pass without correction would be to do you a disservice."

He pulled me up to face him. I didn't resist, but I certainly didn't throw my arms around him. I just stood there, limp as a rag. I was too hurt. Too ashamed. Too humiliated.

He reached out, put a finger under my chin, and lifted my head until I looked into his eyes. I tried to pull away, but he held me fast. When he spoke, it was barely audible. "If thou hast run with the footmen, and they have wearied thee, then how canst thou contend with horses?"

PART TWO

Phase Two

CHAPTER 4

United States Penitentiary, Tucson, Arizona
June 22, 2011, 2:17 a.m.

United States Penitentiary—Tucson is a high-security federal prison for male inmates operated by the Federal Bureau of Prisons, a division of the United States Department of Justice. It is located on a 640-acre site ten miles southeast of the city and about a hundred miles north of the Mexican border. One-story buildings of sand-colored stucco blend in almost perfectly with the surrounding desert. Except for its single guard tower, USP Tucson hardly looks the part of a high-security prison. Among others, it houses a former Colombian drug lord, various organized crime bosses, big-city cops turned bad, international terrorists, and even a former U.S. Congressman convicted of bribery, fraud, and tax evasion.

On this night, under a cloudless sky and bathed by a waning half-moon, a white Toyota Corolla pulled into one of the handicapped parking spots in the visitors' parking area near the front entrance. The driver turned off the lights but didn't open the door. A moment later, a dark figure in a guard's uniform appeared at the front entrance and waved once. The driver opened the door and slipped out. No interior lights came on in the car.

He was an older man, in his sixties, tall, but quite portly. And frail looking. He leaned on his cane heavily as he stood up. His hair and neatly trimmed beard were completely white and gleamed brightly in the soft moonlight. Everything about him signaled elegance and class: A four-thousand-dollar tailored Armani suit and custom-made Italian shoes. Rolex watch. Diamond cufflinks. A gold ring with a large red ruby, worn on his little finger. In his left hand he carried an expensive leather briefcase with combination locks. Moving slowly, he joined the other man and they went inside.

At the main security station, three other men—also in uniform— were waiting for them. They were huddled together, not speaking, watching the newcomer nervously. The overhead lights were dimmed. The tension in the air was almost palpable. That was good, the man thought. He wanted them to be nervous. So was he. At that moment, he was keenly aware that he was in an extremely vulnerable position. And for a man who planned everything with intricate attention to detail so as to eliminate vulnerability, he didn't like that one bit.

Without speaking, the visitor set the briefcase on the desk, worked the combination, then opened it. Every eye was riveted on it—and every eye was filled with greed. He began extracting packets of crisp, new, hundred-dollar bills. Without a word, he handed each man two packets—twenty bills or two thousand dollars per packet. Finished, he closed the briefcase again and locked it. He looked up, letting his eyes move from face to face. "You'll have the rest when I'm on my way out and everything is still quiet." His voice was soft, his accent strange, perhaps Eastern European.

He looked up at the camera mounted on one corner. Seeing that, the first man quickly spoke. "The tapes will be erased before you're out of the parking lot."

He nodded curtly. He looked around. "Gentleman, I have a legal right to be here. I am Armando Mendosa's legal counsel." There were vigorous nods. "The only illegal thing we are doing tonight is making sure that I come and go without anyone knowing it." *That,* he thought, *and the ten-thousand-dollar bribe I'm paying each of you to help me get in and out without detection.* But he didn't say that, of course. His face turned hard. "If this ever becomes known to anyone outside the five of us, you will die. Slowly and horribly. Do we understand each other?" No one said anything. They didn't have to. They were thoroughly frightened men. Which was as it should be.

"All right. Take me to him."

"We already have him waiting in one of the interrogation rooms," the first man said quickly.

"Good. As agreed, I'll be no more than fifteen minutes."

———

Armando Mendosa, the man who chose to call himself El Cobra, was a beaten man. He sat on a chair across the table from the attorney—who was no attorney at all—in an interrogation room where they could not be overheard. His head was down, his hands massaging his temples. He was still trying to throw off the effects of being awakened from a dead sleep. Finally, the older man leaned forward. "All right. Talk fast. Start from the first. What went wrong?"

El Cobra began, quickly becoming more and more agitated as he spoke. Soon he was bouncing back and forth like a tennis ball at a Wimbledon match. He would remember a detail he'd forgotten, or break off the narrative to try to defend his actions. The words poured out, and he grew more desperate as he realized just how utterly insane it must all sound to this sophisticated stranger.

After nearly ten minutes, Mendosa finally stopped. "I know it sounds fantastic, but that's the truth of it."

The man's hand moved so fast that it was barely a blur. His palm caught Armando fully on the left cheek so hard it snapped his head back. "And that is what you expect me to tell your employers? That it was all the girl's doing?" He openly scoffed. "She's a sixteen-year-old kid from a town that's no more than a pimple on a map. And her boyfriend's what? A year older? Come on, Armando. What game are you playing here?"

El Cobra leaped up and started pacing, wringing his hands. "I swear to you, *Señor,* it is God's truth. Ask Eileen. Ask Raul. They will confirm everything I say."

His inquisitor went on as if he hadn't spoken. "Your employers are fully prepared to keep their part of the agreement. Fifty thousand Euros have already been transferred into private bank accounts in each of your names. Those funds will be released when it is fully clear that you have fulfilled your part of the agreement, which is total silence. Should your case ever come to trial—and plans are already under way to ensure that will never happen—my firm, one of the largest and most prestigious law firms in America, will represent you. And rest assured that none of you will be spending any significant prison time."

He suddenly jerked forward so quickly that Armando recoiled. "But all of that will be withdrawn in an instant if I go back and tell them this ridiculous story. Do you think they are fools?"

"I swear it, *Señor*. It is God's truth. You have to believe me. Ask Eileen. She was in the boat with me when it sank."

The lawyer stood up and picked up his briefcase. "Your wife is in a separate women's facility up near Phoenix. I cannot get to her right now."

"Do you really think I would be such a fool as to make up a story like that?"

A thin smile came, then quickly vanished again in the thickness of the older man's white beard. "Funny you should suggest that. I was just asking myself that same question."

The payoff of the remainder of the ten thousand per guard went quickly. They were as anxious to see him gone as he was to be gone. Their leader escorted him to the front entrance, then stood behind the glass and watched until the car pulled out of the parking lot and disappeared.

Five miles down the road, the old man slowed, watching closely for the spot he had scouted out yesterday. When he found it, he turned off onto a gravel road. Two miles to the south, he stopped and got out. A quick look around told him that he was no longer in sight of the highway, and there was not a light within miles of where he was.

With a sigh of relief, he began stripping off his suit and tie. Next came the wig, then the false beard and eyelashes, then the padding in both cheeks that had fattened his face. Finally he unwrapped the three towels around his waist that had given him bulk. Beneath all of that he wore the kind of lightweight athletic clothes that runners prefer. He had also shed about thirty years in age.

He glanced up at the eastern sky. The first blush of light was defining the horizon. It had taken him about fifteen minutes longer than he had planned, and he was tempted to find a rubbish bin—what the Americans called a dumpster—somewhere back in Tucson and chuck his things. But the temptation didn't last long. *Leave nothing to chance.*

He grabbed a short-handled shovel from the trunk and buried everything under two feet of sand. Satisfied, he returned to the car and headed for Tucson, where a chartered plane was waiting for him.

Schloss von Dietz, Bern, Switzerland
June 22, 2011, 3:24 p.m.

From the huge desk in the library, one had only to lift one's head to see one of Switzerland's most spectacular views. In the foreground were the deep blue waters of Lake Thun. Behind it, like towering ramparts, were the snowcapped peaks of the Bernese Alps.

But the woman seated at the desk was not looking out her window. She was totally focused on what lay on the enormous mahogany desktop before her. This kind of concentration was not uncommon for Gisela Decker von Dietz. It was a gift she had learned early in her life that still served her well.

The desk was massive and was clearly a working desk and not just an expensive piece of furniture. To one side, a slightly lower cabinet constructed of matching wood held a desktop computer with two monitors, a combination fax/printer/scanner machine, and a desk organizer. On the desk itself, which was covered with custom-cut glass, there were only four things: a small reading lamp, a multiline phone, and two framed photographs, side by side. The first of these was a grainy, faded, eight-by-ten photo of a woman in a servant's uniform outside an elegant English manor house. Standing beside her was a girl of nine or ten. One didn't have to look too closely at the girl to see that she was a younger version of the woman behind the desk.

The second photograph was also of mother and daughter, only this time they were seated on upholstered chairs in front of a huge Christmas tree. The older woman was but a shadow of herself, and she seemed lost and confused. It had been taken nine days before she had passed away. It was the last photograph taken of her.

Although Gisela often got distracted by the two photos, today she had eyes only for the two sheets of paper that lay before her. They had come by overnight mail less than a quarter of an hour before. About a month ago, she had been reading one of the dossiers prepared by the security company in London. Something odd had caught her eye. After closer examination, she had called London and given her team a very specific set of instructions on what she needed. This was the result.

The document was written in English and formatted in three parallel columns. As she pored over it, her lips moved, but there was only the faintest murmur of sound.

FAMILY HISTORY
CHEVALIER/LAROCHE FAMILY

Name/Birth	Pertinent History	Le Gardien??
1. **Alexandre Chevalier.** 1801, Le Petit Château, France	Grandfather of Angelique Chevalier (#3).	Notation in family Bible: "Keeper of the Pouch." Unconfirmed family tradition says he was the 3rd or 4th in the line of keepers.
2. **Jacques Pierre Chevalier.** 1828, Le Petit Château	3rd son of Alexandre; married Angelique Bertrand of Strasbourg. Purchased farm in Rhine Valley, Germany.	1871. Killed by mob allegedly seeking magic purse. Wife accused of witchcraft, killed same day near French border.

Name/Birth	Pertinent History	Le Gardien??
3. **Angelique Chevalier**, 1863. Rhine Valley	Daughter of Jacques (#2). Escaped mob by fleeing to France where she lived with her grandfather (#1). Married Jean Baptiste LaRoche of Strasbourg, 1885. Died at Le Petit Château, 1932.	Family records list her as "Keeper of *Le Gardien.*" First known use of that name. Parents killed on her 13th birthday as she fled to France to live with her grandfather (#1). Some rumors of strange happenings with her.
4. **Pierre Baptiste LaRoche.** 1902, Le Petit Château	Youngest son of Jean Baptiste and Angelique Chevalier (#3). Married Monique Bourchard of Moselle, France. Member of French Resistance in WW II; arrested by Gestapo, 1944. Taken to Paris for interrogation and execution. Liberated by American forces.	No written references to pouch. Villagers at Le Petit Château still refer to him as *Le Gardien.* Still remembered and greatly revered in the village. More rumors of miraculous happenings.
5. **Jean-Henri LaRoche.** 1934, Le Petit Château	Only surviving child of Pierre (#4) and Monique LaRoche. Aided in 1944 rescue of American airman that led to his father's arrest. Family immigrated to Boston in 1947. Married Kathleen Carruthers of Boston in 1958. Retired French history and literature professor.	Likely the next in line of pouch keepers. Colleagues and friends speak of remarkable gifts, which he passes off to being an avid amateur magician.
6. **Angelique Carruthers LaRoche McAllister.** 1969, Boulder, Colorado	4th child of Jean-Henri (#5) and Monique. Married Lucas (Mack) James McAllister of Butte, Montana, 1993.	No evidence of her either having the pouch or being its keeper.
7. **Carruthers Monique McAllister.** 1995, Ann Arbor, Michigan	Oldest child of Lucas and Angelique (#6), granddaughter of Jean-Henri (#5). Current residence, Hanksville, Utah	No information available at this time. Under further investigation.

Finished, Gisela looked up, letting her eyes rest on the framed photographs. Reaching out, she briefly touched the most recent of the two pictures. "Soon, Mama. Very soon."

———◆———

Half an hour later, the phone rang. Turning from her computer, she snatched it up. "Yes?"

"*Guten Morgen,* Mama," said the voice on the other end of the line. The German was flawless, something he knew would please her.

"Or *guten Tag,*" she said happily. "It's after three in the afternoon here."

"I am well aware of that," he groaned. "I haven't slept in twenty-four hours."

She dropped back into her chair, her face a study in joy. "Ah, Niklas! I'm so glad it's you. I've been very anxious to hear how it went." She glanced at the large grandfather clock in the corner behind her. "Are you still in Arizona?"

"No, no," he said quickly. "I was out of there before the sun was up. Actually, I'm back in Utah now. But yes, here it is still morning."

She checked her phone to make sure the encryption light was showing, then went on. "Any problems?"

"None, other than it cost us forty thousand U.S. dollars. There were four guards who had to be bought off instead of two. But I was in and out in just over half an hour."

She chuckled. "And in that wonderful disguise of yours?"

"Of course."

Then she couldn't resist poking at him a little. "So you agree now that taking that special course on makeup and disguises was not such a bad idea after all?"

"Once again, Mama, you were right."

"Oh, I love those words. So, did Armando suspect anything?"

"No. There wasn't a flicker of suspicion. But then, he had never seen me before, either."

"And that's good." She took a quick breath. "So tell me everything. How was Armando?"

He sighed, and she could sense his frustration. "Troubling, and that's putting it mildly."

"What went wrong? How is it that we get this exuberant phone call saying the whole thing is a done deal and we are twenty million dollars richer, then an hour or so later, the whole thing has unraveled and half the team is in custody."

"More than half, Mama. All but three. The ones we kept on station out in the desert."

"Where are they now?"

"They're in place and waiting. We hope to start Phase Two any day now."

"Isn't that a little dangerous? Someone's bound to stumble across them."

He snorted softly. "You have no concept of how utterly desolate that land is, Mama. You can drive a hundred miles without seeing a sign of human habitation. These guys are not fools. No one is going to stumble across them. And besides, I've called in a couple of 'sightings' to the FBI. They think they're headed for Mexico."

"Are they?"

"No, we'll bring them out by way of Vancouver, in British Columbia."

"Excellent! When?"

"I thought you said you didn't care about all the details, Mama? But just so you know, originally we planned to pull them out after a few days. But now that everything has fallen apart out here, I want to keep them on station in case we need them."

"I agree. This has been a disaster. So, what's El Cobra's story?"

Niklas had a remarkable memory, so he repeated Armando's account with a lot of detail. He fully expected to be interrupted as he made reference to the so-called magic purse and the fantastical things it supposedly had done. But to his surprise, she accepted it all without comment. She stopped him only once to ask him if Armando had said if the pouch had a name.

"Yes," he said, puzzled that she would ask. "He said that the words *Le Gardien* were embroidered on the flap."

"*Le Gardien?*" There was sudden excitement in her voice.

"Yes. It's French for 'The Guardian.'"

She hooted softly. "My dear boy, I do speak French, you know."

"Sorry, Mama. I—" Feeling sheepish, he went on quickly, adding details now about the pouch that he had planned to skip over because he hadn't given them any credence. The only time she interrupted him was when he came to Armando's account of the gold bars.

Gisela jerked forward, hunching over the phone. "Really? That's what sank the boat?"

"No, Mama. That's what Armando claims sank the boat." He was incredulous. "You surely don't believe him. Gold bars out of nothing. That's Dark Ages stuff, what they called alchemy. Pure nonsense."

"How many?"

There was a weary sigh. "Armando wasn't sure. Somewhere around forty. Enough that the boat swamped when another boat came close to them."

"Do you know how much a full-sized gold bar is worth?"

"Actually, I do," he said tartly. "Remember, before I took my new 'job' with you and Granny, one of my responsibilities was managing our gold reserves. Forty bars would come out to about twenty-five million Euros, or around thirty million U.S. dollars."

"Oh, my," she breathed. "That would balance out the loss of the twenty million nicely."

He made a sound of disgust. "Even if it were true, Mama—which I think is about one chance in a million—don't start counting your Euros yet. Not only is the gold at the bottom of a lake, but there's no way the FBI is going to leave it there."

"What if I told you the FBI knows nothing about the gold?"

He openly scoffed. "Of course they know about it. The girl and her grandfather were in the boat with Armando, remember? They would have told them." Then her words sank in. "Wait. How do you know the FBI doesn't know about the gold?"

"Because I received a copy of the FBI's report on this whole matter just a few hours—"

"You what?"

She chuckled softly. "Just because I'm seventy doesn't mean I'm stupid. I happen to have a working agreement with a key staff member in the Paris Interpol office. I pay her a lot of money, and she sends me copies of whatever information I need. There was no mention of any gold in the FBI report. Not a word. They say only that Armando's boat was swamped when a larger craft came too close to it."

"Then . . ." She could almost feel the wheels turning in his brain. "Either Armando is lying, or he's gone mental on us."

"*Or* the girl and the old man didn't tell the FBI so they can keep the gold for themselves," Gisela suggested.

"No way," he said. "You know what we learned about the McAllisters. They're Mr. and Mrs. Straight Arrow. And besides, they would have to assume that the FBI would eventually learn about it. But there is a third option. The FBI didn't tell Interpol because they didn't want to become the joke of the law-enforcement community. Who is going to believe that kind of a story?"

"You're stretching, Niklas. Assuming that Armando has fallen off the apple cart may be the most comfortable explanation, but it leaves you with another question that is just as thorny, if not more so."

"What question?"

"How does some kid who's still wiping her nose with her baby blanket outwit, outfox, and outsmart a whole team of professionals? You answer me that."

Niklas said nothing because he had been wrestling with that very same question and had come up with nothing.

"Niklas, we have to know."

"Know what?"

"The truth. I don't care how you do it, but find out. Get someone in to see Eileen. Find out what the girl's saying to her friends on Facebook. See if she kept a journal. Do you need me to tell you how to do your job?"

He sighed. "I'm going to try to get some rest now, Mama. Our three guys are waiting for directions."

"Niklas! I don't care what else you have going. Find out about that pouch and do it now."

"Bye, Mama. I'll call you later."

She softened. "You're tired, Nikky. Go to bed. We'll talk more tomorrow."

"Bed? I wish. I'm a long way from that. There's work to do here before anyone sleeps."

"When will you be home?"

"Not for a few more days. Even if we finish by tomorrow, I've still got to get out of the country without detection. I took four days making my way here, changing identities four times. I'll do the same coming back."

"You are really quite astonishing, Son. You know that, don't you?"

To her surprise, he laughed softly. "Actually, I do. I just may turn my leave of absence from the bank into a permanent resignation."

She laughed. "I won't tell the board of directors that just yet. Go to bed, Niklas. Call me again tomorrow."

"I will, Mama. I'm glad you're pleased."

After hanging up the phone, Gisela von Dietz sat there for several minutes staring out the window at her magnificent view, seeing none of it. Finally she leaned forward and pulled the two sheets of paper toward her. She read the last entry again, the one that described Carruthers McAllister in this way: *No information available at this time. Under further investigation.*

She reached for a pen from the desk organizer, drew a heavy line through the entry, and with swift, sure strokes penned: *Existence of Le Gardien tentatively confirmed. High likelihood that Carruthers Monique McAllister is the next keeper of the pouch.*

After reading what she had written, she took the pen and lined out the word *tentatively.*

CHAPTER 5

As I came I out of my bedroom the next morning and turned toward the stairs, I nearly stumbled over Grandpère. He was seated on the floor, his back against the wall. I gave a little yelp and fell back a step.

"*Bonjour, Mademoiselle* Danni."

"Good morning, Grandpère. What are you doing out—wait. How long have you been here?"

Mom's voice came floating up from below. "He was there when I came out about 5:45."

"Really?" And then, since he hadn't gotten up, I sat down beside him. I poked him softly. "If you had something more to say, you could have just knocked on my door."

"It wasn't what *I* had to say. It was what Grandmère had to say."

I gave him a quizzical look. "Grandmère?" My grandmother had died some time before.

"No," he said, chiding me a little. "I'm not saying I actually saw her and talked to her. But for a long time before I went to sleep, I could hear her voice in my head. What she would have been saying if she was here."

"Like what?"

"She would have taken me to the woodshed, that's for sure."

"The woodshed? I don't understand."

"It's an old saying. In earlier times, when a kid misbehaved, his parents would take him out to the woodshed and give him a good whipping across the bottom."

"I see," I said, smiling a little. "Kind of like you verbally did with me last night."

"Yeah, pretty much."

"And what if you were right? What if that was exactly what I needed? Would Grandmère still say you were wrong to do it?"

He turned and smiled at me, but it was a sad smile. "Grandmère had a little poem she liked to quote to me on occasions like this."

"A poem?"

"Yes. It went like this:

"Here lies the body of William Jay,

"Who died maintaining his right-of-way.

"He was right, pure right, as he sped along.

"But he's just as dead as if he were wrong."

And then he did something totally unexpected. Tears sprang to his eyes as he turned and swept me up in his arms. "I love you, Danni. More than you can possibly imagine."

"I never doubted that, Grandpère. Never!" I was crying now too.

"It's just that . . ."

"What? What is it, Grandpère? Something's worrying you. What is it?"

He blew out his breath very slowly as he shook his head. "I think it just may be physical, emotional, and spiritual exhaustion. That was definitely part of what happened last night."

I stood up and pulled him up. "But today's a new day." I reached up and touched his cheek. "I needed that last night, Grandpère. And I love you for caring enough about me to say it, even though it hurt. A lot."

"And that's the problem. I regret *how* I said it. And *when* I said it. In that, I was dead wrong. And I'm sorry." Then, blinking back the tears, he took my elbow. "Now, we'd better get downstairs before your father starts those omelets without me. He has a tendency to think, just because he has watched the master chef—namely me—make omelets, that he knows how to make omelets too. Which is another example of being dead wrong."

Laughing, we went arm in arm down the stairs. Life was good. I felt like humming. I didn't, of course. Not when anyone was around. But I was tempted. And why not? I had slept for nearly eleven hours straight and felt great. I had on a set of fresh clothes that had not been worn anytime in the past nine days. The smell of bacon filled the house. And I had decided that right after breakfast I was going to go over to Lisa Cole's house and ask her and her joined-at-the-hip friends if they had been successful in getting Chris Hemsworth's autograph.

———————

"Go ahead and sit down," Grandpère said. "This is about ready."

"Carruthers," Mom said, "will you get the ketchup for Dad?"

"Ugh," I said, but headed for the refrigerator. I had always found it both mysterious and disgusting that Dad smothered his eggs—fried, scrambled, over easy, it didn't matter—with ketchup. Maybe it was a Montana thing.

"Where's Code?" I asked as I set it before him.

"I'm not exactly sure. I checked his bed earlier and found only a petrified log there."

"We decided to let him sleep," Mom added. "He was so tired."

Grandpère brought the first of the omelets and gave it to Mom, then sat down.

"Danni," Dad said, "would you give our blessing on the food this morning?"

I did, and to my surprise, about halfway through it, I suddenly choked up. I should have known better than to try to put my feelings into words. The more I thought about all that had happened this last week, the deeper was my sense of gratitude. We had skirted disaster so many times. And Rick had almost been killed. I hadn't planned to say any of that last part, of course. That would have left me blubbering like a baby. But even when I started to say how grateful we were to be home again and to be safe, I had to stop.

I heard Mom sniffing, and then I felt Grandpère's hand laid on mine. We sat there quietly for what seemed like a full minute. Then I decided that even though none of us spoke, this was probably prayer enough. So I asked that Rick's leg would heal quickly and said amen.

As Grandpère got up and started two more omelets, Mom turned to Dad. "What did Clay have to say this morning?"

"He actually called for Danni, but since she was still in the land of the dead, he talked to me instead." He turned to me. "Mostly he wanted to know how it went for you yesterday. And if he was still on your hit list."

"No, but don't tell him that."

Dad smiled. "Then he gave me an update on things. The FBI and the Utah Highway Patrol put out a joint statement about the 'Lake Powell incident' yesterday. They said since they are continuing to investigate the case there will be few details released. They did confirm that one family had been involved briefly but had extracted themselves without harm. But no names were given and no further details were shared."

I had another question. "Did they find those three guys in Big Water?"

He frowned. "No. There was no trace of them. And what is even more strange is that now they're wondering if the tip was a hoax."

"A hoax?"

"Yes. When Clay's agents got there, they couldn't find the man who supposedly called in the tip. No such person by that name in Big Water. Nor was there a service station with the name he gave to them."

"I don't understand," Mom said.

"They got another tip last night, this time from a woman, reporting that three suspicious-looking men had checked into a cheap motel down in Flagstaff, Arizona. This time there was a motel by that name, but no one there had called the FBI, and no one had seen three men."

"How strange," Grandpère said.

"Strange, but not unusual," Dad answered. "Clay says they get these crank calls from time to time. Some people hate law enforcement and like to send them chasing after shadows."

"So they're still at large?" Mom murmured.

"Yes, but Clay's convinced they've left the country by now. And with that, let me change the subject." He turned to Mom. "So, how about a painting trip up in the mountains today?"

She had been about to put a bite of omelet in her mouth. It stopped in midair. "I thought you were going up to seal the mine."

"We are. But you've been talking about painting some mountain scenes up in the Henrys for months now. We could drop you off wherever you choose, then come back for you later."

"And this has to happen today?" Her eyes were troubled. She took the bite, then started moving the food on her plate around with her fork. "I had another idea."

"Oh?"

"I called Jan last night to see what was going on with the houseboat."

That caught my attention. We owned a houseboat with another family. We kept it docked down at the marina at Bullfrog. We laid out a schedule each year, blocking out the times when each family got first grabs on the boat, but it was all pretty flexible and we often traded times. It had worked out really well, actually.

She put her fork down. "They're not using the boat either this week or next."

Dad was watching her closely. "So what are you thinking?" he finally asked.

"I was thinking we need to get out of here. You know what's waiting for us the minute we go into town. We have so many friends and neighbors here, and they are going to want to talk to us, hear the whole story. They mean well. And, of course, they don't understand what's really behind the shooting. But I'm not sure I want to keep on talking about it."

"I'm sure," I said. "And I don't want to. I don't need any more Danni Oakley cracks."

"So," Mom said, really quite earnest now, "what if we got out of here for a week, or even ten days? We talked about doing it in July. Why not now instead?"

Dad's expression was thoughtful; then he started to nod. "Why not?"

"What about Rick?" I asked. "Could we ask him and his family to come?"

It took me back a little when Mom shook her head.

"But—"

"I don't think we *could* ask them. I think we *should* ask them. The attention is going to be even worse for Rick, and besides, a week on a houseboat would be a great way to let his leg heal. And we owe that family a lot. Maybe we could rent a couple of extra Jet Skis."

This was great. "Charlie doesn't work Saturdays and Sundays," I said, "and I'll bet Kaylynn and Raye would be ecstatic. I'm not sure they've even been on a houseboat before."

Mom was looking at Dad. "Think about it. No phones. No visitors. No FBI or Danni Oakley. Could we do that, Lucas?" Her eyes were pleading now. "Please."

Dad was nodding his head. "It's a great idea, Angelique, but—"

"No, Lucas," she exclaimed. "No buts. Let's just do it."

"I wasn't going to object to going. But Clay said he wants to leave an agent down here with us for the next few days."

"He does?"

"Yeah, he's not really worried about us, but with those three guys still loose, he just wants to be super cautious." Seeing Mom's expression, he went on quickly. "But I'll call him. Going to Lake Powell might be a good alternative. With more than two thousand miles of shoreline, we'd be pretty hard to find."

"No," she said. "I'm not objecting to that. In fact, I like the idea. I like him being cautious. We can even take someone along if Clay wants. But let's go, Lucas. Let's just get out of here."

That made up Dad's mind. He glanced at his watch. "I'll call Charlie. He's probably to the mine by now, but maybe they haven't gone down the shaft yet."

I jumped in. "Rick told me that his dad has accumulated a lot of overtime. He can either take it as time off or be paid for it."

"I'll ask him about that," Dad said. "But if the Ramirezes go—and I hope they will—they're going to need some time to get ready. As are we. If Charlie can get the whole day off tomorrow, we could be on our way by ten or eleven."

Mom's face fell. "Is there no way we could go today?"

Dad sighed. "Not really, Hon. They need some time. And Jean-Henri and I need to secure the mine, especially if we're going to be gone for the next ten days."

"What about Green River?" I asked.

"If we go to Lake Powell, that will have to wait," Dad said. "But your journal's locked in the safe. We can do that when we get back."

Grandpère came over and put a hand on Mom's shoulder. "Angelique, you and Cody could get your painting things together and maybe pack us a lunch while Mack and Danni and I load up the four-wheelers. If we work at it, we could be out of here in an hour or two."

"Okay," she said. "But I don't need to go. I'll stay here and start getting things ready for tomorrow."

Grandpère reacted quickly to that. "You are *not* staying here and having everyone dropping by to say hello. And doing some painting would be good for you about now."

"It does sound wonderful." Her head bobbed. "All right. Lucas, you call Charlie. Danni, go drag Cody out of bed. I'll call Jan and tell her we're trading times with her."

"And call Bullfrog and reserve the Jet Skis," I reminded her.

"Of course."

After we had the four-wheelers loaded, I started back for the house. I was thinking about Mom being glad that Clay was going to send us someone. I guess I'd just figured this whole thing was over and was ready to put it out of my mind. Then I remembered Grandpère's nervousness, and I started getting a little uncomfortable myself. Why did those three guys have to get away? That was what was causing it.

In keeping with Grandpère's advice, I had _Le Gardien_ with me now, even though we weren't leaving for another half an hour or more. But what about the journal? Would it be okay in Dad's safe? Of course it would. His safe was only about three feet square, but you'd need dynamite to get it open or a crane to carry it off.

Then another thought came to me. I broke into a trot and went inside. I went straight to Mom's craft room and found her box of thread.

"Whatcha doing?" Cody asked from right behind me. I jumped, almost knocking over the box. "Geez, Code, stop sneaking up on me."

He grinned. "A little jumpy, are we?"

Which gave me another idea. "Hey, Code. Come help me."

"Whatcha doing?" he asked again.

"You know how sometimes in spy movies, you'll see the hero take a piece of thread and put it across the door to his room? So he can tell if anyone comes in while's he's gone."

"Yep. I think Jason Bourne did that once."

"Who is Jason—oh, yeah. In the Bourne trilogy. Yeah, that's it. Well, uh . . . I don't want Mom or Dad to know about this, or they'll freak out, but I thought maybe we could do that before we leave. You know, just to be sure. See if anyone's been around while we're gone."

"Cool. What do you want me to do?"

"Get the ladder and meet me at the back door. Then we'll take turns making sure no one sees us doing it."

CHAPTER 6

We left the pickup truck and the trailer at the Lonesome Beaver Campground and took only the four-wheelers from there. Cody rode double with me because Mom had her easel and painting stuff on the back of her vehicle. Dad pulled a small trailer loaded with lumber and fencing with his, and Grandpère's four-wheeler was loaded with tools and stuff.

Dad found a little two-track road near the top of Bull Creek Pass. It led off the main road for several hundred yards and stopped on the top of a ridge that provided Mom with a spectacular view of Mt. Ellen to the north. It was pretty amazing. At more than eleven thousand feet, Mt. Ellen was the highest point in the Henry Mountains. Even this late in June, the peaks were still snowcapped.

I watched Mom while she helped Dad get her stuff off the ATV and set up. I noticed that when he wasn't looking, she kept looking around. I walked over to her. "Mom, why don't I stay here with you?"

Her head reared back. "Why?"

I shrugged. "Just so you have some company."

She peered at me with those wide, gray eyes of hers, searching my face. "I'm all right."

"Really, Mom, I don't mind."

"Or I can stay," Dad said, coming over.

"What is this? A let's-babysit-Mom conspiracy?" She looked around. "I . . ." She shook her head angrily. "In all the years we have lived here, I have never felt unsafe before. I hate it." But before Dad could answer that, she waved him off. "No. I'm all right. You know how I hate having people hanging over my shoulder when I'm painting." She smiled at me. "No offense intended."

"Yeah, right," I said, pretending to pout.

"Really," she said to Dad. "We've got our satellite phones, so we have coverage up here. I can call you."

"And we'll check in with you, too. We'll probably be gone a couple of hours."

"Perfect," she said, smiling and looking more comfortable now. "So go."

—————

The turnoff to the faint two-track that led up to the mine was another four or five miles on. We nearly went past it because someone had cut down a five- or six-foot-high pine tree and laid it across the entry.

Dad gave Grandpère a strange look but said nothing. He dismounted, dragged the tree out of the way, then motioned for us to come through. To my surprise, he put the tree back in place before we started forward again. We hadn't even gone a quarter of a mile up the road when Dad pulled to a stop again, holding up one hand. The track was too narrow for us to pull alongside one another, so we stopped in single file. Dad got off and, to my further surprise, reached back and got his rifle from the scabbard attached to the side of his ATV.

Goose bumps in places I didn't know it was possible to have goose bumps suddenly popped up all over my body. I instinctively clutched at the pouch, which was over my shoulder. "Dad! What is it?"

He didn't answer. He walked a short distance up the track, staring at the ground. I saw immediately what had gotten his attention. We had last been up this road on my birthday. That was now ten days ago.

But the tire tracks here were fresh, not more than a day or two old. Dad dropped to one knee and touched the side of one of the tracks.

"Today?" Grandpère asked.

That question started my pulse pounding, but Dad shook his head. "No. I'd say yesterday." He turned his head and quietly asked, "Are you feeling anything, Danni?"

You mean other than a serious case of the creepies? But I didn't say that. I knew those feelings were just a normal reaction to my seeing Dad going for his rifle without warning. I focused inwardly for a moment, then shook my head. "Nothing."

He straightened and moved forward a little, little pinch lines forming around his mouth now. "Look how deep the tracks are. They were heavily loaded, either with people or something else." He pointed to another place. "It looks like a dozen or more ATVs came through here, but if you look more closely, you can see that several of the tracks are made from the same tires. I'm guessing it's two or three vehicles that made several trips in and out."

"Kids just exploring?" I asked.

"Hopefully. People are always looking for new places." He didn't sound convinced. And yet, as I focused inward, I still didn't feel like anything was out of the ordinary.

He stood there for a long moment, staring up the trail, then made up his mind. "Grandpère, you wait here with the kids. Give me ten minutes. If it's clear, I'll fire one shot and then you come up. If there are any concerns, I'll fire two. If I do that, call for help immediately. But don't come up before then." He looked at me and Cody. "You hear me?"

We nodded, and Dad started away. But then he had another thought. He unbuckled his gun belt and handed it to Grandpère without a word, climbed back on his four-wheeler, put it in gear, and started moving forward. If the pistol was meant to comfort us, it wasn't working.

The next ten minutes seemed more like half an hour, but finally we heard a single rifle shot. Grandpère, who had said nothing during all that time, motioned to us, and in moments we were back on our vehicles and headed up the two-track path.

The mine was a little over a mile up the road. When we came out of the last of the pines into the small clearing, I was hugely relieved to see Dad standing by his four-wheeler. He still held the rifle, but it was in the crook of his arm and the muzzle was pointing at the ground. He was scanning the hillside above him where the tailings from the old mine were clearly visible.

As we shut off our vehicles and dismounted, I looked around quickly. It was a familiar scene—lush meadow grass, lots of wild flowers, the old tree stumps scattered here and there, and pine-clad mountains all around us. Here there were a lot of tracks, far more than we had made on my birthday. But I could see only one old campfire site, and that was ours. It didn't look like anyone had camped here. That was good. Maybe it *was* just kids.

I scanned the ridge directly ahead of us. This was the one where earlier I had felt like someone had been watching us. I was touching the pouch with my left hand. Listening. Everything was perfectly still. Our coming had even silenced the squirrels for the moment. But there was also no inner tingling.

"What do you think?" Grandpère asked.

Dad didn't turn. He raised his free hand and pointed at the slope above us. "You can see that someone climbed up to the mine, but from here the fence looks like it's still intact. Can't say about the locks till we get up there."

"Then let's go," I said, anxious to put this to rest.

Dad led, Cody and I were behind him, and Grandpère brought up the rear. Though it was only about a hundred feet up the slope, it was pretty steep. And we were loaded. Grandpère carried an armful of short two-by-fours. Dad had a forty-pound sack of cement on his shoulder. I had a small bucket of water in one hand and a shovel over my other shoulder. Cody was carrying our toolbox and three burlap bags. So we were all puffing pretty heavily by the time we reached the top.

Dad immediately went to the chain-link fence he and Grandpère had put across the entrance to the shaft a month or so before. The gate was closed and the lock was in place. He rattled it with one hand, then grunted in satisfaction. "It's not been cut." Taking keys out, he unlocked it, and we swung the gate open. Moving through it, he went right to the heavy plank door that sealed off the shaft. Here, too, the lock was in place and the door secure.

Setting the rifle down, Dad unlocked the second padlock, then stopped and looked around. "What do you think, Jean-Henri?"

Squinting, Grandpère looked around. I could see him calculating things in his mind. "I'd say the first thing is to reinforce the door. Put in those U-bolts to secure the metal plate around the lock so no one can pry it off with a crowbar." He turned. "And I think we need to cement in the fence posts so someone can't just rip them out of the ground."

"And double padlock the gate?"

"Definitely. With tempered steel locks. Maybe bring up some razor wire the next time we come and string it along the top of the fence. That should help."

Dad was nodding as Grandpère spoke. "Okay. Then let's get to work." He turned and unlocked the door and pulled it open. It squealed in protest. "All right. Danni, you and Cody take those mining picks and start cutting out enough ore to fill the three bags. Come on. I'll show you the best place to start."

We stopped a few feet inside to let our eyes adjust to the darkened tunnel. I was directing my headlamp at the ceiling above us, looking for spiderwebs. There hadn't been any when we were here before, but spiders were hard workers. No telling what they could have done in ten days.

Cody started to push his way past Dad, but Dad's arm shot out and held him back. "Jean-Henri," he cried. "Look!" He was pointing forward, directing his light at the floor. I moved up to see better. Suddenly the chills were back, only this time they were hitting every cell in my body. The dirt floor was covered with footprints. No, not footprints. *Boot* prints. And none of us had worn that kind of boots when we were in here before.

Dad moved quickly forward, swinging his headlamp back and forth to illuminate the floor of the tunnel ahead. He called back over his shoulder, "I'd say at least three men. Maybe four." We were into the tunnel now, probably two hundred feet or more.

"But how did they get in?" Grandpère asked. "There were no signs of forcible entry."

Dad started to shake his head, then gave a low cry and raced forward. He trained his light on the side wall and groaned. I knew exactly where we were. This was the place where Dad had shown Rick and me the long, diagonal vein of rhodium. I moved forward slowly, not sure what Dad was seeing.

It didn't take long for me to find out. There was a pile of rubble on the floor below where the vein was. The pile was much deeper and longer than the one we had made when we were here last week. Then I saw something that hit me like a blow. Where the vein of rhodium had been visible before, there was now a deep channel cut out of the solid rock. It was about three feet in width and cut at least two feet into the wall. The channel followed roughly the same angle as the vein had before.

Dad stood there, as rigid and lifeless as the heavy timbers around us. Slowly, he reached out one hand and felt along the channel. He turned around, and in the light of our lamps we saw that his face was white with shock. "They've stripped the seam." He focused the light onto the pile of rubble. "They must have taken thirty or forty bags of ore out of here. Maybe fifty."

I rocked back. Fifty bags! I had to reach out and steady myself against the wall.

"How much would that be worth, Dad?" Cody asked.

Dad didn't even hear him. He just stared blankly at the wall in front of him. Grandpère came over. "Danni," he said quietly, "take Cody outside. Wait for us at the entrance."

Too dazed to protest, I took Cody's hand and we started back the way we had come.

We had only gone a few steps when Dad's cry stopped us. "What's this?"

When we turned back, he was leaning in, looking at the wall just above the channel. I hurried back and shined my light on the same spot. There, chiseled into the stone wall, were two words. *PHASE TWO.*

Dad let his fingers run across the letters as he read them aloud. Then he turned to Grandpère. "Did you do that?"

"No." He was peering at it too. "Could it have been here before and we just missed it?"

"No way," Dad said. "It's freshly cut. Like the channel."

"What's it supposed to mean?" I asked.

He shook his head. Grandpère motioned with his head for us to go again, so we turned and headed for the entrance. Suddenly, I was very eager to get out of there.

———

Once outside, Cody and I found a couple of large rocks to sit on. Still reeling, we settled in to wait for Dad and Grandpère. It was a beautiful summer afternoon. Azure blue sky. An occasional puffy, white cloud. Mountainsides lush with towering pines. And yet it felt like there was this huge black cloud hovering right over our heads.

I could tell that Cody had a thousand questions as we sat there, but I guess he sensed that I didn't feel much like talking. I was asking those questions of myself. Who did this? And why? (Well, that was a pretty stupid question. If our four bags were worth half a million dollars, then forty or fifty were worth ten times that.) But who? El Cobra and his gang were in prison. My head came up with a jerk. All but three of them.

I shook that off almost immediately. That didn't make sense. They were on the run. And this had happened probably just yesterday. I finally gave it up. There were no answers, and asking the question only made me feel worse.

The sound of footsteps brought us both to our feet. A moment later, Dad and Grandpère appeared, walking slowly, heads together in deep conversation. When he saw us, Dad came over. I had never seen him quite this shaken before.

"Who do you think did this, Dad?" I asked.

His face was grave. "I don't know, Danni. Nothing makes sense."

"Could it be those three men who are still missing? Think about it. We cost them twenty million dollars. Why not come and get some of it back?"

"I wondered that too, but it's highly unlikely. Whoever did this had at least three ATVs. You can take only three or four bags of ore at a time on those machines, which means they probably had someone down at the road waiting with a trailer or a panel truck to get it out. This was preplanned and carefully orchestrated. Doesn't sound like something three men on the run could do."

"Well," Grandpère said, "whoever they were, they're gone now. Nothing here is fresher than yesterday."

Dad took out his phone and punched in a couple of buttons. A moment later, he was talking to Mom. "Hi. How's it going?" Pause. "Oh, good. I'm glad. Yeah, Grandpère was right. You needed this." Then, very casually, "Had any company?" Another pause, then relief lit up his face as he shook his head at us. "No. We've seen no one either. Uh . . . Angelique? Securing the mine is going to be a bigger job than we thought. We're going to have to come back another day. Yeah, I'm sure. We'll unload our stuff and come on back down. Probably be there in about ten or fifteen minutes. Okay. Love you too. 'Bye."

"Is there even any need to secure the shaft now?" Cody asked as Dad put his phone away.

Dad didn't seem to hear him. He was staring at the dark square of the mine shaft entrance. So Grandpère answered for him. "They got the richest ore, Cody, but that doesn't mean they got it all. Yes, we need to secure it."

Dad turned back. To my astonishment, he was smiling. It was pretty sickly, but it was a smile. "Not our best week ever, eh? Twenty million dollars one day, and another five million a week later. This keeps up, and first thing you know, we could see some serious losses." Then he clapped Cody on the shoulder. "Let's go eat."

———

We unloaded the rest of our stuff from the ATVs and carried it into the trees where it couldn't be easily seen. Finally, Dad looked around. "All right, let's mount up."

While we worked, I had removed the pouch from my shoulder and laid it on the seat of my ATV. Now I reached over, picked it up by the rope strap, and slung it over my shoulder. As I did so, I froze. The pouch was warm through my shirt. I jumped to my feet and jerked it around to the front of me, grasping it with both hands. It wasn't warm, it was hot.

I spun on my heels. "Dad! Something's wrong."

Both he and Grandpère jerked around. "What is it?"

It wasn't just *Le Gardien* that was hot. In one instant, my whole body felt like it was on fire. Every cell seemed to be aflame.

Dad raced to his ATV and grabbed his rifle. Grandpère strode over, taking me by both shoulders. "What are you feeling, Danni?"

I gasped as the answer came with perfect clarity, like a jolt of electricity. "We have to go!" I cried. "Now! Hurry, Dad. We have to go."

"Is it Mom?" he cried.

"No. It's here. We're in danger."

Bless my father for trusting me when he had every reason to stand there and demand to know what in the heck I was doing.

"On the machines," he cried. "Go! Go!"

The next thought burst into my head. "No! Not the machines. Run! Run for the trees."

Dad grabbed Cody's hand, nearly yanking him off his feet as he broke into a hard run, keeping low, darting back and forth, as if he were dodging bullets. Grandpère was between me and the trees, but he waited for me to pass him, waving me on and shouting at me. The four of us raced across the meadow, dodging tree stumps. In moments, we plunged into a thick stand of old-growth timber and were instantly in deep shadow.

"This is far enough," I cried when we were about twenty or thirty feet in. Dad darted behind the trunk of a large pine tree, pulling the rifle up to cover our retreat. Grandpère pushed Cody behind another tree, keeping him close. Using a tree trunk as a shield seemed like a good idea, so I found one where I still had a clear line of sight to the meadow.

We held our breath, trying to hear anything over the sound of our hammering hearts. I kept my eyes pinned on the mine shaft, expecting men with rifles to come running out. Thirty seconds went by, and suddenly I was feeling like an absolute idiot. There was nothing. Not a sound. No movement. Nothing. I reached down and touched the pouch. It was cool again. Dad lowered the rifle and stood up. He turned to me. "Are we okay?" he said in a low voice.

"I . . . I'm not sure. I just had this awful—"

KA-BOOM!

The deafening blast and its accompanying shock wave came so closely together as to be one simultaneous experience. At the same instant as I saw the hillside disappear in a billowing cloud of smoke and dust, the shock wave came crashing down the mountain into the meadow almost more quickly than the eye could follow. I saw one of the four-wheelers tossed violently onto its side. I ducked just as the concussion slammed into our grove of trees. Smaller trees sheared off at the base and went tumbling wildly through the air. Bushes were flattened. Above us, baseball-sized rocks zipped through the trees like bullets, cutting off whole pine branches or gouging out great chunks of bark from the trunks. A deluge of smaller rocks and rock fragments began to shower down on us from the sky.

"Cover your mouths," Dad yelled.

I looked up. Like a wall of muddy water, a cloud of thick dust was rolling toward us. It had reached the meadow and was flattening out. Just before it enveloped the ATVs I saw that the machine Cody and I had come on was on its side and gasoline was trickling from the gas cap. Before I could even process that, the machine disappeared. Moments later the roiling cloud was on us and we instantly began to choke.

We waited almost for a minute, huddled over with our eyes closed and our mouths clamped shut. Gradually the dust cloud passed and began to dissipate. I opened my eyes and slowly straightened, looking around.

"Danni, are you all right?"

It was Dad. He stepped out from behind his tree and started toward me. "I'm okay," I sang out. "I'm okay."

He turned the other way, but Grandpère and Cody were already coming toward us. Huge relief flooded over me. We looked like ghosts coming out of some haunted mist. I began to brush the dust off my shirt and arms. And then I realized how lucky it was that we had stepped behind the trees for protection.

Dad joined me. He looked down at my hand. I did too and saw that it was bleeding. "It's all right," I said. "Just a cut from a flying rock." Then I pointed at our ATV. "It's leaking gas." I started forward.

"No, Danni. Not yet."

That brought me up short. Was someone out there? I didn't think so, but I sure didn't want to be wrong. But at the same time, I knew we couldn't end up with an empty gas tank. We still had a long way to go to get back to our truck. I took *Le Gardien* in my hands and held it tightly for several seconds, half closing my eyes. "No," I finally said. "It's okay. We're alone."

CHAPTER 7

When we came wheeling in on our vehicles to Mom's little painting spot, her surprise quickly turned to annoyance. "I thought you said I had another hour or two."

"Um . . . yeah. Something came up."

What an understatement. The amazing thing was that Mom had heard the explosion but decided it was a sonic boom and thought nothing more about it.

I wondered how much Dad would tell her. I shouldn't have. Holding something back from her would have suggested that she wasn't strong enough to handle it. So, after asking Grandpère to call Clay and give him a report, he sat her down and told her all of it.

I watched the blood drain out of her face, but she remained calm. "Help me pack up my things," she said when he was through. "I think we need to go home."

Just then, Grandpère finished with Clay. "Hang on," he said. "Clay's got a team of four agents down at the dive site at Lake Powell. He's sending two of them to us. He wants them to go up to the mine and treat it as a crime scene. I told him we'd wait for them at the campground where we left our truck. They won't have ATVs, so we'll leave two of ours with them."

"That's good," Dad said. "Where's Clay?"

"Actually," Grandpère said, "he's almost to Price at the moment. He was already bringing a man down to be with us at Lake Powell. So they're about two hours out. He'll meet us at home."

"Very good." Dad turned to me and Cody. "All right. You two help your Mom pack up her things. I'm going to take a look around." He got his rifle out and started back toward the main road, moving quietly, on full alert.

Mom watched him go, her face somber. "If that's meant to make me feel better, it isn't working."

———

Clay's team still hadn't arrived by the time we had the two ATVs refueled and the other two loaded on the trailer. So Dad suggested we break out our lunch—totally forgotten until then—while we waited. There were a few people in the campground and occasional traffic going back and forth on the road, so we didn't feel like we were in any danger. Mom agreed, and we got the coolers down from the trailer.

While we ate quietly, we avoided talking about what had happened for a time, but inevitably our conversation turned back to it. "So the mine is gone?" Mom asked.

Grandpère nodded, face grim. "And half the mountainside with it. There may still be a lot of rhodium up there, but the Danny Boy Mine has, for all intents and purposes, ceased to exist."

Dad spoke softly. "Judging from the hole, they must have planted the explosives farther into the tunnel than we went. I assume they left a trip wire or some other triggering device. We were very lucky that we didn't go in any farther."

When Mom shuddered, he instantly saw his mistake. "I'm sorry, Angelique. Let's not talk about it."

"No!" she said firmly. "I want to talk about it. I want to try to make some kind of sense out of all of it. Why would they blow up the mine?"

I thought that was obvious. "To hide the theft of the ore."

But Grandpère shook his head. "I don't think so."

We all turned in surprise. "Why do you say that, Jean-Henri?" Dad asked.

"Think about it. I agree that's the most obvious reason for destroying the mine, but if that's the case, why not blow it up immediately when they finished? And why carve 'Phase Two' into the wall? No, they wanted us to know the rhodium was gone."

"Say that again," Mom said. "Phase Two?"

"Oh, I forgot to mention that." So Dad told her quickly about the strange words we had found carved in the rock face.

"But that doesn't make any sense. What does it mean?"

Grandpère shrugged. "It only makes sense if we assume they wanted us to see it."

Dad drew in a sharp breath. "But . . . hold on. If there was no trip wire inside, then the detonation had to be controlled from outside or by some kind of timer."

Grandpère's head came up slowly. "Or by cell phone. That would be simple enough. Bury the detonator just inside the shaft where it could still receive a signal, then run a wire from there to the explosives."

"Which meant they had to be watching the site. They had to have seen us come out of the mine. Maybe they were up on a ridge."

"No, I would have felt that," I said. I wasn't positive of that, but I was pretty certain.

"They didn't have to be close," Cody said. "Not if they had binoculars."

"Which means . . ." Grandpère was shaking his head in wonder again. "They wanted us to actually see it blow."

"Maybe they *were* trying to kill us."

"Oh, Danni," Mom cried. "Please don't say that."

But I was already correcting myself. "No, if it was that, why not do it while we were inside the mine? But think about it. I had this terrible feeling of danger and shouted at you guys to run. But . . ." I couldn't believe where my mind was taking me with this.

"But they didn't set off the blast until we were safely into the trees," Dad finished for me.

I was feeling sick to my stomach. I glanced sideways at Mom and saw she was feeling the same. Dad went over and pulled her close. She buried her face against his shoulder. "Who are these people?" she whispered.

None of us had an answer to that.

＊

We were still a few minutes out of Hanksville when Dad's phone rang. It was Clay. Dad mostly listened and said "Yes" or "Okay." Finally, he broke in and asked a question. "What does this mean about our trip down to Powell?" He listened for another moment, then, "Right. I totally agree. See you in a while."

He hung up and turned to us. "Clay just passed us. He's left his guy at the house to check things out. But he's meeting one of his dive team members down at the junction that leads to Lake Powell. Says there's something he needs to get from him. He'll be back to us in about an hour."

"What did he say about Lake Powell?"

"He thinks it's a great idea for us to get away. Now more than ever. But he's sending a man with us, just to be sure. He has a tent and sleeping bag and will rent a boat of his own. For all intents and purposes, he won't appear to be with us, but he'll be close enough to keep watch."

I saw Mom visibly relax. "Good. Very good." Then her shoulders straightened. "We're going to need supper for all of us tonight, as well as a lot of groceries for tomorrow. Since we have some time now, let's stop at the store."

That made me smile. Who but Mom? Always the perfect hostess. And at that moment, I loved her all the more for what she was and for her courage.

But when we came into town, we went right on through at my request. I remembered our experience at the Chevron station the day before and wasn't too keen on seeing anyone right then. When I told Mom and Dad that, they agreed, saying they would take us home, then come back for groceries. I ducked down as we passed. Good thing. We had three cars honk and wave, and other people called out to us as we passed.

I straightened as we cleared the last houses. "Dad? Can I call Rick and tell him what happened?"

He seemed surprised that I would ask. "Of course," he said. "He's a member of our consulting firm. Why wouldn't you?"

"In fact," Mom said, "why don't you see if he wants to come over to the house? We can pick him up after we finish our shopping. That way he can be there and hear what Clay has to say. And tell him Lake Powell is still on." She looked at Dad. "I'm really glad they're going, Lucas. They need to get away from here too."

Good point. I was thinking about them coming because it would be fun to have them. Now I realized that there might be danger for Rick's family too. "Great. I'll call him as soon as we're home."

———

When we arrived home, Dad pulled up behind the barn and turned off the engine. Clay's agent was sitting on the porch in the shade. He waved, then came over and introduced himself.

Cody was, as usual, the first one out of the truck. "Gotta go to the bathroom," he called. He headed for the keypad on the garage door.

"Remember to turn off the alarm," Dad called.

I was sliding across the seat to follow him, feeling the need for a potty stop myself by now, when I remembered something. I jumped out of the truck. "Hey, Code. You can go through the garage, but don't open any of the outside doors yet."

He slowed, then called back. "Got it. The doors, right?"

Grandpère got out beside me. "Doors? What about the doors, Danni?"

Mom was instantly beside me. "What is it, Carruthers?"

"I . . ." As Dad came over too, suddenly I was feeling pretty stupid. "It's nothing."

He took me by both shoulders. "What?"

I could feel my face getting warm. "Well . . . um . . . you see, I had this kind of dumb idea. I guess I've been watching too many spy movies. But anyway, you know how it is when the good guys leave their hotel room or wherever they are, they . . . um . . . put a little thread or something across the door."

"So they can tell if someone has been inside while they were gone?" the agent asked.

Mom sighed, clearly exasperated. "And you did that? My word, Carruthers, you scared the heck out of me." She whirled and started after Cody.

Dad was still eyeing me with this funny look. "Stupid, eh?" I said.

He shrugged. "So let's go check out your handiwork. See if your instincts were correct or not."

A couple of minutes later, as that familiar prickly feeling started crawling up and down my back, I changed my mind about being a dingbat. The front door thread—even harder to see because the porch was in shade now—was still there and intact, as was the one on the French doors that led into the family room. But as we came around to the back door that opened into our laundry room, I pulled up short. The thread was dangling in two pieces, blowing softly in the light breeze.

———

Dad, Grandpère and the agent, whose name was Donald Rasmussen, searched the house for five minutes. They didn't go in with guns drawn, but they moved pretty cautiously as they checked things out. What they were mostly looking for was any sign that something was missing, or that someone had gone through our stuff. But there was absolutely nothing out of the ordinary. They called us in, and Mom, Cody, and I went up to check the upstairs.

We gathered in the living room a few minutes later. Grandpère turned to me. "Did you check the duplicate pouch?" I had, of course, taken the real pouch with me.

"Yes. It's right where I left it. Bottom drawer of my chest of drawers."

"What about your new journal?" Mom asked.

"Under my pillow, right where I put it this morning."

Dad looked at Cody. "And your piggy bank?"

"On the top shelf of my closet." Which was also right where he always left it.

There was silence for a moment. We were all perplexed, but I could see that Grandpère was the most bothered by this. He looked at Dad. "What about the safe?"

"Perfectly normal. I opened it up. Danni's journal is still there. Nothing else was touched either."

"I'll check the outbuildings just to be sure," Donald said, "but those threads are pretty flimsy. A gust of wind rattling the door would be enough to snap it."

"Keep talking," I said sheepishly. "I like your explanation."

He smiled. "It was a wise thing to do, Danni. Good thinking on your part."

Instantly, I knew Donald Rasmussen and I were going to get along just great.

———

Clay drained the last of his glass, then waved Mom off as she lifted the pitcher of lemonade to refill it. "Thank you, Angelique, but no. You've already got me ready to bust. I haven't had anything since a fast-food burrito somewhere around noon, so this was much appreciated."

"Yes," Donald said. "It was great. Thank you, Mrs. McAllister."

"It's Angelique, and you both are welcome. Thank you for coming so quickly."

"I'll be outside," Donald said. "I'll call if anyone is coming."

When he shut the door behind him, Clay turned back to Mom. "I'm sorry I didn't see this one coming. That's got to be a terrible blow to the family, especially coming on the heels of the cancellation of the mine sale."

"We've had better weeks," Dad admitted.

"Can you ever reopen the mine, do you think?"

"Sure." He started ticking off on his fingers. "*If* we had several million dollars in capital. *If* we could get heavy equipment up there. *If* the Forest Service would give us a permit to take heavy equipment up there. *If*—" He shrugged. "Well, you get the picture."

Clay looked genuinely anguished. "Hopefully, we can find the perpetrators and get some of the money back for you." He drew in another deep breath. "By the way, thanks for loaning my two guys the ATVs so they could get up to the mine."

"No problem," Dad said.

Clay set his glass down and pushed back from the table. "Can I ask you a few questions?"

"Of course."

"I'm really puzzled by all of this. The first thought that comes to mind is that this was done by our three escapees."

"I wondered about that too," I said.

"But . . . I don't know. It doesn't make a lot of sense. Aside from the fact that they're on the run, there are all kinds of logistical questions. If you're right in thinking they got away with forty or fifty bags of ore, then—"

"Weighing sixty, maybe seventy-five pounds each," Dad jumped in. "We're talking more than a ton of ore."

"Which they had to take out on four-wheelers, right? You can't get a truck in there?"

"No, not for that last mile or so. It's heavy timber. That means they had to have either a truck or a trailer waiting for them out at the road. They could only take two or three bags at a time on the ATVs."

"Could they have done all this in one day?"

I was watching Clay closely. It was interesting to see how his mind worked. He was very sharp. One more evidence of how lucky we had been to get him as our agent for this whole mess.

"If they had a portable pneumatic drill. They couldn't have done it with picks and shovels in less than three days."

"Didn't know there was such a thing."

"They're a chunk to lug around, but they do make them."

"Which means," Clay concluded, "that either it wasn't our three guys—my first conclusion—or, if it was, they had someone helping them."

"Definitely."

Mom raised her hand. "Has there been any word about them?"

"Actually, yes. This morning we got 'positive confirmation'"—he made quotation marks with his fingers in the air—"that they made it to Mexico. Three men matching the description of our three fugitives were seen getting into a single-engine plane just before dawn Tuesday morning. This was at a dirt airstrip near a small rural village in northern Mexico. Probably one of the drug cartel's landing strips."

"You don't sound convinced," Mom said.

"After two false tips, no, I have some doubts. But it is promising. Several villagers confirmed the sighting and gave the authorities the plane's registration number. About an hour later, that same plane landed at the Benito Juárez International Airport in Mexico City. We're pretty sure they're on their way to Europe by now."

Mom's shoulders slumped, and the relief on her face was evident. Grandpère looked as skeptical as Clay. "That is pretty convenient."

"Exactly." He shrugged. "We've also put out the word on the rhodium ore. That can't be easy to get rid of, not if it's as rare as you say."

Dad agreed. "There are probably fewer than a dozen places that can refine it."

"And we'll check them all out."

Mom had been growing increasingly impatient. "All I want to know is this: Are there more people out there waiting to do us harm?"

"Highly unlikely, Angelique," Grandpère soothed. "They're not going to be sitting around on that much potential money to worry about coming after us. They've got what they want. They've had their revenge. Now they're scurrying for safety."

"Totally agree," Clay said. "One thing is for sure: Whoever did this is long gone out of Utah."

Mom bored in on him. "How sure of that are you? And remember, a piece of coconut cream pie rides on your answer."

"Ninety-nine point nine percent sure. Maybe still in the U.S., but not in Utah."

"That's more like it. Do you want a big piece or a small one?"

Clay suddenly had a little-boy look on his face. "Since my wife is not here at the moment, feel free to make that a fairly generously sized piece." He smiled. "No, forget the 'fairly.'"

Mom tipped her head back and laughed. It was wonderful to hear her do so again. "I like a man who thinks like my husband," she said as she cut a piece double the normal size. She handed it to him with a fork, then cut another one and handed it to Cody. "Run this out to Donald," she said. "And take him a glass of milk, too."

As he left, Clay said to Mom, "I hope you're all right with Don going with you tomorrow. I really don't think you'll need him, but I like to be sure."

She started cutting more pieces. "I like you to be sure, Clay. Are you sure he can't just stay with us on the boat? We don't mind."

"No. Unless someone is watching very closely, they won't know he's with you at all, and that's what we want."

———

"So," Dad said about ten minutes later, as we sat back all fat and comfortable. "You're going on down to Lake Powell now?"

"Not now. Actually, I'm pulling the diving team out. We got what we needed."

"You did?" Dad said. "That fast?"

"Yes." A grin filled his face. "In fact, I brought you a little gift. Something I thought you might really enjoy."

"What kind of a gift?" Cody blurted.

He got up and went to where he had left a small duffel bag. When he returned and set it on the table, it made a dull, metallic clunk. Something definitely heavy.

"Wow!" Cody said. "What have you got in there? Your pistol?"

"Not quite," came the answer. "But let me say first that Danni's and Jean-Henri's description of where El Cobra's boat sank was right on. The diving team found it right off. And with the underwater metal detectors, we have the location of all the bars pinpointed, forty-two in all."

"Oh," I said. "So I was close. I guessed about forty." And then I guessed what he had in his bag. "Did you bring one for us to see?"

"No," he drawled, obviously enjoying himself. "Actually, I brought one for you to keep. To add to your souvenir collection."

My mouth fell open. "Really?"

"Really?" Mom cried.

"Really. If I had thought, I could have brought one for Rick, too. Maybe even one for Cody here."

Cody was confused. "Bars? What kind of bars?"

"Gold bars," Clay said solemnly.

Now Cody's jaw dropped about two feet. But suddenly, I was suspicious. A gold bar was worth a ton of money. Plus, it was evidence in a crime case. "You're kidding, right?"

"Nope. I'm dead serious." He stood up and unzipped the bag.

"The pouch made gold bars?" Cody cried, finally starting to catch up. "How come nobody told me that?"

Clay reached into the bag and with both hands removed something that gleamed like the morning sunlight. He set it down on the table with a solid clunk. "There it is, folks. Twenty-seven and a half pounds, or about 440 ounces. At gold's current selling price of about $1,600 an ounce, what you have before you is . . ." He stopped, grinning broadly. "Wait for it." Then he did a little drumroll on the tabletop with his two hands. "Seven hundred and four thousand dollars! Or"—another drum-roll—"with forty-two bars, that's a grand total of twenty-nine million, five hundred sixty-eight thousand dollars!" He laughed aloud. "Which is about ten million dollars more than you lost the other day."

Good old Cody, always one to cut through the clutter, was the first to ask, "So is it all ours?"

Clay found that uproarious. "Why not? The pouch made the bars, and Danni owns the pouch. Once we no longer need it as evidence, they're all yours."

I wasn't sure what was going on, but it was obvious that Clay was really enjoying himself. He slid the bar across the table so it stopped in front of me. It was so heavy I almost dropped it. So I set it down and stroked the brilliant metal with my fingertips, totally enraptured.

"Can I feel it? Can I?" Cody cried.

I handed it to him. "Pass it around the table," I suggested.

Even though I had seen the bars being made, I have to admit, it was still pretty amazing.

"It's incredibly beautiful," Mom said in awe as she took it.

"Amazing," Dad breathed.

"I agree," Clay said. "So, Danni, you get the very first one. That seemed only right."

"No way!" I shouted. "You really do mean it?"

"Of course I mean it. Would I joke about something like this?"

"I want one," Cody cried.

"Okay. Next time I come down."

"You're giving my children seven hundred thousand dollars each?" Dad said. "What's the catch?"

"Well," Clay said, still obviously enjoying himself immensely, "There is one little thing." He reached in his left front pocket and brought out a red Swiss army knife. He unfolded the blade and walked around to Mom. The bar had come back and stopped in front of her. He reached down and picked it up with one hand. "Danni, I think we can conclude that *Le Gardien* has a rich sense of humor."

I just looked at him, not sure what that meant. A pouch with a sense of humor? I didn't think so. But even as he said that, he turned the gold at an angle and ran the knife blade along one edge. The metal was soft enough that a sliver peeled off, like when you're peeling an apple. Then he shut the blade and returned the knife to his pocket. "Notice anything unusual?" he asked.

It was then that I saw that where he had made the cut, the bar was not gold, but a dark, metallic gray.

Dad, being the metallurgist, understood it first. "Oh. My. Word!" he breathed.

Then Grandpère started to laugh. At first it was just a deep chuckle; then it exploded into a full roar of laughter. "Would you look at that!" he exclaimed, slapping the table with the flat of his hand.

"What?" I cried. Mom was looking confused too.

Dad reached out and took the bar, running his finger along the cut. "What you are looking at, ladies and gentlemen, is a bar of solid lead that has been immersed in gold-leaf paint."

Clay was laughing so much now that tears were forming at the corners of his eyes. Finally, he got control enough to say, "The asking price for lead on the open market right now is about a dollar per pound. The good news for El Cobra is, he didn't lose some vast fortune after all. Only about eleven hundred dollars."

Then he turned to Dad, the smile fading. "I am sorry, Mack. At first I thought this might be an answer for you, but . . ."

Dad merely shrugged and looked at Mom. "Sorry, hon. I think we just lost another twenty-nine million dollars. Darn! That's the third time this week."

CHAPTER 8

Schloss von Dietz, Bern, Switzerland
June 24, 2011

Gisela von Dietz was going over the latest quarterly reports of Von Dietz Global Financial when the fax machine beeped three times. That was the signal for a secure fax coming in. Almost immediately, the first sheets began to print.

She waited a moment, then took the first sheet. As expected, it was from Niklas. Relieved to finally get it, she leaned back and began to read.

Dear Mum,

 Sorry I haven't called. In addition to things being pretty hectic here, since there is a remote risk of having one's mobile phone conversations monitored, I'll keep my calls to a minimum. Am on the road now, making my way back to Europe as previously described. Hopeful to arrive by Saturday night or Sunday. Here are a few items of interest pending my full report when I arrive:

• Our three remaining assets successfully extracted 55 bags of rhodium ore from the McAllister mine. The ore is now on its way to British Columbia, where it will be put on a freighter bound for Vladivostok, Russia. Russian Mafia—ever discreet in sensitive matters—offered 7M Euros, about half its estimated worth. But

extraction of rhodium is very expensive and risk of detection is high, so offer was accepted. Money transferred to Cayman Island accounts. This does somewhat soften the loss of the twenty million dollars.

• *Destruction of the mine went off as planned. Took the family longer than expected to go up there, but timing turned out perfectly. I asked the team to take in a video camera with zoom lens to verify mission success. Thought you might like to see what 500 kilos of Semtex (or C4) can do in a tightly enclosed space. (Sending video clip via secure email.)*

• *Since we will not need our three assets again until we launch Phase III, I was planning to extract them immediately. However, the FBI has launched a widespread search for possible vehicles involved in the mine explosion, so they will go to ground for a few more days.*

• *While the McAllisters were in the mountains, I sent Enrico (our in-house cat burglar) into their home. Following this brief note you will find high-resolution photos of (1) a fabric pouch found in the girl's bedroom, and (2) a copy of the personal journal of Danni McAllister, which was locked in an office safe. I trust you will find both of much interest. Especially the last few pages. I was wrong. The gold does exist. Not that we can get to it. But she confirms Armando's story in every detail.*

• *As always, Enrico left no trace of his entry and exit.*

Enjoy, Mama. You owe me big on this one. We'll talk tomorrow.
Much love, N.

Gisela laid the note aside and turned her attention to the photos that were already coming out of the fax machine. The first one caused her to draw in a sharp breath.

For the next half an hour, she barely moved as she studied the photos of the pouch, then read the scrawled handwriting of a silly, empty-headed, young American female.

When she was done, she unlocked one of the drawers on her desk and removed the two sheets outlining the family history of the Chevalier and LaRoche families. She focused on the previous cross-out and its correction, which read: *Existence of* Le Gardien ~~tentatively~~ *confirmed. High likelihood that Carruthers Monique McAllister is the next keeper of the pouch.* Once again, she crossed it out and rewrote it:

Existence of *Le Gardien* positively confirmed. Carruthers (Danni) Monique McAllister as keeper of the pouch, 100% confirmed. Mystical powers of pouch 100% confirmed.

She sat back, read what she had written, then added: *THIS CHANGES EVERYTHING!!!*

Oregon Trails Inn and Restaurant,
Interstate 80, North Platte, Nebraska
2:41 a.m.

Niklas von Dietz came partially awake as the ring tone penetrated his consciousness. He rolled over, grabbed his mobile phone, and held it front of his face. When he saw the number, he groaned. "Aw, Mama. There's seven hours difference between you and me, remember?"

Falling back on the pillow, he tapped the ACCEPT button. "Hello, Mother."

"Did you see the video footage?"

"What?"

"The video footage you sent me. Have you watched it?"

"Of course I watched it. Why?"

"You could have ruined everything."

He went up on one elbow. "What are you talking about?"

"Don't play stupid with me, Niklas. You know what I'm talking about. After all the promises you made to me and Granny, you go off and totally risk everything."

He could tell how angry she was from her breathing. He sat up. "All right, Mama. It's almost three in the morning here. So start over and go slow. What is the matter?"

"You nearly killed them with that explosion."

"First of all, *I* wasn't there. I don't go out on the actual operations. I was forty miles away in a truck, waiting for them to bring the ore. Second, who are you talking about?" Then it dawned. "Oh. You mean the family?"

"No," she said, her voice dripping with sarcasm, "I'm talking about the squirrels. Of course I mean the family. I told you and told you. No one gets hurt. Not physically. Not in any way. This is a war against the mind, not the body."

"No one did get hurt," he said, fighting for patience. "Those were my specific instructions. That's why the guys waited until they ran into the trees before they set it off."

"And sent rocks flying like cannonballs. You could see trees being cut in half. What if one of those had hit the boy? Or worse, what if the grandfather had been killed?"

There was a weary sigh. "Ah, Mama, you and Granny. Your ethics are something else. You say you don't want them hurt. This while you are dedicated to totally destroying them in every other way—mentally, emotionally, financially. Don't you find that a bit contradictory?"

"This is about *suffering*. Never forget that. There were times when your grandmother and I longed for death, even begged for it. But it never came. We had no choice but to endure. That's why they can't die. It puts them out of our reach."

"But, Mama, no one *was* hurt. Now, good night. I'll be in touch by fax again tomorrow."

PART THREE

Crosby Canyon

CHAPTER 9

Oak Canyon, Lake Powell, Utah
June 26, 2011

I'm the first one up this morning, don't ask me why.

What a waste. Church doesn't start until 11:00 and I could have slept in until 8 at least. But here I am, up and wide awake at this ungodly hour reserved only for the dead. Bummer! But since I am, and since no one else is, and since I can't make any noise until the others are up, I'll use this time to write some more here.

Quick catch-up. We were supposed to leave on Friday morning to come down here to Lake Powell. Didn't happen. Rarely does. We didn't get much done the day before due to losing the mine and finding out we are the owners of a small fortune in lead. Emphasis on small. It was after noon before we actually got away. Driving to Lake Powell, picking up the rental Jet Skis, transferring all of our stuff to the houseboat, and getting under way took until nearly 3:30, so it was almost 8:00 by the time we found a spot and got the houseboat beached and secured. We had snacked on junk food most of the way down, so we skipped supper and were in bed by 9.

We are in Oak Canyon, which is farther downstream than we usually go. But Mom wants to paint Rainbow Bridge this week, and this is closer.

So Friday was a get-there-and-get-set-up kind of a day.

131

But yesterday was great. It was mostly sun and water all day long. Rick's sisters, Kaylynn and Raye, got to drive the Jet Skis—with an adult on behind them, of course—for their first time and thought that was the best thing ever. Rick was kind of bummed because he couldn't get on them. Doctor says he can't get his wound wet for a few more days. But he and Mom took the boat out, and Mom insisted he drive, so he was cool with that. So we went cliff jumping and swimming, made sand castles on the beach, went for a short hike to the top of the bluffs, chased lizards, drank enough pop to keep the bathrooms busy, and ate enough Cheetos to turn the water orange when we washed our hands. Now, that's what I call a perfect day.

Oh, and one really special thing. While we were cliff jumping, I got in the boat with Mom and Rick. To my surprise, Rick was very quiet. I could tell he was kind of emotional about something. So, with my usual feminine sensitivity, I dug my elbow into his side and asked him what was wrong. I was really shocked when he turned and I saw that his eyes were glistening. Then, with some difficulty, he pointed to where his father and his Aunt Shauna were about to jump off the cliff, each with one of the girls in their arms, and he said, "I haven't seen Dad play with Kaylynn and Raye like that since they were little girls. And I can't remember the last time I heard my sisters laughing so hard."

I thought Mom was going to start bawling right on the spot. Not me, of course. I am way too unemotional for that. O.K., O.K. So I choked up a little bit.

Sadly, Charlie and Shauna and the girls have to go back today since he has to be back to work tomorrow, and Shauna is going to Moab tomorrow with the girls. Shauna's going to move here and live with Rick's family.

Well, I just heard someone out in the main area of the house-boat—probably Grandpère—so I'd better stop for now. Besides, I don't want to get the page wet with my blubbering.

With ten people, there wasn't enough room for all of us to sit at the table at the same time, so for our big meals, we'd load up our paper plates, grab a can of pop or a bottle of water from the fridge, and find a place to eat. Breakfast, however, was a little different. By Mom's decree, there was no set time for breakfast. We were to sleep in as long as we wanted—or, to be more accurate, as long as we could. A houseboat is not built to be soundproof. So whoever was cooking that morning prepared something that could be eaten as people woke up.

Since it was Grandpère's turn to cook, when I came out I was not surprised to see the counter filled with eggs, tomatoes, sliced ham, shredded cheese, green onions, bacon bits, and the like—all the makings for customized omelets. What did surprise me was that Kaylynn and Raye were there helping him cut things up. And chattering away at him like a couple of chipmunks. I got a cursory wave and smile, and then I was quickly forgotten. I sat down to watch. Kaylynn was cutting a tomato into small cubes. Raye was grating cheese. They kept looking at each other; then suddenly they'd break out in peals of giggles.

I couldn't help but join in the laughter. It was a musical sound, infectious and joyous. They were darling girls. With their long, jet-black hair and their enormous brown eyes, they could have passed for twins, except that Kaylynn was a head taller than Raye. I had always thought of them as being very shy. That impression was gone. They were delightful.

Raye finished filling the bowl with cheese and took it over to Grandpère. "Here you go, Mr. LaRoche," she said. Grandpère was breaking eggs into a bowl. "*Merci beaucoup,* my dear," he said with a slight bow.

Raye wrinkled her nose. "Mercy what?"

He chuckled. *"Merci beaucoup.* It's French for 'thank you very much.'"

"Oh." She climbed up on a chair beside him. "Are you French?"

"Oui, ma petite fille, which means, 'Yes, my little one.'"

Kaylynn came over with the tomatoes. "You're weird," she said. It was a matter-of-fact statement, not a criticism.

"No," Grandpère laughed. "Not weird. Just French."

He picked up the whisk and starting whipping up the eggs.

"What are you making, Mr. LaRoche?" Kaylynn asked.

"*Omelette au fromage.* The food of the gods." He said it with great solemnity. Then he winked. "That's an omelet with cheese to you mere mortals."

Reaching for the milk, Grandpère poured some into the eggs, then whipped them vigorously.

"Why are you doing that?" Kaylynn wanted to know.

"Because the milk creates air bubbles, and that is what makes an omelet light and fluffy."

"Really?" I asked.

He sniffed haughtily. "Americans! You are such barbarians when it comes to food." He turned his back on me. "Pay Danni no attention, girls. It is time to begin. Tell me what you would like in your *omelette au fromage.*"

———

Mom was the last one up. For the second day in a row. It was almost nine when she came out, still in her pajamas and slippers. She came to a stop as she was caught in the simultaneous grip of a yawn and a stretch. "Oh my goodness," she cried as she finished. "That's the first time I've slept clear through the night in almost two weeks." Then she looked around. "Oh, something smells good. What are we eating?"

Kaylynn turned. "The food of the gods," she said with reverent awe.

We all laughed.

"Grandpère's been indoctrinating the girls about French cuisine," Dad said.

"And French superiority," I added. "And without shame, I might add."

"But of course," Grandpère retorted. "There is no shame in truth." He waved at the counter behind him. "Come, Angelique. Your omelet awaits you."

———

As we did the dishes, Mom seemed thoughtful. She finally glanced at her watch. "If we're going to church, we'd better get going. Even in the ski boat, it will take us over an hour to get there."

I whipped around. "*If?*" I echoed. I looked at Dad. "Did I just hear my mother use the word 'if' in the same sentence with the word 'church'?" We *never* missed church when we came down here. No matter how far away the houseboat was from Bullfrog. There was no church at the marina itself, but there was one at Ticaboo, a short distance up the road.

She looked around at the chaos in the room—towels, a life jacket, paper cups left from last night's late-night snacks, Cody's swimsuit draped over the back of a chair—and sighed. "The thoughts of getting cleaned up and our hair done and getting everyone dressed in Sunday clothes and . . ." She let it trail off.

Dad waved a hand. "If you're looking for an excuse, Don called a bit ago and asked about our plans. I told him that church was a good likelihood, but he counseled against it. He would have to go with us, and in a small church like that, he'd be pretty conspicuous. He talked to Clay, and Clay agrees."

"Well, then," Mom said, "if it's a matter of following the FBI's counsel, I don't think there is a choice."

"Try not to look too devastated, Mom," I said.

"Me? I'm brokenhearted," Cody said with a grin.

"So," Dad said, "I thought we could just hang out this morning. Have some quiet time. Just visit. Maybe have our own little informal worship service."

"That would be great with us," Charlie said.

"Yeah," the girls echoed. "We want Grandpère to tell us about France," Kaylynn added.

Mom rubbed her hands together. "I think we have a plan. So, I'll have one of Dad's divine omelets, then we'll clean this place up a little. What say we gather back here at eleven? That will give us time to take a shower if we want." She turned to Charlie. "If we leave here about four, that will put us to Bullfrog by five, and you back home by six or six-thirty. Is that soon enough?"

Charlie agreed with a quick nod. Rick's Aunt Shauna was in the process of moving to Hanksville to live with Rick's family. Charlie had to work at the mine tomorrow, so Shauna was taking the girls to Moab for the next several days to help her pack. Rick would stay with us. He had protested that, of course, saying he could help Shauna, but his father had been firm. He was to rest that leg, and that was that.

I could have kissed him right there in front of everybody. I mean his father. Not Rick.

To call what we did just before lunch a "worship service" was probably a little generous. We didn't get into Sunday clothes or anything—though it definitely wasn't swim attire, either. We gathered in the main room of the houseboat, some on chairs, some on cushions on the floor. We did open with a prayer, but then Dad kind of looked around and said, "I think it would be a good idea to get to know each other a little better. So, nothing formal, let's just talk. Tell us about yourself. What you like. What you don't like. Your talents. Whatever. Charlie, why don't you start. I know that your parents came here from Guatemala many years ago. Were you born in Guatemala too?"

"I was," he said. "But I wasn't even two when they came to California. Shauna was born the following year, so she is a native-born American. My parents and I became citizens when I was fourteen."

With a little prodding, Dad kept him talking about their early life. It was amazing to learn about him. He had worked as an itinerant laborer for many years, eventually becoming a foreman. He married Rick's mother when he was twenty-two and she was seventeen. Eventually, he came to Hanksville to work in the coal mine because the wages were much better and it was permanent, year-round work.

The whole discussion was wonderful, actually. Shauna opened up after some initial shyness, and we learned that she had a delightful sense of humor, in spite of having had a tough life. Kaylynn and Raye blushed a lot as we asked them questions, but you could tell they were loving it.

Rick balked when I said, "Okay, your turn."

"I'd say it's time to hear something from the McAllisters," he said. "We can come back to the Ramirez family later." I tried to protest, but Cody interrupted. "I'll go," he said. And then, with his usual shyness—not!—he kept us laughing for the next five or six minutes.

"You're next, Danni," Rick said.

Ha! He thought he could get away with that? Dodge it himself, then turn it on me?

"I've got a better idea. I think our guests need to hear the story of how Lucas McAllister and Angelique LaRoche met and fell in love."

Both of them started to protest, but they were drowned out by our applause. As they finally agreed, to our surprise, Grandpère stood up. "I shall provide some background information, since I am largely responsible for getting these two together."

"No," Mom cried, laughing. "What are you going to say?"

He ignored her. More applause. He did a little half bow, then gestured at my parents. "Feel free to add commentary or correction as you see fit."

They surrendered with good-natured smiles, and so he began. "All right. To begin with, you have to remember that Lucas McAllister, the man most of us know as Mack, was born in Butte, Montana, where his father was a mining engineer. They lived on a small cattle ranch outside of Butte. Thus Mack grew up with a cowboy heritage as well as mining experience. During his high school years, he worked in the mine with his father. So by the time he graduated, he knew enough about mining that he got a full scholarship to the Colorado School of Mines, in Golden, Colorado. He got a bachelor's and a master's degree there, and then went on to Michigan for his doctorate. While he was in Colorado, he supported himself at school by working as a cowboy at a nearby ranch.

"Now," he said, "let's go down the road from Golden about twenty miles to the south, to the city of Boulder, Colorado, home of the University of Colorado."

"Where Grandpère was a professor of French History and Literature," I called out.

"That is correct," Grandpère acknowledged. "And where my oldest daughter, Angelique Carruthers McAllister, was a junior in fashion and design. So . . ."

I had to smile. He loved to tell a story, and he was a master of the pause, to build suspense.

"So about this time in my career I was getting bored. I have always loved to learn new things, and I like to keep busy. So one day, I decided I wanted to study mining engineering. Where I grew up in France was not far from a large coal-mining area. This had always fascinated me, so I started taking classes at the School of Mines."

"And met Dad," Cody supplied, in case any of us had missed that obvious connection.

"Exactly. We met in a metallurgical chemistry class. I think we were both surprised at how well we hit it off, in spite of our age difference. Anyway, the more I got to know this cowboy from Montana, who was getting straight A's in his college work, the more I started to wonder if he might not be the one for my Angelique."

"Okay," Mom said, standing up beside him. "I'm coming in here. I knew none of this, of course. But I did know two things for sure. I wanted to study fashion and interior design in New York City—maybe even do a master's degree in Europe—*and,* I had a strong aversion to cowboys and the so-called Wild West."

"*Strong* is an understatement," Dad murmured. We were all smiling by now. This was great. I loved this story, and to have the three of them telling it together was a first for me and Cody.

"So," Grandpère came back in, "I knew that no matter what I said, there was no way that Angelique was going to go out with some guy in a cowboy hat and manure on his boots."

Rick was chuckling. He leaned over to me. "They really are different," he said.

Mom again: "What my father has neglected to tell you is that he didn't like the idea of fashion and interior design and had been trying to talk me into studying art, especially oil painting, for quite a while. He thought I was much better at it than I did, so I was kind of resisting him on it. But it did raise questions, and so I started praying about it. I asked God many times what I should do, but I couldn't seem to get an answer."

She turned and looked at Dad. "Then one summer day, this handsome-looking guy in a cowboy hat and cowboy boots came walking into the restaurant where I was working. When he saw me, he just stopped and stared at me, like he'd seen a ghost or something."

She laughed merrily. "I thought he was crazy. He didn't move. He didn't say anything. He just stared at me with those huge, green eyes of his."

We were all looking at Dad now, who was grinning like some lovestruck kid. "Well, before we talk about that," he said, "let me back up a bit. Jean-Henri had said nothing about having a daughter. Especially one so beautiful."

"Thank you, dear," she sang out.

"He just kept telling me about this really great burger place down in Boulder that wasn't too far out of my way when I was headed out to work on the ranch. So finally, one day I had a little extra time, and I stopped in. And Angelique's right. When I saw her, I was struck dumb. I mean, she was beautiful and all that, but there was something else about her. I couldn't take my eyes off of her."

Mom chuckled. "Finally, some guy bumped into him and nearly knocked him down. So he finally came out of it and found a table. But it wasn't one of the tables assigned to me. That didn't stop him. A few minutes later, one of the other waitresses told me that this cute guy over there wouldn't let anyone wait on him except me. Well, there was no way I was going over then. I had my friend tell him that either he left now, or she was calling the cops."

"How's that for romantic?" Dad said, pulling a face.

"So what did you do?" Kaylynn blurted. Her face was wreathed with genuine concern.

"I thought about it a lot," Dad said. "That was while I was pacing back and forth outside. Then I called the ranch and told them I wouldn't be there that day. And I found a bench where I could watch the door, and I settled in to wait."

Now Mom's eyes had a faraway look in them and her voice was soft. "When I got off work a couple of hours later, there he was, waiting outside the restaurant. Which seriously freaked me out. I tried to get around him, but he stepped in front of me and asked me one question." She turned to Dad. "Go ahead, you tell them." She shook her head. "I still can't believe this."

To my amazement, Dad was actually blushing. "I'll admit, it wasn't the brightest pickup line a guy has ever used on a girl, but I asked her this: 'Do you believe in love at first sight?'"

Rick burst out laughing. "You didn't!"

"I did," he said. "I was smitten. No doubt about that."

Incredulous, Rick turned to Mom. "And you bought into a line like that, Mrs. McAllister?"

"Oh, no. I thought it was the stupidest thing I had ever heard. I was taking a marriage and family class at that time, and I remembered something my teacher had recently taught us. So I said to him, 'No, I don't believe in love at first sight. But I do I believe in *attraction* at first sight, which, if it's strong enough, can keep a relationship going until love develops.'"

"Which was a pretty cold slap in the face, you have to admit," Dad replied. Then he too went a little mushy in the knees as he looked at her. "All I could of think of to say to her was, 'Angelique'—I had gotten that off her name tag—'if that's the case, then we'd better start spending a lot of time together so this attraction I'm feeling can turn into love.'"

"And I was a goner," she said. "Just like that. There went my aversion to cowboys. There went New York City. There went fashion and design." She walked over to him, put her arms around him, and kissed him a good one. This time we clapped and whistled and shouted.

When she straightened again, her face was flaming red and she had tears in her eyes. "And we've never looked back. It's almost nineteen years now and we're still in love as much as we were when we were married."

Dad took her hand. "More."

She moved closer, then shook her head. "That's not possible."

CHAPTER 10

After hearing that story, I think we all knew there was no way anyone could top it, so our little meeting broke up and we just sat around talking for a few minutes before we started a light lunch. After lunch, Rick and I volunteered to clean up, and, to our surprise, Grandpère came over to help. Shauna took the girls and Cody outside and started a game of Monopoly under the deck umbrella. Mom decide to lie down for a while, and Dad went in to help Charlie pack up.

Seeing that we were alone, I decided this was my chance to ask Grandpère something that had been bugging me for a couple of days now. Maybe with Rick there, he wouldn't go through his usual dodging, teasing routine with me.

"I have a question," I said abruptly. "For you, Grandpère."

"Fire away."

"Remember what you said on the phone the other day, about the footmen and the horses?"

He gave me a look. "I know I'm getting old and senile, but I am able to remember what happened two days ago."

"Good. Then tell me what it means."

To my surprise, he picked up a dish towel and dried his hands. Then he turned and walked over to the small bookshelf in the corner. When he came back, he had a Bible and was thumbing the pages. "It actually comes from the Old Testament," he said. "From the book of Jeremiah, chapter twelve, verse five." He sat down at the table, still looking for his place, then he motioned for us to join him. We did.

When he found what he was looking for, he bent down and read it to himself, his lips barely moving. "Here it is. 'If thou hast run with the footmen, and they have wearied thee, then how canst thou contend with horses?'"

"Yeah, that's it." I looked at Rick. "He texted me that the other night." Back to Grandpère. "So, what does it mean?" I asked.

"What do you think it means?"

I pulled a face at him. "No, Grandpère, don't do that. Just tell me what it means. I want to know why you sent that to me."

"Because I thought it might be of value."

"But how can it be of value when it doesn't make sense? Footmen and horses? What man in his right mind would try to race against a horse? The horse would always win."

He looked thoughtful. "You make a good point." Then, catching me off guard, he picked up the book again, pushed it down the table to Rick, and tapped on the verse. "What do you think, Rick? Does this sound to you like Jeremiah is talking about a race here?"

Rick took the book and read again where Grandpère had indicated. "If thou hast run with the footmen, and they have wearied thee, then how canst thou contend with horses?"

Grandpère cut in. "That's good. Don't worry about the rest of the verse. So? Do you think Jeremiah is talking about a race between man and horse?"

Rick read it again silently, then shook his head. "I don't think it's talking about a race at all. I think it's talking about war."

"Wait," I exclaimed. "Really?" I took the book from Rick and read it to myself.

Rick went on as I did so. "It sounds to me like the footmen would be what we call the infantry, and the horsemen would be the cavalry."

"The Israelites didn't have cavalry back then, but they did see horses used in times of war in another important way." Again he looked at Rick rather than at me. "Think of the Romans."

Rick's head came up as understanding dawned. "Chariots! He's saying that if you have trouble fighting against men on foot, how can you possibly fight against chariots?"

"Ah," Grandpère said in satisfaction, "very good." He turned to me. "Any more questions?"

"Yeah," I said, feeling the familiar exasperation starting to rise. "You still haven't told me why you sent it to me."

He stroked his goatee thoughtfully. "To be completely honest, I'm not exactly sure." He smiled. "Maybe it will come to me sometime." And with that, he got up and went back to the sink. Rick and I exchanged looks. Then I shook my head, giving up.

———

Rick's family left right after supper. There were tender farewells and renewed promises that we'd do it again once or twice more before the summer was over. Dad permanently wormed his way into Raye's and Kaylynn's affections when he leaned over to their father and said, "Charlie, would it be all right with you if the girls helped me drive the boat on the way back?" Then he turned to them. "Are you all right with that, girls?" As if he had to ask.

We stood and waved until they disappeared around the bend; then we turned and started inside. As Mom pushed open the sliding glass door, Rick said, "You know, don't you, Mrs. McAllister, that you have witnessed a little miracle."

We all turned, but Mom spoke first. "In what way?"

"My dad, actually taking time to play, to laugh, to sit at the table and just talk. It's incredible." He sighed. "Thank you for insisting that all of us come with you."

"You are most welcome, Ricardo," Mom chuckled. As his eyebrows lifted at the use of his formal name, she shook her head. "The next miracle I'm looking for will be when you stop calling me Mrs. McAllister. You make me feel like I'm an old woman, Rick."

"And that could be dangerous, Son," Grandpère said somberly.

Rick grinned. "I certainly don't think of you as old, so I guess it will be Angelique, then."

She slipped her arm through his. "That, my boy, just earned you as many warm peanut-butter bars as you can possibly eat. They're supposed to be warmed in the oven, but that's one of the nice things about Lake Powell. Everything's an oven down here." To me: "Get them out, Danni girl, this calls for a celebration."

Celebration indeed. *Danni girl?* Her calling me *Danni* was starting to happen with increasing frequency. It was just one little miracle after another tonight.

———

The Colorado Plateau is a vast area of high deserts, deep canyons, and several small mountain ranges in America's Southwest. Its center is roughly in the Four Corners area, and the plateau spreads across parts of Colorado, New Mexico, Arizona, and Utah. Because of its elevation and isolation—there isn't one large city in it—the air is spectacularly clear. Get on some of the high spots, and there are places you can easily see things a hundred miles away.

And that makes for spectacular viewing of the heavens at night.

I had spent most of my life in this country, but it still completely dazzled me when I lay on my back and looked up into the night sky. I had read somewhere that the naked eye can only see about six thousand stars, but I questioned that. It felt more like six million. As I looked up, I remembered something Dad often says: "If you get to feeling like you're really something, sleep out under the stars. That will cut you back down to size."

Cody, Rick, and I were lying on our air mattresses, quiet for the moment, humbled into silence by the vastness that spread out above us. We had asked Mom and Dad if we could sleep up here on the top deck of the houseboat, but Mom shook her head. It was a sobering reminder that there was still a potential threat. But we had all slept late this morning, so she and Dad said we could go up there until eleven or so. We lay side by side, with Cody in between Rick and me.

I half turned my head and raised up enough that I could see Rick. "Penny for your thoughts."

He turned and smiled. "Not for sale."

"You can have mine for free," Cody said.

I pretended that he didn't exist right now. "Aw, come on, Rick. What are you thinking?"

He sighed. "I was thinking about Leprechaun Canyon and . . ." His voice trailed off.

I came up on one elbow and looked directly at him. Just exactly what part of Leprechaun Canyon was he thinking about? Gordo and Doc coming after us? Him racing forward and grabbing Lew's rifle? Or . . . a kiss in the near-total darkness? I often wondered if he ever thought about it. I know I sure did. But I wasn't about to ask him that now. Especially not with my little brother lying between us.

"And I was thinking about your mom and dad, too."

"What about them?"

He turned and looked at me. "I don't think you and Cody know how lucky you are."

"Yes we do," I said. Then I remembered what he had once told me about his mother. It was the night she told his dad and Rick and the girls that she was leaving. One of the things she said was that when it came to custody of the children, if they went to court it would be over who had to take them, not who got to keep them.

"No, Danni. You really don't. They are so much in love."

I let out a slow breath. He was right. Cody and I just took that for granted. Today had been a good reminder for me. "You're right."

"Your mom is amazing."

I lay back down again. "You know, Rick, calling her 'your mom' isn't going to go over any better with her than calling her Mrs. McAllister. You may as well get used to it. It's Angelique."

"I know. It's just so . . . weird." He sighed again. "I'm working on it."

"Hey," Cody broke in, "I've got a question for you."

I went up on my elbow again. "What?"

"Now, don't laugh. Think about it before you answer." He paused. "What do you see when your eyes are closed?"

I laughed. "What kind of a stupid question is that? You don't see anything."

"Is not stupid," Cody said hotly.

Rick sat up. "I think I'm going to side with Cody on this one."

"All right!" Cody yipped.

"Oh, please," I muttered. "Not more male bonding."

Cody sat up now too and turned to me. "Close your eyes."

I did, deciding to humor him. After a moment, I said, "Guess what I see?"

"What?"

"Absolutely nothing. A whole lot of black."

Rick: "Are you sure?"

"I think I know black when I see it."

"Shut them real tight," Cody urged.

"They are shut tight," I snapped.

"Tighter."

I complied, feeling ridiculous. "This is ridiculous. I still don't—" I stopped. "Oh."

"Ha!" Cody yelled. "What are you seeing?"

I didn't answer. I was concentrating. But Rick did. "I see patterns of colors swirling around in the center of the blackness. Like when you wash out a watercoloring brush."

Cody was delighted. "Press the heels of your hand against your eyes."

I did. For a moment, nothing changed; then I leaned forward, as if I were taking a closer look. Suddenly, all kinds of things started happening. At first there were quick pinpoints of white in the upper part of my vision; then light surged upward in shimmering waves.

Without realizing it, I was describing what I was seeing. "I've got white checkerboards, only they're kind of rubbery and they're kind of rippling. Oh, wait! I'm back to solid black."

"Ooh!" Code exclaimed. "I'm getting flashing purple dots."

I know it sounds stupid, but it was actually quite fun. For five minutes we sat there like kids at a circus, calling out to each other what we were seeing. Finally, tired of it, I lay back down. Cody and Rick did the same a few seconds later.

"I'm waiting," Cody sang out a moment later.

"For what?"

"For an apology."

"In your dreams!"

He and Rick both laughed, and a moment later I heard a sharp slap. I didn't have to ask what it was. It was my two male companions giving each other a high five.

A few minutes later, Cody checked out on us. He was like that, churning away at warp speed, then all of a sudden, BAM! his system would shut down and he would be gone. With a huge yawn, he excused himself and climbed down to the main deck.

Remembering Mom's feelings about us being up there alone, Rick and I went down too. Mom and Dad were still there, but they excused themselves and followed Cody down to the bedrooms. Rick asked me if I was tired, and I started to say that I wasn't, but then a huge yawn cut me off. He laughed, nudged me, and said, "Good night, Danni."

June 29, 2011

"Do you dread going back tomorrow?" I asked.

Rick turned to me in surprise. "Not really. Do you?"

"Kind of. These ten days have been great. Nothing but family, friends, fun, and relaxation. I think we all needed that. Going back to Hanksville sounds kind of boring."

"I can handle boring," he said with a smile.

Rick and I were sitting on the beach about twenty or thirty yards up from the houseboat. Though the sky above us was still light, here in the narrow confines of Oak Canyon, the sun had disappeared behind the cliffs hours ago, and we were in deep shadow. Down the beach from us, I could hear the murmur of voices from another houseboat. Inside the main room of the houseboat, we could see Cody and Grandpère at the table playing some game or another. There was an occasional yell of triumph from Cody, or laughter from Grandpère. It was a soothing and pleasant sound.

Up on the top deck, barely visible in the evening light, Mom and Dad were in deck chairs, holding hands and talking quietly. I supposed that they, like us, were talking about going back to the routine of life. Were they dreading it too? No, *dread* was too strong a word. I didn't dread going back. It was just that this had been such a wonderful time, and it was ending tomorrow.

"It has been great," Rick said. "I need to thank your parents for including me and my family. We'll never forget it."

"Nor will we. And your leg seems to be doing really good. I am so glad." I laid a hand on his arm. "Every time I think of—"

A sound came across the water to us, cutting me off. It was Dad's rich tenor voice. He was singing. We both turned to listen, and I recognized the song instantly.

> *Oh, Danny boy, the pipes, the pipes are calling*
> *From glen to glen and down the mountainside.*
> *The summer's gone and all the flow'rs are dying,*
> *'Tis you, 'tis you must go and I must bide.*
>
> *But come ye back when summer's in the meadow,*
> *Or when the valley's hushed and white with snow.*
> *'Tis I'll be here in sunshine or in shadow,*
> *Oh, Danny boy, oh, Danny boy, I love you so.*

And if you come, and all the flowers are dying,
If I am dead, as dead I well may be,
I pray you'll find the place where I am lying
And kneel and say an "Ave" there for me.

And I shall hear, though soft you tread above me
And all my grave will warm and sweeter be
And then you'll kneel and whisper that you love me
And I shall sleep in peace until you come to me.

Oh, Danny boy, oh, Danny boy, I love you so.

I suddenly found myself needing to wipe at my eyes. The song brought back a flood of memories and so much happiness. Then, in the faint light, I thought I saw Dad lean in and kiss Mom, and that made the tears come all the faster.

Rick evidently sensed what has happening to me. He reached out and took my hand and squeezed it. "That was beautiful."

"That's what Dad sang to me almost every night when I was a little girl," I whispered. "That's where my nickname comes from. I love that song, but it's so sad."

"It's a beautiful song." He took a quick breath, and I could tell it had gotten to him too. "Tell me what it means," he went on. "What are the pipes it talks about?"

"The bagpipes. There are Irish bagpipes as well as Scottish ones. No one is exactly sure what the lyricist had in mind. Is it a young girl speaking to her true love who is about to go off to war or to America? Some say it's a mother speaking to her son as he leaves Ireland during the great Irish potato famines, perhaps never to return."

"I think it's the former. Two young people in love. I like that."

I gave him sharp look, but turned away before he saw it.

"And what does she mean when she says, 'I must bide'?" Then it came to him. "Oh, like in abide."

"Yes. She has to stay behind. And she's afraid she might die before he returns. If that happens, she asks him to kneel at her grave and say an 'Ave' for her. *Ave* meaning *Ave Maria*."

"I caught that. Remember, we've got a lot of Catholics in our family,"

"Of course, sorry. They often play bagpipes at Irish funerals, so maybe she's afraid the pipes are for her. That's the part that always makes me want to cry."

"Do you know the words by heart?"

"Oh, yes."

"Will you sing them to me?"

I jerked around and stared at him. "I don't sing solos unless I'm sure there's no one within a hundred miles. I don't even sing in the shower unless I'm the only one home."

He took my other hand. "Please. For me."

"Don't say that," I said. "That's not playing fair."

He didn't smile. His eyes were searching mine. "If it helps, pretend that I'm going off to war and that you may never see me again."

I jerked one hand free and slugged him on the arm. "Don't even joke about that."

He found my hand again. "Please, Danni. I want to hear the words again now that I understand them better."

I hesitated for a long, long moment, then finally nodded. "I might not get through it all."

"That's all right."

And so I began, very softly at first, then more loudly as I gave myself to the song. And then, to my surprise, on about the third line, Dad's voice came in to join me. And a moment later, Mom began to sing too. I made it through, but when the last words slowly died and the night was still again, I broke down and started to cry.

Rick put his arm around me and pulled me in against him, I threw my arms around him and buried my face against his shoulder. And then, though the tears still came, everything was all right.

CHAPTER 11

At breakfast the next morning, I was feeling a little grumpy. Well, maybe even more than a little. Even though we slept with all the windows open and the lake helped cool the air by morning, I wasn't used to sleeping when it was so hot. As I came stumbling out into the main room, dressed but barefooted, I saw Rick and Cody smirk at each other. I ignored them completely. They could be so juvenile at time. Mom, Dad, and Grandpère smiled at me, but said nothing.

I went over to the stove and loaded a paper plate with eggs, sausage, and toast, then grabbed the cup of orange juice someone had already poured and went back and sat down next to Grandpère. Without looking directly at me, he started reciting in a singsong voice, "Good morning, Merry Sunshine, how did you wake so soon? You've scared the little stars away, and shined away the moon."

Cody openly sniggered. Rick covered his mouth. Only Mom came to my defense. "Leave her alone." I shot her a smile of thanks. Too soon, I realized, because she went right on, "Remember that old saying: Never approach a growling dog."

"Funny, Mom. Very funny." Then I swung on Rick, who was fighting hard not to laugh. "And you? Keep it up, Ramirez, and I'll massage that leg of yours with your crutches."

But in five minutes, with some food in my tummy and the sleep out of my eyes, I was back. I wasn't smiling yet, but that would come eventually. "So what's the plan for today?"

Mom answered. "As you remember, as Clay was leaving the house on Thursday, he asked if he could buy one of my paintings."

"Yeah, that was way cool," Cody said.

"I told him I wouldn't do that, but what I would do, in grateful appreciation for all he did for our family, is paint something just for him and his wife and bring it up on the Fourth of July."

"Did he say what he wanted?" I asked.

"He said it was my choice, so I've decided to do Rainbow Bridge."

"Great choice," I said.

"I've never seen Rainbow Bridge," Rick noted.

Dad stood up and started clearing the table. "Mom will need several hours there, so I thought we'd do some exploring while she works. We don't get down this far on the lake very often. I'd like to check out a few of the canyons. Maybe do a little hiking." He looked at Rick. "As much as your leg can stand. "

"It's really doing quite well," Rick said. "I'm putting more and more weight on it."

"Okay, then," Mom said. "Dad called Don, and he'll go with us."

"He'll stay there at Rainbow Bridge with Mom while we go exploring."

"So, let's get this cleaned up," Grandpère said. "Angelique would like to leave as soon as possible so she can catch some of the morning light."

Rainbow Bridge is one of the world's largest known natural bridges. Jutting out from a solid red-rock cliff, it majestically spans the dry wash below at a height of nearly 300 feet, about the same length as its width. Though our family has been there many times, I never grow tired of it.

You have to leave the boats a ways from the bridge and hike in. We went far enough from the boats so Rick could see the bridge, and we took a few pictures. Then Dad helped Mom find a good place that wasn't visible from the trail and got her set up with a beach umbrella. Don, our guardian agent, as Cody called him, took up a station where he could see her but not be too intrusive. Dad promised we'd be back in about three hours, but Mom said she wanted four or five, and so he quickly agreed. Since Don had come in his own boat, it wasn't a big deal either way. If Mom finished early, they could go back on their own. Leaving them both plenty of water and some snacks, we were on our way again in less than an hour.

Back out in the main channel, Dad turned the boat left and we started downstream. Only a few miles downstream from Rainbow Bridge is Dangling Rope Marina. Roughly halfway between the dam and Bullfrog Marina, it is an important facility in the Lake Powell support system. We stopped there to gas up, go potty, and replenish our water, pop, ice, and snacks.

As we got back in the boat, Dad got out our Lake Powell map and spread it out. "Where do you want to go?"

We all bent over the map and studied it. Then I had a thought. "Hey, Dad. Do you remember the name of the place where Clay said they found the boat those three guys abandoned?"

"Uh . . . it was . . . I remember it was in Warm Creek Bay, but . . . no, I don't."

"It was Crosby Canyon," Grandpère volunteered.

"Yeah, that's right," Dad agreed. "Crosby Canyon."

We found Warm Creek Bay on the map and started searching. Cody saw it first. "There. Almost to the end of the bay."

"Show me," I said.

"Yeah, look," Rick said. "There's a road that comes right down to the lake."

Cody was looking at the channel marker numbers. "It's only about twenty miles from here," he said. "Let's go check it out."

"What's on your mind?" Grandpère asked me.

I knew if I tried to pass this off as just a whim, they would never buy it. So I decided to be straight with him. "If I was right there on site, maybe I could get some impressions about those guys. You know, like I did when we were near Robbers Roost that time."

"Even if they're not there anymore?" Cody clearly thought this was a dumb idea.

"Butch Cassidy has been gone for more than a hundred years, but I still felt something when we got close to Robbers Roost. So, it's worth a try, isn't it? Maybe, with the help of the pouch, I might sense which way they went. Where they are now. Then we could call Clay and tell him. We're just killing time anyway waiting for Mom." I turned to Grandpère. "Think how relieved Mom would be if they caught those guys."

He and Dad exchanged looks, and then finally Dad shrugged. "Why not? I'll call Don and let him know what we're thinking. If for some reason he says no, then that's the end of it, agreed?"

I nodded. Happily, Don said everything was quiet there and that Mom had already told him she wanted about four more hours. So I won out.

The lower end of the lake was much busier than up around Bullfrog, I guess because Wahweap Marina is the largest of all the marinas. Houseboats were parked along the beaches of Warm Creek Bay, and the water was dotted with all kinds of watercraft. But as we went farther north into the bay, it thinned out quite a bit. I was studying the map as we went.

Identifying Crosby Canyon was easy. The gravel road coming down to the beach was visible from the lake. Dad turned the boat that way, and soon he had to slow down as the water rapidly grew more shallow. Cody and I went up on the bow, making sure he wouldn't hit any big rocks as we approached the shore. About twenty feet out, Dad cut the engine, hit the button to pull the props up out of the water, and gently nosed the boat up onto the sand.

Cody stood up and grabbed the anchor and was about to toss it over the side, but Dad stopped him. "Hold on, Bud." He turned to me. "Are you feeling anything, Danni?"

That caught me by surprise. I was so focused on what we were seeing that I had forgotten why we had come. I let my hand drop and touch the pouch, turning my mind inward. After several moments, I shook my head. "Nothing."

"Good. Rick? You up to walking a bit? Near as I can tell from the map, that little side road Clay talked about is about a mile in."

"I've got calluses in my armpits by now," he grinned. "I'm good."

"Okay, but you set the pace. And when you start getting tired, we turn back. Check?"

"Check."

We lathered up with more sunscreen and took time to eat another snack. Then each of us grabbed a bottle of water, at Dad's insistence. The thermometer in the boat showed that the air temperature was now 102 degrees, and it was still early afternoon.

As far as scenery goes, there wasn't much here. Much of the land around Lake Powell consists of towering red-rock cliffs, deep canyons, sculpted sand dunes, and high mesas. No such luck here. There were some medium-sized cliffs off in the distance, but mostly it was low bluffs and small bumps for hills. The colors were dull, with mostly whites and grays and an occasional splash of light brown.

"Let's go," Cody said, throwing the anchor onto the beach and jumping down after it. I followed, then took Rick's crutches and helped him down. Grandpère got into one of the boat's compartments and retrieved the binoculars and two of our handheld radios that we always carried with us. A couple of minutes later, we were off.

———

The road alternated between hard gravel and patches of sand, but it didn't have a lot of steep places, so it provided easy walking for the most part. The heat was brutal, but having grown up in Hanksville, it was something we were all used to. We moved along, letting Rick set the pace. I watched him, relieved to see that he was putting more and more weight on his leg, which allowed him to move right along.

It's hard to judge exactly how far you've come when you're on foot, but at about a mile, we found the turnoff that Clay had talked about. It turned to the right and headed for a pretty high mesa with steep cliffs, which was another half mile away. "This has got to be it," Dad said, and we turned off onto it.

Almost immediately after leaving the main road, the turnoff climbed up one of those little bumps of a hill. I glanced at Rick. He would never have said anything, not in a lifetime, but I could tell even this mild climb was more of a challenge for him. "Let's go up to the top," I suggested. "Then we can decide whether to go any farther or not."

Bad idea. It was actually a pretty gentle hill, but by the time we reached the top we were all sweating profusely and puffing pretty noticeably. We stopped by unspoken agreement and opened our water bottles. While we drank, Grandpère lifted the binoculars and scanned the area out ahead of us. After a moment he said, "This has got to be it. The road definitely goes through the wash over there, which is probably where they hid their truck."

"Can I look, Grandpère?" I asked. He nodded and handed me the glasses. As he did so, he asked, "Feeling anything?"

I shook my head. "Hot, sweaty, and a little foolish that I thought this was a good idea."

He smiled and opened his bottle and took a deep swig. I lifted the glasses and started at the bottom of the hill, following the road slowly. There was nothing to see other than flat, dull, whitish sand and rock. Then I found the line of willows and brush that marked the path of the dry wash. They weren't terribly thick, but I could see that if you pulled off the road far enough, you could get a vehicle out of sight.

"Let me see," Dad said.

I handed him the binoculars and took another long drink. We had liter-sized bottles, and I had already drained about half of mine. I decided I'd better save the rest for our walk back.

After a moment, Dad spoke. "It looks like the road comes out of the wash again right at the base of the cliffs." He lowered the glasses. "Not a bad place to leave your transportation for several days and not have anyone bother it."

"I think we ought to go take a look," Grandpère said.

"Really?" I said, not trying to hide my total lack of enthusiasm. "It's probably another half a mile."

Grandpère gave me one of his looks. "Are you wimping out on us? This was your idea, remember?"

"I don't remember that, but it does sound like sooo much fun. Let's do it."

Dad handed Rick one of the handheld radios. "Why don't you stay up here with the glasses so you can tell us which direction to go? You'll have a better perspective than we will."

It said a lot that Rick only nodded and took the glasses. But to my surprise, Cody volunteered to stay with him and immediately started looking for a rock to sit on.

———————

The road was obviously not one that saw a lot of traffic, but there had been a vehicle or two up and down it recently. About ten minutes later, we found the place that we were pretty sure Clay's agents had said they had found tire and boot tracks. It was pretty hard to miss. The brush wasn't that thick, and there were several places where there was room enough to back in a vehicle. I turned and looked back. The brush couldn't hide a truck if you passed right by it, but from the hill it wouldn't have been seen. Dad lifted the radio. "This is it," he said. "Can you still see us?"

"If you stand in the road," Rick answered. "Smile, Danni," he said. "You're supposed to be having fun."

I started to take the radio from Dad to make some smart comment, but then Grandpère nudged me. "Try the pouch."

I sighed. I wasn't feeling anything except hot, sweaty, and tired right now. But I took it off my shoulder and held it in both hands, half closing my eyes.

Nothing. I opened my eyes, looked at Grandpère, and shook my head. "Sorry. Maybe this wasn't such a good idea after all."

"Can you even feel any presence?" he asked.

"No," I said, somewhat surprised. "I feel nothing."

Dad was looking around. "Why don't you two start back? I'm going to walk up the road a little farther. Take a look around."

Thanks to the heat, my curiosity was sufficiently satisfied. "Okay," I said.

Then the radio crackled. "Mack?" It was Rick's voice.

Dad raised his radio and pressed the transmit button. "Here."

"Um . . . I'm seeing a cloud of dust off to the north of you, moving along where the road follows the base of the cliff. But it's behind a hill and I can't see what it . . . uh. . . no, wait. It's a pickup truck. A white one."

A chill shot through me. The false report of the sighting at Big Water had said there were three men in a white pickup. "Let's go," I cried, pointing back toward where Rick and Cody were.

Dad was staring up the road. Now we could see the dust, but we were too low to see what was making it. "No," he said. "That will put us out into the open. Quick, into the brush. Get down."

Heart pounding, I ran off the road, and Dad spoke again into the radio. "Rick. You and Cody find a place and get out of sight. It's probably just a couple of campers, but let's not take any chances." He jammed the radio into his pocket and raced in after us.

We chose the thickest patch of brush we could find and crouched down behind it. "They'll see our footprints in the dust," I said. My alarm bells were clanging like crazy now.

"Not if they're moving very fast," Dad said grimly. He had his pistol on, and I saw that his hand rested on the butt. That didn't help how I was feeling.

We heard the truck less than a minute later and could tell it was coming at a pretty good clip, but the wash twisted and turned enough that we wouldn't see it until it came right past us. As the sound grew louder and louder, we grew smaller and smaller. The brush now felt like no more than a few blades of grass.

And then it was on us. It appeared to our left, swaying back and forth and bouncing hard on the rough hardpan of the wash. I saw immediately that it was especially equipped for off-road travel—big, knobby tires, a lift kit to give it higher ground clearance, three lights across the top of the cab. It flashed by us, leaving a swirling, choking cloud of dust. As the sound died away, we got slowly to our feet, covering our faces with our elbows.

"Two people," Grandpère said. "Both men I think, but I couldn't be sure."

"But not three?" Dad asked.

"No. I'm sure of that. Only two."

I said nothing. My heart was hammering like a freight train. My mouth was dry (and not from the dust), and I could feel my hands trembling. Only then did I realize how frightened I had been. I had convinced myself it was our three enemies.

We stepped out into the road and started moving forward rapidly. As we cleared the brush, we had a good view of the hill again. The truck was just coming up on the bottom of it. Dad spoke into the radio. "They're coming fast, Rick. Stay down. We're on our way."

We started walking as swiftly as we could, watching the truck ascend the low hill and disappear. Dad lifted the radio again, thought better of it, and increased the pace.

But two minutes later, a huge wave of relief washed over me as the radio popped again. "Mack?" It was Rick. "It's okay. They went on by. They didn't see us."

I thought I could hear his voice trembling a little even through the radio. Good. Maybe Iron Man had been just a little bit scared too.

"We're coming, Rick," Dad said. "Hold tight. We'll be there in a few minutes."

———

As we hurried along, sweating profusely, we didn't say much. The sudden appearance of the truck—a white truck—had really rattled us. I was sorry I had ever suggested this. I wanted to get back on the boat and head back to Rainbow Bridge as fast as we could.

Up ahead of me about four strides, Dad raised the radio to his mouth. "Rick? You there?"

After several moments, the radio crackled. "Here."

"Can you still see the truck?"

Long pause. "Uh . . . not really. When they . . . um . . . reached the main road, they turned north."

Something in the way Rick said that didn't sound right. I was suddenly feeling uneasy.

"We're down low enough that we can't see you anymore," Dad said. "You two still okay?"

"Um . . . yeah. My leg's hurting a bit, is all."

I pulled up short. Rick complaining about the pain? "Dad," I hissed, "something's wrong."

He and Grandpère jerked around.

I pulled *Le Gardien* close to my body, hugging it tightly. I was expecting to feel this sudden sense of danger, or the presence of evil, but there was none of that. Just this deep uneasiness. Like all was not what it seemed or should be. Then I realized that instead of a sense of danger, what was coming was a flood of thoughts. It was as if random thoughts and events were suddenly connecting together, with the same rapidity and clarity that I had experienced during our battles with El Cobra.

Dad started to say something, but Grandpère held up his hand and shook his head.

I closed my eyes, listening inside myself, standing perfect motionless. Finally, I opened my eyes. "We know that El Cobra and his people never left anything to chance. They planned out everything to the smallest detail. So what if Crosby Canyon wasn't an escape route? What if it was a place for them to hole up? What if they left their truck full of camping gear and supplies and—and what if it was them who blew up the mine?"

It was almost taking my breath away how quickly things were coming together, and how right it felt. "That would explain the phony tips the FBI kept getting." I stopped, my eyes widening in wonder. "They wanted us to think they had escaped and were no longer a threat."

"But why?" Dad asked.

I gasped. "Because the kidnapping was only half the plan." Suddenly, I wasn't asking "what if?" Suddenly, I knew. "They planned from the beginning to come back and strip the mine, then blow it up. That's why they wrote 'Phase Two.' Their plan wasn't just to steal twenty million from us. It was to steal everything—the cash and the ore." I stopped, taking in short breaths, my sweat suddenly cold as ice.

Dad was nodding slowly, watching me intently. "It's a stretch," he mused, "but . . ." He reached down and took the satellite phone off his belt. "I'm going to call Clay."

"And I'll call Angelique," Grandpère said. "Tell Don to be particularly alert."

The pouch was suddenly so hot, I had to pull it away from my body. "Mom's okay, Dad! But we're not. We are in danger. Hurry. Tell Clay where we are."

CRACK! The blast of a rifle broke the stillness, echoing off the cliffs behind us. A bullet kicked up a spurt of dust about five yards to the left of us, then whined away in a sharp ricochet.

"Nobody move!"

About fifty yards away, from behind a low clump of brush, a man in lightweight camouflage dress, like the kind worn by soldiers in Iraq, stood up. He held an assault rifle up to his shoulder as he started forward. "Drop the phones. All of you. Hands above your heads. Keep 'em where I can see them."

We looked at each other, stunned into silence.

BLAM! This time the bullet hit no more than two feet to the left of Dad.

"Come on, people! We're not playing games here." He was walking swiftly now, cutting the distance between us rapidly. He looked like something out of a special-ops movie—the military dress, a waist belt with ammunition pouches, a holstered pistol, and a hunting knife in its sheath. I squinted more closely. And gloves. Weird. He was wearing gloves. Not the kind you wore when driving four-wheelers or playing sports. These were more like ski gloves. Double weird. The temperature out here was over a hundred degrees now.

He stopped about thirty feet away. "You, little girl!" he shouted. "Drop your purse on the road and step away from it. If you so much as twitch, you're a dead woman."

Make up your mind. Am I a little girl or a woman? But even as that totally irrelevant thought came, I realized something else. His accent was distinctly British, and I recognized him from the houseboat.

"Set the radio and the phones down in the road. If you are carrying a weapon of any kind, do the same with it."

We had only brought two radios, the one Dad had and the one we had left with Rick. But Dad had his hunting knife on his belt, as always. Keeping his hands in sight, he slowly removed all three items and dropped them on the ground.

Grandpère kept both of his hands high. "I carry nothing," he called.

"Get in single file. Stay at least five feet apart and start walking slowly toward me." He moved farther off the road as he said that so he could keep us all clearly in sight. Then he unclipped a handheld radio from his belt and spoke into it. "Cover me, Geoffrey. I'm going to get the pouch."

"Copy that. I've got your back."

My heart sank. Up on the crest of the hill, about a hundred yards away, another man appeared. Same kind of special-ops look.

"Keep moving," our captor barked as we approached him. "All the way up the road to where my associate is waiting. Don't stop."

It was an unnecessary command. As we filed past him, I glanced quickly back and saw that the man was stuffing the radio and knife into *Le Gardien*. But he held the pouch out at arm's length, as if it were some rabid dog that might bite him. I also saw that he still had those silly gloves on.

Were the gloves for the pouch? Did he think they would somehow protect him from its powers? I laughed bitterly. *Don't worry, Mr. Special Ops. Right now, the pouch is as dangerous as a wet mop.* And why was that? Why hadn't *Le Gardien* told me to back off when I first got this stupid idea to check out Crosby Canyon? Why hadn't I sensed the presence of evil as I had that day near Robbers Roost? Why hadn't I felt the uneasiness before it was too late to get away? Why had the pouch remained silent until the very last moment?

Why? Why? Why? The questions just kept hammering at me.

And for that matter, why hadn't Grandpère felt anything? He was my failsafe, my backup guy. The steady one. The wise one.

My thoughts were interrupted as Grandpère spoke right behind me. In our little single-file line, Dad was in the lead, Grandpère in the rear. "Danni," he said, so softly I could barely hear him, "don't look back. Keep your head to the front."

I stiffened, my eyes fixed straight ahead. I could hear that our guy had fallen in behind us, staying back far enough that we couldn't try anything. "Okay," I murmured.

"These men may be of greater danger to us than El Cobra was."

"So why didn't the pouch—"

"Just listen!" he hissed.

That shocked me. I don't think he had ever spoken to me that sharply before.

"*Le Gardien* is not the problem here, Danni. *You* are the keeper of the pouch. *You* have the gift. This is not a child's game any longer. You must step up."

The rebuke was like a lance in the back. There it was again. The reminder that little-girl time was over. *Don't you understand? I don't know what to do. I don't have the pouch. He does.*

It was as if Grandpère were hearing my every thought. There was more rebuke in his voice. "That kind of thinking only diminishes you, Danni. Don't you see it? These guys are only the footmen. What are you going to do when the chariots arrive?"

Oh, really? The bitterness was bile in my mouth. *You're really going to throw that quote at me right now?*

I quickly glanced around, wanting him to see how deeply he had hurt me. But I saw our captor moving up quickly. "No talking," he barked. "Step it up. We don't have all day here."

I turned back, feeling more bleak and more hopeless and more abandoned than I had at any time during our days with El Cobra.

Behind me, the man spoke into his radio again. "I've got the pouch, Geoffrey. It's secure."

My head came up. So the pouch had become an objective now? First El Cobra, now these guys. But even as that thought came, another really strange thing happened. Our guard pronounced the guy's name as *Jeffrey*, but somehow I knew in my head that if the other guy was British too, the spelling of the name would likely be *Geoffrey*. I gave a low grunt of disgust. *How very helpful. Thank you, Nanny, for the spelling lesson. If you're done with that, how about having a rattlesnake jump out of the bushes and strike him down? Or, better yet, why aren't you turning this guy's rifle red-hot and—*

And then came understanding. I couldn't remember if this man had been one of those at Cathedral Valley or not. But even if he wasn't, word of Doc's pistol instantly turning red-hot would be known to the whole gang. That explained the gloves.

If that insight was supposed to make me feel better, it didn't even come close. So, head down, I plodded on, trying to ignore the pain and the shame and see if I could somehow turn off the blame game going on inside my head.

———

As we reached the top of the hill, the man called Geoffrey stood like a stone pillar, rifle trained on us. He too wore gloves. They made him look ridiculous, but not any less threatening. I saw that, in addition to all his other gear, he had a satellite phone on his belt. He jerked his head toward the truck. "Take them over there, Malcolm. Cuff them. Keep them separated from the two kids. Call Jean-Claude on the radio and tell him to come on in."

"Right." Malcolm turned to us. "You heard the man. Move!"

So it was Malcolm, was it? And Geoffrey spoke with an English accent too. The tiny details continued to register. As we started away, I saw Geoffrey pull the satellite phone off his belt and start punching numbers.

Pushing all that aside, I looked around anxiously. The truck had pulled off the road about twenty yards away, out of sight of the main road below. Then I saw Rick and Cody sitting on the ground a little behind the truck. They looked like they were okay. The important thing was that Nanny was functioning again, even though our captor had it slung over his shoulder several feet away. Which was a huge relief.

Not Nanny. Le Gardien. *Will you never learn?* And of course the pouch was functioning. The problem here was not *Le Gardien.* It was my nanny attitude. Maybe it had been functioning all along, and I was the one who couldn't hear it because I was moping around like some bubbleheaded teenager. Grandpère was right. The problem was not my age. It was my maturity. *So grow up. When the third man shows up, what then? Take us out and shoot us? Drive us into the desert and leave us to die? Come on, Danni. The footmen are here.*

Malcolm took his radio off his belt. "Jean-Claude? Do you read me?"

The radio crackled instantly. "Copy that. What's going on? I heard rifle fire."

"We've got them. Everything's under control here. Come on in."

"Ten-four. Be there in about ten minutes."

So our third guy was out on watch somewhere. That made sense. How else did they know we were here? It wasn't like the five of us were kicking up this huge plume of dust. And then another piece of trivial information clicked in my head. This must be the Belgian. Most of Belgium spoke French, and *Jean-Claude* was definitely a French name. Not that it mattered a lot. Except that . . .

My thoughts turned back again to Geoffrey and the satellite phone. If he wasn't calling the third member of their team, then who was he calling? Not El Cobra or any of his gang. Not unless they had phone privileges in the jail. *Does it really matter?* My inner voice was mocking. *Maybe he's ordering pizza. Come on, Danni, focus.*

Malcolm moved in beside me. "What are you muttering to yourself about?"

"Nothing," I murmured. I lowered my head, staring at the ground, not daring to look at him. By this time, we were nearly to the truck, and I pulled myself back to our current circumstances. Rick and Cody were seated on the ground behind the truck, as I had guessed. Their hands were behind their backs, and I assumed they had been either handcuffed or tied up. They looked pretty miserable, and yet both also looked defiant.

Dad saw them too and increased his pace. "Cody? Rick? Are you all right?"

Malcolm leaped in front of Dad, shoving the muzzle of the rifle right into his face. "They're fine. Now get back. Move over there." He pointed to an open, mostly rocky area. "Sit down on the ground. Stay at least ten feet apart." He gave us each a hard look. "We have instructions not to hurt you. Unless you give us trouble." He leaned in and sneered at me. "And frankly, after what happened at the houseboat, I would very much like to hurt you."

"The feeling is mutual," I said pleasantly, without thinking. I was suddenly shocked at how brazen it sounded. But to my huge relief, he only threw back his head and laughed.

As I sat down, feeling the heat of the rocks burning through my shorts, I saw Rick watching me. I gave him a wan smile. He smiled back, and though he never spoke a word, that look gave me a huge boost. He might be in cuffs, but he wasn't quitting yet. Two weeks ago I had seen what this guy was made of, and it was a huge comfort to me now to have him close by.

Malcolm walked over to the truck and emptied the pouch of our stuff. He then took Dad's belt with the radio and knife and tossed them through the open window onto the front seat. Then, stuffing the pouch in his belt, he moved back a step or two and started fishing around for something in the back of the truck. When he straightened, he had three pairs of nylon handcuffs.

Great. Another set for my growing collection of memorabilia.

"Malcolm?"

We all turned. Geoffrey, who still stood near the road, was motioning for his companion to come back up and join him.

"Be right there," Malcolm called back. "I still need to cuff them."

"*Now,* Malcolm!" Geoffrey snapped.

With a shrug, he turned and went over to join his companion. But he positioned himself so that as they talked, we were in his direct line of sight. And he kept his rifle up. Geoffrey, on the other hand, turned his back on us and began speaking in a low voice.

"All right. Here's the deal. Change of plans. We're being pulled out."

"About time. How soon?"

"Now. The plane will be waiting for us as agreed. But we've got to get moving."

I realized with a start that I was hearing every word they spoke, as if I were standing right there with them. I glanced at Dad and Grandpère. Dad was tracing patterns in the sand with the heel of his hiking boot. Grandpère had his arms folded on his knees, and his head was down. Neither gave any sign that they were hearing what I was hearing.

"What about them?" Malcolm gestured toward us. I held my breath for a moment, straining to hear what Geoffrey's answer to that would be.

"The instructions haven't changed. They are not to be hurt unless they pose a direct threat. He made that very clear."

Huge relief flooded through me. So Grandpère was right. Whoever this "he" was, I was grateful to him at that moment.

"So what do we with them?"

"We're taking them with us."

No! Any gratitude instantly disappeared.

"I'll wait here for Jean-Claude and get them secured. You go down to their boat. Take it out far enough so it won't be visible, then open the drain plugs so it will sink."

Geoffrey turned and looked at us. "Who has the keys to the boat?"

Dad raised his hand and, without waiting to be told, he fished the keys out of his pocket and tossed them a few feet away. Malcolm trotted over, picked them up, and then returned to huddle with Geoffrey, who was talking again even as he came back. He pointed down the hill toward the lake. "Head straight down from here. It will save you half a mile or more if you don't take the road. We'll come down and pick you up there. Just hurry up and get it done. I don't want to be sitting on that beach waiting for you."

Malcolm slung the rifle over his shoulder, then removed his gloves. Once that was done, he pulled *Le Gardien* out of his belt and handed it across to Geoffrey. "Whatever you do, keep it away from the girl."

"Yes, Mommy," Geoffrey sneered. "I'll look both ways while crossing the street, too."

I turned my head as I felt something hit my shoulder. Grandpère still had his head down, but even as I watched, he picked up another small stone and flipped it at me.

"Are you hearing what they're saying?" he whispered.

I nodded. "Every word. Are you?"

"No."

"Neither am I," Dad said.

I glanced quickly at our two captors, then looked away again. They were standing toe to toe now, speaking in angry whispers. Quietly and urgently, I summarized their plan as quickly and concisely as I could.

"You have to stop them, Danni," Dad said before I had finished. "Once they put the cuffs on us, or put us in the truck, our chances of escape drop to about zero. And remember, we've got Mom and Don waiting for us at Rainbow Bridge. If we don't show up, they'll go back to the houseboat, thinking we're just late. It could be hours before they sound an alarm."

Oh, man. I had totally forgotten about Mom. "But how?" I cried. "They have the pouch. There's no way I can get it without—"

Grandpère flipped another rock. It hit me on the cheek, stinging the flesh. I jumped a little. "Ow!"

"Hey!" Malcolm shouted. "No talking over there."

Grandpère's eyes were boring into mine. "Stop telling us what you can't do, Danni." And then, to my surprise, before I could answer, he got to his feet.

Malcolm gave a shout and started toward us, his rifle coming up. "Sit down, old man," he shouted. "Sit down or I'll put a bullet through your leg."

Geoffrey was right behind him. He grabbed Malcolm's arm and jerked him around. "I'll handle this. Get down there and sink that boat. We'll be there in no more than a quarter of an hour."

Malcolm was watching me, his eyes dark and angry. But finally, muttering something under his breath, he handed the cuffs to his partner, turned on his heel, and started down the hill. As he did so, Geoffrey chambered a round into the rifle, took quick aim, and fired. We all instinctively jumped, but he wasn't aiming at us. The bullet kicked up sand a few feet away from Cody. "Sit down, Grandpa, or your grandson dies."

CHAPTER 12

Regardless of who it was who had told Geoffrey we were not to be hurt, at that moment, I could see it in his eyes. He not only was ready to hurt us—he wanted to.

In addition to that fact, several things registered in my head all at the same time. Malcolm had whirled around at the sound of the rifle and was coming back. Geoffrey screamed at him to get down to the lake and sink the boat. The third man had also come into sight down below. He was crossing the wash not far from where we had hidden and coming up the road in our direction at a fast trot. Most of all, I saw Geoffrey coming toward us in long strides, his eyes murderous. Grandpère stood there, regal as a king. And now I feared for Cody's life.

I leaped to my feet, holding my hands high above my head. "Stop where you are!" I shouted. "You are in grave danger."

Grave danger? The voice in my head was filled with derision. *From what? The terrible look in your eye?*

But to my surprise, what I had said was so totally unexpected, Geoffrey's stride faltered for a moment. Then he laughed raucously, raising one hand and fluttering his fingers. "Oooh," he cried, "please don't curse me, O wicked witch."

With absolutely no idea of what I was doing—I mean, totally no idea at all—I raised my right hand and pointed it at him, my fingers splayed out and pointed at his heart. It was just what you saw witches do in the movies. "Stop or die!" I yelled.

That actually brought him to a halt, and for a moment, I saw a flicker of fear in his eyes. Then he raised the rifle, aiming at my chest. "You are starting to really irritate me."

"If you take another step, you will deeply regret it."

Oh, really? What will you do, Danni? Spit in his face? Cripple him with the old evil eye?

"One. Two." His voice was low and menacing. "When I say 'five,' *you* die. Three."

Then another image clicked in my brain. I was looking at the pouch on his shoulder. I pointed my right hand at it, concentrating every ounce of willpower, every thought, every wish I had in me and aiming them at the pouch. *Come to me,* Le Gardien. *Come now.*

I don't know what I expected. I guess I was hoping it would fly from his body and I would snatch it out of midair. That didn't happen. But I was right in one way. The pouch did keep coming toward me because Geoffrey started forward again, rifle steady against his shoulder, one eye closed as he sighted on my chest. "Four." His face was a mask of fury. "I'm not bluffing, girlie. Sit down now or die."

But again that ridiculously stupid thing came into my mind. "You are in grave danger," I blurted. "Do not come any closer." And, having zero faith that my words would make even the slightest difference, I sat down so hard I could feel the rocks jar me all the way to my teeth.

BRRRRR. The sound was so soft as to be almost missed. But Geoffrey heard it clearly. He froze in place, one foot suspended in midair. His eyes jerked downward, wildly looking around for the source of the sound. BRRRRR.

There aren't many sounds more chilling than that of an adult rattlesnake coiled and giving warning.

Dad jumped to his feet. "Don't move. Stay perfectly still and it won't strike at you."

I don't think Geoffrey even heard him. He was swinging the rifle down, half turning as he did so. This brought the foot that was suspended in the air down hard. That did it. There was a gray blur, low to the ground. Geoffrey screamed and fell back. The pouch dropped as he clutched wildly at his rifle and blasted off three shots in rapid succession.

I heard Malcolm yelling and a moment later he came tearing back up the hill. "Geoff! What's wrong?"

But Geoffrey was in total panic mode now. He threw the rifle aside and scuttled backwards, rolling away wildly, screaming, "Snake! Snake! I'm bit!" His face was contorted with pain and horror as he clawed at his pant leg.

Seeing the pouch on the ground, I started inching toward it. But Malcolm saw me and fired off a shot in the air. "Stay back!" he screamed. And then he skidded to a stop, staring at the ground around him in pure terror.

BRRRRR. BRRRRR. BRRRRR. BRRRRR. The rattling sounds were coming so fast as to be barely distinguishable one from another. Some were high and shrill. Some deep and sonorous. Falling back, firing blindly at the ground in fully automatic mode, Malcolm was screaming like a madman as he stumbled and went down.

"Rattlesnake nest!" Dad shouted, racing forward. Grandpère and I followed. What I saw was something out of a fiendish nightmare. A three-foot-long rattlesnake was slithering away from where Geoffrey lay on the ground, clutching at his leg. His pant leg was up enough that we could see the two puncture wounds from the fangs. They were already starting to ooze blood.

But much worse than that, ten feet beyond him, the ground was alive with snakes of every size. Malcolm was frantically slapping them away, screaming and moaning and writhing on the ground. As I came up, I saw a snake flash out and sink its fangs into his right cheek. He shrieked, then screamed again as a larger snake went for his bare arm.

Dad bent down on the run and snatched up Geoffrey's rifle. BLAM! BLAM! BLAM! He blasted away at the ground, and body parts of snakes went flying everywhere. Grandpère looked wildly around. He grabbed a dead sagebrush branch about three feet long and ran forward. Snakes started flying through the air as he scooped them up and flung them away. Finally he had the ground cleared enough that he could move in. He grabbed Malcolm by both arms and started dragging him backwards. "Get the pouch, Danni," he yelled at me. "Then cut Rick and Cody loose. Your dad's knife is in the truck."

As I leaped away, I saw Grandpère drop Malcolm, snatch up his rifle, and start blasting away alongside Dad. Covering the ground in great strides, I snatched up the pouch and slung it over my shoulder, then sprinted for the truck. A moment later, I was kneeling behind Cody, carefully cutting through the nylon cuffs. "There," I said, as they finally snapped. I moved quickly over to Rick and started sawing on his.

He looked at me as he reached for his crutches. "Did you do that?" He jerked his head toward Dad and Grandpère and the two men writhing on the ground.

My eyes widened. *Did I?* No. All I had done was . . . was tell Geoffrey he was in grave danger. I hadn't asked for rattlesnakes. That thought had not even entered my mind. My eyes widened. *Except earlier, you wished for a rattlesnake to bite Malcolm.*

Then came another realization. I knew enough about rattlesnakes to know that rattlesnake nests or dens were rare, and even then they occurred usually only when the weather was cold. Snakes gathered together in the wintertime to share each other's warmth. Right now, the temperature was over a hundred degrees. That ended any question.

I reached down and touched *Le Gardien*. *It was you, wasn't it?* I didn't expect an answer. I didn't need it. I got to my feet marveling, totally astonished once again at how this strange companion of mine worked.

And that was when I saw the third man come into view just below the rim of the hill. His rifle was slung over his shoulder, but he had a wicked-looking pistol in one hand, and it was up and pointed at the three of us. "Hands up," he hissed. "Don't move." I instantly recognized what was clearly a heavy French accent.

Jean-Claude had arrived.

———

Keeping the truck between himself and where Dad and Grandpère were dealing with Malcolm and Geoffrey, Jean-Claude came quickly over to the three of us, the pistol rock-steady in his hand. "You, boy. Come here." He was motioning with his other hand at Cody.

Cody hesitated, then moved over to him. Jean-Claude stepped behind him and put a hand on his shoulder, then turned to Rick and me. "All right. You two will go ahead of us. Please do believe me when I say that I will not hesitate to shoot one of you if you disobey me."

While he was not as horribly frightening as Doc, his manner was cold and ruthless, and I knew we were dealing with a very dangerous man. I didn't doubt that he meant what he said. Rick moved forward, and I fell in beside him.

If Jean-Claude's plan was to stay undetected as long as possible, it was too late. Grandpère, who was squatted down beside Malcolm, examining his wounds, suddenly looked over in our direction. His head jerked up, and he slowly straightened. "Mack?" I heard him call softly to Dad.

Dad was on his knees beside Geoffrey. He too stiffened. For a moment, I thought he was going to grab for the rifle, but he caught himself and put his hands in the air as he stood up.

"Step away from my comrades," Jean-Claude called. "Stay clear of their rifles."

Both Grandpère and Dad did so, moving back toward us. Jean-Claude gave Cody a little shove. "You! Go over there with your father." As Cody gave a sob of relief and took off running, our captor stepped behind me, jamming the pistol in my back. "Move. I want to see what happened here." Then to Rick, "You. Cripple. Stay right there."

I looked over my shoulder. "They stepped into a rattlesnake den."

His eyes widened for an instant and then went dark. "I do not believe you."

I shrugged. "Go see for yourself."

"You show me!" he snarled, pressing the muzzle hard against my back.

I didn't have to say anything. The blood and scattered body parts of a dozen snakes bore silent witness, as did the multiple puncture wounds—now dark with blood.

Malcolm was incoherent with fear, rolling back and forth and howling in pain. Geoffrey was sitting up now, holding his leg, moaning softly. His face was white with shock. Malcolm's cheek was already turning dark. I knew what that meant. A rattlesnake's venom is injected directly into the bloodstream. Rodents, birds, and other small animals are a snake's primary food. Venom doesn't kill instantly, but it does contain toxins that cause paralysis. This slows the animals down enough for the snake to follow their scent until they cannot move. It also starts breaking down fleshy tissue so it will be easier for the snake to digest. Both of those processes are extremely painful.

"They've been bitten several times," Dad said. "We need to get them help as soon as possible." He started slowly toward us. I could see the shock in Jean-Claude's eyes and wasn't surprised that he didn't object.

Dad's voice got Malcolm's attention. He opened his eyes. When he saw Jean-Claude, he started yelling. "I'm dying, Jean-Claude. Help me! Help me!"

Geoffrey turned too. "You gotta help us, Jean-Claude."

With hands raised in the air, Dad went to Malcolm, giving Jean-Claude a wide berth. He knelt down and put his hands on Malcolm's shoulders. "You're not dying," he said. "Most rattlesnake bites are not fatal. Thrashing around only pumps the poison into the system more quickly."

"You lie!" he screamed. Then to Jean-Claude, "He wants us to die. I need a tourniquet. Get me a tourniquet for my leg."

Dad stood up again and spoke to Jean-Claude slowly and calmly. "About eight thousand people are bitten by rattlesnakes in the United

States each year," he explained. "Fewer than ten of those die. But those who do, do so because they didn't get help. If you put a tourniquet on his leg, it cuts off the blood to the limb and he will likely lose it. We keep antivenom shots in the first-aid kit in the boat. Malcolm has been bitten at least half a dozen times. If we inject him and Geoffrey now, that will stabilize them until we can get them to a hospital. But if we don't do something immediately, they *will* both die."

Jean-Claude's head swung back and forth between Dad and the two men on the ground.

Grandpère spoke rapidly in French. Jean-Claude seemed barely to hear him. "Come on!" Grandpère snapped in English. "It's over. Your friends need help and they need it now."

To my surprise, Jean-Claude held up his hand, as if to ward off the words. Then he started backing up, waving the pistol at all of us. "Stay away from me."

"No!" Geoffrey shrieked. "Don't leave us."

The Belgian stopped, staring down at his two partners. Then, catching us all off guard, he leaped forward and snatched up first Geoffrey's rifle and then Malcolm's. He waved us back with them. All the time his eyes kept flicking to the ground, watching for any more snakes. Finally, he looked down at Geoffrey. "Sorry, *mon ami*. I can do nothing for you now." And with that, he spun around and sprinted for the truck.

Geoffrey tried to get up, but his leg collapsed and he went down again. He started swearing and cursing, shaking his fist at the disappearing figure. Malcolm began to sob hysterically.

Jean-Claude did not turn back. In seconds, he was to the truck. He threw the rifles in the back, jerked the door open, and roared off in a cloud of sand and dust.

As I watched the truck bounce down the hill and turn north on the road that led away from Lake Powell, I felt a curious mixture of emotion. It was a blow to know that he was getting away. One more enemy still on the loose out there. But to have him gone had removed a tremendous complication from our lives. Now all we had to do was—

"Rick." Dad's voice cut into my thoughts. "Is your leg up to a brisk hike?"

"Yes."

"Good. Okay, then. I need you and Cody to go to the boat. Go straight down the hill there, like Malcolm was going to do. It's the shortest way, and while it's a little rougher, it won't tire you out as quickly. Cody, you get me the first-aid kit and get back up here as fast as you can. But you need the keys to the boat first."

Dad dropped to one knee and fumbled at Geoffrey's waist. He unbuckled the ammunition belt with its pistol, holster, hunting knife, and phone attached. Then he rolled Geoffrey onto his side and pulled it free. The man screamed out. Dad ignored him, tossing the belt aside. He looked up. "Grandpère. Get Malcolm's belt off too. And get the boat keys from his pocket for Rick."

Rick spoke up. "Mack, I left my phone in the boat. You and Danni and Grandpère had yours, so I left mine. Do you want me to call Don?"

"No," Dad shot right back. "That will just frighten Mother. But call 911. Tell them where we are, and that we have antivenom. Then call Clay. His number's on the speed dial. Tell him what happened. Tell him about the white truck."

As Rick and Cody started toward Grandpère, Dad looked at me. "Danni, check and make sure there are no more snakes lurking around. Once you're sure it's clear, help Grandpère bring Malcolm over here by Geoffrey."

As I moved gingerly forward, searching the ground for any sign of movement and making sure that I wasn't stepping on dead snakes, Dad started trying to calm Geoffrey down. By the time I reached Grandpère, he had retrieved the gun belt and the boat keys out of Malcolm's pocket as Dad had asked. He removed the pistol and handed it to me, then tossed the belt aside and the keys to Rick. Rick and Cody set off immediately.

Gratefully, I saw nothing moving as I looked around. I guess all the rifle fire had sent any remaining snakes running—or slithering—for cover. That was the one nice thing about rattlesnakes. They weren't aggressive unless confronted. "We're clear," I called.

I rejoined Grandpère and helped him lift Malcolm to a sitting position. He howled in agony. I stared at the puncture wounds on his face and arms and nearly lost it. I swallowed quickly to keep the bile from coming up. I didn't want to think about what must be going on in his body right now. Concentrating on Grandpère, I moved in and took Malcolm's legs. Together we lifted him as best we could and half carried, half dragged him over to where Dad was working on Geoffrey. He screamed and cursed and bit his lip so hard it started to bleed.

Dad looked up as we joined him. "Get the knife, and—"

Geoffrey's head jerked up. "Are you going to cut the wound open and suck the blood out?"

"No, I'm not." Dad tossed me the shirt. "That's pure Hollywood stuff."

"You have to get the poison out!" Geoffrey screamed. "My leg's going numb."

Dad just shook his head. "Danni, use the knife to cut the laces on his boot. The foot is already starting to swell. Get the boot off of him."

At that, Malcolm's eyes flew open, and he gripped Grandpère's arm. His fingers bit deeply into the flesh, causing Grandpère to wince. "Don't let me die. Please don't let me die."

"You're not going to die," Dad snapped. "More people die of wasp and bee stings than from snake bites. We're going to get you both a shot of antivenom, then we'll get you to a hospital as quickly as possible. Now shut up and try to stay calm."

━━◆━━

The chopper from Page, Arizona, arrived in just under fifteen minutes. A sheriff's deputy was with it and put both men in metal cuffs. As soon as it was gone, we all headed for the boat.

As we approached, waving to Rick to let him know everything was all right, I was thinking about Grandpère's rebuke down there on the road. I wanted to apologize, to thank him for verbally slapping some sense into me. But I didn't trust my voice to speak quite yet.

Dad was a few feet away, speaking rapidly into Rick's phone, giving Clay more information on how to find us. "Hold on," he said after a moment. He lowered the phone and turned to us. "Did either of you happen to get the license plate number of the truck?"

We both shook our heads. "It was an Arizona plate," Grandpère said. "I did notice that."

"And it was a late model Ford F-350," Rick added.

"Yeah," Dad said glumly. "I told him that. The only problem is, more white vehicles are sold than any other color, especially in Arizona. Jean-Claude could go any one of several directions from here." He started to explain that to Clay, but I suddenly cut him off.

"Wait," I said. A thought had just popped into my head. Don't ask me why, but I was suddenly remembering last night up on the top deck of the houseboat when Cody had asked us his question. "What do you see when your eyes are closed?"

"What?" Dad asked.

I shook my head and clamped my eyes shut. For a moment, there was nothing, but I was concentrating hard. After a moment, a shadowy, white shape began to form. I felt a thrill of exultation. It was the truck, and I was looking at it from behind. I squeezed my eyes even more tightly closed. Slowly the image grew larger, like I was zooming in on it with a camera. I held my breath, staring at the place where the license plate would be.

And it happened. First it was a blur of color, but then it continued to resolve and grow larger and larger. In a moment, it blotted out the truck and filled the entire frame of my vision. I swung around, my eyes flying open. "It *is* an Arizona plate," I cried. "Number 942, ATG. Expiration tags are November 2011."

Staring at me in open amazement, Dad started to repeat it into the phone.

"Wait," I cried again. I didn't have to close my eyes this time. This was something that I was suddenly feeling. Very strongly. "Tell Clay he's not going out by way of Big Water. He turned north, heading for Escalante."

This was amazing.

"Remind him he has our phones. Track 'em, and they've got him."

Dad spoke rapidly, repeating what I had said.

Just then, I felt an arm go around my shoulder. I turned to look up into my grandfather's face. It was very grave. He took me by both shoulders and turned me to face him directly. Only then did he finally speak. "Well done, *ma chérie*," he murmured.

Then Dad called out again. "Clay is sending someone for Mom and Don. But he has a question for you, Danni."

"Oh?"

"He wants to know if it would be all right if when he gets here, he gives you a huge bear hug and then kisses you on both cheeks."

Grandpère laughed. "Tell him it is the French thing to do."

"Yeah," Rick said. "And then it's my turn."

I was grinning so big that it felt like my cheeks were going to split. "Oh," I drawled. "I see no reason why you should have to wait for him to get here."

———

It is way past my bedtime and I am so tired that I can barely keep my eyes open, so I am going to do it backwards. I'm going to write some conclusions tonight, then tomorrow I'll write up everything that happened. It's my journal, so I guess I can do it however I like.

I will also write about this totally awesome experience we had tonight after we got back to the houseboat, where we sat around and talked about all of the feelings we had about all the things that have happened to us. But I will just say this now.

I have the most incredible parents in the world, and tonight, I decided that, number one, I want to be as strong as my mom when I grow up. And two, I want to marry someone as strong as my dad. That's the best way I can make sure I am strong enough to help my children be strong for whatever is coming.

I think I have a candidate in mind for this. It's still a long way off and I know a lot of things can happen, but like it or not, I've got him in the crosshairs of my hunting rifle. I mean, when a guy takes a bullet for you, he's a keeper. Don't you think?

Anyway, here's a quick summary of what we have learned about today:

1. Our two Englishmen, Geoffrey Campbell and Malcolm Birdwhistle, are going to live. The antivenom Cody brought back from the boat was instrumental in saving their lives, especially Birdwhistle's. (I kid you not. That is actually Malcolm's real name, according to Interpol.)

2. Clay already has an interrogation team on its way to Page. He hopes that grilling the two of them while they are still pretty traumatized will yield important information about their European connections. He's not wildly optimistic—they seem to have a good cutout system—but he is hopeful.

3. When we told Clay that Geoffrey had called someone on his satellite phone, they checked the phone and found the number. Using a GPS tracking device, they were able to locate the phone and send in a team. However, it turned out to be in the trunk of a car rented in Denver but left at the Toronto airport two or three days ago. Phony name and address.

4. As for Jean-Claude, whose last name is Allemand and who is from Belgium, he was captured a few miles south of Escalante after a brief but fierce gun battle with FBI agents and officers from the Utah Highway Patrol. He was shot once in the chest and was flown to the University of Utah Hospital. According to Clay, he is in serious but stable condition.

5. For all his professional competence and his position of importance in the FBI, Clay Zabriskie is at heart a great big teddy

bear of a man. He gave me that hug that he asked for, and kissed me on both cheeks, not once but twice, while Mom, Dad, Grandpère, Rick, and Cody—and a couple of FBI agents—looked on and applauded.

6. Speaking of Mom, Clay was absolutely charmed by Mom's painting of Rainbow Bridge. She hasn't finished it yet, but she showed it to him anyway when he begged to see it. The fact that she broke her inflexible rule—never show a painting until it is finished—says a lot about how relieved she is to have this whole thing over.

7. And speaking of Clay, he did confirm that we are to be with him and his family on the Fourth of July and that the Deputy Director of the FBI will be here from Washington.

"Hey, Danni boy. You're supposed to be in bed."

I jumped and gave a little yelp, then sat back. "Grandpère! You scared the heck out of me. You're not supposed to sneak up on people."

"Sorry. Writing up the day in your journal?"

"No, not the whole day. Just a quick summary. I'll say more tomorrow."

"What have you said about the pouch?"

"Not much, why?"

He shrugged. "Just wondered."

"Would you rather I didn't?"

He thought about that. "Maybe. I'm not sure it's wise, particularly when it could be subpoenaed for evidence in a criminal trial."

My mouth fell open. "Are you kidding?" He shook his head. From his expression I could tell he wasn't. "Oh, that would be awful."

He sat down at the table beside me. "I don't know, Danni. I told you before that writing it all up was important. Now, I'm not so sure."

"Why not?"

"Not sure. Just been thinking about it."

"Me too. Not about writing in my journal, but about *Le Gardien*."

"Some strange things happened today, that's for sure."

"Yes," I said. "Can I ask you a couple of questions?"

"Only a couple?"

"Okay, a bunch of questions. And before you answer, remember, I am really, really tired tonight, Grandpère, so don't tease me. Please."

He frowned. "The very accusation wounds me deeply."

"See?" I exclaimed. "That's what I mean."

He laid a hand over mine. "All right. After what you did today, I think you are entitled. So, fire away."

Wonderful. Maybe I could finally get some answers. "All right. First question. Why did the pouch wait so long to work today? I mean, why didn't I sense the danger before we were actually caught in the middle of it and it was too late to get away?"

"I'm not sure. There are several possibilities. One, maybe it did warn you and you were just too insensitive to feel it."

"Thanks."

"Do you want me to answer you or to make you feel good?"

"Answer me. Sorry. Go on."

"Two. Remember when we talked about whether the pouch was your nanny or not, back a year or so ago?" When I nodded, he continued, "I told you that I felt like the best analogy of the pouch was that of the tutor in ancient Greece. Though he was a servant, his purpose was far more than just to teach and protect a child. He was to prepare the child in every way for adulthood, when it would no longer need his services. To do that sometimes requires the tutor to step back and let the child learn from its own experience, whether foolish or wise."

"Ouch again."

"Three. The tutor may see other aspects of a situation that the child does not either see nor appreciate. For example, if you had been warned back at Dangling Rope when you first suggested we go to Crosby Canyon, we would have been kept out of harm's way, but . . ."

"Oh," I said, surprised that I could have missed something so obvious. "But then tonight, there would still be three men out there who were a threat to our family."

"That's right. There may be other reasons, too. Just remember that when the pouch is helping you, you may not be the only person involved nor your needs the only ones that are being met."

That was a marvelous insight. "Thank you, Grandpère. That is very helpful." He waited, so I went on. "Second question. I think we all agree that the rattlesnakes today were the pouch's doing, right?"

"I think that is a safe conclusion."

"But at the time, I no longer had the pouch in my possession. Can it work when someone else has it? Or would it work for them?"

"It wouldn't be much of a guardian if it only worked when you were holding it. Early on in your experience, it serves as a tangible aid that can bolster courage or bring insights. But you are called the *keeper* of the pouch, not the *owner,* not the *holder,* not the *possessor,* not the *controller.* So no, you don't have to actually touch it. As for the question, can someone else use it, that would be up to the pouch, now, wouldn't it?"

He leaned in. "Let me ask you a question. Did the pouch work for El Cobra when it made the phony gold bars?"

"I . . ." My first impulse was to say yes. He had it in his hand. He commanded it to make gold. But then, it didn't make gold. It made lead. And it led directly to his capture. "I'm not sure."

"Nor am I. Danni, I think you still have it in your mind that the pouch is a possession, something you own, something you control. It is not. It is an inanimate object that has remarkable powers, powers that can bless you or curse you. It is something entrusted to you to be used for good and to help others. But even then, it decides what it will and won't do, what it will and won't share. The key is to open yourself up to it and its powers and not do foolish things that turn it away from you. To be grateful for when it does intervene in your behalf. *And*"—he stabbed his finger at me—"maybe to be grateful when it doesn't."

"I understand." I quickly caught myself. "Or rather, I think I am *beginning* to understand. Next question. Is there more than one pouch?"

"I would think so—it would be a strange thing if our family happened to own the only one in the world. But maybe it's not a pouch in every case. Maybe it is some other object, like a necklace or a book. I frankly don't know. But I like to think there is."

"I really appreciate this, Grandpère," I said, touching his arm. "One more?"

"Of course," he smiled.

"When evil people see what the pouch can do, they want it for themselves. This can bring danger on the keeper of the pouch and on those she, or he, loves. Since it isn't blessing the world in general, only our family in particular, maybe it would be better to not have it, to—"

He was shaking his finger at me and giving me a chiding look. "There you go again. All you've seen is the pouch working for you and your family, but why do you assume it is restricted to that? I mean, what if the pouch holds a 'second job'? What if it has more than one keeper?"

"But how could it, when I have it with me all the time?" But I saw the flaw in that reasoning right away. "Okay, maybe while I'm sleeping."

"Or when you don't take it with you. Or you leave it on the bus. Or maybe during your 'down times,' you know, kind of like more than one person using the same computer." His eyes were alive with intensity. "The key is, Danni, to remember that you don't get to decide what the pouch does, when it does it, for whom it does it, or how it does it. That's not your privilege. You can influence it to one degree or another, but you do not control it. *Est-ce que c'est clair?*"

I lowered my head, appropriately contrite. "Yes, Grandpère. It is very clear. Thank you."

His face softened. "You look very tired. We can talk more in the morning."

I stood up, bent down, and kissed his forehead. "No. You have given me much to think about. Thank you for being so clear." I kissed him again. "I love you so much, Grandpère."

"And I you, my precious child," he whispered huskily. "And I you."

PART FOUR

Anonymity Lost

CHAPTER 13

Sandstar Motel, Sandy, Utah
July 4, 2011

One of the nation's largest Fourth of July celebrations takes place each year in the town of Provo, Utah. Known as the Freedom Festival, the festivities culminate in the spectacular Stadium of Fire concert and fireworks show, held in the football stadium of Brigham Young University.

Though I had lived in Utah most of my life, and though we had talked many times about going up for the celebration, the McAllisters of Hanksville had never quite pulled it off. Until now. We pretty much did it all, or, at least, everything major—hot-air balloon festival, pancake breakfast in the park, old-fashioned Fourth of July picnic at noon, potato sack and wheelbarrow races, Utah Symphony Orchestra concert. There were also various "runs"—10K or 5K "Freedom Runs" and the mayor's mile-long "Fun Run."

Mom ran the 10K with Clay Zabriskie's wife, Helen. They asked me, but I begged off, saying that it would only make Rick feel bad, him still limping around and all. (Rick just rolled those big, innocent eyes of his and said, "This from the girl who is always saying things like, 'When I see my first happy runner, then I'll consider it,' or 'Fun Run is a contradiction in terms,' or 'I collect articles on the dangers of running.'")

It all started Friday night with a BBQ at Clay's house. Clay

189

and Helen have four children, all married, and 13 grandchildren, ranging in age from 9 months to 18 years old. You would have thought we were national celebrities the way we were welcomed. Clay hadn't told them much, except that we had been instrumental in helping the FBI break a major case.

Today we enjoyed the biggest two events of the festival—the Grand Parade in the morning and the "Stadium of Fire" concert and fireworks show tonight. Rick's dad has to be back to work at the coal mine tomorrow, so he didn't stay for the evening show, but the rest of the family did. It was fun to be together again. We've become good friends since our time together on the houseboat. Rick, Shauna, and the girls will go home with us tomorrow.

The fireworks were amazing, but what was absolutely awesome was that David Archuleta performed at the concert. He's from Utah and won second place on American Idol. He's way hot, and when he sings, oh my. . . . I felt like I was going to melt into a pool of butter right there. Fortunately, I had the perfect cure for that. I was sitting next to a guy who also has dark black hair and large brown eyes and a smile to die for. He won't ever sing for me, but the scar in his upper leg kind of balances that out.

Afterwards, the traffic was awful and we didn't get home until about 11:40. Everyone instantly crashed. But you know me. Danni the insomniac. The good news is, we don't meet with the Deputy Director until about eleven tomorrow morning, so there's plenty of time to sleep in. Cody wanted to go with Shauna and the girls to a water park tomorrow rather than meet with the DD. Mom and Dad decided that would be acceptable.

It has been a great weekend. Amazing in so many ways. And it's great for us and the Ramirez family to just have fun and not have to worry about saving the world. So with that, good night.

——◆——

When Rick, Cody, and I came back from the breakfast in the restaurant next door to the motel, Clay was already in the room with Mom,

Dad, and Grandpère. Typical. If he said he would be there at 9:30, you could count on him at 9:25 or earlier.

He waved to us as we came in, but since they were deep in conversation, Cody backed out and went to his room, and Rick and I went in and sat down. Mom was sitting on the edge of the bed, leaning forward, and looked very much in earnest as she listened to what Clay was saying.

"I'm picking up the Deputy Director at the executive airport at 9:45."

"And Officer Blake will be there too?" Mom asked. "Is that typical?"

A frown creased Clay's brow. "Officer Blake has been assigned as our liaison officer for the Utah Highway Patrol because she was the one involved with the case."

"Which is great," I said. "She's cool."

"Agreed, and a fine officer, too. But . . ." He blew out a long breath. "But I didn't expect the DD to ask her to join us for this meeting."

"Oh?" Dad said. "What's up?"

"I think I know, and that worries me. Anyway, Joel—that's his name, Joel Jamison—wants to spend an hour with us first, so we'll have you all come in about 11:30. He's staying at the downtown Marriott. Do you know where that is?"

Dad nodded. "I've met clients there before." He looked more closely at him. "You look worried, Clay. What's wrong?"

Clay sighed. "I think he's out for blood."

We were all surprised at that, but Grandpère spoke first. "Blood? I thought he'd be pleased that you have the whole gang in custody now."

"Oh, he is that. But Joel Jamison doesn't miss much. That's how he got to be Deputy Director over the western region. He's not happy with my report. Or Shayla's either. She'll be on the hot seat too."

"But why?" Mom broke in.

He turned and looked at me. "Well, Danni created this little problem for us both."

"Because of the pouch?" Grandpère guessed.

"You got it," he said glumly. "In my first report, I wrote up everything as it happened, often quoting Rick and Danni directly. When I was through, I read back through it all and I said to myself, 'Clay, you turn in this report and Joel will have you committed to a psychiatric facility before the sun goes down.' So, I locked that report in my private safe and wrote a second one—what you might call a 'sanitized' version. No mention is made of the pouch, or red-hot pistols, or packets of hundred-dollar bills appearing out of nowhere, or a toy pistol blasting away with real bullets . . ." He shook his head. "Or a boat being sunk by forty-two bars of gold-plated lead."

"Does he not know about the dive team you sent down there?"

"Uh . . . no. When I pulled them out as quickly as I did, I felt I could get by without mentioning it. Did you write about the gold in your journal?"

"Um . . . yeah. The full story."

"And this second version is a problem?" Dad asked.

"Oh, yes. I quote: 'Your report is filled with vague generalities. It glosses over important elements of the story, seems openly evasive at times, and leaves many questions unanswered.'"

"Like what?" I asked.

"Like how you and Officer Blake communicated with each other when Gordo was in the backseat holding a gun on you."

I smiled. "I can see why that could be a problem. So what does the sanitized version say?"

He looked as if he had just bitten into something sour. "I said that the two of you somehow managed to communicate with each other in a nonvocal fashion by looking at each other in the rearview mirror."

Dad chuckled. "No wonder he smells blood."

"Yeah," he said glumly, "and I'm still wrestling with how to answer him. I—"

"That's simple," Grandpère said. "Take him the full report. Let him read it. Then talk."

"Are you kidding?" he blurted. "This guy has his law degree from Harvard. He graduated third in his class. He's a hardheaded realist. He's not going to warm to the idea of a pouch creating things out of nothing. If I give him the full report, Officer Blake will be busting jaywalkers in Hanksville, and I'll be lucky if I can stay on as janitor at the Federal Building."

To my surprise, Mom jumped in. "You have to tell him the full truth, Clay. That's the only solution."

Grandpère was nodding. "You can't explain things away and you can't keep hiding them. So, there's no other choice."

Clay was massaging his temples now. "You don't know him."

Rick leaped in. "How come *you're* a believer?"

His head came up. "What?"

"You were highly skeptical at first. What changed your mind?"

Eyes narrowing, Clay peered first at Rick, then at me. I could see that his mind was working hard, remembering that day in the motel when he first met Rick and me. He had scoffed too—until his wallet kept disappearing and the clip for his pistol loaded and unloaded itself.

"So, I'll bring the pouch tomorrow," I said. "Let's see what happens."

"Careful, Danni," Rick said. "You keep saying that you don't control the pouch. So, what if nothing happens?"

No one had an answer for that. He was right. I kept forgetting that. I kept committing *Le Gardien* to some form of action, and sometimes *Le Gardien* fired right back at me and said, "Now, tell me: Who are you again?"

Clay shook his head. "That's what I thought. I like the idea, but it had better work."

Grandpère moved in closer and looked him right in the eye. "The truth is the only answer, Clay. Trust me on that."

Clay stood up, clearly not convinced. "Let me think about it."

—————

Joel Jamison surprised me a little. I guess after what Clay had said about him, I expected this bulldog-faced, hard-nosed, crew-cut, Navy-Seal-looking kind of a guy. Instead, he was shorter than I expected—probably about five feet ten—stocky in build with a bit of a paunch, partially balding, and had a very forgettable face. I guess *plain* was the best word to describe him. I glanced at Rick to see what he thought of him, but he gave me one of his I-don't-know shrugs.

As we filed into the small conference room where he, Clay, and Officer Shayla Blake were waiting for us, all three stood up. Clay came over and shook hands quickly, then introduced us to his boss. Jamison's handshake was firm, but not quite the viselike grip I had expected. As he greeted the others, I noticed several things at once. There were pitchers of ice water on the table with glasses all around. Small paper plates were in front of where the three had been seated. They were soiled and had crumpled napkins on them. A tray with breads, cheeses, dips, and assorted fruit sat in the middle of the table, which explained the smaller plates. Most notable, however, were the three folders lying side by side on the table in front of where Jamison had been sitting. Two had FBI logos, the third the shield of the Utah Highway Patrol. I assumed the first two were Clay's two versions of what had happened, and that he had gone with our recommendation to tell all.

Shayla, dressed in her UHP uniform, murmured a greeting but stayed where she was. She looked pretty subdued. I glanced at Clay. It was hard to tell what he was feeling. He was all smiles as he greeted each one of us, but it did seem a little strained.

When we were seated, Clay poured us water and offered the tray to us. All of us, having had a late breakfast, declined. Which kind of ended Clay's efforts to stall any longer. He returned and sat down at Jamison's left.

"Thank you all for coming," Jamison said. "Knowing how far away you live from here, I appreciate you making the effort to come to Salt Lake."

I was tempted to quip that we had been bribed shamelessly to do so, but decided at this point it was better for the mouse to keep her head down while the elephants were tromping in the meadow.

He took a quick breath, and I thought I saw a flash of anger behind his eyes, but then he smiled. "Let me begin by saying that we are in your debt. What your family has done with this dangerous team of criminals is nothing short of astonishing. I commented to the Director of the FBI the other day that Danni and Rick should be drawing a salary."

We all smiled and murmured our thanks. He leaned forward. "I really mean that. There are several people in Washington marveling about it as we speak." He turned to Shayla. "And that goes for you as well, Officer Blake. I am drafting a letter of commendation to the Superintendent of the UHP in your behalf."

She was clearly taken aback. "Thank you, sir. I appreciate that very much. But, as you say, I just kind of hung back and gave backup to Danni and Rick while they did the heavy lifting."

"Yes." He paused for a moment, then went on. "Let me give you a quick report on where things stand. As Clay has told you, we are disappointed that our investigation into who is the real force behind El Cobra and his team has not borne more fruit. We think they are connected to this international gang of kidnappers but so far cannot confirm that positively. But one thing is certain: We nailed this gang completely, thanks to you guys. And that relieves us of a great deal of anxiety about your safety. We are hopeful that the capture of the last three will prove to be a significant breakthrough. We are particularly encouraged by the two men who were bitten by the rattlesnakes. Their ordeal left them deeply shaken, and they were furious that the Belgian essentially left them to die. So, thus far, they're singing like canaries, but they don't know much. All kinds of information on El Cobra and the rest of them, but nothing on who's behind it all, or even for sure if there is a 'behind it all.'"

Mom tentatively waved a hand. He nodded at her.

"Isn't it a little strange that El Cobra and the others still don't have an attorney?"

"It is. We're not sure why that is the case. But knowing how sophisticated this organization is, they've probably drilled three things into the heads of all their operatives: One, if you talk, you're dead. We'll get to you. Even in prison. Two, if you don't talk, there's a large sum of cash waiting for you. And three, if you keep mum, you'll have the best attorneys in the business. So we expect that one of these days, someone will come forth to represent them."

"But being promised money is not very comforting when you're in prison, is it?" I asked.

Clay spoke up. "Oh, you'd be surprised. They can access those funds to some extent from prison. Use them to bless their families. Invest them so they're earning money."

That seemed logical, and once again I felt a sense of wonder that little Danni McAllister, the girl with the enchanted pouch, was able to stop such a sophisticated gang as this. With help from Rick, of course. It really was quite remarkable.

Clearly finished with the soft stuff, Jamison picked up the thicker of the two FBI folders. A deep furrow creased his brow. *Here we go,* I thought.

But then he evidently had another thought, because he set it down again and turned to Clay. "If—or, more likely, when—they get an attorney or team of attorneys, that could change everything. Not only will we not know what their clients are telling them, but there's no way we can stop the attorneys from making whatever statements they want to the press. Which means it is likely that our drug bust cover story isn't going to hold up for much longer. So, Clay, I want you and Officer Blake to start working on a joint statement. Perhaps you'll even have to hold a press conference sometime in the near future."

"Yes, sir." Clay made a few notes on his pad.

"Okay." He picked up the folders again, and from his expression, we sensed that the game was on.

The room was totally quiet as Jamison opened the thicker of the two FBI folders—which I assumed was the "full" report—and quickly scanned down the first page. As he did so, I watched his eyes closely. And this time there was no mistaking it. This wasn't a flash of irritation.

This was hard, cold anger. He glanced at Clay, but Clay was staring at his hands and missed it. Well, I take that back. He may not have seen it, but I'm betting that he felt it. The rest of us surely did.

Finally, Jamison closed the folder and set it down. Then he turned to me, his eyes boring into mine like they were spear points. "Okay, Miss McAllister. Clay tells me that you—and possibly your family—have a statement you would like to make."

"I do. We do," I said meekly. Though I had no idea what that statement was going to be.

"Before you start, I need to make two things perfectly clear. First, Clay Zabriskie is one of the outstanding agents in the Bureau. Obviously, you don't become a regional AIC otherwise. He has many years of commendable service behind him." He stopped, glaring at Clay, who finally had looked up and was following his every word.

"But you need to know, all of you, that his career is in serious jeopardy at the moment. What you are about to say could make or break the career of one of our finest agents. Is that clear?"

Perfectly. Does he even have to ask?

"Second, and equally important, is this." Now he turned and looked directly at me and Rick. I felt like one of those high-powered searchlights had just been focused on us. "This is a federal criminal investigation of a capital crime. We are presently in the process of collecting evidence that we hope will lead to the conviction of the perpetrators."

He stopped, letting his gaze rake across every one of our faces, stopping again on me and Rick. "Interfering with this investigation in any way is a federal crime with heavy penalties. It doesn't matter whether this is done by giving false information, withholding information, tampering with evidence, embellishing the facts, adding half truths or untruths to place yourself or your family members in a better light, or just plain, straight-out perjury. Any of these constitute a felony. So be very careful what you say—or don't say—because you are flirting with felonious behavior. And I will not, and cannot, ignore that behavior, no matter how commendable your actions of these past two weeks may have been. Do you both understand me?"

I tried hard not to flinch as I met his gaze. My heart was hammering inside my chest, my mouth was suddenly dry, and I was finding it hard to breathe. But I managed to answer him. "I understand clearly, Mr. Jamison."

"Yes, sir," Rick said.

I glanced down the table at my family. Mom was very sober, but she nodded at me. "It's all right, Carruthers. Just tell him the truth."

Right! I think the truth may be part of the problem here, Mom.

Dad also leaned forward and smiled his encouragement. Grandpère was staring at his hands and didn't look up. I didn't dare look at Rick because he was right beside me. But I guessed that he was thinking that everything Jamison said to me applied to him as well.

"All right," Jamison said at last. His eyes bored into me. "I see that you have a purse or a pouch over your shoulder. Is this the pouch I have been reading about this morning?"

I squeezed the pouch with my elbow, pressing it against my body. "It is." It felt cool. Which was not a good sign. "If I may, Mr. Deputy Director, I would like to begin by—"

His face softened a little. "You may call me Joel, Danni."

Oh, really? Maybe sometime in the twenty-second century, but not when I am about to become the first felon in McAllister history. No way.

My shoulders lifted and fell as I took a deep breath, my mind racing. There was nothing. I was blank as a board and blind panic was swelling up inside me. Finally, I cleared my throat. "Uh . . . perhaps I should start by . . . um . . . telling you a little bit about how I got the pouch."

He nodded and sat back.

No! That's not the answer. I looked at the floor. *Then what is?* Nothing came.

I got to my feet, stalling for time. I felt a little dizzy, like I might faint. *Oh, that will impress him. The lady felon faints on cue.*

And then came one simple, little, teeny thought. I reared back for a moment, caught totally by surprise. Then I pushed back my chair enough that I had some maneuvering room and took the pouch off my shoulder. Very solemnly, ignoring the sudden surprise on his face, I walked around to where he was sitting. As he half turned to face me, I reached out and laid the pouch on the table before him. Then I stepped back.

He reached down and picked it up, exploring it with his fingers. Then his head dropped, and he examined it more closely. As he started to unbutton the flap, he saw the embroidered words. "*Le Gardien,*" he murmured. His pronunciation was perfect.

"Do you speak French, Mr. Jamison?" I asked.

"A little."

"Then you know what it means?"

"Yes. The Guardian."

Okay. This was good. No bloodletting so far. So what next?

"You can open it if you like," I said.

He did so, unbuttoning the flap and looking inside. He held it up and shook it slightly so that if there had been anything inside, it would have fallen out. I wondered then if Clay had included his first experience with the pouch back in the motel that first day Rick and I met him. I guessed no, but I wasn't sure.

Jamison was waiting, and I could see that his patience was quickly evaporating.

Come on, Le Gardien. *Do something before he skewers me and puts me over the fire to roast.*

Nothing happened. So I plunged in blindly. "Sir, if I may, I should like to tell you a little bit about how I came to—"

He ignored that. "And this is the pouch that supposedly made you and your brother invisible. That produced a pistol out of thin air? A toy pistol, right? Which then began firing a whole clip of bullets?" He slammed the pouch down on the table. "Don't you start down that path, young lady. It's a very slippery slope, and I would advise you to have an attorney present before you make any further statements."

His warning knocked me back, and I just stared at him blankly. Rick stood and came over beside me. He didn't say anything, just moved up until we stood shoulder to shoulder.

Fortunately, someone else responded. "Actually, it was more than one clip," Grandpère said, speaking up for the first time since the introductions had been made. "The clip held eight rounds, I believe. But nearly two dozen shots were fired."

Jamison swung around, his eyes blazing. "Don't you start too," he began, "or I'll—"

Grandpère shot to his feet, and it so startled Jamison that he stopped in midsentence.

"Is it true you graduated from Harvard Law School before joining the FBI?" Grandpère demanded.

"I . . . yes. So what?"

"Since you're trained in the law, answer me this. In the eyes of the law, how many credible eyewitnesses does it take to get a conviction on charges of unlawful conduct?"

Jamison was glowering at him, not sure what this was all about. Grandpère just waited patiently until he settled back in his chair. Obviously suspicious, he thought about it for a moment. "Technically, only one, *if* he or she is a credible witness and *if* he or she actually saw something directly relevant to the charges, with his or her own eyes."

"You say *technically*. Does that suggest that two or more eyewitnesses would be better?"

"Of course."

Grandpère turned to look at us. "Would you each raise your right hand, please?" As we did so, he looked at Shayla Blake. "You too." Her hand came up slowly. She was as confused as the rest of us.

Grandpère was calm and unruffled, speaking as if he were lecturing a graduate class in French literature. "Do each of you solemnly swear to tell the truth, the whole truth, and nothing but the truth, so help you God?"

We were totally baffled by this, but after a moment, we all said in a ragged chorus, "I do."

Jamison started to get up. "I'm not sure what you're up to, Mr. LaRoche, but I'm running out of patience."

Grandpère merely smiled. "I'm sorry, sir, but you can't do that. You're the judge here, and you are required to hear the evidence."

He sat back down, grumping something to himself. Grandpère immediately turned back to us. "All right, then. I am going to ask several questions. If you have personal, eyewitness knowledge concerning the question, I want you to raise one hand if your answer is yes, or shake your head if the answer is no. Clear?"

We all nodded.

"All right. First question. How many of you were actually present when Danni and Cody became invisible?"

I raised my hand, as did Grandpère, Dad, and Mom. Rick, Clay, and Shayla shook their heads. "If Cody were here, he'd raise his hand too," I said.

Jamison stirred, but at a look from Grandpère, he sat back again.

"And how many of you were present in the room when the pouch, which had been previously searched and found to be empty, produced a toy pistol that started firing real bullets when El Cobra tossed it on the table?"

Same hands went up; same heads moved back and forth.

"How did you know it was a toy pistol?" Jamison cut in.

"Because," Dad said, "El Cobra identified it as such, then held it up for all of us to see. There was no hole in the barrel."

"Ridiculous," Jamison muttered.

Grandpère went on as if he hadn't spoken. "And who was present at Cathedral Valley when the man known as Doc had to drop his pistol because it turned red-hot and burned his hand?"

This time Rick raised his hand along with the rest of us. Then he squirmed a little. "Actually, I was about a hundred yards away, but I saw him drop it and heard it all on the radio."

"As did I," Clay said quietly.

"Sorry, Clay," Grandpère said. "You have to have actually seen this for yourself."

The Deputy Director stood up. "I'm not going to sit here and—"

Grandpère turned and stared him down. "Sir, you said you wanted the truth. As a judge, if the truth doesn't fit your preconceived notions, are you allowed to cut off further testimony being given under oath?"

He sat back down again. But we all could see he was fuming. I half expected smoke to come out of his nostrils at any moment.

"Just a couple more questions," Grandpère went on. "Officer Blake, will you explain something to the judge? Tell him how it was that you and Danni were able to communicate with each other about stopping at Leprechaun Canyon when you had an armed man in the car with you."

Shayla spoke up clearly and without hesitation. "I glanced at Danni in the rearview mirror. The angle was such that our captor could not see us. Suddenly writing appeared on the mirror. It was Danni speaking to me."

"Oh, come on," Jamison snapped. "This has gone far enough."

"I swear it's true," Blake exclaimed. "We carried on a conversation with each other for several minutes and the guy beside Danni never suspected a thing."

I spoke up. "That is exactly what happened, sir."

Turning back to face Jamison, Grandpère made his point. "So there you have it, your honor. Eyewitness testimony from credible witnesses—not one, but six, if you count Cody. Doesn't that create some reasonable doubt in your mind that maybe what you've read is not a false or deliberately evasive report?"

"Not if this is a conspiracy among the six of you," he shot right back. He turned and glared at Clay and Blake. "Though I cannot fathom why one of my top agents and an experienced UHP officer would be part of that. But I promise you, I will find that out."

Grandpère sighed. "Then let me ask you one last question, your Honor, since it appears that your mind is made up. Which of the following three options do you think best describes my granddaughter: One, she is telling the truth."

Emphatically shaking his head, Jamison started to answer, but Grandpère cut him off. "Two, Danni is a fraud. She is a liar and a cheat, a clever con woman engaging in an elaborate deception for reasons we do not fully understand. As are all the rest of us. Or three—" he turned and looked at me, then back to Jamison. "Danni is wildly delusional. She is mentally deranged, out of touch with reality. She's either schizophrenic or possibly even wildly psychotic." He leaned in and punched out the next words. *"As are her parents, her grandfather, her brother, her best friend, a top FBI agent, and a UHP officer."*

He abruptly sat down. "That's all I have to say."

For a long time, there was not a sound in the room. Then Jamison started shaking his head, and I could see we had lost. "You make an eloquent case, Mr. LaRoche, and I admit that I am perplexed. But if there is a conspiracy, then that would explain—" He stopped and blew out his breath, clearly very much frustrated. He turned and looked at Clay.

"I will admit that part of me wants to believe you. I do find it troublesome that six of you who are, as nearly as I can determine, perfectly normal and trustworthy citizens are engaged in some wild conspiracy, or some grand con scheme. And for some reason that I cannot fathom."

Now he looked at me. "My heart wants to believe you, Danni, but my head refuses to. It is simply not possible. Yet . . ." Deep sigh. "The same rational part of me that says there cannot be an enchanted pouch, that the things which you have described are simply not possible, also refuses to accept that you are delusional or perjuring yourself."

"Thank you. Mr. Jamison," I said. "I fully understand how you must feel." Suddenly I had another thought. "But don't you see that your unwillingness to believe changes the whole dynamic of this situation?"

His face hardened perceptibly. "Meaning what?"

I stalled. I wasn't sure myself. I focused inwardly and was filled with wonder as understanding flooded into my mind. It was like suddenly I had this teleprompter inside my head, and all I had to do was read from it. I took a quick breath. "My grandfather has a story that he occasionally tells us about believing what you see. I think it is true." I turned to Grandpère.

"That is what I was told," Grandpère said.

I went on. "There was a Christian missionary who went to India many years ago to bring those of other faiths to Christ. He worked among a people who had a great reverence for life. They wouldn't eat meat. They refused to harm any animal. They would even go to great lengths to avoid stepping on insects on the ground. When the minister tried to teach them about Jesus, they refused to listen because he did not have the same reverence for life as they did.

"Highly frustrated, one day he decided to show them that their position was not logical. So he got a glass and filled it with water from a tap. He offered it to one of his most vocal critics. After the man took a drink, the missionary said: 'You say you refuse to harm any living thing, but come and look at this.' He then took an eyedropper, put a drop of water on a microscope slide, and asked the man to look through the microscope. He saw that the water was filled with tiny life forms.

"'That is what you just drank, my friend,' the missionary said. 'Now what do you have to say about your belief?'" I stopped, watching Jamison closely but saying nothing.

"And?" he asked. "What did the man do?"

"He broke the microscope."

Jamison rocked back, his face instantly darkening.

I decided I had to press my advantage. "Meaning no disrespect, Mr. Jamison, but it does seem to us that this is what you just did. You refuse to believe what your head and your heart are saying is true."

At that moment, the door to the conference room opened. A woman in a hotel uniform stepped inside. She was carrying a tray with fresh glasses and two pitchers, one of water, one of punch. "Excuse me. I'll just—"

"Not now!" Jamison barked.

Her mouth dropped and she started to back away. "I . . . I'm sorry, sir. The manager asked me to—I'm very sorry. I'll come back later."

"Wait!" I cried. I peered at her name tag. "Wait, Lani." I was on my feet and to her in moments. I took her elbow and gently pulled her forward. "Please come in. It's all right."

Jamison's eyes were shooting daggers at me at the rate of about ten per second, but I ignored him. "It's all right, Lani. I think we all would like something to drink."

Clearly understanding that I was not the one in charge in this room, she looked at Jamison. After a second, he nodded. "It's okay."

As she set the tray on the table and started distributing the glasses, asking each person if they preferred punch or water, I moved around to stand behind the Deputy Director. I leaned down. "Do you know this woman?"

He looked up in surprise. "No. Should I?"

"No. Neither do I. I have never seen her before. In fact, I have never been in this hotel before."

"So?"

"Tell me her last name."

He jerked up. "What?"

Lani came to an abrupt halt. She had evidently heard what I said. "Are you talking to me?"

I held up a hand. "Hold on a second." Then back to Jamison. "Tell me her last name."

His eyes suddenly widened. "Lani *Kinkaid*."

The maid almost dropped the pitcher. "How do you know that?"

I pointed at her. "I think he read it off your name tag."

She looked down, then gasped. She wasn't the only one. Her last name now appeared on her tag below her first name. She set the pitcher down and grabbed at the tag, turning it up so she could see it more clearly. Beside me, I saw Jamison jerk forward. I couldn't see his eyes but I hoped they were bugging out of his head.

I bent down again. "Put your hands on the pouch."

Jamison looked up, as if he had forgotten I was there. "Why?"

"Just take the pouch. Hold it in your hands."

After a moment, he took it from the table and put it in his lap again. His eyes widened. "It's warm."

Oh, thank you, thank you, thank you. But all I said was, "Yes, I know. So tell me her birth date."

"I . . ." He turned and looked at the woman. "April twenty-third, nineteen eighty-two."

The maid still had her name tag between her fingers. She gave a little yelp and fell back a step. As she let it go, we all saw it plainly. Just beneath her name were seven numbers—*4/23/1982.*

Shocked to the core, Jamison got to his feet, speaking slowly. "Is that true? *Is* that your birth date?"

She started backing away. I thought she was going to throw up her hands, like she was warding off evil spirits.

"Is that your birthday?" Jamison said, more forcefully now.

She nodded numbly. "Yes, but how—"

"Where was she born?" I asked.

"Ely, Nevada." He said it without hesitation.

She was thoroughly frightened now. "How are you doing this?"

"The name of her first boyfriend?"

"Elwood Franklin, nicknamed Woody."

The woman gave a little cry, ripped off her tag, and flung it at Jamison, then fled from the room, half sobbing. The tag hit the table, bounced twice, and sailed off onto the floor. I reached down and picked it up, then handed it to Jamison. Besides the Marriott logo, only one word was now on the tag. *Lani.*

He turned slowly, clearly dazed. His mouth opened, then clamped shut again. "But—"

He didn't get a chance to finish. The door slammed open and a very large black guy in a dark suit burst into the room. He pulled up, looking quickly at all of us, then focused on Jamison. "What is going on here? What did you just do to Lani? She's hysterical."

"I . . ." Jamison held out the name tag. "There seemed to be some problem with this. We didn't mean to upset her."

I leaned closer. "What's her husband's name?"

The manager's eyes went very dark. "That is none of your business, young lady."

"Because she has no husband right now," I shot right back. "She has been married twice, but is currently living with her boyfriend, whose name is Roger, and—"

The manager spun on his heel and headed for the door again. "I'm calling the cops," he called over his shoulder. "You all stay right here." And he was gone.

Clay was instantly on his feet. "I'll go straighten this out," he said, trying hard to keep the glee out of his voice. As he went past me, he turned his back on Jamison and gave me a thumbs-up and mouthed, "Thank you."

I turned as Jamison sat down heavily in his seat again. I moved back around the table and sat down across from him. I leaned forward, gazing into his troubled eyes. "Like I said. Sometimes we have to see to believe. But other times, we have to believe in order to see."

———

Five minutes later, we all sat quietly as two different maids cleared our table. The manager hovered nearby, glaring at each of us in turn. No one said anything, but I can say this: It was a very different Joel Jamison who sat before us now than when we first entered the room.

Finally, the girls finished and left. The manager, whose name tag read *Joseph,* followed them to the door. But he stopped and turned back. "Will you be needing anything else, Mr. Jamison?" It was polite, but very cool.

He shook his head. "No. Thank you. We'll be through here in a few minutes. Thank you, Joseph."

"You're welcome." He turned and started for the door.

"Joseph?"

He half turned back. "Yes, sir?"

"Please give our apologies to Miss Kinkaid. We didn't mean to upset her. And add a fifty-dollar tip for her onto my bill."

He thawed a little. "Thank you, sir. I'll tell her that."

After he left, we all sat there. All eyes were on Jamison, who seemed far away. He straightened and looked down at the folders before him, his face a study in perplexity. Finally, he reached out and took the fattest one, the one that contained Clay's full report. He handed it to Clay.

Clearly surprised, Clay took it. "What would you like me to do with this, sir?"

He sighed, and then a little twinkle appeared in his eyes. "I would definitely recommend that you not publish it. I'll make a few tweaks to your—uh—sanitized report, and that will go into the official files."

We all laughed.

"If it were me, Clay, I'd lock it in my personal safe and—" He shrugged. "Well, you get the picture."

"Yes, sir."

"Did you write a full account, Officer Blake?"

Shayla shook her head. "No, sir. I . . . I didn't dare."

"Good. I commend you for your good judgment."

Then he turned and fixed his eyes on me and Rick. "And what about you two?"

Rick was quick to respond. "I've written nothing about it."

"I've written a full account in my journal, Mr. Jamison, and I—"

He cut in, half smiling. "I'm not going to throw you in prison now, so you can call me Joel."

Laughing, I said, "Yes, Joel. And thank you for that. Anyway, I wrote it all up, including details that Clay didn't have in his report, because they were things that happened that didn't directly have to do with El Cobra and his gang."

And please don't ask me more, because I'm never going to tell you about the speed limit sign, or the cutie in the BMW, or the guy with a neck like a tree stump.

He was watching me closely, almost as if he were reading my thoughts. But finally he smiled. "And is that journal in a safe place?"

"Yes, sir—uh—Joel."

"We have it in a safety deposit box in the bank," Mom said.

"Good. Very good." He abruptly stood, glancing at his watch. "Well, I have a plane waiting for me at the airport. I'm sure they're wondering where I am."

Clay stood too. "I'll go get the car and bring it around front." He gave us a happy wave and called his good-byes as he left.

Joel came around the table and began shaking hands, first with Rick, then Grandpère, then Mom and Dad. But when he came to me, he totally caught me off guard by brushing aside my outstretched hand and giving me a big hug. When he stepped back, I looked into his face and wondered why I had ever thought of him as being plain. That was not true at all. He actually seemed like a warm and kindly grandfather. "You're a wonder, Danni. Just like Clay said. It's been a pleasure to cross swords with you."

"Thank you."

He turned to Mom. "We're going to try to keep a lid on this for as long as we can, Mrs. McAllister. So I have an assignment for you."

"You do?"

"Yes. I want you to take these people home. I want you to forbid them to talk about this anymore, at least until we get back in touch with you. And I want you to see if you can't have a little more normal life for a while."

Mom, beaming triumphantly, shot us each a look, then turned back to him. "That I will do," she said. "You have my word on that."

CHAPTER 14

McAllister Ranch, Hanksville, Utah
September 12, 2011

"How was school today, kids?"

I didn't look up. That was Mom. Go ten seconds without anyone saying something and she would ask one of her conversation-starting questions at the dinner table. Knowing Cody would answer—he always did—I kept right on pushing my peas into a line with my fork so they formed a little dam for my gravy.

"Muy bien, Señora."

I put my fork down and shot him a dirty look. He had enrolled in eighth-grade Spanish this year, and on the way home on the bus this afternoon, he'd been showing off to some girls. If you didn't count words like *taco, enchilada, tortilla, burrito,* and *empanada,* his total vocabulary was about ten words. And he slaughtered most of them. So I had leaned over the seat and told him to put a sock in it until he could at least pronounce the words correctly. That had started the girls tittering, and he had gone bright red. He shot me a look that told me he was looking for revenge, then totally ignored me.

But Mom, of course, loved it. "Oh, Code. That's wonderful. Two weeks into school and you're already talking Spanish. And you do it so well."

I rolled my eyes and went back to my construction project.

"How about you, Danni?" Dad asked.

"How about me what?"

"How was school?"

"BOR-ing!" I sang out.

Mom also shot me one of her looks. "I don't like it when you talk like that, Carruthers."

"Well," I fired right back, "Dad asked. And while we're at it, 'How was the bus ride to school this morning, Carruthers?' BOR-ing! 'And how was the ride home, Danni?' BOR-ing!"

Mom's lips pinched a little. "All right, we get the picture." She turned back to Cody. "So is Spanish your favorite class?"

"Nope!" he chirped. "Algebra."

"BOR-ing," I mouthed, turning my head so Mom wouldn't see it.

But Grandpère did. He was watching me steadily. "Now that Rick drives himself to school because he only goes half a day, who do you sit with on the bus?" he asked.

"I sit with Corrie Wallstein or Serena Batista."

"Always the same two?"

"I . . . um . . . yeah, I guess so. I get pretty tired of being teased about being Danni Oakley."

"Are they still doing that?" Mom asked. "I thought that would have died out by now."

"I wish!"

Grandpère went back to his eating, but after a moment, he looked over at Dad. "Maybe you could look into a limousine service for Danni, Mack. You know, something that would help her get to school in the style to which she has grown accustomed."

Cody guffawed loudly, happy anytime he saw me put down.

"With a chauffeur named Dudley," Mom said, trying not to laugh. "Or perhaps McIntosh."

"I am glad that you all find my situation so amusing," I sniffed.

"Do you take the pouch every day?" Grandpère asked, this time serious.

"Yes, I do," I snapped. "Every single day. And I keep it with me in class, and I take it to lunch, and I take it to the bathroom, and I—"

"Danni," Dad said in soft warning.

I ignored him. "*Le Gardien* provides more fodder for jokes than even Danni Oakley."

"Poor Danni," Cody said, with obvious relish.

I nearly told him to shut his mouth, but I was wise enough to bite that back. We had a rule in our house. When one of us—meaning Cody or me—told the other one to shut up, we had dishes that night. And if we really mouthed off, Dad wouldn't let us use the dishwasher to do them.

"Why not do your homework on the bus if you're that bored?" Mom asked.

What was this? Stick-It-to-Danni Day? But I bit that back too and gave her a withering look. "Because I get carsick when I try to read on the bus. Oh, that would boost my popularity with my friends. Upchuck all over them."

"If it's on the bus, wouldn't it be bus sick?"

I whirled around. "Just shut up, Cody! Mom wasn't talking to you."

He grinned and pumped his fist. "YES! Danni's got the dishes, Danni's got the dishes."

"And without the dishwasher," Dad said quietly. "I think you need some time to think."

———

When Mom came in about halfway through me doing the dishes, I didn't turn around. That didn't stop her. I heard a chair scrape, and a moment later she sat down. "Wanna talk?"

"No."

"Good. What would you like to talk about?"

I turned, wanting to be mad, but I wasn't able to. That was my mom, always knowing exactly what to do to tease me out of my bad moods. She patted the table beside her and motioned with her head. I dried my hands on the dish towel and sat down.

We were quiet for a moment, then Mom reached out and took my hand. "This wouldn't have anything to do with the homecoming dance, would it?"

This time I laughed softly. That was my Mom too. Unerring instincts about what was going on in my head. For a moment I considered denying it, but decided that would be pretty stupid since I really did want to talk to someone about it. So I finally pulled a face and bobbed my head.

"It's still three weeks away. Remember, boys are real slow about asking girls to dances."

"Nu-uh. I'll bet half the girls have been asked."

She cocked her head to one side. "Half?"

"Well, a bunch."

"And nothing from Rick?"

"No, Mom. We talked about it. If he starts asking me to every dance, then everyone will think we're dating. Since I'm a junior this year, I really want to go to the Junior Prom with him. So we agreed, no dances until then." I sighed. "So he asked Cherie Averill."

"Oh, she's a nice girl."

"Thanks, Mom. Way to cheer me up."

"Don't give up quite yet. Three weeks is an eternity in the male mind. There's still time."

"I doubt it." My shoulders slumped. "I'm the town outcast."

She said nothing to that, and we sat quietly for a time. "Well," she said, getting up, "I wouldn't give up hope quite yet. You never know."

Something in the way she said that made me whip around. "What?"

She feigned surprise. "What what?"

"Do you know something?"

"*Moi?*" she cried, pointing at herself and sounding very much like Grandpère. Then she hurried out before I could press her further.

It was exactly thirty-three minutes later when the doorbell rang. "I'll get it!" I shouted as I leaped off the bed. Cody was still downstairs, and I heard him race for the door, but Mom's yell pulled him up short. "Let Danni get it."

What I found was quite stunning. Whoever had rung the bell had gone, but they had left a large, chocolate cake on the doorstep. It was covered in swirls of dark brown frosting. What was weird, though, was that brightly colored plastic letters, like from a child's game, were stuck randomly all over the cake.

By the time I got it onto the kitchen table, I had the whole family around me. It took me about a minute to remove the letters, lick off the frosting—and no, I didn't share them with Cody—and lay them on the table. In five minutes more, with the family helping me, we had rearranged them into a short but clear message. *Homecoming? Yes or no? Jason Horne.*

I just stared at them. Mom was much more sedate about it. She clapped her hands, squealed in delight, and said, *"Oh! My! Word!"* It was an almost perfect imitation of me.

Cody looked at them for a moment, then said, "Jason Horne? Who's that?"

I fought back the urge to clap my hands in delight. "He's a senior from Loa. And he just happens to be the best-looking dude in Wayne County High School. Next to Rick, of course."

As soon as the others drifted away, I cornered Mom. "Are you responsible for this?"

"I will say only this much. I received a call two days ago inquiring whether or not you had been asked to Homecoming. I said no."

"Was it Jason?"

"No, and no more questions." She made the motion of zipping her lips. "My lips are sealed," she said and left.

I wasn't sure I believed her, but then had another thought. I shut the door and called Rick.

"Hey."

"Hey, Rick."

"What's up?"

"I got a question for you."

"Okay."

"Did you tell Jason Horne to ask me to Homecoming?"

"Uh . . . no."

"Don't you lie to me, Rick," I cried. "Tell me."

"I don't lie," he said calmly.

"Do you swear you had nothing to do with it?"

"Uh . . . that's not what you asked me."

My heart fell. I felt stupid.

"Danni, it's not what you think."

"Oh, yeah. I know you're good friends. How much did you pay him?" When he didn't answer, I added, "And here I thought someone had actually wanted to go to the dance with me."

"Danni."

"Good-bye, Rick."

"Will you put a sock in it? Geez, Danni. It's like having a conversation with a hornets' nest. Just listen a minute. Jason asked me if you had been asked yet. I told him I didn't think so, but I would find out. So I called your mom."

"And you didn't put him up to it?"

"Don't insult me by making me say everything twice. Oh, and there is one other thing."

I was instantly wary again. "What?"

"He asked if you two could double-date with me and Cherie Averill."

"Really?" I squealed.

"Really, and don't you dare tell him I said anything. He wants to tell you himself."

It was fascinating how quickly the word of my good fortune spread. By the time I got off the bus the next morning at the high school, the word was out. Danni McAllister had a date to Homecoming with Jason Horne. It was on my Facebook page by the end of first period. Rick stopped me after second period to "officially" congratulate me. By lunch I was receiving Tweets every few minutes. Best of all, Lisa Cole sat with me at lunch, literally dripping with envy, even though she had been asked to the dance by the quarterback of the football team.

By the time school was out, things had died down somewhat, and after recounting the details for the umpteenth time, I finally got up and went to the back of the bus, saying that I had to study. Cody snorted as I passed him. "Not!" he mouthed, then laughed.

It was true in a way. But it wasn't schoolwork I was thinking about. Today was September 13. That meant that it was exactly three months ago today that I had celebrated my sixteenth birthday by going up to the mine with Rick, Dad, and Grandpère. And three months tomorrow since we had come home to find El Cobra holding Mom and Cody hostage.

Could it possibly have been only three months ago? In some ways, it was still so vivid in my mind that it seemed like yesterday. In other ways, it felt like a lifetime ago. Part of me felt years older than I had been back then. Another part of me felt more like a little girl. Most of this weirdness, I knew, flowed from my being keeper of the pouch.

What an incredible ride that had been. Wonder after wonder. Surprise after surprise. Lesson after lesson. I had been sorely tempted to ask *Le Gardien* for help in getting a date, but then I tried to picture what I would say if Grandpère ever asked me about it straight out.

I jumped as I felt my phone vibrate in my pocket. I quickly fished it out, swiped the screen, and saw, to my surprise, that it was a text message from Grandpère. It was only four words, but they sent a chill shooting through me.

The horses are coming.

I tried for the next seven or eight minutes to get him back. Nothing. I tried to call Dad. Nothing. Then Mom. Nothing. Cody must have seen my growing concern, because he came back and sat down beside me. "What's wrong?"

I shook my head. "Dunno. I got a text from Grandpère, but now I can't get my phone to work. I've tried texting and calling but it's not working."

"Maybe you're out of the coverage area."

I shot him a withering look. "These are satellite phones, remember? They're supposed to work anywhere."

The bus suddenly started to slow, and I looked up. We were just coming into the western outskirts of Hanksville, and the driver was slowing for our first stop. Kids were already getting to their feet and filing down the aisle toward the door. Including Kaylynn, Rick's sister. She was twelve now and in the seventh grade, so this was her first year riding the bus. She turned around, smiled, and waved. "'Bye, Cody. 'Bye, Danni."

We both waved back. Automatically, I turned to the window and looked for Rick. I always did this, even though I knew he would be working with Dad by this time of the day.

As the bus started again, I turned my phone off, waited about thirty seconds, then turned it on again. Everything came up just as normal, but when I tried to call Grandpère, nothing happened. It didn't go through. I went to Favorites and touched Dad's phone number. Again, nothing. This was crazy. Was Grandpère doing this? Was this his way of rebuking me for last night? Whatever it was, it wasn't funny, and I was starting to get worried. Then came another thought. I went back to favorites and chose Rick's number. But just as I was about to punch his number, Cody's hand shot out and grabbed my arm.

"Look, Danni!"

He was pointing toward the front of the bus. I lowered my phone and looked forward. For a moment, I wasn't sure what he was seeing, but then I jerked upright. Out the front window I could see we were approaching our second stop, which was in the center of town. Up ahead, near the Shell station, there was a dark mass of people milling around.

"What's happening?" Cody asked.

I stood up. "Dunno. Come on."

"But this isn't our stop."

"I'm not getting off. I just want to see." I reached out and yanked him to his feet and started up the aisle. The driver was slowing quickly and pulled off the highway, which turned the bus at enough of an angle that we could see out the side windows. What happened next stunned us both. Hearing the bus, the people all turned to see. Though we were midway into September, down in this country that was still summer, so a lot of the windows on the bus were open. So we clearly heard the cries go up as the bus stopped in a cloud of dust and hiss of air brakes. "There she is now." "Danni McAllister's on that bus." "She's the one you're looking for."

I stopped dead. Then I saw something that really knocked me reeling. Beyond the crowd, parked in the open field behind the Shell station, was a helicopter. Alongside it was a Wayne County Sheriff's car, with Deputy Carlson beside it. I instantly knew what the chopper was because we saw it all the time when we watched the news on TV. Near the rear was a large blue circle with KSL in white letters. Below the door it said, "Chopper 5."

I was stunned. Chopper 5 in Hanksville? What in the heck was going on? Then the cries began to register. They were waiting for *me?*

The bus emptied quickly, leaving me and Cody to be last ones off. As we stepped down, instantly the crowd closed in around us. Leading the charge was a woman with a microphone in her hand; a guy with a video camera on his shoulder was right behind her. I recognized her immediately. It was Kirstin Powers, one of the reporters on Channel 5's *Eyewitness Evening News.*

"Are you Danni McAllister?" she said, thrusting the microphone at me. The cameraman stepped to one side, and I saw the red light on his camera come on.

"Uh . . ." I was too shocked. I couldn't get anything out.

"Yes. That's her." I wasn't sure who shouted it. One of my fellow classmates.

"Um . . . yeah."

Cody pushed in beside me. "Hi. I'm Cody McAllister. I'm her brother." He was grinning like he had just won a lifetime pass to Disneyland.

"Wonderful." She turned to make sure her cameraman was rolling. He gave her a thumbs-up. "My name is Kirstin Powers. I'm part of the Channel Five news team, and—"

"We know who you are," Cody blurted. "We watch you all the time."

The crowd laughed, and Kirstin was obviously pleased. "Thank you, Cody." Her smile was bright and pleasant, just like on TV. I guessed she was about thirty. Her hair was blonde and hung to her shoulders. Her eyes were dark brown, her teeth perfect. She was even more beautiful in person than on screen.

"May I call you Danni?" she said, moving a step closer and holding out the microphone in front of my face.

"Uh . . . sure."

"Go, Danni!" someone cried from off to one side. It was another one of my classmates. The crowd laughed, and a few clapped.

Kirstin was immediately very serious. "Danni, about three hours ago, we received an anonymous phone call at our studio in Salt Lake City." She glanced down at a small notebook she had in her hand. "Are you familiar with the supposed drug bust that took place not far from here earlier this summer down at Lake Powell?"

My heart seized up. "Uh . . . yeah. We heard about it."

"Well, according to our caller, it was not a drug bust at all. It was a home invasion and kidnapping of a local family by an international gang of thieves."

A ripple of amazement spread through the crowd. This was news to them. Me? I was too shocked to do anything but stare at her.

"According to our source, it was your family who was kidnapped and held for ransom. And this because your father was selling a mine to someone in Canada. Is that true?"

If she had meant to stun the crowd, it worked. A collective gasp drowned out all sound for a second or two. Over the heads of the crowd I saw Deputy Carlson jerk to attention and start moving forward to hear better.

"Is that true, Danni? Was it your family who was involved?"

"I . . ." I couldn't get my breath.

"Yep," Cody sang out. "That was us."

The crowd exploded, crying out, shouting questions, looking dazed.

Kirstin turned and held up both hands. "People! Please. We are on camera right now." She turned back to me. "We stopped at your house to speak with your parents, but no one was home. Can you confirm if this story is true?"

There was clearly no point in denying it at this point. *Thanks, Code.* "Yes, it's true."

More noise. Another glare. Then back to me. "Danni, can you tell us what happened?"

And so I did. I told her briefly about me and Dad and Grandpère coming back from a trip to the mountains to find Mom and Cody held at gunpoint. I told them about the planned sale of the mine and how we were to be held prisoners until the mine sale went through. A voice in my head kept reminding me about what Joel and Clay had both emphasized. *This is an ongoing investigation. If this all gets out it will greatly hamper our efforts to find these people and bring them to justice.* So I finished quickly. "Cody and I managed to escape. We went to the FBI, and eventually the gang was caught and we were freed."

"Thanks to Danni and Rick," Cody said. "They were awesome."

I poked him hard as I leaned down and whispered, "No more, Code."

After quickly consulting her notes, Kirstin turned back to me. "Rick? Is that Ricardo Ramirez, your boyfriend?"

"Yes," someone behind her called out. "That's him."

She didn't turn. "He's not my boyfriend," I said. "We're just good friends."

"Whatever. Was he kidnapped too?"

"No. After we escaped, Cody and I went to him, and he and his father helped us."

"This is the boy that was shot in the leg, right?"

"Yes."

"The people here tell me that you accidentally shot him. Is that true?"

I hesitated.

She bored in. "We called the clinic in Page, Arizona. They confirmed that Rick was a patient there in June but they wouldn't give us any information on the shooter."

"It wasn't Danni," Cody exclaimed. "El Cobra shot him."

"El Cobra?"

"Yes. The gang leader. That's what he called himself. The Snake. On the houseboat, El Cobra slapped Danni's face. Rick went after him like a torpedo and El Cobra shot him."

This time it was the cameraman who swung around on the crowd. They had erupted into a low roar. "Please, people. Quiet down."

Well, at least there'll be no more of this Danni Oakley stuff.

"And then El Cobra tried to kiss her, but Danni knocked him on—ow!"

The last came when I stomped on his foot. Hard. "That's enough, Code," I hissed.

For a moment, Kirstin looked like she might turn to Cody as her primary source, but then she changed her mind. "Danni, our source said that it was you and Rick who singlehandedly captured four members of the gang and turned them over to the FBI. Is that true?"

I was reeling. This anonymous source seemed to know everything. Gratefully, at that moment, the roar of a truck's engine interrupted us. There was a squeal of brakes and the crunch of tires on gravel. I swung around and gave a cry of relief. It was Dad's truck, and even as I watched, Dad, Grandpère, and Rick tumbled out and started toward us.

"There's Rick now," someone cried. "That's the boyfriend. That's Ricardo Ramirez."

Waving frantically for the cameraman to follow, Kirstin went to meet them. I reached down and grabbed Cody's shoulder, leaning in close. "No more, Cody. We're not supposed to be saying anything." Without waiting for his answer, I grabbed his hand and ran toward Dad. We easily passed Kirstin and the cameraman before they reached him.

I threw myself into Dad's arms. "Dad! Am I so glad to see you!"

He gave me a quick hug. "Sorry. We got a call from Clay telling us about this. We've been trying to call you to warn you for the last couple of hours and couldn't get through. We finally called the high school, but by then you'd left."

He stepped forward, placing himself between us and the news team. "I'm sorry, Miss Powers, but that will be all for now."

Kirstin made a little twirling motion with her finger for the cameraman to keep rolling. Dad saw it, started to react, then changed his mind. He raised both hands. Kirstin stopped, and the crowd surging in behind her stopped too. "I have just been on the phone with the FBI," he called out. "They have authorized me to make a brief statement."

Everyone instantly quieted. The cameraman moved up beside Kirstin.

"The anonymous source that called KSL-TV gave them information about a situation that happened about mid-June of this year. That was initially reported as a drug bust. In actuality, it was much more serious than that. It involved a home invasion and kidnapping of a local family with an attempt to extort money from them. KSL immediately contacted the FBI and are fully cooperating with their office in Salt Lake on this anonymous tip."

From Kirstin's expression, that was news to her.

"The anonymous information given is currently being studied, and further information will be forthcoming as it is evaluated. I am authorized to say this much. It was my family, including my father-in-law, who were kidnapped and held for ransom."

A cry went up from the crowd, but he went right on, raising his voice to be heard. "With the help of the FBI and other law-enforcement agencies, the perpetrators were captured and are now in prison. Other than the gunshot wound to Rick Ramirez's leg, no one else was injured."

I noticed the cameraman swing around and focus on Rick for a moment before swinging back to Dad.

"Since this is an ongoing investigation, much of what is known is still restricted information." He raised his voice as a moan of disappointment swept through the crowd. "However, there will be a joint FBI/UHP press conference tomorrow afternoon at four p.m. at the UHP station in Green River, which is about sixty miles north of here. Our family, along with Rick Ramirez, will be in attendance at that conference. Until then, we have no further comments."

CHAPTER 15

We were still pretty bummed out that evening, especially after watching me and Cody and Dad on the evening news. By this time, we had retreated into a bit of a fortress mentality. Dad finally had put up a sign at the gate of our property which read:

NO TRESPASSING. MEDIA PEOPLE—THIS MEANS YOU!!!

Which several interpreted to mean:

THIS IS THE MCALLISTER HOUSE. WELCOME.

Out on the highway, at the turnoff into our lane, we ended up with such a traffic jam that we had two deputies from the Wayne County Sheriff's office and a UHP cruiser dealing with it—something unheard of in Hanksville.

One TV truck parked itself on the lane outside our gate. Two more set up on the barren hills behind our house. Our phone rang until Dad unplugged it from its socket. My cell phone was chiming every minute or so, alerting me to incoming texts. Most were from my well-meaning but clueless friends, which I erased without answering. Rick called to say they were being bombarded too, though not to the same extent as us. We tried watching television but couldn't concentrate and finally gave up and sat around the table and just talked.

"What are we going to do about school tomorrow?" Mom asked Dad.

"Let's not go," Cody piped up.

"We can't go," I cried at the same time. "It'll be a nightmare."

"I agree," Dad said. "Besides, we have to be in Green River by four. You wouldn't make it."

Then, right on cue, Dad's phone rang. He took it off his belt and looked at it. Then he swiped at the screen and looked at the number. "It's Clay." He put it up to his ear. "Welcome to McAllisters-Under-Siege. How may I direct your call?"

We heard Clay's burst of laughter.

"Hold on," Dad said. "Let me put you on speakerphone." He punched a button, then set the cell on the table in front of us. "Okay," he said as we got settled, "we're all here."

"*Siege* is not a bad word for it. I hear you're surrounded."

"On every side," Mom said.

"Well, the mayor and the businesses of both Hanksville and Green River thank you. I understand every motel is fully booked and the restaurants have had to set up tables outside."

"Awesome!" Cody said.

Mom pulled a face.

"Listen. There have been some more developments, which require some adjustments to our schedule. With all that's happening, Joel Jamison has decided to fly out for the press conference tomorrow. He's coming in by private jet to Moab. I'm coming down to meet him and then I'll drive him to Green River. If we provide a diversion so you can get out of Hanksville without anyone following you, any chance you could meet us in Moab? Joel wants to make sure we're all on the same page before the press conference."

Dad looked at Mom, who was already nodding. "We'd love to get out of here," she said.

"Good. He's due in at about eleven."

"What about Rick and his dad? Do you want them there?" I asked.

"Not Charlie. He wants to keep Shauna and the girls out of this as much as possible. But Rick has to come. If you could pick him up, that would be great."

"What about school?" Cody piped up.

"No school for you guys tomorrow," Clay said.

"Yes!" Cody cried, smacking the table with his fist.

I felt a huge wash of relief. I was already picturing media mobs at our bus stop and hordes of gushing students when we got off the bus.

Clay went on. "About eight o'clock tomorrow morning, there will be a 'leak' from our office saying that a team of our agents are headed for Cathedral Valley to make a possible arrest."

"Really?" Mom asked. "Isn't all of the gang in prison already?"

He chuckled. "You know that, Angelique, and I know that. But the press doesn't. That should send them scrambling. Tell Rick to be ready. You'll need to pick him up and leave immediately once they clear out. We'll meet you in Moab at the Best Western Canyonlands Inn, there on Main Street. Let's say at about eleven fifteen. Okay?"

"Okay," Dad said.

There was a long silence. "Guys," Clay finally said, "these next few days are going to be rough. This has already been picked up by the national media. Our office has been flooded with calls."

"The national media?" I said.

"Yeah, I'm sorry. This is too hot to ignore. 'Two teens foil international gang of kidnappers.'" He let out a slow, discouraged breath. "We're going to have to deal with it. That's one of the things Joel wants to talk about with you."

"Can't you just make it all go away?" Mom asked, her voice forlorn.

It was Grandpère who answered. "When you scatter a bucket of feathers into the wind, there isn't any picking them up after that."

The GUARDIAN

When Clay and Joel Jamison walked into the small conference room where we were waiting, neither of them was smiling. And they both looked very tired. Jamison's mood lightened, though, as he shook hands with all of us. When he came to me, I couldn't resist. "So?" I asked.

He cocked his head. "So what?"

"Are you getting comfortable with the idea of *Le Gardien?*"

"Ha!" he snorted. "You may have to sleep with a five-hundred-pound sumo wrestler, but you never get quite comfortable with being in bed with him, particularly if it's a soft mattress. He just kind of rolls right over the top of you."

I laughed. "Good analogy," I said. "*Le Gardien,* the five-hundred-pound sumo wrestler. I like it."

He was immediately all business again. "Let's sit down. I have a few things to say before we talk about the press conference."

We all sat down again as Jamison extracted some papers and a manila envelope from his briefcase. He didn't sit down, but plunged right in.

"First, a couple of things of interest. We learned just yesterday that our prisoners finally have legal counsel. A high-powered law firm from New York has stepped up to represent them. We're not sure why it has taken them nearly three months to do so, but we're grateful that it did take that long. It's allowed us to move forward with our investigation without a lot of publicity. So while the press leak is a disappointment, it probably would have come out soon anyway."

He frowned. "Second, there is talk that the law firm plans to file motions for several of the prisoners to be extradited back to their home countries for prosecution for other crimes."

"You mean they'd let them free?" Mom cried.

"That's what they hope, but it will never happen. Our case here takes precedence."

I saw Mom visibly relax.

"Okay, now as to our anonymous caller. We're not sure he's European. He speaks with a perfect American accent. Probably from the East, maybe Boston. We're running it through our voice recognition database to see if we can find a match, but so far nothing. Beyond that, we don't have much, and I predict it will be a dead end. Whoever made the call used some highly sophisticated equipment to make it untraceable, but we think it came from somewhere in Europe. Whoever these people are, they are very savvy and very, very sophisticated."

None of us said anything. We just sat there, looking glum.

"What we haven't told you is that in addition to the anonymous call, an envelope was delivered to the station last night about eight o'clock." He picked up the envelope and hefted it. "Fortunately, we have prevailed upon KSL to keep it under wraps until the press conference this afternoon. But it's not good. It outlines the story of the kidnapping. In more detail than was given in the phone call. I mean considerably more detail."

"Like what?" Dad asked.

"Like what happened in Cathedral Valley—what time it was, who was there, the setup, and how Danni foiled El Cobra's trap. And like—"

"Wait," I exclaimed. "Did they say anything about the pouch stuff, like the pistol turning hot or the doll it made?"

"Or what about the gold bars?" Dad asked.

"No, none of that, thank heavens," Joel answered. "Which puzzles us, actually. If they know so much, why not mention the pouch? Why say only that the boat swamped?" He rubbed at his forehead like he had a headache. "Once the press conference is over, I don't think we can hold the media back from releasing most of what they have. I'm sorry. I'm afraid the spotlight on you guys is going to remain pretty intense for a while."

Mom was drawing patterns on the tabletop with her finger and didn't look up when she spoke. "Then doesn't it have to be coming from El Cobra? Or Eileen? They were the only ones who knew about the boat."

Clay answered. "No. This source has information that none of the prisoners could have known."

"Like what?" I exclaimed.

"Like Cody's hay fort in the barn. El Cobra never found you there, so he knew nothing about that. Or that you got away on an ATV, then went to Rick's house and hid it by the river. Those are details none of the gang would know."

Grandpère cleared his throat. "And no mention of the pouch at all?"

"Not a word. Not even a hint." Joel rubbed at his eyes.

"That doesn't make sense," Rick said. "If they know everything else, why not tell the press about the pouch?"

"None of it makes sense," Joel said gloomily. "And I don't like things that don't make sense."

———

By three o'clock, when we arrived from Moab, Green River was crawling with media people. Cars, SUVs, and vans with their satellite dishes and antennae lined both sides of Main Street for a block in each direction. Men and women milled outside of the small UHP building. There were cameras, microphones, and wires snaking across the ground everywhere. The newspaper people watched with an air of faint superiority.

Clay had warned us that we might have national news coverage, which we did. ABC, CBS, NBC, Fox News, CNN—all of them were there. But what was a surprise was the "local" television and radio stations that were also there—"local" including not just the stations from Salt Lake City, but one from Phoenix, two from Las Vegas, two from Denver, and one from Los Angeles. I have to admit, it was pretty darn intimidating.

Inside, in addition to Clay and Joel and Shayla, we had the Superintendent of the Utah Highway Patrol, four other FBI agents, and the county sheriffs of Wayne County—our home county—and three other surrounding counties. With our family and UHP support staff, we were packed in like pickles in a bottle. But it was pretty organized. I guess that's because they were all law-enforcement officers, and being organized is what they do.

At four minutes to four, Joel called us to attention. "Okay, folks. It's time." He turned to us. "Normally, we don't have victims of a crime participate in a press conference. Especially when it involves an ongoing investigation. But, after much discussion, we decided that where the media already have so much information about you—and are likely to get much more—we think they're going to hound you to death anyway, so we'd recommend you join with us."

"We understand," Dad said.

"Are you going to let them ask us questions?" Mom asked.

Clay and Joel exchanged looks, then Joel answered. "The media cannot interview you if you refuse to be interviewed. But . . ." He sighed. "If you do take questions, we'll limit the time to about ten minutes. It's up to you. Totally your choice."

We looked at each other. Dad spoke first. "What we have out there is like a shark feeding frenzy. And the best way to stop that is to feed them something."

"I don't want to answer any questions," Mom said.

"We can state that up front," Clay said. "You can have one person be the spokesman for all of you if you wish." He looked at me. "But it will be Danni and Rick they're really hoping for." Cody raised his hand. "And Cody," Clay added with a smile.

"Thank you," he said, clearly miffed. He shot me a dark look. "Danni can be a real glory hog when she sets her mind to it."

"Not!" I cried.

But then Cody laughed, and Joel went on. "Are you up to it, Danni?" he asked. "Like it or not, you're the one with the target painted on your chest."

I wasn't sure what to say. I knew he was right. If the information given to KSL was that detailed, they were going to know I took the lead role in all of this. But I did have the pouch with me. That would help. After a few moments, I nodded. "I guess. Yeah, I'll do it."

Joel was pleased. "Good." He consulted his notes again. As he did so, Rick leaned in. "You can do this, Danni. You are the most amazing girl I've ever known."

For a moment, I just gawked at him. Then I wanted to throw my arms around him and . . . well, I decided I'd better not go there. "And if things get crazy," I added, "and I start doing something stupid, will you step on my foot, or knock me alongside the head?"

He laughed. "It will be my pleasure."

I saw that Joel was watching us and had heard the interchange. "You'll be okay, Danni. Clay and I can step in too."

"Thank you."

"Okay." He looked at the papers he held. "Here's how it will work. After Superintendent Callahan reads his statement, I'll speak for the FBI. We will then open it up for questions. At first, only Superintendent Callahan, myself, Agent Zabriskie, and Officer Blake will answer questions for about twenty minutes. Then we'll give them just a few minutes to talk to the family." He looked at Mom. "And I'll tell them you will not be responding."

"Thank you."

"Okay, then, let's do it." He looked at all of us. "The important thing to remember is to limit yourself to the information we will give in the official statements. They will all be given copies of those statements. But we're going to stress that this is still an active criminal investigation. The most frequent answer you're going to hear from me and the Superintendent is, 'Sorry, we cannot comment on that at this time.'"

We nodded, but there wasn't much else to say, and so Joel motioned to one of the agents, who moved to the door. "Here we go," Joel muttered, "into the jaws of hell."

I looked at Rick. "You ready to become a rock star, Ramirez?"

His look said it all. I'm sure he was wishing that after I had bloodied his nose back in the fourth grade, he had given me a wide berth from that point ever after.

The moment we came out the door, a wall of sound blasted at us. Camera flashes started popping off so fast that even in the brightness of the afternoon sunlight, they were quite annoying. The men and women behind a line of cameras on tripods jumped to attention and started rolling their equipment. Journalists of all kinds started pushing in for better positions.

Beyond the inner circle of media people, a large crowd filled the parking lot. I saw a couple of uniformed officers at the back, making sure the spectators didn't spill out onto Main Street into traffic. I assumed that most of Green River had come to hear this. Then I stopped as I saw several hands waving and people smiling at us. I shaded my eyes and saw that half of Hanksville had come too. The joys of small-town living. We were the only show in town—or in about three counties too, for that matter.

It quickly became obvious that Joel Jamison had been through this many times before, because things transpired pretty much as he predicted. He stepped to the portable lectern and held up his hands. Gradually, the mob quieted. He introduced himself and Clay, then Superintendent Callahan and Officer Blake. He also acknowledged the county sheriffs who were behind us, looking like a corps of bodyguards. He then briefly outlined the program before turning the microphone— or microphones, as there were more than a dozen of them attached to the podium—over to Callahan.

His statement took no more than two minutes. He explained how the Utah Highway Patrol had become involved when Officer Shayla Blake was caught up in the drama and played a significant role in helping capture two of the perpetrators at Leprechaun Canyon. He thanked the Deputy Director for keeping him informed and assured him that the FBI had the full cooperation of the UHP. "That concludes my statement," he said, and stepped back.

The FBI's statement was thorough but terse. Joel read it in a near monotone, without any emotion. He briefly outlined what had happened, not going into much detail, promising that the written statement included more. He said at least four times that since this was an ongoing investigation, etc., etc., etc. It was a pretty sterile outline of events. There was no mention of El Cobra by name, only that there were about ten perpetrators involved, who now were all behind bars. He mentioned the ransom demands without giving the actual amount. He did say that Cody and I had managed to escape, but gave no detail about how we had done that.

I have to admit, it was a bit disappointing because it all came out pretty flat. I was hoping he would at least mention how I had taken Gordo out by hitting him with the butt of my rifle. To be honest, I was still pretty pumped about that. That had been my idea, and it had worked perfectly.

The rest came in quick succession. The houseboat at Lake Powell, Cody and me going to Rick's house for help, the exchange of Cody in Cathedral Valley.

Here again, I felt a little touch of irritation. He was really vague about Cathedral Valley and made it sound like Rick and I just did whatever we were told by the FBI. However, he did say that I was the one who did the actual negotiating with the leader of the gang, which led to the capture of two of their men.

Negotiating? Rick was blasting away at them with his rifle and I had mine pointed at El Cobra's chest. Some negotiations. But at least Rick and I finally got a little credit.

He made no mention of Leprechaun Canyon but jumped right to the final day on the houseboat. When he paused to take a drink of water, several hands shot up. He ignored them. He finished drinking, wiped at his brow, and went back to his paper.

"Agent Zabriskie had several teams on the ground by that time," he concluded, "but unfortunately, the head of the group had acquired one of our radios and was monitoring our communications. Things kind of fell apart there for a few minutes as the gang made plans to escape, taking Danni and her grandfather as hostages. That was also when Mr. Ramirez was shot in the leg by the gang leader.

"Fortunately, through some clever maneuvering, Danni and her grandfather managed to throw the gang off their stride, and we were able to move in and put an end to the whole situation."

By this time, the corps of media people were stunned. He had just dropped about thirteen bombshells in his bored, tired voice, and they were totally blown away. They kept staring at me and Rick until I felt like a bug at a birdbath.

Lowering the paper from which he had been reading, Joel looked up. "That concludes our official statements. Copies will be made available to each member of the media at the end of the conference. Superintendent Callahan, Agent Zabriskie, Officer Blake, and I will now take questions."

I thought that was an interesting way to put it. *Take* questions, not necessarily *answer* questions.

"Please, no questions for the family at this point. You'll have that opportunity in a few minutes. Okay, let's begin."

———

I started counting. In the next fifteen minutes, I heard this phrase at least fourteen times: "We cannot comment on that aspect since this is still an ongoing investigation." Not that it stopped the dumb questions. Where had these people gotten their journalism degrees? At the Walmart Customer Service Counter?

On the other hand, some questions were pretty insightful. For example, a scruffy-looking guy with a heavy beard asked: "Why would the FBI allow two teenagers to serve as bait to entrap professional criminals? Didn't that put them in real danger?"

Joel calmly handed that one off to Clay, who fielded it with ease. "Let me make a couple of points. First of all, you have to remember that Danni and Cody were the only access we had to the rest of the family. The leader kept in touch with Danni via her cell phone. Second, we had credible evidence that it was counter to the gang's interest to hurt the family in any way as long as they cooperated. Third, had we tried to intervene directly, we might have lost the family. So we assessed the risk, then set up a complete backup system so we could inject ourselves into the situation at a moment's notice. If we hadn't kept Danni and Cody free and in contact with them, this would have turned out very differently. "

I stepped forward. "And fourth, that's the way I asked that it be. They wanted to keep me out of it, but I knew if they did, I might lose my family."

Joel frowned at me, but fortunately a hand shot up near the front of the crowd. Clay pointed to her. She had a KUTV-4 logo on her blouse. "This is for Danni. Tell us about Leprechaun Canyon. Is it true that you and Rick trapped two more of the gang members there?"

Joel stepped forward. "Hold on. Before we switch to the family, are there are any more questions for the four of us?"

It looked like there were, but I think they were more eager to have at us, so no one raised their hands. Joel waited for about ten seconds, then nodded at me. "Go ahead. But please note that Mrs. McAllister would prefer not to answer any questions at this time, so please honor that request." Then he nodded at me to continue.

Remembering his advice about keeping things short, I explained how Doc and Gordo had intercepted us and taken Shayla Blake hostage as well, then briefly described what had happened in the slot canyon. I was careful to praise Officer Blake and Rick for the roles they took in all of it. Of course, I made no mention of the mysterious writing on the rearview mirror. Or of a kiss that occurred somewhere deep inside the canyon.

I had barely finished before hands were up, waving wildly, and everyone was shouting at me. Joel pointed to a man near the front with the logo of one of the Denver television stations on his shirt pocket.

"This is for Miss McAllister. Danni, could you describe how you and Cody managed to escape from your house when there were half a dozen men holding guns on you?"

Cody stirred beside me, but I hurriedly spoke up before he could blurt out something about invisibility. "I think there were eight in the house with us, and one of them was a woman." I glanced quickly at Joel to see if he thought I was giving away too much, but he nodded for me to go on. "Actually, we escaped twice. The first time, my grandfather created a diversion, and Cody and I ran out of the house and hid in the attic. But they found us. The second time, El Cobra tossed a pistol on the table and it accidentally went off. When everyone dove for cover, Cody and I took off again. This time we hid under some hay bales in the barn, and they couldn't find us."

I was sorely tempted to tell them about Gordo and our brilliant little trap, but I pushed it away. "When the gang finally gave up and left, taking Mom, Dad, and Grandpère with them, Cody and I waited for about an hour, then took one of our four-wheelers and headed for Rick's house."

"Grandpère?" he asked, looking puzzled.

I smiled at Grandpère. "Yes, that's French for Grandfather. Since my grandfather is French, that's what we all call him."

He started to ask another follow-up question, but a woman about three rows back was waving her hand and shouting. Joel pointed at her. The others moved back a little so we could see her better. I was surprised at how young she looked—in her early twenties and probably out on her first big press conference. "Mr. McAllister, did you agree with the FBI's decision to actively involve your children in the rescue attempt of you and your wife?"

Dad gave her one of his quirky looks. "Well, as has been stated, my wife and I and my father-in-law were taken hostage and rushed away to a houseboat on Lake Powell. So, it would have been a little awkward for the FBI to call and ask for our permission."

She flushed as laughter erupted from those around her. "But—"

"But," Dad went on smoothly, "my wife and I are completely satisfied that the FBI made the right decision."

Obviously angry and embarrassed, she shot right back. "But what if things hadn't turned out as they did?"

To my astonishment, Mom spoke up from behind Dad. "I'm not sure that speculation constitutes valid content for the six o'clock news. Are you?"

The reporter went bright red as there was a smattering of applause from the crowd.

Mom came forward to stand beside Dad. "I will say this much. As Carruthers has told you, she took an active part in that decision. Though she is only sixteen, she's got a good head on her—" She turned and looked at me, and I saw that her eyes were glistening. "And she is incredibly brave. And, Rick—" She turned to him. "Rick is like a boulder in the middle of a rushing river. Always there, always steady, no matter what's going on around him. Knowing he was with Carruthers was a great comfort to us."

Rick the Rock, I thought. *Not bad.* I wondered if the media would pick up on that.

As other hands shot up, she went on softly, "And to be honest, we felt that they were not alone. My husband and my father and I were all praying pretty hard for some divine protection, and I think our prayers were answered."

Out of the corner of my eye, I saw Joel tense a little, wondering if she was going to be more specific and mention *Le Gardien,* but she stepped back and refused to respond to the questions being called out to her.

And so it went. Someone asked Dad if we were wealthy, and if not, why we were targeted for kidnapping and extortion. Without mentioning rhodium by name, he told them briefly about the sale of the mine. "Somehow, they knew about that, and that was what they were after."

The next question was for Rick. From Kirstin, anchorwoman of KSL-TV. "We know now that it wasn't Danni who shot you, as originally reported. Could you tell us why you told everyone that it was Danni?"

He shrugged. "At that point, there were still some gang members at large, so we felt it best to pass it off as an accidental shooting."

There was an instant eruption. Joel held up his hands and called out, "One at a time, please." Then he pointed to someone in the back.

"How did it feel to be shot?" More groans. Another graduate of the Dumb-It-Down School of Journalism. With his usual laconic drawl, Rick said, "It hurt. A lot."

"Why did the gang leader shoot you?"

Much better question. Same laconic answer. "Because I made him mad."

"How?"

"I got in his face." And he refused to give any more details.

Cody was next and quickly became the star of the show. He was funny, quick, droll, and delightful. And—no surprise—loving every minute of it. Clay finally stepped up beside him and would lay a hand on his shoulder and give it a little squeeze if he started saying too much. The media people loved that, too. No question about who was going to get the most air time out of this.

I was a little surprised that not a single question was directed at Grandpère. It was like he was a nonentity. Which was as he wished it, I'm sure.

The session came to an abrupt halt about five minutes later, when the same clueless young woman reporter blurted out a question without being called upon: "Danni, did anyone in the gang ever threaten you sexually?"

Joel quickly stepped up. "The answer is no, but that ends our conference." Groans. Dirty looks thrown at the woman, whose head was up in defiance now. "Be sure to get your copies of the two statements before you leave. We'll let you know when the next update will be."

And just like that, we were done.

CHAPTER 16

Outside the Highway Patrol office, things were finally quiet. The media people were gone, the Hanksville people had left for home, and the Green River locals had finally decided that Joel was serious and there really would be nothing more happening today. Shayla Blake had already taken off. She was going south to coordinate handling the crowds with the Wayne County Sheriff's office.

Inside, Superintendent Callahan had ordered in pizzas and soft drinks for us while we had watched the five o'clock news coming in from Salt Lake City. There wasn't much. Even though they had the capability to upload their feeds via satellites in real time, the editors and producers back in studio would have to put things together.

We were the lead story. There were brief clips of Callahan and Jamison, then quick shots of me, Rick, and Cody answering questions. Kirstin Powers closed the segment with a promise of much more to come on the six o'clock and ten o'clock broadcasts. Then they went on to other things—all of which seemed deadly dull after our segment—so we turned it off.

At that point, Joel went into one of the offices and started making phone calls. Clay and Superintendent Callahan took the other office and started talking strategy. Mom and Dad and Grandpère moved over in the corner and began talking quietly. I could tell they were troubled by all of this. I thought I knew why, but I was still tempted to go over and tell them to chill out. It hadn't turned out to be nearly as bad as I had feared.

I looked up as Superintendent Callahan and Clay came back out to join us. "You did well," Callahan said. "All of you." He looked at Cody and laughed softly. "I think I'll request you for every press conference we have. You're a natural."

"Amen," Clay said. "You handled yourself like a pro, Cody."

Cody blushed a little—not because he thought they were overstating things, only because the compliment had caught him by surprise. I could tell that he was pretty pleased with himself.

"Unfortunately, it's not over yet," Clay said. "We didn't give them much this afternoon, but that won't stop them. These people are good at what they do, and you can bet they're already out there digging hard for more details. By tonight, you'll be the lead story on virtually every channel, and I predict you'll be on the front page of the morning papers. This is too big—too hot a story—for them to simply let it die."

Clay picked it up. "Not only that. I'm sure by now you three are burning up the Internet on Facebook and Twitter, and I predict that Cody's portion of the conference will be viral on YouTube by morning."

Cody was beaming like the fox who just got into the henhouse. Mom, who had turned around to listen, was not. "I guess there is no way to stop all that from happening?"

Both law-enforcement officers shook their heads. "Not now," Clay said.

Callahan spoke up. "I know this is upsetting, Mrs. McAllister, but you're going to have to face it sooner or later, so I would think sooner is better. Your husband was right. This is a feeding frenzy, and until they're satiated, we have to be sure it doesn't get out of hand. Officer Blake is on her way to work with the local deputies to keep things in hand. I've also asked for a couple of our officers from Richfield to come over to Bicknell and be there at the school before the kids arrive. We'll also post someone near your home and Rick's home to keep the media at bay. Oh, and there will be a deputy on the bus both going to and coming from school."

"What about school tomorrow?" I asked. I was picturing what would happen when Cody and I stepped off the bus at Bicknell. To be honest, it wasn't a totally unpleasant picture. It was time that Danni Oakley was put to rest and Danni McAllister got a little share of the glory, before Cody hogged it all. I felt a little stab of guilt. No question about who was the real glory hog here, but he had been awesome. And I was proud of him.

"Is all of that necessary?" Dad asked. "You're not worried about physical threats to them, are you?"

"No, not at all. This is more like crowd control. We can't stop a crowd from forming; we just want to make sure it doesn't get out of hand."

There was a knock on the door, then another highway patrolman stuck his head in and spoke to Callahan. "Sir, we have the mayor of Hanksville here. He is requesting a brief audience with the McAllisters."

We all turned at that. Mayor Brackston? That seemed a little odd.

Clay turned to my parents. "Any objection?"

Mom and Dad exchanged puzzled looks, then Mom nodded and Dad shrugged. "Why not?"

Callahan nodded at his officer, and we all got to our feet as he turned and went out again. A moment later, Mayor Brackston entered the room. John Brackston owned one of the two restaurants in town, and, as with many in the food preparation industry, the benefits of good cooking showed around his waist. He was about fifty, a jovial man with a ready smile and a strong handshake. Everyone liked him. But something about him was a little strange now, and for a moment I wasn't sure what it was. Then I had it. He was wearing a suit and a string tie, along with his ever-present straw cowboy hat and cowboy boots. As he swept off his hat, I saw that his forehead was shiny with perspiration.

"Hello, John," Dad said, going over to shake his hand. "Didn't know you were here."

"Wouldn't have missed it for the world," he boomed. "Big day. Very exciting." Then he instantly sobered. "What a shocker. We had no idea what you were going through. No idea."

Dad gave him one of his crooked grins. "Wasn't much time to stop by City Hall and report."

He barked with laughter. "No, I suppose not. But it all turned out well, thanks be to the good Lord for that." He turned to us kids. "And you three. My, my. Who would have guessed that we had heroes right in our very own town?" He corrected himself quickly. "Well, two heroes and a heroine. That's amazing. Well done."

"Thank you." I was beaming a little now too, finally.

Then he got right to business. "Sorry to interrupt. I know you're busy, but we wanted to talk to you about a proposition."

As he said that, I noticed that Joel was now off the phone and standing at the door of the office watching.

"A proposition?" Mom said.

"Yes. We would like to declare Saturday as 'Honor Our Heroes' day in Hanksville. I've already spoke with LaVere—" He stopped to take a breath, looking at Clay and the Deputy Director. "He's the high school principal over in Bicknell. He's agreed to bring over the marching band. He was thrilled, actually. And I was just talking to the mayor of Green River, and he thinks their high school will come too. Heck, I wouldn't be surprised if Moab doesn't want to join in as well. I mean, this is a big deal, people. There'll be a free hotcake breakfast in the morning and a barbecue that night. We've already called a fireworks place in Salt Lake, and they think they can put up a fireworks show by then."

He was almost bubbling as he looked around at us. "It'll be a real celebration."

"Awesome," Cody whispered beside me.

I looked at Rick. He looked pretty much like I expected—like someone had just jabbed him in the backside with a very long needle.

"Well, well," Clay said to Mom. "How about that?"

Mom was frowning. "I . . ." She shook her head. "Sounds like a lot of fuss over nothing."

"Nothing?" John was shocked right down to his boots. "This is hardly nothing, Angelique."

"I know, but . . . it just seems like a little much. We were hoping to let this all die down."

My mind was racing. A parade? Fireworks? Just for us? It was pretty dizzying when you stopped to think about it. One part of me was thinking about how ridiculous I was going to feel. And what did one wear on a float? I pictured me and Rick and Cody waving and throwing candy to the kids. Then it hit me: No floats. Not with just two days' notice. On the other hand—

Behind us, Joel cleared his throat and came forward. "Joel," said Dad, "this is Mayor John Brackston, from Hanksville. He has—"

"I heard." He turned to John. "That's a wonderful idea, Mayor. However—" He took a quick breath. "I'm afraid the McAllisters won't be available this weekend."

"We won't?" Mom and I said it almost exactly together.

"They won't?" the mayor cried in dismay.

"No, I'm sorry. Something's come up," Joel said, looking at Dad. "I was just coming out to talk to you about it." Then he turned back to the mayor. "But hold that thought, Mayor Brackston. I think when the time is right it would be a wonderful thing to honor this family."

Then Grandpère, who had been strangely quiet since this whole thing had started this afternoon, spoke. "It's kind of you to think of us, John. Thank you."

———

As our mayor left, you would have thought someone had just burned down his restaurant. Joel waited until he was gone, then motioned for us to sit at the table. As we did so, I saw that he held several slips of paper in his hand. He didn't join us, but stood at the head of the table.

"Mack, Angelique, I apologize. I should have conferred with you before saying no, but there has been a new development." He looked at Cody, who was in half a pout. "Sorry, Son. But I think we can compensate for your great loss."

"He'll get over it," I said, with some satisfaction.

"What is it?" Mom asked.

Joel was clearly not happy with what he was about to say. "This is not unexpected, but things are happening much faster than I thought." He lifted the papers and waved them back and forth. "I've just been on the phone with my executive assistant in Washington. She's been fielding a stream of phone calls and emails. We're barely an hour past the news conference and already excerpts are being aired in the national news media—Fox News Channel, CNN, MSNBC. The word is out and spreading like a wildfire."

Mom sighed. "I'm not sure I want to hear this."

He looked at his papers. "What I have here are invitations for you and your family, Angelique."

"Invitations?" she said warily.

He began reading the slips one by one. "All five of you are invited to be on the *Today Show* with Matt Lauer. Ditto for *Good Morning, America.* Fox News has offered Danni and Rick their choice of appearing in the morning with *Fox and Friends* or on *The O'Reilly Factor* that night."

"Me?" Rick exclaimed. "I'm not part of this."

I gave him a pitying look. "You're the one who got shot rescuing a damsel in distress, Cowboy. Of course you're part of it."

"What about me?" Cody asked.

"The Disney Channel wants to do an exclusive with you," Joel said with a smile.

"Awesome!"

Joel went on. "David Letterman wants all three of you kids on, as does Jay Leno."

"Jay Leno?" I exclaimed. "Shut up!"

Evidently Joel had raised enough teenagers to understand the meaning of my last exclamation, for he took it without a blink. "Leno could be a problem because his studio is in California. All the rest are in New York. And these are just the main ones. We have four or five other inquiries, and we think that number will double by morning."

"I warned you," Clay said. He made quote marks in the air with his fingers. "'Teenage Kids Outwit International Kidnappers.' This is the kind of stuff journalists dream of."

Joel set the papers on the table and sat down. "Before you decide how to handle all this, here's something to consider. In addition to paying all travel expenses, several are offering 'incentives' if you agree to be on their shows."

"Define *incentives*," I said.

"Picking you up in their private jets. Luxury hotel accommodations. Perhaps an extended stay in New York. A couple of producers are even offering to set up education trust funds for the three kids. Danni, Cody, and Rick could come out of this with ten, maybe even fifteen thousand dollars each, salted away for their college educations."

Judging from Cody's eyes, you would have thought an alien had just walked into the room. "Ten thousand dollars? Seriously? For just talking to people? You're kidding, right?"

Joel solemnly shook his head. "You'll find that in our business, we don't kid much, Cody." He leaned forward, focusing on Mom and Dad now. "I know that you have reservations about all the glitz and the attention, but you can't just wave your hand and make it go away. The Wayne County Sheriff's office called to say news crews and paparazzi are already swarming Hanksville. Motels from Price to Blanding are booked solid. Every van and SUV at the Salt Lake International Airport is rented or reserved. We heard from Capitol Reef National Park that their phone lines have been swamped all day. They expect lines of cars to show up by tomorrow. Guess what the number-one inquiry is?"

"Leprechaun Canyon," Rick said quietly.

"Exactly. The BLM says their website on the Irish Canyons can't keep up with the traffic. They already have a request to film a reenactment of the events that took place in Cathedral Valley with Danni, Cody, and Rick starring as themselves."

"Cody wasn't there," I noted for the record.

But then I saw Mom's face. She looked deeply dismayed, so I jumped in before she made up her mind. "It's New York, Mom. How many times have you and Dad talked about going there? So let's go. We'll do five or six shows—bam, bam, bam—and then stay on for a few more days. Go to some Broadway plays. Visit the Metropolitan Museum of Art."

"See the Statue of Liberty," Cody added.

I could see Dad watching Mom closely, trying to gauge how she was taking it. "Danni's right, Hon. It would be a great experience for us and the kids."

Then I had an absolutely brilliant idea. "What if I promise that while we're being interviewed, I just happen to mention the fact that you are a successful western artist? You'll have New York galleries begging to show your works."

She shook her head. "Bribes from the producers. Bribes from my own kids. Pressure from my husband. The FBI telling me that it's only going to get worse." She turned to Clay and Joel. "So what happens if we just say no? What if we don't care about their incentives? What if we just say that we are not going to put our family in the national spotlight?"

"It's too late for that," Clay said gently. "You are in that spotlight, and all you can do now is try to control it as much as possible."

She swung on Grandpère. "What do you think, Dad? And you don't need to remind me that the feathers are already scattered on the wind. I get that, okay?"

He was thoughtful, obviously carefully considering her question. "Tempting as your solution is, my dear, I fear that Clay is right. It could create an even bigger problem."

"Like what?" Mom said.

"If we refuse to talk to the media, then they'll go elsewhere for their information. They'll be interviewing every kook, goofball, airhead, and ditz from here to New York. And what they'll get from them will be wild speculation, half-truths, opinions—"

"Even pure fabrications," Clay added.

"So," Grandpère finished, "I say let's go to New York and give them the truth. Let's not turn this into a worse sideshow than it already is."

Mom's gaze was locked with Grandpère's for a long time, but still she didn't relent. "I—I don't know, anymore. I don't want this to change our kids. I don't want it to change us. Can it never be the same again?"

Grandpère got up and went around to stand behind her. He started massaging her shoulders very gently. "I know it is discouraging, but it is not hopeless," he said. "If you'll pardon another metaphor, we need to remember that the media are like California surfers. They're out there, offshore, sitting on their boards, searching the horizon for signs of the next big wave. When they spot it, they start paddling madly out to meet it. The race is on to see who gets there first and who catches the longest ride. But even as they catch that wave and start riding it into shore, they're already looking over their shoulders for the next big one."

Joel looked at him with renewed respect. "A perfect analogy, Jean-Henri."

Bending down, Grandpère kissed the top of Mom's head. "All we have to do," he said to Mom, "is pray that the next wave is not far behind ours."

We sat there watching Mom, not making a sound. I don't know about the others, but I was holding my breath. Finally, there was a slow nod, followed by instant relief. "All right, I agree."

"Wicked!" Cody cried, leaping to his feet.

I started to punch the air, then stopped halfway up. "And Rick too, right?"

Rick had his head down and was examining his hands. "I think our family would rather face the media back here."

"I understand," Clay said. "But back here it will be your whole family, Rick. Go to New York and get this over with, and I think they'll leave the rest of your family alone."

"When would all this take place?" Dad asked.

"Well, that's why I suggested to Mayor Brackston that you might not be available on Saturday," Joel said. "Here's what I've been thinking. You head home tonight—with an escort, of course—and get a good night's sleep. In the morning, pack your things—let's say enough for a week—and then drive over to Moab. I've already told *The Today Show* that there's a good chance you would accept their offer for a private jet. They're just waiting for your approval. With that, you'll be in New York by late tomorrow afternoon. That will give you Friday, Saturday, and Sunday to see New York before you start the first interviews Monday morning."

Cody was up and doing a little dance. I was in much better control. I turned and punched Rick hard on the shoulder. "Seriously wicked!" I said. "Rock stars, Ramirez. That's what I'm talking about. Just like I said."

Mom was still less than excited about this. "How many shows?"

"Good question," Joel said. "We'd recommend you accept five, maybe six of the invitations. The ones who will give you the best and widest coverage. And we'll say no to all the rest. Let's say that would take Monday through Wednesday. You'd be back home by Thursday night."

Mom's head was down. "In time for the parades, the paparazzi, the news crews, the crowds." She shook her head. "Will it never end?"

Clay answered this one. "We'll keep deputies and highway patrol officers there until the frenzy dies away."

Grandpère raised one hand. "What if we were to just disappear instead?"

That got Joel's attention. "What was that?"

"Angelique's right. All those interviews on national television are only going to pour more blood into the water. The feeding frenzy is only going to intensify."

"Disappear where?" Mom said.

He smiled that mischievous little smile that was so French it always made me laugh. "Well, a strange thing happened this last week, before all of this burst upon us. I got an email from Le Petit Château, of all places."

Mom's head jerked up. "Le Petit Château?"

I shot to my feet. "You mean the one in France?"

"I know of no other. It seems that someone has purchased the old homestead, which has been empty for several years now, and they have turned it into an exclusive bed and breakfast and guest house. And they are looking for guests. As an introductory offer—I'm sure to get a guest list started—they are offering half price for up to six guests for the first month."

I sat back down, my head spinning.

Grandpère went on. "For years I've wanted to take Cody and Danni there. Let them see the place of their ancestors. So why not now?"

"Omigosh!" I cried. "France? We're really going to France?"

He turned to me. "For you especially, *ma chérie*. I would like to be the one who shows you the home of your namesake, Monique LaRoche, my mother and your great-grandmother. Maybe even find that Gestapo headquarters in Paris where my father was held prisoner."

"Oh, yes, Grandpère. Yes! Yes! Yes!"

Cody was actually struck dumb and just stood there gaping at him.

But Grandpère had eyes only for Mom. "You have a graduate degree. I think you could home school the children for a month or two, don't you?"

Eyes filled with wonder, Mom finally nodded. "I think I could manage that."

Joel interrupted our celebration. "When would you go?"

"The day after the last interview. We'd pack for more than a week, then simply get on a plane and disappear."

Clay spoke to his boss. "In a way, this is like putting them into a witness protection program. If we sent them on one of our planes, there would be no way the media could track them."

"I like it," Joel said. "I like it a lot."

"Good," Grandpère said. "I thought you might, so I took the liberty of reserving us five rooms, beginning a week from tomorrow."

"Don't forget Big Ben," Cody said. "We have to stop and see Big Ben and Parliament."

"Maybe on the way back. But I think we need to go right there, keep the profile down."

"Wait," I said. "You said five rooms?"

"But, of course," Grandpère said, turning to Rick. "I also took the liberty of calling your father after the news conference. I explained our dilemma, and he agreed that it was best that you disappear for a time too."

"I can't go to France," Rick said. "No way!"

I whirled. "Why not?"

"I—um—because I don't have a passport?"

"*Not!*" I cried. "That's not why you don't want to go." He was thinking about how much it would cost.

"But he makes a point," Clay said. "Do the rest of you have passports?"

Dad nodded. "We got them a couple of years ago when we took a trip to Canada."

Joel looked at Rick. "We can work out the passport, walk it through by hand while you're in New York. Is there another reason you can't go?"

His face turned red. "I . . . I can't just leave my family. Dad needs me."

Grandpère went on. "Rick, our family owes you an enormous debt. Mack and I agree that part of the money from the sale of those bags of ore is yours. That is what's paying for our trip, and that is what is paying for yours."

"But—"

I leaned in and whispered in his ear. "Ramirez, this would be a very good time to shut your mouth and nod your head up and down vigorously."

Which he did.

PART FIVE

New York, New York

CHAPTER 17

Marriott Marquis, Times Square, New York City
September 20, 2011

Sorry that it has taken so long for me to finally get around to writing in my journal, but these last five days have been amazing—incredibly wild and incredibly wonderful. Once again, Night-Owl Danni is up and awake while everyone else has crashed and burned.

Since this is probably going to be my only chance for a while to write, and also because our next appearance tomorrow isn't until 1:00, I'm going to try to catch up on all that's happened since we got here.

THURSDAY: We were up most of the night packing after getting back from Green River. Knowing we were leaving for a month or six weeks instead of a few days put Mom in a real panic. But Dad finally said we could buy things as we needed them and for each of us to take only one large suitcase and a travel bag. We had an extra suitcase that we gave to Rick. Who, BTW, is still pretty much in a daze.

Late that morning, we drove to the airport north of Moab, where we met Clay and a couple of his agents. Shayla Blake was also there. They came to see us off, but also to make sure we weren't hassled by any media—which we weren't. The private jet was already there waiting.

Cody thought the jet was way awesome. I told him to settle down. After all, if you've seen one private jet, you've seen them all. LOL. Rick, who's only flown on an airplane once before, got pretty excited about it—though you have to know him pretty well to tell when he's excited.

We arrived in NYC about 7:30 Eastern Time. Our hotel is the Marriott Marquis, right on Times Square. How cool is that? Even the name is French. But this is seriously wicked. I can look out our window and see the big ball they lower on New Year's Eve here in the Square. Anyway, it was about nearly 11:00 by then, so even though that's only 9:00 Utah time, we were all exhausted and totally crashed.

FRIDAY: All day sightseeing. Amazing day. We started with a visit to The National September 11 Memorial on Manhattan Island. That was deeply moving, especially since we celebrated the tenth anniversary of the attack on the twin towers of the World Trade Center just nine days ago. It was a powerful reminder of what Mom has said many times. Us kids are facing some pretty challenging times and we'd better be prepared.

Next we took a ferry out to the Statue of Liberty. I expected to be wowed by the statue (whose real name is "Liberty Enlightening the World"), but it was even more amazing than I expected. It was totally awesome. Cody, Rick, and I decided to climb the steps to the top. I guess you need tickets to do that, which are sold out months in advance, but good old Clay had enough for all of us. Mom went with us. Dad and Grandpère said they thought the view was better from the bottom. Right! All I can say is, "Wow!" It was a beautiful clear day and we could see the skyline of Manhattan just like you see it in the movies.

We then went to Ellis Island, where millions of immigrants from Europe were processed before they could enter the country. Grandpère told us about the day he and his parents sailed into New York Harbor in early 1947. He was only ten or eleven but could remember every detail. He said his mother had tears running down her cheeks and his father couldn't speak as the statue came into view. Having the statue be France's gift to America made it all the more special to them. We found Grandpère's name in the Ellis Island registry, and those of my great-grandmother and great-grandfather. When I read the actual name, Monique LaRoche, my great-grandmother, I started to cry.

SATURDAY: We split up this morning. Mom and Grandpère went to the Metropolitan Museum of Art, while Dad, Cody, Rick, and I went to the Museum of Natural History. Talk about wow! It's the largest natural history museum in the world. We could have spent a week there, so we almost had to jog through it, taking pictures. Rick, always Mr. Cool-and-No-Emotion, actually got quite excited. Sometimes he and Cody would race ahead to this display or that while Dad and I caught up.

That afternoon, we went to the matinee of Phantom of the Opera, which is the longest running musical ever. Our hotel is close to Broadway, so we walked there. Then that night we went back and saw Wicked. (Same thing. Clay had gotten us these fabulous seats, even though Wicked is sold out months in advance.) Mom loves Phantom, and so do I, but I thought Wicked was really wicked ☺. Rick continued to surprise us when he actually gushed over Phantom when it was finished. It's the most animated I've ever seen him. He liked Wicked too, but nothing like Phantom. Another big day, but a great one!

SUNDAY: Quieter day today. Church services in the morning in a church across from Lincoln Center. It was amazing to see how diverse the congregation was. Blacks, Asians, Puerto Ricans, Jamaicans, and who knows what else were there. It was really different, and way awesome. After lunch, we visited St. Patrick's Cathedral, which is the largest Catholic cathedral in America. (You seeing a pattern here? The largest this, the biggest that. The most famous, the longest running, the most beautiful, the best. That's New York for you. I would hate to live here—the noise and the crowds are awful—but what an awesome place to visit.) That afternoon, we took a long walk in Central Park, then spent a quiet evening at the hotel.

MONDAY: This morning, the McAllisters of Hanksville, Utah, went to Rockefeller Center (by limousine, I might add) to make their national television debut on Today with hosts Matt Lauer and Meredith Viera. Now, that was pretty darn intimidating. I even wore a dress ⌒ . All the lights, the studio audience, and the cameras were overwhelming, but Matt and Meredith (that's what they insisted we call them) made us feel right at home as we visited with them before the show. Because the story was such big news by this time, they gave us an unprecedented fifteen minutes on air, breaking only once for commercials.

They began by having Mom recount the night that El Cobra came to our home. Then they had me and Cody describe how we escaped (without any mention of invisibility, of course). From that point on, it was mostly me and Rick and Cody that they wanted to hear from. Matt was particularly interested in the details of Leprechaun Canyon and had us both tell our side of the story. The audience roared as we talked about Gordo getting stuck in that first narrow slot. Not sure where they got them, but they had videos of Leprechaun Canyon they showed on screen as we talked. From their reaction, most of the audience had never seen a slot canyon before and were pretty amazed. Quite different from the "canyons" of Manhattan. Being here has made me appreciate the desert country of Southeastern Utah more than ever.

But I have to admit that Rick stole the show. Meredith asked him about how he got shot. He was quiet for several seconds, staring at his hands, as usual thinking carefully before he spoke. (I know, I know. Just the opposite of me.) I thought he was going to do what he did at the press conference—a couple of short, one-word sentences—and quit. But he blew me away. As much as I can remember, here's kinda how it went.

MEREDITH: We've heard how the actual shooting took place, but can you give us a little of the setting that led up to it? What happened that made you go after a man with a gun?

RICK: Well, for one thing, Danni had gone swimming over to a rock fall so she could contact the FBI by radio. So when she came back, she was still in her swimming suit.

I was shocked. Where was he going with this?

RICK: El Cobra kept staring at her. As did the other guards.

Eileen, that was El Cobra's wife, didn't like that one bit. (He glanced at me and smiled.) Danni looks pretty good in a bathing suit. So she told him to make Danni put on some more clothes.

I'm blushing about fourteen hundred shades of red by that time. Then someone in the audience whistled, and everyone laughed. Make that fifteen hundred.

MEREDITH: Then what happened?

RICK: El Cobra didn't like Eileen telling him what to do. He was raging at her. Told her to search Danni for the radio. When she couldn't find it, he went after Danni himself. He grabbed her by the hair and yanked her head way back.

By this time, Rick's voice had gone soft. Any embarrassment I was feeling was gone, because suddenly I was back there on the houseboat, reliving it all. I couldn't look at Rick or our hosts or the camera. Just listening to Rick made me feel like I was going to vomit. I could feel El Cobra's hot breath, smell the liquor and cigarettes again, feel the cold clutch of fear as he started to lean in to kiss me.

MATT: Go on, Rick.

RICK: When he leaned in, his face just inches from Danni's, I knew he was going to kiss her. And I just lost it. I charged at him, fists flying. So he shot me. And I went down like a rock.

I was fighting with every ounce of strength I had not to lose it. "You're on national television, Danni," I kept saying to myself. "This is not the time nor the place for an emotional meltdown. Pull it together."

MEREDITH: (who evidently had been watching me closely) And what you were feeling at that point, Danni?

I opened my eyes. The first thing I saw was Rick's face. He was worried. I think he sensed how close to the edge I was, so he told me with his eyes to get ahold of myself. So I finally turned to our two hosts. "I'm just glad Rick was there," I managed to choke out.

To my surprise, I saw that Matt was struggling with his emotions. Meredith was teary eyed. I looked at the audience.

Handkerchiefs were out everywhere. Even Mom was crying, evidently remembering it all over again too.

Anyway, we got a standing ovation when we finished. Afterwards, we had to be escorted to the limo by staffers because the crowds outside were so huge. It was really a great experience except for two things. I nearly lost it on national TV. And now half of the country's female population, from tweens to grandmas, are all aflutter over Rick Ramirez of Hanksville, Utah.

TUESDAY: Just me and Rick appeared on Fox and Friends. Ugh! They do things mostly live there and they start at 6, so we had to be there by 5:30. That's a.m., not p.m.! There are three cohosts on that show, and it's not a big set, so I think having all five of us would have been kind of crowded. So they asked that only Rick and I be on set, which bummed Cody no end. I figure it's about time he got his ego cut down to size a little. BTW, Gretchen Carlson, one of the hosts, who is very beautiful, sure wears short skirts. As we were getting ready, I leaned over and told Rick he'd better keep his eyes to the front or I was going to smack him right there on national television. But it turned out that Gretchen was as articulate and personable as she was beautiful and it was a great experience.

From there we went straight to Good Morning, America, whose studio is in Times Square, near our hotel. Pretty much the same thing, only with Mom and Dad being asked more about what the impact on the family was during the ordeal. Cody made up for being cut out that morning. I have to admit, he even had me laughing. He's a charmer, and in spite of all I say, I love him a ton.

By this time I was getting more comfortable with this whole national TV thing. I was able to mostly forget we were being watched by millions of people and just talk to our hosts. It's actually kind of fun. And even the cab driver recognized me as we drove from Rockefeller Center to Times Square.

Next up was the David Letterman Show. I had dreaded this one, because on the East Coast, his show plays at like 11 o'clock at night. I stay up that late all the time, but I'm not very sharp. But we were much relieved to learn that they tape it live that afternoon, then replay it later that night. Letterman asked if he could interview all of us in the first segment, then just bring me and Rick back for the last part. So Clay's prediction that Rick and I were going to get the most attention was proving to be true.

Since Letterman's and Jay Leno's shows are so late back in Utah, our family didn't watch them much, but we had enough to have a pretty good idea what to expect.

Letterman really is a very charming and really funny guy. He had us kind of summarize our whole story, asking questions and making funny quips as we did so. He had us laughing a lot—even Grandpère. I was surprised—and pleased—when, at the last of that first segment, he focused a lot on Mom. I was really proud of her. She looked so beautiful on screen. And when she opened up and tried to describe her feelings, I could see that even he was touched. And I'm sure she had half of America bawling their eyes out before she finished.

One of the big things on the Letterman Show is what he calls his "Top Ten List." I'm sure about everyone in the world—well, maybe not the world, but in the U.S.—has heard him do one of those. They're a big hit on his show and I could just picture what he'd do with our story. So, without telling anyone—not even Rick—I decided to do what my dad calls one-upmanship. You know, kind of give back as good as you get, only do it first. So I wrote out my own Top Ten list. So imagine my disappointment when I asked one of the producers if he planned to do one with us, and she said no. They did Top Ten on most shows, but not all.

But that didn't stop me. While we still had two or three minutes left, I reached in my pocket. "Excuse me, Mr. Letterman," I said, "but I love your Top Ten List, so I made one of my own. Would you like to hear it?"

It kind of knocked him off his stride, but when everyone broke out in applause, he graciously agreed. When I took a bunch of 3x5 cards from my pocket, the audience roared. That was how he always does it. I looked over at the band leader—I can never remember his name—and, laughing, he gave me the usual drumroll.

"Okay, here we go. Ten Reasons why El Cobra does not want

to continue his relationship with Danni McAllister." Laughter and some applause. Even Letterman couldn't hold back a chuckle.

"Reason number ten. Danni already has a boyfriend with a Spanish name."

Drumroll. Laughter. Applause.

"Number nine. He can never remember Danni's real name, Carruthers, and that really chaps her mother."

More of the same. I saw Mom was laughing too.

"Eight. Her grandfather wears a French beret, and El Cobra thinks French berets are for sissies."

We had monitors strategically placed in the studio so we could see what the television audience was seeing. The camera cut to Grandpère, who dutifully doffed his beret and waved to the audience.

"Number seven. Danni is still trying to get him to pay the bill for patching up the bullet holes in their living room."

That won a few cheers along with the applause.

"Six. He doesn't know how to ride a horse, and he can't drive a four-wheeler or a houseboat."

The audience was roaring now. I couldn't repress a smile. This was fun.

"Fifth reason why El Cobra is not interested in maintaining a relationship with Danni McAllister. He asked her to be his tour guide to Cathedral Valley and she pulled a gun on him."

From Letterman's face, I knew I was on a roll.

"Fourth reason why this relationship is done with. After their first kiss, Danni knocked El Cobra across the room."

"Number three. She keeps taking the battery out of her cell phone so he can never call her when he wants to talk with her."

Pause. More drums. More cheering.

Number two: The last time he asked if they might go for a walk, she suggested they go to Leprechaun Canyon.

I waved the last card at the audience. "And the number-one reason El Cobra does not want a relationship with Danni McAllister is: . . ."

Long drum roll with much banging.

"There is no bus service between Hanksville, Utah, and the federal penitentiary in Tucson, Arizona."

Well, I got another standing ovation. Even Letterman seemed impressed.

A favorite quote of Dad's is from Dizzy Dean, who I guess was a great baseball player when he was growing up. He said: "It ain't bragging if you really did it." So, if you'll pardon a little bragging—since no one will ever read this journal, at least not while I'm alive!—I'll just say this much. My Top Ten List was a huge hit and made the front page in a couple of evening papers tonight along with leading several television news shows.

To celebrate, we had dinner in "The View," a revolving restaurant on the top of the hotel, which has fabulous views of the city. It was an awesome, amazing, tiring day.

And so, good night.

CHAPTER 18

Crossroads American Kitchen, Marriott Marquis Hotel
September 21, 2011

To my surprise, when Cody and I came down for breakfast, Clay Zabriskie and Joel Jamison were already there eating with Mom, Dad, Grandpère, and Rick, the early risers in the family. Both agents stood up, but Clay came over to greet us. He shook my hand vigorously. "Well done," he said. "That was brilliant last night, Danni. A perfect way to keep him from asking too many questions."

"That's what I decided too," I said demurely. Which wasn't exactly true. That thought hadn't entered my head. I just thought it might be a lot of fun for the audience.

We went back to the table, and Joel shook our hands too. "Totally agree with Clay's assessment. Did you write those yourself?"

"Yes."

"Very funny. Maybe I'll get a clip of it and send it to Arizona. Let El Cobra watch it in his cell." That made me hoot loud enough that several people turned to look.

"And Eileen too," Cody said. "She never did like Danni. Not one bit."

As we started to sit down, Mom pointed to the far wall. "There's a fabulous breakfast buffet over there. Get some food, and then Joel and Clay want to talk to us about what happens next."

Cody was already gone before she finished. I was a little more reserved, but I was hungry enough that I wasn't far behind him.

As a waitress refilled Joel's coffee and moved away again, he sat back. "Before we get to today, let me tell you what's going on tomorrow. Since we want to make this 'disappearance,' as Grandpère calls it, as clean and complete as possible, the limo that picks you up from the hotel tomorrow will be rented. Clay will be your driver. We're going to take you across the Hudson to New Jersey, where we have our plane waiting at an executive airport."

"Wow," I said, "we're leaving for France that soon?"

"No. We're still working on getting Rick's passport. And we want to make sure all arrangements are in place. So we're taking you to Washington, D.C., for a couple of days. Then we'll send you on to France."

"D.C.?" Cody blurted from a mouthful of French toast dripping with syrup. "Can we go see things like the White House and the Lincoln Memorial and the Smithsonian?"

"Sorry," Clay said. "You're too high profile now, so that will have to wait. But we've got lots of video games for you."

"Well," Mom said, reaching out and stopping Cody from stuffing the next bite in, "this has been wonderful. I love New York. It's all I thought it would be."

"We hope we can have you on your way across the Big Pond by Saturday morning." Joel turned to Grandpère. "When do your reservations at Le Petit Château begin?"

"On Monday, but I mentioned that we might be a day or two earlier than that and they said it would be no problem."

"Good." He took a sip of his coffee, then sat back. "Okay, then, let's talk about today. This may prove to be the most challenging one you've done." He was looking at me and Rick. "The hostess has already made it clear that she wants to put only you, Rick, and Cody on camera."

"It's about time somebody remembered who the real crowd pleaser is," Cody piped up.

"Cody," Mom said, shaking her head in apology at Clay and Joel, "let Joel continue, please."

"In what way challenging?" I asked.

"*Life Is Real* is a show whose primary audience is women between the ages of twenty-one and forty. It is highly popular and for a cable show gets a remarkably large number of viewers. But the hostess is an ardent feminist. She has a reputation for being confrontational, sometimes even downright combative. That's part of what makes her popular. She's known for ambushing her guests, chewing them up into little pieces, then spitting them out on the floor."

"I watch it from time to time," Mom said. "I think you're being a little hard on her. I would use the word *provocative* rather than *confrontational*. And I like that. She doesn't let her guests get away with the usual platitudes that other hosts do. And she's very funny."

"She is that," Clay agreed.

Rick was frowning. "If she is what you say, why did you agree to do her show?"

"Because the whole country is focused on your story right now," Joel said. "We don't want anyone to think that you are taking only 'soft' appearances to make yourselves look better. That might suggest that you have something to hide."

"Which we don't, of course," I said, not liking what I was hearing one bit. "I mean, other than the pouch, and the twenty-million-dollar ransom, and a blown-up mine, and a nest full of rattlesnakes, and a whole boatload of gold. Right?"

"But she doesn't know any of that, Danni," Dad said. "You'll do fine."

There it was again. The word *fine*. Catch all. Cover all. Without meaning. It didn't help. I was starting to feel uneasy because I could see that both Clay and Joel were worried. Enough to warn us about it. That's not my definition of *fine*.

Mom slipped her arm through mine. "Dad's right. It will be all right. The audience is going to love you three. If you can hold your own against Letterman, you'll do okay. Just don't let her goad you into saying more than you should." She was pointedly looking at Cody as she said that.

I had a sudden insight. "Are you and Clay coming to the show?" I asked Joel.

"Just Clay. I'm going to the New York office and catch up on where the investigation is. But I'll see you after the show."

"But you're sending Clay to make sure I don't screw it up?"

They both laughed. "Oh, Danni," Joel said. "You are a piece of work." But I noticed he didn't really answer the question.

"What's her name again?" Rick asked.

"Cierra Pierce."

"Sierra, like the mountains?" Cody came in.

"Yeah, only she spells it with a C."

"Pierce?" I said dryly. "Like through the heart?"

Clay laughed. "That's right." Then he punched me softly on the shoulder. "You're going to be fine."

"Fine?" I shot back. "Thanks, Clay. I've always dreamed that someday I might be fine."

———

Life Is Real Studios, New York City

When Rick came out of the makeup room, he shot me a look that made me laugh. "You look great," I said. "Maybe you ought to ask her what she uses. Get some and take it home with you."

If he could have, he would have turned me into burnt toast with his eyes right there. There was not even a wisp of a smile.

"Come on," I said. "This is the last one. Man up, Ramirez."

"I'm here, aren't I?" he grumbled. Then he gave me a sharp look. "You know something? I think you like this. Maybe even too much."

My temperature flared up. "What's that supposed to mean?"

"I'm sick of these dog and pony shows, marching out on the show floor, letting everybody have a good look at us, jump through the hoops, maybe do a trick or two."

"Man," I said. "Who put the burr under your saddle this morning?"

He looked at me for several seconds. "I guess maybe you did, Danni. I'm here because of you. And I'm playing it straight because of you. But I don't like it. The whole thing is a farce. So why are you lapping it up like it was warm milk?"

"What are you talking about? I don't like this."

"Aw, come on, Danni. Remember what you said last night on the way back to the hotel. 'It's too bad we're going to France. I might have asked Joel if we could do the Jay Leno show.'"

Before I could answer that—or give him a good, hard pop on the nose—Mom came bustling up. I saw instantly that she had heard most, if not all, of it, but she was pretending not to have heard anything. "You both look good." Then to Rick, "You can't tell you've got makeup on. It just takes the shine off your forehead and your nose."

"I'm glad for that," he grumped. "I've always been quite bothered about my shiny forehead."

I stepped back and watched as he and Mom bantered back and forth. And, for the ten-thousandth time, I thought how lucky I was to have Rick as my friend. So many of my friends were doing royal battle with their parents over who they hung out with, who they dated, and so on. To watch them now, you might think that Mom liked Rick even better than she did me. I knew she didn't, but it was close. And today, maybe it was switched for the moment.

There was a fleeting moment of doubt. Was this all going to my head? But there was no chance to answer that.

"Well, good morning."

We all turned to see a woman in a gray pantsuit and red scarf come striding toward us, a female assistant on either side of her. She was tall—probably five eight or nine—and had long, dark hair that curled naturally in soft waves. She was lean and obviously very fit. No. As I watched her stride toward us, I realized she was much more than that. She had the hard, muscular body of a marathon runner.

She wasn't what you would call strikingly beautiful—wasn't everyone in television strikingly beautiful?—but she had pleasant features and two small dimples when she smiled, as she was doing now as she came toward us. It was her eyes that caught and held you. They were a dark brown, almost black, large and without makeup, and with a penetrating intelligence that seemed to take in everything in one quick glance.

Watch it, Danni. According to Joel, she's a people-eater. Don't get sucked in by her charm.

She came right up to me. "You're Danni. Hi. I'm Cierra." She stuck out her hand. It didn't surprise me that her grip was hard and confident.

I gripped it back. "Thank you for having us on your show."

"Are you kidding?" she said with a short laugh. "Every seat in the auditorium is full, and there are hundreds more outside watching on the monitors. No, we thank you."

She came up to Cody. "Ah, the charmer. Cierra Pierce, Cody. Delighted to meet you." Before he could respond at all, she turned to Rick. "And you're Ricardo." She smiled. "You're even better-looking in person than you are on the little screen."

I stared at her. Was she hitting on him? Rick barely smiled. "Call me Rick. And it's the makeup," he drawled.

"I'm sure," she said with a short laugh. As I watched his eyes, I could see that he did not like this woman. And it was more than her fawning comment. He was wary of her, like when you approach a dog with its lips drawn back and the hair on the back of its neck raised. They shook hands quickly, but Cierra was already turning to Mom and greeting her. "Well, well," she laughed. "It's not hard to see where Danni gets her good looks from."

And I decided she wasn't coming on to Rick any more than she was coming on to Mom. This was just her way. Speak what's in your head as it comes, no filters, no holding back. "Mrs. McAllister, thank you so much for coming and bringing your family to our show."

"Our pleasure. I watch your show all the time. I love it."

Oh, this was rich. Yesterday it had been "from time to time." Today it was "all the time." Even Mom was intimidated by her.

"We can get you a chair back here, if you like," Cierra said. "Or would you prefer to be with your father and husband in the audience?"

"The latter," Mom said.

"Good." She looked around. "We have about six or seven minutes." She pointed to a table off to one side. "There are drinks and snacks over there. Help yourselves. I'll be right back."

As she walked away, I heard someone call my name and turned around. Dad, Grandpère, and Clay were coming quickly toward us. Clay motioned for us to join them. We did, and he formed us in a little huddle off to one side. "I just got a call from Joel," he said, speaking low. "Bad news. Someone broke into your home. Totally ransacked the place."

"What?" Mom gasped.

"Joel is furious. This evidently happened two nights ago, but it wasn't discovered until this morning. Seems like when you guys came east, the sheriff's office pulled off the round-the-clock watch and started doing random patrols instead."

"But why?" I cried. "What could they possibly be after?" I felt sick to my stomach.

He looked at me. "Did you leave the duplicate pouch at home?"

"I . . ." I was gaping at him. "Of course. I left it in the bottom drawer of my chest of drawers."

"Well, that's gone. And Mack's safe was opened, obviously by a professional." He turned to Dad. "Did you have anything of value in there? Money? Bonds?"

"No. It's mostly to protect important papers in case there's a fire."

"What about that 'gold bar'?"

"No," Mom answered. "I made him put that in the safety deposit box along with Danni's journal a couple of months ago."

"Why would they want the duplicate pouch?" I exclaimed. "That doesn't make sense."

"It does if they think it's the original," Grandpère said quietly.

That shocked me deeply. "It's a battered, worn-out old purse. Except for us and those who are now in prison, no one knows what it is."

Just then one of Cierra's assistants came hurrying over. "Two minutes to air time. We have to check the sound levels on their microphones. The rest of you will have to return to your seats. Danni and Rick, please come with me."

Clay nodded and started backing away. "I'll try to find out more while you're on."

"Good luck," Dad said and quickly kissed me on the forehead. "Don't let her rattle you, Danni. Keep it cool."

Another odd warning. And suddenly I was feeling very uncomfortable. I reached down and clasped the baggy leather purse I had over my shoulder closer to my body, feeling the reassuring lump that was the real *Le Gardien* inside. And the feeling immediately left me. The Guardian was here. It would be okay.

———

"One minute, Cierra," the producer said as we got settled, holding up one finger. "Sound test is good. Stand by."

She nodded, then turned to us. "I'd tell you two to relax, but after watching you on the other shows, especially Letterman, I can see there's no need for that." There was an unreadable smile. "And remember, the producer has decided to let you have the whole show. You've become so famous, he postponed the other guests until tomorrow." We must have looked alarmed, because she smiled sweetly and said, "Oh, didn't I tell you that?"

No, she hadn't. Our commitment was for fifteen or twenty minutes tops, but I could see that it gave her great satisfaction to see that she had caught us off guard. Then I understood. This was her way of throwing us off balance just before we went on.

"We requested that your first appearance in New York be on *Life Is Real,*" she said, clearly irritated, "but since you chose to put us last on the schedule, everyone pretty well knows your whole story now, so we're going to quickly summarize the details and then focus on—"

Rick cut her off. "We didn't set the schedule. The FBI did."

She was genuinely startled. "What?"

"Thirty seconds, Cierra," the producer warned.

"This is still an active investigation," Rick noted. "We have to be careful what we say and what we don't say." He gave her an innocent look. "Which probably applies to you as well." He imitated her smile perfectly. "Oh, didn't they tell you that?"

Perfect! From the flash of anger in her eyes, I could tell that now we weren't the only ones who had been knocked off balance. And I forgave his earlier sour mood. I could have hugged him right then for not being sucked in by her oozing charm.

———◆———

After the usual brief introduction to the show, Cierra introduced us to the audience and the viewers. Though she mentioned that my actual name was Carruthers, there were no cracks about it—thank you, very much—and thereafter she called me Danni. Nor did she call Rick "Ricardo" again. We received a warm and enthusiastic applause from the studio audience, which helped me relax a little.

She then explained that since most of the world now knew the basic outline of what had happened to us, they were going to cover the main elements of our story with a short summary of events in a two-minute video. As a narrator summarized the key events, they filled the screen with still shots and short video clips that supported the narration. It included a Google Earth zoom-in on Hanksville and our little homestead, and the same for Rick's house on the river. They had video footage of Cathedral Valley with the Temples of the Sun and the Moon, and both aerial and ground shots of Leprechaun Canyon. Somehow they had found the actual houseboat that El Cobra had rented and had both exterior and interior pictures of it. They also had a video taken of Iceberg Canyon from Jet Skis, which brought more gasps of admiration. It turned out to be remarkably good, and I was amazed at what they included. The segment closed with mug shots of El Cobra, Eileen, Raul (or Doc), Lew (Gordo), and Jean-Claude. I hadn't seen these before, and I felt a twist in my stomach as I looked at them.

The final image was me, Cody, and Rick standing outside the medical clinic in Page—him leaning on his crutches, me with one arm slipped through his, Cody grinning at the camera. When the image froze, Cierra called out, "Ladies and gentleman, let's hear it for Danni and Cody McAllister and Rick Ramirez, three very remarkable and courageous young teens."

The reaction was loud—applause joined with whistles and cheers—and sustained. It only subsided when the image faded out and the lights came back up again.

We turned back to face Cierra, who was smiling triumphantly. "So, Danni, thank you so much for being with us today. If you don't mind, let's start with you. How does it feel to be the new—" she paused and her hand did a little flourish in my direction, as if she were presenting a member of the royal family—"Katniss Everdeen?"

Talk about being blindsided. For a minute I wasn't sure if I had heard her right. Even the audience was taken aback and didn't immediately react.

She turned to Rick. Another roll of her hand. Another grand cry. "And with her is our very own Peeta Melark."

And as the cameras zoomed in to catch our faces—flaming bright red, I'm sure—and the audience reacted, she cried out even more loudly, "Don't you agree, people, that what we have here is our own version of the *Hunger Games*? Two young people fighting back against an evil world."

The response was instantaneous and thunderous.

"Only this is even better, right? *Because this story is totally true!*"

She had them. And from the satisfaction in her eyes, I could tell she knew it. And loved it.

As it died down, her mouth pulled down. "Sorry, Cody, but I just couldn't quite see you as filling the role of Prim, Katniss's little sister. But welcome to the show anyway."

She let the applause roll for ten or fifteen seconds before raising a hand. It almost instantly ceased. She turned back to us. "Well, I can't fully express how delighted I am to have the three of you on our show today. That little summary we just saw says much, but it also raises many questions. So let's get right to it."

She picked up a notepad from the lamp table beside her. I hadn't noticed it there before, but saw now it was filled with lines of handwriting. She didn't look at it, just placed it in her lap. "Cody, tell me about Hanksville. As we saw from that Google Earth view, it seems pretty isolated. Tell the audience how far you ride the bus to school."

"Fifty-eight miles. A little over an hour one way."

"Wow!" someone on the audience gasped. "My kids walk a block and a half." Everyone laughed.

"And how many people live in Hanksville?"

Cody shrugged, so I answered. "As of the 2010 census, the population is 215."

"So basically, you know everyone in town."

"Heck, yeah," I drawled, "and about half the county. We even call the lizards and scorpions by their first names."

That brought another wave of laughter.

To Rick: "So what do you do when you want to order in pizza?"

Rick didn't hesitate. "If you want it hot, you call Denver and they drop it in by parachute. If you don't mind reheating it, UPS delivers in three days."

Cierra laughed with the audience. She was liking this too.

Not waiting for her next question, I spoke up. "It probably sounds pretty awful to a New Yorker, where your population density is 27,532 persons per square mile. But in our whole county, we don't even average

2 people per square mile." I had checked this out on Google earlier this morning, wondering if she might talk about Hanksville.

"Really?"

"Yeah. Even on a windy day, you can spit in any direction and not worry about hitting anyone. I wouldn't try that in New York City if I were you."

As the audience roared, I saw Clay flash me a thumbs-up. I could even see a touch of respect in Cierra's eyes. I was learning how to play an audience too. And my little "cowgirl-from-Hanksville" routine was working like a charm. I could see she didn't like being upstaged.

Cierra let the laughter die, smiling and seemingly enjoying the moment too. Then suddenly she went serious and leaned in toward me. "Is your family wealthy, Danni?"

"I—" I looked at her more closely to see if she was serious. She was. "Heavens no," I exclaimed. "Why would you think that?"

"Well, if you're not wealthy, why would El Cobra and his gang ask for a twenty-million-dollar ransom for your family?"

Several things registered at once. The audience reaction was that of shock. But it was nothing compared to what I saw on Clay's face. His jaw was slack. Dad was clearly dumbfounded. Grandpère was staring at her. The amount of the demanded ransom had never been made public. "Substantial" was all the FBI had ever admitted.

"Well," Cierra prodded, a touch smug now. "That was the amount they asked for, right?"

"I . . ." I glanced at Clay and saw him nod. "Yes. But that was not money my family had. My father is a mining consultant, and he and my grandfather discovered a mine with a rich seam of precious ore and—"

She glanced at her notes. "Rhodium, I understand. Which has sold for as much as ten thousand dollars an ounce. Correct?"

Whistles of amazement from someone out in front of us.

I went on doggedly. "We had arranged to sell the mine to a large Canadian firm for twenty million dollars. Somehow El Cobra learned about that, and his plan was to have the money transferred to an off-shore bank account once the deal was completed."

"But you and Rick thwarted that plan. El Cobra never got the twenty million. So haven't you become a very rich young woman?"

"No. The Canadians backed out. And besides, it's not my money," I blurted.

She went right on as if I hadn't spoken. "This is a part of the story we haven't heard about. Cinderella times twenty million. Every girl's dream. Poor little girl from Hanksville, Utah, suddenly becomes fabulously wealthy. Better gear up, Danni. You're going to have a string of suitors from Denver to Los Angeles."

"We don't have it anymore," I said, feeling my face growing hotter. "There was an explosion at the mine. We cannot get the ore. What's left of it."

That startled her. Her eyes narrowed. "An explosion?"

"Yes," Rick broke in, and I could see he was trying to hold his temper. "An explosion. You know, like 'Boom!' The mine was totally destroyed."

We had thrown her off her game and she didn't like it. She flashed an angry look at her producer, who was as surprised as she was. She took a quick breath, assessing quickly. Again she glanced down at her notes for a moment, then went on. "Rick, in the closing picture of the introductory segment, you were on crutches. It was mentioned that you were shot. That was on the last day, right? Just before El Cobra took off with Danni and her grandfather?"

"Yes."

"Tell us what happened."

"I have told that story several times now on national TV. Is there something I haven't already said that you're interested in?"

There was a flash of irritation, but she nodded. "Was Danni injured in any way in that attack?"

"No. He knocked her around a little, but—oh. He did strike her with the back of his hand and cut her face with his ring."

Without conscious thought, my left hand came up and touched my cheek. I jerked it away as I saw they had my face on the monitors.

"And so you went after him?"

There was a brief nod.

"And he shot you."

"Yes. With a pistol."

"Did you actually see that happen?" she asked me.

"Of course."

"And what did you do?"

That was a condescending question. "What do you think I did? I screamed. We all screamed. My mother leaped up to help Rick. I tried to get to him too, but Armando stopped me."

"Armando? Is that El Cobra's name?"

"Yes."

"You were on a first-name basis with him?"

"What? No, of course not. His wife called him that several times. I didn't."

"Oh. Just wondering. We learned from Rick yesterday that you were still wearing your swimsuit at that time. Correct?"

I was reeling. What was she after here? Alarm bells were clanging in my head, but I wasn't sure why. "I was. So what?" I shot back.

"Was this a bikini?"

I just stared at her. "No, it was a tankini. It looks more like a one-piece bathing suit."

"I know what a tankini is," she said dryly.

"Does that matter?"

"Was *Armando*—" she emphasized the first name deliberately— "coming on to you at that point? Was that why Rick went after him?"

The question shocked me, even though I should have guessed that was where she was going with this. "How would I know that?"

"Oh, come on, Danni. A woman just knows. Don't play coy with me."

"She answered your question," Rick broke in tartly. "Let's move on."

She had expected the hot-button reaction from me—even seemed to be deliberately goading me for a reaction—but Rick going on the offensive took her by surprise. She chose to ignore him. "You said he kissed you. But it wasn't a kiss of passion. It was a kiss of domination."

"Yes."

"And that's when you knocked him flying. Your words, not mine."

"That's right." I was wary now. She was leading me again, and I wasn't sure where or why.

"So just how did you do that?"

"How did I do what?"

"How did you knock him flying? Did you strike him with your fists?"

"Uh . . . no."

"Did you shove him with your hands?"

"I . . . um . . . things were happening so fast, I just remember him stumbling backwards and falling over a chair and . . ."

"Wait. On the *Today* show you told them you knocked El Cobra flying. Now you're saying he just stumbled backwards? Which is it?"

Before I could answer, she held up her hands. "Never mind. It was an incredibly brave thing you and Rick did, Danni. Incredibly brave. I don't mean to push you on the details."

The applause signs came on and the audience erupted. She and I looked at each other, me breathing hard, her calm and unruffled. And in her eyes I could see that she was setting me up for the next surprise.

She smiled at the audience and the cameras. "We have to take a commercial break, but when we come back, we would like to introduce you to the third hero in this unbelievable story of courage and resistance. I think you'll find him as delightful and amazing as Katniss and Peeta." As the applause began, she waved and called out, "Don't go away. We'll be right back."

CHAPTER 19

"So, Cody," Cierra said with an engaging smile. "Welcome to *Life Is Real.*"

He shot her a wide grin. "Thank you, Cierra." The audience laughed. You would have thought he and Cierra were old buds from the chatty tone of his voice.

"How old are you, Cody?"

"Thirteen."

"And you were with your mother that night when El Cobra's gang came? I think you had been to Denver that day?"

"Yes. They were waiting for us when we got home."

"And what were your first thoughts when you saw them?"

He looked surprised by the question. "What the heck are these guys doing in here?"

She laughed, as did the audience. "And Danni and your grandfather and father were not with you at that time."

"No. They came about an hour later."

"Tell us about how you and Danni escaped from the house. I understand that it happened twice, actually. How were you able to do that?"

He glanced at me, and I tried to warn him with my eyes. *No mention of being invisible. No mention of the pouch.*

His answer was to turn back to our hostess. But I shouldn't have underestimated him. We had gone over this with Clay. Cierra didn't interrupt him as he described our first escape to the attic, then being caught again. All he said about the pistol was that it went off by accident, which allowed him and me to take off and hide in the barn.

Finally, Cierra broke in. "So you and Danni hid in this fort that you and your friend had made, while the gang was tramping right over the top of you."

"Yep. It was a dang good fort."

"Amazing," she said, looking out at the audience. They took that as their signal and warmly applauded. Cody gave them a little bow. The ham.

"This story has so many astonishing aspects." She was speaking to the audience. "Some years ago, Larry King of CNN interviewed Tom Clancy, the best-selling author of such techno thrillers as *The Hunt for Red October.* Since Clancy had also written some nonfiction books, King asked him if there was a difference between writing fiction and nonfiction. Clancy's answer was classic. He said, 'Yes, there is. Fiction has to be believable.'"

We all laughed at that. Cierra let it die, then focused on Cody again. "If this were a novel we were talking about, people would say the whole thing was too fantastic, too unbelievable to sell. But it really happened to you, didn't it?"

"It felt pretty real when it was happening," Cody said soberly.

"I'll bet it did," she said. She leaned forward. Not good. I was learning that was the sign that she was going for the jugular. "Can I ask you a couple of questions about all this, Cody? See if we can clarify some things for our viewers."

"Sure." He was jaunty as he smiled at her. "Ask away."

"Is it true that you and Danni hid under some old blankets in the attic the first time?"

"Yes. It was a playhouse me and Danni had made when we were younger."

I was watching her closely. *Here it comes,* I thought, tensing.

"But didn't El Cobra come up into the attic looking for you?"

Now even Cody saw where she was going with this. "Yes?" he said slowly.

"And he didn't think to look under those blankets?"

"We were in a corner of the attic," I broke in. "For some reason, the lights in the attic wouldn't turn on."

She glared at me. "I'd like Cody to answer if you don't mind, Danni."

Cody shrugged. "It was really dark and all they had were flashlights."

"And they didn't think to shine them in your direction?"

"Yeah . . . they . . . um . . . they did, but they didn't see us."

"Really?" There was no mistaking the disbelief in her voice. But she let it pass. "So they caught you again, and took you back in the house. Tell me more about this pistol that you said went off. Where did it come from?"

"It was in Danni's purse."

Her eyebrows shot up. "Her purse?"

No, Cody! No. No. No.

"Tell me about this purse of hers. No one has mentioned that before. Is that the same as the pouch we've heard about?" She turned to me. "Is it?"

"Pouch?" I echoed dumbly.

"Yes, Danni," she said with a condescending sneer. "The pouch that was given to you by your grandfather on your thirteenth birthday. I believe it is a family heirloom passed down from generation to generation. The pouch that your friends call the Nanny Pouch. The pouch that has the French words *Le Gardien* embroidered on the flap, which in English means, 'The Guardian.'" Her eyes bored into mine. "That's the pouch I'm talking about. Would you care to comment about that?"

I felt like the room was spinning around me. How could she know all this? Had they sent someone to Hanksville to talk to my friends? But if that were the case, my friends would have told me. I was still getting texts and posts on Facebook and Tweets all the time from back home. The whole town was following our every movement in New York.

Cierra was triumphant as she turned back to Cody. "Since Danni seems to have lost her voice at the moment, I'll ask you, Cody. Is that the purse you mean?"

He looked at me. I nodded at him to continue. There was nothing we could do about it now.

"Yes," he said.

"And why hadn't El Cobra found this pistol before? Didn't he search Danni when they first caught her and brought her into the house?"

"I . . ." He shrugged. "Things were pretty crazy about then, Cierra, so I'm not sure."

Good answer, Code.

She grudgingly acknowledged that. "Okay. So how did this pistol come to start firing bullets, which allowed you and Danni to escape a second time?"

"El Cobra decided it wasn't loaded and tossed it on the table, and it went off."

"How many times?"

Rick jumped in again. "Do you really think they were counting at that point?" he asked in disgust.

"All right," she said, her mouth hard. "Let's stop playing games here, shall we? We've got all kinds of things that don't seem to add up in this story, and either this is because the story is fictional"—there was a collective gasp from the audience—"or because Danni and Cody and Rick are holding information back. I think the latter is the case."

I was in full panic mode now and looked out at the front row of the audience. Mom and Dad were rigid with shock. Clay's seat was empty, and I wondered when he had left and where he had gone. To call Joel, maybe. Grandpère's head was down. He was making a steeple with his fingers and staring at it.

Cierra picked up the notebook and waved it at the audience. "Okay, let's see if we can't get to the bottom of this. About two hours before our

show began, this notepad, along with an explanatory note and some sub-
stantiating documents, were delivered to our studios by FedEx messenger.
The note is signed by a man claiming to be El Cobra's personal attorney.
It is a summary of testimony given to this attorney by El Cobra himself."

El Cobra? I felt sick. No wonder she knew so much. I wanted to
look away, to close my eyes, to bolt and run. But I couldn't take my eyes
off the pad.

"According to El Cobra, this pouch of Danni's is an enchanted
pouch." Over the instant eruption of noise, she cried out all the louder.
"That's right. Supposedly this pouch has strange powers that allowed
you, Danni McAllister, to do amazing things." She swung back around
to Cody. "Isn't that why El Cobra and his men didn't see you and your
sister in the attic, Cody? Isn't it true that they were inches from your
face and shined the light directly in your faces, but somehow you and
Danni were rendered invisible?"

The audience exploded. She paid them no mind. Now it was me she
zeroed in on. "And isn't it true that you literally did knock El Cobra flying after he kissed you—not with your fists, not with your hands, but by
some invisible power emanating from the pouch?"

She sat back, her chest rising and falling, her eyes bright with triumph. The producer was directing one of the cameras to swing around
and film the audience. A woman in the audience jumped up and bolted
from the room, a pocket-sized notebook in hand—another journalist,
come to watch the Katniss and Peeta show, now racing off to call her
editor?

I turned back to Cierra. She wasn't looking at us any longer. She was
reveling in her triumph. She had done it. She had orchestrated it perfectly.
After today, *Life Is Real* would be the most talked-about show in America.
America, heck! The world. Her dark eyes glittered with excitement.

And there I sat. What would Cierra say if she knew that I had *Le
Gardien* folded up in my purse right now? That it was right here in the
studio with her? I was tempted to yank it out and wave it in front of her
face. Maybe hurl a few curses at her to see if I could rattle her.

I didn't, of course. I just sat there. Numbed. Speechless. Reeling like a drunk.

———

And then, the calm came. Beneath my elbow, where I clutched the purse tightly against my body, I felt a gentle warmth on my skin. The calm flowed in—and with it came an idea.

I took the purse off my shoulder and unzipped the center zipper. Cierra was instantly suspicious. I ignored her. And seeing what I was doing, the audience instantly quieted too. Every camera focused in on me. I reached inside and withdrew *Le Gardien,* then spread it out on my lap.

Cierra leaned forward, her eyes glittering with excitement. "Is that it?" she exclaimed. "Is that The Guardian?"

"Yes, it is." I held it out to her, nearly laughing aloud as she actually shrank back a little. "Go on," I urged. "It's not cursed. It won't bite you."

She took it, somewhat gingerly, and held it up to examine it more closely. Then she remembered where she was and turned so the cameras could focus on it. After a moment, she looked at me in wonder. "It's warm."

"Yes, I know. That's what it does when it is about to work its magic."

Her eyes doubled in size, and she held it away from her. "Really?"

I laughed. "Don't be silly. It's warm because I've had my purse against my body." The audience laughed, and they weren't laughing at me. They were laughing at her. I saw she knew that, and she didn't like it.

"And this is the very pouch of which we have been speaking?"

"It is. Because it is a family heirloom, I always carry it with me. It was part of my instructions when my grandfather gave it to me."

She held it out toward the nearest camera. "Zoom in here. If you look closely, you can see the embroidered letters where it says *Le Gardien.*" One of the cameras moved in.

I half closed my eyes, willing *Le Gardien* to help me get this situation back under control. As I did so, a lock of her hair, which was brushed back from her forehead, came free and fell down over one eye. It made her look ridiculous. Absently, she reached up and pushed it back. It stayed for only a second, then dropped again, but this time down the side of her face where she didn't see it. One of her assistants, off camera, started motioning to her, making sweeping motions with her hand, trying to get her attention.

I heard a few chuckles from the audience, but Cierra was totally engrossed in her examination of the pouch. Finally she looked up. "So, you admit that this is a magic pouch?"

"Of course!" I crowed. "Look in the inside pocket and you'll find a magic wand."

That really startled her, and for a moment she hesitated. Then she unbuttoned the flap and opened it up. She started to reach inside, and then it hit her. She jerked her hand back. "You're mocking me now?" she snapped.

"No," I fired right back. "I'm only mocking the idea that this is a magic pouch. Do you see a magic wand inside? Is it stuffed with packets of ground toadstool, or dried bat wing, or lizards' gizzards?" I laughed merrily. "I ask you, Cierra. Do I look like an enchantress to you? Some kind of teenaged witch? Come on. That's Harry Potter stuff. Surely you don't believe . . ." I shrugged, my eyes widening innocently. "Do you?"

Bless *Le Gardien*. The thoughts were marching in one right after another. I even knew exactly what tone of inflection to use in my voice.

Out of the corner of my eye, I saw the assistant talking to the producer. He nodded, and the monitors changed to a closeup of me. The assistant rushed in and quickly fixed Cierra's hair, then darted back again.

By now, Cierra was starting to smolder. This was not going quite as she had planned. "You seem to view all of this as a joke, Danni. Are you saying that this pouch played no part in the events that led to the capture and arrest of El Cobra and his gang?"

"No," I said easily. "I'm not saying that at all. This pouch was very important in what happened. So let me explain. Angelique Chevalier was my fourth great-grandmother. She was supposed to receive this pouch for her thirteenth birthday. She was to become what is known as a keeper of the pouch. But on that day both of her parents were killed because the local villagers thought she was a witch. She had to flee to France to save her own life, even though she was still a young girl.

"My great-grandmother, whose name was Monique LaRoche, was another keeper of the pouch. She was a young mother when her husband was arrested and taken to Paris by the Gestapo in World War II. Demonstrating tremendous personal courage, she went into war-ravaged Paris on her own to try to save him. He was on his way to execution when the United States Army liberated Paris and freed him. Monique was there when that happened."

Now I looked Cierra squarely in the eye. "My middle name is Monique. My mother's name is Angelique. We were named for those brave and courageous women."

"So are you the current keeper?" she broke in.

"Yes, I am. I received *Le Gardien* from my grandfather on my thirteenth birthday. And when he gave it to me, he charged me to remember several important things."

"Ah, yes," she said. "The Four Remembers. Tell us about those."

"They are quite simple, actually. First, 'Remember that there is purpose to your life.' Second, 'Remember that you are unique.'"

"Well, you certainly are that, Danni."

I went right on. "Third, 'Remember that you are free to choose who you are and what you become.' And finally, 'Remember that you are not alone.'" My head came up, and my voice rang out. "That is the 'magic' the pouch holds for me, Cierra. When El Cobra was threatening to kill my family and ruin us financially, I thought of Angelique and Monique. Those two women exhibited great courage in very dangerous circumstances. And that inspired me to try to do the same."

To my surprise, my voice was suddenly husky. "There were times when I was frightened to the point of paralysis. But I would cling to the pouch and remember what my ancestors had done. I would remember that I too had unique gifts, that I could choose to act with courage or with fear, that I too had a purpose to fulfill, and that I was not alone." I paused to catch my breath. "So, you ask, is the pouch magic? Is it enchanted? Yes, in its own way." I reached out and took the pouch back from her. "And I treasure it more than you can know."

The audience once again erupted. I saw several women get to their feet, applauding wildly. Others quickly joined them, and soon everyone was on their feet. Cierra saw it too and had no choice but to acknowledge it. She began clapping as well. "Bravo, Danni. Bravo."

Rick leaned over and touched my arm. "Way to go," he whispered.

"Thanks." To be honest, I was soaring. I was amazed at what I had said. And I was touched by it, too—which was a good indicator that those words had not come from me. But for the moment, I was happy to take the credit. I had turned back the Cierra tide and I guessed there wouldn't be any more questions about the pouch.

I looked at her and smiled. She was watching me, her eyes hooded. We sat quietly for several moments until the applause died and people sat down again. Then she smiled pleasantly. "Let's leave the question of the pouch for a moment. It's time for another break, but when we come back, we'll still have about fifteen minutes. Can we talk some more about how the three of you worked together to pull all of this off?"

"Of course," I said.

Rick only grunted.

"Always happy to be of help, Cierra," Cody sang out, making her laugh again.

———

During the break Mom, Dad, and Grandpère came up and joined us. I wanted to ask Grandpère what he thought of how I had handled it, but he pulled me aside and started talking quietly before I could say anything. "She knows, Danni. She knows it all."

"But how? So you think those really are the notes from El Cobra?"

"Perhaps, but it's more than that. How does she know details like it being the Nanny Pouch? El Cobra never knew that."

That set me back. Good question. "Maybe they sent a team to Hanksville looking for background information on us. Any of my friends could have told them."

"Only some details. She has them all. It's almost like . . ." He shook his head.

"Like what?"

"Like they had your journal," he said slowly.

"But that's not possible. It's in a safety deposit box."

"I don't know. I just know that there is something more going on here than meets the eye."

Just then, Cierra came back into the room and started toward us. Grandpère turned to Dad. "Stall her for a minute, will you?" he whispered. Dad nodded and headed off to intercept her. Grandpère lowered his voice, moving closer to me. "Watch yourself. She's not done with you yet."

"I can handle it," I said. "The pouch is helping me, and—"

He grabbed my arm. "Listen to me, Danni. If she starts in on the pouch again, don't play games with her. Here is what I want you to say."

I listened with growing concern and widening eyes as he spoke urgently in a low voice. I was barely able to nod and tell him I understood before Cierra broke free from Dad and came over to join us.

"Okay, folks. We've got about ninety seconds." She laid a hand on Cody's shoulder. "Thanks, Cody. You were delightful, but I think for this last segment, we're going to focus on just Danni and Rick. You can sit with your parents out in the audience."

As she moved off, ignoring the crestfallen look on his face, I grabbed Dad's arm. "Where's Clay?"

"He got a phone call. I think from Joel. From the look on his face, something's come up. He didn't look happy as he left."

"Come on, folks," the producer called. "We're down to about one minute."

"All right, Rick. I'd like to get a little more of your perspective on all this if we can."

"Whatever," he said, seemingly bored. But I knew better than that. Down deep he was seething inside. Most of that was directed at Cierra, but I couldn't help but wonder how much of it was aimed at me.

"Early the next morning, after Danni and Cody escaped from El Cobra's gang, they came to your house."

"That's right."

"When you heard their story, you and your father realized very quickly that they had just put your family in danger." When he nodded, she went on. "How did you and your father feel about that?"

"I'm not sure what you mean."

"You have two little sisters, right?"

"Yes."

"You said your father immediately knew that it wasn't safe for them and decided to take them away. How did that make you feel?"

He leaned back, considering that. Then finally he leaned forward again. "I don't know how it works in New York," he said softly, "but where we come from, when friends are in trouble, you don't stop to ask if it's a convenient time for you."

A murmur of approval rippled through the audience.

"My father immediately sprang into action to help Danni and Cody," Rick continued. "Getting my sisters to safety was only part of that. He told me to stay with Cody and Danni and do whatever I could."

"Very commendable," she said. "And that turned out to be a lot. You really were Danni's Peeta, weren't you."

He shook his head. "Peeta Melark is fiction. Katniss Everdeen is fiction. I think the whole *Hunger Games* analogy is a stretch. I'm surprised you are so taken with it."

Ouch! One zinger straight to the forehead. Way to go, Rick.

"Well spoken," she acknowledged. To my surprise, she didn't seem too irritated by his answer. She actually seemed pleased with how this was going. She smiled sweetly. "So, you and Danni have been friends since you were in fourth grade?"

"Yes."

"Would you consider yourselves as BFFs? Best Friends Forever?"

"I think that's a dumb way to put it, but yes. We're best friends."

She was watching him closely now, and I felt the prickles start along the back of my neck.

"Are you lovers, Rick?"

There were audible gasps from all over. I happened to be watching the producer, and I saw him rock back. Then I looked at Mom. She was horrified. Dad was furious. Grandpère just watched her steadily, his eyes unreadable. My face felt like it was on fire. Then I glanced at the monitor and saw that it was my face that filled the frame.

But almost instantly, the cameras cut back to Rick. He was staring at Cierra with open hostility. "I beg your pardon?" he finally managed.

"It's a simple question," she oozed. "Are you and Danni *more* than best friends?"

His head came up a fraction. "Do you really think that is any of your business?"

"I think it is a question millions of Americans are asking right now, Rick."

"It's none of their business either."

"So can we take that as a yes?"

Eyes dark as thunderclouds, Rick stared at her for several very long seconds. "You are something else, lady," he said. Then he calmly stood up, ripped the microphone off his shirt, and turned to me. "You coming, Danni?"

I just gaped at him.

"Fine. I'll see you outside." And he stalked off the set.

The sounds were coming at us from every side. Some were clapping. Others booed, and for a flickering moment I wondered if they were booing Cierra or Rick. I was too shocked to do anything but stare at his back as he disappeared.

"Well, well," Cierra, clearly shocked right down to her little buttons, said after a moment. "You should have warned me that your Ricardo was so temperamental. The Latin temperament, I guess."

I barely heard her. I was thinking of all the people back in Hanksville who were watching this—neighbors, friends. Lisa Cole! I wanted to crawl into a hole and pull the ground in after me.

Cierra broke into my thoughts. "You don't have to answer that question, Danni, but if you don't . . ." A sleepy smile. "Well, most people will assume that is your answer."

"It's not," I cried. "We are not . . ." I couldn't bring myself to say the word. "We're best friends. That's all. We—we've only kissed one time."

Shocked at hearing those last words, I stared down at the pouch in my lap. Why had I said that? I glanced up and saw a pleased smile stealing across her face.

"Ah, yes. The kiss. I believe it took place in Leprechaun Canyon, did it not? While those two men—the ones you called Doc and Gordo—were coming after you." She scoffed openly. "And you really expect us to believe that after being friends for so long, that was your *first* kiss?"

"It's true," I whispered.

Cierra was shaking her head. "Come on, Danni. We've got school districts in Boston handing out condoms in junior high school and you're claiming that you weren't even kissed until just a few months ago? I'm sorry, but I find that very hard to believe."

My head jerked up as my Irish temper kicked in. "Well, Cierra, perhaps that is because we tend to judge others by ourselves."

The audience's reaction to that was pure delight. Cierra's face was instantly even a brighter shade of red than mine.

"Excuse me for being a little skeptical here, Miss McAllister, but it's not just me who's wondering if you may not be playing a little loose with the truth here. So let me follow up on that." She glanced off camera. "Since Rick is not here to confirm that, please tell us more about it. Where exactly did it take place?"

"Well, it was in a very narrow spot in the slot canyon and we could hear Doc coming. We were both pretty scared." I was suddenly back in that narrow space. I could almost smell the dust again.

"Was it a passionate kiss?" Cierra asked, breaking in, jarring me back to reality.

I didn't answer her. I wasn't about to share that moment with twenty gazillion viewers across America.

"Was it a French kiss?" she asked, this time very gently.

"No!" I burst out. "It was nothing like that. It was . . ." I sighed, bringing the memories back. "We were just sitting there. Waiting. And suddenly I realized that Rick's shape was looming closer to me. I . . ." I half closed my eyes. "It was totally unexpected. But he leaned in and kissed me on the forehead."

"On the *forehead?*" she exclaimed incredulously.

"Yes," I murmured.

"And what did you do?"

"I . . ." I looked up at her. "I tipped my head back. Then I told him that he missed."

"And?"

I couldn't meet her gaze any longer. And I didn't want the camera to show my face. So I dropped my head and kept it down when I answered. "He didn't miss the second time."

There was absolute silence in the studio. I couldn't bring myself to look up. Then finally, Cierra spoke. Her voice was hushed and filled with respect. "I owe you an apology, Danni. I have misjudged you, and I'm sorry for that. You are a remarkable and very sweet young woman." Then she spoke to the cameras. "Tom Clancy was right. The truth is sometimes more unbelievable than fiction."

I glanced up at the clock behind the producer. It was approaching seven minutes to the hour, which meant that our time was nearly up. I turned and looked to the side where Rick had disappeared. Where was he? Was he still in the studio? Had he watched her goad me into sharing the details of our kiss? Or was he on his way back to the hotel? Whatever it was, and wherever he was, I knew it was going to take some doing to repair what had just happened. And that made me angry. Not at him. At Cierra.

I turned back to our host. "May I ask you a question, Cierra?"

She was looking at the notepad, and my question startled her. Before she could answer, someone—a man—called out from the audience. "Yes. Let her. I think it's her turn."

Another smattering of applause. She didn't like it, but Cierra was smart enough to know that she needed to redeem herself somewhat with her audience. "Of course." She gave me a thin smile. "Go ahead."

"This packet that FedEx delivered to your studios. You say that it was from El Cobra's attorney?"

"Yes," she said slowly, "that is what the cover letter said."

"And do you have any confirming evidence that this is true?"

"We're checking on that now. It arrived only a couple of hours before taping. Why?"

"Doesn't it strike you as odd that an attorney would reveal details from his client when those details are protected by attorney/client privilege?"

"Not at all," she retorted. "If El Cobra gave his permission to share them, it's not a problem."

"Do you think he would do that when some of these details actually provide evidence of his guilt?"

That one caught her alongside the head, and momentary confusion crossed her face. I felt a little thrill of exultation. *Thank you, Grandpère.* She shot a look at the producer, who was shaking his head frantically.

When she turned back, she was less sure of herself. "It's nothing that you and your family haven't already testified to. We're not revealing new information here."

Oh, really? But I let it go. "Here's another question. I think you are aware that this is an ongoing investigation being conducted under the direction of the FBI."

"Of course. And we contacted the FBI immediately after receiving the packet. We will be fully cooperating with them in this matter."

"Did the FBI give you permission to go on air with this information?"

"No," she shot back. "But the public's right to know is protected by the First Amendment, which guarantees freedom of speech." She took a quick breath. "Look, our time is nearly over, so unfortunately we have to wind this up, Danni. I—"

I was searching my mind to remember all that Grandpère had told me. I cut in quickly. "You seemed especially interested in this pouch of mine. Evidently, in his statement, El Cobra claimed that it had strange and unusual powers—even magical powers?"

"Yes. So?"

"Did it ever occur to you and your producers that this might be a very clever way for his attorney to set up a possible plea of not guilty by reason of insanity?"

"What? No. That doesn't make sense."

"Sure it does. He's gone round the bend. He's off his rocker. Delusional. Out of touch with reality. And now, everyone in America knows it. It's actually quite brilliant, when you think about it."

"That is pure speculation," Cierra snapped, "and totally unsubstantiated."

"Or maybe," I mused, "maybe this is a clever way for that attorney to discredit *my* testimony. Show that I'm the one who's delusional. After all, I have a magic purse, right? How much credence can the court give to a girl like that?"

I stood up abruptly, catching her totally off guard. "Since this discussion now has legal ramifications for me and my family, I think it's best if we end our interview here and now. Any further questions should be directed to our attorney."

And with that, I finally found the courage to follow Rick's example. I stood, removed my microphone, laid it down on the side table, and walked off the set.

CHAPTER 20

One of Cierra's assistants hurried up to us and suggested that we go out the back door to avoid the crowd waiting out front. While her motives were almost certainly to protect Cierra from further embarrassment, it was appreciated nevertheless. I didn't feel like facing anyone right now.

None of us spoke as she led us through the labyrinth of passageways to a back alley. She pointed the way back to our hotel, thanked us, started to shut the door, then opened it again. To my surprise, she smiled at me and said, "Nicely done, Danni." She looked quickly over her shoulder, then lowered her voice. "And tell Rick that I thought he was perfect." Blushing, she quickly shut the door and disappeared.

When the door clicked shut, everyone started talking at once. Mom and Dad were furious. Cody was griping about how rude Cierra was. He started to say something to me, but I held up my hand, cutting him off. I grabbed my cell phone. "I've got to find Rick."

Mom reached out and put her hand over mine. "He texted us a few minutes ago. He's waiting at a small sidewalk café about a block south of the studio. It's called the Blue Bistro." She leaned in and gave me a quick but heartfelt hug. "You did brilliantly, Danni. But you're right. Go talk to him. We'll meet you back at the hotel."

That didn't require any persuasion. I jammed the phone back in my pocket and took off. As I ran, I just kept cursing myself. Had I crossed a line in our friendship that was nonrecoverable? What had possessed me to tell them about our kiss? It was a good thing I was out of the studio because right now I wanted to claw that smug smile off Cierra Pierce's face. She did this. And she did it deliberately.

———

Rick barely looked up when I slid into the chair across from him. "Hi," I said softly.

"Hi." He was using his fork to trace circles on tablecloth. "So, it's over?"

"Yes." Silence. "Did you watch the rest of it?"

He didn't look up. "Yes."

"I'm sorry about what happened. I had no idea she would ask those kinds of questions."

"Oh? I thought that was what the pouch was for."

I stared at him, stung by what he was suggesting. "*Le Gardien* doesn't make me a mind reader, Rick."

"Oh?" he said again. Thankfully, he didn't start listing all the times the pouch had done pretty close to exactly that. I started to change the subject, but suddenly it all came out.

"This was all a game to her, Danni. She set you up. She set *us* up. It was an ambush from the very first. I had that feeling before we ever went in. But you didn't?"

I wasn't sure what to say to that. "No, I didn't see it coming. The pouch gave me nothing."

"I wonder why that is?" Then he waved it off. "Forget I said that. I guess the only question I really have is this: Why did you feel compelled to give her every detail about our kiss? I thought that was between you and me."

My head dropped. "I . . . I'm sorry, Rick, I—"

"How many others have you told?" he asked, and now the bitterness was evident.

"No one. I swear. I wouldn't do that."

"Except to twenty or thirty million viewers," he said softly. Then he burst out. "I guess I can see why you admitted we had kissed. That got her off the lover thing. But why tell her everything? Who said she gets to set all the rules?"

"Because . . ." I felt the frustration welling up inside me. *Because the reason she asked me about the kiss was she wanted to prove her point, that our relationship was more than just friends. That was why she wanted to know what kind of kiss it was. Can't you see that?* But all I said was, "I couldn't think of what else to say."

He sighed. "How about, 'None of your business, Cierra'? That would have shut her up."

"Really? It didn't shut her up when you said it."

"Forget it," he said. He sighed, looking away again. Neither of us spoke as we retreated into our respective emotional corners. I was thinking of what to say that might allow us to come out and shake hands and declare the fight over. But another part of me was smoldering too. I knew he was ticked, but why had he walked off and left me—*No, Danni! You go with your pride here and you could lose him.*

So I started again. "Rick, I am really, really sorry. When you kissed me, it was . . . well, I'll just say it was one of the best moments of my entire life. And now I've ruined it, cheapened it, and I would do anything to take back what I said."

"Well, you can't, Danni. You just threw twenty or thirty million feathers to the wind. There's no picking them up again now."

I had to look away. I couldn't let him see the pain. Not now. Oh, how I wished he would just take me in his arms and hold me. Stroke my hair and tell me it was all right, that I was forgiven.

I could tell he was watching me, but I didn't look up. Finally, he touched my shoulder. "Danni?"

I didn't answer. I didn't move.

"Talk to me. Please."

"If talk is just feathers in the wind, what difference does it make?"

"I'm sorry for that. I didn't mean it. Now it's me that cheapened you by tossing your apology back in your face."

I finally looked up at him. "I meant it, Rick. I feel horrible. I can't believe I did it."

"I know. It's just that . . . I don't know. Suddenly, here we were in New York, living this fairy-tale experience. Only I felt like you were here trying on the glass slippers and I was outside cleaning up after the horses."

I wanted to laugh. My Rick was using a princess metaphor? And yet I was touched, because I guess I never thought about how the guy felt who was always outside the palace.

"Rick, it's over now. No more shows. So can we just kind of start over and—"

I stopped when I saw Rick's eyes lift and look up at something behind me. Before I could turn to see, I felt a tap on my shoulder. I half turned in my seat and looked up. A woman was standing just behind me. "Excuse me," she said in a rich Southern accent, "but aren't y'all that McAllister girl?" She was about twenty-five and wore shorts and a halter top, even though it was a bit of a brisk September day.

"Yes, I'm Danni McAllister."

"I thought so," she crowed. She dove into her purse, which looked big enough to house a cattle truck, and came up with a cell phone. "I saw y'all on the show. We couldn't get tickets but I was outside watching. Y'all were wonderful."

"Thank you." I glanced at Rick, who was intently counting the threads in the tablecloth.

"And y'all are the boyfriend, right?"

He managed a pasted-on smile. "Yes. Melark. Peeta Melark."

"Oh, you," she said, waving a hand at him. "I know your real name. It's . . . uh . . . Ricardo. Right? Yes. Ricky Ricardo." Up came the camera. "I just loved what y'all did, putting Miss High and Mighty Cierra in her place. Can I take a picture of y'all?"

"Of course," I said, putting on a bit of a drawl myself. "Why don't I take the picture while y'all sit there by Rick."

"Oh, no," she cried in horror. "I want one with all three of us." She swung around to the couple at the table just to our left. "Could y'all take our picture for us, please?"

The guy—a young black guy with a shaved head and neatly trimmed beard who was already laughing—stood up and held out his hand. "I'd be happy to."

She handed him the camera. "Oh my, they are nevah gonna believe me back in Louisiana." As Rick and I slid our chairs closer together, she squeezed in between us.

"Smile," our photographer said. The flash went off and he checked the screen. "Looks great."

"Do another one," she cried. "Just to be sure."

He did, but as he finished, the young black woman with him was up and beside him, her cell phone up too. "I saw you on David Letterman last night," she said. "You two were awesome." She handed the camera to her guy. "Jason, take one of me with Danni." Then to me, "Is that all right?"

"Sure, why not?" Rick said. He quickly got up and stepped back.

Before we were through, six other luncheon customers or passersby had gotten in on the act. When we were done and the last thank-yous were given, I turned around to see how Rick had fared.

I didn't learn much. Rick was nowhere to be seen.

Ah, man! Did you just walk out on me?

After confirming he wasn't just standing nearby waiting, I looked at his plate. There was a napkin folded neatly on it, hiding the portion of his lunch he hadn't eaten. I reached over and picked it up. Scrawled across the paper diagonally was a message from Rick:

THIS IS YOUR FAIRY TALE, NOT MINE. I'M SORRY, BUT I WON'T BE GOING TO FRANCE WITH YOUR FAMILY. MY FLIGHT BACK HOME LEAVES AT SEVEN FIFTEEN TONIGHT.

CHAPTER 21

My mind was in so much turmoil by the time I got back to the hotel, I walked right into the arms of the waiting crowd of media. I heard someone shout, "There she is!" then saw people sprinting toward me. Only then did I realize my mistake.

"Ms. McAllister, tell us about the magic pouch." "Show us *Le Gardien*." "Have you and Rick ever discussed marriage?" "Are you going to sue Cierra Pierce for defamation of character?" "Where's your boyfriend?" "How does your enchanted purse work?" They were coming so fast and furious that it registered more as a dull roar than individual questions. Cameras were clicking. Microphones were shoved at me. I ducked my head, lowered my shoulder, and pushed into them.

Suddenly I heard a voice roar out, and my heart leaped for joy. "FBI! Stand back. FBI! Coming through. Get back, people! Move! Move!" And a moment later, Clay and two of his agents appeared as if the Red Sea had divided and opened up a path for me to escape. Clay took my elbow. "Let's go." And with the two agents opening up the way before us, we pushed our way through and entered the hotel.

"Thank you, Clay. I—"

He still had my elbow and was steering me toward the elevators past the gaping lobby crowd. "Why didn't you answer your phone?" he asked in a low voice. "We were going to bring you through another entrance."

I shook my head. My phone hadn't been ringing. Then I remembered. I had turned it off as we started the show, and everything since then had been so crazy, I had started to turn it on, then hadn't when Mom told me where Rick was. I slowed my step. "Is Rick here?"

"Yes. He's upstairs."

"I—"

"Let's go upstairs. Joel is there with your family." He frowned. "We need to talk."

———

The first thing I saw as my family swarmed me was that Rick was not there. "Where is he?" I asked, looking over Mom's shoulder as she came and threw her arms around me.

"He's in his room," she said. She looked away. "He's packing."

"*No!* You don't know what happened. I have to talk to him."

Dad came up right behind me. "Rick told us what happened," he said. "You can go to him in a minute, but we need you to sit down now."

"Danni?" Joel called from the far side of the room. "Please come in. There have been a couple of new developments we need to talk about."

With Mom and Dad escorting me, we all sat down. Joel, who remained standing, began immediately. "We learned about two hours ago that the law firm we talked about earlier sent an attorney in yesterday to represent some of the members of the gang."

"Only some?" Mom asked in surprise. "Which ones?"

"Just four. Armando Mendosa and his wife, Eileen; Raul Muñoz, or the one you called Doc; and the Belgian—Jean-Claude Allemand."

"Doc," I whispered. That familiar creepy feeling when I had been around him was instantly back. And I was thinking of Jean-Claude, too. The two worst ones. Both were more frightening to me than El Cobra had ever been.

"Not Gordo?" Cody asked.

"No. Only the four."

"Wonder how the rest feel about that?" I said.

"Madder than you-know-what," Clay said, "which we think will work to our advantage. Word has already reached us that they have asked for court-appointed attorneys. We have a team on its way to interrogate them and offer them a deal if they tell us everything they know."

"That's wonderful," Dad said.

Joel shook his head. "Probably not. I think whoever is behind all this was willing to sacrifice the ones they did because they knew those particular gang members don't know that much. Anyway, that substantiates that the source for the notebook sent to Cierra was El Cobra."

Grandpère was shaking his head before Joel finished. "No."

"No?"

"She had too many details that none of the gang members knew."

"Like what?"

"Danni's nicknames for them. Raul was Doc, and Gordo was Lew. Did you ever call them that to their faces, Danni?"

"No."

Grandpère turned to me as if to speak, but then he hesitated a moment. "And there was one other detail that came only from Danni's journal. Even we in the family didn't know about it until we heard it today."

My face flamed, and I ducked my head.

"The kiss," Mom said, nodding.

"Then how . . . ?" Joel exclaimed.

Dad saw what Grandpère was suggesting. "Tell them about the broken thread, Danni."

I snapped up my head at that. I had forgotten all about it. So I explained how I had put a thread across the top of each door the day of the mine explosion, and how the one on the back door had been broken. I turned to Grandpère. "But my journal was locked in the safe."

Clay was nodding now too. "A simple task for a professional burglar."

Mom was clearly perplexed. "But why would whoever this is release that information to the media? Did they ask for anything in return for this packet of stuff they gave Cierra?"

"No, nothing."

"But that doesn't make sense," Mom cried.

"Not to us," Grandpère answered, "but you can be sure that it makes perfect sense to them."

I was barely listening. A deep groan rose up from somewhere inside me and burst forth. "Not my journal! Please don't tell me some stranger is reading all the stupid, ditzy stuff I wrote in there." But I knew instantly that Grandpère was right. It explained everything.

Joel was pulling at his lower lip. He looked to Dad. "Is your safety deposit key somewhere in the house? We'll need your permission to have the bank let us get it." When Dad nodded, he turned to Clay. "Send down a team. I want Danni's journal checked for prints."

"If they can open a safe without us knowing it, they won't be foolish enough to leave prints," Dad noted.

"I know," Joel replied, "but we have to try."

"But you can't read it," I blurted.

Clay laughed softly. "You have my word."

Suddenly all business, Joel straightened. "All right, that explains a lot. But on to the next thing." He took a quick breath. "Because we no longer have to wait for Rick's passport to clear, Clay and I agree that you ought to skip Washington and go directly to France in the morning."

"No! He needs a passport. I need to talk to him."

His eyes filled with compassion, Joel looked at me. "If you can convince him to go with you, we're all for it. We told him it will be very difficult if he goes back to Hanksville, but . . . you two are going to have to work it out."

I turned to Mom. "Will you help me?"

She shook her head gently. "No, dear. I'm afraid this one is up to you."

Rising slowly to my feet, I turned and started for the door.

The first thing I noticed when I came out into the hallway was that the agent who had been outside Rick's door when I came in was gone now. Good. I was in no mood for a hassle. As I lifted my hand to knock, I saw the door was ajar. "Rick?"

No answer. I pushed it open and went inside. The light was still on, but no one was in the room. "Rick? You in here?"

Silence. I looked around. The doors to the closet were both open, and the closet was empty.

And then I saw the note. It wasn't in an envelope. It was a single sheet of paper propped up against his pillow on the bed. I went to it in three quick steps and snatched it up. I saw what it was, and my stomach fell through the floor. "No!" I cried. "No!"

It was printed in capital letters. There was no introduction, no "Dear Danni." Not even a "Hi." It took a moment for me to understand. When I did, I found it suddenly hard to breathe.

> OH, DANNY BOY, THE PIPES, THE PIPES ARE CALLING
> FROM GLEN TO GLEN, AND DOWN THE MOUNTAIN SIDE.
> THE SUMMER'S GONE, AND ALL THE FLOW'RS ARE DYING.
> 'TIS YOU, 'TIS YOU MUST GO AND I MUST BIDE.
> BUT COME YE BACK IN SUMMERTIME TO HANKSVILLE;
> OR WHEN THE DESERT'S HUSHED AND WHITE WITH SNOW.
> AND I'LL BE THERE IN SUNSHINE OR IN SHADOW.
> OH, DANNY BOY, IT BREAKS MY HEART THAT YOU MUST GO.

By the time I read it a second time, my vision was so blurred, I could barely make out the last line.

> SORRY, D. I'M JUST NOT A FAIRY-TALE KIND OF A GUY.
> WITH DEEPEST AFFECTION, RICK

PART SIX

Le Petit Château

CHAPTER 22

Le Petit Château, France
September 28, 2011

It is an unbelievably glorious day. Finally!

We landed at Strasbourg late Thursday night—that's last Thursday—in a heavy drizzle, and it has rained steadily until last night. For a couple of days, that wasn't all bad. We were all pretty wiped with jet lag and were content to sleep, unpack, explore the château, sleep, eat our meals together, and sleep. In spite of having a lot of time on our hands, I didn't even write in my journal until yesterday. (To be honest, I tried, but every time I started, I thought of Rick and put the pen away again.)

But Monday, when our internal clocks were finally adjusting to the eight-hour time difference (well, six from New York), I was at a point where I was feeling caged. I wanted to get outside, to go for a walk or explore the estate, even in the rain. (That seemed to fit my mood.) I don't think Hanksville has had this much rain in the ten or so years we've lived there.

It was night when we drove through the village of Le Petit Château, which is about a mile from the château itself. This was a disappointment to Grandpère, who has been so anxious for us to finally see where he grew up. He was pointing out things to us as we drove through, but we could barely see what they were. So I was anxious to go into the village and see it in daylight, and reminded Mom and Dad of that wonderful invention called the umbrella.

But I was voted down. Joel and Clay reminded us that our story had been so sensational, it had jumped across the ocean. Clips of the Today show, Fox and Friends, David Letterman, and especially some of Life Is Real had been played quite a bit in the major countries of Europe—which, of course, included France.

Grandpère agreed with them to a point, but assured them that the chances that our story would have gotten much play in a little village like Le Petit Château were small. And he noted that at the château, the new owners had refused to put in television because they wanted to maintain a mid-twentieth-century atmosphere in the facility. We compromised and agreed to stay in the château for a week, and then, when we did venture out, to alter our appearance somewhat. Mom and I were to wear our hair up or put on scarves. The men were to always wear a hat of some kind. We would also wear sunglasses when appropriate. The idea was to avoid looking like American tourists and to blend in more with the European style.

All of that seemed a little much to me and Cody, but Mom was adamant that we honor our commitment to Joel and Clay. And, as she pointed out, there really was no need for a trip to the village quite yet. We haven't met the people who own the château; they are out of town until tomorrow. They have two servants—we would call them employees. One is the cook/housemaid. The other, her husband, is an overall handyman and maintenance guy. So the kitchen is fully stocked. There are lots of books in the library, and they have a pretty impressive collection of table games in what they call the drawing room.

At first, having no television was a bit of a bummer, but now, it's okay. In fact, it feels right not to. The cook is great. She prepares our meals, and all of our needs are cared for. Except the beds. Mom says no way is she having someone make our beds. That would be "too corrupting"—her words.

We have also sat around a lot just talking. It sounds boring, but it's actually been pretty cool. Especially sweet is when Grandpère talks about what his life was like growing up here.

Yesterday, Mom started home schooling me and Cody, with Dad and Grandpère helping occasionally. (Dad is teaching us math, which Mom hates.) That is turning out to be much more fun than I thought it would be. Mom is amazing. We laugh a lot together, but she really challenges us, even as she makes learning a lot of fun. The best thing—at least for me, Cody is less enthusiastic—is that she started teaching us French. And here, of course, Grandpère is the "senior professor."

I love it here. It is so beautiful and peaceful. Even this late in the season, things are so green and lush. What a contrast from Hanksville! And the fall colors are stunning in the sunshine.

Okay. I've put it off long enough. So I'll just say it. Rick hangs over me like a black shroud. It's like every time I breathe in and out I sense his absence. Part of that is knowing how much he would love this place. And France. To share it together would have been amazing. I text him or Tweet him every day—he refuses to have a Facebook account—and he answers. But his responses are pretty short, pretty noncommittal. Even knowing how I hate the word "fine" that's how he answers a lot of my questions. How's things at home? Fine. How is your last year of high school going? Fine. That's not a big surprise. He's never been one to run off at the mouth. That's one of the things I ~~like~~ love about him. But in light of what happened, it feels like what he's really saying is, "I'll be polite, but if you think things are back to normal between us, you are wrong."

Mom keeps saying that I need to give it some time, but it depresses me more than I can express. It's not the same without him. Even Cody says so.

Thank heavens today is finally sunny. I'm looking out the window right now, and it truly is a glorious day. When Grandpère listened to the forecast last night on the radio, it predicted this, so we're planning a long walk in the woods today. I'm going to try to push Rick back to the "contain-the-pain" corner of my mind and have a good time.

———

We were approaching the hillsides I had seen several times since our arrival, though they had always been barely visible through the rain or mist. Now, in full sunshine, and with the autumn colors coming into full leaf, they were stunning. Cody had raced ahead and was disappearing into the trees. Mom and Dad were behind us, holding hands and talking quietly. I had my arm through Grandpère's and leaned against him as we strolled along at a leisurely pace.

"It is so beautiful," I said. "It's everything you promised it would be."

"But of course," he said with a smile. "The land is enchanted, no?"

"I love it." I looked around. "And you played here when you were a boy?"

"*Oui.* Almost every day in the summertime." He pointed off to the left. "And we had a grand sledding hill over there. Often, the children from the village would come out. Papa would build a great fire and Mama would have sandwiches and sausage and hot cocoa and we would sleigh ride all the day long."

We looked up as Cody came running back and joined us. "This is great. Isn't it great?"

"Yes, it is."

"Grandpère. Are these the woods where that American pilot was shot down?"

"*Oui.* The very ones."

"Do you remember where you found him?" I asked in excitement. "Can we see it?"

"But of course," he said again. "Where else would we be going? Before we ever left New York, I determined this was the first place I wanted to show you."

Mom moved up to join us and slipped her arm through Grandpère's as well. "Don't forget that your daughter has never seen it either."

He pulled her close. "This is for you, *ma chérie,* as much as for Danni and Cody."

We stood in the shade of an enormous beech tree that had to be at least a hundred years old. The trunk was easily ten feet in diameter and the lowest branches were huge, as much as two feet thick. We were all looking up as Grandpère talked softly. He pointed to a dead log off to our right in the trees. It was decaying and covered with moss. "That was where Louis and I sat down to rest. We were very discouraged. Night was coming on quickly, and we knew if we didn't find him soon, we would have to wait for morning. And that was bad. There were already German patrols searching for him."

"And that's when Louis saw the blood?"

"Cody," Dad warned gently, "let your grandfather tell the story."

Grandpère smiled, pleased with Cody's eagerness. "You have to remember, Mama had given me *Le Gardien* before Louis and I left. I didn't understand why then, of course, but for some reason, as we sat there, I clutched it close to my body."

I was nodding. I knew exactly what he meant.

"And that was when we heard a soft moan coming from this direction." His eyes had a faraway look in them now as he pointed. "We came forward, not sure where the sound had come from."

"And that's when Louis saw the blood?"

"Cody?" Mom warned.

Grandpère just laughed. "Yes." He moved a few steps. "Right here, actually. And we looked up and there he was, hanging unconscious in his parachute. I'll never forget the relief I felt when we realized he was still alive."

"And you still haven't heard anything from Louis?" Mom said.

He shook his head. "No, the foreman at his manufacturing plant would say only that he was on an extended business trip. He promised to send word to him that we are here."

Suddenly, he clapped his hands. "Come. Since we don't have to get Lieutenant Fitzgerald down out of the tree today, let us go. I will show you the path we took and where we met the French Resistance." He looked at Cody. "And I should like to see if that hiding place my father built in the barn is still there. Would you like to see that?"

"But of course," Cody said, nearly perfectly imitating Grandpère.

——

The half wall in the hayloft was still there. Grandpère and Dad had to take pitchforks and move the hay back from it, but there it was. It looked like an extension of the main wall, but it bumped out about halfway down to accommodate some structural need.

Grandpère walked to one end of it, reached down, and pressed on the bottom of a board with the toe of his shoe. It swung out, revealing a small door and a narrow passage behind it. It looked far too small for a grown man to enter, but then I realized that was probably what made it such an excellent hiding place.

"It was nearly morning by the time Papa and the other Resistance members were able to get him here. And by that time he had lost a lot of blood. He was unconscious, and we weren't sure if he would live through the day." He looked at me. "But Monique, my mother, was a very good nurse, and by that evening, we knew that he would be all right."

"And then the Gestapo came?" Mom whispered.

His face was grave and his eyes dark. "Yes. In the middle of that next night. Colonel Horst Kessler. I shall never forget his name nor his face. He arrested Lieutenant Fitzgerald and took my father away, too. Later, he struck my mother with his ring. She wore the scar the rest of her life." He took a deep breath. "I was absolutely devastated, of course. I had talked a long time with the American that afternoon. I learned about his family. He showed me the picture of his girlfriend. It was very hard for me to . . ." He shook his head. "Very hard."

He straightened, and shut the door again. "When Clay and Joel say it's safe for us to travel, I should like to go to Normandy to see if I can find his grave in the American cemetery there."

Mom's head came up. "But I thought he died under interrogation in Strasbourg and was buried there."

"Yes, in an unmarked grave. But after the war, his family came over here, and with the help of an archivist in Berlin, they found a record of where he was buried." He shook his head. "That was one thing about the Germans. They kept very good records, even of their crimes. The family received permission from the French government to have his body moved to Normandy."

"Can we go too?" I asked. I was quite amazed at how deeply this morning had touched me. I had even forgotten Rick for a while. And now, I wanted very much to see the grave of this American boy, only two or three years older than me.

"I would have it no other way," he said.

Mother moved up beside him and started to say something, but just then a voice called out. "*Allo,*" it said. "You must be my new guests."

The woman who stood before us was slender and petite, shorter than me by two or three inches. Her eyes immediately caught my attention. They were a pale blue, like the morning sky, and had deep wrinkles around the corners. My first impression was that they were "smile wrinkles," as my Grandpa Mack called them, but as I looked closer, they looked more like they were the mark of sorrow and pain. Her hair was honey blonde, with a touch of gray around her ears. With a start I realized that it was naturally blonde and not dyed. You didn't see that much anymore. Her dress was simple and straight but looked expensive. She had two gold bracelets on one wrist. On her left ring finger was a pretty impressive diamond ring, which seemed a little odd for someone running an inn. It was in sharp contrast to the rest of her jewelry. On her feet she had black clogs with no heels. That too seemed a little out of harmony with the rest of her dress, but then perhaps she had put them on to come out to the barn.

She stepped forward, extending her hand to Grandpère. "*Monsieur* LaRoche?"

"*Oui.* You must be *Madame* Dubois." He gave it the French pronunciation, making it Doo-BWA. He gave a slight bow. "I am indeed Jean-Henri LaRoche." He took her hand and held it for a moment. Then he turned to us. "This is our hostess, the owner of Le Petit Château." Then back to her. "May I present my family. This is my daughter, Angelique McAllister."

Mom stepped forward and took her hand. "I am very pleased to meet you, *Madame* Dubois."

"Oh, please," came the response. "Call me Juliette. *Madame* is much too formal, and I have great hopes that we shall quickly become good friends."

"I hope so too," Mom said graciously. "And this is my husband, Lucas McAllister."

He grinned as they shook hands. "I'll call you Juliette if you'll call me Mack."

"Very good, Mack," she said with a wry grin.

Grandpère pulled me forward a step. "And this is my granddaughter, Carruthers Monique McAllister. She is sixteen."

I did a little curtsy. "And you can call me Danni, Juliette."

"Dannee?" she said, looking puzzled. She accented the last syllable.

"Yes, like in the Irish song."

"Ah, *oui*. 'Danny Boy.'"

"Exactly."

"And last, but certainly not least," Grandpère said, "my grandson, Cody."

"Very pleased to meet you, *Monsieur* Codee."

He grinned at her. "And you can just call me Cody. Or Co-DEE, if you like."

That won him a laugh. "You are our very first guests, you know," Juliette said. "We just finished preparing the château a few days before you came."

"When you say *we*, do you speak of your husband?" Dad asked.

Her face fell. "Ah, no. My husband has been dead for a few years now."

"Oh," Dad replied. "We're sorry to hear that."

"It is all right. I speak of him as if he were present because this was his idea. He bought it several years ago as an investment and planned to sell it again once we turned it into a guest house. But then he got cancer, and . . ." She smiled sadly. "My children were horrified when I told them I was going to move here and see the project through to its completion, but it is a good way to get through my old age. And I wanted him to know I didn't just abandon it."

Grandpère spoke softly. "I lost my wife to cancer too. Keeping busy was the only thing I found that lessened the pain."

Her head raised. "Yes, exactly. My children think it is demeaning for me to be an innkeeper, but it has been wonderful. I love France, especially out here where it is so quiet. I suppose, come spring, we'll put it back on the market and hopefully get our investment back, but for right now, it is perfect for me."

We didn't say much. Her words touched us all.

"And what is this?" She moved forward toward the wall we had uncovered. "Have you found something in my barn of which I am not aware?"

Grandpère was immediately apologetic. "I apologize, *Madame*—" He quickly corrected himself. "I apologize, Juliette. If I had known you had returned, I would have asked your permission before poking around."

She waved that away. "You are our guests. You are free to go anywhere on the grounds or in the house. My wish is that you think of it as your home now."

"But it is," Cody blurted. "Or, I mean it was. Grandpère used to live here. This is where he was raised as a boy."

She spun around. "No! That cannot be. This was once *your* home? I knew you were from the village, but not . . . I cannot believe it. That is wonderful. All the more honor for me."

Grandpère nodded. "It was. I was born in the upper east bedroom. And this barn was my favorite place to play as a boy."

"But why did you not tell me?" she cried. "I would have let you stay for free."

Grandpère laughed. "You have already given us a wonderful discount, and that is enough."

She dismissed that with a toss of her head. "The first two weeks are free, *Monsieur* Jean-Henri LaRoche, and I will hear of nothing less." Then she shook her head in amazement. "Your boyhood home? I cannot believe it."

And then, with our encouragement, Grandpère explained about the half wall. He told her the whole story of how he and Louis had watched the American plane shot down, and the events that followed.

To my surprise, she seemed deeply moved. "Those were terrible times. Terrible."

"Were you alive during the war?" I exclaimed. Then I immediately blushed. "I'm sorry, *Madame* Dubois. I . . . I didn't mean to pry."

She laughed merrily. "If you think I am not old enough to have been alive during the war, there is no need to apologize, Danni. I'll take that as a compliment. But actually, I was born in 1940, so, yes, I lived during the war, though I was very young."

"You do not speak with a French accent, Juliette," Grandpère said. "Are you not French by birth?"

"Very perceptive, *Monsieur* LaRoche," she said, clearly impressed. "No, I was born and raised in England. But I have lived on the Continent now for many years. France is my adopted country."

"You're seventy-one?" Cody exclaimed. "Wow! That's almost as old as Grandpère. He's seventy-seven."

"*Cody!*" Mom cut in, her face coloring. "Please."

But Juliette was eyeing Grandpère more closely. "You hold your age very well, *Monsieur.* I would have guessed you were not yet seventy."

"*Merci,*" he said with a laugh. "Either your eyesight is failing or you are overly generous with the truth. But, please, call me Jean-Henri."

She smiled demurely. "Perhaps." Then, almost shyly, she added, "I think we shall get along very well together."

I looked at Mom in amazement. She nodded. She had seen it too.

Juliette was actually flirting with Grandpère. I nearly laughed out loud. This was an unexpected twist.

Juliette went on. "I hope that you are not disappointed in what we have done with the château. It needed much work."

"*Au contraire,*" he answered. "I am very pleased to know my former home has been given a new life. We look forward to a delightful time here."

CHAPTER 23

Le Petit Château, France
October 5, 2011

Freedom! Yippee! Hallelujah!

After nearly ten days in our bonds, we have been unchained. Our shackles no longer hold us. Clay called this afternoon. After consulting with Joel, they have agreed that we no longer have to be restricted to staying right around the château. He didn't tell us this before, but Interpol had one of their operatives waiting for us when we landed in Strasbourg. He is now living in the village, posing as a biologist from the University of Strasbourg doing a study of the forests surrounding the village. He has reported that no one is watching us, no one has taken an interest in us, and no one has made any inquiries about us. So Clay thinks we are safe to start roaming farther abroad. Sweet!

Don't get me wrong. I adore Le Petit Château. It is lovely and perfectly charming in every way. But the only place we've gone is into the village and back. Not that that's bad. It's been wonderful to have that time together as a family. Grandpère has talked about his childhood and told us things that even Mom didn't know. And walking through the village with him was like stepping back seventy years.

Clay said that the FBI issued a statement to the media the day after the fiasco with Cierra Pierce. They said that due to the

316

release of confidential information, our family was being placed in a witness protection program and would not be available for further comment until the trial begins early next year. That doused the media firestorm in a hurry, and, just as Grandpère predicted, the California surfers were soon off chasing the next big wave.

They're not ready to give us free rein to roam all over Europe, but we can go anywhere in France as long as we keep a low profile in the big cities.

Another great thing happened today. I got to talk to Rick for the first time since we left. The FBI has been super cautious about our safety—and no one is complaining about that— so they've restricted our contact with home to texts, Tweets, and good old-fashioned letters (which we send to a P.O. box in Washington, D.C., and they forward them on home). The satellite phones Clay gave us are secure for texts and Tweets, but he wanted us to avoid phone calls for a while. With the Interpol report, he thinks we're fine now.

So the minute Dad told me that, I asked him if I could call Rick. It was sooo good to hear his voice again. And I could tell that even though there was a little strain between us, Mom's right. Things are a little better. And now that we can talk two or three times a week, I think they'll get better and better. However, when I started to apologize to him for what happened with Cierra—yet again—he cut me off. "I don't want to talk about that, Danni," he said, and it was pretty abrupt in how he said it.

So, things are not all better, but I'll take what I can get. It's tons better than texting or Tweeting. He talked about school and what's going on at home and told me that Mayor Brackston asks him all the time when they're going to get to have our parade. I also asked him how the homecoming dance with Cherie Averill went. His answer was classic Rick: "It was fine." And he would elaborate no further. But he did tell me that he called Jason Horne and explained why I wouldn't be able to go.

It was so good to talk to him again, but it was hard also. I've always been able to tell him anything, everything. Just be myself around him. That's not back yet. And I know that's my

fault. I'm bossy and headstrong and stubborn and mouthy and
. . . I miss him. I feel so empty without him. Every night I pray
that he will somehow understand and forgive me. Tonight was
the first time I've had hope that it might come to that sometime.

Oh, one good thing came out of that phone call. When I hung
up, I didn't want to talk to anyone, so I ran up to my room and
threw myself on the bed and started to cry. When I heard footsteps in the hall, I blew my nose with a Kleenex and called out,
"I'm all right, Mom. I'd just like to be alone for a while." To my
surprise, it was Dad who came in.

Bless him. He didn't say anything. He just lay down beside
me and took me in his arms and let me cry it out. Finally, after
enough tears to cause our water bill to double, we sat up. "You're
a guy, Dad," I said. "Tell me what to do."

"Just what you're doing," he said. "Give it time. You've been
best friends since you were ten. Friendships like that don't just
collapse. They just need time to heal."

"You really think it will?"

"Absolutely, and maybe even something more. . . ." He stopped,
giving me the oddest look.

"What, Dad?" I said, instantly giving him my full attention.

"Nothing."

"No, Dad, you just can't toss me that ball and then turn
away. 'Something more' what?"

With a soft smile, he just shrugged. "Dunno. You'll have to
just wait and see." He kissed me on the forehead, held me tight
for a few seconds, then got up and started for the door.

I wasn't about to let him off with that. "Wait. Here's a hypo-
thetical question."

"Okay."

"Let's suppose this mysterious 'something more' you referred
to just happened to become reality. How would you and Mom
feel about that?"

He laughed right out loud. "Are you kidding?" he said. "I'm
not supposed to tell you this, but your mother and I have been
bribing Rick to be your friend since you were ten. We had to. You

punched him in the nose, remember? You surely didn't think all of this happened just by chance." I guess my mouth dropped open about a foot, because he laughed again. Then he winked at me. "Luv ya, Danni Bug. See you in the morning."

I am sorely tempted to say much more about that, but I am able to restrain myself.

So, back to Clay loosening the shackles. We had a debate about what we wanted to do first. What we finally settled on was awesome. Dad, Mom, and GP borrowed Juliette's car and went into Strasbourg this afternoon, where they rented an eight-passenger van for a month. Mom thought that was a little big. Dad said he didn't want us to travel like we were peas in a pod. Dad won.

Tomorrow, we're going to Moselle, which is a few hours to the north of us. That was where my great-grandmother Monique was born. It was also where she took GP and left him with her parents when she went to Paris to find my great-grandfather during the war.

Next week, if the weather is good, we're going to take off for a week, maybe even ten days, and go to Paris. In addition to the usual tourist sites, GP is going to take us to the building that used to be Gestapo headquarters in World War II. Since that's my heritage, and after reading Monique's account of her visit there, I am way pumped to see it for myself.

After Paris, we'll go north to the Normandy coast. GP wants to see the World War II sites, like the beaches where the Allies landed and the huge German shore batteries built along the cliffs. Cody is way hyped about seeing those. Knowing my ancestors were part of that history, including Grandpère himself, is totally awesome. I am way excited to go. Only wish that Rick was here to go with us. ☹.

It's getting late, but maybe a word or two about Juliette before I quit and go to sleep. Juliette Dubois is our landlady—I guess that's what you would call her. Anyway, she owns the château and runs it as a bed and breakfast. We have other people staying here now too—a couple from Holland, who are older and on holiday for a month, and a family from the south of France with a boy who is twelve and a girl seven. Cody and the boy have become good friends already. And with that, suddenly Cody is interested in learning French, much to Mom's delight.

On that first day we met her, Juliette said she wanted to be friends. That has proven to be the case. We are really good friends now. She often joins us for our meals—and the cook is excellent, BTW. (Grandpère insists that there is no such thing as a bad French cook.) Juliette and GP have hit it off famously. It is fun to watch him when he's with her. I think she's pretty lonely and is glad for company closer to her own age. Me and Cody often go on walks with her around the estate or into the village. She's just a really fun person. She has a quick sense of humor and makes us laugh a lot.

She doesn't say much about herself, but we have learned a few things. Her father was a pilot in England's Royal Air Force and was killed in the Battle of Britain when she was still a baby. Her mother never remarried, so Juliette grew up in pretty humble circumstances. But she eventually met a banker from Paris and they married, which meant she was no longer poor. No surprise that she could attract someone like that. She has a picture of them on their wedding day, and she was beautiful. Still is, of course, but back then she was stunning.

She and I have become especially close. She has two children, a son and a daughter, and three grandchildren. We haven't met any of them yet, but she talks about them all the time. It is strange that we have hit it off like we have, her being seventy and me only sixteen.

One of the things I like about her is that she's very honest. Sometimes to the point of being downright brutal. For example, the other day, Cody called something totally awesome. She waggled a finger at him. "Awesome is a word that should be reserved for things that are truly awesome. To call something which is trivial awesome is a contradiction in terms. And totally awesome is an unnecessary redundancy."

Cody, with his usual charm, said, "That's a totally awesome

concept, Juliette." Which made her laugh. She and Cody get along really well too.

But here's another example. I always have the pouch with me when I leave the house. I had noticed her studying it several times, but the other day while we were getting some hay down for the two milk cows, she finally asked me about it. But the way she did it was pretty blunt. "Do you know what the French word gauche means?" she asked. Gauche is pronounced like "gohsh."

"Sure. It means awkward, kind of like a klutz."

"Yes, but it's more than that. It means that one is lacking in the social graces, that something is crudely said or done. In French, it literally means 'left-handed.' Since most of us are right-handed, it implies clumsiness, but socially more than physically."

"Okay," I said slowly, not sure where she was going with this.

And then she hit me with it. "So why do you carry that old purse around with you all the time?"

I laughed right out loud. "What? You think it's gauche?"

She was immediately embarrassed. But she went on to say that the French had invented the concept of chic (pronounced "sheek"), and that she considered me chic in so many ways (which made me feel good). Because of that, however, she found it strange that I would carry around that old pouch all the time. And then she added, "In France, we have chic. And in America, you have what? Grungy?"

I just laughed. By this point, I was getting used to the faint condescension for anything American that is common in Europe. So I ignored that and explained that the pouch was a family heirloom which I had received from GP and which had been his mother's. She was instantly apologetic, but I assured her that no offense was taken.

The next day she apologized again and I asked her if she wanted to see it. She did, so I let her hold it. She hadn't noticed the four fleurs-de-lys on the flap, or the words Le Gardien embroidered there too. She seemed quite fascinated by it. When she handed it back to me, she smiled. "I was wrong. It is not gauche. It is quite appropriate that you wear it."

"But not chic?" I teased.

She laughed. "No, definitely not chic."

Well, it's nearly ten thirty and we're leaving for Moselle early. Closing off for tonight.

Le Petit Château
October 7, 2011

"Dad?"

"Yes?"

"Do you think French cows are more gentle than American cows?"

He gave me a funny look.

Mom laughed. "Are you serious?"

I shrugged. "They seem like it." We were in the barn, putting fresh straw in the stables for Juliette's two milk cows. I reached through the slats and rubbed the nose of the nearest one. "These two are so gentle. And I love their big brown eyes."

Mom hooted. "You're in a particularly odd mood today." Then she snapped her finger. "Oh, that's right. You talked to Rick again."

When I realized what had just happened, I laughed merrily. "What? You think their brown eyes remind me of Rick?"

She gave me one of her looks. "Just an observation."

Actually, I *was* thinking of Rick, but I didn't think it had anything to do with the cows. This was our third phone call in three days. Yesterday's was better than Wednesday's. Today's was better than yesterday's. I was starting to sense what felt like the tiniest thaw in that wall of wounded pride. But I was forcing myself to be very cautious. Not get my hopes too high and all that.

I looked at Mom and grinned. "They do look a little like Rick, now that I think about it."

Mom left a few minutes later to go help the cook with supper. Juliette had gone into the village and wouldn't be back for another hour or two. While I finished with the hay, Dad went up to the loft to get some grain for the horse.

"*Excusez-moi.*"

I jumped and whirled around. There was a dark silhouette standing in the doorway. The hairs on the back of my neck were suddenly standing straight out. I fell back a step.

"*Pardonnez-moi, mademoiselle.* I didn't mean to startle you."

I took a quick breath, then another, forcing myself to calm down a little. "It's all right . . . uh . . . you just . . . um . . . startled me." *Duh! He just said that.*

"I am very sorry," he said in perfect English as he started coming toward me. I fell back another step and he stopped. There was amusement in his voice when he spoke again. "You must be Carruthers. The one they call Danni."

"I am," I said, realizing that his accent was British. "Can I help you?"

"I am looking for my mother. I could not find her in the house."

Dad appeared above us with a sack of grain on his shoulder. "Hello," he said. "I'm Lucas McAllister. But everyone calls me Mack. You must be Philippe."

"Yes, I am. Philippe Dubois. Has my mother been talking about me?"

"Only seven or eight times a day," Dad said. "She went into the village. Said she'd be back about four. Was she expecting you?"

"Ah, no," he said. "Actually, I'm on my way back to Paris from a conference in Zurich. We finished earlier than I thought. So I thought I'd pop in and say hello."

He was fully inside the barn now and at an angle so that the door was no longer behind him. This allowed me to see him better. No question about it. This was the same man as the one in the picture Juliette kept on the fireplace mantel. He was tall, probably six two or more. His face was narrow and the features finely shaped. I guessed he was in his early thirties. There was no mistaking his resemblance to Juliette.

He was dressed in a three-piece business suit with a dark maroon tie and matching handkerchief in the breast pocket. His shoes gleamed in the subtle light, and I guessed they were Italian, or something similarly expensive. Definitely looked like a man of means. Rich like his mother. And very chic, if that word applied to men.

Dad set the sack down and came down the ladder. When he reached the bottom, he walked over to Philippe, sticking out his hand. "We can call Juliette if you like," he said as they shook hands. "She has her mobile phone with her."

We learned very quickly that in Europe you didn't call them cell phones. They were mobile phones, which was pronounced not as "MOH-bull," but "MOH-bile," so it rhymed with "no tile."

"No, no," Philippe said quickly. He lifted an arm and glanced at his watch. It looked like a Rolex. "That's not that much longer. I'll wait inside." He turned back to me, and the smile he shot at me was very warm and open. "I must say, Danni, Mum has told me all about you. She says you are becoming fast friends."

I bobbed my head. "I'm glad she feels that way because that's how I feel about her."

Philippe looked around and a small frown creased his brow. "Anina and I—that's my sister—have tried and tried to talk Mum out of all this château nonsense, but she just won't talk. So I'm glad her very first guests have turned out to be so pleasant."

As dinner progressed, I found it interesting to watch Philippe and Juliette together. There was a comfortable easiness—almost an equality—between them, unlike what you saw between many mothers and sons. He wasn't married yet, but that was not unusual for European men.

Once we finished with dessert, Cody quickly tired of the adult conversation and excused himself. Dad left a short time later to get online with Rick to deal with some problems in the consulting business. After ten minutes, I almost left too because it soon became a four-way conversation between Juliette, Philippe, Mom, and Grandpère, much of it conducted in French. And even though the topics were absolutely fascinating—French literature, French Impressionist painters, the European economic climate, the strength of the Euro against the dollar, and the like—I was bored stiff in about two minutes.

But Juliette had this way of bringing the conversation around to Philippe, no matter what the topic happened to be, and I kept learning interesting things about him, so I stayed on. He spoke several European languages, including French, Spanish, and German, in addition to his English. He could slip back and forth between a clipped British accent and a slow Bostonian drawl with perfect ease. After graduating from an exclusive prep school in England, he came to America and attended one of the Ivy League schools. When Mom asked him which one, he modestly admitted it was Harvard. Juliette informed us that he had received a full scholarship there. He was now a vice president at his bank, the youngest in the company. And so on and so on. I was beginning to think that Philippe Dubois had an enthusiastic fan club of two people—his mother and himself.

I'm not sure why, but Juliette's attempt to impress us with her son actually had the opposite effect on me. Philippe was too polished, too suave, too sophisticated—I don't know—too "packaged," I guess, to suit me. As they talked, I kept making the comparison between my dad, the cowboy from Hanksville, Utah, and Philippe, Mr. Slick from Paris, France. And between Philippe and Rick. And I decided that being gauche maybe wasn't all that bad after all.

I came back to the conversation when Philippe asked Mom a question about running in the mornings.

"Yes," Mom said. "Since we're early risers, Lucas and I often go running before breakfast."

He nodded. "I, as well. I try to run ten kilometers each morning. Perhaps I might join you tomorrow?"

Ten kilometers? That was six miles.

Mom turned to Grandpère. "How early are we leaving for Strasbourg?" She turned back to Philippe and explained. "Since we've stuck pretty close to home since our arrival, we thought it was time to see the city."

Grandpère shrugged. "Not until after breakfast. You would have time for a run, if you like."

Philippe looked surprised. "But Jean-Henri," he said, "Mother has told me that you were born and raised here at Le Petit Château. Surely you know Strasbourg."

Nodding, Grandpère explained. "The last time I was in Strasbourg, other than the night we landed at the airport when it was dark and rainy, was in early 1947. My family and I walked to Strasbourg, then caught a train for Cherbourg. There, we took a ferry across the English Channel and left two days later by steamer from Southampton for New York City. The last image I have in my mind of Strasbourg is mile after mile of bombed-out buildings. I am anxious to replace that image with something more pleasant."

"But of course you must do that," Juliette said. "It is a most beautiful city now."

"I agree," Philippe said. "We have a Strasbourg branch of the bank and I'm often there." He snapped his fingers and turned to his mother. "What would you say to that, Mum? Should we offer them our guide service? Show them our beloved Strasbourg?"

No. We can do it on our own.

But Juliette loved the idea. "But of course," she said. Then to Mom, "If you would not see that as an imposition on your family outing."

"Are you kidding?" Mom said. "Lucas has been worried about driving in the city."

"We would be delighted," Grandpère said, even as he saw the look on my face.

"Then it's settled," Philippe said. "We shall spend the day together in Strasbourg." Back to Mom. "So, will you and Mack still run in the morning?"

"Yes. I think so."

Juliette turned to me. "What about you, Danni? Are you a runner too?"

I had already seen it coming. I smiled sweetly. "I am, but I was lucky enough to find a young boy in the village who likes to run. I'm paying him twenty cents for every mile he jogs for me. And so far it's working out great. He's making money and I'm getting in twenty-five miles a week."

Juliette's mouth dropped open, something I hadn't often seen in her. "Really?"

Philippe laughed. "It's a joke, Mama. She's just kidding you."

CHAPTER 24

Le Petit Château
October 9, 2011

A quick report on yesterday, then to some great news.

Strasbourg was amazing! And it turned out to be more fun than expected, even with Philippe along. We left right after breakfast with Philippe driving the other six of us in the van. It was a perfect fall day with clear blue skies and temperatures in the low sixties.

Strasbourg is the largest city in eastern France and is very beautiful. It sits on the west bank of the Rhine River, which forms the border between France and Germany, so it is a wonderful mixture of both French and German culture. We saw some really amazing and awesome things, which I won't detail for now.

More puzzlement about Juliette and her son, Philippe. With almost every day that goes by, we see more and more evidence that Juliette is quite wealthy, and yet she is perfectly content to be hosting a bed-and-breakfast guest house in a little village in Eastern France. And Philippe? Well, he can be insufferably arrogant at times, but he was also enormously charming and very funny. Overall, it was just a fun day.

We came back and had dinner together, but I slipped out early—with Mom's and Dad's permission—to call Rick. We talked for over an hour and it was wonderful. Maybe a little awkward at first, but soon we were laughing and joking with each other like nothing had happened between us. It felt so good. The only reference we made to New York was that he told me he had gotten a five-thousand-dollar check from the Today show. That wasn't a surprise because me and Cody had each gotten one too. Rick said he tried to give it to his dad, but he wouldn't take it. Made him open up a savings account at the bank in Green River. Good on you, Charlie.

Then, stupid me. I told him that Clay and Joel were now saying there was a possibility of us staying through Christmas, since Interpol wasn't making much progress in their investigation. This was just to be super safe. Rick had already heard that. I guess Clay calls him regularly too. So I worked up my nerve and asked if he wouldn't come over and join us, just for Christmas. Mom and Dad had told me to ask him, and said they would pay for his tickets. I assured him he didn't have to stay very long. Just come and see us for a few days. Maybe see some of France.

He went very quiet for a time, and I knew I had blown it. He finally said that he'd think about it. Translation? "No way." When we finally hung up, I lay on the bed and cried myself to sleep.

Okay, enough of that. Today was better. To our surprise, and Juliette's irritation, Philippe was gone by the time we were up. He'd left a brief note saying that he had to get his report of the conference prepared for a meeting first thing on Monday, but promised he would return as soon as he could get free to spend more time with her. I wasn't too broken up to have him gone. Though I had warmed up a little toward him, he still left me feeling uncomfortable, and I wasn't sure why.

We went to the little church in the village this morning and I got to attend my first Catholic mass. The church is over two hundred years old. It was way different from our church services, but kinda neat in its own way. Most of those there were older people, especially older women. Dad said that's the trend all over Europe. The younger generation just doesn't care much about religion.

But what was really super cool was what happened after the services. Grandpère took us out behind the church to the old church graveyard. We walked around and found the graves of several of our ancestors. But the neatest of all was that we found the graves of Angelique Chevalier and her grandfather, Alexandre Chevalier. Angelique is the one who fled Germany with her mother when men killed her father trying to get the pouch. Mom was named for her.

It was this really weird thing to stand right where their bodies now lay in the ground. It made them seem so real to me. I don't know why, but suddenly I got pretty emotional.

And then Grandpère dropped his little bombshell on us. He put his arm around Mom and pulled her close. "You know," he said, "this Thursday is October thirteenth. That will be exactly one hundred and forty years ago that Angelique turned thirteen years old and had to flee Germany for her life. I was thinking that might be a good day to see if we can't retrace some of her journey. What do you think?"

Wow! What a question. We leave early Thursday morning. Grandpère has promised us we can actually walk in the same creek she did. And we'll come all the way back to Le Petit Château, just like she did.

<hr />

The Rhine Valley, Germany
October 13, 2011

Our reenactment of the flight of Angelique Chevalier from her little village in Germany to Le Petit Château turned out to be more deeply stirring to me than I expected—and my expectations were pretty high. Grandpère had stressed that what he hoped for was not just retelling her story but actually reenacting the key parts of her experience.

The village of Schwarze Kirche was hardly a village at all. There were maybe five or six small farmhouses with their outbuildings set amidst the vineyards that filled the valley. Black Church seemed like an odd name for a settlement to me, but Grandpère explained that it took its name from Black Creek, which ran nearby, and had nothing to do with the idea of evil.

The cottage in which Angelique had been born and lived the first thirteen years of her life had never been rebuilt. But we did find the site, which was about a quarter of an acre of land knee-high in grass. One of the villagers told Grandpère that some people believed the site to be cursed, and that was why it had never been rebuilt. But Grandpère said it was much more likely the result of little villages like this slowly dying as the younger generations moved to the cities.

But it was really strange. After one hundred and forty years, I could feel the presence of evil around me, just like that day out near Robbers Roost. As Grandpère read Angelique's account of how the men had come that morning, I found myself shivering in spite of my warm clothing. I guess Dad saw that too, because he came up and put his arms around me and held me tightly until we finished.

We didn't attempt any kind of reenactment there, of course. But we stood together in a circle as Mom held the umbrella and Grandpère read Angelique's account of that horrible day. Then, with the help of a local vineyard keeper, we did find the path that led to the forested hillsides in the distance. Dad drove the van across the valley to meet us while the four of us followed the path mother and daughter had used to flee from their attackers.

Leaving the van at the base of the hill, we followed the path into the forest and actually found the place where the trails split, one going up the ridge, the other crossing over to the next valley. This was the site where Angelique's mother had sent her on alone, taking her coat away so she could draw the dogs after her. For our reenactment, Mom took the mother's role; I became Angelique. We didn't have to pretend very much. Suddenly, I could hear the distant baying of dogs, and I desperately clung to Mom as she told me to take off my coat and give it to her. Both of us sobbed and sobbed as Mom finally pried my hands loose from hers and told me to run. It was so real, I had to keep reminding myself that it had happened a long time ago.

We also found about a six-kilometer (or one-mile) stretch of the creek. Mom had thought to bring flip-flops for us, so all of us but Dad—who had to drive the van—changed our shoes for flip-flops and plunged in. Even Grandpère wanted to do it. It was raining lightly by then, and the water was freezing cold, so we were shivering pretty badly by the time we got out again. But I will never forget how I felt as I walked that mile hand in hand with my great-great-grandmother's memory.

———

After we crossed the bridge over the Rhine into France, we drove north on the main highway that led to Strasbourg until we could see the city in the distance. But as we passed a sign showing an exit for Ostwald, one of the suburbs of the city, Grandpère called out to Dad, "Take this exit, then stop as soon as you can find a place to pull off the road."

To my surprise, once we were stopped, Grandpère asked only me and Mom to get out. "Okay, you two. Remember, this is a reenactment of that day so many years ago. Though Angelique carries her name, I should like you, Danni, to continue to take her part since you are much closer to her age then." He focused in on me. "I know there are many distractions, but try to let yourself go back a hundred and forty years ago. While the road is paved now and much wider, you'll pretty much be following the same route she took. To do that, go straight on this road to the next intersection, then turn right, or north. It's a much smaller road. Follow that for a couple of miles until you see the sign for Le Petit Château. We will meet you there."

One part of me wanted to protest. I had several blisters by this time—one on each heel, and a big one on the ball of my right foot. From the way she walked, I suspected Mom did too. But we said nothing. Blisters seemed appropriate, lending authenticity to our experience. Angelique had said nothing about blisters in her account. Back then, people walked much more than we do now. But if she had walked twenty-six miles that day, she almost certainly had her own cluster of blisters.

The rain had mostly stopped, but I was still shivering a little and my feet still felt like blocks of ice. That was not all bad. It helped to numb the blisters. By choice, neither Mom nor I had worn hats, and our hair was wet and stringy. It seemed important to both of us that we not be too well prepared for our trek. We didn't say much as we walked along. We were passing large vineyards and small clusters of forest. Everything was still mostly green, though the grapevines were mostly wilted or gone. I was glad Mom was walking this with me. I knew it would create a bond we would share for the rest of our lives. I think Grandpère knew that too and had planned accordingly.

About half an hour later, Mom nudged me. "There's the sign for Le Petit Château."

The rain had started again in earnest, and I had to wipe my eyes to see better. Sure enough. It was a small metal sign bolted to a post on the side of the road. An arrow pointed left, and underneath, it read, *Le Petit Château, 3 km.* We increased our pace and walked up to it. I looked around.

"So this would be the place where she found the little wooden sign, right?" I said.

Mom was peering through the rain in the direction it pointed. "Yes. The château is about a kilometer up the road, and the village about a mile beyond that."

I started as a figure stepped out from between the rows of grapevines into the road about fifty meters away. "*Bonjour,*" he called. It was Grandpère, of course, but in that instant, he was a mysterious man who had suddenly appeared out of nowhere, causing a thirteen-year-old girl to shrink back in fear. I was thinking of Angelique's account of this day.

"*Allo,*" I called to him.

"Are you the one I am supposed to meet?" he called back.

Mom and I smiled at each other, and she nodded for me to respond. "*Pardon?*" I cried.

"I know it sounds strange, but a short time ago I had a strong impression that I needed to come out here to the Strasbourg Road to meet someone."

I felt the tears welling up again. "What is your name, *monsieur?*" I called back.

"Alexandre Chevalier. And yours, *mademoiselle?*"

I choked back a sob of joy. "I am Angelique Chevalier. I believe I am your granddaughter."

———— • ————

We didn't arrive back at Le Petit Château until after eight. Juliette had retired to her room by then. The cook had left a note saying she had left supper in the oven. We ate quietly, not saying much, still caught up in the power of the day's experience.

As we finished, Mom turned to Dad. "I'm going to take a hot bath, then it's off to bed for me."

"Me too," I said.

Grandpère held up his hand. "One more thing before you do. I checked the weather forecast for next week. By Tuesday, high pressure is supposed to start coming to most of northern France again. They're predicting at least a couple of days of cool but pleasant weather."

Mom, who had started to get up, sat down again. "Are you saying . . . ?"

"I am saying that maybe early Monday we head for Paris. Finally take that trip we've been talking about. We'll spend Monday and Tuesday seeing all the usual sites—Notre Dame, the Louvre, the Eiffel Tower. Then Wednesday, we'll spend the day down at the Palace of Versailles."

"Oh, yes," Mom said. "We have to see Versailles. Unbelievable."

"We're also going to see the museum at the former Gestapo headquarters in Paris," I said. "Right, Grandpère?"

To my surprise, Mom frowned. "I'm not sure about that."

"Yes," Grandpère said. "That is as much our heritage as the walk from Germany. And then on Thursday, it's on to Normandy. I hope we can stay at least two days, maybe three."

"And find the grave of Lieutenant Fitzgerald?" Cody asked.

"Yes."

We turned in surprise as the door to the dining room opened and Juliette came in. "Is that the American pilot you and your parents saved, Jean-Henri?"

"Yes. The same. He's buried at the cemetery there."

"I have an uncle, my father's brother, who was in the Royal Air Force on D-Day. He was shot down on the third day of the invasion."

"Really?" Dad said. "Is he buried at the cemetery too?"

"No," Juliette answered. "Not the American one."

Grandpère spoke up. "The British have their own war cemetery at Bayeux, not far away. Is he buried there?"

"Yes, that's the one. I promised my mother before she died that sometime I would go up there and put flowers on his grave. But I never have."

"Then come with us," Mom said. She turned to Dad. "We could do that, couldn't we?"

"Yes, of course," he said. "We have room in the van. We'd love to have you."

Juliette was immediately embarrassed. "Oh, no. I wasn't suggesting . . . no, it is too much of an imposition. This is your family's holiday time."

"Nonsense," Grandpère said. "The promise must be kept."

"I . . ." She was clearly wavering. "Do you mean that? Truly?"

"Oh, yes, Juliette," I exclaimed. "All your other guests have gone home. Come with us."

She hesitated, then brightened. "I could stay with Philippe while you tour Paris. I also have some business at the bank. Then whenever you are ready to go north, I could join you."

"Excellent idea," Grandpère said. "Sounds like we have a plan."

PART SEVEN

Return to the Past

CHAPTER 25

Marriott Courtyard Hotel, Paris, France
October 20, 2011

"Where's Grandpère?" Cody asked. "I'm hungry. When are we go-ing to go down for breakfast?"

"You're always hungry," I said.

"He's on his way back right now," Mom said. "He called and said he'll meet us in the dining room at eight thirty."

"He's gone?" I asked. "Where did he go this early?"

She chuckled. "This is hardly early for Grandpère. But he decided to go to Louis Girard's office in person. Be there right at seven thirty to see if he could get some answers as to Louis's whereabouts."

"Oh?" Dad said. "I thought Louis's electronics factory was in a sub-urb of Paris."

"The factory is out to the east somewhere," Mom explained, "but the corporate offices are here in the city."

"Maybe Louis doesn't want to see Grandpère," I suggested. "Maybe that's why he isn't returning his calls."

"Why would you say that?" Mom said, frowning at me. "They are lifelong friends."

"Because Grandpère has been trying to get together with him since we first arrived. That's almost a month now. Doesn't that strike you as a little odd?"

"Not if he's out of the country," Dad said.

"So he couldn't call? What country doesn't have telephone service? I'm just saying, it seems a little strange to me. And I think even Grandpère is puzzled by it all."

Mom shrugged. "I'm sure there is some logical explanation for it. But your grandfather wanted to go to his office in person. Give them our itinerary in case he returns." She stood and started for the bathroom. "I'll brush my hair, then we'll go down."

I had another thought. "Have we heard from Juliette? Did she make it to Paris all right?"

"Yes. She called Grandpère last night. Her board meeting was today. We're picking her up at her hotel on our way out of town."

"Good. With Paris traffic, Grandpère might not make it back by eight thirty."

"On the other hand, he just might." We turned as Grandpère entered the room. He was wearing his wool coat and beret and his cheeks were red.

"Oh, good," Cody said. "Let's go to breakfast."

Mom went to Grandpère and helped him off with his coat. "Is it cold out there?"

"Pretty nippy. But the sky's clearing, and I think we'll have a good day."

"Any luck with Louis?" Dad asked.

He shook his head. "No. His executive assistant did say he has been traveling extensively, but assured me that he has received my messages. He's promised to call as soon as he returns, which will be tomorrow."

More stalling, I thought. "For a guy who is a successful and wealthy businessman, doesn't it seem odd that he can't call you from wherever he is? Or send a note?"

He gave me a long look. After a moment, I began to squirm. "Sorry. Just wondering."

In Roman times, the area that is now France was called the province of Gaul, so the French are often referred to as the Gallic people. And today, there is a thing known as a Gallic shrug, because the French have perfected this gesture. The shoulders lift and fall slightly; the hands are held up, palms out; the head is tipped slightly to one side; the mouth is pulled down in a slight frown and the lower lip is stuck out. And that simple action can convey all kinds of meanings, like: "I don't know what you are talking about," or, "I don't understand this matter, so why should you?" or, "Why blame me? It's not my fault," or, "Why are you asking *me* these questions?" or, "I don't agree with you, but I won't embarrass you by saying that."

Grandpère was a master of the Gallic shrug, and he gave me one now. I knew there was no use pushing him any further on the matter. He took his coat from Mom and hung it up in the small closet by the bathroom door. "So," he said, "who's ready for breakfast?" Before Cody could respond, he added, "And don't give me any lip about not being hungry, Cody. You're going to eat no matter what."

Cody was up and moving for the door. "Finally. Someone in this family who is talking my language."

As the waitress cleared the last of our dishes, Mom started to get up. "All right. Let's try to be out of here in the next fifteen minutes. We have a full day ahead of us."

Grandpère reached out and caught her hand, pulling her down. "I have something I'd like to say before we start today."

"Okay," Mom said, sitting back down again.

He turned to me and Cody. "In a way, what we are doing this week is like some grand vacation. But I want Danni and Cody to remember, this is a school day for you. What we are doing is part of your schooling."

"I'm cool with that," Cody grinned. "Let's do school like this every day."

"Just remember, we are here not just to see but to learn and to feel."

Both Cody and I nodded, though I'm not sure either of us was sure what he meant by that.

"Um . . . Dad?" Mom said.

Grandpère turned to her. "Yes?"

"I'm not sure taking Cody to the Gestapo Museum is a good idea. I'm wondering if he and I maybe should find something else to do."

Cody reacted quickly. "No, Mom. I want to go. I think it will be way cool."

"It will not be way cool!" Grandpère snapped, the sharpness in his voice catching us all by surprise. "It will be sobering. It will be depressing. In some ways it will be awful. But it will definitely not be way cool."

"Sorry, Grandpère," Cody murmured.

"We do not go there out of some morbid curiosity. We will not be visiting just another museum. This is where my father was tortured to the point where they broke every bone in his hands trying to get him to betray his resistance comrades. This is where my mother was captured by Colonel Horst Kessler and taken out to be shot and dumped into the same mass grave as her husband. Since coming here, we have tried to immerse you two in the culture and heritage of France and the heritage of our family. This afternoon and the next few days we are immersing ourselves in *our* heritage as Americans. And you, Cody—and you too, my sweet and tenderhearted Angelique—need to be there. To see it. To feel it. Yes, even to relive the horror and the pain to some small degree."

Mom's head dropped a little. "You're right, Dad. I'm sorry."

He smiled. "Having said that, we will not be visiting the Gestapo Museum today."

Back up came her head. "Really?"

"There's a snowstorm coming in from the North Sea. They're saying it will get here late tomorrow afternoon or evening, so we're going straight to Normandy to have as much time there as possible while the weather is good. We'll have to do the museum on the way back or some other time."

Mom was happy, though she didn't say it. For me, that was a slight disappointment, but it was Normandy I wanted to see the most, so I was okay with it.

Grandpère went on soberly. "Lieutenant Arnold Fitzgerald left his comfortable home in Nebraska and came to France. He came to help us fight the Nazi tide. He came with hundreds of thousands of other Americans and Canadians and Australians. And many of them never returned to their homes. France was made all the richer because of their sacrifice, and the soil of France became their final resting place."

His voice went very soft. "Today, we shall stand amongst their graves. I hope we shall do so in humble reverence and in deep gratitude and take a moment to thank them in our hearts for giving their all that we might be free."

As we got up from the table and started away, Cody suddenly gave a little cry and pointed. "There's Juliette."

He was right. Juliette was standing at the entrance to the dining room, looking around. Cody waved. "Over here," he shouted, turning several heads in our direction.

Mom took him by the shoulder. "Cody, remember where you are. You're not out in the back pasture now."

He nodded but shot away and went over to Juliette, then escorted her back.

"This is a pleasant surprise," Dad said as she approached.

To my surprise, Grandpère just grunted something. I looked at him and was surprised to see that he didn't look too happy. But he put on a smile and greeted her warmly, as we all did.

"I thought it might be," she said. "Philippe had to leave early for a conference in Bordeaux, so I thought I would save you a trip and have him bring me by. My luggage is out with the concierge."

"And how was your board meeting?" Mom asked.

She gave her a wry smile. "You mean the BOR-ing meeting." She shot me a quick smile. "Isn't that how you say it, Danni?"

I grinned. "You got it."

Dad spoke up. "Have you had breakfast?"

"No. I didn't want to miss you."

"Then why don't you stay here and eat while we go up and get our stuff. It will take us about twenty minutes or so. Charge it to our room number. Room 4329."

"Thank you."

As we started away, she called after us. "Oh, Mack?" We all turned back. "Do you have plans for lunch today?"

"Uh . . . not really. Jean-Henri heard there's a storm coming in tomorrow, so we thought we'd head straight up to Normandy. Maybe just grab something along the way."

"The Marriott prepares box lunches for their guests. Will you let me order one for each of us? Then we can just eat in the car if we choose."

"Excellent idea. Thank you."

"Just give me your orders. It will be sandwiches, crisps, a drink, and—"

"Crisps?" Cody blurted.

Mom laughed. "That's potato chips to you. In England, *chips* are what we call *French fries*."

Juliette nodded and went on. "The sandwiches are ham, turkey, or cheese. The drinks are the usual brands of canned pop or bottled water."

It surprised me a little that she was so familiar with the options; then I decided she had probably talked to someone before coming in. We gave her our order—which she noted without writing anything down—and then went to our rooms.

As Cody and I came back into Mom's and Dad's room, I saw two things at once. Grandpère was already there waiting for us. And Dad was on the phone. And he didn't look happy. As we set our luggage down, he said good-bye and rang off.

"What's wrong?" Mom asked.

He glanced at us. "That was Clay."

Mom sat down slowly, and I had to grab for the back of one of the overstuffed chairs. The feeling of darkness was suddenly back.

Dad sat down and took Mom's hand. "Late Tuesday night, El Cobra's attorney showed up with extradition papers issued by a federal judge in Arizona. They were orders to extradite two of our prisoners to Argentina so they can be tried for crimes they committed there."

"*What?*" It was a collective gasp from me, Mom, and Grandpère.

"No advance notice was given either to the FBI or to the prison that the orders had been issued. When they came to the prison, they were accompanied by two men with Argentine papers and documents."

"And the prison just let them go?" Grandpère cried. "Didn't that seem a little suspicious?"

Dad nodded. "It was a setup. Four guards at the prison released them without clearing it with any of their supervisors. Those four, as well as the federal judge, have now disappeared. Half an hour later, a private jet with several passengers took off from Tucson with a flight plan for Mexico City. However, the plane diverted in flight and disappeared."

"Which two?" I asked in a hoarse whisper.

I saw Dad swallow hard before he answered. "Raul Muñoz and—"

"No!"

"And Jean-Claude Allemand."

I wanted to sink to the earth. Doc and the Belgian. The two men I feared the most.

"Not El Cobra or Eileen?" Grandpère asked.

Again Dad shook his head. "Clay and Joel think they have become a liability and thus they were dumped. Sacrificed for the good of the cause."

Dad started to get up, but Mom pulled him down again. "Wait, Lucas. Does this mean we're going to have to go into a witness protection program?"

He frowned. "Clay said they're almost certain that they flew to Argentina, though it's not clear yet whether Argentina actually knew about it in advance. Interpol is still checking on that." Reaching out, he laid a hand over hers. "I asked him specifically if we needed to cancel going to Normandy. In turn, he asked me a question. He wanted to know if we were being recognized by people when we were out."

I spoke up. "Did you tell him no? I haven't had one person stop me." Mom, Cody and Grandpère were shaking their heads too.

"That's what I told him. I also told him that when we do go out, we try to change our appearance as he suggested. With that, he said we're fine to go ahead with our plans. He's bringing a team over to work with Interpol on this. Witness protection will be on the table for discussion. But right now he's pretty sure it won't be necessary."

And then, Dad got the strangest look on his face. And he was looking me as that happened.

"What?" I said.

"Clay asked how you were doing. I told him you were still a little bummed about the whole Rick thing, but other than that you were fine."

"I am," I said.

"He wondered if you needed cheering up."

I scoffed at him. "Like what? Send me more roses?"

"Oh, I think this is even better than roses." He stood up, ignoring our questioning looks. "Come with me."

Totally confused, we all followed him as he went out the door and into the hallway. But he didn't turn toward the elevator. He turned to the left. To my greater surprise, he stopped at the door next to ours and knocked.

"What is going on?" I cried. But he just stepped back. A moment later, the door opened and Clay Zabriskie stood before us. I couldn't believe it. He was here in Paris? I started to hug him, but he held up his hand, stopping all of us. Then he bowed, gave a little flourish with one hand, and pushed his door wide open.

For one very long moment, I just stared through the door at what was waiting for us in the center of the room. I gave one piercing shriek, screamed out one word—"*You!*"—then I launched myself across the room at Rick, who was standing there with the silliest grin on his face I had ever seen.

I nearly bowled him over as I threw myself into his arms. Mom came in right behind me, with Cody on her heels.

Poor Rick. He never knew what hit him.

CHAPTER 26

Clay finally came in to break us up, probably because he was afraid that Rick might suffocate under the combined weight of our family. "Look, guys," he said, "wish I could stay and enjoy the reunion, but my team has a meeting with Interpol in less than an hour, so I'm taking off. We're setting up our operations here in Paris to begin with. You have my mobile number. I'll keep in touch."

He moved up to Rick, arms extended. They hugged, and Clay patted his back. "I think you can tell from the reaction you're getting that you did the right thing."

"I know," Rick said.

"With you gone, we really don't see any threat to your family, but we're going to put them under surveillance for a while, just to make sure."

"Thanks, Clay." They separated and shook hands. Clay then shook our hands. "I'll call you tonight. Mack's given me the number of your hotel in Caen." And then he was gone.

Mom had us all sit down, with Rick in the center and me beside him—of course. "All right," she said. "As you can tell, you've pretty much knocked all of us off our feet. So tell us how you have come to be here."

Rick was still grinning; he was obviously still getting used to the idea too. "Well, Clay called me early yesterday morning to tell me about

Doc and Jean-Claude getting out of prison. He said he didn't think there was any direct threat to me or my family, but he just wanted me to know. But even as he was talking, suddenly I had the strongest feeling that I had to go to France and I had to go now."

"Just like that?" I said, still holding his hand.

"Yeah, and what was really weird, when I hung up, before I could tell Dad what Clay had said, he gave me this funny look and said, 'Rick, you need to be with the McAllisters.'"

"Really?" Mom said.

"Cool," Cody exclaimed.

"Yeah. I mean, he was adamant. He said I had to go right away. So I called Clay back, grabbed a suitcase, and was in Salt Lake City by that afternoon. He and Joel had gone ahead and finished getting me the passport, so when I arrived in Washington, Clay was there at the airport with his team. I ran to the bathroom, washed my face, and then I was on a jet to Paris." He reached up and rubbed at his eyes. "I'm still a little dazed by it all."

"We are so glad, Rick," Mom said. "So happy you're here."

"I think *ecstatic* might be a better word," Grandpère said. "Eh, Danni?"

"You have no idea," I whispered, suddenly feeling that stupid old lump in my throat again.

"How long do you get to stay?" Cody asked.

"Yes," I said. "And you'd better not say just a day or two."

He squeezed my hand. "I go back home when you guys go back home."

Snuggling in against him, I said, "Good answer, Ramirez. In fact, that's the perfect answer."

Normally, according to Juliette, getting out of Paris with morning traffic could take as much as an hour and a half longer than normal. But by the time we got back down to the dining room, introduced Rick to

Juliette, got the box lunches—including an additional one for Rick—checked out, loaded the van, and finally got under way, it was nearly ten. Traffic had thinned out.

Juliette seemed genuinely pleased to meet Rick. And why not? She had surely heard nothing but glowing reports about him from us. In the van, Dad drove with Mom beside him, Grandpère and Juliette were in the middle seat, and Rick, Cody, and I were in the third seat. Our luggage filled the back of the van clear up to the ceiling.

For the first half hour or so, Juliette half turned in her seat and peppered Rick with questions, giving me hardly any chance to talk with him. Then Cody, with his usual machine-gun style of conversation, picked up from there, talking about all that we had done in France and asking a hundred questions about things back home.

So I had virtually no chance to talk to Rick. But that was all right. He was beside me and he never let go of my hand—his choice—and he had his other arm around me, so everything was good. I knew we likely wouldn't be alone anytime this day, but that gave me plenty of time to plan out what I was going to say when we finally did get some time together. And that was a lot.

Outside, I watched mile after mile of green fields and hedgerows and tiny villages and small towns roll by. The sky was overcast—typical for this time of year—but the weather didn't seem to be threatening yet. I saw out of the corner of my eye that Rick was looking out the window too, so I nudged him. "What do you think?"

He shook his head. "I have to keep telling myself. 'This is France. You're driving through France.' Sorry, but that's going to take some getting used to."

"It's wonderful. You're going to love Le Petit Château. It's got the cutest little village nearby, and woods and meadows." I leaned my head against his shoulder. "Oh, Rick," I whispered, "I am so glad you're here."

He squeezed my hand. "So am I, Danni."

"You must be exhausted. Did you sleep on the plane at all?"

He flashed me a big grin. "Are you kidding? No way."

He started to say something, but just then Grandpère turned around and looked at me. "You have the pouch with you. Right?"

A little surprised, I nodded. "It's in my suitcase."

"Good."

Juliette gave him a strange look. "Why this strange obsession with that old purse?"

That was worthy of another Gallic shrug, with no accompanying comment.

We all fell silent, but then Grandpère turned and looked at Juliette. "I have a question."

"Oui?"

"How much farther would it be if we were to visit Dunkirk after we've done Normandy?"

For a moment she was confused. "Dunkirk? But Jean-Henri, Dunkirk is in Belgium, far to the east of Normandy."

He smiled. "I am aware of that. I'm just wondering how much of a side trip it would be if we went there on the way home."

"What's at Dunkirk?" Cody asked.

Dad answered. "It's one of the most famous sites of World War II. It's where nearly all the British Army—about 300,000 troops—were trapped when the Germans overran Holland, Belgium, and France early in the war."

"Actually," Grandpère said, "it was closer to 340,000 men, including many French troops."

Dad glanced back at Juliette. "Dunkirk isn't that far into Belgium, is it?"

"No. It is only about twenty or thirty kilometers north of Calais. But it is in the opposite direction from how we would go home. It would add five hours or more."

"Is Dunkirk that important to you, Dad?" Mom asked.

"Well, I've always wanted to see it."

Mom, who obviously knew the story well, looked back at us kids. "It was a pivotal point not only in World War II but in world history as well. In one of the most controversial orders of the war, Hitler ordered his armies to stop for nine days rather than pursue their military advantage. They had the Allies on their knees. But that delay gave England the chance to rally a massive rescue effort. Boats of every kind—from navy ships to small fishing boats—raced across the English Channel and ferried the troops back to England over a period of several days. Many people called it a miracle."

"It was a miracle," Grandpère said. "The Germans could have virtually destroyed England's ability to resist and ended the war right then. It was a colossal blunder by the Third Reich. Had they pressed their advantage, the British Isles might be speaking German today."

To my surprise, a look of irritation flashed across Juliette's face. "It wasn't a blunder. It was a marvelous concession on Hitler's part. He always had a great respect for the British people, partly because he considered them to be another branch of the Aryan peoples, the master race. He was greatly disappointed when England declared war on Germany. So when he had England on the ropes, he ordered his army to halt. He knew he couldn't persuade England to join Germany in the war, but he hoped that they would at least stop resisting Germany's efforts to conquer Europe and purify the Aryan race."

Grandpère politely cleared his throat. "Sorry to correct you, Juliette. What you say is a common misconception, later fostered by the German propaganda ministry, but it is simply not true. In point of fact, the decision was not made by Hitler, but by his two senior commanders, Generals von Rundstedt and von Kluge. They wanted to stop long enough to consolidate their victories and prevent a possible Allied breakout from their encircling armies. Hitler later sanctioned the order, but it did not originate with him. And it had very little to do with sparing the English Aryans in order to soften Churchill's heart."

Mom made as if to speak, but Juliette was quicker. And when she spoke, her voice had taken on a slight edge. "Not so. Remember, Jean-Henri, I am from England. I think I know *our* history."

Dad chuckled. "Sorry, but with World War II history, I think I'll side with Jean-Henri."

Suddenly she was bristling. "There is an old adage that says, 'The victors write the history.' I know it has become popular to demonize Adolf Hitler because of what he did to the Jews, but he was a political and military genius. I did my doctoral dissertation on the economy of Germany between World War I and II."

I caught Mother's eye. Juliette had a doctoral degree? She had never given any hint of that. But we were both puzzled by this sudden confrontation going on between her and Grandpère. I guessed that Juliette was not used to being contradicted, especially not in front of others. But, surprisingly, any sign of Grandpère's usual graciousness was also gone.

"In the early twenties," she continued, "hyperinflation was rampant in Germany. The government was printing money so fast that its value dropped like a rock. By 1923, to eat breakfast in a restaurant could cost you as much as three trillion marks. That's *trillion!* A man could sell his farm for a good price on Monday and by Saturday not be able to buy more than a suit of clothes with the proceeds. A common saying of that time was, 'We used to go to the market with our pockets full of money and return with our wheelbarrows full of food. Now we go with wheelbarrows full of money, and return with pockets full of food.'"

Wow! I had never heard the word *hyperinflation* before, and what she was describing seemed like an exaggeration. But Grandpère was nodding in agreement.

She went on. "There was vast unemployment. The German people were in deep despair. And that is how Hitler came to power. He not only halted the inflation and put people back to work, but he restored Germany's national pride. As I say, he was a political and a military genius. He would never have made such a 'colossal blunder,' as you call it, Jean-Henri. He was brilliant. This is why the German people elected him as their leader and followed him in his efforts to restore Germany to her former glory."

She sat back, her chest rising and falling as she glared at Grandpère, daring him to further contradict her. The rest of us just sat there, pretty well stunned by this passionate outburst. Not Grandpère, however. He was watching her steadily, his face expressionless.

Seeing she was finished, he countered, "All of what you say is true, Juliette. Hitler was highly popular with the people, but that was because in those early stages, they didn't yet know about the death squads. They didn't know about people being torn from their homes in the dead of night and being shot without a trial of any kind. They didn't know about the labor camps, the political assassinations, the rewriting of German constitutional law, the euthanasia of the mentally ill or mentally handicapped or any other 'undesirables.' Nor of the disenfranchisement of whole segments of the German citizenry, such as the gypsies and the Jews."

He was breathing pretty hard when he finished too. They sat glaring at each other. The atmosphere in the van had become very tense.

"Whoa," Mom broke in. "Time out. Maybe it's best if we change the subject." She shot a warning look at Grandpère. "I believe the question at hand was, how much longer would it take us to go back to Le Petit Château via Dunkirk? Let's get back to that, shall we?"

Juliette sniffed haughtily. "It is a mistake to go to Dunkirk. There is nothing to see there. Only a large, empty beach. It is not worth the time."

Grandpère said nothing. He just continued watching her, his expression thoughtful now.

Mom, trying to be the arbitrator here, intervened. "Dad? We're doing this whole trip for you. What do you say?"

He took a slow breath, his eyes never leaving Juliette's. "I agree," he finally said.

"You do?" I exclaimed in surprise.

"You do?" Juliette said.

"I do," he said dryly. "I agree that Dunkirk is to the east, and that Normandy is to the west." Her head snapped up, but he went on smoothly. "And I also agree that perhaps now is not the best time to make such a wide detour, especially if there is a snowstorm coming. So, as important as Dunkirk is to English-speaking peoples everywhere, I say we do it another time."

"And I agree with his agreement," Juliette said, trying to lighten the mood, but clearly enjoying her triumph. Then she looked around at the rest of us and smiled. "I apologize for letting my emotions get the better of me. It was a very long day yesterday, and I am still quite tired." She touched her abdomen. "And I have a bit of an upset stomach. Something I ate at breakfast, I suppose." Finally, she looked at Grandpère. "I apologize, Jean-Henri. I didn't mean to sound so testy."

"Nor did I," he answered graciously.

Sensing a chance to change the subject, Dad glanced back. "We're just about thirty miles from Caen. I have a suggestion. Rather than eating our lunches on the road, why don't we stop at the hotel? I'm sure it's too early to get into our rooms, but I think we could leave our luggage there, which would give us more room in the van. And perhaps they would let us use a room where we could eat our lunch."

"That would be much easier than eating our lunches on our laps," Mom said, obviously relieved to be onto a less explosive subject.

Dad turned out to be wrong. This was the off season and not a weekend. The hotel said we could check into our rooms immediately, and they offered a small private dining room for us to eat in. That was good. Nobody had mentioned taking a potty break, but I think all of us were thinking of it.

As we started for our rooms, Dad said, "Let's try to be down in the dining room in ten minutes. The staff will bring our bags up while we're eating. We need to be on our way pretty quickly because it gets dark so early now."

I don't know if the desk clerk thought Grandpère and Juliette were an item, but he put them in adjacent rooms and us down at the other end of the hall.

As we reached our rooms and started trying our keys, I lowered my voice and asked, "Wow! What just happened in the car?"

Mom shook her head. "I'm not exactly sure."

"Was she actually defending Hitler?" Rick asked.

"I wouldn't say that," Dad responded. "I think she was only trying to make the point that Hitler was too smart to give a stupid order like that."

"I don't know," Cody said. "Sounded to me like she thought Hitler was really something." He paused, then said, "Do you think she's really got an upset stomach?"

Mom nodded. "Oh, yes. The question is, was it breakfast or Grandpère who brought it on?"

Chuckling, we opened our doors and started into our rooms. I looked at Rick just before he entered. "Don't lie down, Buddy, or you're a goner."

He yawned a mighty yawn. "That's for sure. I'm honked out of my zed."

I laughed. "I think 'zonked out of your head' makes a little more sense."

"That's what I said."

"Right. You can sleep in the car. Just don't do it now."

CHAPTER 27

*Normandy American Cemetery and
Memorial, Colleville-sur-Mer*

"Omigosh!" My hand shot out and grabbed Rick's upper arm, my fingers digging into the flesh.

He jumped about a foot, his head snapping up and looking around wildly. "What? What is it?"

Everyone else in the van turned around to look at us. I was instantly contrite. "Sorry, Rick," I said in a low voice. "I didn't know you were asleep. I'm sorry."

Gradually he came back to reality. "Where are we?" He was obviously still a little spaced.

"We're just coming up on the cemetery and memorial," I said, waving to the others that everything was all right. "We'll be there in just a minute."

"Oh." He straightened and gave his head a quick little shake. "Thanks for waking me up."

"You're welcome," I sang out. Then I leaned in close and whispered in his ear. "Actually, that wasn't it. I just remembered something bad."

"Oh?" He was fast coming fully awake. "What?"

"Shhh!" I lowered my voice even more. "I just realized that I left *Le Gardien* in my suitcase in my room. We were hurrying and I totally forgot about it."

"Oh, boy," he whispered back. "Your grandfather's not going to like that."

"Are you kidding?" I hissed. "He's gonna kill me."

"No, he's not going to kill you."

"All right, Mr. Literal. But when he's done, I'm gonna wish I was dead."

He nodded. "Now, that's very possible."

"You can't tell him, Rick. Hopefully, he'll think it's under my parka. When we get back tonight, I promise I'll sleep with it tied around my neck."

"I won't say anything," he said.

I felt a nudge on my other arm. I turned to see Cody grinning at me. "Hey, Sis. You know that hoodie you bought with the Eiffel Tower on it?"

"Yeah, so what?"

"I really like that."

I gave him a strange look. What was he looking so cocky about? "Yeah, so?"

"You give me that, and my lips are sealed about *Le Gardien.* I heard every word you just said."

Originally, we had planned to make our first stop to the east of the memorial and visit the line of German coastal shore batteries that lined the bluffs along the Normandy coast. Cody had been really excited about seeing those, with their massive cannons and their three-foot-thick cement bunkers. But as we reached the coast, the sky to the north was visibly growing darker, and Dad and Grandpère decided they would have to wait until tomorrow. We'd go first to Omaha Beach, where American forces had landed, and then the cemetery. The visitors' center was close to both, so if the weather turned on us, we could get inside pretty quickly. There weren't a lot of cars in the parking lot, so Dad parked the van close to the gate and we went inside.

As we started down the path that leads from the bluffs to Omaha

Beach, the first flakes of snow came skating down on the light breeze off the water. To the north, out across the channel, the clouds were darker, but above us they looked okay, so we decided to press ahead. We stopped and read the interpretive signs as we made our way down to the beach.

The water looked like gray slate because the sea was surprisingly calm. Fortunately, there was not much wind. In a way, it looked like any other beach. But knowing what had taken place here some sixty-seven years before made it so much more than that. The beaches of Normandy were heavily defended. Hundreds of men had died in the water without ever reaching the beach. Many of the wounded drowned in the surf because there was no one to pull them out. Grandpère softly described what took place in the early-morning hours of June 6, 1944, which only added to our somber mood.

Unfortunately, we had only been down on the beach a few minutes when Cody started complaining of stomach cramps. Mom was asking him how bad they were when he suddenly gave a low cry, then darted into the bushes and started heaving up his lunch. When he finally finished, he was pale as the gray skies above us. Mom admitted that she was feeling kind of queasy too, but at first we thought it was from seeing Cody barf up his lunch. But then Dad admitted that his stomach was also a little unsettled.

We had no choice but to turn around and head for the visitors' center and its restrooms. By the time we were back up on the bluffs, Mom was pale as a ghost, Dad kept swallowing hard, and Cody was half bent over holding his stomach. All three of them made a dash for the restrooms. Then, to our further dismay, Juliette began complaining of nausea and stomach cramps too, and we knew that this was more than just a touch of the stomach flu. Fortunately, to this point, Grandpère, Rick, and I were all feeling fine.

With Cody lying on a bench with his eyes closed, and Mom sitting beside him, her head in her hands, we held a council. Juliette, who so far had managed to hold her lunch down, leaned heavily on the back of the bench behind them. Dad had gotten some Pepto Bismol from his overnight bag in the van, but it wasn't doing any of them much good. He had thrown up a couple of times too, so things were not looking good. So the question was, what now?

"I think we just load up and get our walking wounded back to the hotel," Grandpère said to Dad. "Even if we get the vomiting stopped, you're too wasted to be sightseeing, especially on a day like this."

Cody raised his head in protest. "We're not sightseeing, Grandpère. This is school, remember."

We couldn't help but laugh. But for me, the disappointment was like a blow. I had been looking forward to this particular part of the trip almost as much as Grandpère. I could see that Rick was pretty bummed too.

Mom's head came up. "No, Dad. This is what you've been waiting for. We'll wait here for you. We'll be fine." She managed a wan smile. "As long as we are close to the bathrooms."

"I agree," Dad said. "Take what time you need."

Juliette spoke up. "I think it is something we ate, probably the box lunches. We kept the car pretty warm coming up. Chicken and mayonnaise don't do well in heat."

"I didn't have chicken," Cody said.

"It could also be a touch of stomach flu," Mom replied.

"Perhaps," Juliette went on, "but the fact that it came on so suddenly suggests food poisoning. Which means we should be fine by this evening. So I have a suggestion. Four of us are sick, three of you are well. It is a shame that the three who are fine should have to quit because of the rest of us."

She paused for a moment. "You probably noticed a few taxis out in the car park. Many people don't like to drive in an unfamiliar place, so they come out here by taxi. I'm sure some of them out there are waiting for returning passengers right now."

"Are you saying . . . ?" I stopped.

"Yes." Then to Grandpère. "We'll take a taxi back to Caen. You and Danni and Rick stay here for as long as you wish."

"I may need a plastic sack," Cody said.

Thanks for that vivid image, Code. But all I said was, "We have some in the glove box of the van."

Mom straightened. "That's a great idea. We'll be all right. This is what you've been wanting to do for years, Dad. So do it. We'll go back to the hotel. Then we'll be fine."

"I think that's a good solution, Grandpère," I said. "You need to do this."

He was torn. You could see that in his face, but finally his head bobbed. "All right. Yes. Thank you. We shall do that, but only on the condition that we all come back tomorrow and do it right."

———————

As the taxi drove away, Grandpère turned to Rick and me. "I need to get something from the van. You go on to the visitors' center. Get out of the cold. I'll catch up."

I shook my head. "We'll wait. I'm not cold."

"Me neither," Rick said.

Which was true. Both of us were bundled up pretty well—winter parkas, gloves, scarves, and stocking caps. The snow had increased slightly, but not enough to stick on the ground yet. I wanted to be at Grandpère's side for every part of this experience. He shrugged and started for the van.

When he returned a minute or two later, I was a little surprised to see that he carried a small duffel bag that was stuffed full and, judging from the way he carried it, somewhat heavy. "What's this?" I asked. "More winter clothing? We're fine. Really."

He shook his head but said nothing more.

———————

Nearly two hundred acres of land on the bluffs above Omaha Beach were donated to the United States by a French government grateful for the sacrifice that freed them from German occupation. On that two

hundred acres, America had built the Normandy American Cemetery
and Memorial with an accompanying visitors' center. The visitors' center building is a long, one-story building with a flat roof. It is nestled in
a wooded area east of the memorial pavilion. Once inside, Grandpère
indicated that he needed to go into the restroom and left us to wander.

We started with the exhibits, which took up almost a third of the
entire building. It was fascinating. There were excerpts from accounts
from various participants in the invasion, dozens of pictures, short videos of actual war footage, and many artifacts from the war.

About ten minutes later, as I was leaning over a display case, Rick
poked me. "Uh . . . Danni. You may want to see this."

I turned in the direction he was looking, then gave a low cry.
"Grandpère?"

For a moment, I barely recognized the man coming toward us. The
beret was gone. His winter coat and scarf were gone. In fact, everything he had been wearing just moments before was gone. What I saw
before me now was a man fully decked out in the World War II combat uniform of an American GI. My grandfather had somehow trans-
formed himself into a man identical with the dozens of pictures we saw
all around us: round metal helmet; field jacket with a sergeant's stripes
on the sleeves; ammunition belt around his waist; khaki trousers tucked
into heavily scuffed, brown combat boots. All he lacked was an M-1 rifle
over his shoulder.

All around us people were pointing at him and calling for others to
look. I saw one of the staff members nodding in approval. One couple,
who looked American, called their teenage boys over, and the father
started explaining something to them as he pointed at Grandpère. To
their delight, Grandpère saluted them, and they saluted back. Through
it all, Grandpère stood there quietly, his face impassive, almost as if he
were one of the mannequins on display.

When we finally joined him, I said, "Grandpère! This is incredible.
Where did you get the uniform?"

"I bought it a few years ago, when your parents and I came over for the sixtieth anniversary of D-Day. There were a lot of groups doing re-enactments that year, and I decided I wanted to be part of them."

"So this is authentic?" Rick asked.

"Right down to the brass belt buckle."

Then a thought struck me. "But why an American uniform? You're French. And your father was part of the French Resistance. Why not a French uniform?"

"Think about it," he said softly.

My forehead wrinkled. "Is it because you've been an American for all these years?"

He sniffed in disgust. "I may have lived in America for all these years, but one never ceases to be a Frenchman at heart." Then he shook his head. "Have you forgotten so soon? On August 24, 1944, my father was being taken out of Paris to be executed by the Gestapo. And my mother, who had come to Paris to look for him, had been captured by one of the officers in the Gestapo and was destined for the same fate."

My eyes widened. "Monique and Pierre. Of course. And that was the day," I whispered, "that the Americans entered Paris and saved them both."

"Yes," he replied softly. "I wear the American uniform—as do many of my countrymen in these reenactments—as a way of saying 'Thank you' to America for coming to France."

———

It took almost a half an hour for Grandpère to get the exact location of the grave of Lieutenant Arnold Fitzgerald from the sexton's office. When we went outside, we found the clouds darker and the snow coming down more seriously now. With that, and knowing that the cemetery closed in less than an hour, Grandpère suggested we go right to the cemetery and see the memorial on our way back if there was time. And if not, we would see it tomorrow.

We did pause briefly at the base of an impressive bronze statue that was more than twenty feet high. It was of a young man, his muscular body naked except for a loincloth, arching upward as he rose from the sea. One arm was raised to the sky, the other outstretched to the side, and he was looking over his shoulder at the heavens. It was as if he were leaping free from the grasp of the water. On the base of the statue were the words: MINE EYES HAVE SEEN THE GLORY OF THE COMING OF THE LORD.

Grandpère spoke from just behind Rick and me. "It is called *The Spirit of American Youth Rising from the Waves.* It symbolizes all of the young soldiers, sailors, and airmen who gave their lives here. They are rising from the sea in the Resurrection. Thus the lines from 'The Battle Hymn of the Republic.'"

"It's beautiful," I breathed. And I meant that in so many ways. It was pretty amazing, actually, especially once I knew what the figure signified.

We continued on past the long reflecting pool to where the cemetery itself actually began. Without any of us saying anything to each other, we came to a halt. What an incredible sight lay before our eyes. Stretching away from us in three directions were row after row after row of crosses, brilliant white even in the subdued light. The rows were perfectly aligned and the grass surrounding them was so immaculately trimmed it looked like a putting green.

Something swept over me that I can only think of as a mixture of awe, reverence, and humility. I just stood there, letting my eyes take in the perfect symmetry of each row while my mind tried to comprehend what the crosses represented.

According to the signs we had seen, there were 9,387 Americans buried here—almost ten thousand men, two thousand of whom had died either in the water or on the beaches. It was more than I could take in. Hanksville had a few more than two hundred people. Here before us were fifty Hanksvilles.

Rick and I hung back as Grandpère led the way into the cemetery. We moved more slowly, reading inscriptions as we passed. Some were not actually crosses but Stars of David, signifying that a Jewish soldier was buried there. Here and there, clusters of flowers had been placed at the base of the markers. Some were freshly cut. Some were silk. Some were plastic. But all were meant to honor and remember the fallen.

I stopped in surprise at the grave marker just before me. Without consciously being aware of it, I had been thinking of the dead as being men. Now I read, ELIZABETH A. RICHARDSON, AMERICAN RED CROSS, INDIANA, JULY 25, 1945. I'm not sure why that hit me so hard, but I stood there staring at it, wanting to cry. How old was she when she went to war? She had to have been a nurse. I was thinking more and more seriously about being a nurse. Did she leave a boyfriend to go off to war? A little brother, like Cody? And did she recognize that by choosing to go she might never return, never find someone to love, never be a wife, mother, or grandmother? Of course she did. How could she not have known all that? And yet, she came. Those thoughts swirled in my mind as I stared at her name.

I turned as Rick called to me softly. I went two rows over and joined him. This was a different inscription, but it hit me with a similar emotional impact. HERE RESTS IN HONORED GLORY, A COMRADE IN ARMS, KNOWN ONLY TO GOD. Hard enough to die, but to not even be identifiable? How sad for them. How sad for their families.

I shook my head, trying to grasp the enormity of their sacrifice.

Up ahead of us, a movement caught my eye. Grandpère was holding the piece of paper he had been given by the cemetery sexton's office. He studied it for a moment, his head lifting now and then to check his surroundings. Finally he moved four rows to the left and started down the row, walking more slowly now. About five crosses down, he stopped, then half bent down to peer at the marker. After a moment, he slowly straightened. He folded the paper and put it back in the pocket of his field jacket. Then he came to attention and saluted the grave marker before him. With that done, he removed his helmet and went down on one knee.

"I think he found it," Rick murmured.

"Yes." I started forward, but then stopped. "Let's wait for him back at the statue."

That took Rick by surprise. "But I thought you wanted to see the grave too."

"I do. But it can wait until we come back tomorrow." He nodded, then took my hand, and we started back the way we had come.

———

"If you're cold, we can go inside the visitors' center and wait there."

I was cold, but not terribly so, especially not with him holding my hand. "No. I'm okay." I took out my phone and checked the time. I looked to my right, past the reflecting pool to where the cemetery was. With the swirling snow, I could barely see the dark shape of my grandfather, but he was still standing motionless in the sea of crosses. "We've still got twenty minutes until closing time. Are you okay? I don't want to go inside."

"Sure."

We sat together on one of the stone benches near the statue of the American youth. Rick had turned now and was studying it. "What are you thinking?" I asked him.

"Did you notice how most of those buried here were our age or a little older—eighteen, nineteen? I even saw one who was seventeen."

"I know. And their lives ended here on the fields of France." Then I decided to share something else with him. "Last night, when I was trying to get to sleep, I was thinking about Thanksgiving. Usually my Grandma and Grandpa McAllister come down, and Mom's brothers and sisters, and we have this huge Thanksgiving dinner. And it made me sad that we might not be back for that this year."

"Yes." I could tell he wasn't quite sure where I was going with this.

"So, as we were passing all those crosses, I started thinking about Thanksgiving Day, 1941."

"Why 1941?"

"Because that was about two weeks before Pearl Harbor."

"Oh." He began to nod very slowly.

"And I was thinking that there were kids our age all over America having dinner with their families. Eating turkey and pumpkin pie. Everything would have seemed perfectly normal to them. They were going to school, playing baseball in the sandlots, hanging out at the local soda shop. They had jobs. Girlfriends. They were preparing for college. Some were even getting married. They had no idea that the entire world was about to change for them forever."

"And two weeks later it did," he murmured.

I turned to face him. "What if something like that is waiting for us, Rick? Not two weeks away. I'm not saying that, but sometime in our future. Like what if someone smuggled a nuke into the U.S. and exploded it? That would be so much worse than Pearl Harbor or 9/11."

He thought about that for a moment, then nodded. "If that did happen, I'd go down to the Army recruiter the next day and enlist, just like they did."

"I would too, especially if I were a nurse."

Man! This was heavy stuff.

Part of me wanted to change the subject. And yet, strange as it may seem, I wanted it to be heavy right then. I wanted to know what Elizabeth Richardson had felt like. Or Lieutenant Arnold Fitzgerald. I wanted to know if I had the courage to offer my life for the freedom of others. "But I'm not sure if, when it came right down to it, I'd have the courage to do it," I said aloud.

"This from the girl who knocked El Cobra rolling and foiled a whole gang of international kidnappers? This from the girl who—"

"Why did you come back?" I cut in.

That totally startled him. "Um . . . because your grandfather asked me to."

My head popped up. "Wait. I thought it was because you had a strong feeling that you needed to come."

"I did, and so did Dad. But this was a few days before. I had been wondering if I had done the right thing, and how you were doing, and . . ." He shrugged. "You know, all that kind of stuff. So I called your grandfather to see what he thought."

"Why Grandpère? Why not Dad? Or Mom?"

He shrugged. "Dunno. It just felt right to call Grandpère."

"And what did he say?"

"Four words. That was all."

"Four words? Let me guess. 'Danni really needs you.'"

"No. All he said was, 'The chariots are here.'"

I just stared at him. "'The chariots are here'?"

"Yes. That was it. Then he told me to trust my feelings and that if I did come, you would probably be in Paris by then."

I started to cry. "I do need you, Rick. After all that happened, I thought it was over for us."

"What do you mean by 'all that happened'?"

"You know what I mean. I'm talking about me being such a total jerk. Me feeling like I was the hottest ticket in town. Me treating you like dirt. Me, the new and wonderful Katniss Everdeen. Me not even seeing you leave the restaurant because I was so busy with my adoring fans." I had to stop for a moment. "Me telling the whole world about a very special kiss."

There was a smile behind the gravity of his eyes. "Oh, yeah. That is quite a bit."

I almost punched him as I laughed. "That's not the right answer. You're supposed to disagree with me."

"No, I'm supposed to help you."

I had to turn away. "I don't know if you can. Not anymore. Remember who you're talking to. The girl who, even after being chewed out by her grandfather for treating the pouch so casually, goes off and leaves it in her hotel room. The girl who was so chapped because no one even questioned whether she could actually shoot her best friend in the leg that she sent her friends on a hundred-mile goose chase to see Chris Hemsworth."

He said nothing when I finally shut up. Those dark brown eyes, now almost black in the gray light, were unreadable as they searched my face. After what seemed like a full minute, I finally snapped at him. "Well, say something."

His breath came out in a long, slow sigh. "I think I got here just in time. I think Danni McAllister has been, once again, beating up on herself." He took me by the shoulders and looked deeply into my eyes. "And I don't like that, because I think Danni McAllister is too hard on herself. And it's time she stopped."

I looked up, my eyes swimming with tears. "And what if she doesn't?"

He leaned in very slowly, drawing me closer, and kissed me very gently. I felt my body go weak and nearly slipped out of his grasp. He held me tighter and kissed me again. "Then she's going to have to deal with me."

"I'm not sure I understand what you mean," I whispered. "Tell me again."

He did, and this time I put my arms around his neck and kissed him back. It was a kiss filled with longing, with hope, and with pure joy. Back at Leprechaun Canyon, I thought that there would never again be a moment as sweet and precious as when Rick kissed me.

I was wrong.

When we finally leaned back, we were both a little breathless. I found a smile somewhere deep inside me. "Bring on the chariots," I said. "I think I'm ready."

CHAPTER 28

By the time Grandpère rejoined us and we made our way to the visitors' center, the security guard was ushering everyone out and locking the doors. I told him I thought the guard would let him in long enough to change out of his uniform, but he shrugged it off. "It's not a big deal. I'll change at the hotel."

It was almost full dark and snowing steadily as we left the memorial and headed for the parking lot. There was now about an inch of snow on the ground. If it kept up like this, by morning there would be six or seven inches.

Another guard was waiting for us and a few other stragglers at the gate. He called out in both French and English as we passed by him, "Thank you for coming. Take care. The roads will be getting slick soon."

The parking lot was nearly empty and partially obscured by the snow, but as we started for our van, I pulled up short. There was a sudden prickling at the back of my neck. "Grandpère?"

"Yes?"

"There's a car parked near our van, and the engine is running."

His head came up and he stopped. So did Rick. We peered through the gloom at the black Mercedes sedan parked just two spaces from our van. There was still enough light that we could see clouds of steam coming from the exhaust. I gave a low cry. "Look. There's another one just like it. It's just outside the parking lot, on the narrow road that leads to the highway." The prickling became a slow crawl down my spine.

As we stood there peering at the nearer vehicle, the back door opened and a dark figure in an overcoat and dress hat got out. With the overhead light on, we could see that another man was at the wheel. One hand came up and waved. "Jean-Henri LaRoche? Is that you?"

"Oh my word," Grandpère breathed.

"Who is it?" I whispered.

He swung around, a huge smile wreathing his face. "It's Louis. Louis Girard." And he broke into a rapid walk, waving back and calling out.

———

It was with great enthusiasm, much hugging, backslapping, and kissing on the cheeks that these two boyhood friends greeted each other. Rick and I stood back and watched the warm reunion. Grandpère kept two faded black-and-white photos on his dresser at home. One was of him and Grandmère on the day they were married in Boston. The other was of two boys outside Le Petit Château with their arms draped around each other's necks. Grandpère looked like he was ten or eleven. That was a long time ago, but there was no mistaking the resemblance between the men before us now and the boys in the picture.

Louis was an inch or two taller than Grandpère, with broad shoulders and a wrinkled but kindly face. Unlike Grandpère, he was clean shaven. His heavy eyebrows were perfectly white, as was what hair I could see beneath a black homburg hat. His overcoat and black shoes looked expensive, perhaps even custom made.

When they finally let go of each other, Grandpère took Louis by the elbow and turned him toward us. "Louis, I wish to introduce you to my granddaughter. This is Carruthers Monique McAllister. But we all call her Danni."

Louis stepped forward, beaming happily. "Yes, I know. I saw you and Rick on television. How do you do, Rick?" They shook hands. "And I must say that when I saw you, Danni, I was shocked. You look so much like your great-grandmother, Monique."

"*Merci*," I said with a slight bow. "I take that as a compliment."

"As you should, my dear. As you should." He took my right hand and raised it to his mouth. His lips brushed the back of my fingers lightly. "*Enchanté, ma petite Monique.*"

It was seriously one of the most romantic things that had ever happened in my life, and I think I went as red as a rose. I didn't have to ask what it meant. *Enchanté*—literally, "enchanted"—was a common French greeting—their equivalent of saying "I'm pleased to meet you." But I thought "Enchanted to meet you" was much more lovely. The rest meant, "my little Monique."

I did a little curtsy. "*Merci, Monsieur* Girard. I am very pleased to meet you as well."

Louis looked around. "But where is the rest of your family, Jean-Henri? Where are Angelique and Lucas? And your grandson? They are with you too, no?" His English was very good, the French accent very light.

"They got sick," I explained. "Some bad food. They went back to the hotel."

"Oh?" He didn't seem happy about that. "We were watching. We didn't see them."

"They took a taxi back to Caen," Grandpère explained. "We are just headed back to see how they are doing."

"Dad called about an hour ago," I volunteered, "and said they were feeling much better."

"So why don't you follow us back?" Grandpère said. "Angelique and Mack would love to see you again and you could meet my grandson as well. We'll have dinner together."

His face fell. "I would like that very much, but I'm afraid we must go back to Paris tonight. I apologize, Jean-Henri, for not making contact sooner. But I've been in hiding. I had to be absolutely sure it was safe for me and for you to make contact."

"Not a problem," Grandpère said. "I'm just glad we finally connected. But why in hiding, Louis? Is something wrong?"

He frowned. "Actually," he went on, "I was at the office yesterday morning when you came to see me. But I did not want to reveal myself. First of all, I wanted to make sure it was really you. Second, I wanted to see if you were being followed."

This was starting to creep me out. In hiding. Being followed. Making sure it was safe. We had already played a starring role in one action movie. We didn't need another one.

"You'd better tell us what is going on, Louis," Grandpère said.

"*Oui, oui.*" Louis turned and motioned toward the car. "Come. It is warm inside. I want you to come see me as soon as you return to Paris, but I will give a quick summary now."

———

As we slid into the Mercedes, I decided that Louis had done much better financially than my grandfather. I don't know cars all that well, but I guessed this was the largest of the Mercedes models, the kind that was just one step short of a limo. Inside, it was top of the line in every respect. The leather seats felt almost like we were seated on carpeting. Walnut paneling was everywhere. What I guessed was a minibar was folded into the backseat. Louis got in the front with the driver. Grandpère, Rick, and I sat in the back. Louis didn't introduce us to the driver, who never even looked in our direction.

When we were settled, Louis half turned so he could look at us.

"I was out of the country when you first started calling," he began. "Actually, I was in New York, looking for you."

We gaped at him. "But why?" Grandpère asked.

"Well, it all started one morning back in September. When I come to work each morning, I always turn on the news and listen to it as I start my day. So imagine my surprise when *Fox News* announced that a family from Hanksville, Utah, including the grandfather, Jean-Henri LaRoche, were going to be their special guests that morning.

"Imagine how shocked I was to hear what had happened to you." He looked at me. "And to hear how you and Rick were able to free your family. I was stunned. And not just because it came out of the blue like that. I'll explain what I mean in a moment. So I immediately left to go and find you. To warn you."

There it was again. "Wasn't it a little late by then to warn us?" I asked. "I mean, by the time we were in New York, it was all over with."

"Was it?" he shot right back. Then he held up a finger. "*Un moment,* Danni, and I shall try to answer your question." He turned back to Grandpère. "But when I got to New York, you had disappeared. Without a trace. Poof! You were no more."

"Thanks to the FBI," I said.

"Yes, I thought as much. I went to Utah, but you were not there either. But then, my office called to say that they were receiving calls from you. That you were in France. I could scarcely believe it. I was elated, of course, but cautious. I had to make sure this was not a trap."

"A trap?" Grandpère asked.

"Yes. I had to be sure it was really you. So I had my security team start investigating. They quickly confirmed it was really you, but I had them continue to investigate, to see if you were being watched or monitored down in Le Petit Château. You were, but only by one of Interpol's officers, which was good. And by the way, not to be critical of Interpol, but they had no idea my team was in place."

He gestured toward the other Mercedes outside the car park. "The other car is the security team that has been following you, making sure all was okay. I was greatly relieved to learn that it was. So when you came to the office this morning, I decided it was time that we meet. And so here I am."

He leaned in a little, looking at Grandpère. "When will you be back in Paris?"

"We had planned on heading back Saturday morning. But with the family being sick, they missed the cemetery experience today, so I think we'll extend that another day. Why?"

"You must stop and see me before you return to Le Petit Château. It is imperative. There is so much I have to tell you. And show you. And things we need to put into place for your protection. But for now, let me share the essentials."

"We're listening," said Grandpère, who by now looked as grave and worried as Louis.

"Perhaps I should begin by saying that your family was not the first to be kidnapped."

"*What?*" Rick and I cried out together.

"Who else?" Grandpère asked, his voice low.

"My granddaughter was kidnapped about two years ago."

I fell back against the seat, sick with shock.

"It cost me a million Euros to get her back safely. But that is not all. Eighteen months ago, Jacques Rousseau was kidnapped from his office in broad daylight. He paid two million Euros to his captors."

"Jacques too?" Grandpère whispered.

"*Oui.* At the time, I thought it very odd that two former Resistance members from Le Petit Château should be the target of criminals, but I assumed it was just a strange coincidence. But I immediately hired a highly professional security company to investigate. I had to make sure this was more than blind chance. I also went into seclusion, fearing that something else might happen. That's why my people were so evasive with you."

"Have your security people found out who is doing this?"

He held up his hand. "Let me answer that in a minute, Jean-Henri. First, let me say that I had them look up some of our old comrades and see if there were more instances of kidnappings."

"And were there?"

"No, not exactly. Except for yours, of course. But listen to this. Last January, André Villeneuve had his supermarket in Bordeaux burned to the ground under very suspicious circumstances. When he filed a claim, the insurance company had no record that they had ever insured him. He was financially ruined. Still hasn't recovered. A few months later, Étienne Giroux was accused of embezzling from his company. He's the chief financial officer there."

"Étienne?" Grandpère exploded. "Impossible!"

"Agreed. But the proof was 'irrefutable.' He was convicted and is still serving an eighteen-month prison sentence. No trace of the money he supposedly embezzled was ever found. It was a high-profile case and generated a lot of terrible publicity. His wife divorced him and his children now refuse to visit him. The evidence was so strong that even they believed he did it."

"So five of us from Le Petit Château?"

"*Oui,* and that's only the beginning. Do you remember Célina Chastain? From Strasbourg?"

"Of course." He turned to me and Rick. "She was our courier. She was just sixteen. Your age, Danni. She had the face of an angel and could talk her way past almost any German patrol." There was a fleeting smile. "Both Louis and I had terrible crushes on her, but she was older than we were and barely knew we existed." Back to Louis. "What about her?"

Louis's face was filled with sorrow now. "Célina, now Célina Morneau, worked in the French Civil Service for many years and retired on a small pension a few years back. Last November, her grandson and granddaughter were arrested for the sale and possession of cocaine, methamphetamine, and heroin. The police got an anonymous tip and found several bags of cocaine in the boy's apartment and more in the girl's car. At their trial, people they had never seen before swore that they had been their suppliers."

He sighed. "I know that family well. The boy was one of my employees for a time. He was not a drug user. Neither was his sister. I sent my corporate counsel out to represent them. Because it was a first offense for both of them, they finally got three years of probation. But they cannot get jobs now because they have felonies on their records. It has nearly killed Célina."

"So all of those targeted were former Resistance fighters?"

"That's what I thought at first. But then the security people started finding other puzzling cases where seemingly innocent people were set up, framed, and convicted of fraud, embezzlement, or other crimes. Three had their assets totally stripped by professional identity thieves. Another was convicted of manslaughter after a barroom fight that he didn't start. A bloody knife, which he had never seen before, had his fingerprints on it."

Louis stopped, his eyes far away now. "Are you seeing anything strange about these last examples?"

Grandpère thought a moment, then shook his head. "Not really. What?"

"These brought no financial gain for the perpetrators. In fact, there was another kidnapping two months ago in Le Mans. Same mode of operation. A lot of evidence to suggest it was the same gang. But the man they captured was a factory worker, the son of a retired factory worker. Guess what the amount of the ransom was? Two thousand Euros. That wouldn't even have covered their expenses. Who kidnaps people for two thousand Euros?"

Rick spoke up. "Why else would they do it, if not for money?"

"*Exactement!*" Louis exploded.

"For revenge," Grandpère said quietly.

"Yes," Louis answered. "That was my first thought too. But revenge for what? That was the question. So I sent my team to find out."

"And did they find some kind of common link between all of these crimes?" I wondered.

"Oh, yes, a couple of things. In the first place, no one has ever been physically harmed." He glanced at Rick. "Except for you, but that seems to have been not by preplanned design."

"That's right."

"But that seems strange if the motive is revenge. Second, in every case, with only one exception, the targeted families were devastated by the crimes. They were utterly ruined—mentally, emotionally, socially, economically. And where money was not a factor, that devastation seems to have been the primary motive behind the crimes. For example, one woman in Toulouse tested positive for sexually transmitted diseases. She was a nun in a Catholic girls' school. It was later proven that she was a virgin and that the lab tests had been falsified. But by that time the story had been leaked to the media and went viral on the social networks. She finally asked to be transferred to South America where she could start over."

Louis turned back to Grandpère. "By the way, as you sit here in my Mercedes, being watched by a very expensive security team, you may have guessed that I am that exception. But this is only because I had the money to fight back, to hire security. And we have blocked several attempts to destroy or steal my assets. But those without my resources have not fared so well.

"You are very wise, Jean-Henri," Louis went on. "It is revenge. Of that I am sure. But it is revenge of a very different kind. It is a war of the mind more than a war against the body." He shook his head, a sense of horror evident in his voice. "Their purpose is incredibly simple and absolutely devastating."

Grandpère turned to me. "Like waiting for us at the mine so they could blow it up before our eyes. Like an anonymous person who kept feeding the media sensational information. Look what that has done to our lives."

This was making me literally sick. It was too horrible to contemplate.

"They destroy hope," Louis said quietly. "That is their real target."

"Exactly," Grandpère sighed.

"And the other common link?" Louis said. "This, I think provides us a possible answer to our questions. I had my investigators dig more deeply into the backgrounds of these victims, and one thing turned up again and again. They had all had some role in the war."

"Like what?" Rick asked.

"Two weeks ago, while I was going over all the reports from my security team, I saw something that about bowled me over. I saw a name in one of the reports. That was such a shock that I just stared at it for a long time, not really believing what I was looking at. Two documents later, I saw it again." The pain etched deep lines into his face. "I sent the investigators back to look at every individual case. And without exception, every person is linked to this same name."

"Who?" I cried out. "Who is doing these awful things?"

"No, Danni. This man is not responsible for the crimes. He cannot be . . ." He let the pause hang there in the air for what seemed like forever, " . . . for he has been dead now for over sixty years."

"Dead? How can that be?" Rick exclaimed.

"May I guess?" Grandpère asked, his voice so low I barely heard him.

Louis nodded. "Yes. You know, don't you."

He nodded. "The name is Horst Kessler of Munich, Germany."

I gasped. Rick was confused.

"*Colonel* Horst Kessler," Louis answered. "Commandant of the Strasbourg branch of the Secret State Police, which in German was called the *Geheime Staatspolizei,* which is usually shortened to *Gestapo.*"

For the longest time, none of us spoke. Finally, Grandpère visibly pulled himself together. "Have you told Interpol this yet?"

Louis shook his head. "No. My security firm is pretty sure there is a leak in the Interpol headquarters in Paris. So we cannot let these people know that we are closing in on them, or they will simply disappear."

I turned to Rick. "Horst Kessler is the man who arrested Grandpère's mother and father."

"And who struck my mother across the face, cutting her cheek with his ring," Grandpère added. "I was there. I saw it happen."

"And because you were there," Louis came back in, "your parents—and you—were called to Nuremberg, Germany, to testify in the war crime tribunals of 1947. As were my parents and I. As were Jacques Rousseau, Étienne Giroux, André Villeneuve, and Célina Chastain

Morneau. It was our testimonies that led to Kessler's conviction and sent him to the gallows."

"But wait," I said. "That doesn't make sense. If it was Célina Chastain's testimony that led to his conviction, why not go after her? Why frame her grandson and granddaughter . . . ?" I stopped. I already knew the answer. What better way to destroy hope than by bringing pain and loss on those most loved? My eyes widened. Like me and Cody and Mom and Dad.

"There's more," Louis said quietly. "And this, I think, helps us better understand what is going on. Once we saw the link to Kessler, I sent an investigative team to Munich. Here is what they have learned so far.

"Horst Kessler was the oldest son of a very wealthy and influential family in Munich. He was married and had two children, a boy and a girl. When the war broke out, he was given a commission in the German army and eventually became a colonel with the SS and the Gestapo. When he was captured by the Americans, I guess some of his old so-called friends and associates back in Munich saw an opportunity to profit from his downfall. They started rumors that he had turned traitor and was cooperating with the Allies.

"The *Gauleiter* in Munich—" He looked back at me and Rick. "A *Gauleiter* was the leader of a regional branch of the Nazi Party. Anyway, the one in Munich evidently was the one who started these accusations. Documents were forged. They even brought forth witnesses to testify against him. His palatial home and bank accounts were all seized and divided up amongst a small circle of his enemies. The *Gauleiter* moved into his palatial villa using forged deeds of title. Kessler's wife and children, now thoroughly disgraced, were thrown out into the cold. Then the *Gauleiter*'s wife spread rumors that *Frau* Kessler had been receiving food and supplies from her husband and selling them on the black market—a crime punishable by death. She and her children had to flee for their lives, living from hand to mouth in the bombed-out ruins of the city. This was in the early spring, when the weather was still very cold. Her son caught pneumonia and died."

"How horrible," I exclaimed.

"Yes, very horrible for her." He leaned forward. "Now, here is where things really get interesting. The *Gauleiter* quickly changed sides and cooperated with the Americans in their search for Nazi war criminals. So he not only escaped punishment himself but he helped give evidence against his former comrades, including Horst Kessler. And by capitalizing on their misfortunes, the *Gauleiter,* whose name was Werner, became a wealthy and influential man in postwar Munich.

"Then, not quite two years ago now, the *Gauleiter*'s wife and two children were kidnapped and held for ransom. This was the first of all the kidnappings here in Europe—"

"Wait," Rick said. "I thought you said there were only three kidnappings."

"No, only three kidnappings among those who belonged to the Resistance. We totally missed the one that involved the Werners at first because it was kept very hush-hush, and also because it took place in Germany. Eventually, they had to pay almost five million Euros to free them."

I whistled softly. "Whoever this is, they're making huge amounts of money, aren't they?"

"Enormous amounts. But that's not the whole story. The oldest Werner daughter was a prominent socialite who married a very wealthy businessman from Frankfurt. But one of the tabloid newspapers broke a story that she was actually living a secret life as a high-class call girl when her husband was traveling. They had pictures and evidence to prove it."

"But she was innocent," Rick said, not making it a question.

"Totally," Louis agreed, "which eventually came out. But by then her husband had divorced her, leaving her with absolutely nothing from him. She eventually had a mental breakdown and is now in a mental institution in Munich. A few months ago, Mr. Werner suffered a massive stroke and died. Doctors attributed it largely to the stress he was under."

I was reeling. It was like some horrid nightmare.

Louis nodded, looking half apologetic. "I'm sorry to take so long, but let me share one last thing, and then we shall discuss what we do next." He took another breath. "When we learned all of this, I asked our research team to try to find out what ever happened to Horst Kessler's wife. It took some digging, but here's what they learned. After *Frau* Kessler was thrown out of her home, one of Kessler's fellow officers in the German army, a man by the name of Manfred Hoffman, went looking for her. It turns out that Kessler had done him some kind of favor early on in his career, and he felt that he had a debt of honor to be paid. So he finally found her in a bombed-out shell of a building. By that point, her son had died. Hoffman risked his own standing and reputation and helped her and her daughter escape to Switzerland and hid her in the home of his sister there. Together, they managed to create new documents for *Frau* Kessler and her daughter and smuggle them out of Switzerland. We're not sure where they went yet, but we're getting closer to finding out."

Grandpère started to say something, but Louis went on quickly. "Let me finish, for this is the most important part. Manfred Hoffman was captured by the Americans in Munich and put in a POW camp. But he was never charged with any war crimes. He was eventually released and went on to live a quiet and respectable life as a college professor in Hamburg. He passed away of cancer in 2004, leaving a wife, three children, and several grandchildren. His sister was married to a Swiss banker and is now a widow. She and her family still live in Zurich."

"So there is at least one happy part to this story," I suggested.

"Indeed. But here is what is fascinating. Several months after the Werners paid their ransom, an anonymous donor deposited five hundred thousand Euros into the account of Manfred Hoffman's widow. And the taxes on that amount had been prepaid."

"Five hundred thousand?" I gasped.

He nodded. "Another hundred thousand tax-free Euros were given to the sister. In all cases, the donor was never identified, but the bank that transferred the money certified to the authorities that these contributions came from a completely legitimate source."

"*Je suis bouche bée,*" Grandpère breathed softly.

It was the French cry of astonishment, literally, "My mouth is agape."

"So, it is not just revenge motivating these people. I think the better word is *justice,*" Louis concluded. "Those who helped the Kesslers have been richly rewarded. Those who hurt the Kesslers are being systematically ruined. It is quite a remarkable story, no?"

Grandpère's head had been down now for several minutes as he stared at the floor, listening. Now it came up with a snap. He yanked his door open, then turned to Rick and me. "We have to go. *Now!* Get in the van." He turned back and extended his hand. "Thank you, Louis. I'll be in touch. We are greatly in your debt, but we must go."

I didn't move. This abrupt urgency left me, Rick, and Louis totally stunned. Grandpère got out of the car and went to shut the door. When he saw that Rick and I were still sitting there, too dumbfounded to move, he barked, "*Now, Danni!* We have to go."

We both scrambled out of the car and ran to the van. I looked back and saw that Louis was out of the car too. He and Grandpère embraced for a long moment. As we climbed into the car, they separated for a moment but were talking earnestly. Or I should say, Grandpère was talking earnestly while Louis listened intently and kept nodding his head.

"*Au revoir,*" I heard Louis call as Grandpère left him and came and opened the driver's door and got in. Grandpère waved back. "*Au revoir. Merci beaucoup, mon ami.*" "Good-bye. Many thanks, my friend."

He shut the door and inserted the key in the ignition, and the engine roared into life. Moments later, we shot out of the parking lot, the back end of the van fishtailing wildly in the snow.

PART EIGHT

The Rumble of Chariots

CHAPTER 29

"Danni?"

"Yes, Grandpère?"

"Try them again."

I did, going through the same exact routine as the previous two times. Hit the "Favorites" button for Dad. Wait. No answer. Hang up. Hit the button for Mom. No answer. Hang up. Hit the button for Cody. Nothing changed. "Still no answer," I said.

"Maybe they're down at the swimming pool," Rick suggested from behind us. "You know Cody. He's a fish."

I shook my head. "Mom would take her cell phone. Maybe not Dad. Definitely not Cody. But Mom would. Dinner?" I said it without much hope.

"Same thing," Grandpère grunted.

I was riding in the front seat with Grandpère. Rick was behind us. I gave Grandpère a sideways glance. "Do you feel like something is wrong?"

His head jerked around. "Don't you?"

"I . . . I'm not sure. I'm worried, of course."

He turned his gaze back on the road, but not before I saw his mouth turn sharply down. I kept my eyes straight ahead. The windshield wipers were starting to have trouble keeping the windshield clean. The highway was still only slushy, but it was snowing hard now, and at this rate, the roads would be slick before we got back to Caen.

Suddenly, Grandpère let off the gas and started to pull over.

"Uh . . . why are you stopping?"

"Where's *Le Gardien,* Danni? I want it out from under your coat. We need help."

I looked away quickly, but not before I saw Rick's look. With shame lancing through me, I dropped my chin and stared at my hands. "I . . . um . . . don't have it with me."

What hurt even more than his expression was the realization that my confession didn't surprise him. It was if he were expecting it. So I rushed on. "We were in such a hurry to get on the road again that I went off and left it in my suitcase. I'm sorry."

Grandpère put the van in gear, checked the rearview mirror, and pulled back onto the road again without saying a word. Not a good sign.

"I'm really sorry, Grandpère," I said in my most contrite voice.

He just shook his head slowly back and forth. "Oh, Danni." There was a deep, pain-filled sigh, then very softly, "Danni, Danni, Danni."

And that was the last word spoken in our vehicle until we turned off the highway and started down the road that led into Caen and to our hotel.

As we stopped at a traffic light about two blocks from our hotel, Grandpère finally spoke again. "If the family is with Juliette, we'll say nothing of this until we are alone."

I turned, caught off guard by his comment. "Why not?"

"Nothing, Danni. Do you understand me?" There wasn't much warmth and affection in his voice.

"Okay. But why, Grandpère? If our family *is* in danger, then so is she, and . . ." My voice trailed off as understanding dawned. "You don't think that . . ." I just gaped at him. "What are you saying?"

"I'm saying I don't want to speak about Louis in any way if she is there. I mean it, Danni. Don't fight me on this."

"I can't believe this. That's not fair, Grandpère. Not after all she's done for us."

"Ah, yes," he mused, the sarcasm thicker than cold bacon grease. "Let's talk about all she's done. She bought Le Petit Château and spent a ton of money turning it into a bed and breakfast, supposedly because she and her husband had an emotional attachment to it, and also to provide her with some income in her retirement."

He had me on that one. I had wondered about that myself more than once.

He went right on. "And how convenient that they somehow just happened to get my name and email so they could offer us this fantastic deal if we would come and stay with them."

"Oh, come on, Grandpère," I said. "I find that hard to believe. She had no way of knowing we would come to France. We didn't know it ourselves until just a short time before we actually left."

"That's right. Not until someone blew up the mine so we would know that the danger wasn't over. Not until someone copied your journal so they knew every detail about *Le Gardien* and about you and Rick. Not until carefully orchestrated leaks to the media led us step-by-step to the point that we had to escape to somewhere."

He blew out his breath in utter disgust. "And all along, we thought we were being so clever. We were so careful every time we went out to dress and look so that no one would recognize us. I can't believe we were such fools."

Rick leaned forward over the seat. "Grandpère, what if the food poisoning today wasn't an accident?"

"Of course it wasn't an accident," he retorted. "That's why she volunteered to provide the lunches. That's why she kept them right with her on the ride up here."

I was getting angry now. "Come on, guys," I pleaded. "If that's the case, then why didn't *we* get sick? And why would she make herself sick?"

"Actually," Rick answered, "she never was really sick. She just said she was sick. We never saw her throw up. And maybe she wanted us separated."

I gave Rick a sharp look, but my uneasiness was growing in leaps and bounds. If Rick had doubts too . . . I turned back to Grandpère. "So what? You think she's *Frau* Kessler? That would make her over ninety years old."

"No, not his wife. His daughter."

I still couldn't make myself accept it. "And you really think she is out to destroy us?"

"Yes, I do," he answered quietly. "Financially. Socially. Emotionally. Spiritually." He said each word slowly and precisely, just as Louis had done earlier. "And we walked right into it." Then, with great sadness, he said, "You do understand why you're having such a hard time accepting this, don't you."

That caught me off guard. "I . . . no, I guess I don't. I like her. We've become good friends. I'm having trouble picturing her as this horrible monster."

"I'm not talking about your friendship. I am asking why *you* are having such a hard time seeing any danger here."

He had me, and I knew it. And the only defense I could see was to go on the offense. "If you are right, then why did I feel so positive about her? Why didn't I have any sense of evil or danger?"

"Maybe because she convinced you that *Le Gardien* was not chic. Maybe you were just a little ashamed of the pouch." He glanced back, and I saw the sadness in his eyes. "And maybe that's why you 'forgot' and left it in your room today." He quickly held up a hand. "I'm not saying you did it deliberately, Danni. But it's like she has somehow convinced you that *Le Gardien* is something to be a little bit ashamed of."

Deeply stung, I struck back. "Oh, yeah. What about you? Why didn't you see this coming? Why didn't you see her as the dragon lady?"

In a voice so quiet I could barely hear him, he said, "Because I am not the keeper of the pouch."

That hurt. More than anything I could remember. It cut me like a knife.

On the defensive now, I changed the subject. "And I suppose Philippe is part of this sinister plot against us as well?"

"Of course. He's a banker, Danni. How do you make several million dollars in ransom money disappear? How do you fund complex, international operations or bribe prison guards and federal judges? It's the perfect cover for him."

"That would explain Juliette's outburst about Hitler last night," Rick suddenly said. It was clear he had accepted Grandpère's theory and was now looking for examples that supported it.

"Precisely," Grandpère said. "What you heard was the Nazi line of propaganda."

More and more it made sense, which only wounded my pride all the more. "And what about being innocent until proven guilty?"

"I didn't suggest we call the police and have her arrested. I just asked that we say nothing about Louis in front of her."

I threw up my hands. "All right! I accept the possibility. I admit it makes sense in a lot of ways, but I hope you're wrong and that you are going to owe her a very big apology."

"If so, I will make sure you are there when I offer it to her."

⸺◆⸺

I was a total basket case by the time we entered the hotel lobby. My fear for my family—in spite of all my protests—was gnawing at my gut like a pack of ravenous rats. My confidence in Juliette's innocence was eroding very quickly. Grandpère's suspicions had a lot of merit, no matter how vigorously I wanted to believe in her. And even though it made me mad, in a way, that Rick didn't take my side, I had always trusted his instincts. He had that gift of what Dad called "an enormous amount of common sense," and for now he was standing solidly with Grandpère. Most of all, if I was right and there was some simple explanation for all of this, why weren't Mom and Dad answering their phones?

I hung back, letting the two of them go through the revolving doors first. Once inside, I stepped to one side, scanning the lobby for any sign of my family or Juliette. There were quite a few people in the lobby, either sitting in the various lounge areas or coming and going. Everyone stared at Grandpère in his uniform as he strode quickly across the lobby to the front desk. He was oblivious to them. Seeing that I had stopped, Rick came over and joined me. He started to say something, then evidently thought better of it and turned to watch Grandpère.

I couldn't bear to watch, and yet I couldn't take my eyes from him as the front desk clerk kept shaking his head as Grandpère asked him question after question.

The chariots are here. Sick at heart, I finally understood what that meant.

Grim as death, Grandpère turned away from the desk, motioned to us to follow, and headed toward the bank of elevators. As we joined him, an older couple waiting there got on the elevator with us. So we said nothing as we ascended to the fourth floor. As we got off and started down the hall toward our rooms, I started to say something, but Grandpère shook his head. "Let's get inside," he murmured. "Make a quick trip to the bathroom, then we'll meet in your suite. Hurry!"

The first thing I did had nothing to do with the bathroom. I went right to my suitcase, which was still lying on the bed where I had tossed it. I threw it open. Everything looked exactly as I had left it. I dropped to my knees, pawing through it like a wild person. Not there. *Le Gardien* was gone! I jumped up and looked frantically around the room, trying to remember if I had put it somewhere else. But I knew I hadn't.

I dropped back down on my knees and buried my face against the bedspread. "Oh, dear God," I cried. "Help me. Help me find our family." But all that came out was this deathly silence—in the room, and inside my heart. And then I realized that what I had done earlier today might turn out to be the biggest mistake of my life.

———

My room was joined to Mom and Dad's with a connecting door. I opened it and then let Rick in to join me. Two minutes later Grandpère knocked softly. He was back in his civilian clothes. He also had his phone to his ear, speaking in a low voice with great urgency. "I'll call you if we learn anything," he said in a clipped voice, then he tapped the phone to end the call and put it in his jacket pocket.

"That was Clay in Paris. He and his team will be on their way to Caen within the hour."

"Did you tell him not to contact Interpol?"

"I did. They're also going to look into that possible leak. They'll come here by helicopter. I also gave him Louis's number, and he's calling him right now to get a full briefing."

"If Mom and Dad have been abducted, we have to call the police, Grandpère. Now!"

He came over and took me by the hand. "No, Danni. If it is an abduction—and we're still not one hundred percent sure that it is—then we don't dare call the police. We are dealing with a highly sophisticated group of criminals. It likely they have someone on their payroll among the *gendarmes* here in Caen. It's too great a risk. We have to wait for Clay."

"And the desk clerk hadn't seen them at all?" Rick asked.

"No, and he's been on duty since noon."

The buzz of a cell phone cut into my growing despair. For a moment, I thought it was Grandpère's, but then I realized it was mine. I leaped to where I had dropped my parka and clawed at the pocket. "Maybe it's Mom."

It wasn't. I saw from the display that it was a French number. One I didn't know. I tapped the screen and jammed it up to my ear. "Hello."

"Danni?"

I instantly recognized the voice. "Philippe? Is that you?"

I turned. Both Grandpère and Rick moved closer. I quickly tapped the button to put it on speakerphone.

"Danni? Is my mother with you?" It came out blunt and hard.

"No, Philippe. She and my parents and Cody got sick up at Omaha Beach. They came home earlier. We just returned. We can't find them."

"When did you last see her?"

"Uh . . . it was about three o'clock. They took a taxi back to the hotel, but—"

"I just received a call from a group who claim they have kidnapped Mother."

I gasped. "No!"

"They are demanding ten million Euros in ransom. I thought at first it was some kind of a sick joke, because I knew she was with your family."

Grandpère snatched the phone from me. "Philippe, this is Jean-Henri. Our family are not here either, though they should have been by now. Did these people say anything about them?"

"No."

My hand shot to my mouth and I bit down hard.

"They told me to come to Caen and find your family as quickly as possible," Philippe explained. "They will call us with further instructions at nine p.m. sharp. I'm at the airport now, just boarding an air taxi. I'll be there in an hour."

"Can we pick you up at the airport?"

"*No!*" He literally shouted it. "Their instructions were very specific and related to you as well as me. You're to wait for me there at your hotel. You are not to leave for any reason, or they said the direst consequences will follow." There was a momentary pause, then, "Have you made any phone calls since you got back?"

Grandpère shot me a puzzled look. "Why do you ask?"

"They said you are not to make any phone calls. Especially not to the police. From what he said, I think they're monitoring all of our phones. Did you call the police?"

"We talked about calling the *gendarmes* here in Caen but decided it was better not to."

"Good. Don't call anyone."

I was staring at him. The look on his face was one of anger. And why not? He was sure that Philippe was part of it. But if Juliette had been kidnapped, then . . . I was stricken. I no longer knew who to believe and who to trust.

"Stay put," Philippe commanded. "I'll bring help with me and we'll sort this out." And he hung up.

As Grandpère turned to face Rick and me, I burst out in tears. "Not again, Grandpère. This can't be happening again."

Grimly, he nodded. "We don't know for sure, Danni." He handed me back my phone, his face deeply troubled.

We stood there for a moment, almost paralyzed. Then he suddenly straightened. "I want you and Rick to go back to your rooms. Put on your warmest clothes. Then pack your things as quickly as possible. I want you back here in three minutes. Hurry."

"Pack? Where are we going?"

"Just do it, Danni," he cried. "Something's not right, and staying here is not the way to find out what it is."

"But where will we go?"

He suddenly looked very sad. "Why don't you ask *Le Gardien* that?" And with that he herded us into my room, shutting the door behind us.

———

I grabbed blindly at Rick's hand. "Oh, Rick. The pouch is gone. What have I done? What have I done?"

Before I could answer, the door jerked open again and Grandpère stepped in. Through the blur of my tears, I saw that he was holding something in his hands, and my heart leaped for joy. He was holding *Le Gardien*.

In one leap I was to him, but as I went to take it from him, he pulled it away. "*You* took it?" I cried.

"Yes, I did," he murmured. "I thought someone ought to."

"I know," I wailed. "I'm so sorry, Grandpère! I'm so sorry."

His face softened. "I know you are, my dear, but have you forgotten Humpty Dumpty so soon?" He quoted softly, "'All the king's horses, and all the king's men, couldn't put Humpty together again.'" He looked away in frustration. "I tried to warn you. When I said that the chariots were here, Danni, did you think that it was just the ravings of a senile old man?"

I looked away, stifling a sob.

"But all is not lost, my dear. The *fleurs-de-lys* have been passed to you. *Le Gardien* has made his choice. He is your blessing and your burden now, my child." And he handed the pouch to me.

I had never known that shame could bring such physical pain. I wanted to thrust it at him, make him take it back so the guilt might lessen even a little. But I couldn't. It was our only hope, and I was desperately in need of hope. I clasped it to my body in quiet urgency.

Then, suddenly, Grandpère stepped forward, his arms outstretched. I fell into them with a wrenching cry. He crushed me to him, which only made me cry all the harder.

And suddenly, he was crying too. "Ah, Danni, Danni. You remind me so much of myself when I was your age. So don't give up. And if something were to happen to me . . ." He had to stop and take a deep breath. "Just remember. I love you with every fiber of my being."

He started to pull away, but I clung to him. A cold, dark feeling was shooting through me, and I was terribly frightened all of a sudden. "Grandpère, don't leave me. Please."

He lifted my head and wiped away the tears with his thumbs. Then he kissed me softly on both cheeks. "I will never leave you, child. Remember that. No matter what you may think. You are not alone. *Adieu,* my love." He wiped at the tears. "Now go! You must hurry!" He whirled and went back into my parents' side of the suite. I saw him take his phone out of his pocket as he shut the door behind him. To my further surprise, I also heard the lock click, and moments later the murmur of his voice.

———

Rick and I came out of our rooms at almost the same instant. I was in my parka again, and this time *Le Gardien* was on my shoulder outside of it. "You ready?" he asked.

I nodded. "Rick, I . . ."

"It's all right." He grabbed my hand. "This is why I came." One of his crooked little grins broke out across his face. "Nowhere I'd rather be right now, even if I don't get much sleep."

We walked down the hall to Grandpère's room. I set my suitcase down, tapped on the door, and called softly, "Grandpère? We're here."

I came back over to Rick, standing close enough that our shoulders touched. He reached down and took my hand. I grasped it like it was a lifeline thrown to someone who had just washed overboard. We stood there that way, not speaking, for almost a minute. Then, puzzled, I went back to the door and knocked a little louder. "Grandpère? We're here. Can we help you?"

I leaned in to listen. There was no sound. I looked at Rick. He came over and joined me, then rapped sharply with his knuckles. "Grandpère?"

Nothing. Rick reached down and turned the handle. To our surprise, the door was unlocked. Rick gave me a questioning look, but I was already pushing it open and moving through it. The first thing I saw was that his suitcase and overcoat were on the bed, but the duffel bag was gone. "Grandpère?" I was fighting hard to keep the panic out of my voice.

"Look, Danni."

I turned to see what Rick was pointing at. On a small writing table, a white envelope was visible. I raced to it and snatched it up. The envelope had hotel letterhead, and on the front there were three words. *Danni and Rick.* The horrible feeling was back. I ripped it open and cast the envelope aside. Rick moved up to read it with me. And what I read pierced me more sharply, more terribly than anything I had ever experienced before.

My dearest Danni and Rick,

My being here is what has put you and my family in extreme danger. It is me they want to destroy, and they know that the most effective way to do that is through those I love. So I must go. The pipes are calling.

Remember this always. Just because there is no flame doesn't mean the fire is out. And just because the pouch is empty doesn't mean there's nothing there.

Adieu.

With great love. GP.

The paper slipped from my fingers and fluttered to the floor. "No, not *adieu*. Please. Not *adieu*." I turned and buried my head against Rick's chest as the shuddering sobs started in yet again.

Rick held me tightly as I rocked back and forth. Finally, he said, "I thought *adieu* just meant good-bye."

I stepped back, shaking my head. Then I wiped at my eyes. "In French, they say good-bye with *au revoir,* which means literally 'to see you again,' or 'until our next meeting.' But *adieu* means 'to God.' The implication is that you believe that you shall not see that person again and so—" The words caught in my throat. "And so you commend them to God's care."

Rick pulled me close as I burst into tears again. He stroked my hair over and over, whispering, "It will be all right, Danni. It will be all right."

━━━━

I'm not sure how long we stood there, numbed and stricken. I was just glad that Rick had come. Otherwise, I would be alone now. Totally and utterly alone.

A sharp knock on the door brought my head up with a snap.

"Danni?"

It was Philippe's voice. I squeezed Rick's hand, then pulled free. "Philippe's here." I walked to the door and unlocked it, then opened it. He burst past me, shoving me aside roughly with his shoulder. "Mother! Are you in here?"

I gaped at him. "She's not here. I told you that she was—" Philippe strode past Rick and jerked open the bathroom door. "Where is your grandfather?" he barked back at me.

"He's . . . he's gone."

He spun around, snapping his fingers. The door to our room had started to close behind me, but it slammed open again with a bang. Four men in the uniform of the *Police Nationale*—the national police force of France—came busting into the room, pistols drawn and looking very ready to use them.

"Seize them," Philippe shouted. "These are the ones who kidnaped my mother."

The nearest man stepped up to me and thrust his pistol into my face, so close that it almost touched my nose. He was smiling warmly at me, and that frightened me even more than the pistol did.

"*Hola, Señorita* Danni. *Es tan bueno volver a verlo.*"

My gift of translation was back. I understood perfectly what he had said. "Hello, Miss Danni. It is so good to see you again." And then I realized who it was wearing the *gendarmes* uniform with its round cap. It was Raul Muñoz, known also to me as Doc. As I gasped, he did two things at the same time. With one hand, he jerked *Le Gardien* off my shoulder. The other came up with a large, wicked-looking syringe filled with liquid. I fought back, kicking at his shins, but he only laughed and tightened his grip. Eyes filled with relish, Doc plunged the needle into my right upper arm. I felt an instant burning spreading through the flesh.

"Sleep tight, *Chiquita.*" he said. There was no time to react, no opportunity to even let the horror of his face register in my mind. The room started to blur. Nausea swept through me, and then the lights began to rapidly retreat. A moment later, all went black.

CHAPTER 30

Schloss von Dietz, Bern, Switzerland
October 22, 2011

My first conscious perception was of my head. It felt like it was in a vise and someone was turning the wheel tighter and tighter. It was pounding so hard I was sure it was going to shatter.

My second awareness was that it was day. And the sun was shining outside. Not sure how I knew that, I pried my eyes open a crack. On the wall opposite, but higher up, was a small window. I could see a corner of blue sky, and sunlight was streaming through the bars to make shadows on the opposite wall.

Bars? Wait. Hotels didn't have bars on their windows. Did they?

Finally, a third and more pressing realization came forth out of the thickness that filled my head. It was cold. Very, very cold. I realized that I was hugging myself tightly and shivering violently.

With a groan, I threw off my very thin blanket and rolled my legs over the side of my—cot? I was on a cot? What kind of a hotel was this?

With a great effort I pulled myself up into a sitting position, groaning as my head screamed in protest. It was so cold! For a moment, I thought I was naked. But when I looked down, I was hugely relieved to see that I had clothes on. Not the parka. Not my shoes or socks. But a blouse, pants—the essentials. But I was shivering uncontrollably. Instinctively, I reached up and felt my hair. Ugh! It was a wild tangle and felt greasy.

I forced myself to ignore the pounding in my head and looked around. This was definitely not a hotel room. Not unless hotels had cots bolted into the wall with nothing but an inch-thick mattress. And a small, porcelain toilet with no seat stuck in one corner. And steel bars for a door. And gray cement floors. And gray cement walls. And gray cement ceilings. And a small video camera mounted on the ceiling in one corner of the room.

I let my eyes move back to the window. It was about seven feet up the wall and about three feet beyond the end of my cot, just far enough that I couldn't reach it from the cot. There was glass in it, but behind steel bars. As if the glass had not been put in until later. I got to my feet, wincing as the cold cement connected with my bare flesh, then walked to where I was directly below the window. It was recessed into the wall, which was about fifteen inches thick. The bars were set in the cement and spaced about four inches apart. The glass was set back a couple of inches from the bars and looked like it was at least half an inch thick.

I could reach the sill with my hands if I stretched, but the surface was too slick for me to get a grip. I jumped up and caught hold of the bars, then pulled myself up enough to look out. What I saw was so totally unexpected, I was momentarily disoriented. I was looking out on an expanse of blue water. I could see a snow-covered shoreline some distance away. A couple of sailboats with brilliantly colored sails were visible about midway across the water. But it was what I saw beyond the lake that stunned me. In the distance, looking very much like a gigantic picture postcard, was a towering wall of snow-covered mountains. It was breathtaking.

I stared at it, trying to make my mind compute how this could be so, but then I realized I was about to lose my grip, so I dropped back down and returned to my cot to try to sort this out.

I had never been to Switzerland, but I knew that was where I was. We had decided as a family that we would go there before we went home. So we had gotten on the Internet and started working out a possible itinerary. We had settled on the area around Bern and Interlaken, which had some of the most beautiful country in the world, and I was pretty sure that was what I had just seen.

I drew my feet up beneath me to get them warm. How could I be in Switzerland? The last I remembered, I was in Caen, France. We had been—and that was when it all came rushing back. My family getting sick. Louis Girard. Grandpère's disappearance. Philippe busting into our room with *gendarmes*.

And Doc and that enormous needle!

I leaped up again and strode over to the steel-barred door, realizing now that I was in a cell of some kind. Like the window, the door was recessed into the wall, and while I was looking out into a narrow hallway, I couldn't see very far in either direction. Directly across from me was another cell, however. From what I could see, it was identical to mine. There was a momentary flash of hope, but then I saw that the door was half open. It was empty. But one thing was clear. I was in a cell block, which meant I was in a prison. My heart plummeted.

I listened intently. There wasn't a sound anywhere. I looked more closely at the opposite door. The door had the usual square metal box that held the locking mechanism, but I couldn't see a keyhole. Curious, I examined my own door, reaching through the bars, feeling for the keyhole. What I found instead was a flat metal box mounted on the door with a slot in it. Then I understood. The door was opened by a card reader, like you see in hotels.

I grasped the bars with both hands, shoved my face as far through the opening as I could, and called out in a loud whisper, "Rick? Rick, are you here?"

I heard a scuffling noise, then, "Danni?"

"Rick! Is that you?"

"Hey!" It was a man's voice and it was angry. "I told you to keep your mouth shut." More footsteps, this time heavy ones from boots, and moving fast. They stopped. There was a sharp clicking sound, a muffled scream, a heavy thud, then the sounds of someone in agony—grunts and gasps, feet thrashing on the floor.

"Rick!" I screamed and shook the bars as hard as I could. "Leave him alone!"

I heard the footsteps start again, this time coming in my direction. I folded myself up as tightly as I could on my cot. A short man with a barrel chest appeared in the hallway, then stepped up to the barred door. I had never seen him before. Then I saw that he held this squarish-looking pistol with wires dangling from the barrel. I recognized it immediately from TV cop shows. It was a Taser—a stun gun—that shot out electrical impulses and shocked a person into immobility.

"Your boyfriend just got Tasered," the man said. His accent was thick and obviously German. "And, just so you know, if I hear another sound from either of you, he will be Tasered again. And again." He spoke with much relish. "Ever had fifty thousand volts of electricity discharged into your body, little girl? It temporarily fries the central nervous system, and all your muscles lock up." His grin was so evil I felt another kind of chill. "I would be happy to give you a demonstration."

I said nothing. As he started to back away, he got in one final barb. "Breakfast is in half an hour. Why don't you take a hot bath before then? You look a little chilly." He thought that was enormously funny. I watched his belly jiggle as he cawed in delight. Then, with those glittering black eyes leering at me, he reached in his shirt pocket and drew out a plastic card. I got a glimpse of a photo on it and guessed immediately what it was. He stepped up to the door and swiped it. There was a distinct snap as the lock opened.

I was on my feet instantly as he stepped inside. My eyes swept the cell, looking for something—anything—to use against him. He took another step. I cringed and fell back. Then he threw back his head and roared. Without another word, he backed out again, clanged the door shut, and started away. He turned and looked over his shoulder at me. "Oh, and by the way, it was stupid of your grandfather to try to escape. Especially in a blizzard."

I straightened, instantly alert. Something had changed in his countenance. This wasn't a game anymore. "What about my grandfather?"

"A couple of our men saw him trying to escape and went after him. Your grandfather took a curve too fast and lost control of the van. It went through the guardrail and into the river."

"*No!* I don't believe you." And yet, even as I spoke, I remembered that as we entered Caen, the road ran parallel to a river that flowed right through the city.

He shrugged. "They haven't found the body yet. The driver's door popped open with the impact. Probably won't find it for several days. When the water's this cold, the body doesn't decompose as fast, and—"

I turned away.

He went right on. "As the body decomposes, gases form inside the body. That's what causes it to float to the surface. Who knows how far downriver he'll be by that time. Maybe even out to sea, where he will never be found."

"Stop. Please."

Another raucous laugh. "Have a good day, little one." He gave me a jaunty wave, then turned and disappeared.

For a long moment, I stared through the cell door at the empty hall. I wanted to scream at him that it was a lie. To ask where Mom and Dad and Cody were. But I knew that would be futile. I dropped back on my cot and buried my face in my hands.

It had to be a lie. Grandpère was gone. He had to have gotten out.

I threw myself down, covering my face with my arms. There was one thing wrong with that reasoning, and I knew it. *Grandpère knew. He knew he was going to die. That's why he bid you adieu.*

———

I'm not sure how long I lay there, wallowing in sorrow. It felt like a long time. I knew I had fallen back asleep for part of it. But I also knew that was partly because they had drugged me with some pretty powerful stuff. When I finally sat up, my mind was clear. And I had exhausted my supply of tears—for the moment, at least.

I forced myself not to think about Grandpère. I was able to do that only because I had to believe that he had escaped from the van. Heck, knowing Grandpère, this was probably another trick birthday candle that wouldn't go out, even if you put it in the punch. I straightened slowly.

Don't assume there is no fire just because something isn't burning or that the pouch is empty just because there's nothing there.

It provided the tiniest glimmer of hope. They hadn't found his body yet, so I wouldn't give up until I actually saw him dead. But another part of me knew I was looking for any sliver of hope to cling to. With a groan, I swung my feet over the cot and sat up. As I did so, I saw a small plastic tray with some food on it just inside my cell door. There was a hard roll along with two boiled eggs on a paper plate, and a paper cup filled with orange juice. No silverware. Nothing else. I ignored it. Food was my last concern right now. I looked around the cell again, seeing if there was anything I could use to get out of here. There wasn't, but my eyes stopped on the small video camera mounted on the ceiling. I turned away, my heart sinking. The thought of someone—maybe even Barrel Belly himself—watching my every movement, my every tear, was both horrifying and disgusting.

Pushing that aside, I decided to focus on Philippe and his lovely mother. What had happened there in the hotel? Did Philippe really think we had kidnapped his mother? No! Not when one of the *gendarmes* was Doc. Which meant that Juliette was almost certainly part of this too, just like Grandpère said. I heard this bitter laugh inside my head. *Almost certainly? Talk about blind optimism.*

Then came another sickening thought. If that was true, then she was the one who had my journal. She had read all of my silly, little-girl entries. She knew what a total airhead I was. Talk about an easy target! She had played me like a fiddle. She had fed Cierra the data required to make me look like a fool. I sighed. The shame was almost more painful than the fear and sorrow.

You are such an idiot! Sweet, innocent, gullible, stupid idiot! And the trap had worked with absolute perfection. She had us all now. More to the point, she had *Le Gardien*. And that made me the sickest. The shame and embarrassment were almost too much to bear. How could I expect any help from the pouch when it had been my own colossal stupidity that had lost it? If I hadn't left *Le Gardien* in the room, I might have sensed that we were in danger. But oh no. Not me. Just waltz off as if it didn't exist.

Then I remembered Grandpère's statement. *What is the difference between intelligence and stupidity? There's no limit to stupidity.* I was living proof of that. And now it was consequence time.

A sound out in the hall pulled me out of my stupor. Someone was coming. I sat up, ran my fingers through my hair—as best I could—and faced the door. A moment later, Barrel Belly appeared, carrying a tray of food. He stopped when he saw that the tray he had brought earlier was untouched.

"Not hungry, *Fräulein* McAllister? I wonder why." Laughing, he bent down and started to pull the other tray out.

"No, wait," I cried. "I fell asleep again. Leave both the trays, please. I'm very hungry." And that was not an exaggeration. I had suddenly realized that I was famished. Also, it was stupid not to eat and keep my strength up.

"Sorry, *Fräulein*. This isn't a hotel. And I'm not your room service." He removed the one tray, slid the other one into place, then left again.

———

Even though the lunch was simple—a small, round loaf of hard bread, some cheese, a plastic cup filled with water, and two very hard cookies—it tasted wonderful and did mountains to lift my spirits. I got up and shoved the tray under the door, then returned to my thoughts. I started pacing to see if I could warm myself up. I decided that it wasn't that the cells were unheated—there was one small vent behind the toilet—but that someone was keeping the temperature at about sixty degrees. That was not enough to cause hypothermia, but sufficient to keep me miserable.

All right. So I had been colossally stupid. I got it. It didn't take a genius to figure out that piling on more stupidity was not going to solve anything. So I sat down again and forced myself to think. The biggest challenge was that I no longer had the pouch. I assumed that Philippe and Juliette—if those were their real names—had it by now. The next challenge, which was another biggie, was that I was locked in a cell. So there was some justification for my feeling hopeless.

And that was when I realized what Grandpère had meant. I finally got it.

I have run with the footmen, and they have wearied me. There was no arguing with that. I was mentally and emotionally exhausted. Frightened. Scared. Worried. Anxious.

My head dropped, and I felt the tears coming as it seemed like Grandpère was suddenly speaking in my head. *Wearied you? That doesn't begin to describe it. They absolutely walked over the top of you. They totally creamed you. And don't blame Juliette and her son for that. Try looking in a mirror.*

———

"Criminy, Danni! Will you shut up for a minute and listen!"

I jumped like I had been stabbed with a needle. It was Rick's voice, but it was inside my head, not coming through my ears.

"I've been calling you and calling you. Geez. Getting through to you is like trying to talk to a high-speed freight train."

I stifled a cry of joy. "Can you hear what I'm thinking?"

"No." He sounded disgusted. "This is all your imagination."

"This is amazing. Are we reading each other's thoughts?"

A brief pause, then, "No, I don't think so. I can't tell what you're thinking right now. But I can hear it when you speak to yourself in your head."

"Incredible!" I was soaring. "Are you all right? I heard the guard Taser you."

"I'm a little sore where I hit the floor, but—"

"Liar!"

"Okay, I'm way sore, but otherwise, I'm fine. The effects wear off quickly."

"Oh, Rick. I can't tell you how good it is to—"

"Danni." He cut in sharply. "We don't have much time. Let's focus."

"Oh. Right. Sorry."

"Danni? Is that you?"

I jerked up. "Cody?"

"Yeah, it's me. Hey, I can hear you guys too."

Tears were instantly back. I couldn't remember ever hearing anything more wonderful than the sound of his voice at this moment. "Where are you?"

"In some kind of jail."

"Are you with Mom and Dad?"

"Kinda. I can't see them, but I can hear their voices sometimes. I called out to Mom and she answered, but our guard yelled at us. We can't talk to each other. But I think they're all right. Is Grandpère with you?"

I closed my eyes. "No. I . . . I don't know where he is right now."

Then I had another thought. "Dad? Mom? Can you hear us?"

Nothing. The disappointment was sharp and keen. That would have solved a lot of problems.

"They're not there, Danni," Rick said softly. "But that's all right. At least we can talk. What do you want to do?"

Excellent question. With no answers. "Um . . . I'm not sure. Let me think about that. You be thinking too. I'll get back to you in a few minutes."

"Roger that," Cody said in this pompous radio voice. "Ten-four. Over and out."

I actually laughed. But I quickly cut it off, forcing myself not to look up at the cameras. I couldn't let them know that I was back.

No, Danni. YOU'RE not back. ALL of you are back!

———◆———

"Are you ready yet?" Once again Rick's voice startled me.

"Um . . . yeah. I guess."

"You don't sound too sure," Cody said.

"You got that right. Okay, first question. Cody, how did you and Mom and Dad get here? Do you have any idea exactly where we are?"

"That's two questions, but yes, I do. We are in the city of Bern, Switzerland, which is about an hour and a half west of Zurich."

I was dumbfounded. From what I had seen through the window, I had guessed that we were somewhere in Switzerland, but it was obvious that he wasn't guessing. "How do you know that?"

"Because we flew into Zurich with Juliette yesterday, then drove here."

Rick came in. "*You flew?* Wait. I thought you guys were sick and were going back to the hotel."

"That's what we thought too. But Juliette had some medicine with her that she said would help. Instead, it knocked us out. When we woke up, we were landing in Zurich. And guess who was waiting for us at the airport with Juliette's limo, Danni? Jean-Claude, the guy from Belgium. What's going on? They handcuffed us and put us in the backseat of the limo. Then we drove to Bern and Juliette's castle."

"Castle?"

"Yeah, it's this really cool, old castle. It's called the *Schloss* von Dietz. *Schloss* is the German word for castle. Juliette must be super rich, Danni."

"And what did Juliette have to say about all this?"

"Nothing. She drove in a separate car. And Jean-Claude refused to say anything to us."

So much for our dear Juliette being the innocent victim. I felt incredibly stupid for arguing with Grandpère about her.

"Focus, Danni," Rick chided me gently. "Beating yourself up about what's now water under the bridge isn't very helpful."

"Right. Sorry."

"What about Grandpère?" Cody asked. "Is he with you guys?"

I barely heard him. My mind was racing. This had all been so carefully planned. The doctored sandwiches. Separating our family into two groups so we would be easier to control. Getting Mom and Dad and Cody clear away before they moved in to take us. But Juliette and Philippe had made one serious miscalculation. Louis Girard. They had no idea that we had met Louis and knew what was behind all this. Nor that we had called Clay and that the FBI now knew what was going on.

"Danni?" It was Rick.

I turned my mental voice back on. "Right. I'm here." I hesitated, then, "Cody?"

"I'm here too."

"I have some bad news. I think Grandpère may be dead."

"*What?* No, Danni. No!" And he started to cry.

So I told him what the guard had said. Which only made Cody cry all the harder. There was no reaction from Rick because he had heard the guard tell me about Grandpère's accident.

"*Code!*" I said sharply. "Listen to me. We have cameras in our cells. They're watching you. You can't let them know we are communicating somehow."

"I . . . I can't stop."

It was strange. This was all going on in our heads, but I could tell that he was having trouble getting his breath. "I know, but you have to. Turn your face to the wall. If they come to check, say you're upset because you are frightened."

"Danni," Rick came in, "you can't be sure. Remember what Louis told us. Their purpose is to take away any hope, to inflict as much mental and emotional anguish on us as possible. So this could all be a big ruse. Maybe Grandpère got away and is with Clay right now."

Good point. "Rick's right, Code. They didn't find his body." I decided not to tell him about the note Grandpère had left me. Gratefully, Rick didn't say anything more either.

"Can you use the pouch to get us out of here?" Cody finally asked.

"I don't have the pouch. Philippe took it. I don't know where it is."

"So?" Rick shot right back.

"So what?"

"So let's get it back."

"That's what I'm thinking too," I said. "But we do have this little problem of being behind bars." I was thinking hard now. "Code, how much of the castle did you see when they brought you here?"

"Not much. We went through a big, fancy entryway, then Jean-Claude led us up this long, curving stairway to the second floor. A short way down another long hallway, he stopped at an open door. It was a library filled with walls and walls of books. Juliette was inside, sitting at this huge desk with a computer and stuff."

"Like an office?"

"Yeah, like an office."

"Then that's the likeliest place for the pouch. Do you remember how to get to that main entry from here?"

Cody thought a moment. "Not really. Jean-Claude told Juliette that we had arrived, but she only nodded. She didn't even look at us. Dad tried to talk to her, but Jean-Claude shut the door again and took us back down the stairs to the entry.

"What way did you turn once you reached the entry?"

"Uh . . . left, I think. Yeah, left, into this long hallway. About half-way down the hall, we came to a narrow set of stairs that led down to the basement. That's where we are. We're in the basement of the castle."

So, not a prison. That was good news. "Great work, Code. I think we must be in a different cell block, because we've heard nothing from you or anyone else."

Somewhere down the hall from my cell, I heard a door open, then shut again. There was a murmur of men's voices, then footsteps started down the hall.

"Omigosh," Rick blurted. "I can see down the hall. It's Doc. Wait. Someone else is coming too. It's Philippe." The footsteps were growing louder. "They're going past my cell, Danni."

And suddenly there they were, standing at my cell door, Philippe in the lead with a key card in his hand. Doc stood back, one hand resting lightly on a Taser gun, looking as mean, as ugly, and as frightening as always. Philippe peered at me through the bars, his face totally impassive. Then he swiped the card, and the lock opened.

CHAPTER 31

"Well, well," I said bitterly. "I thought you might be lurking around here somewhere."

Philippe pushed the door open and motioned for me to follow him. "You are not to speak unless you are first spoken to. Do you understand?"

I said nothing and followed him out. Doc smirked at me as I passed, but also said nothing. We had walked only a few steps down the hallway when Philippe grabbed my elbow and pulled me to a stop. I looked to the left. Rick was standing at the steel door of another cell, watching anxiously. He moved back as Doc stepped past us, ran his own key card through the lock, and pushed the door open. "Don't speak unless spoken to," Doc said, pointing the Taser at Rick. Rick only nodded as he came out and fell in beside me.

We passed one more cell—which was empty—then approached a desk near a metal door. Our barrel-chested guard was standing at attention beside the desk. As we reached him, Philippe held out the card. The guard took it and put it in the top desk drawer.

Our two escorts—Philippe in front, Doc behind—led us out into a wider hallway, then turned up a flight of stairs, just as Cody had described. Which seemed to confirm that there were two separate cell blocks.

Cody hadn't been kidding. As we came up to the main floor, it was evident that this really was a castle. It had high, arched ceilings, stone walls, and cement floors. Our footsteps echoed softly as we started down a long hall studded with paintings of both men and women who I guessed were ancestors. We passed doors on either side, all of which were closed, and then came into this enormous entry hall. It was huge, bigger than our entire house back home. It had two-story ceilings, with marble statues and busts set in tiny alcoves all around. Giant potted plants sat in the far corners. But most spectacular was the grand, sweeping staircase that curved gently as it rose to the second floor.

As Philippe turned and started up the stairway, I decided it was time to stop being the cowed little dummy. "So," I said, "did the police have any luck finding your kidnapped mother?"

He half turned his head. "I told you. Speak only when you are spoken to."

"Ooh." I said to Rick. "Looks like we're being taken before the headmaster for a spanking."

Philippe spun around. There was a blur, then my head snapped back as he slapped me very hard. "No one here finds you amusing, Danni," he snarled. "So keep your mouth shut."

I was reeling. My cheek stung like fury and I had spots swirling before my eyes. I knew I would have the imprint of his hand on my face for the next half hour or so. But it worked. I decided that I'd better stop thinking I was this way cool, wisecracking Super Chick.

"Danni?"

It was Rick, inside my head.

"Yeah, I know, I know. No more being cute."

"No, listen, Danni. I just had two thoughts. First, we can't let them know that we are communicating with each other. We can't. This is our only hope right now."

"Okay," I said slowly, knowing instantly that he was right. And why hadn't I thought of that?

"And, we have to play dumb. We don't know anything about

Juliette. We don't know what is going on. They can't know that we talked to Louis. And that we called Clay."

"Right," I said. "Got it." But I was marveling. Those were two significant points. No, not just significant. *Critical.*

So why is Rick getting this and not you? It didn't take a rocket scientist to answer that question.

At the head of the stairs, a stone-faced man stood at attention, an assault rifle slung over his shoulder. As we passed him and moved down the hallway, I saw another guard posted outside a door. As we approached, Philippe gave that guard a curt nod, and he quickly opened the door.

Cody calling this a library was a big understatement. It was a huge room, with most of the wall space filled with bookshelves from floor to ceiling. There had to be thousands of books here. Many of them looked very old. All were in rich leather bindings. This alone had to represent a sizeable fortune.

A huge fireplace—probably a foot taller than me—occupied the far end of the room. A cheery fire burned several four-foot chunks of logs. The smell of pine in the room was rich and pungent.

Then I turned the other way. "Oh my word!" The words came out without thinking. The wall to our right had no bookshelves. Instead, it had three large picture windows. And what I had barely seen out my cell window now lay before us in full glory. It was a stunning view of the lake and the mountains beyond. The sailboats were gone, but what looked like a passenger ferry of some kind was crossing the lake toward the far side. With yesterday's snowstorm, everything except the lake was a pristine white. It literally was quite breathtaking.

Down the lakeshore in either direction, and also across on the opposite side, there were signs of human habitation everywhere—homes, buildings, a busy roadway. That was good. If we could somehow manage to escape, we wouldn't have to go far to find help.

Dominating the center of the room was a large, round table with elaborately carved mahogany legs and a huge floral piece in the center of it. It sat on a circular Oriental rug that reeked of money. Directly over the table, an elegant, cut-glass chandelier hung from a long chain. Overstuffed chairs and small couches were scattered about the room as well.

Finally, my eyes stopped to rest on the other piece of furniture that dominated the room. Beyond the table, in one corner of the library, I saw the desk that Cody had described. It was huge. What in this room wasn't? It had a beveled glass top that showed not even the tiniest smudge on it. The only thing on the desktop were two 8x10 pictures in elegant gold frames. Attached to the left side of the desk there was a long extension made of the same rich mahogany. Here I saw twin computer monitors, a printer, what looked like a fax machine, and a multiline telephone. A deep maroon leather office chair, the kind that swiveled, was behind the desk, and six matching high-back chairs were arranged in a semicircle in front of it. Desk and chairs also sat on an Oriental rug, only this one had to be twenty feet square. As Philippe led us forward, my feet sank into it like I had stepped onto a cloud.

"Sit down," he commanded, pointing to the chairs. "Rick, you take the end one. Danni, you're next to him." As I passed by him he gave me a hard slap on the rump. "What's the rule of the day, Danni?"

"No speaking unless spoken to." I didn't need reminding. My cheek still burned.

"Very good. Now, sit down."

As we did so, Doc walked over and stood just behind me. Philippe went around the desk and stood behind the chair, his eyes never leaving mine. Behind me, I heard a door open and shut. I turned my head and saw Jean-Claude entering. He too carried a Taser, as well as a regular pistol in his belt. He planted himself directly in front of the door.

Well, Danni girl, the gang's all here. So zip your lip. These guys are not playing around.

What followed next was an eerie silence. No one moved. No one spoke. Rick and I sat perfectly still, not daring to even glance at each other. We were obviously waiting for someone, and I was pretty sure I knew who it was.

Finally, Philippe gave Jean-Claude a questioning look. "Where is she?"

"She's on the phone with Geneva, Niklas," he said. "She'll only be a couple of minutes."

My head came up. *Niklas? Not Philippe?* And not Nick-O-las. Was this the German form of the name? But of course it was. If Juliette—or whatever her name was—had been born in Germany, then why not give her son a German name?

"Are the others outside?" Philippe, or Niklas, asked.

"Yes."

"Bring them in. Let's get everyone seated before she arrives."

Jean-Claude turned and opened the door behind him. He stepped back and motioned to someone in the hallway. A cry of joy burst from my lips when I saw Mom walk into the room, followed by Dad, then Cody. Bringing up the rear, pistol drawn and ready, was yet another guard we had not seen before. This was not good, one part of my mind thought. The place was crawling with armed muscle.

I didn't care about the warning. I leaped to my feet. "Mom, are you all right?"

Doc started forward to cut me off, but Philippe—or Niklas—shook his head. "It's all right."

I pushed past him and flew into Mom's arms. Dad and Cody pushed in too, and in moments we were crushing each other in great hugs. Mom reached up and caressed my cheek where Philippe had smacked me. "Are you all right?"

"Yes. I'm okay."

She looked over at Rick and smiled. Then she looked around the room. "Where's Grandpère? Isn't he with you?"

Before I could speak, Niklas cut in sharply. "That's enough. Sit down."

Mom was obviously surprised to see Niklas here and gave me a questioning look. I didn't dare say anything. I just shook my head and looked away.

Niklas spoke, his voice firm and clipped. "Angelique, you sit beside Danni. Cody, sit on your mother's other side. Then Mack, you sit by Cody. Do not attempt to move. No one speaks unless you are specifically asked to do so by one of us. Please do not make the mistake of thinking we are bluffing here."

As we moved back to our assigned chairs, Jean-Claude shut the door, but now he moved over and joined Doc just behind us. As he did so, two unrelated thoughts popped into my head. One: There were six chairs facing the desk, but only five of us. Was the sixth for Grandpère? I felt a tiny surge of hope rise inside me.

Second, as I sat there, staring at Niklas, I was shocked to see how different he was. There was no sign of the suave, charming Philippe that we had met before. There was not the slightest hint of a smile. He was still very handsome, but his face was like flint, his eyes a glacial blue. And there was this darkness about him, this sinister aura of evil, that was deeply frightening, much like I felt around Jean-Claude and Doc. I realized that we were sitting in a room full of dangerous, violent men, but Niklas was the most dangerous of them all.

We sat there in silence for another two or three minutes. No one moved. No one spoke. Then finally, a side door to the library opened and Juliette swept into the room. Again the impressions came quickly. No one actually snapped to attention, but I saw out of the corner of my eye that Doc and Jean-Claude both straightened perceptibly. Even Niklas stood a little taller.

Swept was a good verb, because as she came across the room toward the desk, her bearing was that of a queen entering the throne room. I thought again how beautiful she was. Her naturally blonde hair was pulled up into a bun at the back of her head, accentuating the sharpness of her features. Her dress was simple—a deep royal blue with half sleeves and a scooped neckline. The diamond choker was gone, replaced with a delicate gold chain that held a single blue sapphire dangling from it. It perfectly matched the dress.

But in all that beauty there was not even a glimmer of warmth. She didn't so much as glance in our direction. She kept her eyes to the front and moved around the desk to join Niklas. As she came up to him, there was a momentary smile. She tipped her head back slightly, and he gave her a dutiful kiss on the cheek. "Good afternoon, Mama," he murmured.

"Hello, Niklas. Is all in readiness?"

"Yes. Whenever you say, we'll bring him in."

I felt my heart leap. Him? Was Grandpère alive? At that moment, I didn't much care what else happened. If Grandpère was still alive, then . . .

Niklas pulled the chair back, and Juliette sat down. Finally, her eyes came to rest on us. They were expressionless, almost disinterested, as if she was looking at a collection of bugs pinned to a board. The change in her was dramatic. There was not the slightest hint of the warm, gracious, grandmotherly hostess of Le Petit Château. This was the Ice Queen—haughty, imperious, distant. And that did not bode well. I had alarms going off in every part of my mind.

She let her gaze move across the five of us, pausing only momentarily to examine us with this oddly curious detachment. It was like she was seeing us for the first time. When she came to me, they seemed to harden even more, and I felt a little shiver run down my back. Finished, she sat back.

"My name is Gisela Elizabette Decker von Dietz." She pronounced her first name with a hard G and emphasis on the first syllable—GEES-a-lah. "It is *not* Juliette Dubois. You will no longer call me Juliette. I detest that name and I detest everything that is French. So please do not make the mistake of calling me Juliette again. If you have to address me, it will be as *Madame* von Dietz or Lady Gisela. Is that clear?"

My gosh. Did she have to ask? It was like she had just nailed it in writing to our individual foreheads. But we all nodded.

"I am sure you have many questions about why you are here and why these terrible things have happened to your family. It is time you know. But I shall give you only the essentials now. The full story will have to wait for later. We have much to do.

"Originally, my name was Liesel Elizabette Kessler. It was changed to Gisela Decker when I was about four years old and had to flee Germany with my mother. My father was Colonel Horst Kessler of Munich, Germany."

Mother gasped. "Kessler? Colonel Kessler? Of the Gestapo?"

There was the briefest of nods. "The same." Then her eyes swung to me. "You are not surprised by that name, Carruthers. Why is that?"

She had me. Stupid me. I was so caught up in her and Niklas and their new identities that I had already forgotten Rick's warning. "I . . . I wasn't surprised because I don't recognize it," I stammered.

There was a soft sound of disgust. "When you lie to me, Danni, that will only cause you pain."

She opened one of the side drawers in the desk and reached down. What she came back with made me gasp, even though I should have expected it. She gave a little flip of her hand, and *Le Gardien* plopped down on the desk just a few feet from me. I almost leaped up and grabbed for it, but I saw Niklas watching me, daring me to move. So I looked away, as if it meant nothing to me.

Gisela reached in again and took out a thick sheaf of papers with a rubber band around them. She dropped them on the desk, then picked up the pouch and put it back into the drawer and pushed it shut. I was watching her closely. She did not lock it. *Good.*

Tapping the papers, she said, "What I have here is a copy of your journal. Which, I must say, provided me one of the dullest and least enjoyable reading experiences of my lifetime. I may as well have been reading the city phone book for all the pleasure it gave me. You prattle on like the empty-headed fool that you are. I found it quite dreary."

I raised my eyes to meet hers. "It warms my heart to know that it was only quite dreary, not extremely dreary." But even as I spoke, my mind was racing. Grandpère had gotten it right again. They had somehow copied my journal. That was how Cierra Pierce had known so much about everything. About the kiss.

Suddenly I screamed out, writhing in pain. Doc had stepped up behind me. Now his fingers were digging into that muscular cord that runs down from the neck across the shoulders to the upper arm. His fingertips dug in, and agony shot through my body. He held it for several seconds as I jerked violently and tried to pull away. Finally, he let go and stepped back.

"My mother wasn't asking for one of your infantile responses," Niklas said.

It was as if Gisela had seen nothing. Her voice was calm and conversational. "I've read your journal, Danni. So I know that you know very well who Colonel Horst Kessler is. So cut the childish games. You are far out of your league here. So I'll ask again. Why weren't you surprised when I said that I was Horst Kessler's daughter? Did you already know that?"

Cursing myself for being so stupid, my mind started to race. No way could I tell her about Louis. Then it came to me. "Say that again? You're Kessler's daughter?" I was happy to hear that I sounded truly amazed.

"I'm warning you, Danni . . ."

But I rushed right on. "I'm sorry. I must have missed that. To be honest, I'm still reeling over the fact that you and Philippe are behind all of this. Our dear friend, Juliette? When I was lying in my cell, I refused to believe it. There had to be another explanation. But now, as I watched you come in here like you were Queen of the Night, I realized it must be true. I am still shocked. I was barely listening to what you said."

To my great relief, Gisela bought it. And I saw both Rick and my father visibly relax again. Returning to her cool and calm persona, she went on. "When my father was captured by the Americans in Paris and was tortured for information, he—"

"That's a lie!" I shouted. "He was never tortured."

Instantly I was screaming again. This time Doc had me by both shoulders, and I nearly fell out of the chair trying to escape. It felt like his fingers and thumbs were actually massaging each other through the muscles. When he finally released me, I was gasping for breath.

Gisela went on as if nothing had happened. "When he was tortured by the Americans and the French, he was forced to give them information about German troop movements and other critical war information. Because of that, he was charged with treason *in absentia* and convicted of being a traitor to the Third Reich. A local civic official used that as an opportunity to seize our property and bank accounts. My mother was thrown out into the streets in the dead of winter with myself and my older brother. We were forced to live on the streets, starving and cold. After a particularly cold winter storm, my brother caught pneumonia and died."

Her eyes swept across ours, daring us to contradict her. None of us took the dare.

"We were forced to flee Germany altogether to avoid arrest and possible death. Through the help of a good and decent man, we eventually were able to go to England, where my mother became a scullery maid— the lowliest of all household servants—in an English manor house. And my mother, an elegant, gracious woman of class and breeding and culture, spent the rest of her life in abject poverty and servitude. She finally died a few years ago, a broken, unhappy, tragic figure of a woman."

I saw Mom lift a hand and tensed. To my surprise, Gisela nodded at her. "Yes?"

"That is a terrible thing, tragic beyond our comprehension. We mourn for you and your mother and your loss." It was said with simplicity and the deepest sincerity. I was watching Gisela, and while there was suspicion in her eyes, she also seemed to sense that Mom was sincere. "But what has that got to do with us?" Mom went on. "I know that my father and his parents met your father during the war, but they had nothing to do with what happened in Munich. Why are you trying to punish our family?"

In an instant, Gisela was trembling with rage. Her face had become an ugly mask. "In 1947, my father was convicted of war crimes in Nuremberg. He was accused of torturing and killing several members of the French Resistance and also an American airman who had been shot down near Strasbourg. It was all a lie. A terrible lie. The evidence was questionable at best."

"And my grandfather and grandmother were at the trial," Mom said in growing horror, understanding at last. "They testified against him."

"Yes. But what really convinced the jury that my father was some kind of a monster was the testimony of an eleven-year-old boy. His name? Jean-Henri LaRoche. So, Angelique, your father, more than any other, is responsible for the death of my father and what happened to my mother."

Dad raised his hand, but she ignored it, so he lowered it again. She was staring at the desktop now, her chest rising and falling. "Two months later, my father was taken to the gallows. A noose was put around his neck." Her head came up, and I saw that her eyes were glistening brightly. "My mother and I were there, though no one knew who we were. The sister of the same kind benefactor who helped us escape Germany made it possible for us to come back and see my father one last time. At the gallows, he refused to have a hood put over his head. And when they asked him if he had any last words, he snapped to attention, saluted the air, and shouted, 'Heil Hitler.'"

"So this is what this is all about?" Mom asked in a bare whisper.

"Yes! It has taken many years. And, after all that time, just as we were about to see justice done, what did your father do? He took the coward's way out and committed suicide."

Mom leaped to her feet. "*What?*"

I shot to my feet too. "He didn't kill himself!" Doc moved in and grabbed my arm, but I jerked free. "You were chasing him. It was an accident. You're responsible for his death."

She waved Doc back. "You are wrong, little girl. Having your grandfather dead is the last thing I desired. I wanted him alive. I *needed* him alive."

I launched myself across the desk at her, but Doc and Jean-Claude had clearly expected that. Strong hands caught me and jerked me back, slamming me down into my chair.

"So now," Gisela said, her voice still strained with anger, "I have no choice but to take it out on his survivors." She leaned forward, looking at me, her blue eyes so chilling that I had to look away. "Especially on his favorite granddaughter, whom he chose to be the next keeper of the pouch."

She swung on Niklas. "Get them out of here. Get them out of my sight."

"I don't believe you," I sobbed. "He's not dead. I know that he is still alive. You just couldn't find the body. And, yes, justice will be done. He will see to it."

To my surprise, after a momentary stare of astonishment, she started to laugh. At first it was this soft cackle, but it quickly became a full-throated roar. It was chilling, because it was almost like there was a touch of madness in it.

"You are such a child," she hissed. "You take all the fun out of it." She spun around to Niklas. "Bring the old man in."

So he was *alive!* Soaring, I laughed in her face. Here it was again, this hideous game of psychological warfare.

Niklas strode to the door, opened it, and called to someone outside. Seconds later the euphoria came crashing down. Two more guards appeared. They were wheeling a hospital gurney. On it, beneath a gray shroud, was the shape of a human body. I gasped as the breath was sucked out of me. I heard Mom cry out and saw Dad leap to his feet. I couldn't move or speak or think. My eyes were riveted on that shape beneath the cloth.

Gisela was out of her chair. She came around the desk and grabbed me by the wrist, yanking me to my feet. Then she jerked me hard forward. In three strides we were to the gurney. With her free hand, she reached down and whipped off the covering.

"No!" I fell back. I started to cover my eyes. I couldn't bear to look. Yet I couldn't not look. It was Grandpère.

And he was cold and stiff in death.

CHAPTER 32

Gisela stood there in imperious majesty. She pulled me forward, then grabbed the back of my head and pushed it down so I was just inches from Grandpère's face. "Look at him!" she shouted. "Is he dead or not?"

I choked out a sob. "Yes." With a soft sound of disgust, she shoved me hard back toward my chair. Mom was sobbing uncontrollably. Dad held her, trying to comfort her. I saw that Cody's eyes were filled with tears and his face was white as a sheet of paper. Rick stood with his head bowed and his fists clenched.

Gisela nodded curtly to Jean-Claude. "Get them out of here. All but Danni and Rick."

As he marched my family out, Gisela walked back and stood behind the desk next to Niklas. She called after the retreating figures, "Jean-Claude, take the parents and the boy back to their cells. See that they get a good dinner and warm blankets."

I guess my eyebrows shot up because she turned to me and said, "Don't even think about it."

Jean-Claude took Mom, Cody, and Dad out the door through which they had entered. I saw Mom shudder and avert her eyes, crying softly as she passed by the gurney. I wished I could do the same, but I couldn't take my eyes away from my grandfather, my lifelong friend.

The sense of loss was spreading through my whole body and numbing me. I wanted to scream out in agony, to launch myself at Gisela and scratch out her eyes. But I couldn't move.

As they left, Gisela turned to her son. "Niklas, you and Raul take Danni and Rick back to their cells. Rick gets dinner and a blanket. She gets nothing. In fact, strip her down to her underclothing. Let her spend the night that way."

I felt a shudder ripple through my body. My underclothing? With Niklas and Doc looking on? The cold would be nothing compared to the humiliation.

She turned to the two guards. "Get that body out of here. We can't leave it in here with the fire going. Put it in the cooler downstairs. We'll cremate him tomorrow."

"No!" I whirled and darted to the gurney, throwing myself between it and the door. "Don't cremate him. Please."

Gisela looked at Niklas. "She's right," she said. "It's not worth the fuel it will take to start up the crematorium. Have the guards take the body to the dump tonight. Make sure no one sees them. Leave it for the ravens."

I leaped forward, my hands coming up like claws. "You horrible woman!" I screamed.

She fell back, but Niklas was faster than I was. He shot in, catching me from the side and knocking me away from her. His arms clamped around me, crushing me so tightly I couldn't breathe. Behind us, the two guards hurriedly pushed the gurney through the door, closing it behind them.

I started to gasp for air. Her chest rising and falling in rapid, short breaths, Gisela stepped in, thrusting her face up to mine until we were separated only by inches. "Get her out of here," she screeched. "Now! Before I shoot her myself."

"With pleasure," Niklas said, a wicked grin twisting his face. Before I could react, Niklas grabbed me by the hair and jerked my head back hard.

"No!" Rick launched himself at him, but Doc evidently had anticipated that. He stepped in, swinging his pistol, and Rick went down like a rock.

I screamed as Niklas pulled my head down. My back arched and I felt like I was falling. But he held me so I couldn't. I reacted instantly, exploding into action. I kicked out, catching him in the shins. He yelped and loosened his grip on my hair. I went after him, pummeling him with my fists, kicking at him, screaming in rage.

It took him a second to recover, but, quick as a cat, he swung me around to face him, then pulled me to him with such force that it cut off my breath. One hand came up and grabbed the back of my head, pulling it down so that it forced my face up toward his. Then he leaned in and kissed me. Actually, he came in with such force that our faces collided and I felt his teeth cut my upper lip as he tried to force open my clenched teeth.

I was fighting him like a wild woman, trying to bite at him, kick at him, knee him in the groin, hit him with my fists. But his grip was too powerful. I was like a child fighting a giant.

Kiss him back!

That stunned me. It was Grandpère's voice, and it shouted at me again, *Kiss him back!*

Though the very thought filled me with utter revulsion, I stopped resisting. I let my body go limp. I could sense his surprise, and he reared back, staring into my eyes. I pulled one hand free from his grasp, reached up, and pulled him in toward me.

His eyes widened. Then he grinned. "Now, that's more like it."

This time he was more gentle, not so demanding and violent. I went up on tiptoe and I kissed him back. I mean, I *really* kissed him back.

Somewhere behind me, I heard Gisela's gasp of surprise. Then she laughed. I opened my eyes and saw Doc standing right behind us. He was shocked. I could see the hunger in his eyes. And at that same moment, Niklas suddenly stiffened. His eyes flew open, and there was sudden panic in them. He released me and fell back, gagging and clawing at his throat.

"Niklas! What is it?"

He waved his hands wildly, staggering now, eyes bulging as he struggled for breath. I stepped back away, wiping at my mouth, spitting out the taste of him. Both Gisela and Doc jumped forward, grabbing him by the arms as he started to sag. Doc started pounding on his back. Niklas fought him off, his head jerking back and forth wildly, his mouth moving, but no words coming out. I could see that his face was turning blue. Gisela spun around and started toward me. "What did you do to him?" she screamed.

Before I could react, Niklas jerked free from Doc's grasp and, clutching at his stomach, started in a lurching run for the door. He only made it as far as the big table. He slid to a stop, dropped to his knees on that elegant Oriental rug, and began to retch. He vomited again and again, gasping in pain, moaning in between the violent spasms that wracked his body. Then he would hunch over as it started again.

Watching someone be violently sick is not a pretty sight. But I have to say that I can't remember seeing anything that has given me more satisfaction than the sight of him heaving his guts out. After Grandpère, it was small payback.

I walked up and stood over him. Gisela looked up, her eyes frightened and yet cold with fury. "What did you do to him?" she shouted again.

Still breathing hard, I forced a bright smile. "Maybe it was something he ate for lunch. A touch of food poisoning, perhaps."

I didn't hear her response. Doc grabbed my arm and pulled me away. I wasn't sure if he thought Gisela was going to kill me or vice versa. But he didn't wait to find out.

——

I had no sense of the passage of time. Outside the window the sky was nearly black, but I couldn't tell if that was because it was night or because a storm was coming. Not that I cared. Curled up in a fetal position, I was like a huge black hole sucking up every shred of grief, sorrow, and pain in the universe. Grandpère was gone. My body ached with pain from the wracking sobs and twisting stomach. Now I was empty. I had no more to give. And, I guess when I reached that point, I had fallen asleep.

A flash of light, followed by a crack of thunder a few seconds later, brought my head up. I turned over on my back and looked up at the window. Then I sat up. There was some fading light still in the sky, but obviously, a storm was coming. Then an odd thought came. A winter thunderstorm? Was that common here? It sure wasn't in Utah.

I wrapped my arms around myself, shivering with the cold, and it was then I realized they hadn't stripped me down to my underclothing. I was still barefoot, but I had my pants and blouse still on. And my single blanket was on the cot. I took it gratefully and wrapped it around my shoulders. In the chaos with Niklas, I guess Gisela's instructions had been forgotten. Or had that been just another shaft in the mind games she was playing with us. Sometimes the anticipation of something bad was almost as bad as the thing itself. Either way, it was one tiny blessing in an otherwise horrible day. I reached up and wiped the last of the tears out of my eyes, then closed them and spoke in my mind.

"Rick? Are you there?"

"Danni! Thank the Lord. Where have you been? Cody and I have been trying to get a response from you for a couple of hours now."

"Longer than that," Cody said. "Where were you?"

"Doesn't matter. I'm back now." Then the oddity of their comments hit me. "Wait. Have you two been talking without me?"

"Yeah, is that a problem?" Rick asked.

"No." Sudden wonder came over me. "But that means the pouch is helping you guys, even though I wasn't part of it." Then I thought of how Rick had received those two really brilliant ideas just before we went into the library. Could *Le Gardien* have changed allegiance? Not that I was complaining. If it was functioning again, I would gladly take second place to Rick. "That's wonderful, guys." Then I had a thought. "Code? Are you still with Mom and Dad?"

"No. I'm in the same cell I was before, but Jean-Claude took Mom and Dad somewhere else after he left me here."

I felt a lurch in the pit of my stomach. What was Gisela up to now? "Did they say where?"

"No."

"We have to hurry, then," I said.

"What happened up there, Danni?" Rick said. "When I finally came to after being slugged, I saw Philippe on the floor with throw-up all over him."

"It's a long story. But one thing's for sure: Even though Gisela has the pouch, I think it's still helping us. Which means we're not alone. So we have got to get out of these cells and find Mom and Dad."

"But how?" Cody exclaimed. "I've got a guard sitting about twenty feet away. He can see me from where he is."

Rick came back in. "We had Doc down the hall from us. I heard him talking on the phone to someone just a few minutes ago. Then he left."

I was trying to remember the exact placement of that desk as Rick and I had been taken upstairs. That must be where Doc was now. And as I pictured it in my mind, something else popped up. Niklas had paused momentarily at the desk. My eyes widened. To put the key card back in the drawer. The key card that he had used to open my cell door.

"I've got an idea," I said, still speaking inside my head. "However, I have to say also that I have no concept of how to actually make it work."

"Leave it to the men to figure that out," Cody said.

"Yeah, right. But here's what I'm thinking. When Philippe came and got me and Rick, he used a key card he got from the guard's desk. Remember, Rick? The guard put it in a drawer. If we could get that, we could get out of these cells."

"Great idea. So how do we get it?"

"I'm still working on that. But here's the thing. If we can get out, maybe we can get the pouch. We know where it is."

"Assuming Gisela hasn't moved it."

I ignored that.

"And assuming that the guards we saw are all taking a nap," Rick added.

"You're not helping here, Rick."

"I understand, but—"

Lightning flashed again, and a second later a crack of thunder reverberated through the hallway. It made me jump a little, but I quickly recovered. I started to ask Rick to finish his sentence, but then I had an idea. "What we need is some kind of diversion." Just like the storm had momentarily diverted my attention. "Any bright ideas from the male side of the team on how we do that?"

There was no answer. I waited, wanting to give them time to think. Finally, Rick spoke. "Whatever we do, we've got the problem of the CCTV."

"The what?" Cody asked.

"CCTV. Closed Circuit Television. We've not only got cameras in our cells, but I saw several of them in the hallways too, both upstairs and down. Which means they're going to see any movement we make, even if we do get out of these cells."

The silence stretched on for another long minute. I could almost hear them thinking. To my surprise, it was Cody who spoke first. "Hey, you guys. Remember that night on the houseboat when the three of us were up on deck?"

"The houseboat? You're thinking of the houseboat?" *Was he losing it?*

"Yeah." His voice lowered a notch. "I asked you what you see when your eyes are closed."

"I remember," I said, a bit tartly. "And what has that got to do with anything?"

"You thought I was nuts then, too, Danni. But do you remember your answer?"

I thought quickly. "Yeah. I said that if your eyes are closed, you can't see anything."

"Exactly. So, let's close their eyes."

"Like . . ." My mind was suddenly racing.

"Like turn off the CCTVs?" he finished for me.

Rick was on that like a buzzard on roadkill. "Cody, you didn't happen to see any kind of room that housed electronic stuff when you came in last night, did you?"

"Not last night. But as they took me back to my cell a little while ago, I was watching more carefully where I was going."

"Good job," I said. "And?"

"We passed a large kitchen area—you know, stoves, sinks, a large walk-in cooler, that kind of stuff."

"Okay," I said, not sure why we needed to know that. But Cody always focused on anything related to food. "If we get hungry, we'll keep that in mind," I said dryly, hoping he would hear the smile in my voice.

"*And*—" he added with obvious irritation—"just beyond the kitchen there was a door in the hall with a little sign on it in German."

Come on, Code. You're killing us here. But I bit my tongue and only said, "And how is your German nowadays?"

"I recognized two words," Cody fired right back. "*Electronische* and *mechanische*. Maybe you're smart enough to figure out what those mean."

"Okay, okay. I'm sorry. I just keep thinking of Mom and Dad. We've got to hurry."

"That's probably where the CCTV central recording equipment is kept," Rick said. "If we could get in there, then we can blind them. Way to go, Code."

"Yeah, Code. Way to go. Sorry for dissing you."

"It's all right." He paused briefly. "I'm used to it." Then he went on bitterly, "But that doesn't do us any good unless we can get out of our cells."

"And we need to do it before Doc returns," Rick pointed out.

Silence. That was the issue, and there didn't seem to be an answer for that.

———

It wasn't two minutes later that Rick came in again. "Okay, I've got it," he said.

"Good," I said. "What?"

"Cody, you're the man. They won't be nearly as suspicious of you as they will of me and Danni. So, let me ask you both a question. What do you *not* see when your eyes are *open?*"

"What?" we both said at once.

"You heard me."

"I have no idea what you're saying," I said.

"Think about that first night in the attic. When you and Cody hid in the fort."

"Omigosh!" I cried.

"You don't see someone who's invisible," Cody blurted.

"Exactly!" Rick said. "Can you do that, Danni?" he asked. "Can you make us invisible?"

That knocked me back a minute. *Could I?* I knew the answer immediately. "No, only Cody." How did I know that? I don't know, but I did.

"Cool," Cody chortled. "I am the man," he crowed.

"Yes, you are," I said. "So here's how I see it unfolding."

———

"All right," Cody said. "The guard's reading a book or something. He's not looking at me at the moment. Are we ready?"

"We are," I said. "Go for it."

"Wait a sec," Cody exclaimed. "How will I know if I'm invisible? When it happened before, you and I could see each other, and we could also see ourselves. We didn't realize we were invisible until afterwards. So how will I know when I am now?"

"It's pretty simple, really. When the guard goes ballistic, you can assume you're invisible."

"Okay, then," he said. "Start the incantations or whatever it is you have to do."

I actually laughed. "Incantations? You have definitely been reading too much Harry Potter. All I can do is try to focus my mind and will something to happen. And Rick, you need to try that too. You seem to have some influence with the pouch now too and—"

Rick broke in. "Somehow, Code, once you're invisible, you've got to turn off that CCTV camera in your cell. They won't see you, but they'll see what the guard is doing."

"How do I do that?"

My mind was racing. "If the pouch can make you invisible, it's going to have to blot out the camera, too."

Long silence. Then, "And how will I know if it did?"

Rick had the answer for that. "You won't. But if it doesn't, we'll know in about five seconds."

At that moment, I almost looked up at my camera, but I caught myself. Pulling the blanket more tightly around me, I closed my eyes, trying to look miserable and defeated. I think I was successful.

"Omigosh!" Cody yelled inside our heads. "He's looking this way. He's staring at me." He gave a little yelp of joy. "It's working. He looks like he just saw a ghost. Okay, here he comes. He's got his Taser out."

"Be careful, Code," I whispered.

"Shh!" A moment passed, taking only an eternity to do so, then we heard, "He's opening the door. Man, is he juiced. Okay, he's in."

"Then get out of there!" I yelled. "Lock him in."

"Hold on. Slight change of plans."

No, Code! Don't say that.

"Okay," Cody yelled in pure exuberance. "Bad guy down."

"What?"

"He bent over to look under my cot. His rear end was too good of a target. I kicked him hard and sent him crashing headfirst into the edge of the cot. He's out cold. I have his key card, but he's lying on his pistol." I felt him grunt. "I'll try to roll him over."

"Forget the pistol," Rick shouted. "Get out of there."

I held my breath, then let it out in a huge whoosh when I next heard, "Okay. I'm out. He's locked in." Pause. "No one else is around. I think I'm okay."

"Unless someone is watching the CCTV monitor of your cell," I cried.

"Not likely," Rick said. "Alarms would be going off by now if they were seeing all this."

"Then get here as fast as you can, Cody. But if you see anyone, make sure you don't make any noise as you pass each other. Oh, and put that key card in your pocket. If they see a card floating mysteriously in midair, they're gonna freak out."

"Right." I could tell he was breathing hard. "Okay, I'm on my way."

"You're amazing, Code."

"Yeah, yeah. You're just saying that 'cause it's true."

Everything went silent for almost a minute, then, "Hey, Rick."

"Yeah, Bud?"

"I'm coming up on that mechanical room," he cut in. "Do you want me to do something?"

"No, come and get us first," I cried.

"Danni's right," Rick said. "They can't see you. But the instant you take out the system, everything is going to break loose. So come get us first, before Doc comes back. Then on the way back we'll have you take it out. Oh, see if the door's open."

"Already did. It's not."

I wanted to scream at him. He was so matter-of-fact. So maddeningly calm. "We'll worry about that later, Cody. Move it. Hurry! I want you back in that cell with the guard out of there before he wakes up again."

"What? I'm not going back in there."

"Yes, you are. When that guard wakes up, he's going to sound the alarm. Everyone will come running. And that's important. I need the upstairs cleared out so I can get in and out of the library without being seen. Remember, I'm not invisible."

Rick cleared his throat. "I've got a better idea."

"Shoot."

"On his way back, Code slips in and destroys the CCTV system. That will wake everybody up, I promise you that. Cody stays hidden in the mechanical room. They find the guard and learn that Cody's gone. Big search ensues, starting in the basement. But the longer Cody stays hidden, the more time it buys you."

"Wow! You're on a roll, Rick."

"No need for sarcasm."

"I wasn't being sarcastic."

"I like it," Cody sang out. "Twist their tails a little. That'll get them."

"Have you reached the stairs yet?" Rick asked.

"Just barely. I see a door ahead. It has bars on it."

"That's us. Hurry."

———

The next minute or two passed swiftly—like it took only about a hundred years. I was listening intently for any sounds. I heard what sounded like a drawer opening down the hallway. A moment later, Cody's voice sounded in my mind. "All right, I've got the second card. Coming to you now."

Careful not to look up at the camera, I tossed the blanket aside, got to my feet, and stretched. Then, trying to look dazed, I started pacing slowly. "Okay, Code," I said in my head, "I'll be at the cell door. If I keep my back to the camera, they can't see beyond me."

I made one slow circle of the cell, then stopped at the door, grasped the bars, and looked out. I was confident I was a picture of forlorn surrender. I had barely gotten there when there was a soft scrape of shoes on cement. "Oooooh," an eerie voice said in my head, "I am the ghost of Christmas Past. Why did you break my new air rifle when I was six years old?"

I stifled a laugh, keeping my back to the camera. "You are a nutcase, Bro."

"Guilty as charged. That's why you love me."

"True. Now get that door open."

He laughed. A card appeared out of nowhere and floated through the bars into my hand. "Here's yours. I've still got mine."

Keeping my movements slow, I carefully took the card and slid it into my pocket. "Perfect, Cody. Now get the heck out of here."

"You can thank me later," he said dryly, but I heard his footsteps moving away.

———

It was another couple of minutes before Cody spoke again. "Okay, I'm at the mechanical room. Any ideas how I get through a locked door?"

"Open the lock. You can do it."

"Oh, really? So I'm a wizard now?"

"Think of *Le Gardien.* Close your eyes and concentrate. You can do it." I had fingers on both of my hands crossed as I spoke calmly and confidently to him. I should have been hyperventilating about now because I was alternating between panting frantically with excitement and holding my breath in fear. At the moment, it was the latter.

"Omigosh!" Cody yelled, startling me. "That is seriously wicked."

"Did it work?"

"Yes, I'm in. Okay, Rick. There's all kinds of stuff in here. What am I looking for?"

"The CCTV system will have all the cable feeds from the cameras coming out of the ceiling into the back of it. So, lots of cables. Do you see something like—"

"Got it. Want me to rip the cables out?"

"Yes. And smash the box, too, if you can. Is there a place to hide in there?"

"Of course. It's no sweat when you're invisible. See ya."

Not even thirty seconds later, a Klaxon alarm started blasting and an electronic voice calmly announced, first in German and then in English, "Attention! Attention! Security breach. Monitoring system down. Attention! Attention!" and it started all over again.

"Okay," I cried. "Here I go."

"No, Danni," Rick shouted. "Not yet. One of the first things they're gonna do is see if we are still in our cells. Sit tight for a minute."

I went rigid. He was right. Again! Where was my head? I had all these great ideas but kept missing the real essentials.

"Someone's coming," Rick hissed about a minute later.

I hurriedly moved to the cot and lay down as the sound of running footsteps grew louder very rapidly. A moment later, Niklas and Doc came running up to my cell door. I sat up, feigning surprise.

Doc stepped forward and shook my cell door hard. It rattled loudly but didn't give way. Without a word, they disappeared again. I heard them do the same with Rick's door; then they raced away again.

"Thank you, Rick. Glad someone's thinking."

"You're doing great, Danni."

"Unlike our little experience with El Cobra," I said, "this time it's much more complex. I think *Le Gardien* has decided it's going to take all of us working together to make it work. And I'm very grateful for that."

"Can't argue with that."

I was already to his door and looking at him. "Wish me luck, Ramirez."

"I can do more than that," came his soft reply. "You sure you don't want me to come along?"

"If you were invisible, yes. But for now, I think it's best if we have only one visible person out there wandering around. I'll call you if that changes."

He touched my hand briefly. "Take care, Danni."

"I will. Thanks." And a moment later I was out the door and running hard down the corridor toward the stairs.

CHAPTER 33

I stopped at the top of the narrow set of stairs that led up from the basement. I could still hear people yelling from down below, but things seemed very quiet upstairs. That didn't reduce my anxiety much. I knew the whole house would be on the alert and that there was a good chance someone was left upstairs to watch things. So I stopped, leaning a little forward, straining to hear anything close around me. Nothing.

I was barefoot, of course, not having seen my shoes since waking up in my cell. But that was perfect for moving quietly on marble floors, so I ignored the cold. Stepping carefully, I started in the direction of the main entry hall. As I passed a window on my right, I could see a thick swirl of snow outside and several inches on the windowsill. In the darkness it was hard to tell, but it looked like it was near whiteout conditions outside.

As I approached the great entry hall, I moved in behind a huge porcelain urn filled with artificial flowers that were taller than me. I listened intently, concentrating inwardly, desperately hoping that if I was about to walk into danger, *Le Gardien* and I were reconciled enough that I would sense it in time to take evasive action.

The sounds from downstairs suggested there was still a frantic hunt for Cody going on, but I thought I'd better check to make sure. "Cody?"

"Yeah?"

"Are you still okay?"

"A little cramped, but yeah. They've looked in here four times now. The one time I thought the guy was going to shove his elbow in my face, but I managed to duck down."

"Okay. Hang tight until I give you the word. I'm going up to the library now."

"Got it."

I darted across the big hall and took the stairs three at a time. As I reached the top, I didn't hesitate, even though the hallway ran in both directions. I turned left and headed for the library. Stopping only for a second to listen, I grabbed the bronze latch and pushed down. It didn't give. It was locked. Just as I had feared. It was time to follow my own advice. I stepped back, focused my eyes on the keyhole, then fiercely concentrated in making it open. Nothing happened. There was no click, no sound whatsoever. I tried it again. Still locked. Great. So much for having *Le Gardien* open the way. For Cody, yes. For me, no way.

I closed my eyes this time and sent a pleading cry through the doorway, picturing the desk and the drawer where the pouch was. *Please!*

Nothing. A huge disappointment, but not a big surprise. Par for the course about now. Just then I heard something that turned my blood into ice water.

Gisela's voice rang out over the intercom speaker above my head. "Raul! He's not anywhere down here. Take your team and search the main floor. Jean-Claude, you take the second floor. Check the library first. He may be after the pouch."

That was almost instantly followed by men shouting and the sound of boots pounding up the basement stairs. Locks not unlocking suddenly dropped to the bottom of my priority list. I had only one choice. They'd be coming up that grand staircase any moment.

I took off and raced to the next door. Locked. Two more. Locked. All of the doors so far were exactly the same. I passed by three more on a run, my heart pounding like those pile drivers you see when they're building bridges. Up ahead of me, I saw that the next door was different. It was much larger. As I reached it, my heart leaped with hope. It was a set of double doors, both much larger than the others. A drawing room, perhaps?

The voices behind me were growing louder, and I knew that at any moment someone would be at the top of the stairs and looking straight down this hall at me. In near panic mode now, I tried the huge, ornate door latch and gave a little cry of triumph. It opened and the door swung inward. I ducked inside and pushed it shut behind me, making certain I made no noise.

Seeing a small brass knob above the latch, I turned it and heard a deadbolt slide into place. Good. But instantly, I changed my mind and unlocked it again. If this door was normally open and they found it locked, it was a dead giveaway. Whoops! Bad choice of words. A *sure* giveaway. I turned and moved through a small alcove into the room.

This was not a drawing room or a sitting room, as some people called them.

This was definitely not that. Two small lamps in sconces on the walls were lit, providing enough light to show me I had entered a very large bedroom. A massive four-poster bed with richly embroidered drapery hung from ceiling to floor dominated the room. Directly above was a large, delicate, crystal chandelier, a smaller version of the one in the library. One wall was filled with a floor-to-ceiling mirror. Several armoires and large wardrobes were strategically placed along two of the walls. There were chairs clustered around a large coffee table off to one side. Here, as in the library, the place reeked of luxury.

All well and good, but none of that helped me. I knew they would search every possible hiding place. What I needed was a way out. I walked quickly to a third door and yanked it open. It led to a bathroom. My warning bells were clanging like crazy now as I checked a couple of the wardrobes. Chock-full of men's clothing in both cases. I could hear doors slamming now, and the noise was rapidly growing louder. Getting more frantic with every second, I moved on, passing a draped section of the wall. Curious, I stopped and lifted the curtain.

Nearly shouting for joy, I yanked the drape aside to reveal a set of French doors looking out onto a small, snow-covered, stone balcony. I unlocked the deadbolt, then pulled down on the twin door handles. The right one gave way, and, with a soft creak, the door opened. Instantly, a cold blast of swirling snow assaulted my face and I felt the cold pinpricks of snowflakes on my bare arms and cheeks.

"Check every room," I heard Jean-Claude shout. "Even if they're locked."

I moved forward hesitantly. On the balcony there was a single ornate metal garden chair and a small table in front of it. Both were covered in snow. I looked at the floor. Five inches at least. Maybe six. I stuck my head out. Beyond the stone wall that enclosed the balcony, I could see a vast expanse of perfectly white snow—lawns, I supposed—and then a line of dark trees barely visible in the lights from the castle.

I stood there, torn with indecision. Before me was an escape. But I was barefoot. How far could I go in that snow with no shoes? And was I ready to leave Cody and Mom and—I jumped as a door slammed very close by and the chandelier above me tinkled softly. That simplified my decision. I pulled the doors open wider, then, bracing myself for the shock, lifted my foot and leaned forward. Then I caught myself, my foot in midair as I looked down. Right where I was about to step, a left footprint suddenly appeared. It was a crisp, perfect impression in the new snow.

I just stood there, frozen in time for a moment. My foot hadn't touched the ground. Then something else hit me: *This print was not made by a bare foot!* I leaned forward. How weird was this? It was a couple of sizes bigger than my own feet and *it was made by a man's athletic shoe!* It looked familiar. Could that be the pattern of the Nike shoes that Cody always wore? I leaned in closer. And there between the sole and the heel I saw the imprint of the Nike symbol.

Even as I stood there gawking at it, another print appeared just ahead of the first. This time it was the right foot. Then another from the left. I watched as the footprints skirted around the table and stopped at the stonework. Then it hit me. For some crazy reason, Cody had come up here.

"Cody? Is that you?" I silently cried out.

"I'm here, Danni. Still hunkered down. Are you ready for me to get out of here?"

"You're still in the mechanical room?"

"Sure. Where'dja think I was?"

"Never mind. Gotta go."

Totally dumbfounded now, I watched as about a two-foot wide swath of snow was brushed off the top of the stone railing. Then, next to it, a handprint appeared, turned sideways, the way you would place your hand if you were going to vault the wall. There was no sound at all, but moments later, in the faint light from the window, I saw footsteps start appearing one after another in long, leaping strides across the grass. They went off into the darkness.

Goose bumps were doing this little dance up and down my arms and my back. And they weren't from the snow or the cold.

"Jean-Claude!" It was Gisela's voice, and very close. Then I realized it was coming through a radio, probably a handheld one. "Be sure you check carefully in the Saxony bedroom."

There was no time to think. Leaving the door wide open, I sprang to one side, jerked open the nearest wardrobe door, and dove inside. It was a wardrobe full of men's coats, and I split them apart like I was dividing the seas. Scrambling wildly as I hit the floor, I pulled a couple of coats down with me, then twisted around and pulled the doors shut behind me. As I heard the heavy bedroom door open, I shrank back into a corner and pulled the coats up over the top of me.

I don't think Jean-Claude and the men with him were in the room more than fifteen or twenty seconds. The footsteps had barely reached my hiding place when I heard him give a yelp of surprise. "He's jumped the window," he screamed. I heard the crackle of a handheld radio.

"Lady Gisela. The boy jumped out of the window in the Saxony bedroom. He's headed for the trees."

Instantly, pandemonium broke loose. Gisela started screaming into her own radio. She called to someone else in English and told them to secure all exits and entrances to the grounds and to send out the dog patrols immediately. She was raging. Me? I was soaring. So what if *Le Gardien* wasn't doing it my way? It was back. And that filled me with enormous relief.

I moved slowly at first, stopping before entering the hallway. I peered out, but there was no one in sight, no nearby voices, no approaching footsteps. I could hear the faint sounds of the pursuit outside, joined now by a chorus of barking dogs. I shook my head, marveling again at how neatly *Le Gardien* had emptied the house.

Moving more confidently now, I started back for the library, remembering that I had a locked door to contend with. Would the pouch open it for me now? But to my further shock, the one door was ajar when I reached it. I guessed that in their haste, Jean-Claude's searchers had not locked it again. I reached for it, then stopped. Leaning in, I put my ear against the panel. The last thing I needed was to bust in and find that Gisela had come to her office to direct the search for Cody.

There was no sound, and so I slowly pushed the door open a few more inches and peeked in. The lights were off, but someone had added a new set of logs on the fire, and the room was dimly lit by the firelight. Almost dizzy with relief, I quickly slipped inside and locked the door behind me. It had been locked earlier, so locking it again now seemed like the thing to do.

Crossing the room swiftly, I went around behind the desk. Offering a quick, silent prayer that Gisela had not locked the drawers since we were here with her, I reached out and pulled the top drawer open. And there it was. Underneath the sheaf of papers—which I saw was the copy of my journal—I saw the braided rope handle. *Yes!* I pumped my fist in the air.

Totally elated, I pulled the pouch out from under the papers and clutched it to my chest. I glanced upward. "Thank you," I murmured. But this was not a time to sit back and revel in my success. I slipped the pouch over my shoulder, shut the drawer again, and straightened.

"Rick! Cody!" I sent my thoughts flying outward. "I got it. I've got *Le Gardien.*"

"Great!" Rick answered almost instantly.

"Yahoo!" Cody cried.

"Are you coming back down here, then?" Rick wondered.

"Yes, but not yet." I quickly explained to them about the footprints and the hunt going on outside. "While they're still out there, I'm going to try to find Mom and Dad."

"Danni?"

"Yes, Code?"

"I want to be with you and Rick."

That wasn't what I had expected. "Uh . . . not a good idea, Cody. Not yet. If I find Mom and Dad, hopefully my key card will open their cell. Then we'll come and get you and Rick and we'll get out of here. But I have to hurry before they give up the search and come back in."

"Uh . . ." There was a long silence, then a forlorn "Okay."

"You all right, Code?"

"Yeah. Um . . . I just have this awful feeling. It's creeping me out."

"I think Cody needs to go back to his cell," Rick said. "Go inside and lock the door again."

I started to protest, then suddenly changed my mind. "Good idea. That way if they do come back, this will totally knock them off their balance. Code? Are you still invisible?"

"I think so."

"Then do it. If I find Mom and Dad, I'll come for you first, okay?"

"I guess." It was said with total lack of enthusiasm.

I started around the desk, but stopped again a moment later. I had been half looking at the computer stuff on her desk. "Hey, hold on a sec." I was staring at the fancy telephone beside the computer's keyboard. I took a step closer, an idea forming in my mind. It came quickly. "Hold on, guys. I've got a phone here. I'm calling Clay," I said. "I'll get back to you."

"No, Danni, wait." That was from Rick.

"There's no time. Gotta hurry. 'Bye."

I picked up the phone and heard the dial tone immediately. On my phone, Clay's number was in my favorites list, but I knew it by heart too. I started to punch in the numbers, trying to listen with one ear for any sounds out in the hall. I jumped when some lady started speaking to me in rapid German. I hung up quickly. What the heck? Then I realized my mistake. I probably needed to get an outside line. So I tried again, punching 9 first. Good. There was a momentary pause, then a different-sounding dial tone started. I keyed in the number again.

The call took a few seconds to go through, but when it finally rang, Clay picked it up instantly. "Hello?" It was cautious and tentative and with no self-identification.

"Clay, it's me!"

"*Danni?* Thank the Lord. Where are you?"

"I've only got a minute," I said. "We are being held captive in a castle in Bern, Switzerland, called the *Schloss* von Dietz. We're by a lake, and I can see the Alps in the distance."

"Switzerland? No wonder. We're still in Caen trying to find out what happened to all of you."

"Me, Rick, and Cody are all right. Mom and Dad are here too, but we haven't seen them for a while now." My voice caught in my throat. "And Grandpère's dead."

"*What?* Is that what they told you?" I heard him cover the phone with his hand and speak to someone.

I went on, "He tried to escape and his car went into the river."

"But the police here haven't found his body yet. Maybe he—don't give up hope yet, Danni."

"Clay, I saw the body. Gisela brought it here. He's dead."

"*What?* No, Danni."

There was nothing to say to that.

He was silent for a moment, then, "Who is Gisela?"

"Juliette Dubois, our landlady at the château."

I was getting nervous now. Since they obviously weren't going to find Cody outside, that search couldn't last very much longer. "Did you get to talk to Louis Girard?"

"Yes, he's here with us. We know the full story now."

"Well Juliette Dubois is the daughter of Horst Kessler. Her name is Gisela von Dietz. She and her son, whom we knew as Philippe Dubois, but whose real name is Niklas von Dietz, are the ones running this whole operation." It all came out in a rush, and I wondered if I was making any sense at all.

Suddenly I realized I could no longer hear the dogs barking. "Gotta go, Clay. Hurry. Things are not good here."

"We're tracing your number as we speak. We're on our way."

"Be careful. Doc and Jean-Claude are here."

He whistled softly. "Not good."

"You got that right. There are other guards too. A lot of them. Please hurry! We need you badly."

I didn't wait for an answer. Slamming the phone down, I took off. I had to get back to my cell before they got back in. As I passed one of the windows in the hall, I saw flashlights through the falling snow, coming toward the house. "Rick. Code. They're coming. Sit tight. I'm on my way."

"Are you coming for me?" Cody asked.

"No, not yet. I've got to be in my cell before they come back. Once I'm there, we can figure out what to do next."

"Where you gonna hide the pouch, Danni?" Rick asked me as I stopped for a moment at his cell door.

"Not sure. They won't know I've been out of my cell, so hopefully they won't search me for it for a little while." Reaching out, I briefly touched his hand. "But I have the pouch, Rick. We're going to be okay."

"Danni, this is Code. My cell door is locked. And the key card's not opening it. I can't get in. I'm coming to you."

"No, Cody. They're coming." But I saw Rick nodding vigorously. "Okay. You're right. We'll hide you in one of the empty cells and hope you stay invisible. But stay where you are until they get back in. We can't have them bumping into you. Give it five minutes."

"Ten-four. But hurry."

I started to back away from Rick's cell. "You'd better be thinking hard, Rick. I have no idea where we go from here."

He pulled a face. "I will. But you did great, Danni. You've got the pouch, and they don't know it yet."

———

Niklas, Jean-Claude, and Raul, or Doc, came to our cells about five minutes later. For a moment, I didn't recognize the latter two. They had weird-looking helmets on their heads and looked like some kind of aliens. Then I realized they were wearing night-vision goggles, like you see army guys wear in the movies. Which made sense if you were searching for a kid out in the night.

Again they said nothing, just peered into my cell and rattled the door to make sure it was secure. Niklas looked especially grim as he glared at me. Obviously, he was still chapped about our first kiss. As he started to back away, he turned his head and spoke into a lapel mike clipped to his collar. "She's here. So's the boyfriend. All is secure." He paused a moment, then, with obvious strain in his voice, said, "I'm telling you, Mama, the footprints just stopped. We followed them into the trees, where they simply ended. There weren't any signs of anyone else. They didn't stop and tramp around. They just stopped. Like someone had snatched him up from the sky."

Another pause, and his frown deepened. "I don't know what it means, Mama. I just know that half of these guys are spooked. They've heard some of the stories about the pouch and they don't like it. I say that we—"

He looked up at me as he stopped. "Yes, Mama. I understand." With a jerk of his head, he backed away from my door and disappeared down the hallway. He spoke to his two lieutenants as they moved away. "She thinks the kid is still inside. She wants the entire castle searched again." Their voices quickly faded as they moved away. "I don't care what you think, Raul," he snapped. "Post a man at every exit. Then we start room by room."

I heard the cell-block door open and shut, and immediately their voices were cut off. Finally, I dared to breathe again. My legs were so weak, I had to quickly sit down on the cot. "We did it, Rick. We did it."

"Danni, we have a problem."

"Only one?"

"Did you see those night-vision goggles?"

"Yes."

"They work off of infrared light, or what they call a heat signature."

"So?"

"So, it doesn't matter if Cody's invisible or not. They can see him."

"Great," Cody cut in. "That's just great. Danni, I'm coming to you guys now. I'm scared."

"You can't yet," Rick shouted. "The three of them are coming down the hall now. Wait until they go up the stairs. Then get here as fast as you can."

"Yes," I cried. "But be careful."

"Okay. I'll wait a minute," Cody said.

"So what do we do now, Rick?" I said. "I mean once Code gets here. There's no way we're going to find Mom and Dad with the whole castle buzzing with guards."

"I think that's easy. We get out of here and find Clay, then we come back for your folks."

"And just how do we do that?" I asked.

Rick answered. "Dad has a favorite saying that I think may apply here. It comes from Will Rogers, a famous comedian from the early twentieth century."

"Go on," I said slowly, baffled by this sudden, totally irrelevant piece of information.

"This was early in World War I when the German submarines, the U-boats as they called them, were sinking huge numbers of American ships. It was a topic on everyone's mind. So one night, Rogers told his audience that he had the perfect solution: 'Just heat up the Atlantic Ocean to the point it gets too hot for anyone to stay in the U-boats.' Since he appeared to be dead serious, someone raised his hand and asked, 'And how are we supposed to do that, Mr. Rogers?'"

"Good question," I noted.

I could almost hear Rick chuckling inside his head. "'Oh,' Rogers drawled, 'I gave you the solution, it's up to you to work out the details.'"

I openly hooted, which was probably the first time I had laughed in a couple of days. It felt good. "Thanks a lot, buddy. Just the kind of help I was looking for. I guess I'll—"

"Danni?" It was Cody again.

"Yeah?"

"Just so you know, I'm coming right now. So you and Rick work out the details. I'll see you in about one minute."

"No, Cody!" I shouted. "You'll run right into them. Just a few more minutes, then we'll bring you in. I promise."

"Danni's right, Code," Rick said. "Hang tight for a few more minutes. We'll let you know."

"You'd better," he said.

PART NINE

Walking with the Dead

CHAPTER 34

I sat for several minutes in complete turmoil. What did we do now? What about Mom and Dad? Did we really just leave them and hope for the best? How soon could Clay get here? How did we get Cody to a safe place? The questions just kept rolling in. If ever there was a time I needed help, especially a clear mind and a certain vision, it was now.

I went back over to the cot, removed *Le Gardien* from beneath the mattress, sat down, and smoothed it out on my lap. I can't begin to express how much comfort it gave me to have it back in my hands. I lifted it and pressed it to my cheek.

As I did so, I felt something inside. It wasn't much, something flat. A paper, maybe, but it was something. Puzzled, I set the pouch back on my lap, undid the wooden button, and opened the flap. I was shocked to see that inside there was a single sheet of paper, folded in half. Wondering if Grandpère had left me another note back at the hotel in Caen, I took it out and unfolded it. As my eyes fell on the ornate letterhead, I suddenly went very still.

Schloss von Dietz, Bern, Switzerland

Dear Danni,
    If you are reading this now, then all things went as planned

and you have Le Gardien in your possession. How very resourceful of you. But based on what I learned from Armando—El Cobra to you—I expected nothing less. At this moment, Niklas and the boys are probably trying to figure out how you did it, but I had complete confidence in you.

I know you will not believe me, but it was never our intent that anyone in Jean-Henri's family be physically harmed. I deeply regret that events turned out so differently than we had arranged. The death of your grandfather—a stubborn and foolish old man—was as much a blow to me as it was to you.

Hardly!

Now he is beyond my grasp, and justice cannot be fully achieved.

Whether you believe this or not is completely irrelevant to me. But know this. I will have my revenge, even if it must be on his family. Please believe me when I say that it is useless for you to resist. And it will only prolong the pain and anguish your mother is experiencing now.

So, I have an offer for you. It is a way for you to spare them and yourself even greater suffering. If you agree, you have my solemn word that you and your family will be immediately released the moment the terms of our agreement are met.

Right. As if I would believe that.

I'm sure your petty little mind is thinking that we would never let you go because you know too much. You can be at ease on that point. Niklas and I have already made elaborate plans to simply disappear and take on new identities in a new country. Even our physical appearance shall be altered sufficiently that we will not be recognizable. So we fear not what you and your ridiculous FBI, or

*our own feeble Interpol, can do. Believe me when I say that with
what I inherited from my late husband, and with the millions we
have obtained from those who did my family such enormous harm,
we have more than enough to live out the rest of our lives in great
luxury. You will never hear from us or see us again.*

Somehow, I felt that she was speaking the truth. With that kind of
money you could make just about anything happen. But what did she
want? Then another thought came to me. She had to have written this
before we were ever brought up to the library to meet with her. Which
meant—I gasped—*she wanted me to find the pouch.* She set the whole
thing up and sucked me in like I was a kid looking for candy. That was
why she had showed me where she kept the pouch. Why she left the
desk unlocked. Why the door was left open. I was like a little bird following a trail of bread crumbs into the trap. And I thought I was being
so clever, so unpredictable.

My mind was racing. She may have been mostly in control, but we
had done two things that I was pretty sure she and Niklas had not expected. We had taken out her eyes when we had destroyed the CCTVs.
And we had turned Cody invisible. There was no mistaking the urgency
in her voice when she thought he was escaping into the trees. It was
panic mode there for a while.

And . . . one more thought gave me great comfort. She also didn't
know I had called Clay Zabriskie. *This is not over yet, my dear Lady
Gisela.* I looked down and continued reading.

*In my pursuit for justice, especially from your grandfather, I
decided that the ultimate pain I could inflict on him was to leave
all of you destitute and without hope. But then, something happened that offered me more than I had hoped for. I learned that
Jean-Henri LaRoche had this remarkable pouch. That it had been
in his family for many generations.*

At first, I assumed it was just some silly family tradition. Then you came along and foiled everything we had so carefully planned. I kept asking myself, "How could such a silly, immature girl thwart such an intricate and careful plan?" When I learned that it was not you at all but this magic pouch you possessed, I knew I had the perfect way to punish Jean-Henri. I would end those generations of tradition held sacred by the LaRoche and Chevalier families. What exquisite guilt that would bring on his head! The great and wise Jean-Henri LaRoche, the destroyer of two hundred years of sacred trust. As you would so crudely put it, "How sweet is that?"

I stopped, lifting my head to stare at the walls of my prison. But why allow me to get the pouch back, then? Surely she could have told me all this without putting a note in the pouch and setting it up so I would find it. It didn't make sense. I shook my head and went on.

Here are the terms of our agreement. You will teach me how to draw upon the full potential of the pouch. Note that I am not asking you to provide me an instruction manual. Your journal has already done that. What I need from you is help in coming to understand its remarkable powers and how to control them. When that is completed, you and your family shall be put in your cells while we disappear. Within twenty-four hours, Interpol will be notified of your whereabouts, and you will be freed.

If, however, you refuse, know this. I will utterly destroy your family. Oh, I won't kill any of you. That would not serve our purposes. But here is just a taste of what you might expect to follow.

1. Your house back in Hanksville has already been prepped. One call from my mobile phone, and your house, your barns, your equipment—everything will burn to the ground. Also know that your insurance on the house was canceled before you left for New York, so you will receive no compensation for your loss. When you return to your pathetic little dust patch there will be nothing but ashes to greet you.

2. We already have access to your bank accounts. They will be stripped of all funds, and those monies, though they be but a pittance, will be transferred to our Swiss bank in Zurich, leaving you not only homeless but penniless.

3. We have prepared credible evidence that your father is guilty of numerous violations of federal mining laws, including the obtaining of claims through fraudulent means. If he's very fortunate, he will only lose his mining consultant business. More likely, he'll spend several years behind bars.

4. Your mother will be accused of selling forged paintings. No gallery will ever touch her work again.

5. And as for you, illicit drugs will be found in the ruins of your home. Cierra Pierce will be given evidence that you and Rick have been sleeping together for years and lied to the nation about it. I am sure your little community will be shocked to the roots of their graying hair.

I share this with you so that you know I can and will utterly destroy your family. I will do to them what your grandfather and others did to me and my family. Your life will become such a living hell that you will long for death. You shall be left with nothing, including that most precious of all gifts—hope.

Again, I knew with absolute certainty that this was not a bluff. It fit the pattern that Louis had described. But something was not right. There was more going on here than met the eye, and I wasn't sure what it was. As I read the next paragraph, I had my answer.

You may be thinking that you will once again, with the aid of the pouch, be able to thwart my purposes, to defeat us in battle. Well, my foolish girl, look closely at what you have in your hands at this moment. Look closely and weep. Then take care. If you continue to resist, I shall crush you like the worthless insect you are.

—Lady Gisela

"No!"

I leaped off the cot, flinging the letter from me. I grabbed the pouch and began to examine it closely. "No," I said again, this time in a bare whisper. But it was true. My eyes focused on the embroidered words, *Le Gardien,* and I saw it instantly. When I first got the duplicate pouch Clay had made for us, I noticed that whoever had stitched in the capital *G* on *Gardien* hadn't gotten it exactly right. The difference was so slight that it hadn't worried me. I knew El Cobra would never have the two pouches side by side to compare them. But I saw the difference now, and the realization of what Gisela had done hit me in the stomach like a fast-moving freight train.

What I held in my hand was not *Le Gardien.* It was the duplicate pouch. The pouch that some "fool"—or so we thought—had stolen from our home.

I let the pouch drop to the floor. I was sick. Devastated. Defeated. It was over. I knew it, and I knew that she knew I knew it. I picked up the letter and read the last line again, and then I did what she asked of me. I wept. And the tears were hot and bitter.

"Danni!"

My head snapped up and I looked around wildly, momentarily disoriented. It sounded like Cody was right outside my cell. "Um . . . where are you?" I asked.

"I'm hiding. Where do you think I am?"

"Are you all right?" I felt terrible. I had totally forgotten he was waiting for us to call him in.

"No. I'm scared, Danni. How come neither of you were answering me?"

"I . . . um, Rick? Are you there?"

Nothing.

"I haven't been able to get him either, Danni. Not for almost ten minutes now. You guys scared the heck out of me. I couldn't get him and I couldn't get you and . . ."

"Maybe he fell asleep." It sounded pretty lame, and we both knew it.

"I'm coming, Danni. I'm not waiting any longer."

I shook my head, trying to shake off the heaviness that gripped me now. "No, Cody . . ." Then I thought about him being alone with Doc and Jean-Claude prowling around and I changed my mind. "Yes. Come now. Hurry. And lie low if you see anyone coming."

"Got it. Thanks. See you in a minute."

I immediately called again to Rick. "Hey, man. You there?"

No answer.

"Hey, Rick. Wake up, buddy. Cody's coming in. I need you."

Total silence.

A wave of fear swept over me. Where was he? Had he fallen asleep, still on jet lag? It hadn't been that long ago that we were talking with each other. Could they have come and gotten him without me hearing them? I didn't think so, but I had been concentrating pretty hard on other things.

"Rick! Please. If you can hear me, please answer."

The silence was complete. Despair came crashing in. Not now. Not after getting him back. He couldn't be gone.

"Danni, I see the door to your cell block. All clear so far. I'm coming in."

Suddenly I had this horrible feeling of danger slam into me. My whole body was tingling, and I started to hyperventilate.

"No, Cody. Stay back."

"Sorry," he sang out, this time in real audio. "Too late. I'm here. Just coming up on Rick's cell. I'll see if he's checked out on us and—" He gasped. "Danni! His cell door is open. He's gone. And there's blood on the floor. A whole lot of blood."

"What? No!"

A moment later I heard footsteps and the key card appeared just outside my cell door, floating in the air again. At the same time I heard running footsteps coming down the hall outside our block.

"Quick, Cody. Get in that other cell. Hide in a corner. Don't lock it behind you. Leave the door as it is now."

I heard the scuffle of his shoes on cement, and the card retreated back into the hall.

A door banged open with a crash. "Stop right there, kid." It was a man's voice, but one I didn't recognize. "I can see you, so don't move." The footsteps started moving closer. The key card suddenly dropped to the floor with a soft clatter. I had no idea if Cody was complying with the guy's command or not because I couldn't tell where he was any longer.

"He *can't* see you," I cried silently to him. "Hide."

Again I heard the soft sound of shoes on cement. Then there was a loud, sharp click. Two tiny projectiles flashed across my vision, trailing curls of very thin wire. To my astonishment, they stopped dead in mid-air. Two things happened at the same instant. Cody screamed in agony, and at the same instant he materialized out of midair right in front of my eyes. It was like his body was being hit by lightning strikes. Violent spasms shook his frame. Then his eyes rolled up, his face contorted, his knees slowly buckled, and he started to fall forward, face-first.

"No!" I screamed as I leaped to the door of my cell.

"No!" Gisela cried as she shot into view from where she must have been hiding nearby, both of her arms outstretched. Cody fell into them. She staggered backwards but managed to lower the twitching, jerking body until it was laid out on the floor. The minute Cody was down, she was on her feet and whirled around. "Who Tasered him?" she yelled. "Who shot him?"

Doc ran up to join her, dropping to one knee beside her. "It was Bruno," he said. "He saw him through the night goggles."

A man stepped forward into view. It was Barrel Belly from earlier. He had a Taser pistol in one hand and a nightstick in the other. He was also wearing one of the night-goggle helmets Rick and I had seen earlier. "I thought he was getting away," he wailed, visibly quaking.

"Idiot!" she raged. "I told you. Not the full charge. Not on the younger ones."

"Cody!" I screamed it out, gripping the bars and shaking them with all my might.

Doc glanced up at me, then leaned down and put two fingers to Cody's neck, just below his jawline. My breath caught in my throat. *Breathe, Cody! Breathe!*

I saw Doc's fingertips press into Cody's flesh more deeply. He held them there for several more seconds as he looked over at Gisela. Finally, he shook his head slowly, then withdrew his hand.

I tried to cry out, to scream, to shout. Anything. But nothing came.

More running footsteps, and a moment later Niklas burst into view, holding a Taser of his own. "What happened?"

"Bruno has killed the boy," Doc said softly. "I think the Taser stopped his heart."

"Someone call the infirmary," Gisela cried. "Tell them to prepare the defibrillator."

"Mother! It's too late for that. He's dead."

"He can't be. I forbid it!" she shouted in his face.

Niklas handed his Taser to his mother, scooped up Cody's body, and started to turn away. Then he stopped and looked at me. "I assure you, Danni, this was not meant to happen." I dropped to my knees, hands clutching the iron bars of the door. Great sobs were torn from my throat as I tried to rip the door from its hinges.

Gisela whirled around, the Taser coming up. For one split second, I thought I was her intended target, but I was wrong. She did a full 180-degree turn, pointing the weapon at the big guard. I heard the sharp clicking sound again and saw the two electrodes blast out of the front of the pistol and bury themselves into his chest, just above the swell of his stomach.

Bruno had seen it coming. I saw that in his eyes. But there was no time to react. He screamed and went down. Gisela moved a few steps closer until she was standing right over the top of him. "Get him out of here," she snarled.

Two more guards, who had been out of my sight line, rushed in, picked him up, and carried him away even as he continued to twitch and moan.

For several seconds, Gisela stared after them, her chest rising and falling; then she handed the weapon to Doc. Only then did she finally turn to me. One finger came up, and she stabbed the air with it. "This is your fault. He was not supposed to be harmed."

"My fault?" I was incredulous.

"You are such a stupid, foolish girl. I read your journal. Did you think I wouldn't know about Cody turning invisible? The second they said Cody had disappeared, I knew what you were up to. That's why some of the men had infrared night glasses on."

It wasn't true. Well, some of it probably was. But not all. Those footprints headed for the trees had created a genuine panic. And if she were *Frau* Know-It-All, she wouldn't have left the equipment room unguarded.

I started to cry again. "You killed him!" I whispered.

"I . . ." She looked away. "This was not supposed to happen, Danni," she whispered. "That's two of you that I've lost now because you and your family have acted so stupidly. The responsibility lies on your own heads." Then she turned and walked slowly out of sight. Doc gave me one last, baleful stare, then turned and followed her out.

———

As I lay on the cot, curled up in a ball, hugging myself tightly so I didn't scream out into the night, I felt the heaviness closing in again. I think I slept for a time—fitfully and with horrible dreams—but I couldn't be sure. Maybe it just seemed that way because of the numbing effects of shock and grief and horror.

Suddenly I wondered if somehow they had drugged me again. Had they come in while I was sleeping? Then it hit me. There had been no food, but another guard—not Barrel Belly—had brought a large plastic cup of water and left it by the door. I had drunk it all. Had they put something in it? But why? Why drug me? I was in a secure cell. And in the emotional state I was in, I was hardly a threat.

My first thought was that with the CCTV cameras not working,

Gisela had sent someone in to check on me, to search me, to get back the key card. But as far as I could determine, nothing had been disturbed. The key card was in my back pants pocket. I had put the duplicate pouch under me when I lay down and it was still there now.

The tears burst forth and started streaming down my cheeks again. *Oh, Cody. My crazy, impish, nutty, maddening, lovable, exasperating Cody. First Grandpère and now you. How can I live without the two of you? This is more than any person should be asked to bear.*

I let the tears flow without restraint. I no longer tried to hold in the shudders that racked my body. I no longer tried to block the images of fifty thousand volts ravaging Cody's body, of Grandpère lying on a gurney, of blood on the floor of Rick's cell. I was too weary to fight it, too numbed to even try to get ahold of myself. I wanted to die. That was the only way I might find peace.

At that last thought, my head came up. Another image had come up in my mind. A paragraph from Gisela's letter was suddenly before my eyes. I actually saw it with perfect clarity.

I can and will utterly destroy your family. I will do to them what your grandfather and others did to me and my family. Your life will become such a living hell that you will long for death. You shall be left with nothing, including that most precious of all gifts—hope.

As I thought about those words, I felt something stirring deep within me. It was like this tiny spot of volcanic heat in the vast coldness. I wasn't sure what it was at first. When I finally recognized it, I opened my arms to it. Here was my saving grace, and I embraced it gladly, fully, completely.

It was pure, undiluted, unrestrained, razor-sharp anger.

———

I sat there for several moments trying to decide what to do. Where did I start? Mom and Dad? Rick? Did I go straight up to the library to confront the enemy? And what if they were waiting for me, as they most certainly would be? I had to have a plan of some kind. I couldn't just go running blindly toward my own destruction.

No! No plans. No questions. No fear. Just do it. Let the anger sustain you.

I got up from the cot, barely aware of the coldness of the floor on my bare feet. I removed the key card from my back pocket and tiptoed to the cell door. For a long moment, I listened to the silence, straining to pick up any sounds of another living human being nearby. Who was out there waiting for me? Jean-Claude? Niklas? Or—I felt a little shiver—Doc? My heart was hammering so hard inside my chest I felt like I might faint.

Sorry! Fainting is not an option. Move! Go! Do!

Reaching through the bars, I carefully slid the key card down through its slot. There was an immediate click, and my cell door swung open about an inch. Again I froze in place, listening carefully. Again there was not a sound. I pushed the door open, stepped through it, and started to shut it again. As I did so, my eyes fell on my cot. There sat the phony *Le Gardien* on top of the mattress. *Leave it,* I thought. *It cannot help you.* But I couldn't do it. If nothing else, I decided, maybe it would serve to give me a little courage, reminding me of what I once had.

I went back in, grabbed the pouch, and slung it over my shoulder.

When I stepped into the hallway, I could see all the way down to the guard station and the desk. There was no one there. And the door into the outer corridor was ajar. Moving forward on tiptoe, I went a few feet. I stopped in front of Rick's cell. My stomach lurched as I saw the smear of dark brownish red on the floor. It looked as if he had been dragged across the floor.

That's your first task. Find Rick.

But where? Then a thought came. With Cody gone and Mom and Dad moved, maybe they moved him to the other cell block. That would be logical—separate us, heighten the shock for me.

I moved into the small foyer where the guard station was. The chair was pulled away from the desk, as though someone had left in a hurry. I moved quickly to the desk. Using both hands, I pulled out the top drawer to see if there was anything there that might be of use—a weapon of some kind, keys. Nothing. In the bottom drawer, I found a small mag flashlight. Since it was still night, I decided to pocket it in case I needed it. Then I moved to the half-open door and swung it fully open.

The lights were on in the hall. I could see all the way down it. It was empty. The whole castle was eerily quiet. I had no idea what time it was. Had everyone gone to bed? *Of course not! There will be guards every-where. Count on it.*

Perhaps Gisela was holding a war council.

Stop thinking! Go! Move!

Running on the balls of my feet, I raced down the hallway, stopping only long enough to peek up the stairs and make sure no one was there. Nothing. I moved on toward the other cell block, passing the kitchen and the large open pantry—both dark and empty. Just ahead, a door was open, half blocking the hallway. Instantly I knew what it was. The metal sign had two words—*electronische* and *mechanische*.

A stab of pain hit me hard as I thought of Cody hiding in there for all that time. I ignored it and moved up to push the door shut. That's when I noticed another door almost directly across from the mechanical room. It was much larger than a normal door and nearly square. The surface was metallic and painted white. A heavy chrome door latch was on the right side. A sign read: KEEP LOCKER DOOR CLOSED AT ALL TIMES.

I had started past it, moving toward the other cell block, when I stopped and turned back. Gisela had told the guards to put Grandpère's body in "the cooler." That was before she ordered them to take his body to the dump. Was this what she meant?

I moved back and gripped the latch. I took a quick breath. Could I do this? Could I take the shock of seeing him again? *Yes! You have to know what they've done with him.*

To my surprise, the door swung outward with ease. A blast of cool air and the smell of food hit my nostrils. Inside it was dark, and the small lights in the hallway didn't penetrate very far. I quickly stepped inside, pulling the door shut behind me. That plunged me into total darkness, and a wave of vertigo swept over me. I groped blindly for something to steady me. My hand immediately found cold, smooth metal, and I leaned against the wall heavily. After a moment, I began feeling along the wall. There had to be a light switch in here somewhere. But as my fingers found the edge of the door, and then the switch, I chose not to turn it on. It wasn't likely that someone would be coming in here, but if they did and found the lights on . . .

A deep uneasiness was settling in now. I wasn't sure why, but I felt I had to hurry. I took out the flashlight and turned it on. I saw immediately that I was in a walk-in refrigerator. Slabs of beef hung from hooks. Large cans of milk lined a wall. There were stacks of boxes and cans on shelves. All were labeled in German. As I flashed the light, I saw that the cooler went back at least twenty feet.

Then my stomach lurched. Halfway back, I saw a table filled with stacks of large cheese wheels and cheese bricks. But just beyond the table, I could see something large and gray. I forced my feet to move forward, the dread rising like a tidal surge within me. I knew what it was. The gray sheet still showed the form of a body underneath it. My mind told me to lift the sheet, that I had to know for sure it was Grandpère beneath it, but my hands refused to obey. Who else would it be? I shrank back, feeling sick all over again. I had to get out of here. I had to. Or I was going to throw up.

But as I started to turn, the beam of the flashlight swept up, illuminating things farther back in the cooler. Horror exploded inside me as I saw what looked like another gurney covered with a gray sheet just beyond Grandpère. I lifted the light a little to see better and fell back with a cry. It wasn't another gurney. It was three more gurneys, lined up side by side with Grandpère's.

Run! The cry in my mind was a deafening shout, but my feet refused to retreat. Instead, to my absolute horror, I found them impelling me forward. Violent shivers ripped through my body. Goose bumps the size of baseballs were popping out on my arms and legs. My whole body was tingling so hard I was finding it tough to breathe.

I had to know, even though my mind was screaming at my body to flee. It couldn't be Cody. They couldn't have gotten him ready that quickly, could they? Dread or not, I had to know. I stopped at the nearest gurney and took a deep breath, telling myself that even if it was Grandpère, this would give me a chance to say my good-byes to him. So I grasped the corner of the sheet, took another, deeper breath, and lifted the corner of the covering enough to reveal the face.

I screamed as I saw that it was not Grandpère who was before me. It was a face I knew even better than his. It was the face of my mother, Angelique Carruthers McAllister.

I fell back, crashing into one of the milk cans. I started to sob hysterically. And then everything went black, and the last thing I remembered was crashing to the floor.

CHAPTER 35

More time passed. Don't ask me how much. And don't ask me how I managed to get to my feet and endure that shock three more times as I pulled back the sheets and looked into the faces of my entire family— Mom, Cody, Grandpère, and finally Dad. Perhaps I fainted a second time when I looked into my father's face. I'm not sure. I do remember pulling myself up to a sitting position on that cold, hard floor, then hugging myself, rocking back and forth and moaning softly. I could feel sanity slipping away from me. How utterly, incomprehensibly horrible was this? I was in a food locker filled with the dead bodies of my family.

But equally devastating was this keen awareness that for the first time in my life I was alone. It didn't matter what the Fourth Remember said. *I was alone.* And facing possible death at the hands of a woman whose hatred for us was boundless.

And then a small, barely audible voice somewhere deep inside me whispered, *What about Rick? Where is Rick?*

I got to my feet again and swung the flashlight beam slowly across the back of the locker. If there was another gurney, I decided I wanted to die right on the spot. Make the loss complete.

And there it was, separated from the others, at the very back of the locker. A fifth gurney with a human figure covered with a gray sheet was half hidden behind some boxes. The flashlight slipped out of my hands and clattered to the floor. I groped blindly for anything to catch me. There was nothing, and I went down hard, hitting my knee on something sharp and gasping with pain. I didn't even try to find the wall. I just curled up on the floor in a ball and gave way to the silent shudders that racked my body.

Not more than a minute later, I stiffened as I heard the click of the door latch behind me. Instinctively, I rolled up against the nearest gurney as the heavy door swung open and light flooded the room. Fortunately, being between the gurneys, I was not visible from the door. Darkness immediately closed in again as the door shut. Had they gone again? Or come in? I jumped as there was a slight buzz and the fluorescent lights above me flickered into life. A moment later, I heard a whisper of feet on cement. My heart was hammering so hard it felt like it must be thundering in the enclosed space.

I was on the floor now, facedown, cheek against the cold tile. I slipped the duplicate pouch off my shoulder and put it under my face, which helped. As the steps came closer, I watched beneath the gurney that stood between me and the center aisle of the locker. I would be able to see the person's feet as he or she passed. If he was wearing Doc Martin shoes, I wasn't sure if I would just die right there on the spot or jump up and commit as much mayhem on his body as possible.

But when I saw the beat-up old pair of tennis shoes moving past me, I shouted with relief and leaped to my feet. *"Rick!"*

He crashed backwards into the cheese table as he screamed and threw up an arm in front of his face.

"Rick! It's me."

For a moment, he just gaped at me, eyes as big as bicycle wheels. It was like he was looking at some spectral spirit from the other world. Then, with a cry, he hurtled across the few feet that separated us and swept me up in his arms. "Danni?" It was a half sob. "But this is not possible."

I forced a crooked smile. "Sorry, but what you see is what you get.

Where have you been? I thought you were . . ." I couldn't say it. I just pulled him close and squeezed him hard enough to make him grunt. Joy was shooting through me like a Fourth of July fireworks show. "I've been looking for you," I said. "What happened to you?"

"What happened to *me*? I . . ." He stepped back, giving me that incredulous look again, like what he was seeing was not possible. "I don't understand." And with that, he started moving away from me. His hand brushed the gray sheets of the four gurneys as he passed them. Baffled by what he was doing, I cried out and got quickly in front of them. "Don't. It's . . . it's my family. Grandpère, Mom, Dad, Cody."

He took me by the shoulders and turned me aside. "I know, Danni. I know. But there's something you have to see."

He moved past me, heading for that fifth gurney. I started to shrink back, but then realized that whoever it was, it wasn't Rick. I followed behind him, thoroughly curious now. Had the guard Gisela had Tasered died too? I shivered. Whoever had heard of turning a food locker into a morgue?

"I don't care who it is," I said as we drew close. "I can't stand to see another dead body, Rick. I can't."

Gently, he took my elbow and pulled me forward. "You have to, Danni. I'm sorry, but you must do this." He stopped as he reached the gurney, then gently pulled me up beside him and took my arm. "Brace yourself," he said softly, "because you are about to see why the sight of you gave me such a start a moment ago." And with that, he pulled back the sheet.

I recoiled like I had been Tasered. For several seconds I gaped at the body before me, unable to catch my breath, feeling like I was going to gag. I had been through shock and grief and loss this day like few people ever know. But what I saw now was a greater shock than Grandpère, Mom, Dad, and Cody all taken together. Horror shot through me like liquid fire as I looked down into the face that I knew better even than my mother's.

It was in perfect repose. The eyes were closed, and the hands were crossed on the chest. I screamed, wondering if I was going mad. For what I was looking at was the body of Carruthers Monique McAllister. *I was looking at myself!* As Rick dropped the sheet again, he pulled me away, putting his arms around me. I felt my legs give way and my eyes roll back. And for the third time that day, I fainted dead away.

———

When I came to again, we were still in the locker with the light on. We were both sitting on the floor. Well, Rick was sitting on the floor, I was lying with half of me curled up in his arms. He was stroking my hair softly, speaking to me in soft, soothing tones. When he saw my eyes flutter open, he stopped. "Hi."

"Hi." Looking around, I realized where we were. And I remembered. I stiffened, fighting against his grip, feeling the bile welling up inside me again.

He didn't let me break free. "It's all right, Danni. It's all right."

"But . . ." I craned my neck. I could see the last gurney just behind us, and I shuddered at the sight. Then I saw that the sheet was pulled back into its original position, and I felt myself relax a little. Rick pushed me up into a sitting position, then got to his feet. Taking both of my hands, he pulled me up to stand beside him. Then he reached down, picked up the duplicate pouch, and slipped it on my shoulder. I kept my head averted away from the gurney.

"Danni," he said, "listen to me. I need to show you something. And I need you to be strong. It's not what you think. But we don't have much time. Okay?"

I managed a sickly nod. How many times was he going to expect me to be strong today? When he stepped forward and reached for the sheet, my hand shot out and grabbed his wrist. "No, Rick! I can't bear to look."

"Yes, you can. This is important."

He pulled the sheet away from my face. Then, to my further horror, he bent over, peering closely at my face. His one hand came up, index finger extended.

"Don't touch me!"

He jumped, then whirled. "Geez, Danni! Get a grip. This isn't you!"

That was easy for him to say. It was me. And I was losing much more than my grip at this point. Looking down at a dead me was seriously freaking me out. I was beginning to wonder which one of us was the real Danni McAllister.

His finger came down and softly touched my cheek. I had to look away. And then I had to look back. As I did so, I saw him press harder against the flesh on the dead Danni's cheek. It didn't give. He gave a soft "Ah," as if something had just been confirmed to him. "Touch it, Danni. Touch the face."

"No!" A shiver shot through my entire body and I tried to pull free, but his grip only tightened.

"You have to, Danni." Then he took my face in his hands, peering into my eyes. "You have to. Trust me."

"No," I whispered, but I stopped resisting. And in a moment, he pressed my fingers against the cheek. My eyes flew open and my head jerked up. I stared at him, my mouth forming a big O. Then, of my own choice now, I laid my hand on my cheek. "But . . ."

"That's right," Rick said. "It's not flesh. Not even dead flesh."

"What is it, then? Why is it so stiff and hard?"

"Because it's wax."

My jaw must have dropped down about a foot and a half. I had no answer to that.

"Remember when your family went to Las Vegas? You told me how you went and saw all those wax statues of famous people at that place— what's it called?"

"Madame Tussaud's Wax Museum."

"Yeah, that's it. Well. This is a wax duplicate of you."

They say that the symptoms of a concussion, which result from a severe blow to the head, are headache, confusion, dizziness, and nausea.

I had every one of them, even though there had been no physical blow. If you had asked me right then what day of the week it was, or to give you my full name, I'm not sure I could have done it.

Rick was watching me with a most peculiar look.

"What?" I said.

"You don't get it, do you?"

"Get what?"

He just shook his head, but now, strangely, he seemed pleased with something. "I think we'd better check the others."

Suddenly my whole body flooded with light. My breath caught in my throat. "Are you saying . . . ?"

He nodded and took my hand. "I think so. Let's go check."

We moved to Mom's gurney. I stood back as he pulled the sheet down, both hands pressed to my mouth, not daring to hope. He laid a hand on her cheek, then turned to me. "Wax. No question about it. This is definitely not your mother."

Tears burst from my eyes as I realized what that meant. I choked back a sob, feeling suddenly light-headed. "Check the others."

He did so in quick succession, shaking his head as he touched the faces of Cody, Dad, and Grandpère, muttering each time, "Wax. Wax. Wax."

Putting my back against the wall, I slid slowly down until I was sitting on the floor. Then I buried my face in the folds of the duplicate pouch and once again began to weep. And with every wrenching cry, the pain receded and light moved in to fill its place.

Rick didn't let me revel in this euphoria for very long. He sat down beside me and took both of my hands. "Danni, we need to talk, and our time is short. As soon as they finish securing the perimeter of the estate, they'll be coming back. And the first thing they'll do is come looking for us."

"What do you mean, securing the perimeter?"

"Okay, just listen. I'll fill you in on what's been happening. I think after the shock of seeing Cody Tasered—and thinking he had been killed—you finally fell asleep for a while."

"I think they drugged me again, Rick. They left a cup of water for me."

"Me too, only I think mine was in my food. I was out for a while as well." Then he shook his head as if that didn't matter. "Anyway, Niklas and Jean-Claude came and took me out of my cell. I thought they were going to get you too, but they didn't."

"Was that when they hurt you?"

He shot me a puzzled look. "I wasn't hurt."

"Yes you were. I saw the blood on the floor of your cell."

"What are you talking about? They didn't hurt me in any way. They just took me back to the library to talk to Gisela."

"Then—there was blood there, Rick. I saw it. That's why I thought you were dead."

"I don't know about that. I just know they took me up to see Gisela. It was just her, Niklas, and Jean-Claude. She started interrogating me about the pouch and how you made it work. She also said that I had to persuade you not to fight her." He gave me a quick look. "For your own safety."

"And what did you tell her?"

"I told them everything I knew." He threw up a hand as I started to protest. "Come on, Danni, she has a copy of your journal, remember? And Niklas went to the prison and had a long interview with El Cobra shortly after he was arrested. You think I told her something she didn't already know? I decided that if I was cooperative, they might relax their guard."

"Go on."

"Well, right in the middle of them hammering at me, suddenly Gisela jerked forward. She was looking at the phone on her desk. She turned to Niklas and asked him if he had used it."

My hand shot to my mouth. "Oh, no. I called Clay."

"Well, you evidently didn't put it back exactly as it was before, and she saw that. When she checked the last number dialed and saw that it was a U.S. number, she dialed it. When Clay answered, she went ballistic. Started screaming orders. Got on the radio to warn the guards outside."

"To secure the perimeter," I added, understanding now.

"Yes. If you had been there, I think she would have shot you on the spot. That really rattled her. I mean, she was seething."

"Good," I said. "I hope they run right smack into Clay and his men."

"She told me to stay where I was and not move; then they all ran out to put out the word."

"She left you alone?"

"Yeah. I'm telling you, she was so livid, she wasn't thinking clearly."

"Rick?" The sick feeling in the pit of my stomach was suddenly back. "I don't care how livid she was. She wouldn't leave you alone."

"Well, she did. When I went to the windows and saw everyone running around outside like someone had just kicked over the anthill, I went looking for you. I stopped at the other cell block first, to see if I could find your mom and dad. There was nothing. I was on my way to our cell block to find you when I saw this food locker. I remembered what Gisela said about keeping Grandpère's body cool, so I came in here. That's when I found all of this." He looked away. "I couldn't believe it. There you were, all dead. I . . ." He had to look away.

I reached out, took his hand, and pressed the back of it against my cheek.

He sniffed back the tears—yes, tears, from Rick! I started to cry again, just like that.

"I was shattered, of course. I thought I was the only one left. After a minute or two, I decided I had better get back to the library before they discovered I was gone. I went back. There was still no one there. But as I sat there, things started coming into my head."

His eyes were filled with wonder. "You had told me how *Le Gardien* sometimes kind of flooded your mind with clarity. Well, that's what happened to me. Everything started making sense all of a sudden."

"Yes, that's it exactly."

"My first thought was about Grandpère and how his body supposedly hadn't yet been found. Then I thought about Cody. He's not a little boy. He's a pretty hefty kid, really a full adult physically. Occasionally you hear about Tasers killing people, but it's pretty rare."

He took another quick breath. "So I came back to take another look. And that's when I found you here."

I was pumped. There was no question about that. I had been to the depths. Now I was riding the heights. I jumped to my feet and went quickly over to Grandpère's body.

"What are you doing?"

"Seeing if by any chance they left Grandpère's phone on him."

He gave a soft hoot. "Danni, this *isn't* Grandpère. He went into the river. This is just a . . ." His voice trailed off as I pulled the sheet back, lifted Grandpère's jacket, and revealed his old cell phone clipped to his belt. Then he gave a low cry. "That's not possible. This isn't his body. And in the second place, Clay gave us all satellite phones, remember?"

"Except for Grandpère. He said he wanted to keep his old one. Liked it better. As for how his phone got here, go figure," I went on. "But remember, this is the phone that works even when it's turned off. That isn't affected by being dunked in water. That can text messages even when Grandpère doesn't have it in his possession."

Rick said nothing. So I turned it on, gave it a moment to power up, then brought up his "Favorites" list and hit Clay Zabriskie's number.

Grandpère answered on the first ring. "Hello, *ma chérie*. So you found it."

I squealed so loudly, I probably woke up half of Bern. "You're alive?"

"I think so," he said, sounding puzzled. "Just a moment. Let me check."

"Stop it," I said, half laughing, half crying. "They said you slid off the road and the van went into the river."

"I did and it did."

"You did it deliberately?" I gasped.

"But of course." He paused for a moment, then, "Ah, now you offend me. I am old, but I still know how to drive."

"They said they couldn't find the body."

"Well, of course not. I'm still using it." His voice became solemn. "Are you all right?"

"Yes. Rick's with me."

"Good. What about Angelique and Mack and Cody?"

"Not sure. No time to explain fully, but we think they're alive."

"So you've found the 'bodies'?" He spoke the last word with disgust.

"You know about the wax dummies?"

"Danni, I'm going to let you go now. I've got to call Clay and tell him you and Rick are all right. But listen carefully. Do not underestimate Gisela. She is absolutely brilliant, which makes her only that much more dangerous. Be careful how you push her. And Niklas too. He's in it for the money and for the game, so he has none of his mother's scruples."

"Then come help us," I cried.

"Sorry. I can't do that. You have Rick, and that's all for now."

"We need *you.*"

"I have to go, Danni. It's critical I call Clay. You and Rick have each other. Trust that. Be wise. Be safe. Be brave. I love you."

"We can't do it alone," I cried, weeping openly now.

"Sometimes that is the only choice."

"Grandpère, please." I was sobbing harder and harder. "Help us."

"*Au revoir,* my dearest."

Stricken, I turned to Rick. "I heard," he said softly. "But, Danni, he's alive! Grandpère is alive!"

He was right, but somehow I was finding it hard to celebrate. But just as I was about to answer him, it was like someone had suddenly opened an outside window and a blast of ice-cold air swept the room. I shoved the phone in my pants pocket. "Rick! Someone's coming. We've got to get out of here. We've got to get back to our cells."

He leaped to his feet and pulled me up. "You go back. Lock the door. I have to go back to the library. That's where they left me."

He jumped to the door and turned off the lights. Easing it open he cocked his head. There wasn't a sound. He grabbed my arm and shoved me out in the hall. "Go, Danni! Go! Go! I'll talk to you as soon as it's okay."

As quickly as I broke into a run, I instantly slid to a halt. Doc and Jean-Claude stepped out from the door to the kitchen. Both had Tasers pointing at me.

"Hello, *Chiquita,*" Doc said with a sneering smile. "How good to see you again."

"Rick!" Jean-Claude hollered. "Come out. Keep your hands where we can see them."

CHAPTER 36

"Rick?" I called in my head.

"Yeah?"

I was in the lead, with Doc gripping my elbow tightly. We had started down the hallway toward the stairwell. Rick was behind Doc with Jean-Claude guarding him. "We don't have much time. There are some things you ought to know."

"Like what?"

"Me getting the pouch was a setup."

"A setup? How do you figure that?"

"She wanted us to see Niklas leave the key card in the drawer. She wanted me to know where the pouch was. And when I first came to the library, the door was locked. When everyone went outside looking for Cody, I went back, and the door had been left open."

He considered that. "I'm not sure that's conclusive. She would never give up the pouch."

"She would if it was not the real *Le Gardien.*"

"*What?* Are you telling me that—"

"Yes! She gave me the old duplicate pouch. And why leave you alone in the library? I'm telling you, she is manipulating us like we were a couple of puppets on strings."

We had reached the stairs that led up to the main floor. As we started up, I pretended to miss the second step so that I almost went down face-first. The pouch slipped half off my shoulder. Doc jerked me back up, causing me to cry out. I took a moment to catch my breath. And to stall for time. "But not everything went exactly as planned," I continued telling Rick in my mind. "Knocking out the CCTV system caught them by surprise. They thought they were prepared for invisibility by having night goggles, but then Cody—or what appeared to be Cody—went out the upper balcony window."

"And your call to the FBI really threw her a curve. I don't think she was faking that."

All of a sudden a thought came zinging in with such swiftness and such clarity that this time I really did catch my toe on the top step. I went down hard, jerking free of Doc's grasp. I yelled as I felt my knee scrape on the marble. "Stop pushing me!" I yelled at Doc, stalling for time. "Now look what you've done." There was a circle of raw flesh just below my knee already turning an angry red. But I was barely aware of it. My mind was still racing.

"And that whole thing with Cody was staged. I mean, I know they really Tasered him, but them making me believe he was dead was fake." I had to rush to keep up with my thoughts. "In our presence, she told the guards to put Grandpère's body in the cooler. They didn't take my key card, even though they had to know I had one. They wanted me to get out. To see your 'blood.' And when I started looking for you, no one was around. The hallways were empty. Allowing me to reach the food locker with a sign on the door warning people to keep the door closed. And the sign was written in English. *Even though the staff is German.*"

"Yeah," he said in wonder. "That's why I looked inside."

"She *wanted* us to find those bodies. It was more terrible than any physical blow."

He thought for a moment. "So you think this is all just messing with our heads?"

478

"Yes! Mind games. Psychological warfare. And it worked perfectly. I was utterly crushed."

I felt something hard dig into my ribs. "Come on," Doc growled. "You're not that hurt."

I got up. A moment later we were upstairs and headed for the great entry hall. I went on with the conversation in my head. "Do you know how long it takes to make a high-quality wax replica of a person, Rick? Four months. That's what they told us at Madame Tussaud's museum. And each figure costs about a hundred and twenty-five thousand to make. They insert every strand of hair individually."

"Four months?" he cried. "But that would mean—" "Exactly," I cried. "They planned all of this *before* El Cobra ever kidnapped my family."

"Unbelievable," he said in awe. "But why let you see your own body?"

"That's easy. It was the ultimate blow to the inside of my head. For a moment there, I thought I was going mad. Even now, it makes my flesh crawl thinking about it."

"What kind of a sicko could do something like that?"

"And it's not over, Rick. In her letter, Gisela said that—"

"Letter? What letter?"

I forgot I hadn't mentioned that. "She wrote me a letter and put it in the fake pouch." I reached out and touched the pouch with one hand. "And one of the things she said was that if I didn't cooperate, she would take away the most precious of all gifts. Hope."

"Ah," he said. "Man, Danni. This is incredible." Brief pause. "So what do we do now?"

That question had been tumbling around in my mind for some time now. But when Rick asked it again, the answer came immediately. "We fight back."

"Good."

"No. Fighting back may put my folks and Cody in jeopardy. We have to end it. Here and now. Somehow, we have to end it."

"I agree," he said slowly. "I like that idea a lot. But . . . uh . . . Danni? How do we do that?"

I actually laughed inside my head. "Hey, I gave you the solution. It's up to you to work out the details."

As we moved into the library, things were pretty much the way they had been before. Once again the logs in the fireplace had been replaced, and now a bed of glowing coals covered the entire area beneath the grate. There were still six chairs in front of the desk. Niklas stood behind the desk beside his mother's chair, dressed in a business suit, looking like he was about to attend a board meeting of the bank. Once they seated us, Doc and Jean-Claude took their places behind us, their hands resting easily on the butts of their holstered pistols. Other armed guards were posted at each of the side doors.

But again, Gisela was not there. Of course not. Get the unwashed masses in their places first; then Her Majesty would make her grand entrance.

As we sat down, heads facing front, Rick started talking in my mind immediately. "We've been studying China in our World Civilizations class this year, and we read a book by a guy named Sun Tzu. He was a famous Chinese general who lived a couple of centuries before Christ. He wrote a book called *The Art of War.*"

I turned and gave him funny look. *Seriously? You're talking about World Civilizations at this point?* But his head was down and he was staring at his hands and didn't look at me.

"He said, 'Pretend you are inferior and encourage your enemy's arrogance.'"

"Well, that should be easy enough. No pretense necessary."

"I mean it, Danni. Gisela thinks you are this silly, immature, foolish American teenager."

"You forgot gauche."

He ignored that. "Now would be a good time to convince her that she is right."

———

As we waited, the only sound in the room was the slow tick-tock of the grandfather clock in the corner. Nor was there any movement. We were like stone statues left in the library as some weird form of decoration. Finally, tired of the games, I looked at Niklas. "I know your mother is an old woman and needs her beauty rest, so why don't we just postpone this till morning?" I yawned, and not just to fake it. I suddenly was feeling the exhaustion of a very long and traumatic two days.

His lips pinched into a tight line and his eyes narrowed. But before he could say anything, Doc moved in behind me. His hand shot out, and once again pain knifed through me as he gripped my shoulder and pinched down hard. "No talking."

"You're hurting me," I cried, trying to pull free of his viselike grip.

He leaned in until I smelt the cigarettes on his breath. "Aw, I'm sorry, little Miss Smart Mouth. Does this help?" He dug his fingers in deeper and literally lifted me up out of my chair, using nothing but that one hand.

Yelling with pain, I jerked free and spun around. "Have you learned nothing from what happened to Niklas?" And with that, I reached out with my free hand and placed it palm down against his chest. I could feel the hardness of his muscles beneath the fabric of his shirt. He grunted, then cried out. Doubling over, he let go of my arm and dropped to his knees, his body jerking violently. His eyes bulged as he fought to breathe. He couldn't do it. His whole body was being hit with violent spasms.

I leaned in until I was looking straight into his eyes. "That's what's known as being Danni-Tasered, Mr. Tough Guy," I said sweetly. "Please don't touch me again."

I swung around. Jean-Claude was moving in to intervene. Niklas was too, but more hesitantly. He was gaping at Raul, who was starting to turn blue. Seeing my face, Jean-Claude stopped, then backed up a step. I sat down, and instantly Raul was released from whatever it was that had hit him. He remained on all fours, gasping and wheezing.

"So much for Sun Tzu and trying to look inferior." It was Rick's voice in my head, and he sounded amused.

"Sorry. You know me. Raise the gun. Fire. Take aim."

"Don't be sorry, Danni. You just proved that *Le Gardien* is not fully in Gisela's power."

Good point! I turned back around to sit down. To my surprise, Gisela was standing next to the side door. Once again, she was impeccably dressed, this time in an elegantly tailored blouse and full-length black skirt. She stood there in regal silence, like the queen she was, looking totally bored with it all.

"Up to your old games again, are we, Danni?" she sniffed, then moved to her chair.

She waited until Raul managed to stagger back to his feet. "Did you search them?"

He nodded, still grimacing with pain, and reached in his pocket. He withdrew Grandpère's phone and the key card and handed them to her. "The kid had nothing. Danni had these. Do you want the other pouch, too?"

She shook her head, but as she took the phone from him, I saw real fear on her face for a moment. "Where did you get this?" she demanded.

That surprised me. "It was on Grandpère's corpse. I assumed you had put it there as a nice touch." I said the last two words with heavy sarcasm.

She turned to Niklas. His hands shot up, as if to ward her off. "I didn't put it there. I've never seen it before."

So who did? I hurriedly sat down, guessing she was asking herself the same question. But the veil came down over her eyes again and they showed nothing more—not surprise, not dismay. "Cuff them," she said to Niklas. Though he blanched a little at that, he nevertheless jumped in, taking two metal handcuffs from his jacket pocket. I quickly put my hands out in front of me, not wanting to have him pull them around to the back. He put the cuffs on. Rick did the same, and then Niklas moved back to stand beside his mother.

She turned the phone on, waited for a few moments, then hit some buttons with her thumbs. When she looked up, I could see I had broken through her reserve. She was angry. That was good news. Not every single thing she had arranged with such meticulous care was going according to plan.

She tossed the phone to Niklas, who looked at the screen, then at me. "So you called the FBI again?" he shouted.

Before I could answer, Gisela smiled. "And I assume you told them you were being held in the *Schloss* von Dietz. Ah, Danni, have you no imagination. You take all the fun out of it."

I had no idea what she was talking about. Which only amused her all the more. "The real von Dietz Castle is on the other side of the lake. And it has absolutely no links or ties with the villa where we are now. But we put a sign on the gate announcing this was the von Dietz Castle so your parents and Cody would see it as we drove in. We figured you would make contact with them sooner or later." She clucked sadly. "You are *so* predictable."

Looking at Niklas, she went on, "Have those guarding the outside perimeter be especially alert. And have them call us at the first sign of any activity. In the meantime, I think we can chat without fear of being disturbed."

So Clay would not be coming. Not in time. And Grandpère's words came back to me, "Do not underestimate her, Danni." Which I had just done. Again.

She leaned forward, opened a drawer, and withdrew something. When I saw what it was, I tensed. It was *Le Gardien.* The real *Le Gardien.* She clutched it tightly in her hands and turned it enough that it was facing me square on, like she was sighting on a target. "Earlier today, I sent you a letter with an offer for a deal between us."

I nodded. "And I am ready to deal. But first I need to know that my family is safe."

She laughed harshly. "But your family is all dead, my dear."

"Show me my family or you get nothing."

She exploded with rage, causing me and several others to jump. "Don't trifle with me, girl!" she shrieked. "You have no idea who you are dealing with."

"Oh, I think I do."

"You think that because you haven't yet taught me how the pouch works, I cannot use it?"

I rocked back as I saw her raise the pouch and point it directly at me. She half closed her eyes. There was a soft POOF! and a cool breeze brushed my cheeks. For a moment, I wasn't sure what had happened. When it hit me, I laughed right out loud. "Whoa! That was impressive."

She stared at the pouch for a moment, her face ashen, her eyes like twin points of glowing lava. Then, quick as a cat, she dropped *Le Gardien* on the desk and yanked the drawer open again. When she withdrew her hand this time, it held a Taser pistol.

"Watch out, Danni!" Rick yelled.

As she raised the weapon and fired, I jerked hard to one side, almost tipping the chair over. Out of the corner of my eye, I saw the two electronic probes flash by me and bury themselves in the fabric of the chair. Instantly I felt a shock pass through the whole backside of my body. It was enough to knock me flying off the chair. Hitting the floor with a crash, I lay there for a moment, too dazed to move.

My next conscious awareness was of Gisela bending over me, her face just inches from mine, her mouth twisted in a disdainful sneer. "Consider yourself Gisela-Tasered," she cried.

Suddenly the anger was back. Every evil thing that she stood for crystallized in my mind. I lunged up, jerking my head forward with every ounce of strength I could muster. Stars shot across my vision as my forehead connected with the bridge of her nose. Blood sprayed outward as she fell back and crashed against the desk.

"Mama!" Niklas darted around the desk as she crashed to the floor, her hands coming up to cover her nose. Instantly, cold steel pressed hard against my left temple. I looked up and saw Raul's murderous expression as he cocked the pistol. I didn't care. I pushed it away with my hand and rolled over onto my knees. When I looked over at Gisela, our eyes met. She was dazed. So was I. Both her hands were clamped over her face. Blood oozed between her fingers, and I could see spatters of it on her immaculate white blouse. She was moaning softly.

"Get the doctor up here," Niklas screamed. Somewhere behind me, I heard footsteps take off running and a door slamming open and shut.

The pistol pressed harder against my temple. "Move again and I will shoot you dead," Raul hissed into my ear.

I ignored him and looked up in Gisela's eyes, now shadowed with pain. "I no longer have the real pouch, but I will not stop fighting you. Right now, I have every reason to believe my family is dead. So show me that they are alive or tell this Spanish dung beetle to pull the trigger."

"Easy, Danni," Rick cried in my head. "Easy."

Gisela and I glared at each other for several seconds, but finally she nodded. "Raul. Stand down. But watch her. One more outbreak and you have my permission to go down and shoot her little brother."

Raul straightened. "Gladly."

Niklas stepped between us. "Tip your head back, Mama," he said. He had his handkerchief out. Jean-Claude was behind the desk now, rummaging in a bottom drawer. A moment later he stood and held out a bottle of water to Niklas.

Working with great gentleness, Niklas wet the cloth, carefully pulled Gisela's hands away from her face, and began dabbing at the blood. The nose was swollen and horrible to look at.

"You broke my nose," she whispered, looking past his hands at me.

"Tell you what. I'll pay your doctor bill if you give us back the money you stole from us."

She said nothing more. From the rigidness of her body and the tightness of her face, I could tell she was in a lot of pain. Having once nearly broken my nose in a biking accident, I was not totally without sympathy for her.

A few moments later, a tall, lean man hurried in with a black bag in one hand. He raced over and dropped down beside her. One look at her face and he began to mutter under his breath. And with that we settled into an uneasy silence, me watching her with loathing, her staring back at me with utter contempt.

I quickly tired of the glaring game and laid back my head and closed my eyes. The throbbing in my head was increasing in intensity and I was tempted to ask the doctor if he might have a couple of aspirin. I resisted the temptation.

I looked over at Rick. His head was down in his handcuffed hands as he stared at the floor. I guessed that he was thinking about Sun Tzu's advice and how little it had affected me.

"Sorry," I said to him in my head.

"For what?" Then he chuckled, though not audibly. "For acting so inferior?"

"Yeah. I wasn't thinking about that when she shot at me."

"Danni, listen to me. Toss Sun Tzu out the window. Disregard what I said earlier. You have to go with your instincts, with what your feelings are."

"Even when it is pure rage?"

"That wasn't rage," he retorted. Then he caught himself. "Well, maybe you were a bit ticked off. But it was also brilliant, Danni. She was treating you like a street punk. You had to come back at her, or she would have completely dominated you."

"Do you really think so?" I said, surprised by his words.

"Absolutely. Look at the way she's looking at you, Danni. She had dismissed you like some annoying bug to be stepped on. But look at those eyes now."

I did. I raised my eyes to hers and willed myself not to look away. Behind those startling blue irises, I saw what Rick was talking about. I saw respect. Not the respect you show for someone you admire and like.

Respect for an adversary. And with it, I saw wariness. She was taking my measure, and she was taking it seriously.

"Thanks, Rick. There is nothing in the world I needed more than that at this moment."

"Go get her, Danni. I'm here. I'm praying for you. And I'm pleading with *Le Gardien* not to abandon you, because I've got a feeling that this war is going to be mostly between you and her."

Gisela suddenly snarled at the doctor, who was just starting to put a bandage across her nose. "That's enough. Get out."

Right on! Get out, and let the games begin.

But as he stood up, closed his case, and started to back away, I flashed him my prettiest smile. "Don't go too far, Doctor. You never know what's going to get broken next."

CHAPTER 37

To my surprise, the doctor followed my advice rather than Gisela's command. He moved to the back corner of the room and stood beside one of the guards. Gisela barely noticed. By now the whole area around her nose was swollen and starting to darken. I guessed that by breakfast, she would greatly resemble a raccoon. Knowing how important chic was to her, that gave me a sort of savage satisfaction.

They had cleaned the blood off her face, but when Niklas tried to send out for a new blouse for her, she waved him off. There were one large, dark smear and half a dozen smaller spots on the front of the one she was wearing. In spite of my anger, it was freaking me out to think that I had done that. Without thinking. Out of pure rage. And I felt zero remorse right now.

I looked directly into Gisela's eyes. "You have just had your first lesson in pouch management. *Le Gardien* is a force for good. It will not respond to your wishes or desires if you seek to make it do something wrong, something evil."

"Oh, really?" she sneered. "What about the handwriting on the windshield of that little sports car with the blonde driver?" she shot right back. "Was that a 'good' thing? You nearly killed that poor woman."

I wasn't sure exactly how to answer that, so I ducked her question. "I didn't say the pouch doesn't let us do stupid things. Just not something that is directly evil. So, as you have just seen, if you're thinking you can use the pouch to carry out your crimes, you're in for a surprise."

"Seeing justice done is not a crime."

"Obviously not in your eyes, even if it violates the law, but it will be from the pouch's perspective." I took a quick breath. "So let's get to it. I accept your proposal. I will show you everything I know about the pouch in return for you getting out of our lives. But first, I need to see my family. After your sick little game with the wax bodies, I need to see for myself that they are all right."

"I think instead I may just have my Niklas take you out and shoot you," she said contemptuously.

"Like your father did with innocent men and women so many times, right? Without a trial. Without remorse."

Her hand flashed out and slapped the desktop with full force. The crack echoed sharply in the room, and both Rick and I jumped. She leaned in, visibly trembling. "If you speak of my father again, I will shoot you myself."

"Don't push her, Danni," Rick said inside my head. "She's near the edge."

Not near enough. I leaned in. "If you want my help, you *will* prove to me that my family is still alive and unharmed. Until then, I will do nothing. And all your empty threats about shooting me do not frighten me."

Again she seemed to be hovering between rationality and rage, but finally, she jerked her head at Niklas. He moved around her to where the computer was and knelt down. He typed something quickly, and both screens lit up. His fingers flew across the keyboard again. Directly behind Gisela's desk, there was a portion of the library's wall that was wood paneling rather than bookshelves. A soft sound was heard as, just above eye level, a wooden panel slid open, revealing a large, flat-screen TV. That screen also flickered into life, bringing up this spectacular view of the Swiss Alps in full summer, obviously a screen-saver photo.

Then it faded away and was replaced by something that made me cry aloud. What we were looking at was a richly furnished room somewhere in the mansion. Dad and Cody sat on a couch. They were handcuffed and blindfolded, with a guard behind them.

But where is Mom?

I saw Niklas's hand move and realized that beside the keyboard there was a small joystick like the ones used in computer games. As if he read my thoughts, Niklas put one hand on the joystick and began to move it. The camera angle changed, panning to the right. I gasped as Mom came into view. She too was blindfolded, but she was sitting in a wheelchair, with both arms strapped down and some kind of metal box on her lap. The camera zoomed in and focused on the box. I had to reach out and steady myself on the desk.

It was like I was watching some fiendish horror movie. What sat on her lap was some kind of electronic device with numerous wires coming out the one side. And those wires were attached to my mother with sticky pads that had electrical connections to them. It looked like one of the machines they use to monitor your heart, an EKG, I think they call it. But I knew, without the slightest shadow of a doubt, that this machine was not a heart monitor. It did not read electrical impulses. It gave them.

I fought back the urge to hurl myself across the desk at Gisela. I guess she saw that in my eyes, because she suddenly laughed in my face. "Go ahead, little one. I would love to demonstrate what will happen to your mother if you give in to your mindless anger."

"You are a horrible monster," I cried.

She leaned in toward me. "Don't you try to bargain with me like some cheap street vendor. Try to withhold what I ask and your mother will suffer the most exquisite pain imaginable. Give me what I seek and Niklas and I and all the rest of us will be gone before daylight and you will never see us again."

Her features were twisted into something fiendish, and the ghoulish effect was only heightened by the swollen face and darkening eyes. "So what will it be, Miss Danni McAllister? I'm done with the games. Must I give you a demonstration to convince you that I am deadly serious here?"

I sank back into my chair. My chest had constricted so much that I was finding it hard to breathe. But I finally managed to shake my head. "No," I whispered. "Don't hurt her. I'll do whatever you say."

"All right!" Niklas crowed. His fingers flew across the keys, and the screen went dark.

I jerked forward. "No! Leave it on," I cried. "I have to see them. And if you hurt her—"

What? What will you do, Danni? Spit in her face? Throw a tantrum?

To my surprise, Gisela shrugged and nodded at Niklas. "Leave it on. I want her to see that we are keeping our part of the bargain."

"Danni." It was Rick, and his voice was urgent.

"What?"

"The machine is a fake. It doesn't work."

I glanced at him, then away quickly. "How do you know that?"

"Dunno. Just do. She's just playing with your head again."

I wasn't quite sure whether to accept that or not, but it did infuse me with a burst of hope. Gisela opened a drawer in the desk, reached in, and brought out one of those little electronic dictation recorders. She turned it on and placed it halfway between us. Then she picked up the pouch and placed it in her lap. Her look was one of pure triumph. "You will speak slowly and clearly."

My head came up. "No."

I thought she was going to choke. "No? You dare to defy me?"

"I will not be party to the corruption of the pouch and its goodness. I will not."

She was momentarily confused. I guess this possibility had never entered her mind. "Then your mother will be destroyed."

"No," I said calmly. "No, she won't. And neither will we. If you try to call down the forces of darkness upon our heads, they will descend only on you and Niklas and those who serve you."

She shot to her feet, her eyes wild. "You dare to defy *me?*" she shrieked.

Niklas leaned on the desk, peering into my eyes. "Don't do this, Danni. She's not bluffing."

I spoke clearly and distinctly, punching out each word with quiet emphasis. "You will not receive one sliver of help from me to work your evil ways. Not one sliver!"

She straightened slowly, then looked at Doc. "She's yours, Raul. Do with her what you wish. Jean-Claude, you can have her when he's done."

BAM! We all jumped as one of the library's side doors slammed open, crashing against the wall. "I wouldn't do that if I were you, Raul," a voice barked.

Every one of us jerked around. And what we saw was totally astonishing. A tall, male figure stood silhouetted in the doorway. My heart leaped within me as I saw that it was a man fully dressed in the uniform of an American GI, complete in every detail except that he wore no helmet. He stepped into the room and came into the full light. I heard several gasps, none louder than Gisela's. "You!" she cried, falling back. She grabbed the pouch and clutched it to her chest as if warding off an evil spirit.

"Yes," Grandpère replied, his voice soft and filled with menace. "It's me. Back from the dead, just as you planned."

All kinds of things happened all at once then. I spun around, joy lighting up my soul. "Grandpère!" I cried.

Rick was up beside me, gaping in astonishment.

Behind me, Doc dropped to one knee. His pistol was already in his hand. BLAM! BLAM! The two shots came so close together as to be one deafening blast. Two bullet holes blossomed in the door just to the left of Grandpère.

"No!" Gisela screamed. "Don't shoot him!"

Jean-Claude was down beside Raul now, taking more careful aim. Grandpère stood there calmly, not moving. Seeing what Jean-Claude was doing, Rick hurled himself at him, both fists locked together in a club. He swung them down with all his strength and knocked Jean-Claude rolling.

Doc leaped to my side, grabbing me with one arm and putting the pistol barrel to my right temple, grinding it in hard. "If you move, your granddaughter dies."

"I wouldn't try that," Grandpère said easily. "Hasn't Jean-Claude told you about the rattlesnakes, Raul? You're over your head here, son."

Gisela's cries pierced the room. "Put down your weapons, you fools!" she shouted. "Don't kill him."

Grandpère came into the room, his hands raised, walking slowly, but still with that same marvelous calm. "Thank you, Rick. Are you all right?"

As Rick got to his feet and nodded, Niklas made his move. In one smooth motion, he reached inside his suit jacket, whipped out a pistol—a wicked looking little automatic—and dropped down behind the desk. BLAM! BLAM! BLAM! The automatic fired in rapid succession. Shell casings went flying and clattered as they hit the desk.

Grandpère never flinched. A vase in the corner shattered. I saw where a book was hit.

"Idiot!" Gisela screamed. "I want him alive."

In a fury, Niklas darted away, using the desk as a shield. He scuttled past me and took cover behind the large table in the center of the room. He dropped to one knee, raised the pistol again, this time clasping it in both hands as he took careful aim.

"No, Niklas!" Gisela was on her feet, bringing the pouch up so it was pointed straight at him. There was this soft WHOOSH! of air. Niklas's hands were knocked straight up in the air. BLAM! BLAM! BLAM! BLAM! Four steel-jacketed bullets plowed into the chandelier directly over his head. Shards of glass exploded, spraying the room. I felt something sting my arm. The guards and the doctor screamed and fell to their knees, throwing their arms across their faces. BLAM! BLAM! Two more rounds went off before Niklas could release the trigger. The second bullet smashed directly into the chain that held the crystal chandelier suspended from the high ceiling.

There was a sharp snapping sound as the chain broke, releasing its burden of several hundred pounds of cut-glass crystal. Niklas barely had time to throw his hands over his head as it crashed down upon him. I saw the center shaft of the fixture hit him a glancing blow on the back of his skull, felling him like a lumberjack's ax. The bulk of the chandelier hit the table with a tremendous crash. Wood splintered. Two of the table legs collapsed. Glass sprayed out in every direction. Then the entire thing went down on top of Niklas with a deafening crash that shook the whole room.

With a cry of anguish, Gisela was up and running around her desk. Totally oblivious to the glass shards littering the floor, she dropped to her knees, grasped Niklas by his coat, and dragged him from beneath the shattered table and chandelier. It was done roughly, but Niklas didn't move. He didn't make a sound. She dropped to her knees and lifted his head and cradled it in her lap. "I'm sorry, Nikky. I'm sorry. I'm sorry."

She looked up as the doctor ran to join her. "Please, Lady von Dietz. Stand back. Let me look at him."

As she got to her feet, I saw that her skirt had a large circle of fresh blood on it just below her waist.

The rest of us were in shock. Everything had happened so fast, there had hardly been time for it to register. I was trembling. Even Doc and Jean-Claude had gone ashen. Grandpère came forward to where Jean-Claude's pistol lay on the floor. He picked it up and pointed it at the two men. "Get over there in the corner." He raised his head, looking at the other guards. "The rest of you too. In the corner."

As Grandpère started forward, I raced to his side. He still had his pistol pointed at the six or seven men moving toward the far corner of the room. "How did you get here?" I cried.

He smiled. "I came by car, with a short detour through the river."

"Oh, Grandpère. I'm so glad to see you."

"And I you, my dearest one." He looked around the room. "It looks as though you've been in a spot of trouble here." Before I could answer, he took my arm and steered me forward, toward where the doctor had Niklas on his side and was examining the back of his head. "There are things we need to attend to," Grandpère whispered, "and then we shall talk."

"Niklas has the keys to the handcuffs," I whispered back. "We need to get those first."

As we approached the two figures on the floor, Gisela, clearly in shock, jumped in front of us. "Don't touch him!" she screamed.

Grandpère ignored her. He reached into Niklas's pocket, extracted a set of keys, and unlocked my handcuffs. As I took the keys over to free Rick, Grandpère said, "Rick, get one of the rifles and cover those men in the corner. Shoot the first one who moves." He turned back to Niklas and the doctor and asked, "How is he?"

The doctor glanced up, then went back to work. He had a pair of what looked like oversized tweezers. He was carefully removing pieces of glass from the back of Niklas's head, which was a mass of blood. I had to look away as I felt my stomach lurch.

"He's got a bad laceration. He'll need stitches and he's probably got a severe concussion. The metal shaft hit him pretty hard."

"Did it fracture his skull?" Grandpère asked.

"I can't feel anything, but we'll need an X-ray to be sure." He took a deep breath. "Do I have your permission to move him down to the infirmary where I can treat him properly?"

"Of course."

"I'm going with you," Gisela said as the doctor motioned for two of the guards to help him.

"Ah, no," Grandpère answered. "Not quite yet, Lady Gisela. We have some things to work out here."

"No, I won't leave my son."

Looking down at the doctor again, Grandpère asked, "Is Niklas in any danger of dying?"

He looked up, shaking his head. "No. He needs treatment, Lady von Dietz, but he will be fine. I'll see to it."

I was watching her face closely. Between the swollen nose, the blackening eyes, and the piercing grief, she barely resembled the lovely and gracious woman we had met some weeks before at Le Petit Château. My own head was pounding like crazy, and I wondered if my eyes were going to go black and blue too.

"We will be done with it now," I spoke up, marveling even as I said it.

"Yes," Grandpère said. "It is time."

"Lady Gisela, you and I shall see this through. I want Grandpère and Rick to be with me. You may choose two to be with you. Everyone else is to leave the room."

She was shaking her head before I even finished. "Not your grandfather. I will not have him in the same room with me."

"No," I started, "he stays or—"

Grandpère turned to me. "No, *ma chérie*. Gisela is right. This is not my battle. This is to determine who will be keeper of the pouch, and that is no longer my decision."

"No, Grandpère!" I was stricken. "You can't go."

"Don't let him go, Danni!" Rick shouted inside my head.

But Grandpère went on. "I would ask only for a brief consultation with my granddaughter before I take my leave."

"Ha!" Gisela snorted. "Do you take me for a fool? I know what you'll do. You'll teach her how to defeat me. You will show her how to trick me."

"I give you my word that I shall not counsel Danni on what she must do. As I say, this is Danni's task now, and I will not—in reality, I *cannot*—interfere."

Gisela's eyes, already nearly swollen shut, narrowed even more as she studied his face.

"I swear it," he said. "We come from families where our word is as good as our bond. If I give my word, I shall honor it."

That seemed to satisfy her. "Then I choose Raul and Jean-Claude to stay with me."

"If I only get Rick," I said quickly, "then you get only one also."

"Then I choose Raul." She smiled grimly at me. "I understand that you affectionately call him Doc."

The thought of that left me feeling slightly sick, but I nodded. Then I had another thought. "Before we begin, you will free my mother from that horrible contraption you have attached to her, even if it is as phony as your wax dummies. And there will be a camera on my family at all times so I can see that they are all right."

It was nice to see that I had surprised her again. She was smoldering, but she finally nodded. Yanking up the phone, she hit two numbers, then spoke briefly in German. Immediately, I saw a woman in a nurse's uniform come into the picture and start unhooking Mom. It gave me great satisfaction to see her start to cry as she rejoined Dad and Cody.

"How long have you been here?" I asked Grandpère.

We stood together, talking quietly. I had my arm through his to make sure he wasn't just a hopeful figment of my imagination. We were standing in the hallway just outside the library. The door, with its two bullet holes in it, was closed behind us.

"Actually, I slipped in a few hours ago," Grandpère said nonchalantly. "I'm not sure what happened, but while I was watching the house from a grove of trees, I saw everyone come pouring out and go chasing after something in the blizzard. It seemed like a good time to slip inside."

A double blessing from Cody's footprints. I told him quickly what had happened.

That seemed to please him. "So," he said, with a wry smile, "in spite of all your weepings and wailings, *Le Gardien* hasn't abandoned you."

"No. Gratefully. And it's been working with Cody and Rick, too.

It's actually been quite amazing." Then I cocked my head. "Why didn't you come earlier?"

"Our time is short, my dear. Is that really what you want to know?"

"I . . . no. I . . . why won't you stay with me?"

"Ah, *ma chérie,* that is not possible."

"You can't leave me. I need you. I can't do it. Not after all that's happened."

He smiled and laid a hand on my cheek. "Are you referring to all the foolish choices you have made in these past few weeks?"

"Yes!"

"Including alienating your best and most trusted friend to the point where his only option was to return home until you came to your senses?"

I looked away. "Yes," I whispered.

"So you were being a real . . ." He left it hanging.

"A real brat. Yes! I was stupid and selfish and . . . and. . . ." He put a finger to my lips. I stopped, seeing the look in his eye. He was teasing me again.

"Carruthers," he said, as sober as I had ever seen him. "We don't have much time, and you are about to face the most difficult challenge of your life. Make no mistake. This is not over. Everything still hangs in jeopardy. So I need you to listen and to listen carefully."

"Are you going to tell me what to do?"

He shook his head. "I gave my word. I cannot."

I had expected nothing less. "Go on," I murmured.

"You asked me the other day why *Le Gardien* did not warn us about Gisela and Niklas."

"Not *us.* I know why it didn't warn me. But why didn't *you* feel anything, Grandpère? Didn't you have any premonitions about Juliette?"

"No. But I never liked Philippe. He was an unsufferable prig."

"I know," I said. "I felt the same way. But nothing on Juliette or Gisela?"

"Not until our conversation about Dunkirk in the car."

"Why is that? Why didn't *Le Gardien* warn you?"

He took both of my hands in his and squeezed them softly. "Danni, let me say it again. The Guardian is like a wise tutor whose purpose is to prepare a child for adulthood. But once we reach adulthood, he must step back. It would go counter to the tutor's core purpose if he solved every problem, turned aside every danger, answered every question, softened every blow that life sends our way."

I was nodding. At last I understood what he had been trying to say all this time. "So, basically, we're on our own."

"*Au contraire,*" he said quickly. "*Le Gardien* is still there, but he no longer treats you as he did when you were a child."

"Okay. I get that, but can't you come back long enough to help me get the pouch back?"

He shook his head. "I have given my word. Also, it goes against the proper order of things."

I turned away in despair. That was not what I wanted to hear.

He grabbed my shoulder and turned me back around again. "Listen to me, Carruthers. *Le Gardien* is but a tangible object designed to help you find your way. The power is not in the pouch, it is in you, as long as you strive to live your life in harmony with the Four Remembers. The pouch is not enchanted. It is not magic. Not in the way people use those terms. But it can be a tremendous aid to us as it helps us draw on our own powers, our own strengths."

I was staring at him in wonder. He had never put it so clearly before. "But what about all those miraculous things it does? Like a toy pistol that fires real bullets. Like making gold bars out of nothing. Like making Niklas violently sick when he tried to kiss me."

"Maybe it was just kissing you that made him sick," he said, absolutely straight-faced.

I slugged him. "You know what I'm saying."

He leaned in, very earnest now. "Danni, you must go back in there. I will stay close by, but I cannot interfere. So there are a couple of things you must know. First, Clay is not over at the real *Schloss* von

Dietz as Gisela believes. He was, but when you called him and got me, that allowed him to trace my phone. They now have the whole villa surrounded."

I gaped at him. "Really? Then tell him to get in here. Gisela and Niklas plan to leave tonight."

Grandpère just looked at me. And then I understood why he wasn't going to. "He won't, will he? Not as long as our family is here."

"That's right. We're not sure how many armed men they have, but enough to make things really ugly. So he can't risk having an open gun battle. We have reason to believe there may also be explosives in the villa. So you and Rick have to convince Gisela and Niklas to leave tonight. Convince them that leaving is the best thing for them. And without the family. Can you do that?"

"I . . . I don't know. Why let them go? Maybe Rick and I can free the family and—" I stopped, knowing how unlikely that would be.

"If they disappear, they will leave a lot of unanswered questions. Clay and Interpol want to nail them not just for what they have done to our family, but for all the others. So they need to believe they have gotten away clean."

"I understand."

"Do you? Do you understand what it is we're asking of you and Rick?"

"Of course. It's not going to be easy to convince them to leave all of us behind."

He reached out and touched my hand. "Especially you and Rick."

For a moment, it didn't register, then my jaw dropped. "Do you mean . . . ?"

"Yes. They will take hostages to make sure they are not stopped. If they take all of you, it greatly complicates things for them and for us." He took a quick breath. "This has been heavily debated, Danni. Clay took it to Joel Jamison, who took it to the Director of the FBI. Under any other circumstances, it would never have been considered. But you're not just any two hostages. What you did with El Cobra's gang is still the talk of the FBI." His shoulders lifted and fell. "Actually, I'm the one who suggested it."

By now I was reeling, and yet one part of my mind knew that it was the right thing to do. It made sense, even though the thought sickened me.

He went on quietly. "The whole thing with Niklas gave me a chance to slip into the room where they're keeping your parents." He reached in his jacket pocket and extracted a key card. "Someone left it lying around," he grinned. "I explained all of this, and I told your mother and father that without their consent, it wasn't going to happen."

"And Mom agreed to it?"

"She knows what you are, Danni. After I explained it all, she closed her eyes for a few seconds, then she looked at me and said, 'Danni and Rick can do it.'"

"She called me 'Danni'? Not Carruthers?"

He laughed. "Yes."

"Then I'll do it."

"You and Rick are together for a reason right now, and it's not just because you're friends. It is going to take both of you to do this."

"I understand."

"I know you two are communicating with each other silently. As soon as you get back in there, tell him what we've said. If he has any hesitation, then—"

"He won't. You know he won't."

"I know." He put his arms around me and drew me in close. "I have searched my heart on this, *ma chérie*. If I felt you were in mortal danger, I wouldn't ask this of you. Not ever."

"I know," I murmured. "And knowing you feel it is all right, makes it all right." I took a quick breath. "Okay, we'll do it. Just tell me how we convince Niklas and Gisela."

"I have no idea. It's not for me to work out. But I think we can safely assume that Niklas and Gisela will dump the two of you as quickly as possible."

"Dump us? Oh, that's cheerful."

"You know what I mean. They are not going to harm you. We are absolutely certain of that, or none of us would be consenting to this."

"So what if they get away scot-free after all they've done?" I grumbled. That thought was bumming me out. I still felt this deep anger and the desire to put an end to the both of them.

"What if I told you that the FBI has asked Louis and me to help bring them to justice?"

"Really? Does that mean you're agents too?"

"Oh, no. We're what they officially call paid FBI consultants." He smiled. "Louis and his security team bring a lot to the table here. Clay's delighted to have them. And incidentally, you and Rick are consultants too, starting tonight."

"Shut up!" I cried. "Really? Me? An FBI consultant?" Then I grinned. "That'll look good on my application for college. Right?"

He laughed. "Probably. But right now we have to focus on tonight. I can't tell you how to make this all work because I don't know. But here is what Clay said you need to do."

I went quiet and focused my full attention on him now.

"Your job," he said, "is to make sure that Gisela and Niklas do *not* get away with all they have done. But at the same time, you have to make them *think* that they have."

My stomach did a quick flip-flop. "Oh," I said, forcing a laugh. "Is that all?"

He straightened. "It's time, Danni. I can't be in there, but I'll be right out here waiting."

He bent down, kissed me on the forehead, and then opened the door and gave me a little push back into the library.

PART TEN

Fool's Gold

CHAPTER 38

To my surprise, the only ones in the room were Doc and Rick. Rick was still in his chair and still holding a rifle on Doc. A few yards to his left, Doc sulked in a chair he had rescued from the shattered table. As I entered, Rick looked up. "Lady Gisela went to the infirmary to check on Niklas. She will be another few minutes."

I bobbed my head to acknowledge that I had heard him, then went over and sat down beside Rick. "No talking," Doc growled.

"Who left you in charge?" I snapped. "From this point on, you are here as an observer only."

He didn't like that and scowled at me with his hard, glittering eyes. I ignored him. Unarmed, he was not much more than background noise. Turning to the TV monitor behind Gisela's desk, I saw that Mom was on the couch with Dad. His arm was around her, and they were talking quietly. Cody was at a table playing some kind of board game with himself. It was a huge relief to see them looking pretty normal.

"Cody?" I called out to him in my mind, but there was no reaction from him on screen. Perhaps where they now were in the castle was too far away to make a connection.

Glancing up at the screen, Rick spoke to me in our mind-talk. "I've been trying to raise him too. No luck."

"He's all right. They're all okay."

"Yeah, I know. I heard everything you and Grandpère were saying."

"You did? Cool? That saves me a lot of explaining."

"I'm in," he said quietly.

I wanted to reach over and hug him, but I restrained myself. "I know. If you weren't, I wouldn't be either."

"So what do we do, Danni?"

"I'm not sure. Maybe just close our eyes and hang on."

He chuckled. "We seem to do that a lot anymore."

"Amen to that." I took the pouch off my shoulder and started to unbutton the flap. Doc was instantly leaning forward. "What are you doing?"

"Relax, Dude!" I snapped back at him, as Rick steadied the rifle. "This is not the real pouch, all right?" I held it open so he could see inside it. "Lady Gisela wrote me a letter. Since it involves Rick, he needs to read it. So just relax until your mistress comes back and tells her lap dog what to do." Without waiting for his response, I handed the letter across to Rick.

"Read it," I said. And with that, I got to my feet, turned my back on Doc, and strode over to the fireplace. "Hey," he said. "You can't do that."

"Oh, yeah." Without hesitation, I pulled the pouch off my shoulder as I approached the fire and tossed it into the flames when I reached it. "There," I said. "Now you have nothing to worry about. Nothing except me."

———

We sat quietly as Rick read the letter. He gave me a long, searching look when he finished, then read it again. Finally, he handed it back to me. I folded it together and tossed it on the desk. "Well, now we know what we're up against," he said, speaking in my head.

I drew in a deep breath, then let it out slowly. "Rick, I have something I want to say before Gisela returns."

"I hate it when you say that."

"Say what?"

"That you have something that you want to say."

"I never say that."

"Except when you have something you want to say."

Laughing softly, I nodded at him. How did he sense that I needed even the tiniest bit of light in this otherwise dark and grim day? "Okay. I want to talk about New York."

"Nuh-uh," he shot right back. "That's ancient history now."

"I take that back. I want to talk about what I *learned* in New York."

"Okay, that is relevant."

"I have decided that the underlying problem—the root problem, as it were—is that I get so caught up in myself that I start unconsciously thinking of you as kind of a supportive spectator, like you were my own personal cheering section. I love having you around. And I trust your judgment so much. But then I keep taking center stage, leaving you in the audience to applaud when I do something right."

He finally looked directly at me and smiled. "Or to boo when you don't."

I didn't laugh. I didn't smile. "I wish you would boo, but you're too nice, Rick. You're too kind and gentle and . . . cool. You are seriously cool." I could feel a lump welling up in my throat, so I hurried on. "That has to change."

"You mean you have to change, or me being seriously cool has to change?" When I looked at him, he held up a hand. "Sorry. I'm listening."

"I don't want to be Danni Oakley any more with you, Rick. Or Catnips Overdone."

He chuckled. "Good one, Danni. You should have used that on Cierra."

"I'm always great at the perfect comeback, as long as I have about two weeks to find one." Quick breath. "But anyway, what I'm trying to say is that I want us to be full partners with equal standing in this relationship. Like a lock and key—they're totally different, but when they work together you get something you cannot get with them separately. You bring so much to our friendship, and I've been an idiot not to recognize that and accept it."

"Danni, I have never thought of you as an idiot."

"That is very kind of you to say that, Rick. Even if it is a bald-faced lie." I raised my hand quickly as he started to respond. "But that's not what I want to say. What I want to say is . . . I mean, I guess what I'm saying is . . ." I stopped again. He was watching me, patient as ever. Unlike me, not finishing my sentences for me.

"At the press conference, Mom said that you were our rock in the middle of the river. Always there. Always letting things just kind of flow around you."

"I remember."

"You know that you're her favorite child," I grumped.

He smiled. "Hardly."

"Rick, will you promise me something?"

"Of course. Name it."

"Don't ever leave me. Even when I'm acting stupid and selfish and insensitive and . . ."

"I won't," he cut in firmly. "Not ever."

My eyebrows lifted. "Ever is a long time, Rick."

"I know," he murmured. "That's what I like about it."

Oh my goodness. How I wanted to explore that further. Just what was he saying? Was this the usual talk about *forever* you heard kids use? But as I watched his eyes, I think I saw what I was hoping to see. He meant it exactly as I hoped he meant it. And suddenly I was tingling with this little current of electricity zinging around in my head.

Finally, he straightened, and the moment was gone. "So, did you and Grandpère come up with a plan on how to deal with Gisela that I didn't hear?" he asked.

I shook my head. "He said he couldn't help me. It was against the natural order of things, whatever that means. So I think it's up to you and me."

"So what do you want me to do?"

I pulled a face. "How about beating the heck out of Gisela—*heck* being the Utah version of the operative word—then throw her at my feet and let me take it from there."

He laughed aloud, startling Doc. I turned to look at this sour-faced enemy of mine. "He's like that when he's under stress," I explained. "He tells himself jokes to relieve the pressure."

"Who cares," Doc growled, raising the back of his hand as if he was going to cuff me.

"Danni?"

"Yes?"

"I want to say something too, something I've been thinking about a lot. But I don't want to make you mad."

"*Moi?*" I said. "Me get mad? I can't believe you said that."

He chuckled. "Right. Anyway—" I saw his shoulders lift and fall.

"Just spit it out. I'm a big girl now."

"All right, I will. I understand why you feel so much anger toward Gisela, but—"

"I know, I know. I've got to keep my cool or she wins, right?"

"No," he said. "That goes without saying."

"Sorry. That's another bad habit I have to break, finishing people's sentences for them."

He didn't comment either way on that. "Earlier I was thinking about what Louis told us. About Gisela and her mother losing everything, being torn from a life of pampered luxury and thrown out into the streets in the middle of a war zone. Losing her brother. What was she again? Four years old?"

I nodded, starting to feel my temper rise.

"And then to be forced to leave your homeland, to live in poverty, to see your mother, once the toast of society, become a household servant. I can't begin to conceive what kind of scars that must have left on these two women."

509

I was incredulous. "Hold it. Are you going soft on her? After all she's done to my family?"

"Of course not. When you have a rabid dog coming at you, you do whatever it takes to protect yourself. But you don't hate the dog because it's sick."

I was trying not to kick back at this. What was he trying to say to me? But I wasn't named Carruthers for nothing. With my voice crackling with indignation, I said, "You're talking about the woman who convinced me that she had killed every single member of my family, right? This is the woman who made me discover my own dead body? A mad dog doesn't know what it's doing, Rick, but Gisela did. She is cold, calculating, and utterly without mercy. And if we show the tiniest spark of weakness, she will eat us alive, and sleep well when she's done."

I had to stop and catch my breath, even though this conversation was only going on in our minds. "We have to stop her. We have to destroy her before she destroys us. We can't let her destroy the lives of any other people. And to do that, I'm going to have to hold on to my anger and my hatred for her for just a bit longer. If you find that distasteful, then so be it. Maybe it's better if you stand back and watch for the next while."

"Okay," he said very softly. "I'll just take my seat over here in the spectator section. Call me if you need me."

I dropped my head in my hands as his words struck me like a blow. I had done it again. Within minutes of telling him I had changed, I was right back at it again. Scalding tears spilled out and trickled down my cheeks. Shame was like a hot wind, parching my soul. "Oh, Rick," I cried. "I am lost. I am lost."

He got to his feet, causing Doc to jump up. With a warning look and a wave of the pistol, he motioned for Doc to sit down again. Then he came over to me and laid a hand on my shoulder. But I couldn't bear to look up at him. I couldn't. So he bent down and said five simple words. "Ever is a long time." His hand brushed at the tears for a moment, then he spoke five more. "I meant what I said." Then he went and sat down again.

When Gisela strode into the room a minute or so later, the pouch on her shoulder, her face grotesquely disfigured, still wearing her blood-spattered blouse and the skirt with the large bloodstain on the front, I sensed instantly that something had changed. Wiping at my cheeks with the back of my hand, I straightened and sat back. I saw that Rick's eyes were fixed on her too.

"How is Niklas?" Doc asked.

Her mouth pinched into a grim line. "Niklas is paralyzed from the waist down. The doctor thinks that he will never walk again."

One hand flew to my mouth. "Oh, Gisela," I cried. "I'm so sorry." And to my surprise, I really was. I wouldn't wish that on anyone.

She stopped in midstride and stared at me, as if she had no idea who I was or where I had come from. Then she spat out her words in a low hiss. "You will not speak his name again in my presence. If you do, you will die. That I swear."

Far off in my mind, I heard Rick's voice. "Be careful, Danni. This changes everything."

She moved around the desk and took her place on her throne/chair. Doc moved around to stand beside her. She glared at me for several seconds, then took *Le Gardien* from her shoulder and laid it on the desk in front of her. She then opened another drawer and took out the dictation device again. She turned it on, laid it on the desk, and pushed it toward me. "You have one hour. If I am not satisfied with what you give me, all of your family is lost."

I sat there, rigid as a stone, wondering what to say to that. I knew without any doubt that there was nothing I could do to give her control of the pouch. And I was just as certain that the pouch was not going to accept her as its new keeper.

She eyed me suspiciously for several moments, then spoke. "I have carefully studied all that you wrote in your journal about the pouch. I have also read what El Cobra had to say about it several times. So let's skip all of the general stuff. Get right to how you make it work. Do I have to actually be holding the pouch to make it work?"

"No."

She smiled. "That's better. If I find you are being dishonest or withholding truth from me, it will not go well with you."

"I meant, 'No, I can't help you.'" Suddenly I heard Rick's voice echoing in my head. "You have to stop a sick dog, but don't hate it because it's sick."

And those simple words opened a floodgate of understanding. "Lady Gisela, I cannot help you. No matter what you do to me, the pouch will not accept you as its keeper."

Color darkened her face, and little drops of spittle formed at the corners of her mouth.

I rushed on. "But I have another offer for you. One that you may find even more attractive than the pouch."

Rick stiffened. In my head, I heard him say, "Danni, what are you saying? What can you offer her that she'll accept?"

Some tiny portion of my words seemed to have gotten through to her, for she was studying me closely now, searching for any signs of betrayal. So I plunged. "Out of the bleachers, Rick. I need you right here beside me."

"I'm here," came the instant answer. And he actually got up and came over to stand beside me, again laying a hand on my shoulder. Doc tensed but then quickly relaxed again.

"Lady Gisela, what if I could promise you that your son will not be paralyzed. What if I could tell you that from this very day he will begin to get the feeling back into his legs?"

She fell back in her chair, her eyes wide with wonder. "You can do that?"

"No, I can't. But the pouch is telling me it will be so if you will but listen to me."

For almost a full minute, those hooded, smoldering eyes took my measure. Finally she said, "Go on."

But Rick spoke in my head first. "I'm here. Can I say something to her?"

"This is an equal partnership, my friend," I said. "You don't have to ask."

He sat forward. "Lady Gisela, will you permit me to suggest a couple of things—"

She turned on him angrily. "You are here as an observer only, Mr. Ramirez. If you speak again, I will have you removed."

I started to protest. Rick beat me to it. "Oh, I am much more than that." And with that, he pointed at the pouch with one hand, his fingers splayed out like a magician's. When the pouch lurched forward several inches, I gasped. So did Gisela. Doc actually fell back a step.

"Touch the pouch, Lady Gisela," Rick commanded.

Gingerly, she reached out and touched it with one finger. Her eyes widened. "It's warm."

"It is warm because I told it to be warm," he intoned solemnly.

"Is that true?" I asked, not sure whether to laugh or to be spooked.

"Don't bother me right now, missy," he said, chuckling, "I'm working here."

"So *you* have the power to use the pouch?" Gisela asked, new respect evident in her eyes.

"Do you have to ask?" he said, waving his hand again. The pouch lurched forward another few inches.

"Holy cow, Ramirez," I cried. "When did you learn to do that?"

"About ten seconds ago, actually." Then, aloud, he added, "Now may I speak?"

Still very wary, Gisela nodded.

"Surely you know that the FBI and Interpol are closing in on you. Your time is over. Your crimes have come to an end. You yourself said that you would be leaving tonight. I think you assumed that you would be leaving with the pouch. But as you can now see, that isn't going to happen. So we have something that will compensate you for your loss."

"We do?" I said in my mind, rocking back.

"Yes, we do."

"What?"

He grinned at me. "I have no idea, partner. Your turn. It's time, Danni. Do it!" And then, to my utter amazement, he leaned forward and laid the pistol on the table. As he sat down again, Doc snatched it up and pointed at both of us.

"Why did you do that?" I cried silently.

"Because that way will get us nowhere."

I wanted to scream at him that while that might be true, it did give us some measure of control in this situation. But I got ahold of myself and asked, "Do what? What am I supposed to do?"

"Whatever Grandpère told you to do."

I sat back, my mind a whirl, trying to remember. And then it came. *Your task is to convince Gisela and Niklas to leave tonight. Not* make *them leave. Convince them that leaving is the best thing for them.* And this was followed quickly with, *Gisela and her son will not get away with all they have done. But it is very important that they think they have.*

But how? And that answer came from Rick as he spoke again to me. "What are they going to need most if they go into hiding?"

That was easy. Protection. Anonymity. My head came up. No, they needed money! Buying a completely new and comfortable life takes money. Lots of money.

"Yes!" Rick cried. "So give it to them."

"I . . ." I was suddenly confused. How did I—and then I laughed right out loud. That startled Gisela and Doc. They stared at me like I had lost my mind.

I laughed again. Oh, I was going to lose much more than that tonight.

Leaning in, I asked one question of her. "Since you have read my journal and El Cobra's report, tell me, Lady Gisela, what was it that sank the boat El Cobra was using to get away? You and I both know it wasn't swamped by another boat."

I could tell from her eyes that she instantly knew what I was referring to. She tried to hide it, pretending nonchalance, but the greed was unmistakable. After a moment, she said, "You cannot offer what you do not have. Niklas sent someone to watch. They saw the FBI diving team at the site. They saw them bringing up the gold." She almost spat at me in disgust. "Do not play me for the fool, Danni."

"Whatever else I may think of you, Lady Gisela," I said, "I have never thought of you as a fool."

"I don't need some old pouch to destroy you," she growled. Her answer was completely off topic, as if I hadn't even spoken.

Which chapped me no end. "Sorry, Gisela, but your record in trying to use the pouch against me or Rick is less than sterling. In a word, you just got your butt whipped."

She whirled and faced Doc. "I will not sit here and be lectured to like some misbehaving child, especially by this piece of American trash. I will not let her set the conditions of what happens next." She picked up the pouch and held it to her. "And I will not let her sit there and try to intimidate me. Now, Raul, either you put a stop to this, or I will."

Raul raised the pistol until it was pointed at my heart. "Danni, you will speak to Lady Gisela with courtesy and respect. You will refer to her as Lady Gisela or Madame Gisela or Lady von Dietz, or you will not speak to her at all. Any more of your caustic comments, and this conversation will terminate. Do you understand me?"

"He's right, Danni," Rick said, speaking aloud. "Danni apologizes, Lady Gisela. She is very sorry."

"It means nothing coming from you, Mr. Ramirez, though I appreciate that your words and demeanor are those of a gentleman. It is she who must apologize."

I will not apologize to this woman after all she has done to me and my family. I will not.

"Yes," Rick said, now back in my head, "you will, or we will lose.

Remember that old saying, 'Hell hath no fury like a woman scorned.' Well, if you scorn her further, she will fight you to her dying breath. And we're running out of time, Danni."

The old temper flared up and I swung on him. "Don't you . . ." I stopped, fuming. I had planned to say, "Don't you lecture me," but I knew he was right, so I bit off my retort and looked at Gisela. "Rick is right," I said meekly. "I apologize for speaking to you in a disrespectful manner, Lady Gisela. I will not do so again."

"You had better not," she said, still seething.

Then I swung on Doc. "But this works both ways, Raul. So you tell Lady Gisela that the next time she calls me American trash, or treats me like I am six years old, all bets are off and it's open season between us."

"Fair enough," he said with a nod. He looked at her. "She's right, Madame Gisela. Your verbal swordplay does nothing for us."

Frowning, she looked away. Raul looked nervous, evidently wondering if he had gone too far. Then, surprising us both, Gisela got to her feet, leaned over the desk and picked up *Le Gardien,* and started to walk away. "Madame Gisela," Raul said, "where are you going?"

I was totally alert now. *Where* was *she going?* Now that she had the pouch, was she going after my family again? But, even as that thought came, I realized that she was not headed for the door. Not the main door, nor either of the side doors. When it finally dawned on me where she was going, I leaped up. "No!" I shouted.

But I was too late. She lunged toward the fireplace and flung *Le Gardien* into the flames. Then, quick as a cat, she picked up the large iron poker and held it up like a sword, prepared to fend me off. But my eyes were not on her. My gaze was riveted on the pouch. New logs had not been put on the fire for some time now, so the fireplace was a glowing bed of red-hot coals. In an instant, there was a soft puff of smoke, and the fabric burst into flames. I stopped, too shocked to go further. In moments, the whole pouch was aflame. I saw the braided rope handle just kind of melt away. Then, a tiny explosion of flame within the flames popped as the hand-carved wooden button caught fire.

I turned away, unable to watch, and moved slowly back to my seat. Rick came to me and took me in his arms. "Remember what Grandpère said. It's only a tangible sign of an inner power," he soothed. "The power cannot be destroyed."

I jerked free of him. "That pouch has been in my family for over two hundred years, Rick. It was much more than a piece of cloth you hold in your hands."

He was instantly stricken. "I know, Danni. I'm sorry."

I watched as Gisela sat back down again, her face radiant with triumph. I saw that Raul was a little shocked by what had just happened, but since she had just eliminated what he saw as a problem, he said nothing. "Okay," she sneered. "Now we can talk."

My answer to that came out quite calmly. "You just lost the right to have the title of 'Lady' connected to you in any way, so like it or not, from now on it's Gisela, or Lady Witch."

She just laughed. Then a mysterious, catlike smile spread across her face. "Now, Danni McAllister, see if you can convince me that when you speak of gold, you indeed have something tangible to offer to us."

Just that quickly, my anger was pushed back. I smiled with genuine pleasure, knowing that I could answer that with complete honesty. "I give you my word, Lady Gisela. We do indeed have much that is tangible to offer to you in exchange for the safety of my family."

CHAPTER 39

We sat there for a moment, two great cats in the same cage, circling each other, looking for any sign of weakness. That was interrupted when the phone on the desk rang. She snatched it up. *"Ja,"* she said. Then she came straight up out of her chair. "What?" Her eyes widened, even though they were now just dark slits in her swollen face. "I'll be right there."

She spun around to Doc. "Watch them, Raul. Don't let them move. Don't let them talk. I'll be back in five minutes." And with that she raced out through the main door of the library.

With a gun back in his hand, Doc was all swagger and dominance again. He glared at us, waving the pistol. "You heard her. Don't tempt me."

I leaned forward, staring at the floor. "Rick?"

"Yeah?"

"I was thinking. Maybe we ought to use this time to think and decide what's next?"

Though I didn't look up at him, I sensed he was laughing. "Way to be in tune, Danni. I was just thinking exactly the same thing."

"Then I'll shut up and give you some quiet time."

———

Gisela was gone a full ten minutes, but when she came back in, she shocked us all. She was wheeling Niklas in a wheelchair. His head was wrapped in gauze, and I could see where blood had dripped on his shirt collar, but his eyes were open and surveying us as she wheeled him toward us. Doc was as stunned as we were. "Lord von Dietz?" He said something in French that I think was a profane exclamation of surprise.

Niklas managed a wan grin. "Hello again, Raul." He looked at us. "I understand you have been busy in my absence."

Wheeling him around the desk, Gisela brought him up alongside her chair and locked the wheels. Only then did she look at us. And her eyes were filled with wonder.

"This is a surprise," I said, risking the wrath of Raul. "You don't look like a man with a skull fracture."

He actually smiled. "Only a mild concussion and a blistering headache. Dr. Bauer is actually quite astonished."

"What about the paralysis?"

"None. I'm a little light-headed and wobbly on my feet, but he thinks it was just temporary numbness caused by the blow to the brain."

"He can walk," Gisela said, her voice husky. "Dr. Bauer gave him a cane to steady him, but he can walk."

She stopped short of actually thanking us, I noticed, but I could tell that she had linked the stunning development with what I had promised earlier. And why not? It was astonishing to see him up and moving.

Niklas cleared his throat. "I understand you were in the process of making a proposal to Mama."

"Yes. And it looks like we have fulfilled the first part of that proposal."

He inclined his head slightly, but made no other acknowledgment. "Your second proposal will be a little more difficult to sell."

"I understand, but we are confident we can do so. Before we do, however, we need to clarify a couple of things. First, I hope you remember that what is given by the pouch can be taken away again. Which includes full body paralysis."

That hadn't come as an inspired thought. In other words, I didn't think I was speaking for *Le Gardien*. It was simply the worst possible threat I could think of to throw at him. But it worked. He blanched. "I . . . I understand."

"Okay. Second thing. We need to know if you really are going to disappear when you leave here in a few hours. Or is this just a change of venue and it will be business as usual? In a word, does this end it between us?"

"Absolutely," Niklas said.

Gisela nodded vigorously. "It is true. All the arrangements are made. New identities. New country of residence. New bank accounts."

"Plastic surgery to give us new faces," Niklas added. "We will simply disappear, and you will never see or hear from us again."

"That must have cost a lot of money," Rick observed.

Surprised a little, Niklas finally nodded. "Substantial funds were required."

"Do you still have the seven or eight million Euros you stole in rhodium ore from us?" Rick asked. "The FBI traced it to the Russian Mafia. They even got the price that was paid."

"That's none of your business," Gisela cried.

Niklas ignored her. After a moment, he nodded. "Yes, most of it."

"And how much do you still have from your various kidnapping and extortion escapades?"

Again Gisela balked; again Niklas didn't hesitate. "A little less than two million."

"Thank you for not lying about that," I came in. "The pouch confirms to me that you are telling me the truth." I felt a little twinge of guilt as I saw the startled look in his eyes. I believed that Niklas was being honest, but I certainly didn't have what I would call a confirmation of that.

Rick picked up the conversation again, and I marveled. It was like we had rehearsed exactly how to do this. "So," he said, "you have about nine million Euros in the bank?"

"Give or take a few hundred thousand," Niklas agreed.

"And how much cash and stock in Von Dietz Global do you own between you?"

Gisela was seething. "What has this got to do with our deal? This is none of your business."

Niklas stood by her on this one. "From the beginning, we all agreed—including my grandmother—that we would not touch a penny of our Von Dietz holdings for these actions. It would put the whole company at risk, which has been in our family for generations."

"Fine. We are just trying to assess how much value our deal holds for you. If your assets are about nine million, then we ask this question. How would you like to triple that amount?"

Niklas's head snapped up so fast it made him wince. Pain flickered across his face. Gisela didn't react at all. She turned to her son. "They're talking about the gold."

"Yes, we are," I said. "Forty-two bars, or about thirty million dollars' worth." That wasn't precisely true—Clay had brought up two of the bars, but what the hay? What were a couple of bars of gold between business partners?

Rick again. "And this comes to you tax free, with virtually no risk to you, with very little out-of-pocket cost to obtain it, and with no chance that it can ever be traced back to you."

"Assuming it is yours to offer, which is highly unlikely, why would you give it to us?" Niklas asked. But the hunger in his eyes was unmistakable.

"Because to get it, you have to agree that these funds will never be used to harm us or retaliate against my family or any of the families that you have been persecuting."

"She's lying," Gisela said. "They would never give it up. Especially after losing twenty million dollars' worth of rhodium."

I knew this was going to be the hardest part of our pitch, so I was ready. "My family is worth more to me than ten tons of gold. I know you find this hard to believe, but we have a good life in little old Hanksville.

We don't need castles and bank accounts and servants running around calling us Lady Gisela or Jolly Old St. Niklas to be happy."

There was a quick flash of anger on Niklas's face, but I hurried on. "If giving you the gold frees my family and gets you out of our lives once and for all, then it is worth every dime of it."

"But it's not yours to give. The FBI has already recovered it."

"That's right," Niklas said. "Once we learned about the gold from El Cobra, we were going to go after it. So I hired a man to scope out the approximate site. He reported that a few days after your escape, an FBI dive team came in and recovered it."

"They brought up two bars," I answered. "That's all. The rest of it is still down there, buried in mud and silt, in about fifty feet of water."

"No way they would leave that down there," Niklas said, shaking his head. "No way."

"You're wrong, and here's why. It makes them very nervous to have thirty million dollars in gold bars sitting around in an evidence locker. Since the gold was generated by the pouch, my family is technically the legal owner of it. Once the case is closed, if no other legitimate owners have come forth, then it all reverts to us."

Rick and I both stopped talking, watching their faces as they looked at each other and digested what we had told them.

Gisela spoke first. "And you're telling us that the FBI is not guarding it right now? That you're not leading us into a trap?"

"If you mean, do they actually have live bodies on site watching it, no. No one except two senior members of the FBI, my family, Rick, El Cobra, and Eileen even know where it sank. Even my journal doesn't tell you that."

Mother and son exchanged quick glances. "She wrote about it," Gisela explained, "but she didn't say exactly where it happened."

I went on, deciding that nothing short of the truth was going to satisfy them. "The FBI set up a hidden, solar-powered video camera in the rocks on the nearest shoreline. The camera is activated by any motion that comes into its field of view. The video feed is then transmitted to the regional office in Salt Lake City."

"And how long would it take them to get a team on site?"

"Between two and three hours by chopper. But you are a couple of smart people. I assume you'll find a way to work around that."

"Do you know where the camera is?"

"Not precisely, but I have a general idea. I don't think it would be hard to find."

"Will the lake be frozen over by now?" Niklas asked.

This was good. These two steel-trap minds were obviously taking us seriously.

"No," Rick said. "Lake Powell is far enough south that only a tiny portion of the northernmost inlets ever freeze. The main lake never does."

"In October," I added, "daytime temperatures are often in the seventies, and at night it's around fifty. You can check that online."

"And what guarantee do you offer that this is not a very clever trap?" Niklas asked. He might have a headache, but his brain was working just fine.

"It's very simple," I said. I looked at Rick, and he nodded. "You take the two of us as hostages. When you recover the gold, leave us behind on the lake. At that time of year, it could take a day or two before someone finds us. By then you'll be out of the country."

They looked at each other. Something unspoken passed between them; then Niklas nodded. "We want one other guarantee."

"What?"

"Your grandfather will be our third hostage."

I hadn't seen that one coming, though I suppose I should have. "I don't know where he is," I stammered.

"Oh," Gisela said with a grim smile, "I think he's not far away."

Rick stood up. "Agreed. If we can find him. But for that, Danni's family will be left here unharmed. The FBI and Interpol will be asked to stay back until dawn this morning, by which time you will be long gone.

And we will neither see nor hear anything from you two ever again. Is that your understanding?"

Mother and son exchanged more glances, then both nodded. Niklas turned and looked up at Raul. "Tell the others. Leave the family locked in their room, but no one—and I mean no one—even goes close to them. We will leave here in three hours. In the meantime, you will handcuff Danni and Rick to their chairs here and keep them under guard until we come back for them."

Raul nodded curtly. "And what about the old man?"

The same side door of the library opened, and Grandpère stepped in. "The old man is right here," he said, baring his wrists as he came forward.

Gisela eyed him with loathing. "Get him something to wear, Niklas," she muttered. "We can't be taking him through airports like that."

CHAPTER 40

The four of us sat on deck chairs on the stern of the houseboat and watched the two approaching watercraft. Grandpère, Rick, and I sat in the shade of the awning. Niklas preferred the afternoon sunshine. Since Europeans rarely saw it in October, I wasn't surprised. Another guard stood like a stone Buddha, his eyes never leaving us.

The fishing boat and the Jet Ski cut their engines to idle and came gliding in toward the beach. Raul was driving the boat and had Jean-Claude and two other guards with him. They had all the paraphernalia of a group of fishermen but were in actuality the diving team. Gisela, wearing a black wet suit, was on the Jet Ski. Her function was to go out into the main channel, well out of the field of view of the camera, and watch for any possible interruption.

Niklas got to his feet with ease. Though it had been only a few days since he was hit with the chandelier, he showed no residual effects. I could still see the glaring white spot on the back of his head where Dr. Bauer had shaved it for the stitches, but that was all. Alvin, who always remained on the boat with us, quickly moved along with Niklas, as he always did.

Of the four other guards who accompanied us, Alvin had the look of being the most professional of the lot, which explained why he was assigned to stay behind and make sure we didn't try anything. He never let us out of his sight. Even when we went inside to go to the bathroom, he followed us in and took up station just outside the bathroom door. I had nicknamed him Alvin because he always wore a red baseball cap tipped way back on his head, like Alvin the chipmunk, and had a round face with puffy cheeks.

Grandpère, Rick, and I didn't get up from our chairs as the boat and Jet Ski gently nosed onto shore. As I watched Gisela dismount and come toward us, I marveled yet again at this seventy-one-year-old-woman. In the sleekness of the neoprene suit, her body was slim enough to cause women forty and fifty years her junior to turn green with envy. Her energy was inexhaustible, and her excitement about their diving expedition was unabashed. Though she still wore oversized sunglasses to hide the ugly bruises around her eyes, the swelling of the battered nose was now all but gone and her natural beauty was almost back to normal. To my pleasant surprise, although I ended up with a noticeable bruise on my forehead from smacking her in the face with my head, my eyes never went black and blue.

"Is that the last of it, Mama?" Niklas called out.

"Not quite. We've got six more bars located, but that still leaves us five short of the forty-two. But one more trip will do it."

Getting up, I walked over to join Niklas at the railing. I leaned on the rail, looking down at her. "Not forty-two," I called to Gisela. "Only forty. Remember? The FBI brought up two bars—one to give to us and one to use as evidence in the trials."

She was instantly suspicious, but Niklas nodded. "That's right, Mama. She did tell us that."

"What's two gold bars among friends?" I chirped.

She didn't think that was funny at all. "At seventeen hundred dollars an ounce, every bar is worth nearly three quarters of a million dollars, so it is not some silly joke."

To an outside observer, exchanges such as this would have quickly revealed that this was not some warm and homey family group out on holiday together. The tension between us was growing each day. But

Grandpère decided to pacify her a little. "I will tell you how to find those other three bars. After Danni and I jumped out of the boat and were on the sandbar, El Cobra and Eileen took off. But by that point, the pouch was producing gold bars so fast, they were afraid the boat was going to swamp. It wasn't, of course, not at that point, but they were in a panic. So they turned the boat around and started coming back toward us, screaming at Danni to make the pouch stop making the gold. Then they started throwing bars of gold overboard."

"How many?" Gisela asked.

"Two for sure, maybe three. Based on your count, it looks like it was three. That took place about fifty to seventy-five yards upstream from where their boat sank."

She was watching him through narrowed eyes. "Are you volunteering to help us find them?"

He nodded. "Anything we can do to get you on your way."

Niklas nodded. "We'll take him and Danni back out with us after lunch. They can show us where they are."

Grandpère nodded. "But of course." Then he turned to Niklas and, in a much softer voice, said, "It was greed that destroyed El Cobra. Be careful you don't make the same mistake."

For several seconds, their eyes locked—Niklas's dark and angry, Grandpère's calm, almost serene. Then Niklas relaxed. "Aren't you forgetting something, old man?" he said. "The pouch is nothing but a pile of ashes now. You don't scare us." He turned and cupped his hands to his mouth. "Raul. Jean-Claude. Get this load of bars onto the houseboat. There are sandwiches and beer on the table. After you get something to eat, refuel both the boat and the Jet Ski. I want you on your way again in no more than twenty minutes. If we're going to be out of here before dark, we need to get this done and start packing up."

—✦—

With our help, Doc and Jean-Claude found the three missing bars in less than half an hour. They had the other six bars in the boat with them in just under another hour after that, and we started back for the houseboat.

I have to admit, this mother-son team ran one slick operation. One of the reasons I had told Gisela and Niklas about the FBI camera was in hopes that they would try to neutralize it somehow and thereby alert the FBI in Salt Lake. We didn't know if Clay was still in Europe heading up the search for us, or if he'd come back. We had no way to contact him, of course.

As it turned out, their solution to the camera problem was very simple and absolutely brilliant. First, they never went near the camera. Second, they made sure the camera saw nothing that would raise suspicion. So Niklas rented a houseboat, one Jet Ski, and one of those aluminum, flat-bottomed boats preferred by fishermen. No speedboat like El Cobra had rented. Nothing out of the ordinary.

Fishing at Lake Powell was good year round, but a lot of the more dedicated fishermen liked the off season the best. The colder waters and the elimination of thousands of watercraft racing back and forth across the surface made for some excellent fishing. So having a group of fishermen, mostly men, hanging around Slick Rock Canyon was nothing out of the ordinary, and I finally had to accept the fact that the FBI wouldn't be coming.

An elated Niklas sensed our dismay and continually reminded us of the motto that drove everything he and Gisela did. "Plan impeccably. Strike boldly. Exit swiftly. And leave nothing to chance. *Nothing!*" And it had worked.

Up to this point, they hadn't taken any of us out to the dive site with them, so I wasn't sure exactly how they were working the actual recovery. Now we had a chance to see it for ourselves. They took me and Grandpère with them and left Rick with Niklas and Alvin. We left in the fishing boat and headed at a leisurely pace back toward the mouth of the canyon. About the time we reached the main channel, Gisela roared past us on the Jet Ski and took up her station out in the main channel to watch for any possible intruders.

Stopping well short of the sandbar—and well out of the field of view of the video camera—we anchored in the deep shade of one of the towering cliffs. The three guards got out their fishing rods and tackle while Raul and Jean-Claude quickly removed their life jackets and clothing to reveal wet suits. They donned scuba gear, grabbed their underwater metal detectors, and slipped over the side, leaving hardly a ripple in the smooth surface of the lake.

We stayed in place until they radioed that they had found what they were looking for. Then the "fishermen" moved down past the sandbar and anchored again. Out came the fishing rods and the beer. Moments later Doc and Jean-Claude came up on the side of the boat opposite the camera. The gold was handed up. When they were finished, the boat started back up the canyon far enough to be out of sight of the camera, where we waited for our two scuba divers to return.

Slick. Professional. Flawless. We were back to the houseboat with the remaining bars before two o'clock.

———

When we had been on the houseboat in Iceberg Canyon back in June, El Cobra had used a simple plan to escape. Disable the houseboat, destroy any ability to communicate with the outside world, then leave everyone but me and Grandpère there while he and the rest of the team disappeared. I knew that couldn't happen this time because they had over a thousand pounds of gold to transport, and only the houseboat could do that. I really believed that they did not plan to harm us, but I was trying to work out in my mind how they would make sure they had time to get away before we could somehow sound the alarm.

Here again, it was so simple that I should have seen it sooner. By the time they got everything packed up and the last of the gold transferred to the houseboat—about three fifteen—the sun was well past its zenith, and Doc and Jean-Claude urged the men on to greater speed. Driving a houseboat on Lake Powell at night could be downright dangerous. Especially on a moonless night like tonight. There were too many obstacles that even the powerful searchlights could miss. Doc took the three of us off the boat a short distance up the beach, where we watched them work. As they took in the mooring lines, started the twin engines, and lifted anchor, Gisela came over to us. She didn't even give us a second glance. "Raul," she said, "take care. Give us at least three hours; then you know what to do."

Man, that comment made my stomach drop like a rock. But her next words helped me relax again. "They are not to be harmed. I mean it. Not unless they physically try to overpower you."

He nodded, his face set in stone as always.

"We'll see you in three days." And she turned and went back to the boat. Five minutes later they were gone, leaving the fishing boat, the Jet Ski, and the four of us behind. Doc didn't utter another a word. Rick, Grandpère, and I sat on the sand together; Doc sat with his pistol on his lap a short distance away. The sun went down about six o'clock, and the air temperature immediately started to drop. By full dark, I was grateful that I had on long pants and a jacket. Even then, I knew that by morning, we might be in danger of hypothermia. The forecast was for lows in the upper forties or low fifties.

I should mention here that once we had walked out of the villa, or wherever it was that we were—my ability to communicate with Rick through the mind had stopped completely. I wasn't sure if this was because Gisela had destroyed the pouch or because our "tutor" was letting us find our own way. Either way, it was a bitter blow. I fiercely missed Rick's counsel, his coaching, and his guidance. Even his occasional gentle rebuke was a loss. As the time dragged on at a snail's pace, how I wished that we could have conversed with each other to keep up our spirits.

Somewhere near nine o'clock, Doc abruptly stood up and motioned for us to do the same. We did so, stamping our feet and hugging ourselves tightly to stop the shivering. Grunting more than talking, Doc herded us into the fishing boat, telling Grandpère that he would be driving and to stay no more than ten feet behind him. Then he got on the Jet Ski and pulled out in front of us. By that time, I had decided that he wasn't just going to leave us stranded on the beach. Too much chance that we might walk out. Now I was pretty sure I knew where we were going.

———

Ten minutes later, we watched Doc drive away into the darkness, towing the fishing boat behind him, leaving the three of us on the same sandbar where Grandpère and I had found refuge before. We stood close together for warmth as the lights of the Jet Ski disappeared and the sound of its engine died away. In moments, the silence was as profound and complete as the darkness.

"Here," Rick said. I felt his jacket slip over my shoulders. It was warm and it felt wonderful, but I immediately tried to give it back. "No, Rick. It's going to get really cold tonight."

He caught my hands and pulled them away. Then he zipped it up for me. "Where I grew up," he said gruffly, "we raised real men, not hothouse plants."

I gave Rick a shove as Grandpère sniggered. "Gimme a break, Ramirez. You are so full of yourself." He just laughed.

Grandpère joined us. "Let's sit back to back, use our body heat to keep us warm until they come."

Turning around, I stared at the dim shape of his face. "Until who comes?"

"Well, Clay, of course. Who do you think? I sent him a text message about an hour ago."

"*What?* How did you send him a message? And when?"

He laughed. "The 'how' is easy." He reached in his pocket and pulled something out. A moment later a light came on, bathing our faces in a soft glow. I saw that he was holding the same cell phone Rick and I had found on his "body" in the food locker.

My jaw dropped. "Where did you get that?"

He seemed puzzled by the question. "Where did you last see it?"

"I found it on your wax duplicate. But Gisela had me searched and took it away from me."

"Well, that would explain why I found it in her desk drawer. And I thought she was just being thoughtful."

"Yeah, right," I said. I was astonished once again. "But they searched all of us thoroughly."

"Of course they did," he replied. He nudged us both. "As far as the 'when,' I did it when Doc stood up and took that cigarette break about an hour ago. I was beginning to think he'd given up smoking. I had hoped to call Clay early enough to tell him Gisela and Niklas were coming out, but I'm afraid we missed that window. Come on. Sit down. I'll try to catch you two up on what's going on."

"I would like that very much," I said, a bit exasperated. Playing this game of coy with me was one of his endearing traits, but tonight I wasn't in much of a mood for it.

As we sat down together, he said, "First, let me let Clay know where we are." He punched a button, and a moment later I heard the phone on the other end begin to ring. Clay answered immediately. I could tell it was his voice, though I couldn't hear much of what he was saying. "Yes, yes," Grandpère said. "All three of us are fine. Where are you?"

I leaned in closer, but I still got only the mumble of his voice. Grandpère nodded. "Good. So you're probably about twenty minutes from our location. It's slow going driving on the lake at night. Especially a night as dark as this." Pause. "No, we're not on the beach. They dumped us off on that sandbar at the mouth of Slick Rock Canyon." Pause. "Yes, the same one. When I hear your engine, I'll turn on the flashlight app on my phone."

More talk from the other side of the conversation. "Yeah, no surprise. They had a three- or four-hour head start on us. What? Oh, of course. Hold on." He turned and handed the phone to me. "Someone wants to talk to you."

I snatched it from his grasp and thrust it up against my ear. "Clay, is that really you?"

"No, Carruthers," said a voice I knew and loved better than any other. "It's Mom. We're coming."

And that did it. I dropped my head and began to cry.

"All right," Grandpère said, "I'm sure you have a few questions, so, since we have some time, let's see if we can't clear a few things up."

"A few," I yelped. "How about a couple of hundred!" We were still seated on the sandbar and getting colder rapidly.

I looked at Rick, who motioned for me to begin. "All right. Tell me about driving the van into the river. How did you do that without killing yourself? They said it went right through the guardrail."

"It did; I didn't."

"But you said . . ."

"Let's go back to the parking lot at the cemetery. Once Louis told us what was happening, I was pretty sure that Gisela and Niklas were behind it, and I knew that we were in grave danger. So, as you two were getting into the van, I asked Louis if we could count on his help. He said yes. You probably didn't notice, but he and his security team followed us into Caen.

"Once we got there, the feelings of danger greatly intensified. I knew that I was their primary target and that the best thing I could do to keep you two safe was to disappear. So as we came back into the city, following along the river, I noticed a curve where the road was right next to the guardrail and there was a ten- or fifteen-foot drop to the river. With the slick roads, I thought that might be my answer. But I was also wise enough to know that I'm too old for grand heroics, so while you two were packing, I called Louis, and we worked out a plan. One of his security guards is a former special forces operative with the French army. So I slipped out of the hotel, making sure that I was seen by the hotel staff, and met this man at the van. He put on my overcoat and got in. He waited until he saw one of Niklas's men come busting out of the hotel, then took off, with this guy in hot pursuit."

"So he's the one who drove the van into the river," I said, marveling.

"Yeah, and a good thing, too. Louis said it was a pretty rough go even for an expert. Bitter cold water. Swift current. Guys watching from the bank." He laughed softly. "That was Louis's way of reminding me how old I am."

"So how did you know we were in Switzerland?" Rick asked.

"Louis was waiting for me in the back of the hotel parking lot. We watched until Niklas came out with you two on stretchers. Their story was that two American teenagers had overdosed on drugs and were headed for the hospital. We followed, of course, and saw they went to the airport and boarded a private plane.

"After the kidnapping of his granddaughter, Louis hired one of the top private security teams in Europe. It costs him almost two hundred thousand Euros per year, but they are very good at what they do. So, while it took them most of that night to track where the plane went, we learned it flew in to a private airport in Paris. There they changed to a different plane and flew to Zurich. Unfortunately, we couldn't get anyone to the airport in time to see where they went from there. So we were stumped for a while."

"Then I called Clay," I said, starting finally to fit the pieces together.

"Yes. We were so happy to hear from you, we were all doing a little dance."

"But it was another dead end, right?" Rick asked. "It really wasn't the *Schloss* von Dietz like they had led us to believe."

"That's right. We checked out the castle, but it was deserted except for a couple of servants. Then someone turned the phone on again, and we were able to track its location."

I looked at Rick. "When Gisela was seeing who I had called."

"Working together, Clay and Interpol and Louis's men put the house under close surveillance. I decided that I would slip into the castle and see if I could learn what the situation was." He grinned at us in the darkness. "I was the sacrificial lamb. We figured if I was caught, I could convince them that I had come alone to save my family and not give away the team outside.

"I went through a basement window and into a storage room. We assumed that there were CCTV cameras throughout, and while I was mulling over how to get around them, the alarm went off and everybody started running around to find who did it."

"It was Cody," Rick said.

"Is that what happened? All I knew was that now I had my opportunity to start looking around for all of you." He sighed. "That's when I found myself and all my family 'dead' in a food locker—a bit of a shock, I must admit. But since I was one of those bodies, I knew that something strange was up. A closer examination showed that they were all wax figures."

"So you put your phone on your duplicate?"

"Yes. By then I could hear them yelling about trying to find you and Rick, so I figured that maybe you two had pulled off the old invisibility trick again. Hoping that you were free and would come upon the food locker sooner or later, I left my phone so you would know I was alive. Actually, I was hiding in the kitchen when you went by, Danni. After you left again, I went back in the locker to get my phone, but it was gone."

"I took it. I thought we could use it. Not very smart. I should have known Gisela would search us as soon as we were caught."

"Wow!" Rick said. "I wish we had known you were there. That would have been a real boost to us both."

"It sounds to me like you two didn't need much of a boost. From what I could hear outside the library, you were holding your own in there." Then, with a sudden huskiness in his voice, he turned to me. "You have fully redeemed yourself, *ma chérie.* Above and beyond what was required."

"But not expected," I teased, my own voice a little strained.

"Never. After all, you come from a line of great and courageous women. And I've also heard that your grandfather on your mother's side is quite a remarkable man."

We laughed. *Oh, Grandpère. How good you are for the soul.*

We fell silent for moment, enjoying the sweetness. Then Rick said, "One last question."

"Shoot."

"I want to know about the phone. When you came into the library, I saw Doc search you. How is it that they never found it?"

"By then Niklas was down, and pandemonium reigned. Doc was distracted. Not that he would have found it if he had been thorough. I hid it in my front jacket pocket."

I leaned back, laughing softly. "Oh, Grandpère. I feel for your poor mother."

"Strange you would say that," he drawled. "That's what my father used to say too."

We lapsed into silence, each of us sorting through all that had happened. Two minutes later, Grandpère's phone buzzed. He turned it on. "Yes?"

He must have hit the speaker button, because Clay's voice boomed out. "We passed channel marker eighty-two a couple of minutes ago. We have you as being close to marker eighty-one, so we're almost there. Give us a light."

"Will do," Grandpère said.

Then, even as he touched the screen on his phone and a bright light pierced the darkness, I cocked my head. It was still distant, but I was sure it wasn't just my imagination. Sound bounces off the water and echoes through these deep gorges in remarkable ways. "I can hear them," I called. "They're coming."

PART ELEVEN

Justice and Mercy

CHAPTER 41

As it turned out, it was not one boat, but two: a rental Clay had acquired and one of the Lake Powell ranger boats from Bullfrog. The ranger boat had some really powerful searchlights and could make better time. Clay, who had three other agents with him, also knew that once he picked up the three of us, we'd be too much for one boat.

What a reunion it turned out to be. As three of the agents transferred to the ranger's boat, Dad gave me a hand up. I thought he was going to crush my ribs when he hugged me. I tried to do the same when I hugged him back.

I then nearly knocked Mom overboard as I threw myself into her waiting arms. And Cody nearly knocked us both down as he barreled into us. Dad helped Grandpère up, then Rick. Then, as best we could, we squeezed together for a smothering group hug. At first, we tried not to cry, but then we thought, "What the heck," and just let it rip.

Clay hung back, grinning widely. After a moment, I broke loose and went to shake hands with him. That's when I saw the man in the seat behind the wheel. He had a crew cut and wore Dockers, a sports shirt under a bomber jacket, and some kind of tennis shoes. "Danni," Clay said, "meet Agent Brett Mergenthaller."

"Hello, Danni. It's a pleasure to finally meet 'The Legend,' as Clay calls you."

Clay shot him a dirty look and quickly went on. "And this is Grandpère and Rick."

Brett extended a hand. "Equally famous, I'm sure."

Mom touched Grandpère's arm. "Dad, Clay also brought a special surprise along." She took his hand and moved past him into the main part of the boat. That's when we saw a dark shadow at the very back of the boat stand to face us.

Grandpère stopped dead. "Louis?" he cried.

Louis Girard took two steps forward, and they fell into each other's arms.

I guess I was staring, probably with my jaw hanging open, because when he saw me over Grandpère's shoulder, he smiled broadly. "*Bonsoir, Mademoiselle* Danni."

I did a little curtsey. "And *bonsoir* to you, *Monsieur* Girard. To see you here makes it a very good evening indeed."

Clay watched for a moment, then broke in. "Well, there is much to catch up on, but I'm sure that you are anxious to find a bed as soon as possible." He called over to the other boat. "You lead and set the pace. We'll follow." Then to us, "Let's get you into life jackets, and then we have some blankets and hot chocolate."

In fact, Brett had already taken his seat and was backing the boat away from the sandbar as the other boat moved away from us. In a moment we fell in behind them, heading back out into the channel.

"There's also a pan of cinnamon rolls next to the jug of chocolate," Clay called over the noise of the engine that was rapidly increasing in power. "Those are thanks to Helen." Turning to Louis, he added, "My wife."

———

We moved slowly. The headlamps of the ranger boat, though powerful, couldn't penetrate very far into the thick darkness, and the last thing any of us wanted was to stray out of the channel and hit a submerged rock or a sandbar. The air was cold, and getting colder, but we were all in pretty good spirits as we chattered back and forth. I snuggled up to Rick, deliberately shivering. It worked. He put his arm around me and pulled me in close.

Seeing that, Dad leaned in closer to us so we could hear him over the sound of the motor. "All right, you two. We want to hear the whole story. Cody told us his part in it, which is quite remarkable. Now we want to hear the rest of it."

"Wait," Clay called. "I want to hear this too."

"So do I," Louis called.

"And me," Grandpère said.

Clay went on. "It's going to be at least eleven before we see a bed. So I—"

"Eleven!" Cody wailed. "Do we have to go all the way back to Hanksville tonight?"

"No, Cody," Clay said. "I had the office reserve rooms for all of us at Ticaboo Lodge."

Grandpère turned to Louis. "That's just ten minutes north of the marina."

"Besides," Clay added, "no one is going inside your Hanksville house until my team gets all that stuff out of there."

"All what stuff?" I asked.

"The explosive and the fire accelerants."

"What?" I felt a little jolt twist my stomach; then I remembered Gisela's letter in the phony pouch. "How did you find out about that?" I said.

"We found the letter on the desk in the library." He pulled a face. "It wasn't an empty threat. I think they would have heard the explosion as far away as Green River. Anyway, there's a good restaurant at the lodge. We'll have breakfast together, then spend a couple of hours debriefing you, and hopefully your house will be all tidied up by then."

He turned to Rick. "We called your father, Rick. We told him it would be late by the time we got you to Ticaboo, but he'll be here first thing in the morning."

"Thank you."

"It seems like years since we were there," I said, snuggling in tighter against him.

Rick nodded, then leaned forward. "Speaking of Gisela and Niklas, were you able to get to Bullfrog to catch them?"

Clay shook his head. "We just got back from Europe yesterday morning. I was down with the team in Hanksville when Grandpère first called." He turned to me. "We had left your family and Louis at a motel in Green River while we checked out the house. I was almost back to Green River when Jean-Henri called. Knowing that it would only take the houseboat about an hour to get back to the marina, I knew there was no way I could get there in time. But fortunately, we had a couple of agents already down here."

Clay reached across the center aisle of the boat and laid a hand on Brett Mergenthaller's shoulder. "I called the Kane County Sheriff's Office and asked if they had any cars down around Bullfrog. They did not, but they had one about forty-five minutes out. Then I called this young man. Brett, let me drive while you explain how it was that you just happened to be down here at Lake Powell when we needed you."

They switched places quickly and Brett sat down in the seat beside Clay, turning to face us. "Well," he began, "this was a very lucky break for us. Yesterday, we got a report from the monitoring center in Salt Lake that there was something unusual going on at the dive site."

I perked up at that. "Really? Like what?"

"No one was actually diving, of course. That would have brought a whole SWAT team running. But we did have a fishing boat come in and anchor not far from the sandbar. They would fish for a couple of hours, then disappear again, going up into the canyon. But then they'd come back in the afternoon. They always anchored in the same spot. Fortunately, one of our guys up there had fished Lake Powell. He said that was not highly unusual, but normally the fishermen liked to stay in closer to the cliffs where the fish were more likely to feed. And very few fishermen are so loyal to one particular spot.

"But there was another thing as well. The camera caught a single Jet Ski going back and forth, too. In the morning, she'd go downstream past the camera, then an hour or two later, she'd come back. That happened several times. I say 'she' because it looked like it might be a woman."

"It *was* a woman," I exclaimed. "It was Gisela. She was the sentry. She would go out and patrol the main channel while the divers were working."

"Divers?" Brett said. "We never saw any divers."

"They had two scuba divers, but they'd change into their gear off camera and then swim in underwater. The boat would only go in when they were ready to load. Which they always did on the side of the boat opposite the camera."

He was clearly dismayed with that. "So did they get the gold?"

"Gold?" Louis yelped.

I feigned a sorrowful, stricken look. "They did. Every single bar of it."

Grandpère sniggered. "Yep. All eleven hundred dollars of it." Then he hooted aloud. "Oh, what I'd give to be there when they discover what they've got."

I don't know who was more puzzled, Louis or Brett. Which caused the rest of us to laugh. Which caused the two of them to look all the more perplexed. Which caused us to howl all the more. Finally, Clay explained the whole thing about bars of lead sprayed with gold-leaf paint. That delighted them both immensely.

"Go on with your story, Brett," Clay said, after the laughter finally subsided.

"Well, so Agent Warner and I came down here to check it out. We got to Bullfrog a little before the sun was going down." He looked a little sheepish now. "That late in the day, almost everything in Bullfrog was either closed or closing. We did manage to rent this boat, but we decided we had to wait until morning to go check things out."

"That's when I called them," Clay said.

"That sent us running," Brett said. "We linked up with the Kane

County deputies and decided to split up. I went down to the house-boat rental area to watch for them. The deputies went to the boat ramp. Warner went up on the ridge by the parking lot to watch for them with the binoculars. This late in the season, we figured it would be pretty hard to miss them."

"And did you see them?" Dad asked.

"Not at first," Brett said, obviously not happy. "Then Warner said there was a houseboat across the lake, almost to Hall's Crossing." He paused to explain that to Louis. "That's across the lake, a little upstream from Bullfrog Marina."

"So what did you do?" Louis asked.

"I was closest to the boat, so we went tearing to the marina and took off. I had one of the deputies come with me. Warner and the other dep-uty called the San Juan County Sheriff's Department. Halls Crossing is in their county, but their nearest patrol car was at Blanding, which is almost ninety miles away."

"Did you find them?" Cody burst out. This was the stuff TV mov-ies were made of, and he was hanging on their every word.

"Not right away. We went to the houseboat rental docks there, but nothing had just come in. So we went looking for them. We finally found them parked on the boat ramp, where they had a panel truck and a car waiting. As we got closer, we could see them using hand trucks to wheel out wooden crates of something very heavy."

He shook his head ruefully. "About then, one of the guys opened fire on us with an automatic rifle. I don't think he was trying to hit us, just to scare us away. It worked. We wheeled around and took off. We then beached the boat behind a low hill and took off running toward the ramp, both of us armed with rifles now too. Unfortunately, by the time we came up on the ridge, they were driving off. And we had no way to follow them."

I slumped back in my seat, the bitterness like bile in my mouth.

"We know now that they had a Lear Jet waiting for them at the Cal Black airport," Clay said. "It took off shortly after six thirty with a flight plan for Mexico City. That means they are well out of the United States by now."

The Cal Black Airport was a modern, jet-capable airport literally out in the middle of nowhere, ten miles east of Hall's Crossing. It catered to the jet set who flew in to Lake Powell in their private planes to go out on their million-dollar houseboats and soak up some sun.

Once again, I heard Niklas's voice in my head. "'Plan impeccably. Strike boldly. Exit swiftly. And leave nothing to chance. *Nothing!*"

As Brett and Clay exchanged places again, Clay turned his head. "We do have one little snippet of good news."

"What?" several of us asked together.

"I just got a text. Agent Warner and the deputies caught Raul Muñoz at the Jet Ski rental dock. He walked right into their arms and gave up without a fight."

"Oh, Clay," Mom cried. "That is much more than a little snippet of good news. That is wonderful news!"

"It doesn't get much better than that," I agreed. "I hope you put him in a cell and let him rot for the rest of his life." Then I had another thought. "Maybe send in a couple of hungry lions to keep him company."

"Danni!" Mom looked shocked. Then a slow smile teased the corners of her mouth. "I was thinking of something a little less invasive. Like maybe a pit viper or two. You know, something that he might feel a little more comfortable with."

We were coming around a bend in the main channel, and up ahead the shoreline was suddenly speckled with lights. We were entering Bullfrog Bay; the marina was just a couple of miles away now. With more visibility, the ranger's boat was accelerating, and Clay pushed the throttle up a little as well. "About ten minutes now."

I looked at Rick. "Do you realize that we haven't had a bath since our hotel in Caen, which is . . ." I gave up trying to remember how long ago that was.

Grandpère leaned forward. "One week ago today."

I lifted one arm and pretended to sniff my armpit. "Whew!"

"I could have told you that you have B.O. without you having to sniff yourself," Cody said.

As I swung at him, he jerked away. I leaped up and horse-collared him, wrestling him down against the seat. "Wanna know what I've got to say to you, Little Brother?"

"No, I don't," he said, trying unsuccessfully to stop from giggling.

I was about to give him a real good noogie when suddenly the image of him slamming back as two Taser electrodes hit his body flashed across my mind. So instead, I bent down and kissed him softly on the check. "I love you, Bro. Like a ton and a half."

He recoiled instantly. "Ew!" he cried, wiping at his cheek in disgust. Then he laughed and horse-collared me back. He pulled me down until we were face to face. "And I love you too, Danni." He grinned. "Maybe about a pound and a half."

———

Ticaboo Lodge, Ticaboo, Utah
October 28, 2011

Once again, all of us were gathered in a hotel conference room discussing—what else?—the saga of the McAllister Family's Ongoing Fabulous Adventures. The only thing that had really changed was that Louis Girard and Charlie Ramirez were there, and that we were finally on the back end of our adventures, not just going into them. At least, we kept telling ourselves that.

Clay stood up and stretched, yawning as he did so. Looking down at the pad of notes he had taken—several pages' worth—he nodded in satisfaction. "Good work, guys. You are amazing."

Louis shook his head. "If I did not know it to be true, I could never believe that it is true."

Sobering, Clay said, "I was expecting nothing less, and still it blows my mind." Then he glanced at his watch. "Let me call the team up in

Hanksville. See if they're finished with the house yet. I assume you'd rather go home than have lunch here first."

"Yeah!" Cody cried. "And I want to call Mayor Brackston. He owes us a parade!"

The rest of us groaned at the thought.

"Just kidding," he said.

Charlie spoke to Clay. "Thank you for letting me be here to hear the whole story." Then to Rick, he added, "Your sisters are very, very anxious to see you."

"And I them," he said.

"Okay, then, let's call this meeting over and—" Clay began.

Dad cut him off. "Not so fast, Agent Zabriskie. We answered all your questions. Now it's our turn."

"Fire away."

"Does the FBI or Interpol have any idea where Gisela and Niklas and the others were going?"

"Not for sure, Mack, but we think it's very likely Argentina. Probably the province of Córdoba. We and Interpol are vigorously searching as we speak."

"Argentina?" Mom asked. "Why there?"

Grandpère, who was seated next to Clay, took a sip of water from his glass. "During World War II, Argentina was a strong socialist country that sympathized with the National Socialist Movement in Germany, commonly called the Nazi Party. In 1946, Juan Perón, an ardent Nazi supporter, was elected president. There was already a large German immigrant population in the country. Since they were mostly a wealthy and influential group, Perón created what was called 'ratlines' to help prominent Nazis and German collaborators secretly escape from Europe. He assisted literally thousands of them to find refuge in Argentina."

"That's right," Clay said. "People of German stock make up the second-largest ethnic group in the country. We think the von Dietzes will choose Córdoba because it has about half a million people of German descent, the highest number in the country. Many of these came from former high-ranking Nazi families, so we think the von Dietzes would be warmly welcomed there, even though no one will know exactly who they are."

"What if they knew they were criminals?" I asked.

"If the crimes targeted those who testified against former Nazis, they would have no problems with it."

"If you do find them, can you go after them?" Dad asked.

To my surprise, Louis spoke up. "Not without the specific permission and cooperation of the Argentine government, which is highly unlikely, especially for the United States."

"That's right," Clay agreed. "They don't take kindly to Americans interfering in their internal affairs."

"And so they get away scot-free?" Mom said in dismay. "After all they've done?"

His brow furrowed. "Louis and I were talking about this earlier. With the information his investigative team has compiled on their illegal activities, especially against those who were only innocent family members, perhaps we can build a strong enough case against them to get the government to file charges against them. Or at least extradite them back to Europe."

"Not likely," Grandpère said. "At most, they might expel them."

I was like Mom. I was feeling a lot of outrage at the moment. "You know that when Gisela and Niklas discover that Rick and I conned them on the gold, that all they have is half a ton of lead worth little more than a thousand dollars, they're gonna go ballistic. Do you really think they won't come after us after that?"

Clay nodded. "We've already considered that. And, much as I hate to say it, we may have to reconsider a witness protection program."

"No!" Cody cried. "No way!"

"Yes, way," I shot back. "We may not have a choice, Cody. Rick and I led them into a trap, and they were nearly caught. They lost thirty million dollars. They lost Raul, their team leader. The FBI and Interpol are hot on their heels. But it's more than that. Rick and I made them look like idiots.

We sucked them in like they were a couple of country bumpkins come to the big city for the first time. To Gisela, the humiliation of that will be worse than losing the money. We have to assume she will retaliate."

"We're not going away again," Dad said quietly. "If we have to carry weapons around the clock, post a guard at night, fine. But we are through running."

Mom was startled by that, but she instantly reached out and took his hand. "I totally agree."

Grandpère began to stroke his goatee, as he always did when he was deep in thought. "Sounds to me like there may be an alternative. Right, Louis? Right, Clay?"

"Are you talking about our FBI consultant program?" Clay said with a smile.

"That is precisely what I'm talking about."

Then Clay turned to me and Rick. "So now that you two have had this three-day vacation on a houseboat, are you ready to go to work?"

"Vacation?" I yelped. But I saw that he was teasing. "What is it that you want us to do?"

"Just what you said. I want you and Rick to start working with us and with Interpol, along with Louis and Jean-Henri. Our task will be to get them out of Argentina so we can get at them."

"But how can we do that if we don't even know where they are? " I cried. "And why us?"

Grandpère decided to answer that. "Danni, remember when we were outside the library and I told you that your task was not just to stop them from getting away with all that they had done, but to make them believe that they had done just that? Well, you and Rick did that brilliantly. I had never even thought of using the gold as bait, but you sucked them in and got them to leave your family behind. I still am marveling at how you did that."

He stopped to take a quick breath. "Louis and Clay and I can provide the backup and the equipment and the support that you need, but we need you two to get into their heads and rattle them so badly that they will start making mistakes. Because if they do that, then we'll have them."

Now I understood. "What you're talking about are mind games. Just like they did to us."

"That is exactly what we are talking about," Clay burst out.

"That's what it's all about with them," I said, marveling at how my mind was opening up again.

"Yes," Rick cried. "That's their weapon of choice. If you don't understand that, you cannot understand them. They don't kill people. They don't torture them. They don't beat them up and leave them lying bloody and battered in an alley somewhere. They're mind assassins. They attack the heart and soul."

"*Oui,*" Louis said in a very quiet voice. Mind games." He seemed far away. Then he looked at me and Grandpère. "I did not tell you this before, but after we paid the ransom for my granddaughter, they told me where to find her. She was in an old deserted apartment building. When we got there, she was on a bed. Her face was pale as death itself, and her body was ice cold. We thought she was dead. My daughter actually collapsed and fainted dead away. But, as it turned out, she had only been drugged with something. Three hours later, she was fine again. But I later asked myself, 'Why drug her?' She was locked in a room. She couldn't get out. So why make it look like she was dead?"

His eyes were suddenly teary. "But now I understand. I shall never forget that moment when I first saw her. It was as if a sword had pierced my soul."

I laid a hand on Grandpère's shoulder, then looked at Rick. "So," I said. "I'm in. How about you?"

"I figure there's a lot of payback waiting to be done," he said. "I'm not sure where we start, but I'm in too."

Grandpère reached up and laid his hand on my hand, which was still on his shoulder. He extended his other hand across to Rick. Then he pulled us together and placed my hand in Rick's. "Then let the games begin," he whispered.

CHAPTER 42

Danni's Bedroom, McAllister Ranch, Hanksville, Utah
November 5, 2011

Well, it's about time, I'd say. The last time I wrote in here was October 7th, almost a month ago now. Wow! So much has happened since then! Way too much to try to put down right now, that's for sure.

Kind of a big day today. We're taking Louis and his wife, Dorothée, who flew out to join him here, on a red-rock tour of Southern Utah. We'll drive over to Moab and see Arches and Canyonlands National Parks. Then we'll continue south through Monticello and Blanding before turning east again. Dad wants to go down and see the Goosenecks of the San Juan and the Valley of the Gods, which aren't that far out of the way, but I don't think we'll have time. After hearing Rick and me talk about Leprechaun Canyon, Louis is pretty keen on it, too, and he and Dorothée go back on Monday, so this will be their last chance to see it.

Big day, but a great one. Fortunately, the weather should be perfect. In the mid-seventies and nothing but sun. I love this country, and I love to show it to others. I've already warned them that once they get this red dirt in the bloodstream, they'll be hooked for life.

Three last things, then I've got to quit. One. I miss Le Gardien even more fiercely than I expected I would. I have left the nail in the wall by my dresser. Seeing that empty place every day reminds me of the pouch—as if I could ever forget—so I think of it several times a day. I've even had a nightmare or two where I saw Gisela throw it into the fire. In one of them, she turned and started hurling fireballs at me, too. It was awful. Anyway, GP keeps reminding me that I am still the keeper of the pouch, even if there isn't a pouch to be keeper of. We'll see if that's true or not, but I miss it. A lot!

Two. First thing Monday morning, we have a big strategy meeting. Joel Jamison, Deputy Director of the FBI, will be here with Clay. Rick and Charlie are coming. Louis and Dorothée will also be there. I didn't think Dorothée would want to, after having one of her grandchildren kidnapped, but she wants to know what she can do. And, of course, all of my family will be there too. Later that afternoon Dad and Grandpère will take Louis and Dorothée to the airport, and they will fly home. There is a ton of stuff Louis needs to be doing back home to help us make this all work.

Three. Rick and I have come out of this closer than we have ever been before. I'm not even sure how to describe it, but our relationship is deeper, more meaningful, more fulfilling than it was before. He's no longer in the spectator bleachers, and I'm no longer the Super Chick waiting for him to cheer me on. It is just super cool. Completely awesome. In a word, amazing. ☺ ☺ ☺

Gotta run. Bye.

I met Rick at the back door, as we had previously arranged, opening it before he could knock. As he slipped inside, I said, "Grandpère's in Dad's office. Everyone else is still asleep."

Nodding, he slipped out of his tennis shoes. "When do Joel and Clay arrive?"

"Nine."

"And this is just him with you and me?"

"Yes. Grandpère said he thought it would be wise if we talked before anyone else gets here."

"I'm glad," he said. "I don't know about you, but I didn't sleep much last night."

"Me neither. I think I got a couple of hours is all." We were approaching the door to Dad's office. "Okay, then. Here we go."

———

We settled in quickly after Grandpère and Rick greeted each other. I saw that Grandpère had one of Dad's yellow notepads on the desk in front of him. It was covered with his handwriting, and I wondered how much sleep *he* had gotten.

"Thanks for coming, Rick," he began. "I thought there might be some value in us talking some things through before the others came."

"We're glad, Grandpère. I can't speak for Rick, but I feel like I'm pretty much in way over my head here."

"Amen to that," Rick said.

"And I as well," he said quietly. He picked up the notepad, looked at it for a moment, then put it down again. "A couple of preliminary thoughts, if I may."

We both sat back. I wished I had brought a notebook or paper or something. No surprise when Rick reached in his shirt pocket and brought out a small notebook and pen. I shot him a look that said, *You're doing it again, Ramirez. Making me look bad.* And he did what he always does. He grinned and lifted his pen.

"I think I need to clarify something up front about my feelings toward Gisela and Niklas," Grandpère began. He stopped, inviting us to comment. Neither of us did.

"I absolutely and without equivocation believe that we cannot falter in our determination to stop these two individuals. The chariots are here, and we are the footmen. They are like an F5 tornado. They touch down here, then jump to another place, skipping some, hitting others.

But wherever they touch down, they leave a swath of destruction and human misery behind."

"And we are storm chasers," I murmured.

"Yes, like it or not. The FBI and Interpol are there and working hard, but they have asked for our help."

"Do you think they'll be more specific today about what they want us to do?"

He shook his head. "I think they're hoping we can give them some ideas about what they need to do. Now that we know for sure that the von Dietzes are in Argentina, their hands are pretty much tied. Our job will be to try to get them out of there."

"You think that's possible?" Rick asked. "If they're safe there, they're not going to be leaving."

"Not unless we can convince them there is no other acceptable alternative." He flashed a grin. "But you got them out of Switzerland without hurting anyone. That's what we need from you again."

"Too bad we don't have another pot of gold to tempt them," I said.

"Danni and I spent a lot of time talking about this yesterday," Rick said. "I think we have some ideas."

"Good. Let's hear them."

"We're going to need a lot of help," I said. "From you and Mom and Dad—mostly in keeping us from doing something stupid—but also from Clay and the FBI. And Louis and his team. We are going to need a lot of information."

"Louis will be delighted to hear that. As you know, he is as dedicated to stopping them as we are. And money is not a problem for him."

"And here's the second problem," Rick went on. "We both agree that the mind games approach is our best strategy. But so far we are baffled. How do we mess with their minds if we can't communicate with them—if we don't have any idea where they are?"

"You don't need to know where a person is to communicate with him," Grandpère pointed out. "We do that all the time on the Internet with people whose real names we don't even know."

"Great," I said. "So can you get us their email address? Or their Facebook account, if they have one? A telephone number would be nice too."

"Oh," he said with a sleepy smile, "I think I can do better than that."

We both stared at him. His smile broadened. "Well," I finally said, "are you going to tell us or not?"

"Are you familiar with what they call keylogger software?"

I shook my head, but Rick was nodding. "Yeah," he said. "It's also called keystroke logging. It's another form of malware or spyware on a computer."

"Explain to Danni what it does."

"Well, I'm hardly an expert, but it's something you install on a computer that records every keystroke made on that computer. I know there are different kinds, some you can buy for under a hundred bucks, and others highly sophisticated and very difficult to detect."

"Why would you want that?" I asked.

"Well, for example, parents can use it to see what their kids are saying on Twitter or Facebook. They can find out what websites they're logging onto." Grandpère shrugged. "They can read their user names and passwords. Actually, it can be pretty handy if you want to snoop around in someone's life."

Rick was nodding. "Basically, it can tell you everything a person has done on his or her computer."

"Or *is doing*," Grandpère added. "The more sophisticated ones can be monitored from a remote site. It's like you have a virtual copy of the other computer at your fingertips and can actually watch what is being typed as it happens. You can ask Louis more. He's the expert."

With a jerk, I came to full attention. "And your reason for telling us this is . . . ?"

Suddenly, he was that little boy again who stared down a Stuka dive bomber, grinning up and waving like he owned the world. "Well, you see, when we got Louis and Clay together, we discovered something kind of interesting. Louis's security company has created this highly so-phisticated and powerful keylogging software. And it turns out the FBI has one of their own. When they . . . uh . . . combined the two—which is highly classified, of course—they created something that is absolutely amazing, as you kids would say."

"And you're thinking that if we could get that onto Gisela's com-puter, then we'd have the information we need? Great, so how do we do that?"

"Well . . . uh. . . ." He was playing the shy schoolboy again, but I could tell that underneath that, he was tickled pink with himself. "Actually, when I slipped into the villa that night, I had with me the very latest version of their combined program. And when everyone was kind of busy that first night after I got there, I . . . um . . . went ahead and installed it on Gisela's hard drive."

I sat back, too astonished to speak. Rick was shaking his head. "You really did that?"

"And we can get access to her computer, see everything that's on it?" I cried.

"That's my understanding. However, it is programmed to stay dor-mant for ten days, so if they were looking for it, they couldn't find it. The question is, would that be useful to you two?"

I laughed aloud. "We have several ideas to put before you. We believe they have a lot of merit. We just weren't sure if they could be implemented."

"So," he said, "what's holding you up now?"

I looked at Rick, and we both shook our heads. "Approval and fur-ther direction from Clay and Joel," Rick said. "That's about it."

CHAPTER 43

Córdoba is Argentina's second-largest city, with nearly a million and a half people living within its boundaries. It is the capital of Córdoba Province, which is in the heart of the region known as the *Pampas.* About three hours west of the city are the Sierras de Córdoba, one of Argentina's more important mountain ranges.

Nestled in one of the valleys at the base of the mountains is the picturesque and serene little town of Mina Clavero. Lying at an elevation of 915 meters (just over 3,000 feet), the valley has more than three hundred days of brilliant sunshine each year. That and its cool nights, clean air, and small-town atmosphere have attracted some of the world's wealthier elites to build second and third homes there. For Gisela and Niklas von Dietz—now officially known as Giselle Mary Elizabeth Smythe and Roger Carlton Smythe III—Mina Clavero was their permanent home.

Two years earlier, they had commissioned a global real-estate agent to start a search for a possible "retirement home" for them. When she found a run-down villa near the head of the valley that had been vacated by a widower returning to Austria, Gisela and Niklas flew to Argentina to see it for themselves. After Switzerland's long winters and England's endless overcast, Mina Clavero held a lot of appeal for the both of them.

557

Though isolated, it was just a couple of hours from Córdoba and its exuberant metropolitan lifestyle. So they made the purchase, spent about a quarter of a million Euros remodeling it to their liking, hired a permanent staff of three to maintain it, and put it all in the name of the Smythes from Herefordshire, England.

They had been there now for just two weeks. After fleeing the United States in considerable haste, Gisela and Niklas split up. She took a circuitous route to South America, changing identities twice as she made her way to Argentina via Guatemala, Panama, Peru, and Chile. Niklas stayed with the gold.

Immediately upon landing in Mexico City, they had taxied their plane to a private and heavily guarded hanger and there transferred the gold to a steel-reinforced cargo container. With Niklas accompanying them, Jean-Claude and his four men drove the truck and the container to a small port on Mexico's Gulf Coast. There the container was transferred to a secure hold on a small steamer and taken all the way around the east coast of South America to Buenos Aires. Using an armored truck escorted by three other vehicles, final transfer was made to the Province of Córdoba, to the villa in the valley above Mina Clavero.

Thus, twelve days after they left Rick Ramirez, Danni McAllister, and Jean-Henri LaRoche on a sandbar at Lake Powell, mother and son were finally reunited. The gold was off-loaded into a vault carved out of solid rock at the back of their underground garage. There it would stay for another six to nine months before they began cashing it in, one bar at a time, through various banks throughout Argentina.

Niklas often went down to the vault and stood there for a long time, awed by the sight of their newly won fortune, and planning how to best maximize the power and influence that it represented.

On this day, after completing an eight-kilometer run through the valley, followed by a few laps in the swimming pool to cool off, he went down to the vault to complete his morning ritual. He considered this as vital to his mental health as the other two activities were to his physical health. It always left him filled with a deep satisfaction. They had pulled it off, and it had gone flawlessly, and that was due largely to him. *Leave nothing to chance. Nothing!*

As he turned and started to leave, he was surprised to hear footsteps in the garage.

"Niklas?"

"I'm in here, Mama. I'm coming."

"No!" It came out sharp and urgent. "We're coming in."

Surprised, he stepped back as his mother and Jean-Claude hustled into the room. Gisela had a single sheet of paper clutched in one hand. Niklas moved forward and bent down to kiss her cheek, but she brushed right past him. He could see that she was highly agitated.

"What is it, Mama?"

She whirled and thrust the paper at him, then motioned for Jean-Claude to join her as she moved over to the neatly stacked gold bars. Thoroughly puzzled, Niklas took the paper. His eyes widened as he saw what it was. It was an email, addressed to both him and Gisela. No sender was indicated, however. He brought it closer and began to read.

To our dear and valued friends:
We have just learned that in recent weeks you have, through a stroke of very good luck, come into possession of a vast fortune.

He exploded in shock. "*What?* Who is this?"

Gisela shook her head. "You'll see at the bottom that they give no names. And somehow they managed to leave no email address."

"But—"

"Keep reading," she snapped.

We regret to inform you that we have also learned—from a totally unimpeachable source—that you may have been the victims of an elaborate hoax, a vast swindle. We cannot absolutely confirm this from our current location, but highly recommend that you immediately undertake a close examination of the "treasure" which is now in your possession.

A concerned friend.

P.S. For your safety and for ours we have chosen not to reveal our identities.

In one savage jerk, Niklas crumpled the letter and hurled it at the wall. "What kind of sick joke is this? No one even knows—" He stopped. "Mama. What are you doing?"

Gisela was bending over the stack of gold bricks. With some effort, she lifted one of them off the top and handed it to Jean-Claude. The Belgian always carried a wicked-looking hunting knife on his belt, along with a pistol. He had it out now as he took the bar from her. Bracing it against his leg, in one smooth movement he put the blade to the edge of the bar and pulled it toward him. It was like he was peeling an apple, only what came out from beneath the blade was not an apple peel, but a slice of dark gray metal.

For one long moment, Jean-Claude stared at what he had just done, then he looked up. *"C'est une catastrophe!"*

As Niklas gaped at what he was seeing, he said, "Catastrophe doesn't begin to describe it." He leaped forward and snatched the bar from Jean-Claude. He felt the sliver with his finger.

"I think it is lead," Jean-Claude said, shock softening his voice.

"Of course it's lead, *stupide*," Niklas shouted hoarsely. "Try another."

He did, with exactly the same results. The third, fourth, and fifth bricks were the same. By that time, Gisela had collapsed on the stack of bars, her head in her hands, muttering over and over, "No! No! No!"

About then, a woman's voice called from the garage, *"Señora* Smythe?" It was the housekeeper. The servants had very strict rules about staying away from the vault, so Jean-Claude darted out to meet her. A moment later he returned with another sheet of paper in his hand. Without a word he handed it to Gisela. In two steps, Niklas was beside her. Gisela started to read it, then had to stop. Snatching it from her hand, Niklas read it aloud:

Greetings from the Red Rock Country of Southern Utah.

We heard that you have found a new home somewhere in South America. Since it is summertime there, we are most envious. We had our first desert blizzard yesterday. The temperature is in the teens, with a wind-chill factor of about ten degrees Fahrenheit (minus 12 degrees Celsius). :) Still keeping up on our metric conversions.

Greetings from Clay Zabriskie, our FBI friend. He asked that I express his gratitude for your excellent work in removing all of the lead bars from Lake Powell. Once the gold-leaf paint wore off, they could have constituted a serious environmental hazard to our water supply. The FBI had a diving team scheduled to remove all of the bars early next spring. :)

Gotta run. A lot going on. If you ever get back to the States, we'd love to have you visit Hanksville again. There are a lot of people here very anxious to meet you.

All the family says hello. Rick too. Give our fondest to Jean-Claude and the gang.

Danni (your gauche friend and former companion)

P.S. Grandpère asked that I let you know that he checked the price of lead on today's commodities market. It is at $1.05 per pound. Experts say the price is expected to rise by two or three cents per pound in the next few weeks. He suggests you wait a little longer before selling so as to maximize your investment.

Gisela was still raging as she paced the large sitting room with its spectacular view of the valley and the mountains beyond. "I knew she was up to something. From the very moment she offered us the gold. I should have slapped her back in her cell and left her there to rot."

Looking up from the computer, Niklas sighed. "Mama, there's no use working yourself up. She played it perfectly, and we were all the more fools for assuming she was a child."

"Oh, no," she snarled. "This isn't her work. She's not that smart. This was the brainchild of Jean-Henri LaRoche. He set it up. He made sure she knew exactly what to say."

"If that comforts you, Mama," he murmured, weary of it.

"So how do we make this right?" she demanded.

He sighed again. "Mama, you saw their bank accounts. Even if we took every penny from them, it wouldn't be a drop in the bucket compared to what we need."

"I'm not talking about their money. I'm talking about making them pay."

"Well, that's wonderful," he snapped. "Let's go on back to Utah and make a frontal assault on their ranch house. Maybe we could rent a tank and an armored personnel carrier. I'm sure it's never occurred to them that we might retaliate. And I'm sure that the FBI thinks they're perfectly safe now and won't have anyone watching them."

"Being cheeky doesn't become you, Nikky. Don't make me slap your face."

He turned around in his swivel chair to face her. "Okay, I'm sorry, Mama. But we have to face reality here. I am in total agreement that we go after the McAllisters for playing us the fools. But not yet. We'll wait six months. Maybe even a year. Let them think they're safe. Let the FBI think it's over."

He could see that she didn't like it but was still rational enough to see he was making sense. He went on quickly, "Here's the bigger problem. In all of our plans for our 'retirement,' we counted on the twenty million dollars from the Canadians and about ten million we'd get for the ore we sold to the Russians. But we didn't get the twenty million, and we only got seven million for the ore. Getting thirty million in gold was the answer to our problems. With that, we could have invested and lived handsomely off the income for the rest of our lives."

He blew out a long breath, massaging his temples with his fingertips. "But we don't have it now. We have a seven-hundred-thousand-dollar mortgage on the villa here. We have a staff of twelve now, if you count the security guards. We also have to start on our plastic surgery right away. That's going to cost us about two hundred thousand each. We needed that money."

"All the more reason to go after them and make them pay."

"They can't pay in money, Mama! That's what I keep telling you. There's a score to settle, but it's not going to put us back on solid footing again."

"So what will? What are you suggesting? Are you talking about more kidnappings? Maybe rob a bank or two? Hire us some highly sophisticated hackers and undertake some major identity theft schemes?"

"And double or triple the risk of both of us going to prison? You know that's not the answer."

"Then sell the castle. Sell the château in San Moritz. Sell the beach house in Barbados. We're not going back to any of them again."

"They're already up for sale, Mama," he said wearily. "But houses like that can take a year or more to sell. And altogether they're worth no more than seven or eight million."

"You keep telling me what we can't do," she exploded. "Tell me something that we *can* do!"

He gave her a thin smile. Finally, he had gotten her to ask the right question. "Between your shares and mine in Von Dietz Global, we have nearly fifty million dollars."

"No, Niklas!" She was out of her chair and glaring at him, her fists clenched, her nostrils flaring. "We swore to Nana. Von Dietz Global is off-limits. We won't put Anina and her children or any of the extended family at risk. We will not."

"And what if I could promise you that nothing that is theirs will be taken or put at risk? The fifty million is *our* money, Mama. We're not stealing from anyone. We just don't have access to it."

"That's the way you set it up. And you did that for a reason."

"Yes, I did. But this is a whole new game. We are up against the wall. We need cash, and we need it now. And since I'm the one who set it up, I know how to get it out. I know how to do it without leaving any kind of a trail or bringing even the whisper of a scandal upon our family."

"I don't believe you," she said, but he could tell she was interested.

"Then come over here and I'll show you," he said, pulling up another chair. "Remember, I'm the one who set up our whole security system. I made sure of that when we first decided to upgrade."

───◆───

Niklas had his mother convinced in under five minutes. She sat back, her face troubled but excited. "And you're absolutely sure?"

"Ninety-nine and nine-tenths percent," he said.

"Not good enough."

"I know. That's why I'm sending for Heinrich Müller."

"Head of Internet Security at Von Dietz Global?"

"The same."

"Is that wise?"

"He's been on my payroll for the last two years. He has been instrumental in setting up several of our operations. He's one of us."

Her brows lowered. "And you never told me?"

"As a member of the board of directors, you needed to have plausible deniability." He hurried on before she could say more. "We need his expertise to eliminate that one-tenth of one percent."

"He's not married either, is he?"

"No. Like me, he enjoys the company of beautiful women too much to settle on just one quite yet."

"How soon can he be here?"

"That's what I'm going to find out."

───◆───

"Niklas?"

He looked up from the *Argentinisches Tageblatt*—the *Argentine Daily*—the country's largest German-language newspaper. "Yes, Heinrich?"

Gisela, working on an intricate needlepoint pattern, looked up, but her fingers kept flying.

"There's a man at the door. He says he is the mayor of Mina Clavero."

"He's what?"

The needlepoint was instantly forgotten. "The mayor?" Gisela blurted.

"Yes. He's got a staff member with him and a journalist with a camera."

"No cameras," Gisela hissed.

"I already told him that," Müller said. "He told the man to put it away."

"What does he want?"

"He wants to talk to you and Lady Smythe. The butler let them in. They're waiting in the entryway. He seems very excited to meet the two of you. He kept telling the butler what a great honor it would be. He apologized for not calling first, but said they didn't have a phone number."

Mother and son exchanged looks, then Niklas shrugged. "Bring the mayor in. Leave the others out there for now."

————

Mayor Javier Roberto Fernández de Arroyo was a short man with a thin, pencil mustache, glistening black hair slicked straight back, darting brown eyes, and an enormous sense of energy about him. As Heinrich formally introduced him to Lady Giselle Mary Elizabeth Smythe and Lord Roger Carlton Smythe the Third, he was effusive in his response. He kissed Gisela's hand, not once but twice. He bowed and bobbed his head as he shook Niklas's hand and apologized over and over for intruding on them without an invitation. He asked his hosts if they preferred him to speak in English. Niklas said yes, not wanting to reveal that his and Gisela's Spanish was near fluent, thus keeping up the idea that they were from England.

Finally, when they had him seated in a chair facing them, with Heinrich standing discreetly in the background, he got to the reason for his coming.

"This is a great honor, *Señor* and *Señora* Smythe. A great honor." He took a sheaf of papers from his briefcase and set them on his lap. "As you may know, our fair city has recently undertaken a campaign to honor some of our citizens. We are very civic minded and seek to encourage service to our community and to the world."

"Oh?" Gisela said slowly, not sure where this was leading.

"Yes. Our campaign is going very well. So, when we received this in the mail yesterday"— he reached down and patted the papers—"we immediately decided that, with your permission, we would like to publicly acknowledge your generous contributions to others. You are an example of the kind of Christian charity that we are all encouraged to practice."

"Christian charity?" Niklas said very slowly, wary now, wondering if this wasn't some huge misunderstanding.

"Yes." He lifted the cover sheet and looked at the paper beneath it. "For example, we have here a woman by the name Célina Chastain Morneau, of Strasbourg, France. Former member of the Resistance during World War II." He held up the sheet and showed them a color photo of a woman in her eighties. "Ms. Morneau had a recent tragedy in her family when two of her grandchildren were falsely accused of possession of illegal drugs. She paid out thousands of Euros to clear their names, even though she was not a woman of means. She recently received a donation of some two hundred thousand Euros in a most generous effort to restore her to financial independence, and—"

He stopped. "Is something wrong, Lord Smythe?"

Niklas managed a fleeting smile and held out his hand. "May I see those, please?"

"*Si.*" He handed the whole packet across to him. Gisela leaned in as he turned to the next page. Here was a black-and-white photo of a balding man with white hair. He read softly. "André Villeneuve from Bordeaux, France. A few years ago, his supermarket burned to the ground. Recently received €750,000 in compensation for his loss from an anonymous donor."

He turned to the next page. "Étienne Giroux. Falsely accused of embezzling from his company. Served eighteen months in prison. Abandoned by his wife and family. Later proven to be totally innocent. Swiss bank transferred in €500,000 two weeks ago."

"It is incredible," the mayor gushed. "In every case, these poor souls were wronged in terrible ways. Now, years later, they are receiving these marvelous gifts."

Niklas barely heard them. He was staring at the opposite wall, a dazed expression on his face. Gisela took the papers from him and continued, moving swiftly now. "Jacques Rousseau. Kidnapped and held for two million Euros ransom. Contribution? Two million Euros. The late Manfred Hoffman, of Munich, Germany. Large contribution to his widow and children for services rendered to refugee families during the war."

She lowered the papers, searching her son's face for some sign of what to do. She didn't even register in his vision. Taking a quick breath, she closed the papers and handed them back to the mayor. "I am terribly sorry, Mayor de Arroyo, but I fear there has been a mistake here. What we see before us is quite remarkable, and I wish I could tell you that we were the ones responsible. But we know none of these names."

The poor man was shocked deeply. "But, Madame Smythe, the person who sent this—"

"Was wrong. I am deeply touched that they thought it was my son and me, but it was not. This will inspire us to undertake a similar program of Christian charity, as you call it, but the credit belongs to someone else." This last was said grimly.

She stood. "Thank you so much for your effort in coming out. We wish you the best of luck in finding the right people so that they can be properly honored. Mr. Müller will see you out. Good day. And thank you again."

———

The entry door had barely shut before the three of them were at the computer—Heinrich at the keyboard, Gisela and Niklas standing right behind him. His fingers flew over the keys, and one window after another popped up and then disappeared. Several times he swore under his breath as he worked. Finally, he sat back, then looked up at them. "It's gone," he said.

"What's gone?" Gisela cried.

Niklas collapsed into a chair. "The seven million Euros we got from the Russians."

"Gone? How can it be gone?"

Niklas dropped his head and covered his face in his hands. "Because they took it."

"*Who* took it?"

He looked up, the bitterness twisting his face. "Who do you think?"

"Somehow they knew all of our passwords and user names," Heinrich explained.

With that, a stricken Gisela sank down into one of the chairs. "How much do we have left?"

Heinrich slowly shook his head. "I'll have to check to make certain, but it's under two million, I'm pretty sure."

Niklas got to his feet. "Change all of the names and passwords. Now! And no more waiting on the von Dietz money. We go for it this afternoon, as soon as the offices in Europe close."

"How long will it take to get it out?" Gisela demanded.

Heinrich shook his head in frustration. "With this amount, as much as several days. We can't take it out in one lump sum or they'll be onto us in an instant. We'll have to create several accounts. We can use the weekend to get it all set up, then start moving the money Monday as soon as things get busy and it won't be immediately noticed."

CHAPTER 44

"Aha!" Heinrich cried, leaping to his feet. "That explains it."

Niklas got up from the desk and came around. "What?"

"Someone installed keylogger software on your machine."

"They what?"

"Do you know what keylogger software is?"

"Of course I know what it is. And what it does. I thought you swept the computer for spyware."

"I sweep it every week. But this is a highly sophisticated program. I mean, top-of-the-line sophistication."

"What is?" Gisela asked as she came into the room from the hallway. Heinrich took a quick breath and then plunged. He told her quickly what he had found and what it did. "I couldn't figure out how anyone could get access to our user names and passwords. Most of those have at least three levels of security, some four."

"I don't understand."

"They can monitor all activity on our computer from their own computer via the web. They didn't need to crack the names and passwords because we gave them to them every time we entered them into the system, including each time we changed them."

"Why didn't you find it earlier?"

He swallowed hard twice. "I have been scanning the system every day and it's never showed up. This afternoon, I specifically went looking for how they were getting the passwords."

"How long has it been on there?"

"That one is easy. It shows that it was installed on Saturday, October 22, at 5:03 p.m."

Gisela and Niklas looked at each other. He spoke first. "Saturday afternoon. That would have been at the villa. It was about the time that Danni got out of her cell."

"But surely she couldn't have done it," Heinrich said. "This is pretty sophisticated stuff."

"Sophisticated to install?"

He shook his head. "No, not really. That wouldn't be too hard if you could get access to the computer's operating system."

"It wasn't Danni," Gisela said flatly.

Both men turned and looked at her. "Why do you say that?" Niklas asked.

"Because she was in our custody from the hotel in Caen on. We searched her thoroughly. She didn't have it. And therefore she didn't do it. He did."

"He?" Heinrich asked.

"Jean-Henri LaRoche. Grandpère. We know he was in the building later that evening. I'll bet he was there earlier."

The men looked at each other; then Niklas's head bobbed. "It makes more sense than Danni."

"It's the only thing that makes sense," she said. Then, in a very low voice filled with hate and menace, she added, "And if it's the last thing I do, I am going to kill that man. Once and forever, he is going to be dead."

———

If anyone in the Smythe/von Dietz household was aware of the fact that Christmas was coming fast upon them, they gave no outward evidence of that fact. There were no Christmas decorations. No special holiday dinner. No gifts. A group of carolers came to the front gate and rang the bell, but when no one answered, they sang one verse of "Silent Night" and went away again.

Gisela brought in a tray of sandwiches and black coffee to the three men working in the study, then joined them as they ate. No one said much. They ate silently, each lost in their own thoughts. On the surface, none of those thoughts seemed to be centered on Christmas. Heinrich asked Jean-Claude where he had lived in Belgium, but when he gave a one-word answer—"Brussels"—they fell silent again.

As they were finishing, the computer chimed softly, the signal for an incoming email message. Heinrich started to get up, but Gisela was faster. "I'll get it." A moment later, the entire atmosphere in the room changed when Gisela yelled out and shot to her feet. "What? What is this?"

The three of them were up and gathered around the computer. She had leaned in to peer at the screen and was blocking their view. Niklas reached out, took her shoulder, and gently drew her back. "What is it, Mama?"

She couldn't speak. All she could do was point. Niklas nearly choked, then fell into the chair next to her and began to read. "It's from Von Dietz Global, Department of Internal Security.

Dear Valued VDG Clients:

We regret to inform you that the VDG financial systems have experienced a serious breach of security from unknown, hostile hackers. All systems have been shut down while the source of this breach is discovered and full security is restored. We apologize for any inconvenience this may cause. At this point we cannot say how long we will be out of service. Clients should be prepared for as much as two to three weeks.

"Two to three weeks!" Heinrich cried. "They can't be serious."

Niklas went on without comment:

Clients in need of immediate, emergency access to funds should contact any regional office of VDG Financial. Please bring at least two forms of government-issued identification. Clearance of funds may take up to three working days. We shall keep you informed of any progress or further developments. Thank you for your patience and understanding,

Ernst von Blankenburg
President and CEO
Von Dietz Global Financial Enterprises

Even before Niklas had finished reading, Heinrich snatched up the phone and stabbed at the buttons. Gisela shot out of her chair. "What are you doing?" she shouted at him.

"I'm calling a friend in Zurich. We need to know what's going on and—"

"Don't you do that on a phone that can be traced to here!"

"Oh. Uh . . . sorry."

Niklas handed him a cell phone from a drawer in the desk. "This is a throwaway. But keep it brief."

Heinrich put it on speakerphone, then dialed the number. He kept the conversation to just under two minutes and asked four questions.

How much was taken from the company? Fifty million dollars.

Do they know how it was done? They're pretty sure it was someone on the inside who came through a back door and circumvented the firewalls.

Do they know where the money is now? No, but there is some evidence that it may still be within VDG's financial system, but well hidden.

How soon will funds be available again? This is such a huge loss to the company and such a serious breach of the multi-tiered security system that the three to four weeks mentioned in the email is likely a highly optimistic estimate. The guys in the know are talking more like five to six weeks.

When he hung up, Gisela gave her son a scathing look. "I told you this was a mistake. What if they discover who's behind the breach?"

"They won't do that," Heinrich said. "I left no footprint."

"The jails are full of men who left no footprints," she said in disgust.

Angry now, he turned on Niklas. "Thank heavens we can get it out sooner. I'm sure all we have to do is take two forms of ID to the regional office in Buenos Aires and see if they won't release the funds to you. I think our situation could be described as an emergency."

Niklas got to his feet, eyes smoldering. "Remember what you said about me being cheeky, Mama? Well, that street runs in both directions."

He stalked out of the room without another word. A moment later Heinrich and Jean-Claude followed after him, not daring to look at Gisela as they skirted around her and exited the room.

<hr/>

Villa del Sol, Mina Clavero
January 17, 2012

"*Señora* Smythe?"

Gisela looked up from her needlepoint. "Yes, Rosita?"

"There are two members of the *Police Nationale* at the front gate asking to see you and *Señor* Smythe."

She shot to her feet, sending the needlepoint flying. "Get *Señor* Smythe. *Pronto.*"

"I already called him, *Señora*. He is coming now."

Even as she finished speaking, Niklas strode into the room, followed by Heinrich, Jean-Claude, and one of the other guards whose name she could not recall.

"What shall we do, Niklas?" she cried. "What do they want?"

"Be calm, Mama. I have no idea. But if they came to arrest us, there would be many more than two of them. Just stay calm."

He was right. They were not there to arrest them. Not exactly.

When the two officers were shown in, the older of the two men stepped forth. "*Señor* Smythe, I understand that you do not speak much Spanish, so I shall speak in English, though I do not speak it very well."

Both Niklas and his mother spoke fairly fluent Spanish, but Niklas didn't want them knowing that. "Thank you," he said. "What is this about, Officer?"

The man carried a leather pouch beneath his left arm. He removed it, unzipped it quickly, and withdrew a sheaf of papers. For a moment, Niklas thought they were the same papers that the mayor had brought earlier. Then he saw that there were more of them. And there was a letter on the top, written on fine linen paper and with an official-looking letterhead on the top. Without preamble he began to read:

January 16, 2012
Office of the President
República Argentina

Mr. Roger Carlton Smythe, III
Mina Clavero, Province of Córdoba

Dear Mr. and Mrs. Smythe,

It has recently been brought to our attention by various law-enforcement officers in the United States of America, France, Belgium, Switzerland, and Germany that there are numerous criminal charges and arrest warrants issued in your names. (See enclosed dossier.) While we are not obliged by the laws of our sovereign nation to comply in any way with another country's demands, it is not the policy of the State of Argentina to harbor known fugitives or suspected criminals. This letter is to inform you that you are, therefore, officially declared persona non grata in any part of the Argentine Republic or any of its territories.

Since none of the alleged crimes occurred on Argentine territory, no further action against you is planned. None of your property will be confiscated, nor will your freedom be restricted in any way until the deadline set below. This declaration hereby revokes or cancels all visas and other documents that grant the two of you the right to maintain permanent residence in our country.

This declaration becomes effective at 12:01 a.m. on 1 February 2012. If you have not left Argentina by that time, a warrant for your arrest will be issued and you will be forcibly ejected from our country.

Capitán Juan Vasquez, the bearer of this letter, has instructions and full authority from this office to assist you in identifying a country or territory willing to grant you asylum and to help you in any reasonable way to remove to that country. All expenses incurred in such a removal will, however, be your personal responsibility.

With deepest regrets,

What followed was an undecipherable signature.

Gisela collapsed in a heap on the couch and began to sob. Stone-faced, Niklas held out his hand. "May I see the dossier, *Capitán?*"

He handed it over without saying a word. It came as no surprise that the first page inside the cover held a picture of Lucas and Angelique McAllister and their two children, along with Jean-Henri LaRoche. Their individual names were typed beneath the photo. Beneath the names, the type read:

Country: United States of America

Charges: Kidnapping, extortion, conspiracy to kidnap, conspiracy to extort, physical assault with a deadly weapon, theft and destruction of property, deliberate creation of extreme mental distress.

Then followed a two-paragraph description of what had taken place back in June 2011.

He went to the next page. It was identical to the first except that the picture was of Rick and his family. The charges were also the same, with the addition of conspiracy to commit second-degree murder.

Niklas suddenly had to sit down too. There it all was in black and white—the names, the charges, the terse, cold summaries of kidnapping, embezzlement, extortion, defamation of character, giving false testimony to officers of the law, arson, and on and on.

When he finally shut the dossier and handed it back to the captain, the officer shook his head. "That copy is yours to keep." He straightened his shoulders. "As noted in the letter, I am at your service, Lord Smythe."

"Where shall we go?" Gisela wailed. "What shall we do?"

"My staff is hard at work trying to answer those questions, Lady Smythe," Captain Vasquez assured her. "That said, I can tell you where you will *not* be going. Inquiries have already been made to all the major countries of Latin America concerning possible asylum. All but four have responded in the negative. The exceptions are Panama, Colombia, Venezuela, and Nicaragua. Of those, Venezuela and Nicaragua require a deposit of one million dollars in a bank of their choosing as a precondition for acceptance."

Gisela's head snapped up. "Not Venezuela. Their president is a pig and I will not live there as long as he is president."

The captain sighed deeply, but spoke to Niklas. "Perhaps you would prefer a European country. If so, all members of the European Union have an agreement that does not grant asylum when criminal activity is involved. You would have to look to Eastern Europe to—"

Gisela looked like a little girl lost in a supermarket at rush hour. "Niklas," she cried plaintively. "Niklas? What shall we do?"

He went to her and took her in his arms. "It's all right, Mama. It's all right. I'm here. I will take care of you." He looked up. "See if Colombia will have us. I have been to Colombia once. It is a beautiful country."

"What about us?" Heinrich cried. "What about his employees? We haven't done anything wrong."

"There is an addendum at the back of the dossier listing those who are considered to be accomplices in all of this. What is your name?"

"Heinrich Müller. I hold joint citizenship in Switzerland and Germany."

"You are not on the list. If your papers are in order, you are free to go or stay as you like." He swung around on Jean-Claude. "What is your name?"

"What does it matter? My place is by their side."

Captain Vasquez clicked his heels together and snapped off a salute.

"I shall return tomorrow morning to provide further assistance. Until then," he said, saluting again, "*hasta luego.*"

✦

On Approach to El Dorado International Airport, Bogotá, Colombia
January 30, 2012

Niklas von Dietz, aka Roger Carlton Smythe III, reached over and went to lay a hand on his mother's shoulder. But he stopped and let it hover over her for a moment, looking at her face, now in repose as she slept so soundly. He pulled his hand back, a wave of sorrow sweeping over him.

He had noticed just in the last week or so how much she was changing. But now, even in the kindness of the soft morning light that just precedes sunrise, he saw for the first time the toll these last two months had taken on her. She looked old, and that was something he had thought he would never say of her. There were dark circles under her eyes. Her skin seemed sallow, almost gray, and the depth of the wrinkles around her mouth left it looking pinched. But his deepest pain came from the blank, momentary confusion that filled her eyes with increasing frequency. This woman, who had been a towering pillar of strength and determination and independence for all of Niklas's life, was more and more becoming the young child—lost, innocent, confused, vulnerable.

He sighed, feeling the bone-deep weariness in his own soul. These last two months had been pure hell for both of them. He could see that in his own face and the premature gray around his temples. Little wonder. But at last, they were coming to the end of it. Two days following their final visit from Captain Vasquez, Niklas had gotten a call from their real-estate agent. She had a buyer for their beach house in Barbados. *A cash buyer.* The house was listed at 1.5 million U.S. dollars. The buyer was offering exactly half that. It didn't matter. It was cash. It was a lifeline that they desperately needed right now.

Niklas accepted it on the condition that they close in no later than ten days. They agreed, and nine days later a cashier's check for the full amount arrived by FedEx. He put it in a bank in Córdoba, under yet another name, using yet another passport. He didn't open an online account. He didn't make record of it on any of their computers. There was no way anyone could get at this. He had made triple sure of that.

So now there was hope again. Never before in his life had he realized what a precious gift hope was. There was a way out. Things would be okay. They had enough now to see them through until Von Dietz Global sorted out the nightmare of their security breach and released their funds. They were saying that could be any day now.

He reached out and laid his hand on her shoulder. "Mama. It's time to wake up. We're almost there."

It didn't come quickly—another sign of the depths of her weariness. Normally she was wide awake and completely alert in an instant. Now he had to shake her several times before she came fully awake. As she stretched and yawned, looking around in some confusion, he reached over and pushed up the window blinds. Leaning forward, she peered out the window. There was a soft cry of surprise and pleasure. "Oh, Niklas. It's beautiful."

She was right. The plane was banking around on its last approach, and the city and the line of green peaks on either side of it were in full view. Bogotá was the third-highest airport in the world, and the scenery surrounding it was spectacular. As they continued to turn, the first rays of the sun struck one of the skyscrapers and its windows glowed like gold. It was like a welcome sign. "Yes, Mama. It is beautiful. And this is going to be our new home."

A momentary flash of fear twisted her features. "No, Niklas. This isn't home. I want to go home. To our real home." But as quickly as it had come, the moment passed. She turned her head away. "Never mind. I remember now," she said softly.

They cleared customs without the slightest complication. Captain Vasquez had done his job well. Jean-Claude was waiting for them in the baggage area and waved when he saw them coming. They were descending one of the escalators, so Niklas had a clear view of the area and saw him immediately. He waved back, but even as he did so, his hand froze in midair. He jerked forward, gaping in astonishment. "Anina?"

"What did you say?" Gisela asked.

"Mother, it's Anina."

"Who?"

"Anina. Your daughter. What in the world is she doing here?"

She was waving now too, pushing her way through crowds and calling out to them, smiling and crying all at once. Jean-Claude was following, trying to keep up with her. As they reached the bottom of the moving stairway and stepped off, Niklas's sister threw her arms around her mother and pulled her in close. "Oh, Mama. Oh, Mama," she kept saying over and over, tears streaming down her cheeks.

Niklas touched her shoulder. "Anina. I can't believe it. You, here?"

But even as he asked the question, a movement caught his eye. He turned and saw five or six men in business suits moving in toward him, forming a loose semicircle as they came. Jean-Claude saw it too. He whirled and bolted away. He wasn't nearly fast enough. Two of the men whipped out pistols and cut him off.

As Niklas stared, totally dumbfounded, he felt a hand on his shoulder turn him around. A middle-aged but very fit-looking man was facing him. He had a small, black leather case that looked like a wallet in one hand. He flipped it open to reveal a gold badge. "Niklas von Dietz. Agent Clay Zabriskie, United States Federal Bureau of Investigation. You are under arrest for crimes committed on U.S. soil."

Niklas jerked free. "That is not possible. We have been offered asylum here."

"Colombia and the United States have come to an agreement based on a cooperative arrangement between our two countries. Your asylum, and that of your mother, has been revoked, and we have permission to take you back to the United States. However . . ." He stepped back.

A taller, younger man stepped forward and flashed another badge. With a sickening drop in his stomach, Niklas recognized it instantly. It was the badge carried by Interpol officers the world over. "Mr. von Dietz. I am Colonel Pierre Pelletier, from Interpol International Headquarters in Lyon, France. You are hereby charged with kidnapping, extortion, fraud, conspiracy, and several other counts of criminal activity. You have the right to remain silent. You have the right to an attorney. However, those rights do not go into effect until we land on French soil." Two of the other men stepped forward, producing handcuffs.

The colonel kept speaking. "A federal judge here in Colombia has signed an order to have you immediately extradited to France, where you will stand trial for the crimes of which you are accused."

A man behind him handed him a paper. He looked at it quickly. "At the request of your sister, we have drawn up a document of confession. If you are willing to take full responsibility for the criminal acts of which you are accused, your mother can avoid arrest and will be allowed to return to Switzerland with her daughter. Is that something you are willing to consider?"

Niklas's face had gone completely white now. His mouth worked, but nothing came out. Clay stepped forward. "If you choose to sign that statement, I am authorized to say that the United States will not take further action against your mother. She will be free to go."

He still couldn't speak. Anina came to him, tears streaming down her face. "Please, Niklas. Look at her. Think what a trial will do to her. Think of the publicity. It will kill her if she goes to prison."

For most of his adult life, Niklas von Dietz had been a decision maker. Big, small, hard, easy—it was what he did. Choking back a sob, he took the paper. "Do you have a pen?" he asked.

EPILOGUE

"Dad. Stop the car!"

He turned his head. "Here?"

"Yes. Rick and I want to walk from here."

He let off the accelerator. I leaned up from the backseat of the van and touched Grandpère's shoulder. "Do you want to come with us?"

"I do," Cody sang out.

"No, I think it is best if just those two go," Grandpère said. He gave Cody a warning look. "You can walk it later, if you wish."

Grandpère scooted his seat up and opened the sliding door of the van. I was out in a second, and Rick was right behind me. "'Bye," we called out in unison as we set off at a brisk walk.

It had been September when my family first came to Grandpère's ancestral home. The fall colors had been glorious. But now? *"Magnifique!"* I exclaimed as we entered the narrow, two-track road that led to the château. We were surrounded—embraced, engulfed, immersed—in a thousand shades of green, and all of them so vibrant and warm. I loved it even more than the fall colors.

581

I slipped my arm through Rick's. "I'm so excited. I can hardly wait for you to see it."

When we came around the last bend in the road and Le Petit Château finally was in full view, we both stopped. "Wow!" Rick said softly. We stood and looked at it for a moment, then started forward again.

We had barely gone fifty yards when the front door to the château opened and a woman stepped out onto the porch. She shaded her eyes with one hand. "*Mademoiselle* Danni?"

I waved. "Yes. It's me."

We increased our pace, closing the distance between us rapidly. We met on the gravel sidewalk near the stone fence that defined the yard of the château. "*Bonjour,*" she said as we came up to each other. "I am Anina. I am very happy to finally meet you."

———

I was quite surprised at how much sorrow we felt as we watched Gisela. We were in the dining room having lunch with Anina and her three children. Grandpère Jean-Henri and Grandpère Louis were regaling her with tales of their boyhood and their wartime memories. Gisela sat on the opposite end of the table from her daughter. Occasionally, she would turn and seem to focus on the conversation, but quickly she lost interest and turned away to stare out the window or twist the tablecloth with her fingers.

This was the woman that I had once hated, that I had once vowed to utterly destroy if I had the chance. Now she reminded me of a child. She was still as lovely and distant as ever, but there was a childlike quality about her that was both touching and disturbing. Disturbing because I had known her before.

Grandpère startled me when he suddenly asked, "Do you take your mother to see Niklas ever, Anina?"

Anina turned, looked at Gisela, then slowly shook her head. "I did on two different occasions. But she barely understood what was going on. And yet, it upset her for days afterwards. So I go see him when my husband can be with her."

"And how is he?" Rick asked.

"Quite well, considering. He has actually taken on a strict regimen of weight lifting in the prison and looks very fit."

Dad spoke up. "If you don't mind me asking, Anina, how did the whole thing with Von Dietz Global turn out? We heard they were talking about awarding all of the family shares to you."

"Yes. I am the only other child, so the full fifty million came to me and my husband." She lifted a hand and waved it around the room. "Had it been otherwise, we would have been forced to sell the château. But Mother loves it here. As do the children. I think we shall spend each summer here from this point on."

Rick surprised me when he suddenly stood up and went around to Gisela. He knelt down beside her chair and took her hand. She turned in surprise, then searched his face with those eyes that were such a startling blue. I watched for any sign of recognition, but saw none.

"Lady Gisela," Rick said softly, "my name is Ricardo Ramirez, but everyone calls me Rick."

She peered at him more closely. "Do I . . . know you?"

"We met a long time ago," he said. Squeezing her hand gently, he said, "Thank you for letting us see your beautiful home. We love it here."

Her face lit up. "It is lovely, isn't it?"

"I envy you," Rick said with a smile. "Where I live, we don't have many trees."

A horrified look crossed her face. "No trees? But how could you stand such a thing?"

He laughed, then glanced at me. "We make up for it by having good friends instead." He motioned for me to join them. "And I have one of my very best friends here with me."

I was suddenly having a difficult time seeing very clearly, but I got up and joined them, kneeling down on the other side of her. I took her hand. It was cold, even in the sunlight. I took it in both of mine.

"This is my best friend, Danni McAllister. Danni, this is Lady Gisela von Dietz."

"I am very pleased to meet you," I said, smiling through the tears, trying to push back the memories.

She looked at me for what seemed like a very long time; then she turned to Rick and leaned in closer. "She's very pretty," she said in what was meant to be a conspiratorial whisper but could be heard by everyone in the room.

"I think so too, Lady Gisela. Very pretty indeed."

She turned to me and searched my face. Then one hand came up and touched my cheek. "Do I . . ." She gave a little shake of her head. "Have we met before?"

I couldn't answer her, so I just nodded my head.

"It's Danni McAllister, Mama," Anina said. "She stayed here at the château with you last year."

"No." She shook her head emphatically.

"No what, Mama?"

"Not Danni."

I gaped at her. She was struggling to remember. "It's . . ." Then she shook her head again. I started to tell her, but Rick quickly shook his head at me.

And suddenly she sat forward again. "Carruthers."

I couldn't believe it. "Yes," I cried. "Yes, Lady Gisela, my real name is Carruthers."

She looked at Rick in triumph. "Not Danni."

He laughed happily. "No, Lady Gisela. Not Danni. Carruthers."

As I got up and returned to my seat, I saw that I wasn't the only one with tears. Anina, Mom, Dorothée. Even Grandpère was misty-eyed. Anina reached across and laid a hand on my arm. "That was amazing," she whispered, tears in her eyes now. "Thank you. I can only imagine how much pain she has caused you and your family, so thank you."

I sniffed back sudden tears myself. "Whenever I find myself feeling bitter," I finally managed, "I try to picture a four-year-old girl in a ragged dress and tattered shoes, holding her mother's hand as they pick their way through the rubble of Munich. And the bitterness goes away."

———

As we drove slowly back into the village, then on to Strasbourg to the airport, all of us were pretty subdued. Even Cody said nothing. When we got to the airport and reached the terminal where Air France's domestic flights originated and ended, Louis reached up and gripped Grandpère's hand. "I had heard that the château might be coming up for sale, and I planned to buy it as a surprise. Thought I would keep it as a bed and breakfast, with an open invitation for free lodging to the McAllisters of Southern Utah to come anytime. But this is better." He swallowed quickly. "This is better."

"*Oui*." Grandpère cleared his throat.

———

*Normandy American Cemetery and Memorial,
Colleville-sur-Mer, Normandy, France*
June 13, 2012

At first, Grandpère talked about doing it at the grave site of Lieutenant Arnold Fitzgerald, but then he decided perhaps that was too sacred a place. Mom suggested the picnic area behind the visitors' center. Too public. Louis settled it when he said, "Why not on the beach, where the young men of Danni's age first came ashore in France?"

We walked down the beach, beyond the paved walkways, and found a secluded spot near the undergrowth at the base of the cliffs. There, Grandpère had us all sit down in the sand in a semicircle facing him. We were barely seated when he looked at me with great solemnity. "Carruthers Monique McAllister, would you come forward, please?"

I got to my feet, not sure what to expect. We had had my birthday cake and opened my presents in the hotel before we left. I was pretty sure there would be some reminiscing about what had happened during World War II here. And I expected to get my usual birthday counsel and wisdom. So I was a little surprised at the formality he was setting up here. But I got up and went up to stand before him.

"Danni, we are gathered together here on the beaches of Normandy on this, your seventeenth birthday. The place where we now stand is hallowed by the blood and sacrifice of literally thousands of an earlier generation. We stand here mindful of the stirring examples of those who have gone before: Angelique Chevalier. Pierre and Monique LaRoche. Lieutenant Arnold Fitzgerald, who never returned home. I believe that they still live, and that from time to time, God allows them the privilege of seeing through the veil and watching us now. It is always humbling to wonder what they might say to us if they were allowed to speak."

That hit pretty hard.

"It was four years ago today that Danni celebrated her thirteenth birthday," Grandpère continued. "Because it fell on a Friday that year"— he shot Mom a quick look and a smile—"we celebrated it the following day and the day after that. On that third day, Danni was presented with a family heirloom that I was given by my father on my thirteenth birthday. It was an old cloth pouch with the name *Le Gardien* embroidered upon it, along with four *fleurs-de-lys,* symbols of the concept of guardianship. Danni was given a most solemn charge to care for the gift and to learn from it. Which she did."

"Especially the learning part," I said. It wasn't meant as a cute quip. I really meant it. *Le Gardien* had been a wonderful tutor, guide, and guardian. More and more now I realized just how much I had learned and grown.

"Unfortunately," Grandpère continued, "last fall, the pouch was forcibly taken from Danni and tossed onto a fire, where it was totally consumed. I know that Danni still believes that was partially her fault, but it is not so. She kept the pouch faithfully and well."

I was looking at the ground now. So many memories were flooding back.

"But, if there is anything that the McAllisters have learned in this last year, it is that there are more important things than battered old pouches."

"I know, but—" I started.

He cut in quickly. "I know that Danni feels terrible that she has nothing to pass on to her son or daughter when the time comes. Therefore—" He stopped and reached around to the back of his waist, lifting up his light jacket to do so. "As her parents and grandparent, we felt there was value in starting a new tradition." He smiled. "After all, even the most ancient of traditions all started somewhere."

And with that, he extracted a package wrapped in lavender gift wrap and extended it to me. For a moment, I just stared at it, not daring to hope. But good old Cody saved me. "Come on, Danni," he cried. "Stop stalling. Open it."

And so I did. And the moment the paper fell away, I started to cry. What I was holding in my hands was another perfect replica of the pouch. There were the *fleurs-de-lys,* one in each corner of the flap. There was the braided rope strap, with the hand-carved wooden button below it. And there were the embroidered words, *Le Gardien.*

I could barely see my family and friends through the tears, and I knew that I was never going to get any words out. But good old Grandpère. Always the one to have just the right touch. He stepped to me, took me by the shoulders, and softly kissed me on both cheeks. Then, in a husky voice, he said, "Happy birthday, Carruthers."